Farewell Berlin

"Have you ever wanted to kill someone?" His eyes were like darts. "I don't mean killing Hitler or Göring. that's easy—shit," he hissed, "they should all be dead. And not just because some son of a bitch on the street did or said something you didn't like, where you'd think, 'What an asshole. If I had the chance I'd . . .'"

Frowning, he waved his hand, then shrugged wearily. "The feeling passes. You cool off. The next time you see the guy—if you ever do—you've already forgotten."

Straightening, he set his jaw defiantly. His eyes flashed as if he'd suddenly become mad. "No! I'm talking blood-on-your-hands killing."

He shook his head, and his eyes wandered past his friend to a distant place. "I'm talking about murderous rage . . . grabs your head in both hands and tightens. All you hear, see, touch, smell, is boundless fury. Uncontrollable anger that won't, can't, release until he's limp, dead at your feet."

His fists clenched so tight his knuckles turned white, his pupils contracted. Then, shoulders relaxed, he leaned forward and asked in a calm, measured voice, "Well . . . have you?"

Farewell Berlin

Steven Muenzer

St. Paul, Minnesota • Alexander Press • 2013

On the cover: Prewar family photo of an unidentified park in Berlin.

This is a work of historical fiction. The author acknowledges these sources for background and several story ideas:

Marion A. Kaplan, *Between Dignity and Despair: Jewish Life in Nazi Germany* (New York: Oxford University Press, 1999).

Rita Thalmann and Emmanuel Feinermann (trans. Gilles Cremonesi), *Crystal Night: A Gripping Documentary of the Nazi Night of Terror That Was Prelude to the Holocaust* (New York: Coward, McCann and Geoghegan, 1974).

Martin Gilbert, *Kristallnacht: Prelude to Destruction* (London: HarperCollins, 2006).

For inquiries or additional copies:

Alexander Press: 651-373-5158 or jmssam@comcast.net

Manufactured in the United States of America

10 9 8 7 6 5 4 3 2 1

Library of Congress Control Number: 2012948264

ISBN 978-0-578-11734-8

Editing, design, production management: E. B. Green Editorial, St. Paul, MN

Printing/binding (paperback): BooksOnDemand.com, Stoughton, WI

To my parents, who bid Berlin farewell in 1939,

to Herman Mahlerman, whose book *The Fugitive* inspired me,

and to Jeanne

Today there passed six oxen, seven swine, and a Jew.
—Rosenthal Gatekeepers' Log, Berlin, 1743

I think of Germany at night.
The thought keeps me awake till light.
—Heinrich Heine

"I'm sure I don't know what makes you want to leave Berlin, all of a sudden, like this . . ."

"No. Even now I can't altogether believe that any of this has really happened."
—Christopher Isherwood

1

What is more agreeable than one's home?
—Marcus Tullius Cicero

Early on a summer morning in Sonny's twelfth year, his father shook him awake: "Get dressed. You're going to learn how to make a living." They were going to the warehouse in Scheunenviertel, Berlin's old barn quarter, cheek by jowl with Spandauer Vorstadt, where they lived. Both were in the Mitte, Berlin's historic center, where most of the city's eastern Jews lived and worked.

Sonny was born Sigmund Landauer in 1909, but no one called him that. He'd been Sonny since his father had dubbed him as a toddler. He took his father's word that he had been a happy child, full of laughter. In any event, the name stuck like chewing gum to the sole of his shoe, and almost no one knew him by any other.

Sonny's skin was light, his eyes nearly sky blue, his nose straight, his lips full but not thick. His golden hair hadn't yet darkened, and as he grew older he grew taller than others in the family. Both a German and a Jew by birth, he realized early that he stood out among the dark eastern Jews of the Mitte. His face could have invited tourism on a German poster.

His father was one of four brothers, all born in Germany, his mother an only child with no living relatives. His grandparents had immigrated to Germany from somewhere in the east, though no one could trace his ancestry to a particular village, town, or city. That unfortunate circumstance forced Sonny to conjure his past, and he imagined a shtetl, or village, a simple place far removed from the Berlin of his youth. Its genesis sprang from a story his father told when Sonny was ten. Sonny later refined the story with pictures he cut from magazines given him by Joseph, the bookseller.

With a broad palette, Sonny painted a dream of simple wood houses, of children playing in dirt lanes among chickens and goats. Looking through the curtained windows into a single room of crude furniture, he saw more children playing on the floor while their mother prepared a meal. The men worked as carpenters, bakers, and farmers; older boys ran to their Talmudic studies; and girls in headscarves giggled as they passed.

Somehow these people had withstood the terrible winters and oppressive governments, then found their way to Germany. But in leaving, they had left all traces of their former home behind. They found safe haven in Germany, settled, and made a life, though Sonny's father warned him that trouble had its way of finding a Jew.

That he was Jewish made Sonny different, though just how that might affect him was unclear. He was different in another way too. He didn't look like the Semitic stereotype. Many acquaintances were surprised to learn he was a Jew.

When his father told him the story generating his interest in the shtetl, Sonny gave little thought to being different. He loved that first story, and though other versions followed, it remained his favorite. Over time, the tale rose to the status of lore—a sort of Landauer myth, endlessly embellished. Finally it became tiresome, a caricature—to his relief rarely told though never completely lost.

Sonny's father, Morris Landauer, was a thin, wiry man with an expressive face, and he drew his young son into his story, asking, "Do you know what a shtetl is?"

Sonny shook his head.

"It's Yiddish for a small village. There were too many shtetls to count in the Pale of Settlement, that immense area in Czarist western Russia and eastern Poland." He threw out his arms to indicate its breadth. "Catherine the Great, in her wisdom, was good to the Jews—well, at least not so horrible as most of the czars—and she granted them permission to live, pray, and raise their families in the Pale. But they were kept under strict control. They remained poor and separate, so that they wouldn't compete with Russian peasants, who had as little as they. In the cities of the Pale, Jewish communities thrived in ghettos."

Sonny was confused. "Is Spandauer Vorstadt a ghetto?"

"No, only Jews lived in the ghetto—separated from the goyim—where they had their own businesses, doctors, lawyers, schools, and yeshivas. Some were prosperous, though most were poor, just like their relatives in the shtetls. Worst of all, those in the shtetls could never be comfortable or make a permanent home. They lived at the whim of the czar's bureaucrats. An entire village could be forced to move, just like that." He snapped his fingers, startling young Sonny.

He continued. "Imagine everyone in the warehouse forced to move within a week's time to some distant place."

Sonny couldn't think of anything more horrible. He shook his head.

"But it happened. All the people and every animal, stick of furniture, every kitchen utensil, were moved. My grandfather's—your great-grandfather's—shtetl was forced to move twice in his lifetime. Entire lives were uprooted, but that was the plan. Jews had to suffer."

The sadness in his father's eyes reminded Sonny of the Polish immigrants he'd seen on the street, but he didn't say anything.

"And there was more—they also had to endure the Cossacks. Yes, Jews were sometimes attacked in the cities, but in the shtetls the Cossacks swept in on horseback to remind them they were nothing, to steal from them and make mischief. They often left with Jewish blood on their swords." He paused to let Sonny think about what he'd said.

"Brave Russian Cossacks drew their swords upon defenseless Jews." His sarcasm bit like the horseradish they ate at the Passover Seder.

Then he leaned close to Sonny and whispered, "Cossacks came with more than thievery on their minds. They took their pleasure on any woman or girl they chose. You don't understand now, but you will, someday." He shrugged. "Our ancestral home is lost to history, its name long forgotten. But among my distant relatives in that unlucky shtetl was a pretty newlywed—still childless, of course."

Sonny's father had him imagine the young bride busy in her kitchen, preparing dinner, washing clothes, perhaps lost in thought about her new husband and their new life together. Then Sonny felt his father's hand tighten on his arm and saw his eyes widen.

"Suddenly the door swung open, and a Cossack stood on the threshold with a glint in his eye." He stopped and took a deep breath. "Thank

God her husband was away, for had he tried to protect her, she might have become a widow. But she was a strong woman, and the two rejoiced when she bore a son nine months later. The Cossack's awful act did not extinguish her youth and vitality. No!"

Then he lowered his voice: "Her husband never knew." His eyes traced the contours of Sonny's face. "That's how you've come to your blue eyes. I'm sure of it."

At age ten Sonny was fooled, but along the way he wondered how his father could know of the attack if the newlywed had remained silent. He never asked; to do so would be disrespectful, almost a sacrilege. The story was surely apocryphal, and over the years it became an abbreviated setup for a punch line: "And that's why you're a blue-eyed, goyish-looking Jew."

But now, on a summer's day in his twelfth year, Sonny was going with his father to learn a trade. Morris Landauer sold whatever he could get at a good price from a stall inside the cavernous warehouse on Rücker Strasse. Their flat was just a short tram ride from Schönhauser Gate in Scheunenviertel, an area of small shops, street vendors, and small-time merchants—many of them poor immigrants from across Eastern Europe, thousands of them Polish Jews looking for a better life after the devastations of the Great War. They were the small vendors, petty criminals, black marketers sharing the neighborhood with orthodox Jews, secular Jews, non-Jews.

Rücker Strasse was just around the corner from Schönhauser Gate and halfway between Alexanderplatz and the Rosenthal Gate. If you turned left instead of right, you'd meet the busy intersection of Hirtenstrasse and Grenadierstrasse, immortalized by writer Joseph Roth. Hirstenstrasse pulsed with tenements, bars, Jewish bakeries smelling of rye bread, kosher butchers, yeshivas (Jewish day schools) with Hebrew writing on the walls, and people selling goods everywhere between, like in a cheap department store. You'd find prostitutes and petty criminals there, too, though most of them were on Schönhauser Strasse, nearby.

Roth's "eastern grotesques" were all there—the fat broker, the shriveled old woman selling shoelaces. The street rarely saw an automobile and it had no streetcar line or buses—just trucks, carts, and a constant flow of humanity. For a drink, you climbed dirty steps to little hole-in-the-wall bars, from which the rubbish piled by the doors was collected only occasionally. It was a Jewish district—not a ghetto, though it was drab like a slum—softened by its eastern Jewish inhabitants and essentially unchanged over the years. Hirstenstrasse was truly the most Jewish street in Berlin . . .

Years later, when Sonny aspired to newspaper reporting, he read Roth's columns from the yellowed newspapers piled in a corner of Joseph's stall. And he read Roth's book *The Wandering Jew*, appreciating the raw seediness along with the dignity of his characters. In the same year Roth wrote of the broker and the woman selling shoelaces, the warehouse and Scheunenviertel became a part of Sonny.

Though not as colorful as Hirstenstrasse, Rücker Strasse had its charms. Punctuated by dead-end alleys full of men and women selling kitchen utensils, clothing, jewelry, hardware, and food, the street offered almost anything for the "very best price!" Young and old, the vendors spoke heavily accented German, Polish, Russian, Hungarian, and, of course, Yiddish. Barter was their medium, haggling their art.

From the crush of people, Sonny heard wheezing, pulsating music. He and his father pushed through. A man played a funny bellows-like instrument—an accordion, his father later explained—and a young couple danced. People clapped, shouted, laughed, their raucous chorus blending into a joyous cacophony. When the song ended, the dancing stopped and people threw coins into a basket at the musician's feet. Sonny moved but a few meters to a display of watches and gaped at the black-and-white-faced wrist and pocket timepieces. He'd never seen so many at once.

When Sonny turned to his father, he wasn't there. Anxious, Sonny looked in all directions but couldn't spot him. He knew enough to stay in one place until his father came back, laughing, and took Sonny's hand. "There's way too much stimulation for a young boy."

Everywhere men huddled, bantered, argued, with gusto and humor. It was as charming as it was foreign. Someone called another a gonif, a thief, then laughed as if he hadn't meant it. His adversary responded, "Feh," as if spitting on the pavement. Another referred to someone as a yold, a dope, but his friend refined the description to schlemiel, a simpleton. Then Sonny heard an anguished cry—"Oi gevalt!" And when he looked to see the crier in a sea of cascading voices, he pleaded, "What are they doing?"

"They're bargaining, haggling, cajoling over the price," Sonny's father said. "They insult, intimidate, and flatter to make a sale. It's the way we do business." Then as he stood in the midst of the turmoil, he smiled, giving Sonny his first lesson: "It's the eleventh commandment: Never pay what they ask. Offer less, or you'll lose respect."

Sonny was contemplating that injunction when the crowd parted, and he immediately forgot the lesson. He'd never seen the majestic old building so early in the morning, never found it so impressive. At four stories tall, the warehouse loomed over its neighbors. Wide and with windows all around, it seemed to go on forever. People coming, going, standing around, jammed its ancient double doorway. Still holding onto his father's hand, Sonny passed through the magnificent wood doors for the first time as a participant—not a casual Sunday afternoon visitor. Eager not to miss anything, he found his head bobbing in every direction.

Thick pillars reached like giant square trees to an impossibly high ceiling, where exposed wooden beams hung magically, creating a chessboard pattern. Sonny imagined huge pawns, knights, and bishops positioned overhead. Released from his father's grip, he ran with eyes skyward, headlong into a man who caught him before he fell, then patted him on the head. Sonny barely noticed, his attention already newly focused on the horizontal planks covering the windows and walls. They were filled with merchandise of every description. More stalls lined the interior of the great hall.

Once his eyes had their fill, his ears began to pulse with the hum and banter of men and women doing business. But what remained most vivid in Sonny's sensory memory of that day was the aroma of accumulated grime, dried wood, floor wax, and sweat.

"These are my friends," his father declared when they reached his stall, "and they'll soon be yours." He was right. Later on, Sonny couldn't remember when he'd first met Mischa; it seemed he'd always been there. Both boys came to the warehouse because it was their fathers' workplace and they were destined to follow similar paths. They became best friends, apart only during school time—Mischa attended a religious school and Sonny a public one. Running through the aisles, dodging pedestrians, hiding behind pillars, playing in the cellar after school, they made every corner of the vast building their playground. And so it remained.

Hidden in a corner or behind the racks, Sonny and Mischa watched the girls who came with their mothers or sometimes helped their fathers. Like adolescent boys everywhere, the two teased and flirted. Making noises with their hands, pushing and shoving one another, they were guilelessly silly. Older girls disdained them, while the younger ones giggled and ran away.

One girl enjoyed the attention and stayed. Her smile was crooked and toothy but pleasing. Her body and her mind more mature than those of the boys, she showed the curves of adolescence. They were interested in that, but to what end neither yet knew. Hands on hips, she announced, "My name is Sophie Seligmann, and I want to join you two."

Pleased that one of their targets had finally responded, the boys welcomed her, and then they were roamers three. Sophie, like the boys, lived with her family in Spandauer Vorstadt, and her parents, like Mischa's, had emigrated from Poland before she was born. As they got older, Mischa and Sophie found a special kinship, spending so much time together that, like a long-married couple, they finished each other's sentences. Eventually, the three friends moved out to explore the streets of Berlin.

In the meantime the warehouse, with its fuss and flurry and mix of people, shaped and molded the three. The vendors were mostly Jews, mostly from Poland, many of them orthodox. Conspicuous with their long beards and ear locks, they dressed like undertakers—white shirt, tie, black suit often shabby, and worn, black hat. They spoke in a pidgin blend of Yiddish, Polish, and German, with thick accents leaving Sonny endlessly perplexed. His father knew most of them by name and was able to understand what they said without asking them to repeat it. But their strange religious customs marked them—among them was Mischa's father, Herr Hager—as different.

Sonny was familiar with the orthodox Jews from the neighborhood. Their sheer number—like a swarm of blackbirds—made them impossible to ignore. Their arcane and mysterious rituals both intrigued and frightened him. Why did they have to pray each morning? Why did they always wear black? Why didn't they shave? Sonny didn't understand or appreciate their refusal to assimilate. They seemed out of place and time.

If Sonny arrived early enough at the warehouse, he would see a swarm of at least ten—it had to be ten—in the corner of the second floor set aside for morning prayer. Upon their shoulders lay colorful prayer shawls as they bobbed and chanted melancholy dirges to an unfamiliar god. Only then did he see them in anything other than black or white. Sonny's family rarely entered the temple, and when they did, it was outside the rigid rules of the orthodox. When his father told him he was a secular Jew, Sonny thought it was a particular branch of Judaism.

Sonny stopped to stare when he saw the orthodox Jews praying for the first time in what he and Mischa later dubbed "the ghetto." His face clouded, and when he reached the other end of the warehouse, he asked, "Why do they act like that?"

His father turned and looked thoughtfully to the corner where they prayed while Sonny waited for an answer. Finally Sonny felt his father's hand on his shoulder, an unfamiliar move, and heard his familiar hum, as if an internal motor were generating what he was about to impart.

"That's always the question, isn't it? If I could answer that, I'd be a great scholar." He looked from Sonny to the men in black. "What we don't understand makes us uncomfortable. If those fellows find comfort in prayer, it's not for us to judge. If Jews have achieved anything in Germany, it's that we can live in peace, pray to our God, and be left alone."

He pointed. "Where those men came from, they were shunned for their beliefs. What they do is up to them. God forbid the day when they can't stand in their corner and pray."

Sonny felt a slight rebuke in his father's words. He wanted to ask why they couldn't just be like . . . like what? Like his father? like him? He didn't know, so he said nothing.

After that day, sometimes when they passed the ghetto corner—but not often enough to render it meaningless—his father looked over his shoulder to smile at Sonny. Once, following his pregnant glance, Sonny's father warned, "Be wary. People and governments have a way of turning on Jews."

The comment seemed to Sonny out of context; it was confusing. Not until the rise of Fascism did he understand. Unlike the shtetl story, the ghetto lesson endured as a reminder of what is really important. He came to accept the orthodox Jews as equals, though he never fully understood them . . . And in the days, weeks, and months following the deaths of his parents six years later, the warehouse became Sonny's home.

He and his mother endured the shock of his father's death by heart attack while he was reading the newspaper. Carrying on a conversation with her husband from the kitchen, she had been annoyed, then concerned, when he didn't answer. When she saw Morris slumped in his chair, the cup she'd been drying shattered on the floor. She wailed . . .

Then her grief turned to depression, her heart and resolve deteriorating until she no longer wanted to live. She clung to Sonny for support that didn't satisfy, and soon she was bedridden.

The doctors shook their heads and strained to make a diagnosis. She suffered from psychological malaise or from a neurological disorder beyond their ability to diagnose. Those months leading to her death were the hardest in Sonny's young life.

Far worse than his father's quick death, her slow descent was inexplicable and demanding for the care she required. His two aunts helped, and Sonny spent as much time with her as he could, but he had responsibilities in the wake of his father's death. He returned after work and sat beside the bed she rarely left, facing her pallor, like that of a broken bone picked clean. Treatment options were few, so family members and friends recommended Old World remedies. The cloying aroma of camphor permeated the air, refusing to leave the premises. Sonny forever associated that odor with his mother's death.

His mother a month gone, Sonny was closing his stall at the end of the day when he heard the sad, muted strains of a guitar. Mesmerized, he followed the sound to a small stall of costume jewelry, cheap watches, knives, and other miscellany bought from the player's family and connections in Slovenia.

Solomon Pestner was Sinti, born in a squatter's camp on the outskirts of Berlin of parents also born in Germany. The Sinti were related to the Romany, and as Solomon liked to say with a wink, "Many lies have been told about my people over the years, and you can believe them all. We're nomads, never stay in one place too long, and that's what gets us into trouble." But for Solomon it was no longer true. He lived in rented rooms near the warehouse with his young wife, Maria, and a son—the first of what promised to be many strong and healthy children.

Sonny admired Solomon's resiliency, easy charm, and prodigious musical ability. Despite his difficult childhood, his family's Sinti camp being forced to move repeatedly due to police harassment, Solomon was never cynical. Though he was short in stature, his self-confidence projected a bigger man. He was dark, with jet-black hair combed back, and he had a prominent nose. Like others, he was surprised to learn Sonny was Jewish, but he laughed heartily, slapped him on the back, and welcomed him to the clan.

Other Sinti men worked in the warehouse, but none of them played the guitar like Solomon.

From the sudden death of his father and through his mother's swift decline, Sonny felt the loneliness of an orphan, though by that time he was coming of age. Searching for an outlet for the grief he could not express, he embraced the sad Sinti strains of Solomon's music. But he looked most for support to Joseph Kay, the bookseller. Joseph's small stall in a corner of the top floor of the warehouse held a bounty of old books, magazines, and newspapers.

Only a few days after Sonny encountered the accordion player and dancers, he wandered into Joseph's musty space. Endlessly patient, Joseph guided Sonny through his collection, letting him sit cross-legged on the floor for hours, reading. During this heyday of photojournalism, dozens of publications displayed pictures of every corner of Berlin—and of the world beyond. Sonny soaked it in and yearned for more. Joseph accommodated his young friend, encouraging him to read and explore. Slowly they grew close, almost becoming family—for Joseph had none—as well as mentor and mentee. That Sonny knew little of Joseph's background mattered little—he knew only that Joseph wasn't Jewish.

He did know that, unlike his parents, Joseph and the bookstall were always there.

2

Without friends no one would choose to live,
though he had all other goods.
—Aristotle

In the seven months from April to October 1931—his twenty-second year—Sonny met Red Otto on Ku'damm, Polly at the little café, and Albert at the warehouse. He also accepted Franco's proposal and began working with Emil. Change was in the air.

Street-corner orators spewed Nazi and Communist rubbish from almost every corner, or so it seemed, and their antics often led to brawls. Because of that, Sonny normally avoided such harangues, but one beautiful spring night, he stopped at the edge of a small group to listen to a passionate, clean-cut, young man in uniform, leather jacket, and small-brimmed worker's cap, a small goatee clinging to his chin. Sonny later asked Otto why all the Communists looked like Lenin, as if they came from central casting. Otto shrugged, pleading ignorance.

That day's chance encounter led to an enduring friendship despite Sonny's refusal to join the party, though his friend Mischa joined.

Standing atop a small wood box, the young "Lenin" delivered his cri de coeur, clutching a small book, probably *Das Kapital,* to his chest. Sonny was drawn not by the message but by the man's fervor and the faces of his listeners. He sensed in them a yearning for something more than dreams and their one suit of clothes.

With fist raised, the speaker denounced industrialists, Nazis, and capitalism in its temple, Kufurstendamm—the regular list of evils. Then Sonny felt Otto's elbow in his ribs. He hadn't paid much attention to the guy in the black leather jacket next to him, who now pointed to two Brownshirts standing across the road. One was fat, the other old, and though their faces were in shadow, Sonny sensed their disapproval.

Waving his hand as if batting a fly, the man declared, "Those farts don't worry me, but they might have some nasty friends nearby."

That should have scared Sonny, but drawn by the stranger's bravado, he took a closer look. The beardless man had a thin, slightly ominous scar on his right cheek, eyes that registered calm self-assurance, not anger.

"They don't take a shit unless they're told to, and then they fuck it up," he said.

Sonny laughed at that, then imagined him as Brecht's Mackie Messer in a bowler hat, singing, "See the shark with teeth like razors . . . and Macheath's got a knife."

Instead he heard, "Name's Otto. Join us for beer, and I'll fill your head so full of propaganda you'll think you were born with a hammer and sickle up your ass." With that, Sonny's new friend laughed, stuck out his hand, slapped him on the shoulder, and directed him to the Hammer & Sickle in Neukölln.

The speaker had finished and seemed to be waiting for Otto.

"I'm Sonny," Sonny yelled.

Otto raised his fist in salute, without a backwards glance.

The fellow with the bravado and easy manner had impressed Sonny, and he wanted to get to know him. Not that he wanted to join the party. But Otto might make a good story . . .

. . . Several days later Sonny exited Hermannplatz Station, repeating to himself the words "Hammer & Sickle," like change jingling in his pocket. He walked onto the open space of the plaza, his footfalls echoing on the cobblestones, and immediately sensed a change in the tone of the neighborhood. Massive unemployment had scarred this already shabby area of the city.

Sonny walked with head down, hands in his pockets, past decaying tenements exhausted by a lack of maintenance, which the dim streetlight barely concealed. Hard faces masked the residents' sense of shame at the squalor there. Passing an alley, he met the stench of uncollected garbage and automatically covered his nose. There was unemployment in the Mitte, Sonny knew, but this was unfamiliar territory.

People congregated on the sidewalks on this warm spring evening, just as they did in his own neighborhood, to talk and pass the time. Not all the faces were hard, and children played about, but something seemed missing. Then Sonny realized there was no laughter here.

Within ten minutes Sonny turned onto Pannier Strasse and saw the familiar symbol of the proletariat and the peasantry above a plain brown door with a small window. Hesitating, he stood on the opposite sidewalk to watch as the door opened. A bearded old man in a worker's cap and navy coat shuffled out of the tavern. Muttering, he rocked for a moment, looked in both directions, hitched up his pants, and slowly moved away. Sonny crossed the street, paused to look at the old man's receding silhouette, took a breath of stale Neukölln night air, pulled the door open, and went in.

Heads turned toward the unfamiliar face, then returned to beer, conversation, melancholy. Sonny took in the Hammer & Sickle's aroma of cheap tobacco, beer, and sweat. He walked by a bulletin board filled with papers but didn't stop to read.

No more than fifteen men and no women sat at the ten or so mismatched tables. This felt different from other workingmen's bars; Sonny sensed a quiet seriousness. KPD posters lined the walls, giving it the feel more of a shrine to a movement than of a tavern. Neither Otto nor the speaker from the park was in sight, so Sonny walked toward the bar. His eyes immediately focused on a big poster in lush red, fervent yellow, and brilliant blue. It showed three attractive young workers, two men and a woman, standing with fists raised, their eyes locked on some distant horizon beyond the smoke-belching factories forming the backdrop. "Workers of the World Unite. Throw off Your Chains," shouted the text above their image.

"What'll you have?"

Sonny jumped as the low raspy voice, sandpaper across wood, broke his reverie. Two small eyes fronting a nearly bald, round head, a menacing forehead scar, and a scowl confronted him from across the bar.

Sonny cleared his throat, managing only a weak response: "A beer." Then softly, "Please."

Grunting unintelligibly, the huge man moved to the end of the bar, filled a mug, returned, and plunked it down, spilling foam. In one motion he reached for a towel, swiped the surface clean, grunted, and walked away. Sonny's face felt hot as he glanced at the bartender, but he was relieved to be so soon ignored.

After several gulps of beer had worked their calm, Sonny began to think about a local KPD cell and the part Otto played in its operation. Somewhere in Berlin the KPD had a central committee taking orders from Moscow. How that related to Otto wasn't clear. Sonny scanned the bar, returning once or twice to the poster as he gradually lost himself in thought. Then, sensing a presence, he turned to see Otto smiling at him.

"Good, I'm glad you came," said Otto. He turned to the bartender: "Fred, a beer please" . . .

. . . In the six months following that first visit, Sonny returned often to the Hammer & Sickle, to his growing friendship with Otto. Mischa, not to be excluded, had tagged along, and feeling a kinship with the men and their message, joined the party. Sonny refused to join, but he figured that Mischa's membership evened the score. And as it turned out, friendship trumped politics. That he was not a comrade mattered little in his banter with Otto and Mischa about art and film, about that damn poster, and occasionally about politics.

Sonny and Otto's meetings were oases in a desert of work for both of them. For Sonny, work meant making the rounds of the warehouse and of his other contacts in Scheunenviertel, looking for merchandise to sell to his regular and walk-up customers in the warehouse and to small shopkeepers and street vendors.

Like his father, Sonny sold whatever turned a profit: clothing, shoes, utensils, tobacco—you name it. His business was close to the ground with low overhead, and he was his own boss. Being a peddler meant living on the margins, and that suited him just fine. His suppliers at the warehouse and beyond were a colorful lot that he'd known for years. They were young and old, mostly Jewish, and wearing the style of yesterday, today, or no style at all. Interaction with these quirky, urban characters was entertaining. If he had to quit tomorrow, he'd miss them dearly . . .

"What do you do for a living?" Otto had asked, taking a long pull on his beer.

Sonny flashed on the warehouse, thought of his sparse room in Herr Wagner's flat, his chronic shortage of cash. Then he gave his little-bit-of-this, little-bit-of-that, just-enough-to-get-by spiel and waited for the hard sell. When it didn't come, he added, "But I want to be a journalist. I've had several reviews published."

"Reviews?" Otto's lips curled into a sneer, and he shook his head. "It's what you do that interests me. That's the measure of a man. Not his unfulfilled aspirations."

Sonny frowned. "But aspirations are important. Certainly you aspire to win the next election! You do contest elections, or am I wrong?"

Otto winced: "Touché." Then he smiled. "Still, how a man houses, feeds, and clothes himself and his family is what's important. Do you have a family?"

Then, discovering they were both orphans, Otto and Sonny raised their mugs.

Otto, scowling, admitted, "There is a seductive romanticism to journalism now that Germany has a free press. Everyone has a mouthpiece: We've got *Die Rote Fahne*, the Nazi assholes have *Der Angriff* . . . and then there's Münzenberg. He's sympathetic to us, but he's a capitalist and can't be trusted." He paused and kept his eyes on Sonny, as if waiting for a reaction.

"And then there're all the rest," he continued. "Pure garbage, nothing but entertainment and exploitation . . . so-called exposés picturing degradation and poverty next to ads for toothpaste and women's panties. It's all bullshit! They don't care. All they want is circulation, and only the loudest voices penetrate the din." Otto looked at Sonny hard, holding his gaze until Sonny felt uncomfortable.

"'Whoever controls the streets controls the masses. And whoever controls the masses controls the state.' Who said that?" Otto demanded.

Sonny considered the question, then answered. "Lenin? Trotsky?"

Otto shook his head, showing his white teeth in a mischievous grin: "That little shit Goebbels!" Then he surprised Sonny again: "I wish we had a devious mind like his."

Otto rubbed his forehead with his fingers as if trying to coax out a propaganda campaign. But he quickly returned to the present: "What are you? Certainly not a Nazi! Maybe a nationalist?" He stared, searching Sonny's face, shaking his head: "No, and not center religious—which leaves social democrat or socialist. Or maybe you're nothing. Are you a political agnostic, afraid of involvement? You go to plays, look at pretty pictures, and write reviews."

Otto turned Sonny's aspirations against him like an accusation: "Are you one of the apathetic sybarites sucking mother's milk from the tit of Berlin?" But he couldn't keep at it with a straight face. Laughing at his own taunts, Otto slapped Sonny on the shoulder and raised his mug: "I should have been a poet."

Sonny, who'd reddened and raised his hands as if to ward off an attack, now relaxed a little. "All right, all right," he said, "I admit I've avoided politics. There's never been time, and money's tight. I started working with my father at age twelve, and I haven't stopped since. Politics are dangerous—all that brawling between your lot and the Nazis . . . Okay, you want an answer? I'm a Jew, so I hate the Nazis. But as to you and the others, I have no commitment. All I know is that nothing ever gets done. There's only stalemate. Unemployment is high. People are suffering. Hell, I saw it in people's faces on my way here. There you have it!"

Otto smiled. "There's always room in the party for another Jew, even if you don't look it." He winked at Sonny and beckoned, "Join Liebknecht and Red Rosa, our martyred Jewish saints!" His smile broadened with his hyperbole. "You're like clay soft for molding." Otto cupped his hands together, slowly kneading.

Sonny laughed, though he knew a hard sell was coming.

Otto leaned in and started, "Ja, times are tough, millions are out of work, and the government's doing nothing. The world economy's in the toilet, and what's left is controlled by the cartels, who keep it all for themselves. Sure, they spread little bits, like manure for the hacks that run the government for them."

Heads turned as Otto's voice rose. "They don't give a shit about the working man and woman. Factory worker or office worker—it doesn't matter—if they're lucky enough to have a job, wages are low, and the boss lords it over them: 'Be grateful to have this lousy, stinking job!'"

Several men shouted, "Jawohl!"

"Law and order is what they want—not what we want. Chaos and disorder are bad for business but good for us." Otto's fingers rapped loudly on the bar; he smiled then sneered, "Chaos is good. It confuses people. The system goes all wobbly, and then it collapses." Like a preacher, he raised his palms—as if it were that simple.

Just like the Nazis, Sonny thought, raising his eyes to meet Fred the bartender's glower.

Franco Romano was a short, rotund, charming Italian in his mid-forties. A fixture at the warehouse, he seemed a peddler like everyone else, though Sonny suspected there was more to him than that. They had never done business until that fall day in 1931 when Franco offered Sonny four cases of Chianti at "a very good price," or so he said.

After five minutes of haggling, the wine belonged to Sonny. Of course, he knew nothing about wine—his purchase was a violation of his father's code of buying nothing he didn't know about—and it seemed too easy. Then Franco surprised Sonny with an invitation for dinner that night at the Veneto, a small café near Alexanderplatz.

His cheerful goodbye left Sonny wondering what that invitation was all about . . . but then he was distracted by Mischa's voice: "Hey, Sonny! I've got some new Swiss watches. Hurry, or they'll be gone. I'll give you a good deal. You don't want to be left out." Mischa's pitch was good. Like Sonny, he was a natural salesman.

"Swiss watches, my ass," Sonny parried. "About as Swiss as a Yiddish accent."

"Not so loud," Mischa admonished.

Sonny was on his way to meet his friend Paul, an American, slumming in Berlin like many of the other foreigners with money. Mischa said he couldn't join them: "Some people have to work!" But he suggested they get together at the H & S that night. Since signing on with the KPD, Mischa had jumped in with both feet. He spent most evenings working on the next election or talking politics.

Sonny waved over his shoulder but didn't answer. Before leaving the floor, he stopped to lean against a column and watch Albert in his stall. After Albert first appeared on the floor that year, Sonny had heard someone called him a striver. And when he first met Albert, he knew what the guy had meant: Albert was constantly on the make.

"There's more to life than this small-time selling," Albert declared, flinging his arms about like a stork about to take flight. "I'm getting to the big time. You'll see." His gaze wandered to the distant horizon, and he repeated the line. Sonny had no idea what he was looking for. He doubted Albert knew either.

Albert was rail thin, with short blond hair and small, darting, blue eyes. Clad in white shirt and a tie, he kept his hands in perpetual motion, a cigarette in one of them or between his lips, the other hand in the air, then into his pocket, jingling loose change, back out, pointing, his head in a perpetual blue cloud. Moving frenetically around his stall, the blond-headed blur arranged pots, pans, and dishes this way and that, attempting a pleasant display. Often he would frown, stop for an instant, dart forward to rearrange, then step back and start again, never satisfied.

That was the essential Albert, a sharp-angled caricature from a George Grosz cartoon. About Sonny's age, Albert sold everything from pots and pans to shoes from his home state of Bavaria. Sonny couldn't imagine anyone more in contrast to the orthodox Jews working at the warehouse. Yet Albert seemed to get along well with his neighbors. Nearly breathless from watching Albert's gyrations, Sonny walked over to greet him. They made plans to get together a couple of days later. Appointment made, Albert said goodbye and returned to his work . . .

Sonny and Paul had first met at the Pink Slipper Cabaret in the West End, as 1930 came to a close. Several young women and men (they were indistinguishable) with very short hair or shaved heads, lips painted black, wearing tight jackets and pants, white shirts and thin ties, worked the tables. They cultivated an atmosphere of sophisticated ambivalence as they moved archly about the club, taking orders. Over the music, Johnny the bartender asked Sonny and Paul what they'd have, thinking the two were together at the bar.

Their startled expressions said that they weren't, so he took their separate orders and seamlessly fetched their drinks. Always in black tuxedo and starched white shirt, hair slicked back, Johnny was the master of his bar. If you needed a girl for the night or a snort up your nose, if you needed to place a bet or get a tip on what was hot in Berlin, Johnny was your man.

When the band took a break, the two young men began to talk, and Sonny detected Paul's accented German. When he asked whether Paul was American, he answered, "Guilty as charged . . . Paul Glaser from Cleveland, Ohio." And he extended his hand.

Paul's grandfather had immigrated to America as a young man, and Paul had learned Deutsch from him. Instead of completing the graduation tour of Europe offered by his father, he had headed straight for Berlin and stayed.

"That was several months ago," Paul noted with a self-deprecating grin. "Life is wonderful. I have a degree in English. And I'm prepared to do absolutely nothing worthwhile." He sighed with resignation: "But it doesn't matter—I'm expected to go into the family business."

When Sonny asked what kind of business, Paul said his father owned a department store in Cleveland. Then he smiled wryly and whispered, "He thinks I'm training in marketing and retailing, but I spend most of my time in clubs. If he ever found out, I'd be on the first ship home. All I'll really be able to do is run a speakeasy."

They laughed, and Paul asked Sonny what he did for a living.

At the end of the night, the two men wandered the streets together, talking and laughing, oblivious to the cold. Finally, Paul left for his boardinghouse on the Louisenplatz, near the Charlottenburg fortress, close to the Kufurstendamm theater district; Sonny, for his room in Spandauer Vorstadt. In the ensuing months, the two young men frequented clubs, cafés, theaters, and the cinema together . . .

Sonny arrived at the café before Paul, took an open table in the back, and waited for his coffee to cool a bit. The din of conversation and clatter of cutlery and dishes formed a lively backdrop. Because of its location—at the edge of the Mitte, near the site of the former Oranienburg Gate—and its delicious pastry, the little café was a popular spot. Sonny scanned the room, noting several middle-aged, middle-class men in cheap suits. Gnawing on the carcass of a once prosperous city, barely eking out a living, they were a world away in outlook and temperament from Otto's Neukölln.

Sonny's eyes passed over the rucksacks and open guidebooks of several tourists to two elegantly dressed women with shopping bags, then to a young woman alone at a small table across the room. She appeared to be reading, and her hair fell over her eyes so that only the gentle curve of her nose and the red pout of her lips were visible. Her profile reminded Sonny of the face on an ancient coin he'd seen in a magazine. He was still staring when Paul sat down.

Following his friend's eyes, Paul remarked, "She's pretty."

After some mild cajoling, Sonny crossed the café and asked the woman he came to know as Polly whether she'd like to join him at their table. She slowly marked her page in Thomas Mann's *Mario and the Magician* and looked up. Sonny smiled and pointed across the room to Paul, who gave a little wave.

"Is it good?"

"What?" There was a hint of laughter in her voice as she craned her neck to get a better look at the interloper.

"The book."

"Oh yes, very good. A book for our troubled times, or so the critics say."

Stammering, Sonny said, "I . . . I don't usually do this."

She cut him off. "You mean accost young women while they're reading?" Her laugh blunted the barb.

Sonny flushed and grinned broadly. "Will you join us?"

She stared up at him, then: "Why not? You look harmless enough."

Mumbling that he'd have to do something about that, he followed her to the table where Paul waited. For more than an hour, they chatted about Berlin, the theater, cinema, and such, while skimming over their personal lives.

When Polly spoke, she gazed directly at Sonny, her eyelashes sweeping up and down to reveal her animated green eyes. Occasionally she glanced away, searching for the right word, then pursed her lips. Her light brown hair framed her earnestly creased forehead, slightly prominent cheekbones, and firm chin.

Sonny became so engrossed in her physical appearance that he lost any idea of what she was saying. He managed to nod appropriately, hoping she hadn't noticed. At one point Polly spoke of Mann's opposition to Nazism, noting that his wife was a Jewess. Sonny approved, then disclosed that the company she was keeping was Jewish. With a questioning look, she studied his face.

"True, I don't look it," Sonny responded with a harmless smirk, "but then, neither do you."

Polly blushed, looking vulnerable and even prettier than before.

The conversation turned serious as the three spoke of their fears of a Nazi takeover. Polly had taken a class in the history of anti-Semitism at the university. "If you already know this, stop me," she began. "Before the Industrial Revolution, merchants needed money to finance their enterprises, but church decrees against usury made that difficult. So it was in that context that Jews with education and savvy—and of course, capital—filled a need."

Neither Sonny nor Paul stopped her; they listened intently.

"Segregated, living in ghettos, Jews were the perfect choice to finance the Christian business community. Someone had to be the banker, or we'd still be mired in a feudal system. Hence the rise of the Rothschilds and the Warburgs." Her voice took on an authoritative edge as she looked from one to the other. "Jews were tax collectors for the crown, which did nothing for their popularity—I'm sure you're well aware. With their tradition of learning and skill in commerce, it's no wonder so many became successful in Germany. Of course, it's more complicated more that."

"Always is," Paul noted.

Then Sonny teased, "Thank you for the insightful discourse, Professor Polly."

She bowed slightly. "You're welcome. I'm so smart that I'm a sales clerk in a department store."

Polly's self-deprecation was charming, and besides being attractive, she was clever. Sonny liked the determined yet feminine set of her jaw, the smile at the corners of her eyes, and the way she held her hands one atop the other on the table until she raised one to deliver a point.

"I'm leaving at the first whiff of a Nazi takeover, but it won't be easy for you," Paul said.

That brought a thoughtful silence . . . Sonny broke it: "The extremes are killing the Republic, and I hate the political violence. I refuse to join a political party, but my friend Mischa recently joined the KPD."

Paul rolled his eyes and sighed sarcastically, his lack of subtlety rivaling the sweet frosting on their pastries. That rankled Sonny, and though he tried not to show it, the atmosphere became frosty. Polly could scarcely miss it.

Paul was a spoiled and committed capitalist, essentially a conservative—not in the German but in the American mold. He was a firm believer in democracy and capitalism. But he found the constant political talk tiresome, and he blamed Mischa.

While Sonny was frequently impatient with Mischa, he didn't care to have Paul criticizing his friend, especially in front of Polly. Taking on Mischa was his job.

While Sonny stewed, Polly jumped in to note that it was hard not to talk about the roiling nature of German politics, especially with so much at stake. Paul grudgingly agreed but didn't elaborate, and another uncomfortable silence followed. Sonny broke the chill, asking Polly why she had quit the university, though he figured he knew the answer.

"Couldn't afford it, so I went to work." Shrugging off her obvious disappointment, she added, "There was nothing to be done about it. Why should I be different from thousands of others? I'm a clerk at Wertheim's—women's glove department. It pays the rent."

That provided Paul an opening to tell her about his study of the German department store model to take back with him to Cleveland. Then he winked and said, "We'll have to see more of you."

Sonny agreed, trying not to sound too eager.

Then Polly turned to Sonny. "It's your turn."

Sonny put his elbow on the table, rested his chin on his hand, and pondered. He settled on a little bit of this, little bit of that. In the end, he glossed over his work as a peddler to speak of his aspirations. As he described the two reviews to his credit, he grew more animated.

"Good luck! Maybe I just had coffee with the next Joseph Roth," Polly responded with a smile. She noted the sudden quiet, and they looked around at the empty café. They'd talked the afternoon away, running the gauntlet of introductory song and dance. Sonny drank cold coffee, and Paul pulled a paper from his pocket to read, while Polly returned Thomas Mann to her bag and moved as if to rise.

"I enjoyed our talk very much, but it's time to leave," she said.

Standing on the pavement with Polly after Paul left, Sonny apologized, "Paul and Mischa don't get on well, sort of an oil-and-water thing."

"Happens in the best of families," Polly said, waving it off.

Since they both lived nearby, Sonny offered to walk her home. A few minutes on their way, he said, "It's all very troubling and it seems to be getting worse." He explained how one friend called him naïve while the other admonished him not to be too pessimistic. "It's confusing. Guess which one is Mischa."

Polly guessed correctly, then laughed, "You must be quite a pair."

"We cancel each other out," Sonny noted sardonically. "I probably *am* naïve." He brightened. "Let's not spoil a nice walk with politics."

So they talked of other things as they moved through the back alleys of the old barn quarter. Sonny learned that Polly came from Zwickau, in Saxony near the Czech border, that she had been in Berlin for several years, and that she rented a room from an older couple. Everything else remained vague . . . but then, she didn't know much about him, either.

When they reached her home, a clean three-story building with curtained windows and a brown door, Polly apologized. "I'd invite you in, but I need to clear visitors first."

"That's not a problem. I have an appointment, anyway," Sonny assured her.

"A hot date," she teased.

Sonny felt his cheeks flush and shook his head. "No, I'm meeting a man for dinner to talk business."

Polly smiled crookedly as he stuttered, explaining in more detail than necessary. He did manage to say, "I'd like to see you again."

"That would be nice," Polly said without hesitation.

They agreed to meet under the Zoo Station clock two days later, at eight o'clock. After they said goodbye, Sonny watched Polly disappear into the building.

As he made his way home, Sonny languidly traced her pleasing profile, from the set of her jaw to the swell of her breasts to the curve of her calves, in his mind's eye. Suddenly he was filled with a longing he hadn't felt for—God, he couldn't remember how long. So many things about her were attractive. The girls he'd known possessed one, maybe two of Polly's better qualities, but their mutual groping was usually what brought him back for more.

He felt lighter and more carefree than he had in weeks, all because of a chance encounter with a lovely, intelligent woman . . .

3

Secret guilt by silence is betrayed.
—John Dryden

Franco took a long swig of grappa, licked his lips, leaned back, and dragged on his cigar. His hooded eyes topped the faint sigh of bacchanalian satisfaction escaping his lips. The detritus of the longest meal Sonny had ever eaten was strewn before him. They'd spent two hours laying siege to five courses, starting with small plates, then bowls, then a large plate: bread, soup, noodles flecked with a green sauce, a steak, vegetables, cheese, and finally a fabulous torte.

Stifling a belch, Sonny tasted the torte a second time and drained the tiny cup of coffee that suddenly appeared. He hesitated as he reached for his glass of the opaque liqueur Franco so enjoyed, afraid to open his mouth to anything else lest he explode.

Crimson spots from the 1927 Chiantis they'd emptied and other bits of refuse littered the white linen tablecloth. Other than a Passover Seder, no meal had taken so long to eat, and other than the coffee, nothing was familiar though all of it was delicious. Sonny silently counted the bottles of wine they'd consumed, reaching three when his ears pricked at Franco's voice coming through the fog.

"How long have we known each other?" Franco asked in a voice dulled by wine—or perhaps it was Sonny's dulled hearing.

He had to think. "Can't say for sure, but . . ." he replied, stifling another belch, " . . . since I was a kid." His tongue felt heavy, words hard to form. His inner voice was muffled, as if his head were filled with cotton.

Franco smiled indulgently at his young dinner companion and said, "Your father was a fine man. I enjoyed doing business with him over the years." Repeating that sentiment, he digressed to the heady time when he'd arrived in Berlin after the Great War, after the Kaiser's abdication and the chaos that followed. His eyes drifted, a memory emerging as he recalled the Spartacan revolt.

Sonny's eyelids were heavy. He strained to follow Franco's words, but only a few penetrated his mind: "Crazy . . . Communists . . . Fascisti . . ." After maybe five minutes of this, he lost track of time. Franco was talking about business—or was it the Communists? Sonny heard him say times were difficult. Then he repeated, "Your father was a fine man."

Sonny suppressed a smile.

Suddenly out of nowhere, as if cued by a lull in the conversation, the proprietor of the restaurant materialized, bowed slightly to Sonny, then Franco, and spoke quietly in Italian before he disappeared.

"Did you enjoy the meal?" Franco asked.

Nodding, Sonny said, "It was delicious. Thank you."

Franco accepted his gratitude with a wave. "My pleasure."

Sonny figured the reason he was there better come soon or he'd fall asleep at the table. Meanwhile Franco talked with animation about the warehouse, the troubling times, and the increasing difficulty of making a living.

What Franco did for a living was the subject of rumor, but Sonny had the feeling he was going to find out. Supposedly Franco had fathered a child by Hildy, a chorus girl at the Pink Slipper—the leggy blonde who was a half-foot taller than Franco—she was what kept him in Berlin. But Franco wasn't talking about her.

Franco looked around the nearly empty room, leaned forward until his eyes met Sonny's: "Your father and I—we did business for many years and learned to trust one another."

Sonny nodded and Franco continued, saying their dealings were mostly off the books—as if Sonny knew what he meant. But wasn't *everything* cash—off the books?

Franco moved on. "We dealt in merchandise that came into Germany through *irregular* channels." He paused to mention Sonny's father's death, to say how sorry he was, how difficult it must have been. Working his lips in and out like a bellows, he said, "I'm looking for someone I can trust, an associate. The last man proved untrustworthy."

Sonny was perplexed, and his face showed it. With the buzzing like mosquitos in his head, he almost missed the raison d'état for being at the Veneto.

Franco's eyes narrowed. "You do not know?"

"Know what?" The wine and Franco's obtuse commentary had Sonny completely confused.

Bemused, Franco drank more grappa and said, "Let me be clear. People can be very inventive when they need to be, and the times required creativity. So after the war, a thriving black market existed in tobacco, alcohol, wine, and other things hard to obtain. Remember—of course, you are too young to recall—Germany was exhausted after losing the war and reparations ate up what capital remained. Smugglers filled a void that benefited both sides, that created opportunity. People got what they needed. The suppliers made a living. We all—your father and I—knew the risks."

Slowly Franco painted the picture of a black market involving Sonny's father. All Sonny had known was that his father was a small-time merchant. Hell, he'd learned the trade from him! Goods with questionable provenance occasionally came his way, but he knew not to ask questions . . . and he had profited. So, what had his father done for Franco?

Suddenly Sonny felt stupid for not knowing, for missing the clues. But what clues? When he was young, running around the warehouse with Mischa and Sophie, missing it was easy, but what about when he was older?

Sonny knew families had secrets—how well could a son ever know his father, especially if he died young? Fearing the direction of the conversation, Sonny asked, "Was my father a smuggler?"

Franco pondered the question a little too long, then, shaking his head, said, "Not really a smuggler." He took another sip of grappa. "He was a fine man, Sonny."

Shit, not that again.

"Others smuggled—not your father. Once the goods were in Germany, I sold the merchandise, through him and others. That was our arrangement for years, and it was all quite regular. You see, we ran it like a business."

"Regular?" Sonny protested. "I doubt the police would agree." Images of his father lurking in dark alleys, making deals with unsavory people, swirled in his head.

"Yes, there's that," Franco acknowledged. "Mussolini made the trains run on time, but everything else runs on money. For a few liras, anything goes. People have smuggled goods into Germany since the end of the war. When the Fascisti came to power, we continued with the blessing of the provincial government, so long as it got a piece of the action. My principals paid more in bribes to keep the operation going, part of the cost of doing a business that was extremely profitable.

"At that time, I was a mere functionary, a foot soldier, in this enterprise. Your father and I came to trust each other, and it worked for years. We never got rich, but through troubled times we made ends meet. There were others, so we cut up the pie and lived in peace and avoided the attention of the police.

"Others, the higher-ups," he pointed to the ceiling, "made big money. Not me. You see, I am a small fish in this rather large sea." Franco drank more grappa, licked his lips, and considered his words.

Then in more detail, he described a network, goods moving from Italy through Austria and into Germany. He said the Swiss were officious and sanctimonious, hard to bribe, so they avoided Switzerland. He shuddered, took another swallow as if to cleanse his distaste, and continued.

"Bribery was the key. It was only a matter of time to find those susceptible, to unlock the border. Over the years I have learned that few can resist." He rubbed his thumb and forefinger together. "Now I run my own smaller, leaner enterprise through sources in Belgium—even more profitable than before."

Franco's eyes revealed little. Absently picking at a hangnail, he said, "Now do you understand?"

Sonny nodded hesitantly, and Franco continued.

"What you see every day at the warehouse is a front. I have to appear legitimate." His shoulders rose in an extravagant shrug. "What if someone talked, and the police got nosy? The wine I sold you was completely legal and came with an import license. But there is much to sell that is not—cigarettes, wine, aged cognac, cheese, caviar, all that and more."

Sonny was still stuck on the notion that his father was a smuggler. The word skipped across his mind like the repeating chorus of an illicit *Hallelujah*.

Franco's proposal silenced the music: "I need an associate to build a relationship, someone I can trust, who will trust me—like your father."

Sonny only half heard, his face screwed to incomprehension.

Franco reiterated, "The business of buying and selling is in your blood." His hand closed into a fist emphasizing his faith in his young friend. "I am inviting you into my organization."

Sonny put both elbows on the table, clasped his hands, and exhaled. Now he understood—Franco wanted him to be his fence.

Franco kept talking, trying to close the deal. "Ironically, the best in my business are the honest ones. That old maxim about honor among thieves is true." A grin spread across his face. "A little bit of this and a little bit of that. That's life, is it not? The money is good, and it is hard to get out." He laughed heartily, took another drink, placed the glass on the table. He stared at Sonny, his smile gone, then said, "I am offering you an opportunity too good to turn down . . . Sleep on it. You can tell me tomorrow."

Still in a daze, Sonny thanked Franco for the meal and said he'd have an answer in a few days. Standing to leave, he felt lightheaded, faint. Putting his hands on the table, he leaned over as if to speak. Instead he heard Franco's voice.

"Two days at the most. I need someone, and I picked you." Franco's fixed and firm tone suggested the deal was done.

Sonny stared at the shadows his body cast on the table. He was in his parent's kitchen with the chairs moved to the windowless wall. The familiar smells of his father's tobacco and shaving lotion wafted in from the other room. His father sat in the corner easy chair in which years later he had died. Sonny thought he heard the ticking of the parlor clock. He looked up into Franco's impassive face . . .

Outside, Sonny took several deep breaths to clear his head. Automobile exhaust from Alexanderplatz perfumed the air. Spotting three SAs leafleting at the corner, he crossed to the other side of the street. Only days earlier, he had watched a middle-aged Jewish man passing a similar group. One SA had knocked off his cap to a hissing chorus: "Fucking Jew." The terrified man ran, leaving his hat in the gutter. Sonny had retrieved and returned it, the man offering quick thanks but smelling of humiliation and fear.

Sonny's mood soured. They could all go to hell! He was more than a little drunk, his thoughts a jumble. He struggled to push the SA from his mind. All he really wanted to think about was Polly, but Franco's disclosure had pushed her aside.

Sonny walked beyond Alexanderplatz, then turned down an empty street. Hearing strange noises as he passed a dark alley, he squinted into the black, barely catching sight of a vague figure. Frightened, he strained to make sense of what he thought he saw and heard—inchoate echoes of "Sonny, Sonny," then indecipherable rambling. He was about to run when the ghost became material—a derelict stumbling from the alley. Sonny laughed nervously, folded his arms across his chest, and kept moving.

Walking along, he conjured the memory of his father talking quietly to his mother in the kitchen. He couldn't hear what they were saying, but he knew it was serious by the way his father stood slightly bent forward, his arms extended. His mother's head was down and her shoulders sagged as if at bad news. His father seemed exasperated by her lack of understanding.

Whatever it was, she'd taken it badly, and annoyance covered her husband's face as he left the kitchen. Sonny was thirteen or fourteen years old, not too young to know something was wrong. His father said he'd be gone for a few days on business. Over his shoulder Sonny saw his mother, small and forlorn, standing in the kitchen wringing her hands on her apron, her eyes moist.

"Where are you going?"

His father refused to answer, saying just that he had to go. Sonny sensed the tension but hadn't a label for it, not then. Years later, as his mother lay dying, he had felt the apprehension, the dependence, what she may have felt at that earlier time. But then Sonny had seen only adventure, and he'd wanted to go, too.

"Please," he'd whined, but his father scolded him and said no. There was school, and he'd be back in a couple days. Now Sonny remembered him saying there was merchandise to be collected from an out-of-town dealer. He'd imagined his father on a train, moving through a countryside filled with trees, farms, and villages. People waved to his father, and he waved back. Upon his return two days later, he was in a sour mood and wouldn't talk about his trip. Sonny's questions had remained unanswered until now.

Franco's offer, the opportunity to follow his father footsteps into a world of petty crooks and smugglers, was a shock, but what he'd learned about his father was truly unsettling. And the charming Italian he'd known all his adult life was really his father's boss in a smuggling ring! Was that why his mother cried? If she'd known, why hadn't he?

Sonny had never known his mother to work out of the home. His father worked alone, except when Sonny helped. But that was later. His father never left—well, just that once. Could there have been other times? And did he really help his father? They walked around the warehouse together, visiting vendors and making friends in his father's cheery way. Was it all an act?

Sonny's thoughts moved to what he had on his plate now—his little bit of this, little bit of that, a meager living while he played at journalism. He'd done little to advance his prospects as a writer. Was it a naïve dream? Should he flush his dreams for money in his pocket, perhaps a bigger flat? The prospect was as startling as it was incredible. And what did Franco mean by "once you're in, it's hard to get out"?

Sonny stopped looking down alleys and imagined what it would be like selling perfume or watches to shops on Kufurstendamm, cigars and cigarettes to tobacconists, lingerie to a women's shop, and good wine, like the Chianti, to cabarets. Hell, that's what he knew—there was nothing dramatic in that. But if all the merchandise was stolen . . . he looked guiltily over his shoulder . . .

So it went, back and forth, until he reached Herr Wagner's flat and dragged himself to bed.

Sonny's father wasn't through with him yet. He returned in the night wearing an expensive, beautifully cut suit and a bright red silk tie . . . Was it really his father? The face was his, they were in the flat, his mother in her simple housedress of muted cotton. Neither he nor his mother took notice of his father's fancy clothes or of his puffing on a big cigar.

"Mother, Sonny is going to be fine. Don't worry. He'll be just fine."

His mother's face melted into the smiling and satiated Franco, smacking his lips. Both men laughed, softly at first, then louder, pointing to a table piled with cash. They fell to their knees, shaking so hard with mirth that they had to clutch their hands to their bellies.

Sonny woke with a start, sat up, and shook his head. Vaguely unsettled, with fragments of the dream poking through his consciousness, he shrugged, rubbed his eyes, and yawned, then looked around his little room. The bathroom was down the hall; farther on was the kitchen where he ate breakfast.

Sonny liked living with Herr Wagner and never complained about his room—it was clean and affordable. The old pensioner was good company, and Sonny was fond of him. If someone got him started, it was 1918 and Herr Wagner's eyes flashed with the anger of a young man railing against the Kaiser. All the generals were liars, and too many fine young men went to their deaths for imperial arrogance. Sonny would miss the old man when he was gone.

Sonny glanced at the clock. It was 7:04. Early morning light showed at the edge of the curtain. He massaged his head with the fingertips of both hands, assuring himself that he'd only had a dream. Sighing, he pulled the curtain aside. Streaks like long fingers lined the window. It had stopped raining, and dawn was turning the sky to a pretty, dark blue. All he had to do today was sell the Chianti. It wouldn't take long, but he had to get it done.

Until now, Sonny had been too wrapped up in work and nightlife to think much about his future. But he was an orphan—who else was there to think about it? He smiled at his mocking self-pity, acknowledging a modest start—a start nevertheless. Where would it lead? His work as a journalist had resulted in just two reviews for small-circulation magazines. He lived day to day with virtually no savings. His finances were a mess, making Franco's offer enticing.

Sonny shook his head with frustration. It was fine for him to live like a bohemian at age twenty-two, but what about when he was thirty? His father had always said, "What does it matter, so long as you are healthy?" Yet matter it did.

Random rays of sunshine found their way through the clouds. The moist, crisp air cleared Sonny's head. He walked in long, steady strides, nodding at familiar faces. There was little auto traffic—the streets were too narrow, and most people were too poor to afford cars. The flats in his high-density neighborhood were small. Many renters, like Herr Wagner, took in boarders to make ends meet. Sidewalks became parlors, crowded with people and gossip. Vitality and camaraderie, if not always joyful, lifted the neighborhood beyond the ethnic divisions and hard times that had Germany in its grip.

Sonny felt a kinship with his fellows in the Mitte, not just of clannish religious affiliation but because he'd grown up among them, played with them, and now worked with them.

He stopped at a coffee shop, ate quickly in the crowded space, gulped down his coffee, and left. Still without an answer for Franco, he decided to stay away from the warehouse until he had one. Closing the deal for the four cases of wine, he'd already known where he'd sell them. In half an hour, he was asking a man with a mop at the Pink Slipper's service entrance where he'd find Johnny. The man jerked his head toward the front without looking up.

Dressing rooms lined both sides of the corridor. A door on Sonny's left was labeled "Stage," the kitchen was to the right, and at the end was a door swinging into the main room, usually filled with voices and raucous laughter, tinkling glasses, and jazz. Its silence now was disconcerting. A single bulb at the far end of the bar illuminated two men. Johnny was one, the other unfamiliar, short, and round.

"Hello," Sonny called out, "it's Sonny." His voice echoed as he walked toward the bar.

Both men looked up, but only Johnny smiled. Holding up his hand, fingers splayed, Johnny said, "Five minutes."

Sonny walked to the front to look at photos of the celebrities who'd performed at the Pink Slipper. He was perusing shots of Claire Waldorf, of the beautiful stripper Anita Berber, and of Josephine Baker, when he heard Johnny call his name.

"Why are you here so early?" Johnny watched Sonny look around for the other man, who was gone. "That's the manager, Herr Blum."

Sonny hadn't put together a come-on. He decided to get straight to the point: "I've got some Italian wine to sell at a good price."

Johnny stared at him, as if sizing Sonny up anew. Then he said, "It depends."

Trying to look as if he did this regularly, Sonny told Johnny what he had. When Johnny's world-weary smile emerged, Sonny had his answer. After several minutes of bargaining, the Pink Slipper had four cases of '27 Chianti, and Sonny had a nice profit. They were both happy. All Johnny had to do was arrange for delivery.

The two shook hands, and Johnny said, "I won't ask where you got it, but if you get more, let me know."

Sonny let most of the day slip by without coming up with an answer for Franco. Yet he knew inside what he was going to do. He'd looked at it every which way, and it looked good. There was the money, and there were useful contacts to be made. Hell, he knew how to sell, and he would be following his father into the business. Still, it was vexing that his father had had little to show for his illicit endeavors. Was the money really that good? Had he stashed it away without telling anyone—or did he make just enough to get by? Too damn many questions . . .

The risks were obvious, but weighing those against the benefits, Sonny, perhaps irrationally, pushed them aside. Franco had said he needed someone he could trust. By making the offer, he'd shown Sonny that he trusted him. Maybe Franco figured that would obligate him, though Sonny tried not to let that be an influence. He wanted to ask Uncle Simon for advice, but he couldn't involve him. No, Sonny would tell no one—not Mischa, not Simon, not anyone, ever.

Franco stood with his hands on his hips and greeted Sonny with a deferential smile. "Good to see you, my boy. I've been waiting for you."

"I'm in," Sonny answered, not wasting time.

Franco grinned broadly and slapped him on the back. "Congratulations! I did not misjudge you." Then he leaned close, whispering, "It is too good an offer to turn down. Your father would be proud."

There were details to work out, like pay—a percentage of the previous month's sales. The more Sonny sold, the more he'd earn. For ten minutes they talked numbers, finally agreeing on an advance and a percentage, subject to renegotiation in six months.

Franco reached into his pocket, pulled out a roll of bills, peeled off several, and handed them to Sonny as an advance. Then he gave Sonny a folded piece of paper with directions to an address in Wedding.

Franco said, "Meet Emil tomorrow morning at 9:00 at our Wedding warehouse. He will explain everything."

The two shook hands, and Franco greeted a customer warmly. Sonny was dismissed, and he walked away with his father's voice in his head: "Whatever you do, do it well."

Too excited to sleep, Sonny paced his little room until it was time to leave. From the subway station at Oskar Platz he headed toward an alley behind a tenement on Schul Strasse. Franco had said, "Emil has been with the enterprise for years, and there is much you can learn from him, so listen well. He is an extraordinary fellow. You cannot miss him."

"Red" Wedding was a well-known KPD stronghold, a working-class district just north of the old Mitte. Like Neukölln, it was a world apart from Scheunenviertel. Blocks of tenements housed both those lucky enough to have work and those unlucky enough not to. The unlucky ones filled Oskar Platz, lined up for bowls of soup. The sullen men in their best clothes, faces pinched, tried to maintain a thread of dignity. Outside the local KPD office opposite the square were more unemployed men, milling about. Sonny could smell their desperation. One man put a leaflet in his hand. He stuffed it in his pocket.

When he turned onto Christiana Strasse, he saw another line, this one of women. At their feet were buckets of potato peels; they patiently waited in turn to see a man standing on a horse-drawn cart exchanging firewood for peels. What would he do with them? Make vodka? Then Sonny noticed the stout grocer standing next to a bin of unsold potatoes, hands on his hips, frowning at the spectacle.

A little early, Sonny walked partway down the alley, then stopped, leaned against a building, and waited with his hands in his pockets for someone extraordinary. Children ran past on their way to school, skipping and laughing, temporarily lifting the gloom enveloping the neighborhood. Otto's comrades must be doing well here.

He felt a hand on his shoulder, heard a low gravely voice: "Sonny?"

Sonny jumped, but the strong hand kept him from falling. "Huh, what?" he croaked. His pantomime elicited a low, rumbling laugh. He turned to see a big man dressed in coveralls and cap, blocking out the sun. His nose was flat, and he wore a big smile.

"Emil Roden," he said, offering his hand. "Did I startle you?"

"Only scared the shit out of me," Sonny answered with a sideways glance.

More rumbling laughter. "Sorry, I was watching from over there." He pointed to a small space between two buildings. "Franco described you pretty well."

Sonny thought the same, now understanding what Franco had meant by extraordinary. Emil had at least two inches and fifty pounds on him, and the hand that kept him upright was big and calloused. He took another look and saw the full mouth softening Emil's menacing face with a smile, the small, bright, appraising eyes.

Sonny followed Emil to a gate, which he unlocked and swung open, then to wide double doors also requiring a key. "Can't be too careful," Emil said.

Light from the alley provided a glimpse of the interior. It smelled of fresh paint and wasn't as large as Sonny had expected. An overhead light came to life, illuminating white walls lined with shelves holding cartons of cigarettes, boxes of cigars, and cases of vodka, gin, and Scotch whisky. Three rows of freestanding shelves rose above his head, evenly dividing the space. One was filled with boxes of women's silk lingerie, handkerchiefs, and nylon stockings; another held perfume, porcelain, pearl earrings, purses. A big table holding more goods squeezed in front. Almost every horizontal space was occupied. And there—a prosthetic arm!

Sonny gaped: "What's with the fake arm?"

"Well, you never know . . ." Emil laughed. "If you're good, you'll sell it. I don't order the stuff . . . just take care of inventory and delivery." Emil's easy banter put his new salesman at ease.

Sonny noticed a wood table with four overturned chairs resting on its top. "We sell furniture, too?"

"No, that's mine . . . Sometimes I barter favors," Emil gestured to the cigarettes. "I got the table and chairs wholesale from a guy's brother who works in a small furniture factory in Neukölln." He nudged Sonny with his elbow. "Let me know if you need anything. You know the eleventh commandment?"

Sonny laughed and thought of his father, who'd often said that. He took a step back, as if to get a better look, and said with mock sincerity, "You don't look Jewish."

Emil smiled. "You'll do fine."

The two spent about an hour going through inventory. Emil explained that, as the warehouse man, he took care of receiving and delivery, making sure everything went smoothly. Others brought the goods to Berlin. Selling was Sonny's job. Emil reached into his pocket, then handed Sonny a piece of paper with an address on Schul Strasse and a telephone number.

"Memorize it. That's where I live," he said, waving toward an unseen building across the alley. "Call that number when you need a delivery, but," he waggled a meaty finger under Sonny's nose, "I don't want to be bothered unless it's a meaningful order and at a reasonable hour. With a wife and two kids, I like to keep things calm at home. We'll get along so long as you respect the rules and maintain security. I've been doing this a long time, and I want to continue. The money's good. Any questions?"

Sonny shook his head.

"Good. I want you to get a good start, because the last guy was a real piece of crap."

"Why?" Sonny asked.

"He couldn't be trusted." Emil left it at that. "Now let's go to the other warehouse."

On the way they stopped for lunch at a tavern on Oskar Platz near the subway. The innkeeper knew Emil and greeted him warmly. Conversation seemed optional while they stood at the bar and ate. But thus far Emil was an easy and amiable partner, friendlier than he looked, though people gave him wide berth.

Sonny took a bite of bratwurst and thought how quickly life changes. Seemingly fixed in one career direction, he'd taken a sudden turn and become a fence, maybe even a smuggler. Just the other day he had told a new girl about his aspirations. Now that was on hold while he learned a new vocation—if that's what it was.

Sonny raised his glass to the wonders of life, but Emil said, "Let's go."

In half an hour they were in Kreuzberg, in a depressed area of unpaved streets. This warehouse was similar to the other, holding the same small, easy-to-move merchandise. After fifteen minutes, Emil rubbed his face with the palm of his hand, and yawned: "We're in the process of shutting this warehouse down."

When they got to the subway, they saw a crowd gathered at the door of the station. A group of SA was inside, blocking entry, handing out its slimy propaganda. Intimidated by the hectoring and with no way to avoid it, people wove their way through, creating a bottleneck and general tumult. Sonny counted at least six SAs as Emil pushed through like a ship creating a comfortable wake for him to follow.

Suddenly in Emil's path was a big, fat man with a florid face and hooded eyes. He looked like an overstuffed Boy Scout in his ridiculous SA uniform. Brandishing a sheet of Nazi filth inches from Emil's face, he urged, "Friend, take this and do your duty. Support the NSDAP!"

What happened next was so quick that Sonny might have missed Emil's sudden and controlled fury. Emil slapped the man's hand, sending the pamphlet into the crowd. It came with such force that Sonny heard its sound above the din, like a hammer striking a nail, surely leaving its mark. The startled, dough-faced Nazi froze in fear.

Emil's snarl cut through the tension almost before it had a chance to take hold: "Out of my face, shithead!"

Still unable to move, the Nazi gaped like a fish in a bowl. Emil thrust the hapless man aside, knocking him into one of his compatriots. When they were past the confrontation, Emil hissed, "Assholes."

When they reached the platform, Emil calmly instructed Sonny to report to Franco early the next morning. Sonny didn't know what to say as Emil extended his hand, winked, and said, "See you later, kid," before turning to catch his train.

All the way back home and for days afterward, the frightened face of the fat Nazi, the sound of the slap, and the taunt "assholes" stayed in Sonny's head. Now enshrined in Sonny's hall of heroes, Emil surely had much to teach him. Everything thus far had been well worth the price of admission.

The next morning Franco greeted Sonny cheerily and leaned close. "Good morning, my boy. I hear you had a productive day. He is an extraordinary fellow, that Emil. Is he not?"

Sonny was about to answer, but Franco kept talking, leaving him just enough room to nod or shake his head. His instructions were simple: Sonny was to sell merchandise as he'd always done. He'd introduce himself as the new representative, Rolf's replacement, and if anyone had a problem, he would mention Emil. That should take care of it. Sonny was never, under any circumstances, to mention Franco's name. Franco paused to let that sink in and waited for Sonny to agree.

"Good!" Franco exclaimed. "It is all about trust, providing a good product at a good price. So long as we do that, there will not be a problem." Franco put an arm around Sonny's shoulder, leading him to the rear of the stall.

"The police have never been a problem, and I do not expect they will be," Franco continued, handing Sonny several sheets of paper. One was a list of customers, names, addresses, and a contact. "Start immediately. Drop in when they are not busy, and introduce yourself."

Franco took some time to go over the list. Sonny recognized among others the Pink Slipper and its contact, Blum. Other sheets listed the inventory at the Wedding shed and of what remained in Kreuzberg.

Franco pointed to thirty cases of Chianti and said, "The price is not negotiable but," holding up a forefinger for emphasis, "if they want quantity, at least ten cases, offer a 5 percent discount. Prices are competitive, and everybody knows it. Do you understand?"

Sonny nodded, and Franco asked, "Do you have a driver's license?"

Sonny shook his head.

"Tell Emil. It is a simple matter to get one. You will drive mostly in Berlin, though on rare occasions you may have to leave town with Emil for a pickup. Be prepared for the possibility of a trip to Aachen, near the Belgian border."

The memory of his father's two-day trip coming to the fore, Sonny got flustered.

Sensing his agitation, Franco smiled and put a hand on his shoulder. "Do not get ahead of yourself. You will do longer trips only when there is an emergency."

"I'm not interested in smuggling." Sonny's words rushed out in a torrent. He was suddenly frightened.

Franco frowned, keeping his eyes on Sonny for several beats, then said, "Do not worry. Relax, my boy. You will do fine. Now, go sell—it is what you are good at—and return in a week." Franco was already on to something else.

Sonny stuffed the papers in his pocket, then went to the café where he had met Polly. Buzzing with talk and general commotion, the crowded café was comforting. There he ordered some coffee and spread out the list of more than fifty cabarets, taverns, and others businesses he'd be contacting that week. His finger moved down the page listing, beyond the Pink Slipper, the Katakombe, through others he recognized—or not. He'd start with Blum at the Pink Slipper and, while he was there, ask Johnny to reserve a table for him and Polly.

He folded the list, returned it to his pocket, then studied the inventory and price list. Besides the Chianti, there was French wine, brandy, and numerous brands of French and Belgian cigarettes and cigars—everything he'd seen in the warehouses. Sonny leaned back in the chair. This was going to be a piece of cake . . .

Sonny left the café to reprise his visit to the Pink Slipper. This time he entered through the front door as the representative of the enterprise. Nearly blinded in the inky foyer, he saw a faint light framing the door to the bar and silently pushed the door open. He moved tentatively toward the sound of voices but stopped short when he saw Johnny with Herr Blum, then retreated on tiptoe. They hadn't seen him, so he rapped on the door.

"Ja, I'm coming," Johnny answered. "Who is it?"

"Sonny."

Johnny, cigarette in his hand, came to the door saying, "This is becoming a habit." Over his shoulder, he said to Herr Blum. "It's the guy who sold us the Chianti."

A voice raspy from too many cigars and too much yelling responded, "Bring him here."

Johnny waved for Sonny to follow, introduced him to Herr Blum, and went behind the bar. Sonny lowered his eyes to meet Blum's penetrating gaze, then got a brief, firm handshake. Blum had an unlit cigar stuck in the corner of his wide mouth. A red tie hung over a precariously protruding stomach. Alert eyes, darkened by circles, gave nothing away as they moved over Sonny.

Blum took the cigar from his mouth: "Doctor said these damn things were killing me, so I had to quit." He looked at it longingly, then up at Sonny. "So you're the kid with the Chianti?"

"Guilty as charged," Sonny answered. "I just took over from Rolf. This is my first call."

Blum stared but didn't say anything. As the silence continued, Sonny felt uncomfortable under the little man's glare.

Finally, Blum said, "I never really trusted that kid, but never mind." He waved the cigar like a baton. "Johnny says you're all right, so sit down and tell him what you've got. He'll pass it on and let you know." Blum waddled away and, without turning, spoke over his shoulder. "I'm sure we'll get along fine. Johnny, see me later."

Sonny watched Blum retreat through the double doors to an office somewhere in the back. Johnny's grin seemed tired, but every hair was in place and his white shirt was spotless. He was behind the bar, the only place Sonny had seen him until two days earlier.

"You've come up in the world," Johnny said. He poured two cups of coffee and took them to a table. "This your first call?"

"Ja, my second day on the job."

Johnny raised his cup. "Congratulations. What have you got?" For the next half hour they reviewed inventory, then the Pink Slipper ordered more Chianti, some Scotch, gin, and tobacco products. Sonny tallied the order. Johnny looked it over and went to run it by Blum. Sonny watched him disappear into the dim of the cabaret hall.

Faint traces of ammonia hovered in the air. The piano and drum set occupied an otherwise empty stage. The tables were covered with chairs, their legs pointing to the ceiling like a stick forest. It felt strange to be in this room, now empty of people, where he'd first heard American jazz. Like a first kiss, the first notes had been heavenly, and he'd wanted more.

For Sonny, jazz was born at the Pink Slipper, not in some joint in Harlem, Chicago, Kansas City, New Orleans, or another American town. Just being in the room was exciting. Drumming his thumb on the table, bobbing his head, he heard bits of an Ellington riff from "In a Sentimental Mood." For him, fiery solos were red and love-soaked ballads a soft blue. Shades of yellow, green, purple, orange, filled the spaces between them.

Lost in a musical dream, Sonny missed Johnny coming to sit next to him. Roused from his stupor, Sonny learned that Blum had signed off on the order. They talked about delivery, and Sonny arranged it by phone. Then he booked a table for two nights hence.

Johnny walked him to the door, putting a hand on Sonny's shoulder. He winked and said, "I hope this will be the start of a long relationship." They shook on it.

4

We have seen the best of our time: machinations, hollowness, treachery, and all ruinous disorders follow us quietly to our graves.
—William Shakespeare

Sonny slid the chair forward as Polly sat down and slowly took in the room, not quite full at 9:00. Light from the candles reflected off the huge glass ceiling globes at the Pink Slipper, winking like a thousand stars. Waiters in black rushed past with trays, and the clinking of glass mixed with laughter made the couple feel gay and cosmopolitan.

This was their second date, for they'd met under the zoo clock after their first encounter exactly as arranged. Sonny arrived early and watched for Polly from across the road. His eyes lit first on a woman not more than eighteen, in a tight blue dress under a shabby, open coat, and in too much make-up, walking toward the clock. She tried to sway her hips provocatively, but her heels were too high to pull it off. Her attempt at a coy smile only made her pathetic. Guessing what she did for a living was easy, but it made it him sad. Whores aged quickly, if they didn't die young.

Then Sonny settled on another young woman, still twenty meters away, her head moving from side to side, searching. Covering her hair was a peach-colored cloche, perfectly matched to the well-cut coat cinched at her waist. Sonny thought her smile expectant, perfect for a rendezvous. She gazed at the clock. Just five minutes late, she put her hands on her hips and moved her head in an arc until her eyes met his, and she brightened. Sonny's pulse quickened as he raised an arm.

They'd lingered on the pavement beneath the big clock, deciding which film to see, finally picking *The Blue Angel*, based on a story by Heinrich Mann, Thomas's brother.

Polly declared, "We must see it," then raised her eyebrows in self-mocking bravado, "after all, I studied literature."

Halfway through the film, Sonny's hand found hers, and he held on to the end. The film disappointed neither of them nor others in the audience, more than half of them standing to applaud. As they filed out, Polly hummed Lola's song: "How will I ever get that song out my head?"

Holding hands again, they had strolled along Kurfürstendamm to the Uhlandeck Café. Once there, they grabbed a table by a window. During the day, floor-to-ceiling windows flooded the room with light. At night, hanging art deco lamps cast shadows soft as kisses. The restaurant's high, scalloped ceiling gave Sonny the feeling of an ocean floor, leaving him a bit breathless. Polly thought it more like floating in an aquarium. To anyone walking, the scene was of two friends holding hands and sipping coffee, a man at the next table dragging on a cigarette, a group of workers sitting in the corner—all fish at play.

Polly had sat with her elbow on the table—chin cupped in her left hand, fingers slowly tapping on her cheek—still humming "Falling in Love Again."

"Have you ever been to a cabaret?" Sonny asked.

"Once with some girlfriends, but it wasn't very good," she answered with some disappointment.

"Then I will take you," Sonny declared. And they made a date for the Pink Slipper.

Later, as they strolled along Ku'damm, gawking at the fancy shop windows, Sonny had asked, "Do you know about the bubble?"

Polly shook her head.

"Mischa and I worked it out," said Sonny. "Everyone moves inside an invisible bubble, about a meter in diameter, unless they're blind or raving mad. No one's allowed inside your bubble without being invited, though no invitation is necessary if you're intimate." Sonny beamed his most winning smile at Polly. "Those breaking the rule are scoundrels, the police, or as previously noted. Certain exceptions are granted, like on the subway, though faces all around register helplessness over the invasion. SAs and some KPDs fall into the scoundrel and mad categories, penetrating bubbles with impunity."

Polly laughed. Sonny's thoughts flipped to Emil in the Kreuzberg station.

By the time they reached Polly's room in the Mitte, the air was crisp and fresh after a brief cleansing rain, the clouds having given way to a clear sky. Standing awkwardly, they looked up at a nearly full moon, neither speaking. Sonny had gently placed his hands on Polly's shoulders, drawn her near, kissed her goodnight . . .

Now Polly took in every corner of the Pink Slipper, put her mouth next to Sonny's ear and murmured, "This is wonderful. I could spend another twenty minutes just looking at the photographs."

"With you next to me, I have the best seat in the house," Sonny said.

Color rose prettily in her cheeks, and she laughed. "Really? Tell me more, so I'll believe it."

"My words don't betray what I see."

Polly's silver dress hung close, neither too tight to be vulgar nor too loose to hide her shape. The scoop of the neckline was just enough to distract Sonny the evening long. A string of lustrous white pearls—they seemed real—caught his eyes and kept them where they belonged.

"Thank you. It took me only two hours to get ready," Polly exaggerated. Then she leaned back to assess him. After a second or two, she nodded, "You look very handsome."

He shrugged. "I put these rags together in half an hour."

"That long?" she quipped and they laughed.

So they sat, her hand in his, flattering one another while Berlin's night prowlers, men and women in all shapes and sizes, flowed past. Several brushed the table, nearly spilling their drinks, and soon the room was filled to overflowing. The unsmiling, androgynous waiters delivered sustenance to the hungry and thirsty Berliners. One floated to Sonny and Polly's table from nowhere and, over the sound of the band, took their order.

Several couples wandered onto the dance floor to sway to the beat of a slow ballad. Polly wasn't disappointed in the crowd around her. Placing her fingertips on the table, her green eyes wide, she smiled: "I feel the table vibrating, like it's alive."

Sonny squeezed her hand. "Welcome to cabaret!"

Polly whispered into his ear, "Up front, near the stage on the opposite side—is that a man or woman?"

Sonny followed her gaze to a rail-thin figure in black with lacquered black hair. He—or she—sat with an elbow on the table, a pale chin cupped in one hand, arm draped over a companion's shoulder.

Sonny shrugged, guessing. "Probably a woman . . . her posture and attitude."

"Posture? That's a contortionist." Polly tried to emulate the position but couldn't. She started to laugh and did so until she fell against Sonny, giddy from the alcohol and the scene before her.

After nearly an hour, Sonny spotted Johnny wading through the crowd to their table. Sonny stood to greet him, then introduced Polly. Taking her hand in both of his, Johnny cooed, "Enchanté mademoiselle. Welcome to the Pink Slipper. Your beau and I go back a bit." He flashed Polly his most charming smile and winked at Sonny.

Polly clearly enjoyed the attention while it lasted. Within seconds, Johnny's eyes began to wander, and soon he was off to another table. After he'd vanished into the crowd, Polly muttered, "That was quite an act."

"Like a benign shark," Sonny said with a laugh. "If there is such a creature."

They ate canapés of pimento, cucumber, and chicken liver followed by crepes and washed it all down with champagne, which tickled Polly's nose. In the background, a young, blond guitarist played Sinti music. Sonny told her how Solomon's music had drawn him like a soulful magnet at the end of his workdays, salving his grief for his parents. Polly took his hand in hers, and they gently swayed, as a sea of people ebbed and flowed around them. They sat close until shortly before midnight, when the music stopped and the band took a break. Loud voices and laughter filled the void, waiters ferrying trays of food and drink and patrons moving from table to table.

Satiated with food, drink, and music, they watched the milling crowd, then heard a faint sound above the din—a thud, barely audible, apparently from behind the stage. Sonny cocked his head and looked at Polly. Within seconds they heard another, louder and more distinct noise, and this time it was unmistakable—an explosion. An uncomfortable mantle of silence descended, the crowd holding a collective breath, a seconds-long calm before the storm certain to follow. Then a piece of ceiling above the stage collapsed, filling the air with plaster dust mixed with smoke moving quickly through the hall.

A woman—maybe their androgynous friend—screamed from near the stage. A second scream and general pandemonium ensued. People already on their feet pushed toward the bar and front door, away from the explosion. Polly's hand gripped Sonny's. Shouts and screams made it impossible to hear, so Sonny mouthed, "Bomb." Polly, dazed, managed to nod back.

Sonny watched as one man grabbed another and pulled him away only to run into another. The frantic crowd pressed one upon another, shouting, screaming, squealing like pigs in an abattoir. Smoke, thick like fog, filled the room, making it hard to breathe, increasing the panic. Survival trumped civility in the frenzy to escape.

Sonny couldn't compete with the mob . . . Leaping to his feet, he knocked the chair against the wall and shouted, "Polly." But her head was turned to the tangled mass of bodies that would soon disappear into the smoke. Sonny knew there was only one way out. He found Polly's hand again and shouted for her to follow. Flames engulfed the wall behind the stage, but he headed into it, pulling Polly along. "Back door," he shouted in her ear.

Clutching Polly's hand, Sonny lurched ahead, dragging her through bluish-white smoke. Coughing, hugging the wall, feeling the way forward, they pushed through the double swinging doors into the corridor he'd entered for the first time only a few days before. Miraculously, the lights were still on, creating with the orange flames a ghostly glow. The heat was so intense he feared the hallway would explode into flame.

Still, he pushed along. Then, after what seemed an eternity, Sonny felt cool air hit his face, the smoke finally dissipating. They rushed through the open door into the alley, falling against a brick wall into each other's arms, gasping for air.

After taking his fill, Sonny pulled Polly from the alley onto the sidewalk. Polly buried her head in his chest and cried, then suddenly straightened and felt at her throat for the pearls. Finding them, she fell back against him.

At the front door played a nightmare vision of the gates of hell. People tripped over others, collapsed on the sidewalk. Blood streamed down one man's face; another fell over him. Others lay still. Sirens pierced the night air, covering the screams. Sonny looked at his watch. It was 12:08. Only minutes had passed since the explosion.

"Are you all right?" Sonny asked, stroking Polly's hair.

She nodded, unable or unwilling to speak. The fire truck arrived with water hoses followed by a police van and more pandemonium. But Sonny was able to spot a lone figure—Johnny—bent behind a fire truck. Was he was all right? Perhaps he would know what had happened. Sonny put his jacket over Polly's shoulders.

"There's Johnny. I'm going to see if he's okay. I'll be right back."

She nodded again.

Johnny's face was streaked with black, his jacket was ripped, he was missing a shoe. His chest heaved as he gasped for air, but he seemed to have no injury. Sonny knelt so Johnny could see him and asked, "You okay?"

Johnny squinted until he saw who it was, coughed, and nodded.

Sonny asked, "What the hell happened?"

"A bomb . . . threats . . ." Johnny's words were barely audible between his gasps.

"By whom?"

Johnny shook his head and wheezed, "Nazis? Gangsters? . . . Don't know. Blum wouldn't tell me." Then he started hacking . . . Finally he stopped, took several deep breaths, and said, "The explosion came from the area of the office . . . We'll be shut down. Shit, I'll be out of a job . . . How's Polly?"

"She's all right," Sonny answered, patting Johnny's shoulder. "Take care." He didn't want to stick around and talk to any cops. He returned to Polly.

"Do you feel strong enough to walk?"

"I think so. How's Johnny?"

"He's okay," Sonny told her as they walked away from the Pink Slipper, his arm around her waist. With their breath returning to normal, the fear of suffocation gave way to relief, then to a more general anxiety, like the smoke, clinging to their clothes and hair. Slowly, by foot and tram, the two made it safely to the Mitte, assuring one another they were okay.

"But my body tingles, and I can't gather my thoughts," Polly moaned.

"You're probably in shock," Sonny said.

"I keep seeing that poor woman fall, then scream when that big guy tripped over her, then the others falling on him. God!" Polly buried her face in her hands and cried so that her shoulders heaved.

In Sonny's head echoed the refrain: "Welcome to cabaret."

5

Let the black flower blossom as it may!
—Nathaniel Hawthorne

The tragedy at the Pink Slipper seemed to leave few scars on Sonny and Polly's growing romance. Neither doubted that difficult times lay ahead, but they were young and life was to be lived, not fretted about. They met as much as they could after work, usually at a café, then walked to catch a play or film. Sometimes they joined Mischa and Sophie over coffee to talk. That terrible night retreated from conscious memory . . . for Polly, at least.

Though Sonny tried to forget, his memory of the chaos lingered. It shattered the illusion that he could glide untouched by the extremism roiling in Berlin. Long familiarity with the warehouse plus his relative youth had contributed to a false sense of invulnerability. But the bombing at the Pink Slipper awakened him to the lengths men would go to intimidate, to create mayhem. Whatever broader pressure the perpetrators may have intended, the Pink Slipper never reopened.

Men like Sonny's contact, Johnny, were survivors, always landing on their feet. Indeed he had emerged from the blast intact to do much the same as before, only now he did it at The Katakombe. Herr Blum, however, apparently had evaporated.

When told of the bombing, Franco frowned and shook his head wearily: "Yes, a horrible waste, but we must move on. Certainly the miscreants must be apprehended and punished, but it has nothing to do with us. We have lost a customer, a regrettable inconvenience." Offering nothing more, Franco never said what had become of Blum.

Sonny was confused—he'd thought Blum to be a close friend of Franco's, perhaps even godfather to his son. And he knew that night had everything to do with him—and Polly. They both might have died. Now Sonny saw a new side of Franco, but he held his tongue.

As to the other part, Franco turned out to be right: the business wasn't affected. And the money Sonny was making assuaged his wariness of Franco enough to overlook his shortcomings. His hard work at the start paid off later, and as Sonny mastered his territory, he found that less time and energy were required to get the job done. In the process, he became more order-taker than salesman.

Backed by a strong inventory, primarily of alcohol and tobacco—"sin staples," Franco called them—Sonny's visits to clubs and taverns were quick and easy. He took inventory at each stop, told his contact what was needed, closed the deal with a handshake, and phoned Emil for delivery.

Franco increased Sonny's commission, and putting together a "little of this and a little of that," Sonny was able to save some money for the first time in his life. Profit margins were high, taxes weren't a problem, and almost everyone was happy. Of course, their operation shorted the inadvertent suppliers and put legitimate competitors at a distinct disadvantage, but Sonny tried not to think about that.

The cartons of cigarettes, cases of scotch and wine, melted into sameness, like the overcast days of winter. Work became increasingly mundane. Even the cabaret and club scene had lost its luster, assuming the pallor of ordinary business from the first time Sonny walked through the Pink Slipper's back door to sell Johnny four cases of wine. Like chancing upon a chanteuse without make-up or costume, seeing things from the inside dispelled their mystique—and his enthusiasm. Sonny became impatient, even bored, and talked to Franco about a change.

Early in 1932, five months after he had come to work in the enterprise, Franco offered Sonny a day trip to Munich with Emil. Sonny had never left Berlin before, and he was more than ready for the adventure. He wouldn't even have to pack a bag; he could just sit and enjoy the ride. Over coffee, Sonny told Polly he had an opportunity to purchase merchandise in Munich, but he had to retrieve it in person. He hadn't thought about her probing deeper, but she only noted how lucky he was to be able to leave Berlin.

Sonny and Emil arrived at Munich's main railway station in mid-afternoon, then walked to an area dense with factories and warehouses, with men loading and unloading all manner of goods. Reaching a warehouse with a truck parked at its loading dock, Emil instructed Sonny to wait and disappeared inside. He returned, inventory sheet in hand, with a man holding a clipboard. They climbed into the back of the truck. Sonny watched the two check off the boxes and shake hands. The stranger nodded curtly as he walked past Sonny into the warehouse, leaving a faint trail of musk.

"Let's go," said Emil, and they got into the truck and drove from the city into a rolling countryside dotted with trees, meadows, and snow-covered farmland. Sonny imagined cows grazing and fields divided into neat rows, but the agrarian scene was as mysterious to him as Einstein's new physics. Country life—without busy streets, cabarets, galleries, cinema, or theater—lay beyond his comprehension.

"What could they possibly be doing in their tidy farmhouses?" he asked.

Emil laughed: "Better not to know."

Shadows lengthened by the dropping sun created dark shapes on the landscape, soon outdone by a staggering crimson glow in the western sky. As the evening grew dark, Sonny became aware of the drone of the vehicle's engine, like a million bees buzzing in his head. The vibration of the cab added to his discomfort. After a while, though, the noise and jostling simply became a part of the trip, like the faint outlines of the trees, farms, towns, and the driver beside him.

Before darkness fell completely, Emil slowed for an old man in lederhosen, carrying a staff and walking slowly behind a cow. Amazed and amused, Sonny noted, "Grandfather's a relic from the last century."

"That's arrogant Berlin talking," Emil said wryly, giving Sonny a sideways glance. "Maybe we're the lost ones." He tone was introspective. "It's good for you to get out of the Mitte, to see how other people live. Not everyone's a slave to the city."

He went on: "Sometimes I think about leaving Berlin, and . . . " but he stopped midsentence, took a ham-sized hand off the steering wheel, scratched at a spot on his cheekbone, and groaned with pleasure. "God,

I hate the city sometimes—the rush and congestion, the chasing after money."

Sonny didn't know whether Emil was serious or pulling his leg. From the day they'd met, he'd been revising his assessment of Emil. His father's advice—"Don't judge people by their appearance"—nearly drowned by the engine, played in his ears. Now Sonny took stock of his comrade again.

Emil liked to read, and he always had a book poking out of his pocket or in his satchel. On this trip it was Alfred Döblin's *Berlin Alexanderplatz*, a popular book about a criminal released from prison into a society he was ill-equipped to handle. "Interesting choice," Sonny mused.

Emil was married to Lisle—a good woman, he said. Thanks to his earnings from the enterprise, she didn't have to work outside their home. They had two children: son Eric was fifteen, daughter Hannah twelve. Both did fairly well in school, far better than Emil had. An indifferent student, he'd gotten into his share of trouble, much to his parent's dismay. But life had turned out pretty good, and he had no complaints. He'd been with Franco nearly ten years; and a lot had changed, he said, though he didn't elaborate.

Politics on his mind—proof of Otto's influence—Sonny asked Emil, "Do you belong to a political party?"

Emil made a guttural sound. Was it a laugh or an expletive? "Ja, the Emil party," he said, holding up a forefinger. "It's just me, and my platform is to keep working and stay away from the prying eyes of the cops. My slogan is 'Don't take any bullshit'—no pamphlets, no rallies, and no brawls . . . Hell! Politics is bullshit. Nothing gets done, not with Nazis and Reds controlling the conversation."

He reconsidered: "What conversation? All they do is scream. I hate politics." Then he yawned, his eyes fixed on the road.

That topic of conversation seemed exhausted, so Sonny asked what he'd meant to ask for some time: "Did you know my father?"

Emil shrugged. "Don't know. What's his name?"

"Morris Laudauer."

Surprised, Emil's eyes left the road to reappraise the man beside him. "Morris Landauer was your father? I'll be damned. Franco didn't say."

There was genuine emotion in Emil's voice. "We worked together for years, took trips just like this one, down and back. I liked your father."

Then he pulled the truck to the side of the road, cut the engine, and faced Sonny. "I was real sorry when he died so suddenly. I wanted to pay my respects to the family."

"If you had, we'd have met four years ago."

Emil nodded. "I talked to Franco about going, but we agreed it was better to stay away. I didn't relish having to explain our relationship to your family. And to be honest, I didn't think your father would have wanted me there. Besides, a mug like mine showing up for shivah might have shaken things up, and I *didn't* want that."

Sonny laughed. "Franco said he recruited me because of my father. I had no idea, and I don't know whether my mother knew." He felt the weight of Emil's hand on his shoulder.

"My kids don't have a clue either," said Emil. "It's for the best. Children are innocent. They like to talk about what the old man does for a living, and you never know who's listening. What do they know about what's legal? They just want to be proud of papa."

"What do they think you do for a living?"

"That I'm a deliveryman." Emil smiled at the truth.

Back on the road, they jostled and bounced in their seats until Emil raised his voice. " . . . That's where my kids get their brains."

"Where's that?" Sonny braced as the truck struck a pothole.

"From their Jewish grandfather—on my father's side. I never knew him. I've been to several shivahs over the years. Papa used to say there's always a Jew somewhere in the woodpile." And they laughed because it was often true . . .

By the time they got to the outskirts of Berlin, Sonny was sleeping against the door. He woke with a start when Emil shook him.

Soon they were at the Wedding warehouse, unloading, storing, the new merchandise. When they finished and Sonny left for his bed in the Mitte, Emil returning to the truck, it was well past midnight. Sonny had enjoyed getting away from the city and his old patterns. That Emil had spoken well of his father was especially gratifying.

By mid-1932 unemployment affected seven-and-a-half-million people nationally, tremendous fodder for the extremists sowing seeds of discontent. Then, just before the July election, a transit strike supported by both Nazis and Communists rallying on the same street corners turned an already unruly Berlin into almost unmanageable chaos. In the city of five million, just moving around became a challenge to most, a nightmare for others. Sonny didn't mind walking, though it sickened him to see Otto's comrades allied with the Nazis.

Otto and his minions, including Mischa, were busy making mischief in the name of electoral politics. There were too many unemployed, queued at soup kitchens, milling about the city squares, with nothing but time on their hands. Franco remained optimistic, even cheerful, seemingly impervious to the growing chaos so long as receipts were maintained.

When Polly asked Sonny how his work was going, he answered in vague generalities. He told her it paid the rent but didn't satisfy his creative side. In truth, he only pretended to find time enough to write. Polly might have lost patience, but instead she implored him to find the time and not just talk about it.

"What's happening in Berlin demands documentation. With so many events and your rich sources—the bombing, Otto's political exploits—how can you avoid it?" she said.

Sonny became an admirer of Joseph Roth, whose newspaper columns had captured the grit and underbelly of 1920s Berlin. Roth's descriptions of Hirtenstrasse and other haunts inspired Sonny to emulate his narrative style. But something dissipated his initial zeal for writing. He came to believe it was nothing but a pipe dream, an immature affectation, a romantic vision of his youth.

Serious writing required commitment and compulsion—both of which Sonny lacked—and he felt guilty for what he considered failure. His writing output did not increase with the decrease in his workload for the enterprise, and he conveniently blamed his failure to write on the malaise related to his work.

Sonny often sat at the small table in his room, pencil poised above empty paper, staring into space. Over time such attempts, almost physically painful, ended in a restless sleep, his head on his forearms, his mouth open, drooling onto the paper. Truth was, he'd rather be on the road with Emil.

Sonny felt guilty on several fronts, and though he wanted to tell Polly the truth, he always stopped short. His father's lesson and Emil's warning kept him quiet. Nobody knew, and that's the way he'd keep it. Travel could become his remedy, he mused, though long absences might be difficult to explain.

Willing to take that chance, Sonny asked for more trips. And about a week later, Franco asked whether he spoke French. Sonny had taken French in school, and though he remembered little, he exaggerated.

"Un peu," Sonny answered—enough to get by.

"Good," Franco chuckled. "If you are interested, there might be a trip with Emil to Aachen, where goods are coming across from Plombieres, Belgium, through Reinartzkehl, a small town nearby."

Sonny jumped at the chance, though his excitement was tempered by Franco saying there was a slim chance they would have to cross the border into Belgium. Sonny's face darkened, but Franco, reading his reaction, shook his head, "I do not expect that to happen, but if it does, Emil has done it often and will lead the way. You need not worry. I will let you know."

Several weeks went by before Franco gave Sonny the word. At seven o'clock on a late-winter morning, Sonny met Emil at the train station. Emil nodded a greeting, clapped his hands to warm them, and complained, "God, it's cold." He indicated Sonny should follow, and they boarded the westbound train.

During the night, a virginal coating of brilliant white snow had cleansed the city. But every Berlin cynic knew that in a matter of hours the exhaust from thousands of automobiles and trucks, the soot, and the garbage of five million messy humans would turn the city to its normal shades of gray. When the train cleared the city, the two travelers went to the food car for biscuits and steaming cups of hot chocolate to warm their hands.

They returned to their compartment to share the ride with a middle-aged man dressed like a businessman and an older woman. Newspapers and a book appeared as if on cue, and they settled in, soon comforted by the gently swaying of the car and the click-clack of wheels on the tracks. Other travelers moved along the corridor to alight in Hanover, Darmstadt, Bad Kreuznach, and others took their place.

Sonny stared at the farmhouses dotting the undulating hills of white satin bisected by darker lanes, leafless trees poking skyward. As the train rounded a bend, the curves and hills melted into the vision of a languorous body. Sonny saw a woman's stomach rising to her breasts, soft and round, like lush alabaster sculptures. Then he saw it was Polly, and he smiled as the image faded. Sighing, he turned his thoughts to the journey ahead . . .

The compartment door opened. Sonny's eyes lit on a swastika armband, immediately souring his mood. Standing in the doorway was a man average in every way, about forty, in a silly SA uniform. He bowed slightly: "Good day, madam and gentlemen. It is a new day for the Reich. Please read this for Germany's future. Heil Hitler!" He offered pamphlets, raised his arm in a stiff salute, and was gone.

Emil, buried in his book, refused to acknowledge the man, though he murmured a gruff "no."

Sonny also declined but added a thank-you. The woman wordlessly took the pamphlet and laid it next to her.

"I'll have a look," the businessman said, and he began to read.

The others returned to their reading. Sonny watched the man over his newspaper begin to nod. When he'd finished with the pamphlet, the man raised his head, his eyes meeting Sonny's. He seemed about to say something, but he remained silent. Whatever he was thinking, he put the Nazi propaganda in his pocket and returned to his newspaper.

In about thirty minutes, the train arrived at Dortmund, and the man left the train. The woman had disembarked several stops before, smiling warmly as she left. Now that he was alone with Emil, Sonny took the unread pamphlet from the seat, holding it at arm's length. He read a few lines, then tore it to pieces, turning to Emil.

"I admire your restraint," he said.

"Couldn't make a fuss on the train, now could I?" Emil growled.

The train reached Aachen in late afternoon. Shivering, Sonny followed Emil to the main plaza and past city hall, overshadowed by the cathedral rising skyward in the background. Local lore indicated it was the result of an order by Charlemagne in the year 786. Supposedly it held his remains somewhere within its vaults. Sonny had read that at one time the church had the largest dome in half the continent.

Emil knew where he was going, and soon they were walking on narrow streets with increasingly fewer streetlamps. Traffic lightened as they moved farther from the square. Affixed to buildings and light posts were tattered political posters, remnants of the election from three months earlier. Sonny stopped and angrily ripped the face of Adolph Hitler from an outside wall, threw it to the ground, and stomped on it.

Emil turned. "Never mind that now. It'll only draw attention."

Sonny smiled as he twisted the sole of his boot on Hitler's face.

"Feel better now?"

"Actually, I do," Sonny answered cheerfully.

Another ten minutes and they reached a line of tired tenements. Emil stopped at one and went inside, telling Sonny to wait. After what seemed a long time, Emil returned with a frown. The two continued on in silence, no explanation forthcoming, toward a dim glow in the night sky. When they rounded a corner, the night became day. Lights by the score revealed railroad tracks bordered by hulking warehouses.

Emil pointed to a warehouse that looked like all the others, and in minutes they faced a large set of doors with a smaller door to the side. Emil brought out a set of keys, opened the small door; they were inside. He pulled a chain hanging from the ceiling, and Sonny saw the outline of a truck against dark empty space beyond.

As they moved deeper into the warehouse, their footsteps echoed off the hard floor. Emil unlocked the cab of the truck and retrieved a package of papers from the seat, gave it a cursory look, and glanced toward Sonny.

"There's been a change in plans. The shipment didn't come across this morning, so we have to get it."

"What do you mean?" Sonny's voice was shrill. He knew the answer.

"We have to get it in Plombieres. It's less than ten kilometers away."

"Ja, but there's a border . . . " said Sonny, suddenly tense. He'd asked for a jaunt in the country, but he hadn't signed up for crossing the border with contraband. Mouth agape as he imagined himself in prson garb, he stared at Emil. It was not his idea of a successful career. And what about Polly? Sonny paced in a circle, mumbling. Then he flashed on his father and stopped. Had this been his father's work, too?

Emil seemed mildly perturbed by the inconvenience but otherwise unconcerned, as if he crossed the border every day. That told Sonny exactly nothing—Emil was always that way. Sensing Sonny's misgivings, Emil said, "Relax. It's just a hitch. It'll be okay."

"Relax?" The word shot from Sonny's lips like a cannonball, the last syllable echoing in the empty space.

Emil laughed, which only made Sonny angry. Emil moved closer and, in a firm voice, said, "Stop!"

Jolted into silence, Sonny waited for an explanation.

"I've done this before. It's not a big deal," said Emil. "I'll explain as we drive. For now it's important to sit quietly in the truck and follow instructions." Emil grabbed Sonny's arm. "Did you hear me?"

"Ja. I understand." Sonny's temples throbbed. His throat was dry, his voice tinny and remote. He regretted asking Franco to put him in this spot, in this cold, empty warehouse. He'd only wanted to get out of Berlin, to see Germany. Hell! It sounded like a travelogue . . . Slowly he climbed into the cab, leaned forward with his hands on the dash, put his head down, and took a deep breath. There was nothing to do but trust Emil.

Sonny jumped at a sudden screeching, only to realize it was the rusty metal wheels of the warehouse door opening. Emil climbed into the truck and stepped on the starter. The engine groaned to life, then sputtered, and died.

"Shit!" He tried again, and this time it stayed, after thirty seconds running smoothly. "Good!" Emil put the truck in gear, drove out of the warehouse, stopped, closed, and secured the doors. "Later I'll explain. Just keep quiet. Everything's going to be fine."

The two men drove slowly through the empty streets of industrial Aachen, until they reached the dark, empty countryside. Twin headlamps threw cones of light over the bits of constantly changing roadway until Sonny read from a sign: "Border checkpoint—half kilometer ahead."

Emil slowed, drove off the road, stopped, cut the engine, and turned off the lights. Sonny couldn't read his expression in the dark.

"I'm walking to the border. Wait in the truck. I'll be back in twenty minutes," Emil said. And he was gone.

Sonny nearly laughed at Emil's admonition. Where the hell would he go? Emil's footsteps receded, leaving him in unfathomable silence. Clouds covered whatever moonlight might have brightened the road, and he strained to see. He'd noticed as they drove in that the forest hugged both sides of the road, sucking up whatever light and sound existed on this empty stretch. How could it be so desolate this close to the border? Surely there would be other traffic. But there was none.

After a few minutes, Sonny's city ears pricked to the unfamiliar sounds of the nighttime forest. He had no idea how deep the forest reached. For all he knew, there were open pastures full of cows on both sides of the road. No, not cows, not in winter. But maybe a border patrol! Sonny stifled the thought—better to think of cows.

What was taking Emil so long? Sonny tried to read his watch, but he couldn't see it in the dark. In Berlin he went anywhere, anytime, but his aloneness in the rural dark was unsettling. Closing his eyes didn't help. Images of gargoyles, talons raised, leered from the hood of the truck. When he opened his eyes, there was nothing to see, and he realized he was paying for his foolishness.

Sonny's head jerked at the sound of a real creature laughing at him. What the hell was that? His breathing was shallow. He straightened in his seat, took a deep breath, exhaled. Slowly, he repeated: "It's only my imagination, playing tricks on me."

Sonny had thought he understood the risk when he signed on, but *danger* and *risk* were only words, like *smuggling* and *sex*. Now the words were fraught with implication. He told himself that feeling afraid didn't equate to being in danger. Sitting in the dark wasn't dangerous; crossing the border with stolen goods was another matter. He replayed Emil's assurances that he'd done it before, not to worry. He had to calm down. He fell back in the seat with his eyes closed.

Within minutes, Sonny's ears twitched at the sound of boots scraping on the roadway, then saw Emil's bulk faintly through the window.

The door opened, and Emil climbed in, saying, "It's all set." He started the truck. "Relax. We're crossing to Plombieres. Then we'll load up the truck and return."

Sonny nodded, still too tense to speak.

Several signs warned of the checkpoint ahead. Then a big sign directed, "Be prepared to stop in 25 meters." Emil brought the truck to a stop beside the guardhouse in front of a gate blocking the road. A guard in the uniform of the Zollgrenzschutz, or German border patrol, walked out of the shed. His tunic was unbuttoned, and a cigarette hung from the corner of his mouth. He squinted as the smoke rose into his eyes.

Without looking into the truck, he said, "Papers."

Emil passed him an envelope. "Pleasant evening, though a bit chilly."

"It's okay." The man took it.

The ferret-faced guard looked into the cab, removed the cigarette from his mouth, and gestured with his chin toward Sonny. He licked his thin lips and, in an unfamiliar German dialect, asked, "Who's that?"

"My helper." Emil turned to Sonny and winked.

Ferret Face bent over the envelope, fingering what was inside, his lips moving as he counted, then nodded. Raising his head, he smiled with his mouth but not his eyes, raised the gate, and jerked his head forward for the truck to pass.

"Don't forget the boys on the other side," Emil said as he drove away.

Ferret Face saluted lazily.

Bright lights revealed a denuded no-man's land that in both directions harbored nothing but an outline of forest that ended abruptly, as if cut by a giant shovel. A dizzying maze of barbed wire cast whirling shadows towards the horizon. Emil drove silently, then stopped under the vertical black, yellow, and red of a Belgian flag, limp in the still, night air. An older man in uniform, with a big mustache but agreeable eyes and smile, shuffled to the truck, slightly bent.

"Papers, please," he said, in French.

Emil returned the smile. "Hello, Claude."

Claude answered in German. "So, it is you. Hello, my friend. What do you have for me tonight?" His warmth was real, but he turned quickly to the matter of lubrication for the wheel of commerce.

Emil jerked his head toward the German border. "He'll be along in a few minutes."

Claude's smile remained; he winked and raised the gate. Sonny looked at Emil with awe, exhaled, and fell back into his seat, thinking, "What a wonderful world!"

The truck wheezed through its gears, and when they were well inside Belgium, Emil smiled broadly at Sonny. "I've known those two for almost as long as I've been with Franco. But now, we'll visit a true friend. You'll like Fritz."

In several minutes they passed the small central square of Plombieres, where at opposite ends a big Gothic church faced down a squat, uninspiring municipal building. Emil drove another five minutes through the town and out, then turned right onto a dirt track bounded by tall, narrow trees shielding it from the road. They bounced and jostled for several hundred feet, then stopped at a sizable barn.

"Come. Let's see if farmer Fritz is awake."

Sonny stared at a modest wood frame structure with a peaked roof. Smoke drifted from the chimney, but the windows were dark. When they reached the door, Emil pounded. No answer came, so he pounded again, until a voice cried out in that Low German dialect.

"Hold on. I'm coming." A light came on. "Who is it?"

"Shit on the Kaiser! Open the door."

The door swung open. "I'll be damned. What the hell are you doing here?" A broad smile showed uneven yellow teeth. "Come in. The heat's escaping."

They stepped into a small, neat kitchen warmed by a woodstove. Shaking Emil's hand like a friend returned from the dead, Fritz told them to sit down—he'd make a pot of coffee. Emil introduced Sonny, as his partner, to Fritz Girardet. On the floor next to the table laid an old brown dog, its tail thumping, and Sonny crouched to scratch its ears.

"That's Bismarck," Fritz called over his shoulder.

"Kurt took ill," Emil said. "Never saw him, but I heard someone hacking and retching in the next room. So instead of driving out of Aachen with a truck full of merchandise, I retrieved the envelope from Kurt's wife, and we came straightaway."

Fritz's frowned. "I don't like it."

Emil shrugged, "Nothing to be done about it. The man was sick."

They sat at the kitchen table drinking coffee and eating homemade biscuits. After they'd chewed over why they were there, they went on to how long it had been. Sonny leaned back to listen. It would make a great story if only he could write it . . . When there was a lull, he asked, "Where did you meet?"

"During the war, we were both stationed in the Lübeck shipyards, and we became friends then. When the mutiny started, we joined in. Everyone knew the war was lost, but the command ordered the fleet out anyway," Fritz said, throwing up his hands in disgust.

"Everyone was sick of war," said Emil, "and with Soviets sprouting like mushrooms in a summer rain, we were caught in the middle. At least for a while."

"Heady days," Fritz agreed.

"Too much so," Emil noted as he massaged his temples, coaxing his memory. "No one wanted to get caught between the Bolshies and the army, so there was no choice but to join the Reds. And their ill-fated revolution."

Fritz sneered, "No one was going to stick with the navy or the army. The war was lost."

Emil agreed, "After four years of war, we were beaten and exhausted. The left had wanted peace for a couple years, and now it was pure chaos. Factions split. No one agreed an anything. Governing was out of the question, and in the end, passion turned to the right. Ebert sided with the army, got its support, and the Freikorps put down the revolt for good."

"The goddamn right still has Germany by the balls," Fritz said with a scowl. "I wasn't a Communist, and sure as hell I'm no Nazi. But that was long ago, before the Nazis. All that mattered was that the Kaiser abdicate."

Emil tapped his index finger on the table as he spoke. "Then the war was over for real, and that was all the relief we needed."

Fritz nodded. "Long before the revolution faltered, we both lost interest—not that we had much—and went home. Emil stayed in Berlin and I returned to Aachen." He brightened. "It was 6 January 1919, and we had just arrived in Berlin. Leaving the Zoo Station, we got swept up in the crowd at the Tiergarten." He looked at Emil. "Do you remember that?"

"Who could forget?" Emil answered. "The *Red Flag*—that was the Bolshie newspaper—said there were two hundred thousand people there that day, and I believe it. People were everywhere—some armed, most carrying red flags, and everyone waiting for hours. The leaders never showed up. Can you believe it? They pissed away the revolution! It was all but over by March. Martial law was declared, and it stayed in effect until the end of the year."

"I was gone by then," Fritz noted, "and getting more sick and tired of Germany by the day. So I came here ten years ago, moved in with my uncle. He never married, and when he died, the farm came to me. My family's Old Huguenot, and they lived in the area for years, some around here, others around Aachen, more in Holland."

Suddenly a gray cat jumped onto the table, heading straight for the pitcher of milk. When Fritz grabbed her and put her on the floor, she meowed loudly. "Marlene thinks she owns the damn place," he said.

There was no mistaking what Fritz did for a living. He looked like a thousand farmers, dirt under his nails, soiled pants and shirt, the fabric thin and mended—the picture of rural simplicity. Years in the sun had weathered his face and given it character, even nobility. Gray hair fell across his forehead. His eyes were tired and red. He struck a wooden match with his thumb to light a cigarette, wistful: "It's a meager living but worth it."

Sonny's curiosity was whetted, "Fritz, how did you get involved in the enterprise?"

Fritz blew out a cloud of smoke and looked at Emil. Suddenly unsure of himself, Sonny's face reddened, and he too looked to Emil for support.

"He's all right, just naturally curious." Emil flipped a hand in Sonny's direction. "He's Morris Landauer's son."

It took some prompting for Fritz to remember . . . "In that case, I guess you're all right," he said, the corners of his mouth rising into a grin.

"We lost touch for a couple years, then exchanged holiday cards, and one day out of nowhere." Fritz gestured toward his big ex-navy buddy. "He just showed up."

Emil wore a "Who, me?" look on his face.

Fritz shrugged. "We talked about old times, and when he was ready, he told me about the enterprise. I signed on without much convincing. Then I set him up with an old school chum, who passed on the name of a German border guard who knew how to take a bribe. It was easy money, no sweat off his ass, and we've been using the crossing at Reinartzkehl ever since."

Emil stood up, stretching. "We better load the truck—we have to cross before dawn."

There were at least a hundred crates, most small enough for one to lift, but several requiring the strength of two. After muscling a particularly heavy box into a corner, Sonny asked, "What are we hauling?"

"The usual—chocolate, cigarettes, French wine, Cognac . . . miscellaneous merchandise," Fritz answered.

After an hour, the barn was empty except for the old tractor, the hay, some cows, and the mice. Emil promised the next time wouldn't be so long, and they were back on the road with hours to spare. Claude waved them through the Belgian side, then Ferret Face through the German entry, and by noon they were unloading in Berlin.

Warm from the exertion, Sonny was pleased that his fear had been unfounded. He had learned that the border was a sieve, at least for those with the grease to slip through. Returning to Berlin, he'd struggled with the idea of telling Polly about Ferret Face, Claude, Fritz, and his anxiety while waiting for Emil, but knew he couldn't do it. His father's voice prevailed—no one had to know, not yet.

He'd wait to see what the new year had in store. But for the first time, he felt pessimistic, even fatalistic about its prospects.

6

Death is better, a milder fate than tyranny.
—Aeschylus

Sonny's apprehension was well founded. On 30 January 1933, Adolf Hitler became Germany's chancellor. That night, Joseph Goebbels, chief Nazi propagandist, organized a massive torchlight parade through Berlin. Depending on the political leaning of the reporter, estimates of the number taking to the streets varied from twenty to sixty thousand Brownshirts (SA, or Sturmabteilung), Steel Helmets (League of Front Soldiers), and SS (Schutzstaffel). Torch-bearing marchers sang, "We want to die for the flag" amid shouts of "Death to the Jews!"

Some onlookers were joyful over this development, but others met the undertone of aggression moving through the city with foreboding. And with good reason, for in the days to come simply failing to return the Nazi salute could result in a beating, or worse. Otto and Mischa, with the rest of the KPD cell, were at the Hammer & Sickle that night, keeping despair at bay. Sonny and Polly comforted each other in the little café.

Almost immediately, Hitler took steps to consolidate power. Using the Reichstag fire of 27 February as fait accompli, he unleashed the SA against his mortal enemy, the Communists. Granted unlimited power to arrest without charge (and no court recourse for arrestees), Nazi goons kicked in doors looking for Reds to settle old accounts. After dealing with the Communists, Hitler turned his ire on the Social Democrats and the trade unions. Then it was the Centre Party's turn.

Eliminating visible opposition, the Nazis began to destroy theater, music, cabaret, clubs—everything artistic. The intelligentsia fled in droves, some just ahead of arrest. And of course, there were the Jews.

Ironically, in the November 1932 election, the Nazis lost seats in the Reichstag, though theirs remained the largest party. The Communists gained and with the Social Democrats held more seats than the Nazis, though that promising circumstance never evolved to a ruling coalition. Instead, two large blocks—Nazis and Communists—intent on destroying the parliamentary system, confronted each other. Government ceased to function, forcing Chancellor Franz von Papen to resign. After months of stalemate and backroom politicking, what so many had dreaded became reality.

Reichstag elections were set for 5 March as a condition of Hitler's appointment. Hitler's campaign presented a clear choice—the Communists or the German people. With party leaders in hiding or under arrest, the KPD could not campaign and thus drew a dismal 12 percent of the vote. The Nazis and their partner, the Nationalists, took just over 50 percent. The republic was dead.

The harassment of Jews now proceeded in earnest. The SA and SS instigated riots. The first concentration camp opened for political prisoners in Dachau, north of Munich. The Enabling Act of 23 March granted Hitler dictatorial powers. On 1 April, the Nazi Party organized a boycott of all the Jewish shops in Germany. Soon, all would be required to display a Star of David or the word *Juden*. The Reichstag passed laws limiting the practice of Jewish physicians and lawyers, placing quotas on Jews attending schools and universities, and limiting their entry to the professions. Even kosher butchering was outlawed.

On 7 April, the "Law for the Restoration of a Professional Civil-Service" dismissed Jews from service. Front-line veterans of the Great War were the lone exception. On 11 April, a government decree defined as non-Aryan "anyone descended from a non-Aryan, especially Jewish parents or grandparents." One parent or grandparent, especially one of the Jewish faith, was enough to classify the descendant as non-Aryan.

On 26 April, Herman Göring, Interior Minister of Prussia, created the Gestapo (Geheime Staatspolizei or Secret State Police), transforming the Prussian political police into an organ of the Nazi state. Then, on 10 May came the crowning indignity—books written by Jews and others opposing Nazism were burned at the Opera House in Berlin and on university campuses across Germany. In July, the government stripped Eastern European Jews of their German citizenship.

In the midst of the mayhem, Otto and his comrades huddled in a Neukölln flat, plotting their next move though it was too late for much but self-preservation. They'd mourned the loss of too many comrades, reaching the end of their possibilities.

Cooped up too long, Otto one evening reached for a cigarette and found the pack empty. Leaving the flat was risky, but longing for the fresh spring air, he still had the swagger, and with a tavern nearby . . .

Returning from the local watering hole, Otto stopped and leaned against the lamppost at the corner near the flat. Cupping his hands against the breeze, he struck a match to light his cigarette. Without damping the match, he took a deep drag.

Suddenly the entrance door of the apartment building flung open and crashed against the wall.

Otto recoiled at the scene before him. Men in uniform were leading his comrades and friends, in handcuffs, from the apartment building he had left only minutes before. Now he noticed the police wagon and staff car parked on the street. Frozen by fear, his eyes remained fixed on the parade before him.

The match burning to his fingertips, Otto hissed, "Holy shit!" Panic told him to run as fast and far away as he could, but another voice said no—running would just draw attention. So he stood as if belonging on the corner, sweating in the cool air.

Otto silently cursed his friends' bad luck, the fucking Nazis, the hard times that brought him to this moment. The door of the police wagon closed with a clank, locking his comrades inside. The vehicle hummed down the street, away.

He stared at the empty space. A short, bespectacled man in SS uniform sauntered from the building onto the sidewalk, his expression smug as he watched the police wagon disappear. He lit a cigarette, took several drags, and scanned the street, at first passing over Otto, then returning for a second look before moving on. Otto's heart leapt, but nothing happened. The officer said something to one of his men, got into the black sedan, and drove off.

Otto's legs felt immovable, imbedded in the pavement. Slowly, he flexed his toes, bent his knees, raised one foot and then the other, and walked away. Luck was on his side today. But what about tomorrow?

From that day Otto stayed in one place no more than a week. He moved from a broken-down shed in Wedding to a basement flat in Neukölln to a fancy apartment in Charlottenburg to Sonny's warehouse cellar to Willy's tiny flat in Wedding—there were dozens of places. He couldn't remember them all. He watched for a sympathetic patron, an empty building, a quiet corner. Abandoned warehouses and cellars were dirty and rat-infested but perfect for permanent transients on the alert.

Safe houses dwindled in number as the Nazis sent their tentacles deep into the neighborhoods via block wardens and informers. Fear of the prospect of arrest kept Otto focused. The guilt of survival, so intense at times he almost wanted to be caught, tormented him. But that, too, passed.

At first, nearly anything—a furtive glance or an open door—triggered his memory of that day, sending him into a tailspin. The image of his comrade's arrest never receded entirely, but as the years passed it remained below the surface for longer intervals. And his shivers of paranoia were—he was grateful—brief.

Otto, reaching an accommodation of sorts, came to see his life as the butt of an ironic joke: Cigarettes saved his life; for that reason he eventually quit smoking. For months, every drag he took brought that day back . . . but he thanked his atheist ass that he'd had an empty pack that day.

Now a day or night rarely passed that Otto didn't dream of escaping his dirty, miserable life. Frustration mounted as he waited for a chance, whatever that might be. That was all he had.

7

Yet I will bring one plague upon Pharaoh, and upon Egypt.
—Exodus

"Thank you, I'd love to," Sonny responded to Aunt Esther's invitation to Passover seder in 1936. Cradling the telephone receiver, he smiled, remembering past seders with his parents, Uncle Simon, and the others.

Passover was Sonny's favorite holiday, actually the only one he liked at all, because it was celebrated at home with friends, good food, and a stirring story. There was no need to attend a long synagogue service; instead the family did an abbreviated reading of the Haggadah. Earlier seders had alternated between the homes of his parents and Uncle John and Aunt Esther.

With his parents gone, Sonny appreciated the invitation. He didn't ask whether Polly could come, not with the Nuremburg Laws in place. Of his family, only Uncle Simon had met Polly, but everyone knew about her, knew she was a shiksa, a non-Jew.

It was more than four years since Sonny had approached Polly at the little café. Something akin to love had grown between them, but they rarely talked of what they meant to each other. When they might have shared a flat or married, neither was willing. Both liked the relationship as it was. Sonny had never proposed marriage—perhaps he was unsure of Polly's response. Now it was out of the question. For a Jew and an Aryan of the opposite sex even socializing was illegal.

Despite the danger, they continued to meet, though less often than they had before. Polly's job occupied her days, and Sonny's work, with more frequent forays from Berlin, took many evenings. Still, they managed one or two evenings each week, some Sundays, and an afternoon or two. They met under cover of the parks—Tiergarten or Hasenheide—in Sonny's flat, or in a distant precinct of Berlin where they were unknown. Sonny could have afforded a larger flat in the Mitte or even in the West End, but he never considered moving. He liked living with Herr Wagner, and frankly, he was reluctant to make a commitment. A larger flat would have signaled that he wanted Polly to join him . . . It hadn't happened, and now it never could . . .

Esther's table was beautifully set, with the seder plate of symbolic foods in the middle of the table, next to the cup of wine awaiting Elijah's mythical lips. Uncle John sat at the head, to lead the ceremony. On one side was Aunt Esther, a plump and pleasant woman who spoiled her children; on the other was their son, Rudy, about four years younger than Sonny. Rudy had been expelled from university in 1933. Now he taught in a religious school.

Next to Rudy was his younger sister, Frieda, less shy and prettier than she'd been a year earlier, apparently unaware of her appeal. Sonny found this charming. Aunt Edith, Simon's long-suffering wife (or so she was known), sat between Frieda and Uncle Georg. Easygoing and somewhat dull, Georg was the third of four sons and a salesman in a men's clothing store. Rumor had it that he'd briefly been married to a blond, blue-eyed Christian woman several years his senior, but the story was deemed off limits. Even Simon was reluctant to speak of it. Sonny knew Georg only as a confirmed bachelor. He couldn't imagine such flamboyance—Georg talked endlessly of the men's retail business . . .

Sonny sat between Georg and Simon, who sat next to Esther. John had been reading from the Passover Haggadah when Sonny felt a soft nudge from Uncle Simon, his father's youngest brother and Sonny's favorite. Simon motioned with a slight tilt of his head toward the head of the table. Uncle John had put down the Haggadah and was decrying the horrible state of affairs in Germany. What better forum for such venting than recitation of the biblical exodus?

In Simon's world, the worst was yet to come. Now his smile was so wry as to be barely detectable, but Sonny read it to say, "The family has finally come to its senses." He detected profound pain . . . anguish . . . as Simon's very essence, visible on his face, present in his words and his tone. Only his sharp intelligence and searing insight, blunted by his sense of humor, kept him from becoming morose.

Immutable as the laws of nature was Simon. The sun appeared in the east, birds flew, and Simon cracked wise. His bleak vision become reality was disconcerting, despite its three years in the making.

During those three years, the familiar, comfortable world of everyone at the seder table had veered dangerously out of control. "All under the guidance of a wickedly funny God, if one exists, which I doubt," Simon had said. Still, the people around the table whispered, laughed, gazed into space, though each at some point listened to, or pretended to listen to, the reading of the Book of Exodus.

Perhaps inspired by the optimism of the biblical tale, John's indignation now erupted like hot lava. His outrage was understandable, but the venom with which he delivered his screed surprised Simon, who then nudged Sonny.

John was a cautious and circumspect man. He looked to the past for inspiration and guidance. He dressed conservatively, never changing to fit the fashion, supported the Center Party because the Social Democrats were too far left, and hated the Communists almost as much as the Nazis. Through the '20s, when Berlin percolated a fountain of new ideas, John had been confused. Like so many others, he was a living contradiction; the freedoms that brought middle-class prosperity also brought excesses that repelled him.

Uncomfortable with abstract daring, John rejected Dada and Expressionism, the new wave in the arts. Should he venture into a museum or gallery, he favored the simplicity of a pretty landscape and abhorred the abstract works of Otto Dix, the social commentary of George Grosz. He hummed songs he'd heard sung by Tauber, disdaining the cacophony of Schoenberg, though he tolerated Weill's "low cabaret melodies."

When the Kaiser called in 1914, John marched off to war, returning—with thousands of others—disillusioned, though not radicalized. Eschewing the call of the Communists, he watched with horror the failed revolution of Karl Liebknecht and Rosa Luxemburg, endured hyperinflation as he had no savings to lose, and cringed at loosening societal mores and the blurring of sexual roles.

Prosperity eventually had raised John to the middle class, where he came to see his newfound status more as a birthright than as a well-deserved victory. Hard work and moderate success confirmed his faith in the new Germany, which embraced him as a secular Jew and kept the hounds of anti-Semitism endured by his ancestors firmly at bay. By the end of 1932, with the Republic mired in rancor and unable to govern, John felt abandoned. But he never gave up hope.

Sonny often had heard Uncle John cite with pride the Jews who, like cream, had risen to the top. But he suspected that the irony of the lives of John's two favorites had escaped him. Albert Einstein, that model of assimilation and advancement, had fled to America. The venerated Walter Rathenau, industrialist cum foreign minister, had preached moderation only to field an assassin's bullet in 1922. The shock of the loss of Rathenau at the hands of the radical right led John to keep his head down, work hard, and move away from the Mitte as soon as he could. Fleeing his orthodox neighbors in Scheunenviertel, he had found refuge in a middle-class neighborhood in the West End.

Tonight John did not refer to the bearded, black-suited Orthodox Jews as failures of assimilation, as the easy targets of a scornful government, endlessly caricatured as the public face of all Jews. To single them out tonight would be cheap and cruel. An attack on them was an attack on them all.

Stripped of citizenship, the people at the table were part of a terrible dilemma, their bourgeois life threatened. John had always been a loyal German, but now his rightful place in society was denied him. Thrashing about like a drowning man, acting out of character, he groped for a hand, any hand. In the relative safety of his home, the thoughts and words long trapped inside burst through his reticence.

Neat in appearance like his father, Rudy had felt the sting of repression when the university expelled him for no reason but that he was a Jew. His eyes, bright with passion, widened as he followed his father's words. Draconian changes had made their way to his uncle's flat in the West End. If John and Rudy were enemies of the Reich, they all were.

There was nothing more for John to say; his anger had run out of steam. He dropped his eyes. Esther forced a smile and put her hand on his. Muttering under his breath, John retreated further into himself as Rudy recounted his loss and the anger over his powerlessness grew. He couldn't let it rest. His eyes briefly meeting Sonny's, Rudy confronted his father.

"Why the anger now, all of a sudden? What does it take? It's been three years since I was expelled for my *destructive Jewish cleverness*." Rudy enunciated each word of the oft-used phrase. His sarcasm oozed like an infection, and the generational divide widened, the Nazi epithet giving voice to simmering family conflict.

Despite the humiliation his son had endured, John, like too many others, was slow to recognize what Simon had known for years. But his anger at the manifest injustice was no less real, and now Rudy's words personalized his anguish. Surrounded by ancient symbols of their people's famous exodus was irony as thick as the honey on their matzo. They were part of a poignant tableau that surely played in thousands of Jewish homes.

From that moment, the seder became even more somber. Each participant halfheartedly read a passage. Coming to the iteration of a helpful God delivering plagues on the Egyptians, they felt an irrational hope. Deliverance seemed possible; the air of foreboding lifted.

With a sudden burst of optimism, Uncle Georg told of a family emigrating to Palestine. Frieda recalled a schoolmate whose thirteen-year-old brother was sent there by his Zionist parents in 1933. Aunt Edith had a friend whose brother had left for America. A lively discussion of the possibilities ensued, and as each contributed, the reality of their dilemma further sobered them. A silence fell, sending each into personal reverie.

Only Simon had been without words other than to read his portion from the Haggadah. He knew what the Nazis intended. His shoulders bore the burden of ancient pogroms, piled one atop the other, era upon era. Czars and pharaohs had long tormented his soul, sending demons in the night. Like the blood on the doorpost, Simon was marked as the one to suffer for the family, and so it had always been.

"It's a wonder he hasn't suffocated under the weight," Sonny's father once said. Maybe he had.

Easily the most interesting and compelling member of Sonny's family, Simon could speak intelligently on a wide range of topics, albeit filtered through his Job-like lens. Long acknowledged as the smartest of the lot, "he could have achieved anything had he only applied himself." Perhaps school had come too easily—he'd lost interest. Instead of going to university, he'd gone to work.

Sonny's father accused Simon of taking the easy way out; unfortunately, that was the family line. Used as a cudgel against Simon almost exclusively behind his back, the accusation stuck like an unwelcome guest. Family history defined Simon as depressive, cynical, underachieving, insecure in his abilities, and too easily distracted to focus on a career, let alone a profession.

A sad shake of the head secured Simon's place in the family, never to be altered. Simon's brothers never saw through to the man as Sonny did. They grew comfortable making Simon their foil, obscuring their own failings in the shuffle of family emotion.

Simon came to accept his role with equanimity, as if he were no longer in control of his life. He greeted all matters with bemused resignation, for it could be no other way. Work was a series of small jobs beneath his ability that finally led to clerking in a company manufacturing electrical supplies. With Simon's keen mind and interest in science, he flourished.

Unsure of what Simon was involved in, Sonny thought it had something to do with the military, probably the air force. Simon never spoke of his work. But he loved to tell a joke, usually at his own expense, and he was a witty conversationalist, especially in regard to humanity's penchant for darkness. Sonny recalled talking with Simon at a family gathering late in 1932, when the Republic teetered on collapse.

"Do you know the story of Felix Mendelssohn's arrival in Berlin?" Simon had asked.

"You mean the great philosopher? I don't think so."

"Yes, who else? . . . I'll get to it." Simon rarely went straight to the point. "Losing the war had its advantages. We got rid of the Kaiser, the military's eye was blackened, and the Republic was born. Not that it's been a smooth journey, but at least we've—by 'we' I mean Jews—had a say in the mishegaas, the madness, of governing."

Sonny laughed. "You mean hyperinflation followed by prosperity, then worldwide depression and the rise of Nazism."

"Stay off my terrain," Simon said with a mirthless smile. "I fear our renaissance in governing will soon be over. Extremists have Germany by the balls, and that's going to kill the Republic . . . but I digress."

Sonny winced, waiting for his uncle to continue.

"For hundreds of years, since Jews have been allowed to live in Berlin, we've gotten the crumbs, after everyone else got a bite at the pie." He waved his hand dismissively. "Then after the Great War, we had a seat at the table. Suddenly Jews flourished, as if by miracle. But we were ready. Now we can attend university if we choose," Simon said with obvious irony.

He continued, "Professions opened, and we took full advantage. Look at the list—Max Liebermann in art, Arnold Schoenberg in music, Max Reinhart in theater, Jakob Wasserman in literature, Albert Einstein, the greatest genius in science. And Sigmund Freud, pioneer in psychoanalysis, philosopher Ernest Cassirer, journalist Joseph Roth. And of course, the late Walter Rathenau in government." Simon counted them on his fingers. "Those are just the most prominent ones."

"So, how does the eminent Herr Mendelssohn figure into this?" Sonny inquired.

"Ja, ja. I'm getting to it." Simon's palm rested on Sonny's chest. "We helped create a culture unmatched in Europe. We're the strongest supporters of the Republic. Sure, there are Bolsheviks in the mix, but that's to be expected. Hell, there were two Jews in the first cabinet! Imagine that, after all those years in the wilderness! Now to Mendelssohn. He illustrates just how far we've come." Simon lowered his voice to a whisper. "And how far we might fall."

Then Simon asked, "Did you know he was a hunchback?"

Sonny shook his head.

"He was frail, but what a mind! Anyway, it was 1743. He was from Dessau, only fourteen years old when he arrived at the Rosenthal Gate, the only entry point allowed for a Jew. On that day, 'six oxen, seven swine, and a Jew' were granted entry. One of Europe's greatest minds listed with the livestock."

"How the hell did you know that?" Sonny was astonished.

"I know everything," Simon said dryly, then regained the thread of his narrative. "From Mendelssohn to today, unimaginable success. And that's our problem."

Simon's face sagged under the weight, but his eyes remained on Sonny's. "That very success presages our demise. Anti-Semites can't tolerate a Germany with so many successful Jews. No matter that we're less than 1 percent of the populace," he paused to reconsider. Then, "Or perhaps it's because of that. Those malignant fascists can't stomach our success. And if that senile old man makes Hitler the chancellor, I fear everything will crash down on us."

Simon's dire pessimism chafed like a permanent rash. He was at nihilism's border, his prescience of the Nazi rise to power scaring him almost as much as the fact of it. Now with apocalypse at hand, it became his obsession. Simon long recognized the adroit use of violence and propaganda as the Nazis' unique language. He might have admired Goebbels had he not been so repulsed by his message.

None of the other parties had had the dark vision or skill to win out, though the Communists had tried. Simon knew the German workers would never go Bolshevik. When it came to a choice, there was no leader to challenge Hitler. The old man had picked him. That it had taken him fourteen years to rise to power didn't surprise Simon. It simply prolonged the agony.

Simon's uncanny ability to see the decline, then the ultimate defeat, of reason and democracy had come at a terrible cost. More than a crushing blow, it was debilitating, irreversible, and the mark of his personal decline. On 30 January 1933, the earth began to rotate backwards. That he had predicted calamity became a stream of self-loathing and guilt—as if his cynicism were responsible for the Republic's death.

Months had turned to years, the cycle of fear and remorse gnawing at Simon's equilibrium and relationships, especially that with Edith. Some lauded her as a pillar of strength, others as an object of pity for what she endured. That Simon was difficult to live with was a given—a priori, like oil and water. But Edith had long since accepted his quirks with good cheer and her own brand of fatalism. Pleasant and full of life, her laughter was a counterpoint to Simon's increasing depression. She loved Simon and dismissed the family's view of him as its problem, not hers, and she refused to be a victim.

That the two had married and flourished was proof of the mystery that bound the sexes. Their odd union produced no offspring, probably for the best. Sonny, for one, shuddered at the thought of a miniature brooding Simon.

At the end of 1935, Simon had been dismissed from the job he'd held for twelve years, a loss that rivaled if not exceeded Rudy's.

"National security," his manager explained, wringing his hands as if removing something sticky. "I'm sorry. It's out of my control. We can't have a Jew in that position." Simon had gone slack, the air knocked from his lungs. He stared, uncomprehending yet knowing full well his predicament. In the time it took to blink back a tear, his worst fear was realized.

No one spoke of his loss at the seder, though the fact hung unpleasantly in the air.

Work had given Simon's life meaning, kept black thoughts at bay. Now that refuge was cruelly gone—through fiat propelled by hate. In the days and weeks following the seder, Simon's depression deepened, his tears flowed easily, and he became increasingly remote. Soon he was deep in a colorless, brooding despondency, shades of gray darkening to black. He no longer cared enough to be a cynic. Worse, his humor shriveled like a grape drying in the sun. That's when Edith got scared.

Through the rest of 1936, Nuremburg Laws in place, the lot of Germany's Jewish citizens stagnated. During the summer, Hitler hosted the Olympics, turning Berlin into a showcase for the entire world to see. Several months before the big event, anti-Semitic graffiti disappeared, making the city seem almost normal. As for the games, Negro athlete Jesse Owens, from America, grabbed the headlines—much to the consternation of the Führer and Sonny's delight.

Once the games ended, the clouds of alienation and fear returned and grew. For the first time, Sonny considered leaving Germany. He thought about writing Paul for help in gaining entry into America . . . Or he could stay in Belgium after a run with Emil, disappear into Antwerp's dense Jewish quarter, get papers on the black market, and go on to Paris or London. But he didn't take the next step. He wasn't ready. He didn't know where to go. He couldn't leave without Polly . . .

Germany was Polly's home, her family was here, and she didn't want to leave. Sonny was the one under attack. She abhorred the current state of affairs . . . but to leave? In that regard she was fooling herself—so long as they were together, she *was* at risk. They couldn't walk freely through the Mitte. stroll Ku'damm, stop at a coffee shop, or take in a cinema. It brought enormous strain. Polly harbored no illusions about their future. In many ways she was more pessimistic than Sonny. Such was their dilemma.

Sonny often heard this Jew or another say, "The craziness will pass; Germans will come to their senses." Some believed it couldn't get worse, that they'd weather the storm. Germany was "too civilized" to continue the horror.

"That's sheer madness," Mischa railed when he heard such sentiments. "Fool! You walk about with a noose around your neck and act as if it's an accessory, a passing fancy."

Sonny couldn't disagree. Even his family saw that it was too late for wishes. With passage of the Nuremburg Laws, there was no turning back. Of that he was sure.

Yet birds sang in the trees, the sun's warming rays felt good on Sonny's face, and Berlin's cafés still served good coffee and sweets. Because of his looks, Sonny escaped the insults that Mischa often suffered, but strangers occasionally confided their slurs as if he were one of them. He bit his tongue and endured the shame of his silence. To fight each insult would be futile, dangerous.

Polly, Mischa, Sophie, and acquaintances met in familiar cafés where they felt safe—to talk, laugh, and cry over coffee and cigarettes. Even Otto appeared when he felt secure enough, and once he brought his old girlfriend, Angela. They'd run into each other somewhere in Wedding and had a tender reunion. Sonny never saw her after that. When he asked about her later, Otto only shrugged.

Talk at the cafés always centered on emigration, and more than once Sonny heard himself say, "If we had any sense, we'd all leave." Every Jew was hurt in some way—expulsion from university, loss of a job, family business damaged by the boycotts, relationships shattered. There was no future for them in Germany.

Late one night, drinking coffee at a small, Jewish-owned café near Rosenthaler Platz, Sonny and Polly shared a few laughs, a few tears, with recent acquaintances:

Helga was an artist without much inspiration. When it did strike, her vision was so bleak and hopeless she couldn't paint. Her uncle had left for London in February 1934, and her parents worked nonstop to join him. Worn down by disappointment and more than a hint of jealousy, she spoke dreamily of a friend with an uncle in New York. The lucky fellow's relative had just wired him the money and papers to emigrate.

Kurt, an unemployed actor, cursed his luck and laughed bitterly over his uncle going to Warsaw rather than to America, but he'd go . . .

Such was their despondency that both Helga and Kurt spoke with more feeling than conviction, their talk of departure often ending in uneasy silence, fidgeting, looking at their hands, avoiding eye contact. No matter how good they felt for those who left, news of another departure was bittersweet, in the end sad. Envy, self-pity, and jealousy stirred in those left behind, as well as horror at what had forced another friend, acquaintance, or stranger to leave home.

Those with resources and the desire to emigrate could leave, but thousands of poor Jews were caught in an ever-tightening spiral. Constant Jew-baiting attacked the soul and occasionally the body. Diminishing opportunity pushed people deeper into a financial hole. Money wasn't enough; documents were required to gain entry elsewhere. A U.S. citizen had to sign an affidavit for an immigrant's legal entry—if he fell within the quota. France, Belgium, and England required visas not easy to obtain. Jews weren't welcome anywhere, least of all in Germany. The truth weighed.

Some had family ties making them hesitate to leave. The entire family went—or no one. Mischa stood between two forces—Sophie pushing to go, his father pulling him to stay. Sonny, with no such constraint, gave short shrift to that anchor. Still, he wasn't ready to go. His work with Emil and Franco kept him from leaving. And there was Polly.

Even the "Nuremburg Race Laws, for the Protection of German Blood and Honor" failed to waken those who could not see, or refused to admit, their predicament. The laws stripped Jews of their citizenship, turning thousands, including Sonny, into medieval serfs. For those confused as to whether they were in fact Jews, the act provided the definition: anyone with at least three Jewish grandparents. Less than that made you a half-breed, a mischlinge. One had only to consult a chart posted by the Justice Ministry in public places for clarification. Sonny and his friends required none.

Rumors spread of the jailing of Jewish men and Aryan females, or vice versa, for "race defilement," the legal euphemism for a romance or even a friendship. The whispered word of an angry coworker or jealous neighbor was the risk Sonny and Polly took to be together. Yet they continued to meet at the warehouse, in Herr Wagner's flat, or at some other clandestine location. Their time together was often uncomfortable, filled with paranoia. Sneaking around took its toll. They were cautions, but no one could tell Sonny whom to love!

Evil's veil had fallen, and few of Germany's Jews could escape the isolation that had plunged Simon and others into despondency. Herded into virtual ghettos of ever-greater economic and social deprivation, they had no legal protection.

In the four months after the seder, Sonny neither saw nor spoke to anyone in his family, a normal occurrence, since he rarely saw them. Then, early on a Tuesday evening in August, the telephone rang in Herr Wagner's flat. Sonny answered on the third ring. He barely finished saying, "Hello," when he heard Rudy's strangely disconnected voice.

"Sonny, it's Rudy. Uncle Simon is missing. He's been gone all day." He stuttered, "I . . . we . . . need help finding him. Ah, um, ah."

"Slow down. Repeat what you said," Sonny said, trying to stay calm. He pushed his dread away, searching his memory for Simon's wry smile.

Long seconds of silence followed. Rudy apparently was organizing his thoughts. "This morning Simon told Aunt Edith he was going to the old neighborhood. He hasn't returned. I thought he might have gone looking for you. Have you seen him?" Anxiety laced every word. Rudy struggled to keep his voice at its normal pitch.

Perplexed, Sonny stared at the telephone receiver. "No, but that doesn't mean he isn't looking for me. He might have gone to the warehouse." His words sounded unconvincing.

"Right," Rudy agreed, willing to grasp at any straw. "Edith is frantic. We all are. We're trying not to think the worst."

How horribly "appropriate," Sonny thought, but he didn't respond. There were voices in the background.

"Every morning Simon leaves the flat to look for a job—he's been looking for almost a year." Rudy's voice was stretched, brittle. "He left about 10:00, and when he didn't return for dinner, Edith got worried. You know how he is, and he's only gotten worse . . . We need help."

Ignoring the cheap shot Rudy didn't realize he'd made, Sonny said, "I'm coming. We'll find him." Again, the possibilities assaulted him like water splashing from a boiling pot. He flinched, overcome by guilt for not having seen Simon since the seder. Heading for the door, he stopped to tell Herr Wagner what to do should Simon turn up.

Simon was Sonny's last link to his father's family . . . What if he were gone? Sonny squelched the fear that he'd seen Simon for the last time. Suddenly, everything was unfamiliar, depleted, anemic. With some effort, he pushed his doubts aside, struggled again to see Simon's crooked smile. Ah, there he was, standing on a corner in the Mitte, not far from the Theater am Schiffbauerdamm. It was two or three years earlier . . . Simon had come to meet a friend in the old neighborhood. Sonny ran into him by accident.

Simon told Sonny a joke: "Two old Jews shared a Berlin park bench, one reading a Yiddish newspaper and the other reading *Der Sturmer*, the Nazi paper. The one reading *Der Sturmer* started laughing, and after a while, this was too much for the other one. He put down his newspaper and said, 'Is it not enough you should read that awful Nazi rag of lies, but that you should find it funny?' His friend looked up to ask, 'What is in your Yiddish paper? Jews are insulted, Jews are assaulted, and it goes on and on, nothing but tears and sorrow. When I read *Der Sturmer*, there is good news: Jews own and control the world!'"

Sonny had laughed long after Simon disappeared around the corner. That's what he wanted now, what he needed to remember. They would have much to talk about when Simon turned up . . . Sonny sleepwalked onto the subway, held onto the strap of the car as it moved from station to station, filled with Nazi banners reminding everyone who was in charge, colorful posters extolling the ethic of hard work and family, and sinister exposés of Jewish-international conspiracy to rob the German homeland of its essence.

When the train came to a stop, Sonny's eyes fell on a graphic showing a fat, hook-nosed, devious, grinning Bolshevik, another of orthodox Jews with distorted features, hoarding money. Jews were to be feared, mocked, and ridiculed, made to play the jester. First the funny hat, then the pointed shoes, the false nose, the self-mocking sign hanging from the neck: unrecognizable, nonhuman objects of derision, perpetrators of "destructive Jewish cleverness."

The obscenities gave Sonny the jitters, so he looked away. Finally the train left the station, and Simon's old Jews on the park bench returned. A smile came to his lips—he needed those two old Jews . . .

Sonny ran from the station . . . He found the door to Simon and Edith's apartment open. He could hear Rudy's voice but not his words. Then Rudy saw Sonny. Face tightly drawn, he nodded curtly.

"Should we contact the police?" someone asked.

Before anyone could answer, the others saw Sonny . . . murmured hello. Someone said Edith was resting in the bedroom.

"No police," Uncle John snapped, and everyone agreed. "We'll look until we find him." Each got a search assignment. All would meet back at the flat in an hour. Almost a dozen men and women filed from the building . . .

As Sonny peered into doorways and alleys for a familiar face that wasn't there, he felt disconnected from reality. He half expected Simon to lope around the next corner or pop up in a window, laughing. The other half filled him with dread. Twice he exchanged hurried glances in passing others on the quest. They just shook their heads sadly and moved on.

Sonny kept going until more than an hour had passed. Before he reached the door to the flat, he heard sobbing. Then he saw Esther's arm draped over Edith's shoulder; she swayed gently.

"It's over. Simon can finally rest." Edith's voice was scarcely above a whisper, her eyes red and dull, her cheeks glistening with tears. She raised a shaking hand and pointed through the wall. "They killed him."

Georg came in behind Sonny and whispered, "What?"

"Simon's dead."

"How?"

Sonny shook his head. "Don't know yet."

Everyone—family, friends, and neighbors—went quiet, as if all had stopped breathing and were waiting for permission to take in more air. Rudy walked to the door, head down. Without looking at Sonny and Georg, he said, "His body was pulled from the river."

"They didn't have to throw him in. He did it to himself." Edith's voice gained strength as she willed herself to speak. "He saw what we didn't. They took away his work and his dignity. For what? The crime of being a Jew! I could do nothing for him." Her voice broke. "He . . . had nothing . . . to live for." Her resolve vanished beneath a river of grief, her wail echoing from the walls.

Two days later, Polly joined Sonny at the small memorial service in a nondescript Jewish mortuary in the West End. When Sonny told her of Simon's death and the service, she insisted, "I'm going—the Nuremburg Laws be damned!"

Members of the family, friends, several of Simon's neighbors—Joseph, Mischa, Sophie, Polly, and Sonny among them—attended the short ceremony. With scant reference to the almighty, it was as secular as Simon would want. They did recite the Kaddish, or mourner's prayer, giving Simon a Jewish farewell.

Then, as Simon had requested, his body was reduced to carbon, and the ashes were placed in a pewter urn to be buried in Berlin's Jewish cemetery alongside the remains of his parents, his brother, Morris, and his sister-in-law, Frannie. After whispered condolences and feeble attempts to convince themselves that Simon was in a better place, the mourners dispersed.

Before leaving, Sonny embraced Edith, who now seemed remarkably composed. She pressed something into his hand, whispering, "Only you understood Simon and never judged him. He loved you and would want you to have this."

Sonny's hand tightened on the object; he'd wait until he was alone to see what it was. When he opened his hand, he saw a silver money clip resting on his palm. It was engraved with the initials SL, for Shlomo Landauer, his grandfather. Because they shared the same initials, it had gone to Simon and now to him. Sonny smiled at Simon's piece of silver, scratched and tarnished, then filled it with Reichsmarks. It pleased him to carry a piece of Simon in his pocket.

After that terrible day, Sonny worked to comprehend Simon's desperate act. What had compelled him to jump into the murky waters of the Spree, to end his life? Simon's despondency had overwhelmed him, but that seemed too glib a conclusion. He was too complicated for that easy answer. Sonny recalled Simon's silence at the seder. What had he been trying to say with his gentle nudge? Sonny took from it that there was nothing left to say. But that wasn't enough.

Had the loss of Simon's job, his tether to reality, pushed him to madness? Was death the only rational answer? It was beyond Sonny's comprehension . . . he grappled with the questions he couldn't answer . . . Yes, history was confirming Simon's bleak vision; the demons were too awful. Sapped of the strength to fight, he had surrendered.

Whatever the answer to his questions, Sonny was losing the battle against his own worst fears. He found no satisfaction in his ruminations. With Simon gone, how could there be? He wanted to see Simon's suicide as an act of mercy, but he could not . . . and of only one thing was he sure: he'd miss Simon's cynical humor and keen insight. There'd not be another encounter in the Mitte.

8

Reason is unhinged by grief.
—John Ruskin

Simon was seven months gone, nearly a year had passed since the seder, and Sonny was still trying to make sense of his uncle's death. He'd grown up with Simon's depressive personality but seen a different side—black humor, his shield against the world gone mad.

Sonny had laughed and failed to see Simon's sinking desperation. They'd seen less of each other during the four years the Nazis consolidated power—Sonny busy working in the enterprise, Simon at the electronics firm that ended his employment in humiliating discharge. Sonny had been forced to look beyond Simon's façade, and in the final tally, the facts bespoke an irrational act that Sonny could not understand.

But it got him to thinking about his parents and their perplexing relationship—his mother's unhealthy dependence on his father, her wasting away within months of his death, his father's brooding, the long silences, the lies. As a child, he must have shoved these things aside. Now, Simon's suicide provoked questions demanding answers. Would his mother be alive had she demanded more from his father? Would she have become more independent, stronger?

Should he have intervened? How? How could he have been expected to know? The more he tried to fit the pieces of his parents' lives together, the more he realized how little he knew them. It was as if strangers had reared him. In many ways, Sonny knew Simon better than he knew his father. At least he felt a greater kinship. As soon as he was old enough, Sonny had run around the Mitte with Mischa and Sophie. Then he'd gone to work, returning home to eat and sleep. And then his parents had died.

The question for which he wanted an answer more than any other, was why his father had lied. Sonny knew he was repeating the behavior —what a depressing legacy! He wrestled with the idea of telling Polly the truth about his work, though after five years it was a bit late for hand-wringing. Sonny sighed in frustration over what he'd never know.

Events forced upon the neighborhood compounded his quandary to the point that he hesitated at the door of the apartment building before opening it to the outside. There, a vile odor pervaded, forcing his nostrils to rebel and making him curse a pleasant breeze. He opened the door and nearly gagged, then quickly shut it. He steeled himself for the plunge outside where mounds of rotting garbage, kitchen scraps, animal offal, and fecal waste waited.

This latest insult had begun with propaganda warning that dirty Jews from the East spread disease. Posters appeared in subway stations, on lampposts and walls, heralding the danger. The devious fait accompli presaged the halt to collecting garbage in Scheunenviertel and Spandauer Vorstadt. Then the maggots, flies, and rats appeared. Would Simon have found some black humor hidden in the refuse? Sonny could not—not with the mountains of garbage stacked in alleys and on street corners, waiting to crash on unfortunate passersby.

The detritus of everyday existence, previously placed in the bin and forgotten, now lay stinking and rotting through the neighborhood. Garbage-filled boxes and paper bags landed in growing piles because there was nowhere else to put them. Guessing where the piles might be smaller, the stench less pungent, the pests fewer, was a challenge, and the answer changed daily. Some piles reached Sonny's shoulders. One false step could spell disaster.

As in Paris during the reign of Louis XIV, people took to holding perfume or cinnamon-and-clove-doused handkerchiefs to their nostrils. But this wasn't the seventeenth century! And now the streets were empty of children, as their parents, fearing disease, kept them inside.

For Sonny, the situation reached a surreal level when he passed an alley and gaped at the shadow of a rat, the size of a child, cast upon the wall. Light from a low window projected the bizarre pantomime—a rat on its hind legs with coiled tail, arrogantly chewing on garbage as if standing at a bar. Mesmerized, Sonny thought he'd wandered into a post-apocalypse landscape. Another rat scurried into the frame.

The corners of Joseph's mouth formed a slow smile when Sonny told him later of the rat cabaret.

"Very funny," Sonny snorted. "I recall that the last black plague killed a third of medieval Europe and made a lot of trouble for Jews—as if we don't have enough already."

Joseph's smile disappeared. "An interesting but flawed analogy. Containing plague would be impossible. I predict the garbage soon will be collected."

"Not soon enough," Sonny complained.

Joseph's words, though logical, were of little solace as the piles of refuse multiplied. Sonny's appetite waned, and he didn't want to leave his room. Melancholy set in, compounded by lingering distress at Simon's death. But like everyone else, Sonny had to work, and that meant leaving the flat. Searching for a street relatively free of garbage, he contemplated mankind's failings much as Simon would have.

On one occasion immersed in this sour exercise, Sonny failed to see a grizzled old man leaning on his cane. Nimbly avoiding a collision that would have knocked the neighborhood archetype to the pavement, he brushed the old man's arm.

The fellow tottered but remained upright, shrieking, "What?"

Sonny, as surprised as the old man, apologized profusely. Walking away, he heard the old man shout, "Ruffian!" A sudden self-loathing, wildly out of proportion to his actions, came over Sonny, adding to his fermenting melancholia. It was a dangerous brew.

Walking as if in a daze, Sonny nearly collided with the sharp edge of an overhanging awning. Lost somewhere in the gloom of Simon's death, his encounter with the old man, and the garbage, he rubbed his forehead where the welt would have been. An image of the old fellow sprawled on the pavement melted into piles of dead bodies, victims of plague—first, on the pavement in front of Herr Wagner's flat, then across the Mitte and beyond, until all of Berlin was afflicted.

Overwhelmed, Sonny stepped into an alley, nearly tripped on a garbage-filled box, and leaned against the wall. He needed comprehension of the world crumbling about him. He watched the people passing by, searched their faces. But what was he looking for?

A man, dark like Mischa, approached but provided no answer.

Sonny asked himself, "What have I become?" He was a smuggler like his father, living a small life, offering nothing to anyone, lying to everyone dear, forced underground with his lover.

In a pile of garbage at the end of the alley, something moved. Was it a body? Simon—floating face down in the river on a pile of garbage! Sonny shuddered and Simon disappeared. After four years of Nazi rule—of fear, alienation, isolation—the price of staying had become too high.

"What the hell am I supposed to do?" he mumbled. He was just one guy against a machine that chewed up people's lives, grinding them down until there was nothing left. What was next? A shiver ran up his spine.

Looking around the corner, Sonny watched as a striking woman, holding a handkerchief to her nose, approached. Her face melted into Polly's, and Sonny mouthed her name. Then she was gone. Sonny rubbed his eyes, but Polly had disappeared. That meant something, he thought, but what? Nothing made sense anymore!

"We Jews own and control the world!" His head jerked at the sound of Simon's voice delivering the punch line. It was no longer funny. The underside of the joke—the irony of the lie—was clear. Of course, he'd understood it the first time he heard it. But that was before all this. A Jew had turned the "Protocols of the Elders of Zion"—what the Nazis now taught in the schools—into a joke.

Sonny buried his face in his hands. His body shook. He pulled at his lower lip until it hurt, sucking air through his nostrils to let the stink in. Peering between his fingers, he was relieved to find Simon's doppelgänger gone. He knew it was all in his head, but he couldn't stop it. A barrage of self-doubt tumbled upon him. He should be writing exposés, something speaking to the struggle—not smuggling. His childhood dream gone, his life was empty of meaning. He was a failure.

Writing was impossible. They'd know who he was, and he would be arrested. They'd send him to Dachau, where he'd surely die.

So if there was nothing for him in Germany, why did he stay? He should leave for Antwerp or Paris. But he wouldn't—because Polly wouldn't. Or was it that he liked the smuggling? Sonny wondered whether, had his father lived, they'd be working together. Would they be driving to Aachen, sharing the Berlin territory?

He flipped back to his dilemma with Polly. He should leave, but she was unwilling. If they couldn't be together, how could their relationship survive? The warmth of her gaze reminded him of his mother. Should he tell her what he was doing? He laughed, then stopped as he realized how he'd failed Uncle Simon—by not seeing, by not giving him hope. Were his father's lies at the core of it all?

The questions in Sonny's head tumbled about like circus acrobats, faces painted with smiles that scared the children. They shrieked and averted their eyes but peeked between their fingers for another look. Sonny felt his seams ripping apart, his insides wanting out, as if he'd drunk too much coffee. Or maybe it was an organism growing beneath his skin, poking for a way out. Sweat trickled from under his arms, and he shivered. He was hot, but it was cold. His back was bent, his head down, like the old man. He was a question mark under the weight of the unanswerable. He stared at his feet, at the cobblestones, bricks and mortar, a confusion of shapes and hues honed by years of traffic. The distorted faces of people he knew appeared, then disappeared. He looked into the cracks for lost coins as he had done as a kid.

Boys played hide and seek, teased the girls, and, in their innocence, were immune to the evils of the world. Were they? Children bore the scars of the wounds inflicted on their parents. Scars fade but never disappear. The hurt remains until you die, until death releases the pain. Sonny blinked. Was that the reason for Simon's end—for his own?

No longer a child, he was an adult playing at a dangerous game. Did his reckless work satisfy an unconscious need to feel, to penetrate deep inside and reach what was missing in his life? A need so great he disdained safety so that he could smuggle trinkets? God! Sonny winced. He'd touched a nerve.

He was trapped inside a Grosz caricature, faces dissipated and mean, darkened by despair. A gray lifelessness replaced the joyful vibrancy of the Scheunenviertel of his youth. Suffocating clouds reached to the horizon. That God-awful stench! His head was a jumble.

Sonny needed assurance that he was all right. Where would he get it? From Polly, Joseph, Otto, Mischa? None of his friends knew . . . He could go to Emil. That momentarily cheered him. Then his gaze rested on the people going in and out of the small shops lining the narrow street. Empty window boxes waited patiently for flowers to offer respite from the gloom. A bird alighted on a sign, jumped nervously from perch to perch, stopped, and cocked its tiny head. Its eyes met Sonny's and he felt a shock, a sudden jolt of insight. Then it took flight. Damn!

Sonny limped out of the alley. He was invisible, like an alien dropped from space into a strange landscape. He gagged and put his handkerchief to his nose. An idea flickered, then disappeared like the bird. He lunged to retrieve his thought, but it lay just beyond consciousness. Struggling for clarity, he came up with a simple question. What do people need most?

He stopped, tried to forget who he was and to become someone else in a sort of existential striptease. Who would he be? No answer. Then he turned onto Oranienburger Strasse and forgot what he was doing. He fell into the orbit of the massive synagogue, not knowing how he got there. Some invisible hand must have led him there, to the answer—or to his breaking point. Stimulated by the grandeur of the setting, an answer came, and he cried out, "Dignity!" So elegant in its simplicity, the answer staggered him.

His relief was brief. Confronted with another damn question, he groaned. Moving from the shadow of the enormous Moorish dome, he tripped on a rogue cobblestone and almost fell. A hundred bells chimed in his head as he lunged forward. Lightheaded, he fell against a doorway. He heard a voice say, "Hope cannot survive relentless humiliation."

He looked around, but no one was there.

"Hope." He heard it again. Yes, of course. That's what was missing. He'd seen it on their faces. People struggled every day to put food on the table, to appreciate a warm caress, to tousle the hair of a child, to watch a sunset and muster the strength to meet another sunrise. Everyone he encountered, every single day, on the street, or at the warehouse, was stuck in a spiral that compressed their lives, diminished their dignity. Sonny counted the assaults on each finger—the reverse of the ancient plagues delivered on the Egyptians, from the ban on kosher butchering to the

Nuremburg Laws, the ultimate symbol of defeat. There were hundreds of decrees, too many to count—plus the boycotts, the destruction of Jewish property, the arrests, the beatings. What next?

With their very existence at risk, had he, had they all, run out of hope? His knuckles were white from clinging to the doorpost, and his chest tightened. He'd skated through life, doing a little of this, a little of that, thinking he was immune from pain. It was just an act. Tears ran down his cheeks as he swung wildly between hope, the light of rational consciousness, and the despair of a dark, bottomless abyss. He sobbed, shaken to the core.

"What the hell am I going to do?" he pleaded, closing his eyes. Slowly, images moved in and out of sync, until finally, like on a cinema screen, they came into focus. He saw his mother in the kitchen and his father reading in his chair, the space between them a permanent gulf. An image of Polly followed, groping through the dense smoke at the Pink Slipper; then Simon, laughing at his own punch line; the sound of Edith wailing; the misery of Simon's death. Now Joseph sorting his books, Otto ranting against everything at the H & S, Sonny chasing after Mischa and Sophie at the warehouse. And Franco licking his lips, the crack of Emil's slap, Paul at the bar, Albert's hands dancing wildly, a cigarette in the corner of his mouth. Being scared shitless at the border, and finally, Johnny huddling in pain, barely able to breathe.

The screen went black . . . then the show started up again. His father, Franco, Emil, and Fritz were at Joseph's bookstall—without Joseph. They huddled together, laughing over some joke. Sonny tried to get their attention, but they ignored him. The more he tried, the harder they laughed. Unblinking eyes crowded them out, and slowly, the image grew, until Albert's face filled his view. He bared his teeth and started to laugh in a cynical, awful cackle.

Sonny recoiled, and the image disappeared. He rubbed his eyes and saw his hand on the doorframe. His breathing was labored, as if he were under water. Slowly, his breathing returned to normal, and his fear receded until it was gone.

"What the hell just happened?" he asked, looking into the street. A pile of garbage reeked nearby.

That was it! Simon's death, four years of Nazi assault, the fucking garbage, had pushed him to the brink. He'd faced his demons and avoided the abyss. But he felt raw and exposed—as if the butcher had sliced him open from sternum to crotch, removed his guts, and hung him upside down. The kosher Sonny.

He laughed, then wiped his eyes on his sleeve and shivered. He had no idea now long he'd been there, but it was time to go. Turning from the doorway, he was relieved to find no crowd gathering to gawk at the fellow writhing there.

Sonny had barely regained his stride when a man, looking vaguely familiar, asked, "Are you all right?"

"Yes, thanks," Sonny answered weakly without looking up. He kept walking.

In the days following, Sonny made some sense of what had happened. He knew the Nazis had finally gotten to him . . . with garbage. He had felt the distress that pushed Simon over the precipice, the despair over what he could no longer control.

Sonny came to look at his experience with the grizzled old Jew as a step in his development, a primer for what lay ahead. He hadn't decided to leave Germany, but he'd been receptive to the idea for the first time. Whatever he decided, life wasn't going to get easier. He'd have to steel himself for the road ahead.

9

Oh! Woe is me, to have seen what I have seen, see what I see!
—William Shakespeare

Sonny had finally come to terms with his uncle's death: suicide hadn't been the easy way out but the only route Simon knew. Sonny also thought long and hard about his parents' early deaths—and about his own life.

Not that he'd done anything to change it. The money he was making in the enterprise was too good to quit. He wasn't ready to leave the country, so what other job could he do? The fact was, he liked the work. The excitement of brushing up with danger every time he crossed the border with contraband was like nothing he'd ever known—except for the risk of his illicit love affair. Danger provided that extra jolt of adrenaline—perhaps he was addicted to the rush.

Cocaine was like that, he'd been told. Years before, at a party near dawn in a dirty flat in Wedding, Johnny had cleared off a table, put some powder on a plate, rolled a ten-mark note into a tight cylinder, put it in one nostril, and sniffed the substance up his nose. Johnny cleared his nostril, then offered the rest to Sonny.

"You'll soar," he'd said, but Sonny hesitated and lost his chance as someone grabbed the note from Johnny. Now he understood.

Emil had been smuggling for years and was damn good at it. Nothing seemed to frighten him, and his steady, even demeanor couldn't help but rub off on Sonny. From the first day, Sonny appreciated Emil's courage, and he soon discovered a keen mind as well. Emil had him covered, so Sonny needn't worry.

Of course, they both did. Despite their precautions, attention to detail, they had to reckon with human frailty and random events. Bribery opened borders today, but there was no guarantee it would work tomorrow. Ferret Face and Claude, both deeply implicated, had much at stake. But if either was transferred or discovered, the game would be over. With so many eyes watching and ears listening, the risk of detection was real.

Sonny began to notice little details he might earlier have ignored or missed. Like the aroma of stew wafting from Claude's shed, a car on the side of the road, a man in a uniform where he wasn't supposed to be. Once, on a lonely stretch of road, Sonny spotted a fox. The wary animal gave a backwards glance, and their eyes met just before it disappeared in the brush. Sonny felt an immediate kinship.

They'd eluded the cops, except for once outside Bergich, near the Rhine. They'd been heading west toward Cologne, when Sonny heard Emil mutter, "Shit, a cop."

Sonny heard the siren.

"He was hiding on the side of the road," Emil said, as he pulled over. "I'll do the talking."

They were driving a small, dark green truck, with no company name on the side, like a thousand others. Their principal cargo consisted of liquor, wine, and tobacco, especially cigarettes—French, American, and Turkish. The size of the shipments had declined and with it the revenue, but it was enough. Lucky they'd been on the way to Plombieres, empty but for several boxes of shirts and other items carried as cover, just in case.

"What is it, officer?" Emil asked. "I know I wasn't speeding."

"I'll decide," said the cop, circling the truck. "What are you hauling?

Emil told him, and the officer ordered him to open the back. The cop took his time, as if looking for something specific. He asked where they were headed. Sonny heard the words but couldn't see the man. He nervously chewed on his lip. Then the truck moved, and he saw the cop, his cap tilted back, leaning against the truck, lighting a cigarette. Emil chatted with him for about ten minutes, even laughed at a little joke. Finally, the cop ground out his cigarette and remounted his motorcycle.

Unnerved, Sonny watched in the mirror as the cop got smaller, then disappeared. From then on, Emil and Sonny drove at night if possible, expecting the worst. They settled into a comfortable routine, which suited Sonny, until October 1937 . . .

They'd reached the outskirts of Aachen, as the setting sun turned the sky to a deep red tinged with purple. Within minutes, traffic on the main road was at a standstill. Wary of roadblocks, Emil turned onto a dirt track. All year Catholic pilgrims flocking to Aachen (as they did every seven years) had provided good cover. He drove south, turning west onto a less crowded road, into Aachen.

That's when they saw the army trucks—and soldiers, thick as flies on a carcass. They'd seen army personnel often in the two years since Germany grabbed the Saar and occupied the Rhineland—but nothing like this. After a convoy of army trucks passed by, Emil pulled into a gasoline station to fill the tank. Sonny heard the attendant say the army had been on maneuvers for the past couple of days. And no, they weren't going to war, at least not yet. He laughed uneasily.

Emil parked on a side street, and they walked to the main square to eat and take a look around. Heavily armed soldiers mingled on every corner. More waved from passing trucks to the gathered city folks. Though there was nothing ominous beyond the blatant militarism, both Sonny and Emil felt insecure.

Several taverns faced the square, and the two men walked into one of them under the sign "No Jews Admitted." It was past the dinner hour; the tavern was half empty. The innkeeper, a stout man with a huge mustache, eyed the two strangers and bid them good evening. They stood at the bar so they could look out the window onto the square. It felt good to be on their feet after sitting all day. After the innkeeper took their order, Emil remarked, "Business must be good with the army in town."

Leaning over the bar, the innkeeper jerked his head toward the square and said with a smirk, "The army may have taken over the town, but it isn't spending any money in my tavern." Within minutes, he brought their dinner and retreated to the other end of the bar.

Sonny and Emil watched the procession of vehicles and men flowing past the tavern. They could see clusters of officers in the foreground; they looked like ducks at the edge of a pond. In the center, high-ranking officers dispensed orders. Behind them, in the center of the square forming the backdrop, was a large fountain dominated by a statue of Emperor Karl.

Officers came and others went as Wehrmacht troop carriers, most pulling cannon and other ordnance, passed by. An officer in the middle of the scrum, his back to the tavern, ignored the commotion. He was the center of attention, and Sonny noticed a flash of light when he turned his head. The Prussian bastard was probably wearing a monocle.

Emil frowned, and Sonny followed his eyes to the left—the Gestapo had arrived. Sonny counted five or six men in leather coats and several more in uniform, standing stiffly with their hands behind their backs, talking among themselves. They gave the impression they were in charge but looked like scavengers after carrion. The general's staff ignored them.

"Why the hell do they have to play their stupid games now?" Sonny whispered as he watched an officer run to the group, salute, and point toward the far end of the square. Whatever he said got them talking. Several other officers arrived, and they all walked in that direction. Their leader turned to watch for several seconds, then resumed his earlier activity. Several more men in civilian garb joined the Gestapo gathered at the fringe. Two separate and distinct groups, like cliques of schoolchildren, vied for primacy. Tonight, the military brass was clearly on top.

"Let's go. I don't like this," Emil said and drained his beer. "Getting caught in the middle of a military maneuver is bad enough, but the Gestapo makes me nervous." They paid their bill and were out the door.

As Sonny's eyes swept the crowded square, something or someone vaguely familiar caught his eye, and he hesitated. Perplexed, he surveyed the faces in the square. What, or who, in that group could have grabbed his attention? Then his eyes rested on a thin, wiry man, part of the Gestapo clique. He wore a long leather coat and stood deferentially to the side, clearly a junior member. Yet he had someone's attention, and his hands moved extravagantly as he talked. Skipping over him, Sonny scanned the others . . . but there was something about that guy.

Emil said something, but Sonny's gaze remained on the square, and he only half heard his companion. Absently, he asked, "What?"

They were alone on the sidewalk. Emil's voice was low, "Let's get back to the truck. We need to figure out whether it's safe to cross."

"All right," Sonny answered, but he kept his eyes fixed on the square, nagged by what he'd seen. Trucks blocked his view. Then upon a lull in traffic, his field of vision opened. The group had dwindled to about ten men, and Sonny's eyes fell on the thin, pinched-faced man in the long coat. Only thirty meters separated them. He seemed to be about Sonny's age, but the poor light created too many shadows; Sonny was about to give up. Then the man turned, and recognition dawned.

Sonny slowed his step; perhaps that's what drew the thin man's attention. Their eyes met, and Sonny felt a jolt. He watched the man's arm rise, as if beckoning Sonny to stop, and he stepped forward.

Time slowed to a stop, and it was quiet, like the hush at sunset. Trucks stopped in place, shouts of orders silenced, and the wind died. Sonny felt frozen between strides, like a photograph of a man with one leg in the air, the other on the ground. Then, as if pushed from behind, he was propelled forward. He heard the gears of a truck engage, men shouting; the world restarted.

"Albert? Fucking Albert!" Sonny spit out the name as if he'd swallowed a fly, then shook his head. When he caught up with Emil, he was panting and sweating. He climbed into the truck and stared out through the windscreen. His shirt stuck to his torso. He smelled fear mixed with perspiration. "I don't believe it," he said, shaking his head.

"Ja, it's crawling with army," Emil calmly responded. "Don't know if we should even try to cross."

Sonny's mouth was dry, and he spoke haltingly. "That's not what I meant." He fell back in his seat.

Emil glanced at Sonny, alarmed. "God, you look awful!"

Sonny didn't answer. He felt faint. He worked his shoulders and swiveled his head, then sat up straight.

"Hey!" Emil grabbed his arm.

Sonny ran his tongue over his lips and moistened his mouth so he could talk without croaking. "I . . . I had a terrible fright." Over the next few minutes he explained about Albert.

"Albert was a different kind of cat, unique, not just because he wasn't Jewish. He was a nervous ball of energy, couldn't stand still. That's probably why he liked the action at the warehouse. Its teeming quality fit his personality, his restlessness." Mimicking Albert, Sonny flipped his wrist dismissively. "He'd make a nasty comment about another vendor and break into a smile, as if it were a joke. He made some people feel the warehouse was beneath him. So, of course, they were offended." Sonny smiled ruefully. "But he seemed oblivious to his effect on others."

He went on. "It wasn't just that. Albert could be funny. We were in a café—Polly, Albert, me, and some others—and I heard something break on the floor. The next thing, Albert was on his feet, rubbing his crotch, where he'd spilled hot coffee. Everyone was laughing. He got all red-faced but started laughing with us."

"Sounds like a real comedian," Emil commented dryly.

"He had two sides. He could be good company or the kind of guy who asks a question, then turns his head just as you start to answer . . ." his voice trailed off. "Over time our friendship cooled. Nothing dramatic, we just stopped hanging out together. My friend Mischa never bought his act. He thought Albert would stab you in the back if it got him to the head of the line." Sonny bit his lip. "Don't know why I didn't see it!"

Emil shook his head. "You must have had some laughs."

Sonny nodded. "Anyhow, he left the warehouse sometime in '32, and I never spoke to him again. Though I did see him once. Rumors circulated . . . someone said he landed at one of the big department stores. Another guy claimed he saw him in an SA uniform on a corner in Wedding. The guy couldn't say for sure because he didn't get close enough to ask. But that would have surprised me . . . I never knew Albert to be interested in politics. But if he could get ahead . . ." Sonny shrugged. "I didn't give him another thought until the summer of 1935."

"What happened?" Emil asked.

"There's a little coffee shop on Potsdamer Platz near the station. I went in to get a quick snack, and I saw him sitting at a table in the back with three men. They were in uniform, Gestapo uniform, and I think they were officers, though I can't say for sure."

Emil exhaled with a whistle.

"Ja, me too. I was dumfounded, but if you could ignore the uniforms, it seemed normal. They were talking, eating, drinking coffee, and I heard them laughing. But it made me sick that Albert was Gestapo. I just stared into a newspaper and waited."

"Did he see you?" Emil asked.

Sonny shook his head. "Don't know, but I knew it was Albert and that he'd have to walk by me when he left. I thought I'd say something, at least greet him. Time dragged on, and finally they were standing, getting ready to leave, and I got nervous." Sonny shook his head in disbelief. "Can you imagine—just saying hello to an old friend?"

"Ja, I can. He's Gestapo. I'd have turned my back and gone as soon I recognized him," Emil said.

"Well, I didn't. Anyway, I watched him approach, then put the paper down, and as calmly as I could, I looked at his eyes. I was smiling, ready to say hello. I opened my mouth to speak. Albert was just there." Sonny stuck his arm out, indicating the distance. "But he kept his eyes straight ahead, didn't look at me, didn't say a word, as if I didn't exist."

Sonny looked into the street and, as if just remembering, said, "No, that's not right. He looked through me, like I wasn't there. I was a nonentity, a ghost, unworthy of greeting in front of his Gestapo friends. He didn't give me a nod or a wink because then I'd have understood."

"I'm not sure why I was so upset," Sonny went on. "After all, he'd become a Nazi. But we'd been friends, and he just thoroughly ignored me. He couldn't be seen talking to a Jew, though they'd never have known—no one ever does." Sonny looked at Emil and took a breath. "I was a friend, and then I was nothing. It's what's behind the snub: I was part of a group of nothings." Sonny rubbed his eyes to exorcize the image.

"He's an opportunist prick, like most Nazis," Emil sneered. "But are you sure it's him?"

Sonny nodded. "I'm sure."

"How could he recognize you at that distance? The light is lousy. It's Aachen, not Berlin, so he wouldn't expect to see you here. People don't recognize the familiar when it's out of context. So why would he recognize you here?"

Sonny shook his head. "It's the eyes—that's how I recognized him. You know that flicker . . . " Sonny snapped his fingers. "He raised his arm like he was going to point, and he took a step toward me. It was Albert, and he saw me. Shit!"

Emil looked over his shoulder toward the soldiers, the Gestapo, Albert. "Let's get the hell out of town. Then we'll decide what to do next."

He pointed the truck in the direction they'd come, headlamps slicing through the black night, to reveal the passing automobiles, an occasional army truck.

Sonny fidgeted while Emil, both hands on the steering wheel, observed, "This is how you get caught—not by fancy police work but by chance. It's pure bad luck to be spotted by that Gestapo asshole." Emil growled and slammed his fist on the steering wheel.

Neither spoke for a while. The only sounds were those of the groaning engine and the rush of air against the windscreen. Finally Emil said, "We'll figure this out." And he began throwing out the possibilities.

Sonny joined in, and in no time they'd whittled the options to three: Albert hadn't recognized Sonny despite his reaction; Albert recognized Sonny but would do nothing; Albert would make further inquiries because that's what the Gestapo did.

By the time they reached Reinartzkehl, Emil and Sonny agreed that only the third scenario was likely. Sonny dispensed with the first: "It's him, and he saw me."

"All right. And we can discard the second," Emil offered.

"We could be in big trouble already."

"No kidding, Einstein." Emil reached over and put a hand on Sonny's shoulder. "Let's not get too far ahead of ourselves." But his words were unconvincing. They drove silently for several minutes until he asked, "When are they going to finish playing their stupid war games?"

Sonny wasn't listening; he wouldn't have noticed had the whole German army surrounded them.

Emil parked along the side of the road, where he'd left Sonny waiting the first time they'd come this way, and killed the engine. Lights from the checkpoint glowed in the sky. There was no traffic in either direction. "I'll be right back."

Sonny recalled his agitation the first time he'd been there and with good reason felt the same way—scared. Everything had changed. His collaboration with Franco and Emil—work that got him out of Berlin and provided a good living—would end.

But that was nothing compared to what would happen should the Gestapo get hold of him. Rumors were swirling through the Mitte of the Nazi concentration camp in Dachau and one more recently opened in Oranienburg, near Berlin. Otto's comrades languished in one of the camps; it was better not to know what happened inside. Hell, as a smuggler and a Jew, he might not make it that far—they'd shoot him first.

Emil returned wearing a smile. "We're all right for now. Army maneuvers don't affect the border crossings. They're playing their games in the forest to the south, and word is that it's ending soon. According to Ferret Face, a high-ranking army officer and some toadies came inspecting when they first arrived, but he hasn't been seen since. All we have to worry about is Albert . . . "

Fritz was pacing the old farmhouse when they arrived. "You're over three hours late. Where the hell have you been? I was scared half to death."

They explained.

Fritz calmed down but still cursed, "Damn it! Fucking Nazis are going to put us out of business."

"Hopefully, that's premature," Emil noted, trying to be optimistic.

"What's he going to do with the information? And why was he in Aachen in the first place?" Fritz demanded.

Emil glared. "How the hell do we know? You're the one with the contacts in Aachen."

Sonny intervened, "Settle down. We're all on edge."

"No kidding," Fritz answered.

"I don't need you two arguing, not with the bull's-eye on my back," Sonny offered.

That brought matters back into focus. "True enough," Emil agreed, then turned to Fritz, and said. "We need information on a Gestapo officer named Albert Schwarz, about Sonny's age."

Sonny described him.

Fritz suggested they walk to the barn to check on the shipment and give their nerves a break. Squinting in the harsh light, they accounted for everything, including several cases of champagne not on the list. Emil pulled out a bottle, and they all smiled. The cold night air had chilled the bottle perfectly. Emil popped the cork and poured the bubbly into mismatched glasses. He raised his glass: "Long live the enterprise, and our dear friend Franco, who won't miss what he doesn't know he had."

They quickly drained their glasses and poured another, letting the alcohol sooth their frayed nerves. Then Emil said, "We need a plan. If they're already looking for Sonny, the border may have been notified. If so, Ferret Face would turn us both over like a potato pancake."

Talking it over, they agreed they needed more information before heading back to Berlin. At dawn, Fritz would go into Germany and contact his cousin Vincent, who worked in Aachen's city hall, the Gestapo's local headquarters. Vincent would know something, or so they hoped. That meant Sonny and Emil had the day to relax at the farm.

All they could do for now was go to bed. At least Fritz did—Sonny and Emil had to make do on the floor. With only a thin blanket, Sonny was chilly. Emil's snorting and his own racing thoughts kept him awake. Could there even be enough information to solve his problem? He came no closer to an answer than they had earlier, but of one thing he was certain: his life was about to change.

Thus far Sonny had skated through the unpleasantness of the Nazi regime relatively unaffected. Hell, he'd flourished. While others suffered under the weight of Nazi edicts, few of them had directly threatened his wellbeing. Sure, his romance was affected, but he and Polly had continued their trysts undaunted. And business was still reasonably good. Of course, there was Uncle Simon's suicide and Sonny's own flirtation with madness—as he'd come to label that episode. Now, he felt the sting, and his life was about to turn upside down. He'd lose his home, the warehouse, his friends, and his job, he thought. And what about Polly?

Damn it! He wasn't ready. Could he ever be? Otto's experience and his own should have taught him the lesson of how life works. He'd had to fend for himself at eighteen after his parents died. Then, years later there was Simon's suicide. Despite the losses, he'd done all right, so the lesson got lost. And what was he going to tell Polly? His friends? "Sorry, I've got to run, the Gestapo's on my ass. Remember Albert?" Otto would understand, but what about the others? What about Polly?

Sonny finally fell asleep to the image of Albert's piercing stare. He woke in a panic, then remembered where he was and cursed serendipity. His neck was stiff, his arm numb, and his back ached from the hard floor. Gingerly rolling over, he got onto his knees and slowly stood, then stretched his aching muscles. Roused by the smell of coffee, he ran his fingers through his hair, wiped saliva from his chin, and shuffled to the bathroom. Throwing water on his face, he felt better.

Feeling Marlene rub against his legs, Sonny scratched behind her ears until she purred. Maybe it wouldn't be so bad to stay in Belgium. She meowed softly in apparent agreement. But he was without papers, and he'd never see Polly or his friends again. Because of his lies, nobody knew where he was—that's how out of control his life had become. No, he had to get back to Berlin, lift the burden, make things right with Polly. Having to meet in dark corners hadn't seemed to matter. They'd been together and they'd leave together, on their terms. Sonny felt a flicker of doubt. Would she leave? He shoved his negative thoughts aside.

Fritz left at first light in his old Peugeot, which rumbled and sputtered but, like his tractor, refused to die. Border guards had never given the eccentric farmer a second look, and today would be no different. He'd be sent through with a nod and return as easily.

Bismarck slept at Emil's feet, and Marlene stretched, then curled into a furry ball near the stove. The early morning sun cast long shadows on the floor, the tranquil scene belying their predicament. Emil looked up from his reading, grunted, and returned to his book. He had nothing new to offer and little use for idle chatter. Sonny ate in silence, then decided to take a walk.

When the door opened, Bismarck slowly got to his feet, stretched and scratched an itch behind his right ear, then followed Sonny out of the house, tail wagging. Though low in the sky, the sun's rays felt warm, and Sonny filled his lungs with crisp, clean air. A soft breeze teased his face as he set off along the path running next to the field and opening onto the pasture. Clumps of black dirt sat in the furrows, like balls waiting for children to kick them, and that's what he did—he kicked them. The fertile dirt exploded like shrapnel as Bismarck ran ahead, his snout to the ground searching for exotic scents, then abruptly changing direction and sending a bird into flight. It was a good day to find solace in nature. Sonny would empty his mind of all things Albert.

Sonny marveled at the quiet. The only sound was the crunch of golden leaves underfoot. Then Bismarck drank noisily from a small puddle, an animal shrieked, a sharp whistle emitted from a nearby tree, then another. A bird sang overhead; whistles and calls followed. Bismarck barked and Sonny laughed.

In the city, the honking horns, whistling trains, and chattering people drowned the silence so rare and coveted. Even in the darkest night, a neighbor laughed or cried, a train clanged in the distance, cats screeched as they fought or copulated in the alley below. Here, now, the lack of those sounds was becoming more comfortable.

Sitting on a fallen limb, Sonny sighed and watched the chimney smoke rise, creating a fragile trail of white. The sun moved behind a giant cloud that looked like a chicken, then turned into Polly's profile. He'd shut her out, and that was going to be a problem. Why hadn't they married when they could? More—why hadn't he trusted her enough to confide in her? But he'd vowed to tell no one . . .

The sky had turned a paler blue, and the birds quieted. He watched as dust rose along the track like a gray snake, until the old Peugeot stopped at the side of the barn. Fritz's small figure emerged, Emil meeting him halfway. Their arms moved with their conversation as they disappeared into the house.

Sonny took his time in returning. At the door, he heard calm voices and took it as a good sign, but when he saw their somber faces, his body slumped against the doorframe.

Fritz nodded at Sonny and said, "There aren't any problems at the border. Vincent overheard a general tell the mayor that army maneuvers—or war games, whatever they're called—would last a week, and they'd keep disruptions to a minimum. That means the army's leaving tomorrow. Mueller the baker, an old friend of mine, said an officer on the general staff ordered pastries yesterday for a party tonight. Of course, nobody knows what the army's up to, and in the end it doesn't matter. They play their games and plan for a war that everyone hopes will never come." Fritz smiled weakly and offered Sonny some strudel, a gift from Mueller.

Sonny took a piece, then asked, "What about Albert?"

Fritz sighed and raised his brow. "That's more complicated, but I don't think it's the end of the game, at least not yet."

So much for the tranquility of his morning walk! Sonny closed his eyes and slowly exhaled. When he sat down to hear Fritz's report, Marlene jumped onto his lap. Sonny laughed nervously as Albert slithered back into the picture.

"According to Vincent, there's been a Gestapo office at city hall since 1934. Like all bureaucrats, they constantly complain of understaffing, underfunding, too much work, all the regular bullshit."

"Maybe they're too busy to worry about a lone wolf like Sonny," Emil surmised.

"Don't know about that. But according to Vincent, most of them can't find their ass with both hands. They're Nazi cronies who didn't know anything about police work. They strut like peacocks in black leather coats, scaring the shit out of people. Most police work is done by regular cops, leaving the Gestapo to internal security, whatever that means."

"Hunting down Jews and other subversives for crimes like racial defilement," Sonny said.

"True enough," Fritz agreed. "Hunting down the distributor of handbills quoting Roosevelt, catching someone listening to Belgian or Dutch radio, keeping tabs on outspoken clergy. Without enough manpower, they rely on informants, just like in Berlin." His frown deepened. "Whatever the staffing issues, nobody wants the Gestapo to detain them. They aren't to be trifled with."

The conversation turned to Sonny and the import of his avoiding the Gestapo web. He looked away, embarrassed by the attention.

"Vincent and I took a walk in the square, to be alone. People have big ears. When I asked about Albert Schwarz, Vincent got nervous." Fritz shrugged. "He's met Albert, a lower-grade officer, an investigator. He's been in the office for several years."

Emil and Fritz stared at Sonny. But he didn't notice, because images of Albert's thin face flashed through his mind. Sunken fox eyes squinting through a blue smoky haze, a cigarette dangerously dangling from the corner of his mouth, Albert fidgeting over his house wares, Albert at Luna Park making a fool of himself in front of two girls, Albert's snub of him in the coffee shop. Now Albert in the Gestapo, self-importance written all over him, a Grosz caricature of a fascist, leering at him.

Sonny leaned forward, sending Marlene to the floor, speaking in a voice barely audible, "But we need to be sure."

Looking at Sonny, Fritz nodded. "Your guy . . ."

"Don't call him that. I hate him!" Sonny snapped, immediately regretting his outburst. "Sorry."

Fritz ignored him and continued: " . . . introduced himself to Vincent as Albert Schwarz the first time they ran into each other at city hall. It's him." Fritz cleared his throat. "But more to the point, Vincent told me there's nothing unusual going on, no flurry other than the army games. There's no special investigation that he knows of, nothing affecting the border. That's all Vincent knows."

"It just happened last night, so it might be too soon," Emil ventured, then quickly asked, "How big an area do they police?"

"I'm not exactly sure, but a fifty-kilometer radius from Aachen, give or take. They have about a dozen men—but only three investigators in the field, gathering scum as they go. Albert's an investigator in civilian clothes."

That's all Emil needed to hear. He turned to Sonny. "We've got a window. Let's go."

"What about the army?" Sonny asked.

Emil nodded. "That's right. Mustn't forget the army. We'll wait until dark and cut a wide berth, go on back roads around Aachen."

. . . Time passed slowly when there was nothing to do but think. Sonny tried to read but was too distracted, so he took another walk with Bismarck . . .

Finally, Sonny and Emil waved goodbye to Fritz, crossed the border without difficulty, got back on the road, and left Aachen far behind. Once back in Berlin, Sonny would lay low. He shivered at the thought of joining Otto underground, but he had to be careful. He'd move out of Herr Wagner's flat and get lost in Berlin. Still, what about Polly?

They traveled through Alsdorf and Ahlen, quiet towns announced by big white signs, the names appearing with a motto or insignia. Next to each was the ubiquitous notice: "No Jews allowed." Using side roads and back lanes, avoiding bigger towns and the police, Sonny and Emil slowly snaked the six hundred kilometers back to Berlin.

10

Heaven has no rage like love to hatred turned,
nor hell a fury like a woman scorned.
—William Congreve

Back in Berlin, Emil told Sonny he was welcome to stay with him a few days: "Just until you find something." When Sonny protested, Emil replied, "You've nowhere to go. Besides, it's only temporary."

Sonny shivered, recalling Herr Wagner's visit from the neighborhood warden, and it was settled. He couldn't put the old man, or himself, at risk. So it was Emil's flat, with Lisle and the kids, until he found something.

Early the next morning, before heading to the warehouse to talk with Franco, Sonny and Emil sat in the kitchen. Lisle was busy in the other room; the children were in school.

"You're not imposing, okay? It can't be helped," said Emil.

"You're both too good to me." Sonny fixed his eyes on his coffee cup.

Lisle stood in the doorway. "Nonsense. You're always welcome here. You can't go home. Think about it, both of you. It's a signal." And she disappeared.

Lisle was a handsome, sturdy woman, hair graying. Unlike Emil, she was unimposing. She didn't get involved in his work but accepted its risks. And to her way of thinking, the risks were no longer manageable.

"She's right," Emil agreed.

Sonny rubbed his fingers on the smooth surface of the table.

"We had a good run, made some money," Emil said nodding toward the little warehouse in the alley. "You gotta know when to walk away."

Sonny smiled at the memory of their first meeting. "Funny how you end up doing something you never imagined." Thinking of his father, he realized it wasn't unimaginable at all.

"Ja, well . . . you never know what's gonna happen."

"All of a sudden I'm homeless."

"Not for long. Get lost in the Mitte. One of your friends will put you up. You'll find a place."

That's what Sonny intended to do. First he'd talk to Joseph. Then he'd hang around the warehouse until something turned up.

"Let's go break it to Franco," said Emil.

It was early, and the warehouse was quiet. Business was off for everyone. The SA, exhorting people not to buy from "the predatory Jews," had frightened away the non-Jewish customers. And so many in the neighborhood were without jobs—and without cash to spend.

Franco, looking calm as usual, put an arm on Sonny's shoulder. "I will talk to Emil first. Then we will talk."

With Franco's arm across Emil's broad back, his head barely reaching Emil's shoulder, they slowly walked away. Emil bent his head to speak into Franco's ear. When they returned, Franco nodded at something Emil said, then spoke to Sonny. "Now then, my boy—you tell me."

Franco listened patiently as Sonny told him everything, his words occasionally tripping over themselves. Twice Franco soothed him down, but otherwise he said nothing, only nodded or pursed his lips, revealing little. He might have been listening to a customer's drone rather than to Sonny's ordeal. When Sonny finished, Franco put a hand on his shoulder. It seemed an eternity before he spoke.

"We have had a good run—Emil, you, and me."

Sonny looked to the big man, nodding.

"But it has come to an end. Business is falling off, and this government is a big pain in the ass. Now those hyenas in leather coats may come calling." Shaking his head, Franco licked his lips and continued. "No, it is time to call it quits, while we are ahead, at liberty."

Sonny felt his face flush, and he lowered his head to hide his shame. "It's because of me, isn't it?" He slumped, his confidence draining. He became the innocent young man who'd first signed on with Franco.

"No, my boy, that is not it," Franco looked to Emil, who nodded. "I agree it is disquieting, but it is not the reason. It *is* a factor."

Sonny didn't know whether to believe him.

"Events and circumstances push little people like us aside, and if we do not take care, we will be swept away. Look around you. Business is down, the warehouse is in the hands of a Nazi, and it is only a matter of time before the Gestapo arrives or war begins. We do not stand a chance. We must move on. Your little brush in Aachen was our first warning."

Everything Franco said was true, but Sonny hadn't expected it. Words wouldn't come; all he could do was nod. He was a schoolboy failing his lessons, forced to stand in front of the class.

Franco tried to comfort him. "My boy, it is too dangerous. We accepted the risks, but now it is foolish to continue. What happened with Albert . . ." Franco shrugged at how life was, how easily you could lose control. "Hitler's Gestapo has no sense of humor."

Franco and Emil snickered, but Sonny was a blank.

"Mark my words, war is coming. These dictators—Hitler, Mussolini, Stalin—they are all the same." Franco waited for Sonny to meet his gaze. "There is no room for honest thieves like us." He winked. "Right, Emil?"

So it ended with a quip and a wink. To show he was a gentleman, Franco gave each of them an envelope with "severance pay, something to tide you over." He handed a second envelope to Emil, "This is for Fritz. As soon as I wind down the business, I am leaving for Bologna with my little family. There, I have only Mussolini to worry about." He laughed, slapping both men on the back, and they shook hands for the last time.

. . . Emil and Sonny stood awkwardly outside, with little left to say. When they shook hands, it seemed they'd never meet again. Emil left for Wedding, and Sonny walked back into the warehouse, up two flights, stopping at Albert's old stall.

A young orthodox man Sonny knew vaguely was there selling socks, probably all he could get his hands on. Sonny stared at the neat piles of black, blue, and gray. The guy was dressed in a black suit and the paraphernalia of the orthodox.

He smiled at Sonny. "Hello."

Sonny nodded, then was suddenly distracted at the sight of a slight, blond-haired man with a cigarette dangling from his mouth, his hands a blur. Sonny's lips moved in silent soliloquy.

The dark young man asked, "Are you all right?"

Sonny blinked at the man who looked nothing like Albert, nodded, and slowly walked away.

As soon as Sonny saw Joseph, he began to ramble, confusing his friend.

"Slow down. I can't follow what you're saying."

Sonny took a breath. "What do you know about the Huguenots?"

Joseph grimaced at the non sequitur. "What do they have to do with anything?"

Sonny sighed heavily, then started at the beginning. He explained Fritz's Huguenot heritage, back to Franco's offer, to Emil, everything.

Tremendous relief came in his telling. The weight of deceit slowly lifted from his shoulders. Calmer, more in control, he stood straighter, and his confidence returned, at least in part. Finally, he turned to what had forced him underground—the problem of Albert.

Joseph's face showed neither disdain nor accusation; it was an inscrutable mask. He said nothing, and as his silence continued, Sonny's discomfort grew. Now he felt judged, betrayed in the telling. Why would Joseph do that?

"I know you don't approve."

Shaking his head slowly, Joseph said, "Well, I don't know what I believe. I'm speechless, shocked, at your revelation. What should I think? All these years, you've led me to believe you were a small-time operator—your words, not mine. Now, it turns out, you're a big-time smuggler. That's hardly a little bit of this, a little bit of that! Of course, I feel misled. Maybe, given your absences, I should have figured it out . . ." Joseph shrugged. "But it's not up to me to figure that out. I know it's a risky business; one has to be discreet. But to lie to a friend?"

Joseph's edge, sharp as a favorite paring knife, was something Sonny had rarely heard. He protested: "As far as anyone knew, I sold stuff and moved it around. That was enough." But his struggle to escape the deceit was blatantly transparent. Joseph didn't respond, and Sonny averted his eyes. He needed absolution.

"Okay, I lied. I'm telling you now. You're the first to know."

"This is too fantastic. I need time." Joseph barely contained his anger.

Sonny suddenly developed a tic in his cheek; his hand rose to quell it. The tic continued; he ignored it. He heard a rasping and realized it was his breath. For an instant, he was back in the shadow of the Moorish dome, leaning against a doorframe, straining to maintain control. Joseph's squint continued, passing sentence on the no-good liar he was.

Involuntarily, as if caught in a spasm, Sonny's arms shot out, palms up, asking for forgiveness. "I'm sorry. I'm sorry! What am I to do?"

Joseph shook his head. "Not now. We'll talk later."

But Sonny couldn't let it go. "You'll help me?"

A strange look came over Joseph's face. "Yes. Stay at my flat."

Sonny was surprised.

Joseph dismissed him with a wave. But before Sonny could leave, Joseph leaned forward to say, "There's much to discuss. But first you must tell Polly."

. . . Sonny paced in Joseph's flat, fretting as to how he'd do it. He'd rather tell her in a café, maybe where they'd first met, or in some other public place—but he didn't dare. In the two years they'd been forced underground, they'd become reticent partners, rarely hinting at the reality of their uncertain future. They'd floated along without commitment in an environment in which the consequences of discovery were severe. Germany offered them nothing but heartache.

In summer they'd met in parks to walk anonymously in the woods. Occasionally, they'd taken the subway to the edge of Berlin, where no one knew them. But once—in a café in Pankow—a woman who'd bought gloves from Polly had come to their table to chat. Neither was eager to repeat that unnerving experience.

Herr Wagner had welcomed the couple to his flat—he didn't give a damn about the Nuremburg Laws. But the prying eyes of neighbors scared them off. They had their hidden corners of the Mitte, but mostly they met in the secrecy of the warehouse cellar. They cuddled and talked for an hour at a time with only a musty blanket and a couple of pillows separating them from the hard, damp floor.

For the past two years, the strain with Polly had slowly grown. Neither of them had fully appreciated its effect. Now Sonny's bombshell would explode in their faces. So many times he'd wanted to tell her, to lay it all out and quit his false life. But he couldn't. Something always said no: Franco's voice in his ear, Emil's advice, his father's legacy, the fear of her response. Now he had to do it.

Sonny had mustered the courage to call Polly from a telephone box. They'd arranged to meet at the warehouse after work like dozens of times before. There he paced, maybe ten minutes, trying to figure out how to break the news. Then he heard footsteps in the corridor. He embraced Polly at the door, burying his face in her hair.

When they separated, his lips moved in disconcerting pantomime. The words he'd rehearsed wouldn't come.

Polly eyed him suspiciously, put her hands on her hips: "What's going on? Why are you looking at me so queerly?

"I don't know," he blurted, then shook his head and looked into the corner, momentarily absorbed by a spider hanging from a thread.

"That's a fine answer."

Sighing heavily, Sonny murmured, "Oh hell!" And, slowly at first, but then in a rush, his words fought for space until he found his rhythm. He told Polly the same story he'd told Joseph.

She stiffened and backed away, the distance between them becoming far greater than the room allowed. Her eyes narrowed and her lips tightened until they seemed sewn shut. At the end she said nothing. The only sound was their breathing, her eyes widening to hot assessment, from rage to incomprehension.

Wilting under her scrutiny, Sonny took a step back, hit the wall, and looked away. In the overpowering silence, he nearly put his hands to his burning ears. He lamely admitted, "I know I should have told you."

"Oh really?" she snapped, her voice slicing to the bone. Her sarcasm dripped and gathered in a pool at his feet. Her eyes opened wide then narrowed, as she seemed to calculate. "How couldn't you tell me? You've been living a double life, a lie, for how long?"

Her questions hung in the air, daring him to reply. When he hesitated, her throat colored to a crimson that rose to her cheeks. "Obviously you don't trust me—or love me."

Sonny tried to answer, but she cut him off. "How long has it been?"

"Ah . . ."

"Don't get cute with me!" She flared. "You know damn well."

"End of '32 was my first trip across the border," he blurted as if suddenly remembering. "I started with Franco around the time we met in 1931."

"You needn't remind me." Her words were an epitaph to a dead love affair. She turned to the wall and wept.

Sonny waited until she turned. Her eyes brimmed with tears; her cheeks glistened. He moved closer to her but kept some space between them. She flailed against his chest with balled fists; again and again she pounded until she could do so no longer. When he tried to hold her, she stiffened and turned away.

Minutes passed before he spoke. "I couldn't tell anyone. There was the lesson of my father, and I was frightened. And once it swallowed me whole, it was too dangerous to tell you. What if I were caught and you knew, if anyone—Mischa or Joseph—knew? You'd be implicated. No, I couldn't tell you."

A mix of venom and disgust in her eyes, Polly stared at Sonny, then turned away. "You shit! How can I ever trust you again?"

Sonny spread his hands and pleaded, "I'm telling you now."

"Now that you've been spotted by that creep and have to go underground. You goddamn liar! While I thought you were in the far reaches of Berlin, you were really in Aachen, risking everything . . ." Her mouth twitched and she nodded, as if coming to a decision. "How blind I've been!"

"How could you know?"

"And why not?" Polly shook her head as if trying to clear a terrible thought, then stopped and changed direction. "It must have been exciting, putting yourself at risk, sneaking over the border, eluding the army and the Gestapo."

Sonny was wary of her change in tone, though he felt a measure of relief and nearly smiled. "I was scared to death the first time, but with each trip it became easier, and then, to be honest . . ."

"A little late for that, isn't it?"

"I didn't see it that way. It was just a job, and I was a driver's helper. Sure, there was an element of danger that made it exciting, but nothing happened until . . ." He paused, his mind racing at the awful consequences of the box he'd put himself into. "Now my world's collapsed. God, Polly, I wanted to tell you! But I made this promise to myself never to tell, sort of a bond with my father. And I was afraid of what you'd think, knowing I was a smuggler."

Polly, face streaked with tears, blew her nose, then looked away. When she spoke, her voice sounded hoarse, distant, as if she were speaking through layers of gauze. "I don't know how I would have reacted. You never gave me the chance."

"Nobody knew except the three guys I worked with, and now you and Joseph."

"Let's not forget Albert," Polly added icily.

Sonny reddened, then recoiled, suddenly frightened.

"Obviously, you didn't think much of me," Polly dared him to answer. "Afraid I'd leave you?"

Sonny would lose however he answered, so he didn't. But he wanted to say they should put this episode behind them, make a fresh start . . .

That evening Joseph asked how Polly took the news.

Sonny grimaced.

"That bad?" Joseph asked.

Sonny told him.

Joseph scratched his forehead, then: "I'm not surprised." He seemed distracted and said nothing further on the subject. Instead he talked in vague generalities about emigration, documents required, people caught in the Nazis' grip.

He continued, hinting at something but never getting to the point. "If only they had the necessary papers," he concluded.

Sonny quickly became resigned to his life underground, though he felt certain of the need to flee Germany. He brooded over his decision to return to Berlin when he could have stayed in Plombieres. His luck had run out. With everything reeking of impending disaster, he'd fooled himself into thinking he could have a life with Polly. He tried to find solace in the knowledge that he had no passport or visa to stay in Belgium . . . little comfort there.

His new life centered in Joseph's small but tidy flat, where he slept on cushions on the floor. When he asked Joseph where Otto would sleep the next time he came around, Joseph shrugged, "You'll have to work it out."

After they'd talked it out, Joseph never mentioned Sonny's secret life again. That was a relief—Sonny couldn't endure Joseph's disapproval. One estrangement was too many.

Joseph insisted that Sonny stay close to the flat. That was like keeping smoke near a fire, and before long the walls of the little flat started to close in. With nothing but Albert and the debacle with Polly on his mind, Sonny needed distraction. After a few days inside, he started taking late-night walks around the neighborhood, then longer forays to the warehouse. He preferred risk to confinement.

Sonny waited several days before calling Polly again. As he'd anticipated, she was cold and distant. Still, she agreed to meet him at Joseph's flat. When he let her in, there was no embrace. They stood in the middle of the room, uncomfortable. Their conversation was awkward, there was no eye contact, and they cut it short.

Not before Sonny could ask a favor. "Polly, would you collect my clock and my clothes from Herr Wagner's flat? The old man deserves an explanation." Sonny missed his little room and his talks with the old man—but there hadn't been time even to say goodbye.

Taken aback by his request, Polly shook her head and said, "That's chutzpah!"

"Please. There's no one else."

"All right," she said with a sigh, then pointed her finger at his heart. "But I'm not doing it for you. I want to say goodbye to Herr Wagner."

The next day Polly went to his old flat and told Herr Wagner that Sonny was in trouble and couldn't return—true enough, though incomplete. But Polly was not a good liar. The old man pinched the bridge of his nose and looked at her quizzically. She stood at the doorway with Sonny's few things in a rucksack and extended her hand.

Herr Wagner took it and kissed her cheek. "I'll miss you both. I'm old, and I'll weather this storm, but you and Sonny have your lives ahead of you. So take care."

Later, Polly dropped the rucksack on the cellar floor and hissed at Sonny, "I feel complicit in your web of deceit." She told him what Herr Wagner had said, then left abruptly.

Sonny made several attempts to get together with Polly after that, but she had to work, she was too tired . . . then finally she agreed.

They met at a tiny café in Scheunenviertel. Polly was already there when Sonny arrived. With chilly formality, she said she could see him no more. The spark between them had flickered and died in the maelstrom.

Sonny accepted her decision with as much grace as he could muster. He'd breached her trust, and her love had died.

11

Out of his nettle, danger, we pluck this flower, safety.
—William Shakespeare

Sometimes a bit of good luck comes your way," Joseph started, beckoning Sonny to a seat a week after he moved to Joseph's flat. Sonny noticed the envelope in Joseph's hand and did as he was told.

"I hold hope in my hand," Joseph continued, his eyes bright. "I want you to think about a mighty river and how it's formed by the confluence of two streams—like the Vorderrhein and Hinterrhein that become the mighty Rhein."

"What are you talking about?" Sonny asked, though he was accustomed to Joseph's lapses into inscrutability.

Joseph appeared lost in thought. He hadn't heard Sonny's question, and he wasn't framing an answer. The only sound was the ticking of the clock.

Joseph nodded toward the clock, but when he saw that Sonny was already there, he said, "That's our greatest impediment. But . . ."

"You're particularly obscure tonight," Sonny observed.

"Yes, I suppose I am." Joseph turned from the clock, wearing a smirk.

Sonny had seen that look on Johnny's face and on Franco's at the Veneto—but on Joseph? He waited for Joseph to rub his hands together like a scheming child, to lean forward and tell him what he'd gotten away with.

"You'd make a terrible poker player."

Joseph shrugged. "I've thought a great deal about your question, and I have an answer, of sorts."

"To which of my many problems do you refer?" Sonny ventured, exasperated.

Ignoring him, Joseph placed the envelope on the table next to his chair. "Using my metaphor, let's say that your recent revelation is one of two streams, say the Vorderrhein. It's relatively insignificant . . ."

Sonny protested, but Joseph raised a hand to stop him.

"Hear me out, and it will all become clear. Your stream is insignificant, but with the addition of a second stream, the Hinterrhein, we've got a valuable commodity."

Curiosity about what the envelope held was burning a hole in Sonny's patience. He rose to take a look, but Joseph snatched it away, raising a forefinger. "Not yet!"

Sonny sat down. "Okay. Have it your way."

"Did you know I used to work as a graphic artist?" Joseph asked. Sonny shook his head, and Joseph continued: "That's an inflated description of the work I performed, but it suffices for now."

"I knew you were an artist, Joseph."

"Yes, but before I aborted that quest and began selling books, I had a job. Can you imagine that, Sonny? I worked for someone—and not just anyone. I worked for the government."

Sonny laughed. "I don't believe it."

"But it's true. Our late great Kaiser saw fit to offer employment to me in the office of government documents and forms. Alas, it was mindless drudgery, bereft of creativity, and I was but a minor bureaucrat assisting the gears of government to properly mesh, or not, as the case may be."

Sonny tried to picture Joseph in that work, but he had no idea what he had really done. "So far, this is more surprising than interesting."

"Don't be impertinent," Joseph snapped, feigning insult. "My work, along with others, was to design and draft government forms to facilitate the orderly conduct of business. Tax forms for the tax department, contracts for the purchase of equipment, that sort of thing. You follow?"

"I think I get it."

Joseph ignored Sonny's sarcasm. "There was no idea too small, no form too ridiculous, for our office to design." He threw up his hands, raising his eyes to the ceiling.

"But I was just out of art school, broke, and I needed a job. I worked during the day and tried to make art at night." His eyes drifted to and lingered on the one painting remaining from that lost period—*Berlin Street Scene*.

"That was still to come. The Great War was about to start, but of course, none of us knew that." His voiced trailed off with a sigh before he continued. "Anyway, the Kaiser's government needed requisition forms, transfer forms, draft notices. You name it, we produced it. That's why I didn't have to fight in that despicable carnage machine. My service to the country was drowning the government in forms."

"Congratulations. You did a superb job, considering the ghastly outcome," Sonny noted dryly. "Perhaps, the Nazis had it all wrong. It wasn't the Jewish-Bolshevik international cabal that lost the war, but you and your minions."

"I'll leave that to the historians. But of course we did a wonderful job, while our youth were sent to senseless slaughter."

Visions of scarred soldiers limping back from the front played in their minds—for Sonny what he'd seen in the photos of old magazines. But Joseph had personally witnessed the tattered and forlorn troops . . .

"Everyone was relieved that the war to end all wars was finally over, though the utter devastation of defeat wasn't then fully appreciated."

They fell silent until the ticking clock drew them back to the present.

"Well, anyway . . ." Joseph waved off a legion of bad memories. "My drafting had nothing to do with art. Hell, it was barely even drafting. All I did was give succor to the bureaucrats.

"As you can imagine, it didn't take long for the mindless detail work, devoid of artistic merit or imagination, to become tedious. Actually, it was worse than that. The work destroyed creativity and robbed me of energy. But I needed the money. We were called designers, the idea being that a title satisfies in lieu of wages, creativity, and self-respect."

Joseph's laugh was mirthless. He continued, "But the only effect was to ensure our cynicism, the ultimate law of bureaucracy. The forms we designed left our office to be lost in the labyrinth. Their hallmark to confuse, obfuscate, obstruct."

Sonny had never seen Joseph like this. "That bad?"

Joseph nodded. "Maybe worse. I came to hate the work, though the passage of time has made me more cynical. I'd like to think some of my work had value, but . . ." he shook his head. "My confidence as an aspiring artist eroded by the day. The work was so unfulfilling that I resigned. But I made lasting friends, so some good came from it. Several remain there to this day, and we get together on a regular basis."

Sonny vaguely recalled meeting one of Joseph's friends at the warehouse several years earlier.

"That's where this document comes in," Joseph said, removing something from the envelope. He handed it to Sonny.

"Document?" Sonny whispered as he took it, perused it for the first time. Now Joseph's meandering became clear. "You could have been more direct."

"And spoiled my fun?"

Sonny conceded the point, while his eyes remained glued on the paper he held. It did indeed provide a glimmer of hope . . .

Joseph continued his story: "My old comrades share a common disgust for the Nazis, a mentality they can't abide but are powerless to combat." His finger tapped a low drumbeat on the table, in synch with the clock, until he realized what he was doing. "Of course, they're surrounded by Nazis, but my friends do their job and go home at the end of the day. Needless to say they lack esprit de corps, and we," he included himself, "have ruminated for hours about supporting a government they despise."

Joseph paused to consider his words. "The question was how to subvert authority—gum up the works, so to speak. Could they use their expertise and position to do that? They felt a calling, a compulsion to do something, anything, to oppose this vile government. But there's a caveat: whatever they do must not jeopardize themselves and their families. Secrecy is paramount. Nothing must be traced back to them." Joseph looked away, then back, and his face reddened. "Ultimately we're timid men, with no stomach for violence—or prison, for that matter."

"Hell, so am I!" Sonny exclaimed, while examining the document. On its cover was the German eagle and swastika, the heading "Deutsches Reich" at the top, "Reisepass" below. He almost forgot to breathe. He gasped, then whispered, "It's a passport. If only I'd had this in Plombieres—and one for Polly." He frowned when he realized what he'd said.

"Impressive, isn't it?" Joseph said, serious. "I worked on its predecessor, from the days of the Republic. It's nearly identical."

"Oh, yes. Your style is unmistakable," Sonny teased.

Joseph smiled.

"Actually, it's the most beautiful thing I've ever seen," Sonny said, as he turned the pages awaiting a name and other vitals.

Clapping his hands, Joseph threw his head back and laughed.

"But it's not enough," Sonny said.

"Yes, of course. We know that. It gets you out of Germany, but you still need a visa for Belgium, or Holland, or France. We're working on that."

Sonny's mouth went slack. He looked at Joseph as if he were a genie offering him a wish. A floaty feeling of unreality overcame him, and he soared high above the earth in a dream. He could walk on walls, the dead came to life, people were suddenly free to cross the border.

A door slammed in the hallway, a voice called out, and Sonny regained solid ground. "Did I hear you right?"

Laughing, Joseph said. "I hope so."

"Okay, what's the plan?"

Joseph gently took the passport from Sonny. "This is a Type 2 passport, which has replaced Type 1, from the days of the Republic. May it rest in peace. It's virtually the same but for the eagle and swastika, instead of the Weimar crest. Also the print on the cover is a little different."

"How the hell did you get it?"

"Seems that several boxes in storage were lost, never accounted for—funny how that happens. Imagine the uproar as they searched high and low, never finding the elusive passports."

"How many are you talking about?"

Shaking his head, Joseph said, "Many, and they're safely hidden. Of course, the right stamps and photos must be attached, and there's the problem of a visa, but that will be surmounted."

"Oh, I see. It's that simple to get your hand on a Belgian visa and make two thousand copies?"

"That's where you come in," Joseph said. "With all your contacts, it shouldn't be hard to find someone with a visa for you to borrow. We'll make a copy, and one of my friends has access to a printing press. It's all very quiet and clandestine."

He sighed, smiled, and continued with unnerving confidence. "It's perfect—your experience and mine—our two streams making a mighty river for boats sailing with Jews, and others, into Belgium and Holland and France."

Sonny was game. "How's this going to work?"

"In due time," said Joseph. "You used bribery in your so-called enterprise, but with well-forged documents it's not necessary. You have a feel for the logistics. You have contacts in Belgium. And you have knowledge of the area."

Sonny was already thinking of Emil and Fritz, though smuggling people would be wholly different from smuggling goods. "I like it as a concept, but I need to talk to someone."

"Your old chum?"

Sonny nodded.

"The beauty of it is that we're not smuggling. No one's lurking in the dark. No bribes."

Sonny thought of Ferret Face. "On paper, anyhow. You never know what a greedy border guard will demand to let you pass."

"We can't control that, but our people will have proper papers, everything in order, the way Germans like it," said Joseph. "The Belgians and the Dutch will open their arms in welcome."

Still there was Albert to think about, dragging Sonny down like a ball and chain. Repelling the thought, Sonny slammed a fist into his palm. "Sure. Why the hell not?"

Joseph poured from the bottle of aged French brandy, a gift from Sonny. "And I thought you paid retail for this . . . To our new venture."

"Salut!" Sonny exclaimed. "Long live the next enterprise."

"L'Chaim!"

The next day Otto and Mischa came to Joseph's flat.

Mischa and Sophie had finally married, and according to Sophie, the Nuremburg Laws had provided the impetus. Mischa's proposal was as outrageous and unconventional as she'd come to expect. With a sardonic grin, he asked for her hand saying, "What the hell? Since I can't marry a blond, blue-eyed shiksa, why don't you marry me?"

Sophie burst into laughter and rolled her eyes. "How can a girl turn down a romantic proposal like that?"

"Finally," said Herr Hager.

The wedding was a small event for family and a few friends, in the little orthodox shul. So Mischa the Red, who railed against everything conventional, married his childhood love, an irony amusing his friends.

A small gathering of men had taken place in the back room of a little café in Scheunenviertel the night before the nuptials. Sonny, Joseph, Solomon, and several other friends from the warehouse were there. Otto risked his neck so that he could toast, and torment, his friend. He raised a glass of Russian vodka and with a straight face congratulated Mischa, "For abandoning all reason—and the proletarian struggle—for the bourgeois institution of marriage."

When the laughter died, Mischa, flushed with good cheer, shrugged with the insouciance of one who cares little for tradition—though he was willing enough to grasp it when it pleased him—and raised his forefinger to the heavens: "Why fight what's known to be decisive?"

Groans followed his obscurity, but Joseph knew his reference. "So you think Pushkin will save you?"

Mischa nodded happily.

"But you omitted the critical part," Joseph had chided, as all eyes moved to Mischa. "Custom is the despot of mankind . . ."

Now Joseph nodded to Sonny, reached under his chair, retrieved a book, and from its pages took the envelope containing the passport. Otto stared at the ceiling, but Mischa noticed the interaction.

Holding his prop as if it were a holy writ, Joseph hesitated, though he'd given the speech once before. To Sonny he looked as if his stomach ached. He seemed stressed. He must be thinking about the enormity of his plan, how everything depended on execution. Despite Mischa's occasionally erratic behavior and Otto's lethargy from years in hiding, Joseph trusted them.

Seeing Joseph hesitate, Sonny was about to prod him when Otto saw Joseph holding something and asked, "What's that?"

That was Joseph's cue. "An answer to that thorny problem of immigration." Suddenly they were students listening to their favorite teacher. Like Sonny, Mischa and Otto wondered where Joseph's meanderings would end. They exchanged glances just as he was about to deliver the punch line, to explain how he came to have the paper he was waving at them.

Mischa broke the drama first. "You look like Moses descending Mount Sinai."

Joseph nodded, raised his eyes skyward, and laughed. "True enough, for I do hold salvation." He handed the document to Mischa as Otto looked over his shoulder.

Their lips moved as they read, the mood in the small room turning hopeful.

"Damn!" said Otto.

"Pffff," Mischa exhaled.

Savoring the moment, Joseph sat with arms folded across his chest. He explained the document, then clapped his hands gleefully, saying a visa was in the works. Clearly dumbfounded, the newcomers stared at Joseph, then at Sonny.

Mischa's eyes narrowed accusingly. "You knew?"

"Wait. There's more." Sonny silenced him.

Joseph regained the narrative, saying that he and Sonny were working on a plan to get Jews out of Germany. He needed them to make the plan work. Secrecy was paramount. The circle had to be closed.

"My God!" Mischa exclaimed. "It's so simple and beautiful. It has to work!"

Joseph extended his arms to the three men, effecting Mischa's metaphor of the biblical Moses.

Otto exclaimed, "It's brilliant." His excitement was contagious. "Open the border a crack, and people will stream out—comrades, Jews, Sinti . . ." He fell back in his chair, closing his eyes, the images of his long confinement flooding over him.

Otto was thin and gaunt but alive and free, surviving on guts and good fortune. Survival came with a price—guilt over his jailed comrades, fear, constant glances over his shoulder. And finding temporary homes—in a doorway, under a bridge, in a dark alley, out of sight. In Wedding, in the vast warren of tenements and warehouses, old comrades like Willy were willing to put him up for a few days. There and in Neukölln, the working-class districts that gave the KPD their greatest support, he found safe haven.

He'd often question someone on a street corner—a face dredged from his fog of memory—to find a place to spend the night. They'd tell him of places to stay alone or crammed with others into a tiny room, a basement cellar, a rooftop shed. They warned of traps, informants, block wardens. Starved for information about the outside world, he read whatever the others gave him if only to make time pass. They'd wish each other good luck and part at first darkness, or just before dawn. Otto spent the odd day or two per month—never more—at the warehouse or in Joseph's flat. It was too dangerous.

At first, his nerve endings were so raw that the slightest provocation—a man asking directions or a woman's gaze—signaled danger. He felt the heat of eyes boring into his back and fought the urge to run. Over time, his paranoia receded to an itch, still enough to keep him alert to danger. Expecting a cop's tight grip on his shoulder or the business end of a pistol, he just muddled through. The cover of night was best, but of necessity he ventured into the harsh light of day, losing himself in the flow of humanity on the pavement, in the subway, on a tram. Safety was an illusion. He knew he could end up in Dachau like his comrades, but he got used to, though he was never comfortable with, the danger. So far he was a survivor!

The dashing Communist agitator, with leather jacket and scar to show for his politics, was long gone. Otto had eschewed Lenin and Marx for a new politics, one of grit to survive. Moving quickly with his collar up, hat pulled low, and head down, he'd move from the doorway, thread his way through faceless pedestrians, cross the street, and walk down to the River Spree, under a bridge where he'd spend the day. Or he'd go to Grunewald forest for days at a time, so long as he had some food.

He'd never forget that evening rush hour at Alexanderplatz station, rubbing shoulders with men and women oblivious to his identity, feeling safety in their number. Pushing forward with his head down, he'd spotted a pair of eyes watching for men like him. Averting his gaze, he noticed a vaguely familiar face a few feet ahead—an old comrade, who didn't see him, thank God. The last thing he wanted was a sentimental reunion. He lost the thought as the watching eyes, joined by those of another, approached the old comrade. Otto froze, and someone ran into him from behind, nearly knocking him down.

There was a shout, and the comrade ran. Suddenly he was in their grasp, but then he broke free.

"Halt or I'll shoot!"

A woman screamed, and people scattered or pressed against the walls. But the moving crowd, unable to stop, edged forward, pushing Otto closer to the confrontation. He watched the comrade's arms flail as if he were drowning. Only meters to the door and he'd be out of the station, thought Otto. "Go, damn it!" he silently urged.

A shot echoed in the small enclosure, mixing with the screams. Otto's ears rang from the sound. His comrade lunged forward and fell, arms outstretched. Then came a deathly still and the stench of cordite. The crowd pushed Otto around the dead man, his face pressed against the floor, his body slumped, a lone arm extended toward freedom. Otto tore his eyes away and escaped outside.

Nobody wanted to get involved, not with the Gestapo, and the crowd melted away. Otto breathed deeply, purging death from his nostrils, walking without looking back. There was nothing he could do. Glad it wasn't him on the floor, Otto shook off any sentiment for his former comrade. Like any other, it was a good day to be alive. A man was shot in the back—you kept going.

Joseph acknowledged Otto's enthusiasm with a nod and ran a hand through his short hair. He was uncharacteristically nervous and didn't want to show it. He managed a little smile.

"Our model is the pre-American Civil War Underground Railroad that freed so many slaves. It'll be dangerous," Joseph slashed a hand across his throat.

Mischa's hand moved reflexively to his own neck.

"But it's the right thing to do." Joseph furrowed his brow, as if he'd reached a hurdle, then said, "We need a coherent plan to make this work."

An excited hopefulness replaced Mischa's normally caustic edge. He asked, "What's our job?"

Joseph turned to Sonny. Otto and Mischa exchanged confused glances.

Mischa looked at Sonny "What's your part in this?"

Sonny cleared his throat, looked at Joseph, then at his two friends, and told his story for the third time. When he finished, he said, "I'm living here with Joseph." Then he borrowed from Joseph's metaphor, saying how each would bring something necessary to a planned migration of Jews, and others, from Germany.

This heady stuff rendered Mischa uncharacteristically speechless. He paced the flat, mumbling incoherently. Then silence descended until Mischa, turning on Sonny, attacked: "Damn you!" He bit his lip to keep from saying more.

Sonny shrugged, now inured to criticism. "You're right, but that's history. You can stay angry, or drop it and join us."

Mischa's jaw slackened, as if he didn't know which way to go.

Otto had no qualms: "Hell, I'm in."

Mischa was too.

12

O conspiracy! Sham'st thou to show
Thy dangerous brow by night,
When evils are most free?
—William Shakespeare

Sonny sat in the comfortable familiarity of Emil's kitchen. A cold wind blew through the open window, but he scarcely noticed. Coffee untouched, he talked nonstop about anything but the plan. At one point, Lisle looked up from her work to catch Emil's eye. He shrugged in bewilderment. Finally, after fifteen minutes of chatter, Sonny said he had a proposition. Lisle sighed.

"Could you leave us for a moment?" Emil asked.

She'd been married to Emil long enough to know the drill. But before she left, she turned to Sonny. "You be careful." Her eyes locked with Emil's and hardened.

When she was gone, Sonny rushed headlong into the plan. "I have access to passports for Jews, and others in need, for getting out of Germany. All we need now are visas. We're itching to get started. Since we'll be moving people, not cigarettes and alcohol, this is more complicated then the old enterprise.

"We're halfway there, but people need documents to cross borders. Security's an issue—people talk too much, and once words gets out that Mischa, Otto, and I are the ones to see . . . well, that's a problem. We have to work out the details, since we're just getting started. I'm thinking of using several guys I trust from the warehouse to act as recruiters, to sniff out prospects—you know—to insulate us.

"I need you to help set up the pipeline to Plombieres, and to Fritz, just like old times. Nazi intent is clear, and that goes to my second fear—that we'll never be able to satisfy the demand. What do you say? Are you in?"

Emil winced under the verbal onslaught, and his undersized chair creaked mournfully. He didn't answer but stood and walked to the open window facing the alley. Standing with his back to Sonny, he cleared his mind of the clutter, and said, "It was down there that we met. I scared the shit out of you." He laughed.

"Sure, I remember. That seems so long ago."

Emil nodded, glanced over his shoulder at Sonny and back out the window. "I'm a fortunate man with a good family. Lisle's a wonderful wife and a terrific partner. She's always understood what I do, and why wouldn't she? I've made a good living. The kids were never a problem—they still aren't. We're comfortable and, frankly, I'm glad Franco shut it down. We lived with the fear that someday things would turn sour."

He looked back, appraisingly, hands clasped behind his back. "Lisle's happy I'm not on the road. We've saved some money, and I don't have to work for a while. So why should I stick out my neck again, take chances I don't have to?" He shivered and closed the window.

Sonny didn't answer right away but stared at his friend. Emil was a bundle of incongruities—a big man with the face of a brute, a thoughtful man with a facile mind. You underestimated Emil at your peril. He had the life experience Sonny needed to make the new project work.

"People desperately need help, and we've got the tools—or we will soon," Sonny started—then went straight back to Emil's question. "Why? Because you hate everything the Nazis stand for! You just reminded me of our first day together. What about that SA man at the subway station?" That's what stayed in Sonny's memory—Emil's contained fury exploding in spontaneous opposition, like the flaring of a match before the flame.

Emil waved a calloused hand, deflecting the memory. "Oh, I see. Because of that, I'm forever the hero, and I have to get back in the game?" He ran a hand over his close-cropped hair. "Put my ass back on the line?"

He took a breath, and whispered, "It's cold in here." But he'd already closed the window. Shrugging, he turned to Sonny. "I told you to stay in Belgium—we both did. You'd be out, away from all this crap and on your way to France, England—even America—by now. I'd be left in peace, not having to decide whether I want to be a savior to Germany's Jews."

Sonny tried to stifle his grin at the thought of Emil as savior.

"What's so funny?" Emil snapped.

"Never mind . . . How could I stay without papers? And besides, I couldn't leave without Polly then."

Emil's eyes narrowed. "What does that mean?"

Sonny explained.

"Sorry to hear about the breakup, but you made your bed with Franco and me long ago."

Sonny jumped on his words. "Haven't you made yours? What are you gonna do? Live like Wedding gentry?"

Emil smiled.

"Join us," Sonny implored. He kept talking about the good they could do . . .

"All right. All right! Show me an example of your friend's handiwork."

"Not a problem."

Emil said, "Fritz will want in." His face darkened. "Can't forget about our old friend Albert."

Sonny squirmed. He'd thought about Albert too, seen his piercing eyes, dancing hands, around every corner. Planning the new venture had papered over his fears only briefly. But having a meaningful mission would get him through.

"I don't think anyone's looking for me. They knew where I lived, and when Polly gathered my things, no one had been to Herr Wagner's flat."

"It's early. Don't be fooled. They're a patient lot. They have priorities but may get to you eventually. Change your appearance—use a disguise, dress different, like a workingman. Grow a beard and let your hair grow long, or cut it all off. Anything but the way you usually look."

"Yes, of course," Sonny muttered. Why hadn't he thought of that? Rubbing his hands along his chin, he felt the stubble and smiled.

"Now what's so funny?"

"Just thinking that I could grow a long beard and dress in black—or maybe grow a mustache and goatee like Comrade Lenin."

"Very funny."

Sonny said he'd bring Emil a passport when one was ready. "Keep an open mind," he implored.

Emil stood, hands on hips, filling the doorway, a faint smile softening his face as Sonny receded down the hallway.

Sonny was impatient. He wanted to move quickly, but they weren't ready. They needed documents and the ability to act swiftly, improvise if necessary—just the opposite of Joseph's detested bureaucracy. And they needed anonymity, which meant silence.

Sonny had worked on an informal organizational outline. Borrowing from Otto, he figured they'd have cells like the KPD, operating independently, each knowing little or nothing of the others. Mischa, Otto, and Sonny would never know Joseph's ministry friends, which is what they demanded. Neither would they know of Emil and Fritz. Joseph would do his alchemy with help from his friends, passing perfect documents to Mischa, Otto, and Sonny, who'd be insulated from the clients by runners recruited for that purpose. Finally, Sonny, Emil, and Fritz would work the trail from Berlin to Plombieres. Only Sonny would bridge the cells.

Who'd be the lucky ones, those anointed to leave? "We can't set up a stall at the warehouse with a sign—queue up for a pass out of Germany," Otto joked.

Sonny chuckled, glad to see Otto emerging from his shell, returning to the man he'd known before. "I've been thinking about that. We'll use runners to generate clients. Once initial contact is made—if we agree and they can pay—we'll approve and take it from there. If we don't approve, no one knows us. We have a buffer. I've got one guy in mind, but we'll need two others. We can train them—just so long as they can be trusted."

Having crossed the border so many times, Sonny had a visceral feel for the project. But losing a shipment of cigarettes was only money—losing people would be tragic. He focused so tightly on the project that he came to see it as his destiny. He was driven to make it work. If it did work, countless Jews, and others at risk, would escape Germany.

With Polly out of his life, he could leave the stinking pile of Germany behind. With documents available, would he ignore the opportunity to do that? The answer was easy. Now that he had the tools to help others, he'd stay—to leave would be immoral . . .

As Joseph predicted, Sonny was able to find Belgian visas. His source also provided a pipeline of false identity cards, perfect for Sonny, Otto, and others in need. Joseph forged new visas, and his friend with access to a press made copies. New identity cards allowed Sonny and Otto to walk the streets of Berlin as new men.

The documents fell into Sonny's lap after he talked with Otto about a group that had provided him shelter. Otto seldom talked about his ordeal—it was too uncomfortable—but over the years he'd given Sonny bits and pieces, including the stories of those who quietly helped from day to day. No names were mentioned; Otto knew few of them anyway. But early in November, the enterprise still in its infancy, Otto recalled in conversation the groups that had helped men like him.

"They usually operated in the back alleys and run-down tenements of Wedding and Neukölln. One in particular, a shadowy church group, was helpful."

"What was its name?" Sonny asked.

"I don't remember—maybe I never knew—but it was real," Otto grinned. "If I'd known the good they were capable of, I might have joined up with them, instead of becoming a Bolshie."

Otto's story rekindled a memory just beyond Sonny's easy reach . . . then it came. "Do you know the name Karl Larson, a Lutheran minister? Or his son with the same name?"

"Doesn't ring a bell," said Otto.

Sonny told him about 10 May 1933—the night the Nazis had burned books at the Berlin Opera and Karl Larson, the son, had appeared at his flat. Polly had introduced the two young men, and through Karl, Sonny had learned a little about the Confessing Church.

"It started as a reaction to the Nazi takeover of the Lutheran Church, then worked to save clergymen who'd converted from Judaism. When the church moved beyond its narrow interests and resisted generally, it was forced underground."

Otto's eyes narrowed as he started a silent litany of half-forgotten places and names, those he'd chosen to remember or couldn't forget.

"God, I'd arrive before dawn, anxious and tired, always hungry, and stay until dark. That was my routine for years. It's all a jumble," he said. But he kept at it, retrieving places and faces, discarding them. He rubbed his forehead and clenched his fists over his eyes.

Finally, he said, "All I remember is a church group that let me stay in a basement for a couple of nights on two or three occasions—could have been more. It was in Wedding, which makes sense, as that's where I usually found refuge . . . though it could have been Neukölln. They gave me shelter, food, and more food when I left. They were good people."

"Were they Lutheran?" Sonny asked, hoping it was Karl's group.

Otto's eyes momentarily brightened, then he shrugged. "What the hell would a devoted atheist know? They're all the same to me, with their fantastic resurrection myth and hocus-pocus . . ."

Sonny felt the thread of a connection and decided to take a chance. He went looking for Joseph and found him cataloging books, keeping up the appearance of his regular work. Vendors had shrunk by at least half, the number of customers by more, and Joseph's business, in truth, had all but dried up.

The familiar aroma of leather and old paper brought a strong dose of nostalgia. Sonny's eyes strayed to the corner where he imagined a youngster, maybe fourteen, cross-legged on the floor, a magazine spread on his lap, dreaming about travel. Then he remembered why he was there—to ask Joseph a question.

"Sure I've heard of the Confessing Church," Joseph answered. "It's an underground splinter off the Lutherans. Why?"

"I have a hunch they can help."

Joseph grimaced, looked around, then grabbed Sonny's arm and led him to the rear of the stall behind a tall bookcase: "Not out there."

Sonny didn't know where the Larsons lived, so Joseph retrieved a well-worn Berlin directory and thumbed through its pages. They narrowed it down to residents outside the Mitte, Wedding, and Neukölln. That left five Karl Larsons, two in the West End, the rest scattered through the city. Suddenly Sonny realized that Polly would know. He thought he could cajole her into a meeting. He had no other option but to try . . .

Sonny reached Polly at the Schmidts' flat, and when he told her it was important, she reluctantly agreed to meet him again at the warehouse cellar. At the appointed time, she arrived flushed and slightly out of breath, glowing with good health. There was no embrace, little warmth, so Sonny got right to it.

"Have you seen Karl Larson lately?"

Polly's head jerked, and her eyes widened as if she'd been unmasked.

Sonny's grunt hid his surprise. "Do you know where he lives?"

"Why?"

"I need to talk to Karl about the Confessing Church."

"What about?"

"I'm working on something that might interest him and help me," Sonny was amiable, not looking for a fight.

Polly looked away, considering. She must have decided favorably because she nodded. But all of a sudden, footfalls echoed against the corridors walls; the two fell silent, waiting until the noise was gone. Once it was quiet again, Polly looked down at her hands and back at Sonny. Still, she didn't answer. She grew uncomfortable under Sonny's gaze and broke eye contact, shrugging.

"It's my turn for secrets."

Sonny felt a chill on his neck. His words were pointed. "Really? Like what?"

She shook her head. "Why do you want to see him?"

"To talk about old times, before the bonfires and mass rallies."

Polly laughed cynically. "Right! Old times you two never shared."

Another silence. Sonny broke it, saying, "I hope you know what you're doing." He instantly regretted his words.

"Don't patronize me!" Polly jabbed his ribs hard enough to make him wince.

"Okay. That was out of line," Sonny admitted, holding up one hand in surrender and rubbing his side with the other. "It's none of my business, but it's dangerous work."

Wanting to make peace, he shot her a halfhearted smile. "Certain tools have dropped into my lap, and I'm going to use them. Karl might be able to help."

Polly's lips moved as if she were silently debating her next action. Within seconds she nodded. "I don't know exactly where he lives—we always meet in the city. All I know is that he has a long ride."

"Then he must live in the suburbs."

"Good boy," Polly said, patting his cheek.

"Can we make a truce?" Sonny asked. She was clearly hiding something.

"I didn't know we were fighting," she said demurely, folding her arms over her chest and looking into the corner as if something of interest were there.

Sonny didn't respond.

Finally, Polly relaxed, and she turned back to Sonny. "If you must know, I was invited to attend a meeting by an old friend from Zwickau. They're working hard to get people out. Church members collect identity cards, visas, and other documents." She lifted her shoulders. "That's all I know."

Sonny gasped, and his spirits soared. Now their dissolving personal relationship seemed only a petty distraction. He pressed for more.

Polly took a breath and shook her head.

"Please. This is critical."

"I've said too much already."

He stared at her, his body sagging with disappointment.

Finally, she sighed and said, "I'll tell you if you tell me.

Sonny nodded. "You first."

"Meetings are small, maybe ten members, always at night, at what they call safe houses." Then she muttered in what seemed an afterthought something that made Sonny's ears tingle: "They're looking to expand the operation to Jews."

Sonny brightened, his hunch right. "I have to see Karl as soon as possible." He hugged her and pulled out the paper with the addresses.

Confused at his sudden burst of emotion, Polly stared down at the paper. "Not yet. Tell me."

Sonny gave a summary of what his group intended.

Polly scrutinized him. "Much better use of your time and energy than smuggling cigarettes."

"Yes, yes. Now tell me."

"He lives near parks," she began, "and there's a castle."

Sonny prodded until she remembered.

"The castle has four towers. Oh, and the family was famous for something, but I can't think what . . ."

Sonny scratched below his ear, looked at the list, then at Polly, closed his eyes and consulted the map of Berlin stored in his head. After a few seconds he said, "Tegel Castle, home of the Humboldts?"

"That's it!"

They stood facing one another, still uncomfortable.

Polly said softly, "Now that you have what you need, I'll go."

Sonny tried to thank her, but she was already in the corridor. He waited long enough for her to exit the building, then left for the subway station. The irony of Polly being mixed up with the guy he was going to see, of their playing the same game, was interesting, to say the least. Were Polly and Karl lovers? He chewed on that awhile, felt a jolt of jealousy, then decided he didn't care.

On the evening in May 1933 when Karl turned up at his door, Sonny had been practicing his English by reading Graham Greene's first novel, *The Man Within*. He was deep into the story of a son's coming to grips with the memory of a dead father, a smuggler.

When he opened the door, Karl, an art student at the time, stood there in a stupor, barely able to speak. Finally he managed to tell Sonny that he needed to get off the street. After wandering through the Mitte, he had somehow remembered where Sonny lived, though he had visited him only once, with Polly.

Sonny liked this gentle, soft-spoken young man who'd had several small gallery showings, but it wasn't art he wanted to talk about that night. When Karl settled down and finally found his rhythm, his eyes flashed with brittle intensity as he described the horror.

"Fire can be a beautiful sight," Karl said, his voice composed and reflective. "Rich red, fiery orange, and tranquil blue mingled and danced against the dark sky, intensifying the colors. I saw the glow from a distance and felt a foreboding, but I never imagined . . ."

His voice hushed. He shivered and shook his head as if exorcizing a demon. "Before tonight I've never felt the presence of evil." He reached for Sonny's arm as if to keep him from falling into an unfathomable abyss.

"This is worse than when the Gestapo came to harass my father. At first I thought it was a burning building. I couldn't make out what was happening, so I asked, actually yelled, until a frenzied young man—his face contorted as if he'd been overtaken by the devil—screamed that now the Jews can see what the new Germany thinks of them—their books were going up in flames.

"I stared at him, unbelieving. I couldn't speak or move. In the shadow of our great opera house, its soaring columns meant to enlarge the spirit and, and . . . " he sputtered.

Sonny suggested he breathe.

Karl nodded, took a deep breath, and went on. "As the fire leapt higher, so did the intensity of the crowd. Negative, wretched energy filled the air, worsened by the smoke; it made my skin crawl. My urge to flee fought the voyeur within me. I was glued to the pavement. Then I heard, 'Goebbels, Goebbels,' and I knew the devil was among us. I ran from the orgy and didn't stop until I was out of breath." Karl breathed again and, exhaling, said, "So here I am."

That night the flames consumed the works of Brecht, Heine, Freud, Einstein, Mann, Grosz, London, Wells, Hemingway, and countless others, perhaps even copies of the book Sonny was reading. The books of any author labeled as degenerate, defined as an enemy of the Third Reich, ended in ashes. How many were lost in the hundreds of fires across Germany that night was anyone's guess. Newspaper photos, in the days that followed, showed strangely smiling men, silhouetted against flames, destroying literature. Carefully planned, the burning had not been spontaneous as it was reported to be.

Reinickendorf was a mix of urban and rural in the northwest corner of Berlin. Sonny had never been there—he'd had no reason until now. Karl's family lived on Pankower Strasse, near Schäfer See, a lake surrounded by a park. Its faint outline was visible in the dark. He turned onto a residential street, its gardens hidden under a patina of snow. It was a world away from the crowded, noisy, pavement-lined Mitte. He passed No. 22, a modest, two-story wood-frame house, its lights glowing behind curtained windows.

He hadn't encountered a soul but for the cat winding around his legs when he stopped. It scurried away when Sonny stooped to scratch behind its ear. He pushed the doorbell at about 8:30 PM, heard faint chimes, then footsteps. With no invitation or warning given, he wondered what reception he'd get. A lock turned, and the door opened to reveal a white-haired, distinguished-looking old gentleman, the image of a gentle theologian.

Pastor Larson appraised his visitor and in a welcoming voice asked, "What can I do for you?"

"Good evening, Pastor Larson, my name is Sonny. I'm a friend of Karl's. Is he home?"

Muttering that it was too cold to stand outside with the door open, the pastor invited Sonny in. Wearing a bemused grin—as if he'd done this before—he asked Sonny to wait, then disappeared down a hallway. Sonny saw a comfortable parlor with a glowing fireplace, a cat sleeping on the floor.

"You're a long way from home, Sonny," Karl's voice preceded his appearance. "I hope you're not seeking shelter from Nazi mischief the way I was." Karl smiled as he studied his old acquaintance and extended his hand. "You look distinguished in a beard."

Sonny took his hand, and said, "Older maybe—and no, just the ordinary Nazi variety of mischief."

Karl's pleasant manner told Sonny it was natural for someone to appear at their door unannounced. Without turning, he introduced Sonny to his father, barely visible in the shadows. "Sonny's the man I told you about, the one who gave me safe haven that dreadful night at the opera."

Stepping forward, Pastor Larson took Sonny's hand in both of his. "I'm pleased to meet you. Thank you for your kindness. That was among the first of many traumatic nights." Deep furrows lined the space between his eyebrows, as if he'd been overtaken by sadness. "I'll leave you to talk."

The cat scampered out of the wood-paneled study past Sonny into the hall. Karl sat in an overstuffed brown leather chair and invited Sonny to its twin. There was a big desk—and two walls of overflowing bookshelves, more books stacked on the floor. Sonny saw several titles that had met their end in the flames. He mused that Joseph would enjoy perusing the collection.

Karl's voice interrupted his reverie. "Would you like a brandy?"

Sonny nodded absently, and a glass appeared in his hand.

"It's a wonderful collection." Karl noted.

"I was thinking how much a certain friend would enjoy some hours here."

Raising his glass, Karl made a toast, "To good books and friendship."

Sonny smiled, adding, "And an end to this horror."

As they drank, Sonny was able for the first time to take a good look at Karl. He looked older, his face more angular, than in their previous meeting. His eyes betrayed something Sonny couldn't quite read—cynicism or worldly experience? Karl wasn't the innocent youth he'd been in May 1933, but then neither was Sonny.

Sonny's eyes strayed to a photograph of Karl against what looked like the sea, perhaps on a holiday on Rügen Island or the Baltic shore. He couldn't have been more than fifteen or sixteen, blond and winsome like his younger sister. Karl's childhood had been worlds away from Sonny's.

Karl followed Sonny's gaze, emitting a short, hollow laugh. "That was so long ago I can barely remember." He sipped his brandy and said, "Polly came to a meeting recently."

Sonny was jarred at hearing her name.

Karl's tone was casual. "I was surprised and pleased. God knows we need the help."

"She helped me find you." Sonny wondered how much Karl knew of his personal woes. "If she believes in the work, why not? So long as she doesn't get into trouble." Now that we're finished, he thought, why shouldn't she go to you?

"We do the best we can," Karl said, waving one hand in a circle, leaving Sonny to interpret his words. "Maybe some good will result, but I'm not naïve. Real change remains too elusive a goal."

Enough idle chatter, Sonny thought. "Let me be frank," he began, expression unchanged. "You're so calm at my unexpected appearance."

Karl's laugh startled him: "Didn't think I said anything funny."

"I'm sorry, but God knows we try to speak the truth in this house, despite the trouble it brings. We get visitors at all hours of the day and night. I can only imagine what our neighbors, not to mention the Gestapo agent usually parked outside, must think! No, a visit is not out of the ordinary, but I'm especially pleased that it's you."

"Gestapo?" Sonny spit the hideous word, almost spilling his brandy as he tried to remember whether there'd been a car outside.

Karl's smile faded. "Yes, unfortunately. I don't usually conduct business here, but . . . ?" He shrugged as if matters were out of his control. "Your arrival is a bit unusual but not extraordinary, and I'm pleased to see you." He raised his glass.

Then with a penetrating stare, Karl asked abruptly, "So why have you come?"

Another damn clock ticking . . . Sonny searched until his gaze fell on the carved wooden beauty on the desk. He felt the burn of the brandy going down.

"Like you, I'm part of a group, but we're just getting started. Our goal is to get as many Jews out of Germany as we can," he said.

Karl's eyes narrowed, his interest clearly piqued. "Very admirable, but why are you telling me?"

"We have a common vision," Sonny began, digressing then to May 1933, when both men had learned what the Nazis were capable of doing. Sonny hadn't forgotten Karl's anguish. "Conditions are worse than ever, but why should we be surprised? It's exactly as they promised."

Karl gestured toward the books. "The Gestapo paid a visit, before the bonfires, to frighten my father. Certainly they saw the library. Perhaps the visit was an unspoken offer—if my father kept his mouth shut, he could keep his books . . . and his life."

Sonny admired Pastor Larson and couldn't blame him for eschewing martyrdom. "Better to take your work underground, where you can do more good. There's little that words can do in a world full of more devils than hell can hold."

"Well said. So, what do you want from me? I presume you didn't come to reminisce."

"No," Sonny admitted with a tight smile. "Not tonight. We share our abhorrence for the Nazis, but for me it's personal given the strangling decrees and Nuremburg Laws. But I don't have to go into that." An image of Polly slipping into Karl's arms, pushed there by his lies, came unbidden. He looked away.

Karl waited.

"I have access to passports and a skilled forger, as well as a route with people at the other end to facilitate immigration. But we need visas and identity cards."

Karl leaned forward. "Tell me more."

"I'm talking about getting as many Jews out as I can, as we can. Like I said, we need visas. Then we'll send Jews and other people at risk, like your friends, out of Germany. We want to start as soon as possible." Sonny leaned back, his burden lifted.

"Congratulations. I admire your goal as I acknowledge your dilemma," Karl said with genuine warmth, his posture creating intimacy, conspiracy. "Like you, it's personal for me, but we too have our problems." He changed tack. "You must think that I can help, or you wouldn't have come."

"I was hoping . . . Now that I've told you what we're doing, I need you to trust me."

Karl's eyes flickered slightly. "Of course, I do."

"Good," Sonny said. "That I came means I trust you."

Karl relaxed. "What do you need from me?"

"Identity cards, and if you can get your hands on several visas, or even one . . ." Sonny let his words dangle for Karl to ponder.

Karl nodded. "I can help. But I'm curious—did Polly tell you?"

"I had a hunch. Polly helped me find you, and she told me enough to make me think I was right." Then he explained what he'd learned from Otto.

"I like your chutzpah." Karl's grin was broad.

That sealed the deal for Sonny. He absently scratched his beard. Then he gave Karl a bit of his history as a smuggler, of his many trips to Plombieres, of how he'd been forced to join the ranks of the underground.

Karl was laughing before Sonny was finished. "God damn, that's beautiful! You son of a . . . " He refilled Sonny's glass, then his own.

Excited, Karl said, "Your plan complements ours perfectly. We started with Jewish converts, helped those like your friend, and have recently started a pipeline to move those at risk. We've got safe houses around the country, several in Berlin. Documents are the missing element."

"How far along?" Sonny asked.

"Not very," Karl acknowledged. "We collect identity cards and visas from church members. They report the identity cards as lost and get new ones. That's as far as it's gone, but access to a forger, well . . . " He didn't have to finish.

"I know we can help each other," Sonny said, elated at the prospect of shared enterprise.

Their meeting over, Karl took him to the back door, "in case our Gestapo friend is out there."

Sonny stiffened, and the house waxed silent, as if holding its breath. "It wasn't a good idea to come here." He wouldn't do it again.

They agreed to meet near the front entrance at Tegel Castle at six o'clock the following evening. After shaking hands, Karl opened the door, and Sonny scampered out. From over his shoulder, he heard a hushed, "Godspeed."

He took several strides, felt something on his leg and froze, then exhaled with relief. The cat again wrapped around Sonny's legs, and he reached to scratch its head. This time the animal let him do it.

13

The artist, like the God of creation, remains within or behind or above his handiwork, invisible, or refined out of existence, indifferent, paring his fingernails.
—James Joyce

Franz, one of three young fellows recruited as a runner, told his cousin, "I might be able to help. First, I have to talk to someone . . . then I'll get back to you. Keep your mouth shut, or it won't happen."

Then Franz talked with Mischa, who agreed to meet his cousin at the café near Alexanderplatz the next morning . . .

When Mischa arrived, he spotted a guy who looked a little like Franz, sitting alone at the far corner table with his back to the door as instructed. His eyes were full of anticipation, a little fear. When he saw Mischa, he rose and followed his path. Mischa was barely in the chair when Franz's cousin leaned close, wringing his hands.

"I don't have much money. How much will it cost?" Before Mischa could respond, he blurted, "I've heard rumors of agents taking your money, then leaving you high and dry."

Heat rose in Mischa's cheeks, but he kept his anger in check. "Not a good start," he whispered.

The man colored, realized what he'd said, and apologized. He was clearly nervous, so Mischa cut him some slack, thinking about his question. No one had told him how much to charge, so he bought some time.

"We'll get to the price, but first we need to talk."

His name was Hans Finckel, and after ten minutes Mischa knew more about Franz's cousin than he needed to, but the telling had calmed him down.

Mischa laid out the risks, told him there were no guarantees. "Do you still want to go?"

Hans nodded and said softly, "Yes. Now how much will it cost?"

Mischa glanced about furtively, trying to look nonchalant. Perspiration beaded on his upper lip. Distracted by some people entering the café, he looked over Hans's shoulder. Then he opened his mouth, and out popped a nice round figure: "Two hundred Reichmarks."

Hans sighed and said he could get it. Then Mischa said they needed photographs. Hans should pass them on to Franz, who'd continue to be his contact. When the documents were ready, Franz would let him know and provide further instructions. Mischa left first. Hans waited several minutes, paid for the coffee, and left.

Two days later, Joseph sat hunched over his desk, ignoring the ache in his hand. Starting at the upper left-hand corner, he moved down the page, studying each letter and line until he reached the bottom, then repeated the examination. This would be their first family and everything had to go perfectly, but that would always be the case. Too much was at stake. Reviewing his notes to make sure of the spelling, Joseph wrote the name Hans Finckel, then that of his wife, Lena, and of their daughter, Lilli. He sat back in his chair to appreciate the flowery German script—hallmark of the bureaucrat.

Since he had started using his drafting skills, Joseph's self-critical neurosis had returned, like a nosy neighbor who wouldn't leave him alone. That nagging trait, together with the numbing realization that he hadn't the talent, had ended his career as an artist. It had been years ago, but self-doubt still sat on a comfortable, albeit dusty, shelf of his psyche.

"This looks good, very good," he spoke to the empty room, then got up and walked to the window. "I should have been a bureaucrat." He laughed to himself.

Joseph never spoke of his life as a young artist, of when he had lived in a garret in the Mitte after art school, trying to find his place in the competitive Berlin art scene. Glancing at *Berlin Street Scene,* his best work, he thought, "Hell, it's the only remaining piece of those forgotten days . . . when I struggled to become something other than destitute."

Well, not exactly forgotten—bits of memory crept back whenever the painting came into view. In those days he'd bartered art for food and drink, then destroyed or sold all but the one piece hanging on his wall. All evidence of his former life, hand poised on hip, about to attack the canvas, had evaporated. He'd turned his back on it as easily as flipping a light switch.

Joseph was there when the Kaiser abdicated and the strictures of the Willhelmine Era crumbled, starting a period of chaotic experimentation. Fearing he'd be left behind, he had abandoned his work at the ministry to become a full-time artist. Once the dust settled (though not for long), the Republic was born. New freedoms and artistic discovery turned Berlin upside down, massive societal change in their wake.

Saved by the bureaucracy from going to war, Joseph had dabbled in Dada, which bubbled up as an antiwar movement but soon seemed anti-everything. That kind of energy was impossible to sustain; the movement descended to caricature. The basket of art forms—art, architecture, cinema, and literature—known as expressionism emerged early in the century and bloomed in the 1920s.

Joseph never thought he was part of the movement, if that's what it was. Given its breadth, it was difficult to categorize. He knew it was modern, sometimes a response to the modern. It was always emotional, intensely so.

Tending to the bookish, Joseph studied impressionism, cubism, all the *isms,* while trying to find a style of his own. He soon realized he was a step behind—emulating, not innovating. Had he possessed the spontaneity, the vision to see clearly, the passion, he might have succeeded. Had he been more like Mischa—exposing his passions, willing to take risk—he might have succeeded, or so he thought. Making bold statements in rich colors or sparse caricatures, sending messages far louder than met the eye, was not for him. He smiled at what might have been.

Joseph's need to maintain control in a chaotic world was his guiding principle. After the horrors of the war and failed revolution, the new republic barely breathed, the shock of staggering hyperinflation yet to come. Some thrived amid the chaos, finding freedom to experiment. Not Joseph, but not for lack of effort. He simply lacked the talent, an admission painful to make. And passion wasn't his mode. Still, he didn't regret a moment of trying.

Now, through stoic self-control, he managed to ignore his aching neck, numb hand, weakened eyes. Locking out the world for hours at a stretch, he performed magic with his pens, a bottle of ink, and a cup of tea for sustenance. He derived immense satisfaction from creating documents that opened borders.

Others provided legwork and logistics, but Joseph's singular skills enabled their private war against National Socialism. Time was fleeting—perhaps his own would be shorter given the circumstances—but he'd continue until he was caught or until his body broke down.

Joseph walked into the dark bathroom and stared into the inner courtyard, where light from the surrounding flats cast an eerie glow. Looking up, he was reminded of his rooftop garret, of the skylight that had bathed his studio in clean, clear light. If he let his imagination run, he might create a world he wanted. Instead, he reached back to the day when he'd found love, if only for a moment.

A man's voice intruded on Joseph's reverie, and he turned his head, heard a door slam and a woman's muffled laughter. The familiar sounds brought back the days of his youthful excess . . .

On a warm summer evening at an opening in a West End gallery, Joseph had threaded his way through preening intelligentsia, pretentious bohemians. A Russian émigré artist, currently in vogue, exhibited there.

One particular piece bewildered and confused him. Barely contained in its frame, the profusion of lines and scribbles was like an unwound spool of wire interspersed with indeterminate blotches. Pure chaos, no apparent theme, perhaps was the artist's intent, but he wasn't sure. Squinting, he stepped back for a longer perspective as if that might provide insight, but none came. For some inexplicable reason, he kept trying to make sense of it, slowly becoming aware of a presence nearby.

A feminine voice: "Pure garbage. I detest it!"

Joseph nodded, turned to the voice, and saw a young woman, her eyes sparkling with mischief. He laughed.

Surprised, she turned her head to take him in, then smiled, and laughed with him. Soon they were laughing so hard that he had to take her by the arm and guide her outside to avoid a scene. Joseph leaned against a wall, tears rolling down his cheeks.

Finally, she said, "My name's Gretchen. I love art, but I saw none in there." Tossing her head insolently toward the crowd inside, she added without guile, "I'm an artist's model and completely independent." The words were etched in his memory.

Joseph told her he was an artist and that he lived in a Mitte garret.

"Wonderful! I will be your model and your muse," she said.

He searched her face for ridicule, for prevarication, but found neither. She'd already started walking in the general direction of the Mitte. She called back over her shoulder, "Take me there." And so it began.

After making a circuit of the studio, Gretchen had stood beneath the magnificent skylight, bathed in its dramatic light, and begun to dance. Such was the whirlwind of her creation that she gyrated to exhaustion, then fell onto the floor in a heap. He contemplated the unusual woman who'd barged into his life.

A wisp of a girl with small breasts and slim hips, she could pass for an adolescent boy, was perfect for the androgyny of the Roaring Twenties. Her dark hair, cut short, framed an unmemorable face—until she smiled and became almost pretty. Her incongruously small nose sat below large, expressive eyes, her best feature.

In constant motion, she posed standing, lying, crawling—usually naked, her lips in a pout or a smirk, eyes wide, narrowed, smiling, scowling, pensive. As promised, she became Joseph's muse, the subject of countless drawings and paintings. And before long Joseph was falling in love, despite his reticence.

Gretchen loved the big rooftop garret, its nearly overpowering daylight flooding the space, then softening to a romantic glow. Dividing the heavens were nine panes of glass, each the better part of a meter square, so porous that, when it rained, water dripped into strategically placed buckets. Gretchen gaily dumped the water out the window into the alley below, occasionally to the consternation of a passerby. For months they were inseparable, he painting and she posing, the two drinking and eating in the taverns, walking arm in arm. That he had little money was of no consequence. Joseph was liberated. At his most productive, he was selling some of his work, enjoying his life as never before.

Gretchen was his polar opposite—the thought pricked his consciousness. That she'd chosen him was inexplicable, but he did not question his good fortune. Not until, without notice and in the same abrupt manner of her entering, she left. Announcing she was no longer in love, she thanked him for a wonderful time and reminded him of what she'd said at the outset. She kissed his check, gathered her few belongings, and was gone. She had set the terms of their affair from the start, but he wasn't prepared. He hadn't understood the danger of succumbing to her charms.

Gretchen's departure devastated Joseph to the point he was unable to work. That she was so self-absorbed, that she had cared so little for him, made the shock of her rejection greater. How could she have inspired him? How could he have fallen in love?

Refusing to leave his garret, Joseph endured the embarrassment of rejection, the wound to his vanity. Eventually, he ran out of food and drink and had to venture outside. He heard rumors she'd taken a new lover, a ghastly abstract expressionist of little talent. Time passed until he heard nothing more of her. She disappeared from his life and, so it seemed, from the Mitte.

But not from his dreams, where she pounced like a feral cat, her red-hot eyes glowing, claws lashing, lacerating, until he turned crimson. These nocturnal forays ended with his easel thrown to the floor, his futile fight to right it. Raw sexuality oozed from her nightmarish visits. At first the spell broke only when he awoke breathless, covered in sweat, gulping air as if he were running from demons, and he was. As the months passed, the frequency of her intrusions diminished, then finally disappeared.

The Gretchen interlude became a metaphor for the failure of the promise of his youth, for his limitations as an artist and a man. Recalling those moments when he'd stood under the skylight at his easel, inspired and cajoled, was exhilarating and humbling. After all these years, he could still summon the image of her posing for long periods without food, drink, or sleep. Then he'd put down his brush and palette and joined her on the floor. That was the memory he wanted.

With Gretchen's inspiration, he had produced what he wanted, not what was in vogue. He painted impressions of his vision, enhanced by color and texture, yet remaining faithful to the subject. If he emulated another, it was Van Gogh, one who had truly suffered and whom he admired. When Gretchen arrived, Joseph was equal parts youthful pretense, self-imposed poverty, self-conscious posturing—there could be no art without suffering! That he'd uttered the cliché now made him cringe.

In the weeks after her departure, Joseph had drunk too much. After several months, the pain receded, his confidence slowly returned, and he finally returned to his art. That's when he began the Berlin series. Focusing on the Mitte, he painted street scenes, bringing the mix of cultures to life on his canvas. And thus he'd produced his legacy—*Berlin Street Scene,* the third of five paintings. Buoyed by the result and too much wine, he proclaimed to friends: "A true artist survives adversity and strives to greatness, not mediocrity, in the pursuit of art." His burst of hubris set him up for further disappointment.

While others found acclaim, Joseph stumbled on rejection. A gallery owner told him his work was prosaic, another that it was pretty, "but pretty no longer sells." Years after he dropped his brush and palette in the bin, he regretted listening to and taking on himself their condemnation of his work and career. He missed the camaraderie of his bohemian friends, the long hours at the easel, and despite his reticence, the easy spontaneity of the time.

He'd willingly given it all up long ago, but from time to time he missed his muse and pondered her fate. Too many years made his memory unreliable . . . Gretchen blurred. Joseph eventually found his calling in the ordinariness and anonymity of books—surrounded himself with ideas crafted in the beauty of words. Books brought solace—refuge from his perceived failings as an artist and a man.

Staring out the window into the darkness, Joseph imagined the clear, bright light from the skylight pouring onto a canvas. Once he'd stood with brush in hand, ready to make something special. Now he used a pen to produce documents far more valuable than spurious works of art.

The years had erased much of his pain; the memory, though faded, allowed understanding, even wisdom, or so he hoped. He'd found a home in the busy Scheunenviertel warehouse among the Jewish merchants, forever the outsider even as he became one of them. Long ago, he'd left the creative arts to others. Now the riddle of a perfect forgery consumed his energies . . .

Joseph returned to his desk to work on the passport. His friend at the ministry had briefed him that passports issued in Berlin carried a series of numbers such as 5611/39/Z. That particular number was on a passport he'd found in a box of books purchased years before. The letter "Z" indicated the location of the office in Berlin that had issued the passport, so he used that designation. Without access to the official government list, numbers were irrelevant so long as they fit the general scheme and weren't flagged. Using the old passport number, he changed the last digit, coming up with 5612/39/Z.

Next, the bearer's photo had to be carefully affixed with two rivets, one in the upper left, the other at the lower right corner. That posed a unique problem. Affixing the rivets by hand made the document stand out like Gestapo at a bar mitzvah. After hours of practice, Joseph still hadn't gotten it right. Holding the passport, he rubbed his fingertips over the rivet, trying to imagine a tool. He thought of tarpaulins, but they were too big. Then he looked down at the floor, to his shoes, and thought of hiking boots with eyelets for lacing. A cobbler's tool! At the first opportunity, he explained what he needed and sent Sonny out to find it.

The third cobbler Sonny visited, an old Polish guy less then a quarter kilometer from the warehouse, had two of the little machines. Business was suffering, and for the right price he'd sell one.

He named his price and Sonny laughed. "Do I look like I fell off the potato truck?"

"Maybe you did, since you don't know value when you see it."

And so it went as they haggled, Sonny having so much fun he didn't want it to end.

Finally the shrewd Pole moaned, "I'm giving it away."

And Sonny complained, "I'm being cheated."

But they had a deal and shook on it. The shoemaker didn't ask why Sonny needed it. He just counted his money and dismissed it with a wave of his hand . . .

Sonny dropped the satchel on the floor. Joseph was elated . . .

Next, Joseph had to insert a stamp with the Nazi eagle and swastika, the phrases "Polizeipräsident in Berlin" and "Abteilung II" scribed respectively above and below. His friends at the ministry had promised to steal such a stamp for him. In the meantime he'd devised a method to apply each one individually. Here his hand would make the passport a thing of beauty—or render it useless. Judging from the passports he'd seen, the imprint needn't be uniform, but it had to have the look of a crisp stamp, not of a shaky hand.

Joseph mixed his watercolors until the shade was exactly right, noting the formula. Then he made tiny strokes with a brush of only several bristles, left from the old days, until his vision blurred and his hand cramped. After fits and starts, he had it mastered. Sonny couldn't tell the forgery from the real thing.

But Joseph still had to transfer the image to the passport. He had to create a stamp. Recalling an offset technique he'd learned in art school, he dipped crumpled newspaper in water until it was pulpy and thick but not too wet. Then he carefully pressed the muck onto the template, creating the image of the eagle and swastika. Now, all he had to do was press it onto the photos. Through trial and error, with skill and a little luck, he got it just right.

When Sonny asked how he'd discovered the painstaking process, Joseph smiled and said, "Trade secret." Still, he'd have to reproduce the eagle and swastika again and again, as it faded. He urged his friends at the ministry to hurry the delivery of a real stamp.

Sonny and Karl's meeting looked from the outside to be unremarkable. Two young men strolled past the stark, white Tegel Castle, its four corner towers pasted on like afterthoughts. Several children ran past on their way to the skating rink. When they were gone, Karl explained, "Soon after Hitler came to power, the regime moved to co-opt the Lutheran Church, to suppress opposition."

He reminded Sonny of the visit paid his father by the Gestapo: "That intimidated most church members, with good reason. Yet many wanted to protect our Jewish converts. Some, with strong anti-Nazi sentiment and the stomach for subversive action, like me, were more aggressive. We grabbed the opportunity to move beyond the boundaries of the church. I've been groping in the shadowy underground for a long time."

He quickly agreed to supply Sonny with as many identity cards as his parishioners could safely lose.

"I know several men who'll be extremely grateful," Sonny said, slapping Karl on the shoulder. "I'm one of them. Now, if you could get me a visa for France, Belgium, or Holland?"

"I'll see what I can do," Karl promised.

Then apparently desirous of educating Sonny on the architecture of German castles, they made plans to meet near the front entrance of Schönhausen Castle the next morning at 9:00. Karl was to bring several identity cards from which Sonny could choose. Joseph's skill would transform the two underground fugitives to citizens in good standing.

The deal was that in exchange for Karl's identity cards and visas, Sonny's group would provide forged documents and assistance in departing Germany. The two had reached a mutually satisfying arrangement without haggling. This was a departure for Sonny, but he did take some solace in not having to pay retail.

Several days later Sonny became Paul Sander, identity card and a receipt for December's rent in his pocket. His new address wasn't far from Karl's place in Reinickendorf. He quite liked his new name; it reminded him of his old American friend.

Now in the middle of December, Sonny was on the train to Aachen to rendezvous with Hans Finckel and his wife and young daughter. Emil had taken an earlier train and would drive them to the border. After weeks of rehearsal, the operation was underway.

Sonny had opening-night jitters. That was to be expected—this was their maiden crossing with human cargo. He stared out the train window at the passing farms and picturesque villages with their "No Jews allowed" signs, trying to harness his anxiety.

Sitting across from Sonny was a dour-faced, middle-aged man with an old briefcase at his side. He looked up from time to time from his newspaper, disapproving. An uneasy quiet ensued, as if one waited for the other to speak. When they reached Aachen, Sonny's imagined nemesis left the train as he did, and as a precaution he stopped and kneeled to tie his boot. When he looked up, the man had disappeared into the crowd.

Aachen's sky was overcast in a midafternoon relatively warm for December. Sonny walked past the square where, only months before, Albert had intruded into and transformed his life. With new name, beard, and the clothes of a working-class stiff, Sonny was a different man. The change in his appearance made him harder to identify, or so he hoped.

Sonny was still swaying gently from the motion of the train, so he stopped in a recessed doorway to get his bearings. The disconcerting sense that he'd been there before washed over him, until he realized he probably had. His nerves were playing tricks on him and probably would do so until the Finckel family was safely across the border. Pulling his dirty cap even lower so only his nose and beard showed, Sonny casually looked both ways, then left his perch.

After walking some twenty meters, Sonny saw several cops coming his way. His heart pounded, signaling danger, but it was a feeling he could handle. As they moved closer, inspiration struck. He smiled and stuck out his right arm: *"Heil Hitler!"*

This unnecessary act of bravado, or stupidity, take your pick, was a test he found exhilarating. Apparently they hadn't noticed him, and the one nearest gave him a quick once-over but never broke stride. The other cop mumbled, "Heil Hitler," and Sonny almost laughed. He'd passed the test, and his nerves settled.

Sonny's cover, should anyone ask and he prayed no one would, was that of a worker in a railroad-parts factory. Such an enterprise did exist, and he could answer a few questions. More would spell trouble. He wore gloves because his hands were those of a smuggler, though he'd nicked them up a bit and dirtied his fingernails. All things considered, he felt good about his disguise, especially after encountering the two cops.

His destination was a small café in a quiet neighborhood, about a kilometer from the main square. Blue letters spelled *Café* above a blue door flanked by blue-curtained windows. Shafts of sunlight shone through a cloud onto the pavement, which Sonny took as a good omen. The operation was finally underway, and it felt good to be at it again, especially with this cargo.

The wait had seemed interminable, but it had been only seven weeks since the day Joseph told him of his scheme. Sonny had had to control his impatience while they obtained Karl's identity cards and visas, Joseph honed his skills, and they put the semblance of an operation in place. That done, everything was covered, the first rendezvous set.

Scanning both streets, Sonny saw nothing that concerned him. He glanced at his watch. It was 4:15, a quarter-hour past the time for contact, though still within the scheduled boundaries. Finckel's instructions were to wait up to an hour. They'd be nervous, so he wanted the family of three to get settled at a table, to be as comfortable as possible. He felt confident about the plan, glad to be working again.

The familiar odor of onions and cooking oil perfumed the warm air as Sonny stepped inside. Heads turns to him briefly, but only the eyes of the family in the corner fixed on him. Taking a seat at the neighboring table with his back to the man, Sonny quietly said, "Welcome to Aachen. I'm Paul Sander. I hope you haven't been waiting long."

Before Hans Finckel answered, his little girl asked, "Who is that?"

Without hesitation, her mother answered, "Our new friend." She sounded hopeful.

Sonny looked over his shoulder at the family and smiled to break the ice. Only the little girl seemed unfazed, insulated by youth from what lay ahead. Dark circles ringed her father's eyes, and when he spoke his voice was raspy.

"Not long. We ordered food."

Sonny also ate, and within a half-hour, they stood on the pavement across the street, waiting for Emil. The little girl held her mother's hand, as the two men quietly talked. Though it was probably pointless, Sonny tried to dispel his fears, recalling his own first time across the border. They had documents, and that made all the difference.

If Ferret Face was on duty, Sonny and Emil would cross into Belgium—probably the last time either would cross the border unless they left Germany for good. If not, Fritz would cross from Plombieres to Aachen, and they'd meet at the little café later that evening to work out future operations.

Darkness made the air feel colder. Where the hell was Emil? Sonny had asked him where he'd get an automobile. Emil, grinning, said he'd steal one. Sonny wasn't sure whether he'd been joking or not. Now Sonny scanned the buildings around him, his eyes passing over the curtained windows. He stopped upon spotting someone, maybe a woman, but it was dark. She watched him like a sentinel. Her outline was jagged in the dim light, but she had the posture of an elderly person. Sonny feared she was an informant, but he squelched the suspicion. He glanced at his watch, looked for Emil—half an hour late—and back to the old woman. She hadn't moved.

Sonny broke eye contact with her and looked at the little girl. Curly black hair hung from under her cap. She sang as she leaned against her mother's leg. There was innocence in her large dark eyes, oblivious to the adventure that lay ahead. What would she make of all this when she was older?

Lost in thought, Sonny didn't see the black sedan stop at the curb, its door open. When the little girl turned, Sonny turned too, towards Emil's quizzical gaze . . .

Sonny sat up front with Emil as they pulled away. He looked up to the old woman; she seemed to smile. It may have been his imagination, but he marked her as harmless, perhaps even sympathetic. Emil nodded to Sonny, then drove, aimlessly it seemed, through Aachen's side streets, his eyes moving constantly from road to rearview mirror. Then they were out of the city, heading toward Reinartzkehl and the border checkpoint.

Before they got there, Emil turned onto a dirt track leading to a forest, brought the car to a halt, and turned off the engine. He caught Sonny's eye, swiveled in his seat, and took in his passengers for the first time. Smiling at the little girl, he said, "Hello sweetheart."

Unsure, she looked up at her mother, who nodded. In a soft, high-pitched voice she said, "Hello."

Her father glanced nervously at the large man in the driver's seat, then at Sonny: "Yes, hello."

"Welcome," Emil said in a soothing voice. "We're very near the border, and I wanted to find a quiet spot to talk." He paused as he scanned two sets of nervous eyes that said they'd entrusted their fate to him, and it was too late to turn back.

The seat creaked under Emil's weight, the engine idling softly. "In a few minutes I'll drive to the border check point and stop fifty meters before the shed. You'll get out of the car and walk to the border." Emil looked directly at the man. "Give your passport and visas to the guard. He'll look at them, then at you, and hand them back. It's as easy as that."

"I can do that," Hans said and let out a breath, patting his wife's knee for reassurance. "Then what?"

"Walk to the Belgian side, and do the same. We'll follow on foot in about five minutes. We'll meet a friend on the other side who'll take us to a farm outside the village where you'll spend the night."

For the first time the man's wife spoke, her voice clear and to the point, "Have you done this before?"

Sonny answered. "Yes, many times. We know the border guards, and there'll be no problem. You have the necessary papers, and if they ask any questions, you know what to say." He nodded to her and then to her husband. "You'll do fine."

Emil and Sonny looked at each other as the family began the walk to freedom, and smiled in satisfaction. Fifteen minutes later they saw Fritz, a broad smile on his face, standing next to his ancient Peugeot, surrounded by the three. All of them barely squeezed into his car for the drive to the farm. Upon arrival, the family stayed outside—father, mother, and child huddled together, savoring freedom. Hans held his wife in his arms; their little girl clutched at her mother's coat.

Fritz poured strong coffee. Sonny beamed with delight. It had gone as planned, without a hitch, like in the old days. Fritz slapped him on the back and said, "This is wonderful, but you've got nothing to take back."

He walked outside and returned holding the little girl's hand. "Lilli, what a pretty name! Let me introduce you to Marlene."

Early the next morning Fritz would take Lilli by the hand to the chicken coop, where she'd gather eggs for their omelet and giggle with delight. Then he'd feed the émigrés a substantial breakfast and drive them to the train station. By the time they gathered their few belongings and piled again into the Peugeot, he'd be "Uncle Fritz."

Long before that, Sonny and Emil would be back in Germany, on their way to Berlin.

There were rumors of other operators smuggling Jews out of Germany, but all they had were rumors. When Hans confronted Mischa about the possibility of being left high and dry, he'd simply been giving voice to the dark side of what he'd heard. Cologne, close to the borders of France, Belgium, and Holland, reputedly was the hub for illicit traffic. There were stories of shady operators leaving desperate people stranded at the border. But there had to be groups like theirs—"legitimate" smugglers—ferrying Jews with regularity, though the numbers were small. How many succeeded was impossible to know; failures were quietly endured.

But getting out of Germany wasn't the problem—the Nazis *wanted* to rid Germany of its Jews. The ugly truth was that nobody else wanted them. Failure meant being denied entry to Belgium, France, or Holland. The forgeries weren't good enough or there were no papers at all, and the would-be émigré melted back into the Mitte to try again. Or if they were lucky, border guards like Ferret Face and Claude held out their hands and waited for the money to pass. What the hell did they care?

Sonny found purpose in following his father's nefarious path. Before Albert had shut it all down, he'd felt a failure: for not writing, for not making an effort at something substantial. But everything changed with the new enterprise. The Third Reich was by now so restrictive to the Jews that there was nothing but to leave, and he was making it possible.

Having reached a certain age, Sonny took stock, his life's markers marching through his head—his parent's deaths, his Uncle Simon's self-destruction, his long friendship with Mischa, his fortuitous friendships with Otto, Emil, and Joseph. Now his painful ending with Polly, his reacquaintance with Karl, his encounter with Albert. Sonny traced what he hoped to accomplish back to that morning at the warehouse when his father gave him the lesson of those strange, exotic birds, bobbing and chanting in the "ghetto."

Sonny's father had bestowed on him an illicit career, the ability to sell, and the lesson of accepting people as they are—all prelude to his stretching into something new and uncharted. His father's secret had become a legacy to be proud of. People wanted dignity, and Sonny could help them get it.

14

Successful and fortunate crime is called virtue.
—Lucius Annaeus Seneca

During the remainder of 1937 and into 1938, a steady stream of émigrés moved toward Plombieres from Berlin. At first the number was small, but it soon reached an average of ten per week—a good beginning. Finding clients wasn't a problem, but keeping a lid on the operation was. Being caught was the operators' worst fear, but they also dreaded creating a demand they couldn't satisfy. Neither occurred in those months, but in March 1938 something changed the enterprise in ways never imagined.

A man named Helmut Dix found his way to Otto through Willy Ehlers, an old comrade from the Hammer & Sickle. Over the years, Willy occasionally had provided shelter to Otto in his one-room flat.

When Willy and Otto met by chance on a street corner in Wedding, Willy moved close and asked, "Do you have any contacts who can help an old comrade get out of Germany?"

Otto, spooked that Willy knew, answered, "Not here. Tomorrow at 10 AM at the Zoological Gardens, in the far corner by the grove of larches. Do you know it?"

Willy nodded.

The big park in central Berlin was a good place for a clandestine meeting, so long as you knew where to go. Otto entered the zoo under the arch at the Elephant Gate and nodded curtly to the stone pachyderms. He was annoyed at the fifteen minutes it took to find Willy standing behind the biggest tree. Willy was hunched against the cold, and his eye twitched.

Willy ignored Otto's displeasure. "Can you help Helmut Dix?"

Of course Otto knew the name. He tried to hide his surprise. "We can, but first he needs an identity card with a new name, so he can move around. Does he have a photo?"

Willy's sideways glance said it was a dumb question.

Otto shrugged it off. "Never mind, we'll take a photo. Then off he goes." He made a sweeping gesture.

"Good," Willy answered. "Dix is eager to leave. He hasn't seen his wife and daughter in five years."

"Hell, everybody wants to leave yesterday, but that's impossible," Otto snapped. "Good forgeries take time. Tell Dix to report at 10 tomorrow morning to Joseph's bookstall on the second floor of the warehouse in Scheunenviertel. He should ask for a copy of Shakespeare's *Hamlet*. We'll take his picture, and his identity card will be ready the next day." He gave directions, reminding Willy, "Everyone pays a fee. Those are the terms. Take or leave it."

Willy shrugged and nodded. Then his eye fluttered, and he covered it with his good hand. As Otto turned to go, he said, "One more thing: Dix won't leave without his wife and daughter."

Otto sighed and simply nodded.

Willy shrugged. "I'm just the messenger."

Otto wanted to know how Willy had hooked up with a big-time Communist like Dix, but he didn't ask. Still, he looked at Willy differently now—especially after what he had done for him over the years.

In the old days, Willy had hung around the Hammer & Sickle, never really fitting in but willing to help with campaigns and to rally in the streets. He seemed always a beat behind, missing the point, laughing at the wrong time. Some of the guys, including Otto, treated Willy in a condescending manner, but either he didn't notice, which seemed unlikely, or he shrugged it off. Without family, Willy had few friends, and no one took the time to get to know him. Yet, when it mattered, he came through.

Late into the night, in his one-room Wedding flat, Willy had told Otto of his arrest and torture—the first of many such stories Otto heard underground. During the Nazi sweep in the spring of '33, Thälmann and thousands of party members had been arrested. Willy was on a list for "re-education." From the very room they were sitting in, rampaging Nazis had grabbed Willy, then held him in detention with countless others at SA Feldpolizei on General-Pape Strasse.

They'd screamed in Willy's face and spit in his eyes, scaring the shit out of him. On the third day, they ordered the prisoners into the first-aid room. One captor yelled for the young guy to step forward. Willy was slow to realize that meant him, and he was pulled from the line, told to drop his pants and grab his penis. The guards laughed as one held him, and another pricked his groin with a syringe, injecting fluid.

Then the captives were ordered back to the cell—by hands and knees, through a gauntlet of kicking thugs, punching them in the groin, buttocks, ribs, head. Finally, they came to a big room filled with inmates lying on their stomachs. They were ordered inside and laid out like sardines in a can, for stomping. Done with that, the tormentors went after their fingernails and hair with pliers.

By morning Willy was bruised, battered, and he hurt like hell—but he was alive. He'd forgotten about the injection, but then his insides began to burn. Expecting he'd rot in prison until he died, he was surprised to find himself released. All he had to do was promise never to get involved in Communist politics again, never to associate with his old friends. If he did, they wouldn't go so easy on him. Willy would have agreed to almost anything . . .

After several weeks, his bruises healed, and he pissed without pain. But he couldn't make a fist with his left hand, and his left eye fluttered like a butterfly anytime it felt the need, which was often—especially when he was anxious.

Living among his old comrades in Wedding, Willy hadn't been able to avoid wading back into the swamp. Over the years he gave shelter to many, including Otto and Helmut Dix. That he had survived the Nazis gave Willy comfort. They could do little more to scare him. Given what happened to so many others, he considered himself lucky to be alive. Dix was looking for a way out of Germany, and he'd asked Willy for help.

As a former high-ranking KPD official, Dix was used to giving orders. He was imperious, difficult, at times disagreeable. After five years underground, his reliance on the generosity of former patrons and comrades had taught him a modicum of humility and patience. Short in stature, he'd grown thin on meager rations, but his health was intact.

But personality runs deep, so when Otto handed Dix his new identity card, Dix demanded a talk with the man in charge. "I have something important to discuss—but only with him."

"Impossible," Otto said.

Dix protested to no avail.

Later, Otto explained the situation to Joseph and Sonny, and after discussing it, they voted on whether to take him on—Sonny against, Otto in favor, Joseph casting the deciding vote. They'd meet at the flat; it was too damned cold to stand outside at the zoo.

Otto and Dix were late. Mischa had been sent home to Sophie. They didn't want him to know, not yet. Recently, he'd been unpredictable, subject to sudden bursts of anger. Finally, there was a knock on the door.

"What the hell happened?" Joseph demanded.

Otto closed the door, nearly falling back on it: "We were nearly arrested." He nodded toward Dix. "He talked him out of it."

Dix smirked but said nothing.

Joseph put a calm hand on Otto's shoulder. "Quickly, tell us. I want to get him out of here."

Otto sighed and began. "We left by the Lion Gate, skirted the Zoo Station, and moved onto Tauentzienstrasse, intending to turn into Marburg Strasse—it's less traveled. That's when I heard a voice command us to stop. The cop was on top of us, demanding our identity cards." Otto cringed. "I can still smell his onion breath.

"We handed him our cards. I think it was the same cop I saw going into the zoo, but he was so far away I didn't think he saw me. He looked at our faces, at the cards, back to our faces. Finally, he threatened to take us in. That's when Comrade Dix took over. God, it was gutsy!

"He leaned into the cop, and said, 'Why are you bothering two good, hardworking Germans out for a walk—when the enemies of the Reich are out there?' He got all worked up, all dramatic with his hands. Then he said, 'We've done nothing wrong. When you go into the zoo and it's open, you expect to be able to get out.' Then he said that he had us mixed up with somebody else.

"I thought we were done for, nearly stuck my hands out for the handcuffs. But the officer didn't say anything, just handed our cards back. Then he said he'd forget it today, but to stay out of the zoo at night, even if the gates are open. But Dix didn't let it go—he said they should warn us before we go in.

"The officer smiled—like they were a couple of working men bantering on the street. He told us to get going and next time to walk somewhere else. Then he left. I said, 'Yes, officer,' to his back. Dix was smiling and snickering, and I nearly fainted. We hadn't walked more then five minutes when the door of a little tavern opened. The smell of beer and bratwurst drew us in. I know we're late, but I was glad to get off the street and calm down."

"No harm done—right, Otto?" Dix winked. Then he stifled a belch and extended his hand to Joseph. "Your identity cards passed the test!"

Joseph shook his hand, "No more meetings in the zoo. From now on, use Tiergarten Park or Hasenheide Forest." Then he turned to Dix. "All right. What do you want?"

Dix didn't answer his question, saying instead, "Blame me, not Otto."

"I'm not blaming anyone," Joseph responded.

Sonny hadn't wanted the meeting: "For Christ sake, let's get this over with."

Unfazed, Dix took in the small room, then, ignoring Sonny, spoke directly to Joseph. "I assume you are the leader."

Bemused, Joseph shook his head. "No, we put everything to a vote."

"In that case, your enterprise is doomed," Dix retorted, laughing. Even Sonny cracked a smile. The sudden mood change gave Dix his opening.

"Democracy! Admittedly a quaint system, the late Republic was a flawed but charming example. I preferred Lenin's revolutionary-democratic dictatorship of the proletariat and peasantry. But, alas, my former party is no longer extant." Dix sighed.

"Our short-lived experiment with elections made Chancellor of the current dictator—an irony of fatal dimensions." Dix's comment hovered like a feather in an updraft. He had adroitly changed the tone and, in doing so, pushed their conflict from view.

Dix leaned back in his chair and scratched his throat. He looked from Sonny to Joseph, asking, "Are you comrades?" But before either could answer, he returned his gaze to Sonny. "I suspect you are not."

The barb worked, and Sonny opened his mouth, but Joseph intervened. "What the hell difference does it make? Enough of these digressions—get on with it or leave."

Dix frowned, looked down at his dirty fingernails, and said softly, "All right. You will be taking my family—my wife, my daughter, my father-in-law, and me—to Belgium." His face softened at the mention of them. "Naturally, I am prepared to pay your price. But first I want to know what assurance you can provide that my family will be safely taken out of Germany? For all I know, you might be frauds." Then he hesitated, smiled, and softened his demand: "Please."

Joseph's laugh was brittle. "There are no guarantees in this new world order—if there ever were. We'll provide you with the tools to emigrate and our assistance in the process, but you know there are too many variables for assurance. Our successes are long gone, and they haven't left testimonials." His words emerged acidly, etching the point.

Dix's eyebrows rose, and he nodded. "All right. I trust you. I have to."

"A ringing endorsement!" Joseph said.

Otto spoke to Dix. "We've gone to a lot of trouble, comrade. If you don't trust us, please leave. We'll forget we ever met."

"Never mind. I know you cannot make guarantees, but I am concerned about our safety. You can understand that?"

His words met with nods of agreement. He licked his lip. "Do you have anything to drink?"

Choosing whiskey over water, Dix murmured his thanks, took a mouthful, winced with pleasure. Then he wiped his mouth with a handkerchief and said, "In my position as KPD money man, I had access to money, large amounts of money. Operating a political party of that size required significant funds."

He flicked his wrist as if he were addressing subordinates: "I will not bore you with the arcane mechanics. You would not be interested anyhow. Unless you are thinking of a political comeback." Dix smiled even as his attempt at humor fell flat, though he didn't seem to notice.

"Hell, we were trying to win elections, and doing a damn good job of it," he said. "Otto worked hard, as did many others. We won 77 seats in the Reichstag elections of 1930, 89 seats in July 1932, and 100 seats in November. We were well positioned to take leadership, at least that is what we thought. Perhaps we were naïve."

Otto admitted, "We overestimated the German worker's willingness to embrace Communism."

"Yes, and we were outflanked by the extreme right. The bad taste from the 1919 failed revolution lingered, and we did not see it coming," Dix agreed.

"But your biggest problem," Joseph cut in, "was obstinacy, hubris." He pointed at Dix. "You spurned coalition with the SPD but worked in concert with the Nazis on the transit strike in '32, the lowest moment of many failings."

Sonny recalled standing on a street corner near Alexanderplatz, sickened at the sight of Nazis and Communists arm in arm. They took turns yelling tired slogans: "Red Front," then "Heil Hitler." From rival teams, they were like chums, even after brawling for most of the year. It was pure farce.

Joseph continued his indictment. "Communists were willing to accept failure before compromise—a terrible tragedy in light of what we face now."

Dix shrugged, "Coalitions, compromise—it is all a dream." Then he looked away and seemed to recite from memory: "We resisted the abyss until pushed, and then we were smothered by defeat. That is when the truth emerged."

His voice was plaintive as he continued. "Yes, of course. There was no chance of compromise, not ever, and when Thälmann finally called for a general strike, it was too late. We were Moscow's puppets, and Stalin would not allow compromise."

Color rose in Dix's cheeks as he defended himself. "We may not have understood the principles of democracy, but I was not alone. Germany was overwhelmed—by reparations, hyperinflation, and finally, worldwide depression. But most of all, we were overwhelmed by the sinister forces of the extreme right, which kept alive the bitterness of defeat, the demonization of Jews and Communists. History was never on our side, but none of us knew that then. Blame the SPD, the army, the workers, the fat and vacuous political center, and you. All of you." Spittle flew from his mouth as Dix pointed a finger at each in turn. "All of us are to blame. If I failed, I failed myself." Dix let out a breath, looked down in defeat, emptied the glass, and licked his lips, searching for the words to finish.

"Our thin democracy was born in the aftermath of humiliating defeat, followed by a failed revolt. And when it reached mere puberty, it was dominated by the extremes. We were destined to fail. The ballot box is a wonderful ideal. Thälmann embraced the dream, and now he wallows in prison."

Dix turned to Otto dolefully. "We built a formidable organization and won elections, only to fall short like everyone else."

Dix's eyes glazed, seeing what his audience could not: Thälmann speaking at a rally in a large hall, pounding his fist on the podium, his tie flung over his shoulder. He had exhorted the party faithful into the streets one last time, in a feat of political will. Off to the side, out of chances, exhausted, and spent were the men of the central committee, slouched in defeat. Thus had ended the good old days, when six million Germans voted for the KPD and membership was more than 300,000 strong. And when Dix had power and position.

Dix sensed his companions' growing impatience and turned obsequious. "Please, I ask your indulgence a minute more. You need background." Then he leaned forward and spread his hands in a gesture meant to draw them in.

They waited silently, the clock ticking in the background. Sensing his time was short, Dix said, "My expertise was collecting and dispersing funds. Party members were generous, and loyal followers of Thälmann and the Communist ideology supported the party with donations to the very end. Besides the members paying dues, others provided for the party with legacies of extraordinary value—jewelry, gold, silver, and precious stones. The money collected was spent on elections, and as you can imagine, there was never enough. After January 1933 when the Nazis put us out of business, they confiscated what little remained."

Dix shrugged at the powerlessness over matters beyond his control. "But they did not take everything, and I know where there are *riches*," he paused, "worth the effort to find." His nostrils flared as he took a breath.

"What?" Joseph asked, his face showing confusion, impatience.

Dix turned to Otto and said, "You know the old KPD office in Neukölln on Thiemann Strasse near the canal?"

Otto nodded.

"In the cellar there was, and I presume still is, a safe where we kept the gems, gold, and silver. I know the building still stands. I have seen it. But its doors are boarded shut, and the neighborhood is worse off than before. Just what the condition of the safe is," Dix shrugged, "I cannot guess. But there may be a fortune."

Facing Joseph, Dix paused to let the information sink in, then said, "*That* is what."

Sonny thought maybe he had Dix wrong. "Why are you telling us?"

"I need partners. Someone to get inside and retrieve the loot." Dix scanned the three men with his eyes.

"Just like that!" Sonny snapped his fingers, the sudden staccato startling them.

Otto was sweating, so he opened a window and looked onto the dark street below. He shivered at the sudden gust of cold air.

Joseph didn't stir but stared at Dix with his lips pursed. Finally, he said, "Why didn't you recruit your underground chums? Like the man who brought you to Otto?"

Before Dix could answer, Sonny asked, "With your connections, why didn't you arrange for a way out of Germany long before now?"

Dix's shoulders sagged, the questions throwing him off. Momentarily deflated, he looked away and sighed. All he could manage was, "Well . . ."

Joseph was about to speak when Dix found his voice. "First of all, I have had no access to papers, and my wife and daughter are here. As for the safe, I have no one I can trust with such a sensitive job. Willy, and many like him, have been a great help, but he is not up to the task. The past five years have been a humbling experience—and I do not tend toward humility," he said without irony, forcing a wistful smile.

"I have a tendency toward bombast, and I can be overbearing, as you no doubt have noticed. Old habits are hard to break." Dix nodded to Joseph. "Living underground is a great leveler, and I have learned much. Men like Willy risked their lives for mine. Unfortunately, those gallant fellows do not possess the talents I need, and, alas, they are not burglars."

"Neither are we," Joseph interjected.

Dix conceded the point. "And I am a washed-up functionary whose best days are past. For all their loyalty, those men are followers, not leaders. They do not have the skills to accomplish what I need or the sources to provide me with documents for which I will forever be grateful to you. In the past five years I have encountered prosperous men—those with money and know-how, who have remained free, their old loyalties well hidden, and agreed to help me for interludes, but no more. Fear is an infection, and if the source remains too long...

"Simply put, I am adrift in a lifeboat without oars, searching for a safe harbor but unable to reach shore. Rumors abound, yet I put my faith in Otto. Through luck and the help of others, I have found you." He looked at Joseph. "With hope, anything is possible."

"We know what Otto has endured, so we sympathize with your plight," Joseph said. "But what you're asking is beyond us."

Sonny nodded, looked at Otto, then back at Dix, and conceded, "Well said, but you haven't answered our questions."

"Surely you understand that I cannot leave without my wife and daughter. So long as I have been at large, I have thought they were safe. Why have they been able to remain in our flat on Agricola Strasse when so many others have been evicted? The only answer is that they are honey to trap me."

"How could the Gestapo know you're still here?" Sonny asked.

Dix shrugged. "Had I surfaced in Belgium or France, even England, it may have become known." His lips pursed immodestly. "After all, I was a big-time Communist, a confidant of Thälmann, a refugee from Nazism. That would be news, propaganda against Germany."

"Makes sense," Joseph agreed. "Still... why us?"

"As I said, you are helping my family out of Germany. You speak of the attendant risks. Why compound them by involving others? You have the ingenuity and resources to provide for my escape—so why not this little caper? If the safe remains full, as I believe it is, there will be plenty to go around. Your share will finance your operations for a long time."

Then he spoke directly to Joseph—the oldest, probably their leader despite his protestations, certainly the most influential. "That is why I ask you. I need help to plan the operation and carry it out, for I cannot."

"What do you want from the safe?" Joseph asked.

"A new life with my family—what all your clients want."

Sonny smiled at Dix's chutzpah. He was warming to the plan.

Dix pulled a paper from his pocket, then opened up a drawing of No. 15, Thiemann Strasse and a diagram of the cellar. "The safe is behind a false wall opposite the bottom of the staircase. It is invisible to the casual observer. Few know of its existence, which is why I believe it is untouched. Please think about it. I have no one else to turn to."

They promised an answer the following day and bid Dix good night. He didn't say where he was headed, and they didn't ask. Otto would meet him the next day at Oranienburger Tor to give him their decision. Getting Dix and his family out of Germany was easy. This other matter was different, more complex.

Before Dix left, he turned to the men, a pained expression on his face. In a voice barely audible, he said, "I must be sure you are sufficiently impressed with the magnitude of my dilemma and that you take my proposal seriously. Please . . ."

Sonny nodded, quietly shut the door, and turned back to the others. "This is crazy."

For the next hour they debated Dix's proposition, punctuating their discussion with periods in which the only sound was their breathing, a cough, chair legs scraping, Sonny drumming his thumb on the table to the percussion of the clock. Their enterprise, like everything else, was hostage to time. None of them knew how much remained, but the treasure could help their cause.

Should war erupt, as rumor warned, the operation would end. Nazi propaganda called for Anschluss—the unification of Austria with Germany. The constant saber-rattling for a Greater Germanic Reich made it seem inevitable, a simmer coming to a boil. With the garbage of the last war still in their craws, would the leaders of Britain and France stand up to Hitler? Or would they condemn Germany publicly while agreeing privately to the sacrifice of a tiny central European nation—a small price to pay for avoiding war?

None of the present company was sanguine at the prospect, but they'd pushed on regardless. No sense worrying about what they couldn't control—such was the reality.

Dix was right—whatever the safe held would fund their operation for a long time. By the end of the evening Sonny appreciated the opportunity with increasing enthusiasm. But to pull it off, they needed help, and he knew only one man who could provide it.

15

I am fond of the truth, but not at all of martyrdom.
—Voltaire

Smuggling isn't dangerous enough!" Emil snapped loud enough that Lisle came to the door.

"For God's sake, keep your voice down. The whole building will know what you are planning," she said.

Emil shrugged as if he were powerless in the presence of a madman. Lisle shot him a withering glance, then disappeared. Emil followed her with his eyes 'til she was gone, then sighed in frustration and continued in a quieter rant. "Now you want to diversify into a second-story man and take on another fencing operation to boot. That's brilliant!"

"Actually, the loot's in the cellar," said Sonny.

Emil ignored the flip comment. He'd glared incredulously through Sonny's description of the proposed burglary of No. 15 Thiemann Strasse. He frowned, aiming an accusatory finger at Sonny. "Have you lost your collective mind? You must think this is a grand adventure!"

"Maybe so, but they can only hang us once."

Sonny's quip was poorly received. Emil muttered and stomped around the kitchen, but Sonny wasn't particularly concerned. Emil liked to beat a proposition to bits, looking for weaknesses before agreeing to anything. He'd ranted this way when Sonny broached the plan to smuggle Jews from the country five months before.

They kept talking, and after half an hour Emil squinted, a faint smile brightening his face. "Sigmund Landauer, you're a rascal!"

A week later, the operators gathered again in Joseph's flat, this time to meet Emil. Beyond the problem of the residents above No. 15, other neighbors, the block warden, and the police, they would have to get in and out of the building and locate the safe without detection.

So far, all they had was Dix's word and a diagram of the office. He'd give them the combination to the safe when they were ready, though it occurred to Emil that if Dix had it, others might as well. Discounting the thought, he tried to focus on how they'd break into the building.

Emil and Otto sat on chairs, Mischa and Sonny sharing the sofa. Willy sat cross-legged on the floor. Joseph worked on a document, listening from his desk. He'd help only with the planning. Before long, the flat was thick with cigarette smoke. Sonny coughed, muttered an expletive, and opened a window despite the chill. Two days earlier he'd introduced Emil to the others. There'd been no need for them to know him 'til now.

But Emil's reputation preceded him. Mischa had retreated when Emil's raw-boned frame filled Joseph's doorway. Emil was used to that, and he smiled pleasantly, extending a hand. Slowly Mischa circled, like a dog sniffing the ground, and they shook hands.

Sonny provided a short history of his working relationship with Emil and an abbreviated version of what he had learned that first night in Plombieres. Emil had started as an apprentice bricklayer, then turned to truck driving, and finally become a butcher's assistant. But the turmoil of the early 1920s, the hyperinflation, the shrinking job market, and the lousy hours had pushed him into larceny. Like so many Germans who'd endured the economic chaos of poverty as the norm, he'd grown cynical. Exploiting the gaps between opportunity and despair, Emil fished the murky waters of illegality.

On one of his first jobs, Emil, armed with a penknife, had broken into a fancy house in Charlottenburg. When its residents arrived home earlier than expected—though he had no clue when they would return—he clambered down a drainpipe with a handful of jewelry for his effort. He'd remained calm until they were all inside, then climbed out the window. From that time until the demise of Franco's enterprise, property crimes—fencing and burglary—had provided his bread and butter.

With the right temperament and steely nerves, Emil had come to enjoy the rush associated with the risk of discovery. "Larceny kind of became my second nature," he noted with understatement. When, on a long drive back to Berlin, Sonny had asked what gave him the edge, Emil admitted that whatever it was—instinct, experience, intelligence, nerves, luck, all of them—it was God-given. While he didn't want his children to follow his path, he emphasized to them as he did to Sonny that whatever they did, they should do it well and heed the lessons of life.

But it was a young man's game, and though Emil wasn't old, sneaking around other people's bedrooms soon *was*. He had married, and his wife insisted he had responsibilities; he must give up second-story work. That had been more than a decade ago, so he was a bit rusty at breaking and entering. Laughing, he told Sonny that smuggling was cleaner, its hours more amiable. More than that, he didn't have to worry about running into a tenant with a fistful of his silver.

Emil's muscular bulk and flat, Slavic features might intimidate anyone meeting him for the first time. But Sonny knew Emil as a calm man who eschewed violence unless pushed, who'd learned early that, given his size, a frown or a clenched fist was all he needed to intimidate another. There were rumors that Emil had started in the enterprise as a "strong arm," but Sonny never asked about it. Some things were best left alone.

At any rate, Emil liked working in the shadows, so the Thiemann Strasse job was a good fit despite his early resistance. And his insight was sorely needed. "Don't get caught. Forget the loot and run. There's always another day—unless you're behind bars," he said.

On that same long trip, Emil, warming to the subject, acknowledged that a copper and a thief were like brothers: "I know several ne'er-do-wells who've ended up in uniform. Both coppers and thieves break the law, and the most successful ones know how the mind of the other side works. Hell, I'd have been a good cop," he laughed, "but the money's lousy unless you're on the take . . ."

Sonny saw No. 15 Thiemann Strasse, Neukölln, Berlin, as a perfect metaphor for the poverty that stood for everything gone wrong since '33—it was neglected and run down. That it was no more forlorn than the rest of the neighborhood offered little consolation to those consigned to live in its midst. Having been there often, Otto knew well the place that had housed the former local KPD headquarters.

Early in the day after Dix broached the plan, Sonny and Otto had made a tour of Thiemann Strasse. Standing at the corner of Thiemann and Weser, Sonny scanned the buildings until he came to No. 15. He read the faded block lettering—MÖBELFABRIK—of the factory above the second-story windows. Sonny had never stood at that spot before, and it had been several years for Otto.

The laughter of an approaching group of schoolchildren startled them. Dressed in heavy tattered jackets and wool caps pulled low against the morning cold, the girls were hard to tell from the boys. Red-faced, the youngsters were too busy pushing and laughing to pay much attention to two men whispering at the corner. But one did take notice, turning to look at them, saying something to the others. More laughter, and they ran away, the lone sign of joy on Thiemann Strasse.

Sonny and Otto watched the children disappear, then Sonny jabbed Otto in the side and pointed to the street sign.

"What?" snapped the startled Otto.

"The Hammer & Sickle was just down Weser on Pannier."

"Ja, I know," Otto answered tersely. "I've only been here a few thousand times, and besides, the H & S is ancient history. Now I'm George Heinrich, member in good standing of the church of the whatever."

Sonny laughed. "The Confessing Church."

"Sure, if you say so." Otto had taken the other identity that Sonny carried from Tegel Castle. For the first time in five years, he could move safely around the city, as his foray with Dix had proved.

"I'll probably never get used to calling you George," Sonny admitted.

Otto stopped and faced him. "You damn well better, Paul. If you call me Otto while a cop's holding my ID . . . "

Sonny grimaced, nodding acquiescence.

The two stayed on Thiemann until they reached the canal, took a right on Weigand Ufer and a quick left on Teupitzer, and walked onto the bridge. Staring at the Kaiser Friedrich Railroad Station in the distance, they talked about the changes following Ku'damm in '31, forgetting about the burglary for a bit.

Then Sonny laughed and said, "Just before we met, I was trailing a stunning young woman with curves that wouldn't quit. She moved like a pendulum, her gait slow and undulating." His hands moved back and forth. "I was really getting into it when she turned into a café and disappeared." He turned to his friend. "God, why am I having those lewd thoughts now?"

Otto shrugged. "You need a woman."

Now, three days later, Sonny was doing surveillance alone—it was 10 PM, and he stomped his feet, turned up his collar, and shivered, more from nerves than cold. He jammed his hands into his pockets and cursed having to walk, endlessly it seemed, up and down every street near No. 15. Hell, he cursed everything for good measure. Like a moth his eyes were attracted to the glow behind the curtained windows. He wondered who lived there. Something stirred in a second-story window; then it was gone. He laughed at his skittishness.

About all that moved on Thiemann Strasse were a fluttering Nazi banner and a shuffling old man. Sonny was bored. He wished that he smoked so he could have something to do . . . He'd lean against a lamppost and take a drag, like he'd seen in the cinema. But he'd been sick the only time he'd ever tried to smoke. The smell of burning tobacco could bring the nausea back.

Half the lampposts were burnt out, including the one at No. 15, which was good if they would be going in at night. Three- and four-story buildings along this part of Thiemann Strasse stood like faded dreams in the dim light, telling him little worth knowing. Each was distinguished, beyond the level of decay, only by variance in width and height.

Paint peeled off No. 15 like dry skin, the denuded stucco exposing bricks and mortar to the harsh weather. Empty window boxes hung useless, and bars covered the windows. On the neighboring building, scaffolding clung like a skeleton, and its cross-hatching timbers sagged, waiting for gravity to finish the job. Pathos flowed through the streets—Thiemann, Werra, Weser, and Treptower comprising the immediate neighborhood. Neukölln was being punished for its Red past, of that Sonny was certain.

In a window below Möbelfabrik, something moved, then was gone, but this time Sonny knew it was real. When he looked again, an image of his father appeared in the window. When Sonny blinked, the image disappeared. His father had been dead more than ten years—why visit now? Laughing nervously, he blamed it on his fatigue and felt foolish. So he walked, out of fear he'd fall asleep on his feet.

Sonny and Otto had already seen the padlock and chain securing the dark brown door to No. 15 and the big boarded-up window to the right—the old KPD office was officially off limits. In the space between the window and the locked door was a big, poorly rendered, faded swastika, probably painted at the time the office was looted. He walked across the street for a closer look and noticed a tattered but legible sign nailed to the door: "Closed by Order of the Police. Entry is Forbidden." The sign was too well preserved to have survived five years, so it must have been recently attached.

A cold gust of wind made Sonny shiver, and he walked faster. Circling the building and the surrounding streets, he passed several taverns, one on Werra, another on Treptower, and others on Kaiser Friedrich Strasse, as well as other businesses. Maybe he'd visit them all, have a beer and talk to a few fellows, learn something. The surveillance was to be accomplished by all participating members of the operation, in four-hour shifts over several days and nights—or until Emil was convinced he had enough information.

Mischa had reluctantly agreed to stay out of the taverns, where his Semitic features might be problematic, but Sonny, Otto, and Willy would venture inside for a beer and some conversation. While they prowled, Joseph forged names onto passports, visas, and identity cards. His small, cramped flat in Scheunenviertel was their base of operations and where Sonny and Otto now lived. One slept on the little sofa, the other on the floor. The arrangement, while not completely satisfactory, sufficed.

Continuing on Thiemann, Sonny walked toward the canal. He passed the power station on his right—a squat industrial cube surrounded by a fence with security lights casting a pale unearthly light. The only human activity that any of the conspirators had observed there came during the shift change at 11 PM and every eight hours thereafter. Otherwise, it was quiet but for the low buzz, like a giant mosquito, emanating from deep within. Behind the power station lay a gas-storage facility serviced by a rail line running north to south along the canal.

The Neuköllner Schiffahrts Canal cut off No. 15 Thiemann Strasse on the north and east; busy Kaiser Friedrich Strasse blocked it on the south. That created a peninsula, with No. 15 in the center. Three bridges —at Treptower, Teupitzer, and Kaiser Friedrich—spanned the canal.

Across the canal shone the bright lights of the massive rail yard, like a city unto itself. Standing on the Teupitzer Bridge, Sonny heard engines churning, cars coupling and clanking in the distance. The passenger station was at the far end, beyond his line of sight. Behind him, buildings bordered the canal on both sides as it disappeared in a straight line to the northwest. He walked along the canal to Treptower, turned left, crossed Werra, turned left on Weser, and came to a small tavern without a sign. He would have missed it had he not known it was there.

It was 11:00 when Sonny walked in the door to the stale odor of beer and cigarette smoke. He counted nine men altogether, scattered at tables in pairs and seated at the bar. The bartender sat on a stool at the end of the bar, talking to someone. Conversation momentarily stopped at his entrance, then started again.

The bartender delivered the beer Sonny ordered, saying, "Haven't seen you before."

"True enough," Sonny agreed. "Someone told me Möbelfabrik was hiring."

The bartender laughed. "That guy was pulling your leg. The place has been closed since '33."

Sonny shook his head as if confused and waited for him to say more.

He did: "The owner was a good man; he put a lot of the men from the neighborhood to work." The bartender nodded toward two older men quietly talking at a table. When Sonny turned back, the bartender leaned over the bar and said, "It's a damn shame they put him out of business."

Sonny muttered his sympathy, then asked, "What about the tavern on Treptower?"

"What about it?"

Sonny shrugged. "Just curious. I don't know the neighborhood."

The bartender eyed Sonny. "It's a place where guys like them . . . don't go." He waved toward the former Möbelfabrik workers.

Sonny nodded, knowing he meant they were former comrades: "I get it."

The bartender leaned in, his tone confidential. "Ja. Cops and guys like Braun, the warden on the Möbelfabrik block of Thiemann, drink over there." Having said enough, he wiped the bar with his dirty towel and walked away.

Back on the street, Sonny admitted he'd learned something—a guy named Braun, a Nazi, appointed like all the other wardens in the city to report "suspicious" activity on their block. It wasn't much, but it was more than he'd known before . . . And at least he was warm. Skipping the other tavern, he turned off Weser into the alley behind No. 15. It turned to the right past their quarry and emptied onto Thiemann Strasse. This gave them access to the back door from both Thiemann and Weser.

As he entered the alley, its darkness almost consumed him. There was only one dim light at the corner where the alley turned, the buildings forming a black canyon. A glow from the canyon walls' windows, some ambient city light due to cloud cover, and that was it—now enough. But they would need torches if they went in at night. During the day the alley, just wide enough for a small vehicle to negotiate the turn, was in perpetual shadow.

Sonny walked to the corner of the alley where he could see both Weser and Thiemann. The rear door of No. 15 faced similar buildings with doors also opening onto the alley. Retracing his steps, he faced the back door of No. 15, flanked on both sides by windows staring blankly through steel grills imbedded in the wall. Unable to see into the building, he saw his ghostly image reflected in the dirty glass. The windows were big enough for a man to get through, but the bars were a problem. The rear door was also secured with a padlock and chain. He could just make out the tattered corners of the police sign: "Closed . . . bidden."

Several meters down the alley was a set of double doors identical and in the same relative position as those in the front, proclaiming it as No. 13. During the day, Sonny and Otto had seen tracks leading to the doors. They figured there was a staircase inside and a freight elevator servicing the floors above. Over the years Otto had seen lumber going in and furniture coming out.

Sonny turned toward Weser and suddenly froze. A figure, silhouetted in the light from the street, approached him. Adjusting his eyes to the light, he realized it was only an old man, back bowed, moving slowly his way. The man moved unsteadily, as if dragging something on the uneven ground, but his pace was constant. Reaching Sonny, he turned his wrinkled face. Sonny bid him good night, then heard mumbling but couldn't make out the words. The old man cleared the corner, and Sonny followed, saw him fumbling with a key at the door of a building across the alley.

Over the next three hours, Sonny repeated the walk, reversed it, and did it again. Three men, one at a time, entered an adjacent building, and one man left the double door at the rear of No. 13 at about 2 AM. It was obvious people lived upstairs. Sonny saw no cops, though the bartender had said they were around.

Several days after their first meeting they met again. Everyone but Mischa reported stopping at the same tavern. Sonny gave them the block warden, Braun. Otto had seen an old comrade, Leo, and joined him briefly at the table where he sat alone.

Unemployed for years, Leo said he spent most of his time scrounging for money for rent and food for his family. The SA didn't bother with him—maybe he wasn't on their list—but he kept his head down and his mouth shut. Though he'd never worked at Möbelfabrik, Leo knew several men who had. He threw out some names, but Otto didn't know them. The owner had been forced out of business because of his ties to the KPD. Leo didn't know what had become of him or whether he still owned the building.

Before the conversation ended, Leo leaned close, whispered that he'd heard about the raid. The rumors flew . . . he was glad to see that at least some of it was false.

Mischa reported next: Outside a building on Treptower, he had run into a comrade he hadn't seen since the rally in November '32. Nicknamed Red—more for his once-fiery hair than his politics—the man now used his given name, Arthur, to avoid trouble. He'd slipped through the cracks like Leo and was working with his brother-in-law, collecting garbage. They picked up in the area around No. 15 and delivered it to a barge on the canal near the gas terminal. Mischa learned that the cops regularly patrolled near the terminal and adjacent power station but not much else.

Arthur had also told Mischa that the cops spent a lot of time in the tavern just down the street, not the sort of place he'd want to frequent. When Mischa steered the conversation to Möbelfabrik, Arthur said he'd lost touch with the workers he'd known . . .

Finally, it was Willy's turn. They'd decided to take a chance on him—he'd brought them Dix and harbored Otto over the years—as they needed the extra body. And by now everyone in the little group was used to the tic in his left eye. Otto's recitation of Willy's ordeal with the SA had conferred on him a level of respect he had never known before. Whether he noticed it was questionable—no one spoke of what he had endured.

Willy covered his errant eye and said he had nothing new. He'd heard of Braun, but that was all. Like Sonny, he hadn't wanted any part of the tavern on Treptower, but he had a beer with some guys in the dingy little bar without a name.

Emil sighed in response. "We know next to nothing about Braun. Is he active? Has he reported any neighbors to the authorities? Are they afraid of him? The last thing we need is a nosy warden." His face screwed into a question mark. "We can watch the area around No. 15 for a year and still not account for the unexpected. Experience tells me to be cautious—it's what you don't know that gets you in trouble. Even the best plan can't provide for the unforeseen." He met his listeners' eyes in turn. "We may have to improvise."

Joseph chewed on the words, careful not to look at Mischa. From his seat at the periphery, he spoke for the first time. "I don't like the sound of that."

Emil leaned forward, his chair creaking in protest. "Neither do I. But things go wrong and you have to compensate. Like anything else, the more you do it, the easier it becomes. We don't have the time to pull a couple of easy jobs first."

They laughed nervously.

"But that's why you're here," Joseph reminded him.

Emil conceded. "We'll plan as best we can and hope it works."

All heads turned as Mischa's voice rose in protest. "Nobody gives a shit about that building, so what's the problem?"

"True," Emil agreed. "But there're cops around—and there's the block warden to worry about. Don't forget the neighbors . . . and how to get into the building and out without being seen. There's human frailty, carelessness, mistakes, especially with so many involved—too many unknowns." Slapping an open hand on his knee, he said, "Damn it! I want more information. Something about that building is gnawing at me. There's something I should know."

Suddenly the room was so quiet Sonny could hear water dripping in the kitchen sink. Apparently, Otto did too as his eyes turned to the sound. Mischa rubbed his hands together, then in a spasm of pent-up emotion, spilled: "I know what you're thinking." His head moved back and forth. His dark eyes widened. "I'll be the mad dog, the one who gets careless and screws it up. Hell! I'll be out of control. You don't have to say it."

No one spoke. Emil and Willy just watched. Someone had to say it: Mischa's erratic behavior was a detriment. They should have put it out there ages ago . . .

Sonny had first noticed the change in Mischa in November '32, days before the election, before the Republic took its last breath. Mischa turned up at Paul's flat after a rally had turned into a brawl. His clothes were in tatters, and there was a bright-red bruise on his cheek. His hand shook holding a cigarette, and he coughed phlegm into his handkerchief. He eyes would not meet Sonny's.

When Paul said Mischa had just turned up and wouldn't say what happened, Mischa launched into a diatribe about the KPD's last stand. He blamed them—Sonny and Paul—and all the others like them, for what was sure to follow. Sonny and Paul stood dumfounded at the vitriol of his misplaced anger. Then Mischa stormed out of the flat, and Sonny didn't see him for days.

While Otto had been forced underground, Mischa, despite being a Communist and a Jew, had not. Still, he felt he was a marked man, and perhaps he was. After the beating he'd become increasingly paranoid—

afraid to venture out in the daytime, to go anywhere outside the Mitte. That he was no different from thousands of others was scant consolation. But when Sonny offered Mischa a new identity—a new name and a clean start—he refused. It wouldn't work, he argued, not with his Semitic features. Mischa clung to his underground persona even as Otto shed his.

One minute Mischa might be laughing and clowning, and the next—without warning—he'd launch into a rant. Spittle flew from his lips as he raged, arms waving—he'd become unmoored. His erratic behavior was wearing thin.

Several days into the new smuggling plan, Mischa and Sonny had walked through Alexanderplatz toward the warehouse to recruit runners. A thin dusting of snow rose like fine flour with each footfall on the early evening streets. Turning a corner, they came upon a group of men in a circle. Inside the ring, one man held another dressed in black, unable to escape. A cop, massaging his nightstick, leaned against a lamppost only a few meters away.

Serious mischief was in the air. Grunts of laughter punctuated mindless epithets: "Fucking Jew . . . stealing Aryan babies for their blood . . ."

The scene unfolded in the time it took Sonny and Mischa to stop, move their eyes from the old man to the cop and back to the crackling hatred. The captor leaned over the petrified Jew—his eyes white with panic. The others, like feral dogs, fed on the old man's escalating fear. "Cut it off," they yelled. Then there was a flash—scissors—and the captor cut the old man's beard..

Recognition struck Mischa an instant before Sonny, and he gasped, "Reb Friedman." He ran forward, but before he could reach the circle, the cop's nightstick met Mischa's neck with a terrible *thwap*. Mischa crumpled to the pavement. With a malicious grin and without taking his eyes from Mischa, the cop told the men they'd had enough fun for tonight. Several protested, but they heeded his order. As they left, one kicked the prostrate Mischa in the ribs.

It was over in less than a minute. The old man, a friend of Mischa's father, sat with legs splayed on the pavement, uncomprehending but apparently unhurt. Sonny just stared. Then he heard Mischa's moan and helped him to his feet so that both could escort the rabbi to his home nearby. When they arrived there, the rabbi's wife covered her mouth to stifle a wail, and Reb Friedman's fear turned to tears of humiliation.

Sonny and Mischa returned to Joseph's flat feeling helpless and angry but most of all deeply humiliated. Nothing they could do would have prevented the attack. Mischa found scant solace in his futile attempt at rescue. But Sonny had hesitated. What had kept him from coming to the old man's rescue? Even accepting his powerlessness, why did he feel so empty? Why did he loathe his inaction? His anger he understood.

Joseph and Otto expressed concern for the rabbi, but given Mischa's intervention, the outcome might have been worse. He might be sitting in a Nazi jail right now. Then, what would become of the operation? Mischa's valor could put everyone at risk. They'd agreed Sonny should talk to Sophie . . .

Surprised to see him, Sophie had hugged Sonny, then laughed in her infectious way. "You look years older in a beard," she said, scrutinizing his face. "I never see you, now that you're busy saving the world." Her tone was resigned, ironic.

"Liberating the Jews is a full-time job," Sonny agreed. He knew it was impossible to keep her from knowing.

With her dark hair pulled back, her bright, intelligent eyes, she was the girl he remembered. She'd scarcely changed, in some ways, since he and Mischa had spotted her in the warehouse so many years before. And he said as much, for a moment taking them back to the days when three young friends frolicked in the warehouse and dreamed of a bright future.

Sophie waved away his comment and said sadly, "Too much has happened." She smiled and looked into a corner. "And you, Sigmund Landauer—all these years leading a double life! Who would have thought?"

Color rose in Sonny's cheeks, and he cringed. "Things took on a life of their own."

She jerked her head back to face him. "That's too glib! Deceive your friends and lay it off as beyond your control? I don't suppose Polly took it so breezily?"

That stung, and his flush deepened. His ears were hot. "No. I paid for my transgression. We're done, but I didn't come to talk about my exciting life."

Hands on hips, Sophie stared at him. She did look fifteen—though fuller in the hips and bust—and her crooked smile looked the same. She shook her head. "I'm not angry with you, though Mischa was, at least a little."

"That's history. It's over and done." Sonny wanted to leave his duplicitous past behind. Too much was at stake to waste time reliving what could not be undone.

Sophie turned and walked away, her arms hanging limply, and said, "I know why you've come." She rounded on him with her hands balled into fists, the young Sophie gone. "Because of Mischa, how he's changed. He's obsessed with this project—I'm at my wit's end!"

Stifling a laugh, she continued. "Half the time he probably wants to be caught, sent to Dachau to suffer like his hero Thälmann. And his Jewish ancestors, his father," she rolled her eyes. "That's where he gets it. Papa Hager won't leave, won't take his family out of this hellhole. So, of course, Mischa won't go. That my family's gone means nothing. I tell Mischa daily I want out, but it's always 'not now, the work's too important.' I'm beyond frustrated."

"What would make him go?"

Raising her arms Sophie almost shrieked. "If only I knew!

Sonny scratched his beard, looking around the flat until his eyes lit on the old clock Mischa had scavenged when they were kids. Its golden hands sparkled. Sonny heard its incessant ticking in the sudden quiet.

Sophie's eyes followed his, and she managed a smile. "That's probably Mischa's tether to the real world. I shudder to think what that clock represents to him."

Nodding, Sonny thought how their lives had divided into little parcels, some neat, others untidy: lost youth, the ever-tightening grip of the regime, Uncle Simon, the ultimate futility of their lives, the single-mindedness of the operation, and all the rest.

Sophie broke through his reverie, pointing to a book on the table. "Since I lost my job, all I do is read, my great escape . . . Mischa may be going mad, and I'm not far behind."

Since she had opened Pandora's box, Sonny took advantage. He told her about Mischa's frequent outbursts—that he argued over trifles, forcing them to walk on eggshells—and of his foolishness in trying to rescue Reb Friedman.

Tears welled at his mention of the rabbi. "It took me forever to extract the story," she said. "And when it finally came, Mischa was inconsolable. He veered from fury to tears."

Sonny carried two disquieting images of Mischa: one nearly six years ago, bloodied and dazed in Paul's flat, coiled tight like a spring; and the other, trying to save the Reb from disgrace. Thrusting a fist into the air in frustration, Sonny told Sophie, "We have work to do, but we're scared of Mischa's unpredictable outbursts. He's becoming a liability."

Sophie looked away.

"We're afraid he'll explode, confront another Nazi, bring the Gestapo down on our heads. Bravery is noble, but not this kind, not while he's part of our operation," Sonny finished, running out of breath.

Sophie walked to the window, her back to Sonny. "I know he means well. You know that, but . . ." She chewed her fingernail, struggling for words. Then she faced him. "I keep telling myself it's just Mischa, that he'll be all right. Everything will be fine, so just let him be. But he's unwinding . . . the gears are loosening, ready to burst." She raised her hands with fingers splayed. "Sonny, I'm afraid."

A lone tear moved down her cheek. She turned back to the window, and in a voice so quiet that Sonny strained to hear, she said, "I've thought of leaving him. Times are hard enough without having to deal with . . ." She bit off her words. "Our little world's gone quite mad. So why wouldn't *he*?" She looked over her shoulder at Sonny. "But not you—you're too rational. Sonny, I'm not a hero. I haven't the nerve."

A child's voice, then the sound of running feet, came from the hallway. More footsteps, then high-pitched laughter.

"We have to get you and Mischa out of Germany!" Sonny said abruptly.

Sophie's eyes were on the unseen children; her mouth formed a wretched angle. She snorted, then wiped her nose. Her words came bitterly: "What the hell do you think I've been trying to do for the past year? You think I don't tell him that every day, that I haven't been pleading? What do you think I'm doing while he's playing martyr?"

She pointed toward the children. "It's become a second hell, the one I'm blessed to live in. Take off the mezuzah. Instead our doorpost should read, 'Abandon all hope, ye who enter here.'"

She wept silently, as Sonny held her in his arms. When they'd met many years ago, her easy manner and good humor, the inquisitive mind that as a girl she'd been raised to hide, had made her one of them. At a certain age, Sonny had thought romantically of Sophie. But it had made him queasy, as if he were kissing a sister. Mischa was not so reluctant; neither was she. Their union seemed natural—two smart, sharp-tongued outsiders, never apart, finally married.

Her profound sadness enveloped Sonny. The children's laughter lent the moment even greater poignancy . . . Sophie gave a stifled yelp.

He held her at arms' length and said softly, "We'll figure this out. I promise." Then he kissed her on the forehead, turned, and left the flat, before she could say more. He weaved his way through the children, who used him as a shield in their game. Outside he shivered, looked up into the window at her and nodded . . .

Five sets of eyes fixed on Mischa as he jabbed a finger into his chest like a woodpecker attacking a dead tree. "Me? The nervous wreck should improvise? All we've done so far is take a nice walk around Neukölln, catching up on old times with the comrades."

Willy laughed nervously at the sarcasm, turning it to a strangled cough when no one joined him. His eye twitched. Emil's lips moved in and out as he waited for Mischa's diatribe to end.

"You've got to be joking," Mischa continued. "If we're to make this up as we go along, we can do it without you." He pointed to Emil. "Knock down the door, go in, open the safe, and run away with the loot. I need a plan, damn it. We all need one, or we're going to fuck this up."

Suddenly Mischa was calm, as if his saying what they'd all been thinking had lifted a terrible burden. He'd penetrated the gates of his personal Bastille and was actually making sense. Several thoughtful nods buoyed his confidence.

He continued, "We're simple folk who smuggle people out of this shit hole. None of us but Sonny knew you until now." He paused, about to digress, but waved it off. "Me? *I'm* the loose thread. Pull me, and I'll unravel." Suddenly spent, Mischa rolled his head forward, his heel tapping compulsively on the floor.

They laughed, and Willy, sensing it was all right, joined them in diffusing some of the pent-up anxiety. But no one was prepared to argue Mischa's larger point: they needed a specific plan to follow because improvising was bullshit.

That Mischa had said what the rest of them failed to was jarring. Sonny couldn't be sure, but perhaps his visit to Sophie had been fruitful. Perhaps she'd confronted Mischa and told him where matters stood. Whatever had happened, it was out of the box and on the table. They had to deal with Mischa—like they'd had to deal with the guardhouse at the border and the lock at No.15—before they could move on. They looked at Sonny; he was Mischa's best friend and the bridge to Emil.

Sonny licked his lips and began, "It's true, Mischa. You've been erratic, and that's dangerous to the operation. What we do requires caution and discretion, but you've been closed to change." He paused, thinking how to phrase what he needed to say. "Your commitment has never been the issue."

Mischa's hands cut him off. "There you go, sidestepping the truth with that commitment shit. Not saying what you should have said before. You all talked and schemed behind my back, didn't want me here when you met with Dix." He looked down at his hands to avoid their eyes but spoke in a measured voice. "You should have said something. You owed me that."

Back and forth they went, flushing it out, and at the end Mischa asked whether he'd been all that unreasonable.

"Yes," Joseph answered.

Mischa's face colored. He sat quietly, nodded. He waved his index finger in a little circle and met Sonny's gaze, then that of the others. With a deep breath, he promised, "Once the job's done—so long as my father agrees—I'll go." He crossed his arms over his chest. Then he stood and walked to the window. With his head down, he looked small and vulnerable.

The rest sat quietly waiting for Emil to take up where he'd left off. "It's never simple. Don't approach it that way, or you'll get caught. Never assume a goddamn thing!" Then his voice became hard and cold. "We'll have a plan. But if we have to, we'll operate by the seat of our pants." He met their eyes. "Understood?"

Everyone nodded.

"Good," Emil said without satisfaction. "I'm uneasy because we aren't ready."

They groaned.

"Dix is getting impatient. He wants a date," said Willy.

"I don't give a damn. I won't risk the operation to satisfy him," Emil snapped, making Willy flinch. He continued calmly, "Something about the building, about Möbelfabrik, bothers me. I can't put my finger on it, but until I work it out, we don't proceed."

Before they quit for the night, Emil said, "Nobody's going to be a hero—all heroes ever get are monuments. We'll sleep in our own beds when the job's done. Fear is okay—it keeps you sharp. Panic gets you in trouble. The guilty run, so always walk." With a shrug, he joked, "Of course, if you're being chased . . ."

Their laughter settled the uneasy mood. They agreed to meet again in two days, same time. No one had questions. The meeting was done.

Mischa left first, then Willy, and five minutes later, Emil. Sonny walked with him, hoping for some fresh air. As they passed through the sleeping tenements of the Jewish quarter, Emil said, "I've got to figure out what's bothering me. Come tomorrow morning, first thing." And he disappeared around the corner.

16

Open-ey'd Conspiracy His time doth take.
—William Shakespeare

Sonny and Polly were finished as lovers. Despite that, Sonny wanted to see her, though not to talk to her, and he didn't know exactly why. So, on his way to Emil's flat in Wedding, Sonny walked through Alexanderplatz to the department store where Polly worked. Winter was waning, and a cloudless blue sky was bringing in a cold, crisp morning. Patches of ice dotted the pavement, so Sonny minded where he stepped. Soon the sun would peek over the tops of the buildings, turning the ice to puddles.

If he could ignore the swastikas flying from every corner, the Nazi banners hanging from the buildings, and the degrading graffiti polluting the walls, Sonny thought, he might convince himself that Berlin was little changed. But he couldn't ignore so much, and his thoughts flipped to the early days of the Third Reich, when he and Polly could still stroll together, holding hands . . .

They'd walked Linien Strasse, passing Herschel's Butcher Shop, when their eyes turned to a dark monochromatic smudge on the window. It had taken several seconds for Sonny to realize that the word *kosher*—in large Hebrew lettering—had been rubbed away. Millennia of religious ritual—outlawed by the malicious stroke of a pen! All that remained of the ancient Jewish dietary laws was a dirty window. They had stood dumbfounded until Polly said how hateful it was . . .

Shortly after the government ban of kosher butchering, Sonny had heard Mischa's father say, "It is in our heritage to expect such treachery—this is Europe and we are Jews." When asked what he would do, Herr Hager answered, "God doesn't make you do what puts you in danger.

Though one has to wonder that being Jewish at all seems to belie His good intentions."

Now Sonny stared at that same window, but all he saw was his sad reflection. He forced his eyes away and kept on walking. In minutes, the familiar odor of boiled cabbage mixed with that of fish, onions, and grease from the corner restaurant assaulted him. The restaurant's windows were so encrusted with the detritus of dirty hands, grease, and steam that the view inside had become distorted, surreal.

Two grizzled Polish laborers exited, blocking Sonny's path. They wore long beards and dirty pants and argued in Yiddish. Ahead, a group of young men in black scurried to yeshiva like a swarm of blackbirds. The old lady who sold shoelaces on the same spot every day had just arrived. She was setting up as if nothing had changed. Sonny found solace among these people against whom the worst vitriol was directed. Strange that among them he felt most secure.

Surrounded by stories begging to be written, Sonny thought about why he hadn't written them—laziness, distraction, lack of commitment. He had swept such thoughts aside—as he usually did with life's unpleasantness—and left his world to enter the other Berlin, the one that treated him indifferently, the one he shared with millions of others. Now that Berlin—arrogant, assured, sometimes dangerous in its experimentation—was long gone. Welcoming places like the Pink Slipper and Katakombe had long since been shuttered, replaced by a culture devoid of creativity, one that shunned him like a medieval outcast.

Startled by an automobile horn, Sonny jumped back onto the curb, barely avoiding an onrushing sedan. He silently cursed the driver. Like all big cities, he supposed, Berlin thrived on constant motion, but its bold spontaneity was a thing of the past, of the old Berlin, of the one he had so loved.

Sonny flashed to the time before he'd known Otto or Polly, before the brawling, before Hitler and his henchmen had wrecked Berlin. To a time of outrageous appetites, of people working and playing hard until the clock ran out. To some that had meant progress, but others feared the new and would not yield. Berlin was all of that. The memory gave Sonny a headache.

From the open expanse of Alexanderplatz, Sonny could see the Red Town Hall, the center of a city government now led by a Nazi mayor. And Israel's Department Store, barely surviving the anti-Jewish boycotts. The Nazis had slowly expropriated Wertheim's Department Store, where Polly still worked.

Sonny closed his eyes, then opened them suddenly, nearly fooled by the street's veneer of normalcy. Berlin looked like a real city on the surface, populated by real people going to work, eating in cafés, shopping in stores, jostling on the pavement. But madness had descended, and the old Berlin—Herschel's butcher shop, Uncle Simon, his parents, Polly, his Jewish brothers and sisters at work—existed only through the prism of memory. Its cultural stew—the clubs, cabarets, theaters, and music halls—was long gone, its creative force strangled. Artists, composers, actors, playwrights, writers, educators, businessmen and women, scientists all had disappeared. Like the woman he'd once loved.

Shielding himself from view, Sonny leaned against a doorframe across the street from the door Polly would soon enter for work. Men and women converged at the door, some lingering, others disappearing inside. Then came a woman, wearing a green coat with matching hat, a purse swinging at her side. Sonny shuddered but did not move as he watched his former lover smile at a coworker, say something. He hadn't thought this out, so when the twin demons—regret and remorse—hit him at once, he felt sabotaged. His own lies had undermined Polly's trust and doomed their romance. There was no more to it than that.

Polly disappeared into the department store oblivious to the voyeur across the street.

They were done, and Sonny didn't care whether she and Karl were now lovers. The book on the seven-year Sonny-and-Polly affair was closed. It was an era ended. The task of closure accomplished, he set out for Wedding . . .

One hand wrapped around a coffee mug, Emil tapped a forefinger on the table with the other. "I knew something was missing," he said with a grin. "But I couldn't put my finger on it."

Sonny shrugged and waited.

"Remember the table and chairs you asked about the day we met?"

Sonny's brow wrinkled as he tried to recall . . . the dominating image was Emil slapping the SA. "I give up. Tell me."

Emil explained, "I bought the table and chairs from a guy who worked in a factory in Neukölln. I made a deal with his brother, who lives in the building." He stopped tapping long enough to point at the table top with a thick forefinger. "It was right here the entire time."

"Right," Sonny murmured, unsure of where this was headed.

Shaking his head and frowning, Emil continued. "I forgot the neighbor's name, but I got it off the mailbox late last night. This morning I contrived a meeting with Adolf Kleinert, the guy's brother. Now I can follow up. Turns out Gustav, that's the guy in Neukölln who made this, lives with his family in one of the apartments carved out of the old Möbelfabrik. He was probably in that dingy little tavern where all of us stopped. I'm going to talk to Gustav today."

"Ah, now I see," Sonny responded. "Good!"

"But it came too easy. I'm leery."

Emil was superstitious that way, but Sonny waved it off. "What the hell? Sometimes you're lucky.

"Ja, maybe . . ."

Later that day, well past the dinner hour, Emil entered the uninviting little place with no name on Weser Strasse. Squinting through the haze of tobacco smoke, he saw half a dozen men—scarred people—in various stages of inebriation. No one bothered to look up, not even the bartender. At the end of the bar, head hanging between sagging shoulders like a sick dog over its bowl, was the man Emil recognized as Gustav Kleinert.

Emil walked to the bar to get the bartender's attention, and when his beer came, he dropped several coins next to the mug. After a long draw, he turned and looked at the bloodshot eyes underlined by dark semicircles, the nose reddened from drink, the slack jaw below the protruding lower lip, the face of the man before him. To Gustav's credit, or that of his wife, his clothes looked clean.

"I know you," Emil said just loud enough.

When Gustav did not stir, Emil continued: "You're the fellow at Möbelfabrik who sold me the table and chairs? Remember? I'm Emil."

Then as if Emil were pulling a string, Gustav's head turned slowly. His eyes brushed over Emil. Staring blankly, he grunted, "What?"

"Are you Gustav?"

The bartender—maybe he was the owner—returned to his stool at the other end of the bar. Gustav and Emil were alone. Slowly, Emil explained their connection, and after some clumsy give-and-take, Gustav waved a hand and said, "Oh, ja. I remember."

But Emil wasn't convinced. Gustav continued to work his jaw, syllables eventually giving way to words. Incoherent at first, he became more lucid as he proceeded. With a gentle but firm touch, like landing a carp from the Lietzen See, Emil reeled in Gustav enough for their worlds to intersect.

Emil learned that Möbelfabrik's owner, an old leftist, had taken to the streets in 1919 and was proud to have the KPD as a tenant. Almost all his workers were party members, and he treated them well, giving them presents on New Year's Day and food packages when they were sick. Gustav mumbled about the good old days until his eyes misted with melancholy. He had been a skilled carpenter, like his father before him, proud of the solid furniture he made. Now there was no work but for an hour here or there as a handyman, sometimes for cash but mostly for barter. "Like them," Gustav halfheartedly tilted his head toward the room.

Emil bought him another draft. Gustav lived with his family in the Möbelfabrik building. His lips moved as he counted the number of flats on his fingers—a total of six, all occupied by former employees and their families. The landlord kept the rent low, since few had steady work.

When Emil said he was surprised that Möbelfabrik's owner still owned the building, Gustav shrugged. "The joke was that no Nazi wanted the dump. But it's home." He glanced at Emil without meeting his eyes. "Uh, uh . . ."

"Emil."

"Right," he muttered. "Got a cigarette?"

Emil walked down the bar, roused the bartender, and bought one.

With an unsteady hand, Gustav put the cigarette between his lips. Emil held the match until it was lit, then asked casually, "What became of the KPD office?"

Gustav took a drag, coughed, spit out a piece of tobacco. "What?"

Emil repeated the question.

"Police locked it up tight." He took another drag, raised the beer to his lips, swallowed, and wiped his mouth with the handkerchief he took from his coat's breast pocket. "They closed that part of the building when they arrested the KPD. It's been that way ever since. Cops told everyone to stay away or else. What the hell do I care?" Gustav made a sound like the air being let out of a balloon. "Pfft."

"Does anyone ever go in?"

"Why do you want to know that? Who the hell cares? Nothing's there that anybody wants." Gustav blinked, then looked at Emil from the corner of his eye.

Emil caught the gesture. "What?"

Slowly, Gustav's eyes met Emil's and held. "They come back now." He rubbed his face with one hand, the other holding the smoke. He squinted, "Don't ask me why."

Emil felt tingling in his temple. "Who comes back?"

"Nobody went in there for years. Hell! They looted the place—took boxes out and burned them in the alley. It was empty for years, but now they're back."

"Who's back?" Emil persisted.

"Cops, who else?"

Emil lingered, stuck on what Gustav had said. Now only half listening, he nodded as Gustav complained that no one cared about him or his old comrades, on and on. But what were cops doing in No. 15? What mischief . . . ?

Finally, Emil had enough. He stuffed several crumpled Reichmarks into Gustav's hand. "Thanks, old friend. Here's for better luck ahead." He patted Gustav on the shoulder and turned to walk away.

Gustav's voice was faint, but his words stopped Emil in his tracks. "Cops don't bother us none. They come at night, real quiet-like, but I pay no attention. It's none of my business. I don't want trouble." Gustav's shoulders rose as he sighed. "They was just back the other night."

"Damn!" Emil thought. He needed time to think . . .

At Joseph's flat the next evening, Emil explained what had been bothering him and what he'd learned from Gustav. An uneasy silence followed.

Then, "What the hell are the cops doing there?" Mischa asked.

Otto shook his head and moaned, "Life ain't fair."

"That's putting it mildly," Sonny noted.

"Better we find out now than when you're coming out with satchels full of loot and the cops are going in," said Joseph. "Maybe we should scrap the plan."

"I know it stinks," Emil agreed. "Cops don't do business in the dead of night. So I asked myself why they would go into a building they shut down years ago in the middle of the night? The only answer is that they're up to no good."

Emil pictured the boarded-up, long-forgotten KPD office, in a depressed part of Berlin, as a great place to warehouse ill-gotten goods. It's what he would have done were he a crooked cop: "They're running a scam and using the building for a warehouse. It has to be. I can't think of anything else. Police go wherever, whenever, it suits them. They don't slink around at night unless they're under cover—or dirty."

He shook his head, scanning the group. "I'm convinced they're doing something that would piss off their bosses if they knew. And Braun's in on it. I'm just as convinced they don't know about the safe. The loot's still there. Otherwise, they'd have cleaned it out and not come back."

His frown deepening, Joseph said, "I'm not willing to put our smuggling operation in jeopardy for a fool's errand. I say forget about the safe—and Dix."

Then everyone but Willy gave an opinion at once.

After about thirty seconds of voice upon voice, Emil raised his hands. "Stop!"

They did.

"I understand your concern, but let's not call it off, not yet," Emil said. "If we can find a safe way in and out, the job can be done. But I need more information."

They moaned at the thought of more surveillance, then quieted as sirens wailed somewhere in the Mitte. They looked toward the window, then at each other.

Emil sighed, absently pulling at a loose thread on his shirt while they waited. "My drunken carpenter may know more than he said. I plan another visit, this time into the factory for a better look. I just need a pretext to gain his confidence."

"Offer him work," Otto suggested.

"Good," Emil said. "I'll hire him to fix the door on the kitchen cabinet that Lisle's been after me about."

The question of whether Gustav could be trusted hung in the air.

An hour after first light, Emil walked past the single door of No. 15 to the dark brown double door with *No. 13* painted neatly to the right and above the mailbox. All but one of the curtained windows on the second and third floors were dark. Nothing stirred. Emil turned the handle, and the door opened.

Emil fumbled in the dark until his eyes adjusted to the dim light coming down the staircase from the windows on the floor above. The entry was smaller than he'd expected. He went up. On the next floor, another corridor ran the length of the building. Emil ducked under the lightless bulb and walked toward the window on the Thiemann side of the building. It was quiet. The children were in school, and the adults had left for work if they had any.

Then Emil heard voices—arguing—a woman and then a man. He pressed his ear to the door and knocked at the first lull.

"Whadaya want?" A man's voice—not Gustav's. Gruff.

"I'm looking for Gustav. Which flat is his? I got work for him." Emil said to the door.

"Who?" Sounding friendlier.

"Gustav."

"Next floor up, on the other side at the rear. But he's probably sleeping it off." Bitter laughter flowed from under the door.

"Thanks." Emil headed for the stairs. He heard the woman shout, "Shut up! Don't talk . . ."

Emil knocked several times, then heard a soft female voice: "Who is it?"

"My name is Emil. I'm here to see Gustav. I have work for him."

There was a long silence, and Emil thought she hadn't heard. "Are you there?"

"Yes." There was skepticism. Emil tried to imagine the woman on the other side of the door, the one who had ironed Gustav's handkerchief and made sure his clothes were clean.

"Are you serious? I mean about the work."

"I am," he answered.

"Please wait."

Emil leaned against the doorframe. There were holes in the wall, and the paint was peeling. Debris and cheap children's toys littered the floor, adding to the pathos he felt seeping from under every door. He waited a few minutes, heard footsteps, then the gravelly voice of a man roused from sleep: "You got work for me?" Gustav was incredulous.

"Ja," Emil answered truthfully, though it wasn't what Gustav might expect. "It's Emil. We talked last night at the tavern. I'm the guy who bought the table and chairs—years ago."

If Emil kept talking maybe Gustav would remember . . . But there was nothing but silence. Finally, a chain slid off its latch, a bolt moved, and the door opened a few centimeters. The line of vertical light revealed a man in shadow. Hovering in mid-air was the glowing end of a cigarette. Smoke obscured the mouth that held it.

"You may as well come in." Gustav's tone was flat, that of a man overwhelmed by life, resigned to another day like every other. He stepped aside to let Emil in.

The room was neat and clean, the furniture well cared for, in stark contrast to the man standing before Emil. Gustav hadn't shaved; there were dark smudges under his murky eyes. From the next room, Emil heard the clang of a pot, the clatter of dishes.

"Would you like a cup of coffee?" she said

"Yes, thank you."

A small, sturdy woman, her gray hair tight in a bun, came into the room and placed two steaming mugs on the table. Smiling, she assessed Emil, then kissed Gustav on the cheek and said, "I'm going to work."

Gustav nodded almost imperceptibly, and his eyes followed her as she walked out the door. He blinked, seemingly unmoored by his wife's departure and the realization that he faced this man alone. They stood awkwardly, like strangers on a street corner waiting for the light to change.

Emil took the lead. "We'd be more comfortable at the table, where we can drink our coffee and talk."

Gustav shuffled to the table, sat heavily, his eyes still on the door.

"Your wife must be a great comfort to you," Emil said.

Gustav didn't respond.

"Your flat's very comfortable. I see you made the furniture, just like our table and chairs." Emil had to tether Gustav to reality or he'd be of no use.

Gustav's bloodshot eyes peered suspiciously over the rim of his coffee mug, his Adam's apple bobbing as he swallowed. Finally breaking eye contact, he spoke in a low voice. "Why did you really come?"

"I have work for you." Emil seemed impressed by Gustav's sudden insight.

Shaking his head slowly, Gustav said, "I don't understand. We meet in the tavern, never seen you there before. Now we're drinking coffee in my flat, and you're offering me a job. It doesn't make sense."

"True enough, and it's unlikely I'll ever be there again," Emil admitted. "But some years ago you did me a good turn, and I want to return it."

Gustav smiled dully. "Okay. It's just that half the time I don't understand how any of the pieces fit together."

Laughter rose from Emil's throat in a low rumble. "You can say that again." His smile fading, he dropped the pretense and said, "I've decided to take a chance on you."

Flustered Gustav stuttered, "Wha-what chance? Wha-what's that supposed to mean?"

"I set up the meeting at the tavern because I need your help."

Gustav scowled.

"Just listen to me. I'm interested in the building, how it's configured," Emil kept it vague.

Gustav's eyes glazed over in confusion; he went for more coffee. He carefully set the pot on a trivet after filling both mugs, then threw out his hands like a man knocking over a house of cards. "You haven't told me anything."

For several seconds Emil did not respond. Then, "Do you remember our little talk at the tavern?"

Red blotches rose in Gustav's cheeks. He looked away, shaking his head.

"Drink does that," Emil said. "But I'm not going to lecture you."

"That's my wife's job," he responded without irony.

Emil took a breath. It was time to wade in. "What I have to tell you is very important, but first you have to promise not to tell anyone—not your wife, not your brother, no one."

Gustav's head jerked, his eyes found Emil's, and his lips tightened. He cleared his throat and stuttered again. "W-w-why w-w-would you do th-that?"

Emil told him. "Because I need your help, and I'll pay you well. It's as simple as that. There is some risk." He let his words settle. "If you're not interested, say so, and I'll leave. As if we never met." Emil's face softened. "On the other hand, if you're interested in some cash, I'll explain . . . but it has to be our little secret." He raised his finger to his lips.

Gustav muttered under his breath, clearly frightened by the conditions. He rose and paced the room—straightening a picture here, dusting off a lampshade there, emptying an ashtray. With a shaky hand, he lit a cigarette, looked down at the floor and back at Emil. With nothing to grab onto but trust in this stranger, he finally asked, "Is it illegal?"

Emil grinned like an old buddy out for some fun. "Of course, it is. Would I swear you to secrecy if I wanted another table and some chairs?"

Gustav shook his head and whispered, "No, no." He sat down, his lips moving silently, and reached for another cigarette. After it was lit, he nodded. "All right. I'll keep your secret."

"Good!" Emil's face was stern. There would be no more joking around. "I don't want any mixed signals—you keep your mouth shut, and there'll be a good payday. If you don't, there will be consequences." His glower enforced what he said.

Gustav flinched. "You have my solemn promise. Now what do you want?"

"I need information about the police interest in the old KPD office."

Gustav's eyes widened. He might not remember their talk, but he did remember the cops. Brow furrowed, he closed his eyes for a moment, then brightened. "You stuck some money in my hand."

Emil nodded.

That seemed to be all Gustav needed—the information Emil had been waiting for gushed forth. "Ja. I've seen them in the middle of the night, in groups of two and three, from the window over the alley. Sometimes with boxes, other times with nothing. Very strange." He pointed to the window.

"That's only part of it," Emil conceded. He leaned forward, staring into Gustav's eyes. "I need the layout of the KPD office. Me and some friends are going to break into the building to retrieve something valuable. We need your help, and there'll be something in it for you. The police are more than a nuisance—a real problem. I need two things," Emil held up his fingers, "their comings and goings, and the layout."

The more they talked, the more animated Gustav became. His eyes cleared, and his jaw tightened as a new man emerged. He was unsure of the date, but men in police uniform had turned up at the rear door of No. 15 several months before. They usually came with crates—he held up his hands to show the size—some were even bigger, requiring two men to carry them. Once he'd seen them leave with crates, and once they came in an automobile, taking some time to unload. No, he didn't know what was in the boxes. Yes, he was sure they hadn't seen him. He'd made sure it was dark in the flat. Whether anyone else in the neighborhood knew, he couldn't say, but it was hard to keep a secret. Even if they did know, people were afraid of the cops.

Emil smiled.

Gustav continued. "Long ago, I did some finish carpentry at No. 15, built tables for the hall and a desk for the top man. I know the layout pretty well. What, exactly, do you want to know?"

"I need a way into the building other than through the doors and windows."

Gustav puffed his cheeks, then exhaled a rush of air. He mumbled, "Must be something pretty important in there."

"Indeed, there is. But forget about that for now. Just concentrate on a way in."

For the first time Gustav laughed. "Don't ask much, do you?"

"It wouldn't be good for the operation if the cops showed up with me and my friends inside." They both laughed.

Gustav lit another cigarette and described the office set-up. "The front door to No. 15 opens into a meeting hall running the length of the building, minus the stairs at either end. At least part of the hall is under us. The rear door's below and to the right, where I saw the cops coming and going. There are two offices on this side—one large, the other small. The big one faces Thiemann, and the smaller one's on the alley side."

"What about the cellar?"

"In the little office, there's a small storage closet—on the wall shared with the other office. Inside is a stairway to the cellar."

"That's a fine summary." Emil was satisfied.

Gustav beamed.

"Now, how do we get inside without attracting attention?"

Gustav became so immersed in his task that his suspicion apparently vanished. After considering Emil's question, he said, "Maybe you can get through the old factory floor and into . . . No . . . the other tenants would know." His eyes widened in excitement. "Down in the corner by the alley, there's a freight elevator." He pointed to the back of the flat. "It was used to bring lumber upstairs and finished furniture down. You passed it when you came in the door. It was covered up. The mechanism was wrecked, but I think the car and shaft are intact."

Emil liked it. He rubbed his jaw, trying to figure how they'd get into the elevator shaft unseen. "Draw a rough sketch of where the shaft is." He watched patiently while Gustav leaned over the table, his tongue sticking out of the corner of his mouth like a schoolboy's.

"Can we get into the shaft from the roof?" Emil asked.

Gustav pointed to the wall facing the alley. "On the fire escape outside the window."

Emil smiled, then carefully folded the floor plan and put it in his pocket. He put a hand on Gustav's shoulder. "I'll return tomorrow morning after your wife leaves for work."

"Come at 9:00. Both my wife and daughter will be gone. I have two sons, one who is in the army. The other one lives with my wife's family in Hamburg."

Emil reached into his pocket and handed Gustav a couple of Reichmarks. "You've done well. Stay calm and keep quiet."

Before Emil stepped onto the pavement of Thiemann Strasse, he had the genesis of a plan, and that night at Joseph's flat, he told the others how it would go. The next day Otto and Sonny were to go with him to the roof of No. 13, then into the elevator shaft. They'd figure out how to get into No. 15.

In the meantime, Frau Kleinert was cleaning up the dinner dishes. After she'd put them away, she was surprised to see Gustav still in the living room, still in his chair. She asked how it had gone with the big man.

Gustav nodded and said, "All right."

Pleased that Gustav was home—and not in that dingy tavern—she questioned him no further.

17

All for one, one for all, that is our motto.
—Alexander Dumas

Gustav seemed nervous, eyeing Sonny and Otto as Emil introduced them: "They're okay or they wouldn't be with me."

"You look familiar. Were you a party member?" Otto asked.

Gustav shrugged. "That's ancient history."

"Forget it," Emil snapped, eager to get started. "Tell me about Braun."

Gustav laughed. "Braun is lazier than Göring. He doesn't get out of bed until after noon."

"All right," Emil said, not particularly satisfied. "We're playing on the roof with tools, so stay low and be careful. We don't want to be seen."

Gustav explained that the shaft was enclosed in a shingled box with a trap door. But he hadn't been on the roof for years, and he didn't know its condition.

"Okay. Let's go," Emil barked, and they were into the corridor, through the window, up the fire escape, and onto the roof.

On the fire escape they were vulnerable from the alley below and from the windows that faced the alley. Once they were on the flat part of the roof, they could be seen only from the floors of the buildings higher than No.15 and facing the alley—just a few. The steeply peaked front roof protected them from the street side.

Thick clouds kept it dark, and there was no wind. They moved quickly, carrying their tools in rucksacks—a crowbar, a keyhole saw, a hammer, miscellaneous hand tools, and three torches to light the way down the elevator shaft and into the cellar.

Otto peered over the top of the box encasing the shaft, found the hatch, climbed on top, and grabbed the handle, pulling it with more force than necessary. The meter-square lid yielded easily though the rusty hinges shrieked. He scampered off to crouch next to his cringing friends. Emil whispered to Sonny to ask Gustav for some oil.

When all remained quiet, Otto climbed back up to peer into the hole. Steel supports held a large wheel; a taut, thick cable hung from it. A wooden deck ran around the perimeter, and a ladder bolted along the outer wall allowed workers to move up and down the shaft. Otto told the others what he could see, only a few meters into the darkness below.

Sonny followed Emil onto the top, and the three men scrambled through the hatch onto the deck. Emil told Otto to give the ladder a few kicks, then put some weight on it. Otto did so and nothing moved. He smiled broadly at Sonny and said, "After you."

"Thanks," Sonny muttered sarcastically and he descended into the black hole, the other two close behind. Closed for years, the shaft was unaffected by the weather or animals, but the men stopped every couple of meters to make sure. They passed covered openings to the second- and first-floor corridors, soon reaching the ground floor. Between them and the KPD office was a dead elevator. Clearance of at least a meter on each side would allow them to stand on solid ground and work on the wall.

With an echoing thud, their bags hit the ground. They'd need a hammer, chisels, and a lot of time and muscle to work through the bricks and mortar. According to Gustav's diagram, the big hall was on the other side. Wood paneling covered the wall, so their plan was to get through the brick and mortar, then cut away the wood in one piece. They would replace the wood to cover their tracks when they left. After that, who cared?

"What are we waiting for?" Emil's question was a command, but only one man at a time could get into the narrow space.

"I'll start," Sonny offered, and he started chiseling—loosening the mortar from between the bricks.

They rotated every fifteen minutes. Afraid they were making too much noise, Sonny scrambled up the ladder after his turn, out of the shaft, onto the roof, and back down to Gustav's flat.

Sonny and Gustav stood, listening, in the darkened corridor on the floor above where the men were working.

"Plink, plink, plink" came the faint sound of the chisel striking brick and mortar. Sonny frowned, and though he knew the source of the noise, others might not, or they might not even hear the sound. The sound of Emil's low, rumbling voice dashed that hope.

"Shit," Sonny cursed, turning to Gustav. "What now?"

After some serious brainstorming they decided that Gustav would finally get to the maintenance he'd neglected. Within an hour, they set up a makeshift table in the corridor, and Gustav made all manner of noise—pounding, cutting, and whistling as he fixed whatever needed mending, and there was plenty. After several days, the ground-floor corridor looked so good that one of the tenants brought Gustav coffee and a biscuit.

Meanwhile, the men in the shaft eked out the genesis of a hole wide enough to accommodate Emil. Dust filled their noses and mouths and mixed with perspiration to sting their eyes. Nerves frayed, arms ached, and painful blisters rose on the palms tightened to claws from constant gripping. They kept at it, the pile of bricks growing.

About noon of the third day, Emil removed the handkerchief covering his nose and mouth, shook out the dust, and stretched. "That's the last of it."

Now, all that separated them from the KPD office was the hole they were about to cut into the wood wall lining the office. Emil drilled a hole, then a bigger one, and again until the saw blade fit. After that it was back and forth, pulling and pushing, until the constantly enlarging rectangle was nearly complete. Emil held onto a big bolt he'd screwed into the wood at the outset, as Otto drew the saw back for a final pull and uttered a soft, "Ah." The opening was complete. Emil stepped through, and Otto and Sonny followed, each holding a torch. Yellowed newspapers and old flyers, along with mouse droppings, littered the floor of the hall. Cobwebs covered the corners, and dust was everywhere. The hall hadn't been used, or entered, for years.

Emil led them into the bigger, then the small office, hurriedly inspecting each room. Turning off his torch, he saw little light away from the windows. To be on the safe side, they had put tape around the edges of their torches to soften the beam.

On the Thiemann Strasse side, the door was secured from the inside, but on the alley door, the bolt lock had been jimmied. The holes that once held the lock onto the frame and door were jagged to the touch. Dirty footsprints led from the door to the small office—few in any other direction. Clearly, No. 15 had seen other visitors. Emil followed the path into the closet, opened the door, and felt the cool, musty air on his face.

The beam from his torch fell on rickety steps. There was a wall to the right, but he saw little else.

"Let's take a quick look."

He moved sideways down the steep, narrow stairs, the treads creaking painfully under his weight, the other men following. At the bottom he pulled a string, but no light came on. The electricity had long been shut off. Relying on their torches, they saw a small, damp room perhaps five meters square. Rough wood planks softened the walls. The low ceiling was made lower by pipes sprouting from an ancient boiler in the far corner and crisscrossing overhead. The boiler sagged like a squat, multi-armed warrior, its armor a tangle of cobwebs stretching onto the wall. Emil scanned the opposite wall, which gave no hint that something lay beyond it. In the center of the paneled wall, four planks formed an invisible door with a hidden hinge.

Sonny and Otto had turned their attention to stacked wooden crates in the corner to the left of the stairs. "What do we have here?" Otto asked.

Emil cursed under his breath, showing no satisfaction that his hunch was right. The cops were storing stolen goods there. He quickly counted about a dozen boxes.

Something glittered under the beam of his torch, and Otto reached into the crate. He came out with something long and slender. Holding up the ornate object he asked, "What's this?"

"Let me see it," Sonny answered. His eyes widened, then quickly narrowed. Sleek and elegant, the shaft was the length of his arm from elbow to fingertips, nearly half a meter. Made of solid silver, it was layered with gold filigree and set with gemstones. At the top was a sapphire evoking a deep-sea pool, deeper and richer in color than anything he'd ever seen in a museum. Emeralds, rubies, diamonds—others he couldn't identify—

led in a dazzling maze of color to a perfectly proportioned miniature hand, forefinger extended. He'd never held anything so magnificent.

Observing Sonny's reaction, Otto asked again.

Shaking his head slowly, his mouth tightening so that when Sonny answered his voice sounded hoarse, "It's a yad." He swallowed. "A pointer for reading the Torah." He kicked the wall, creating a cloud of dust. "You're not supposed to touch the holy scroll. You need a pointer." He paced, trying to stay calm.

"Put it back. Let's get out of here," Emil ordered.

"But . . ." Sonny protested.

"Leave it," Emil said. "If it's here when we come back, maybe then."

But Sonny slid the yad into a deep inside pocket when Emil turned to leave.

The men retraced their steps back to the elevator shaft and onto the roof.

"Careful. Look over the side to see if it's clear," warned Emil.

Sonny crept around the big box to the side of the building and slowly looked over the edge into the alley. Nothing. He scanned the buildings until he found himself looking into the face of a boy no more than ten. Smiling at Sonny, he waved, and Sonny waved back.

"Great!" Emil responded. "There's nothing to do but get the hell off the roof. If he's still there, wave at him again, and hope he thinks we're just working up here."

They climbed onto the fire escape, waving to the boy before disappearing through the window. "Don't tell Gustav," Emil warned, as he cursed their luck.

He did tell Gustav they'd finish the job in the morning, saying nothing about the boy or the crates.

At Joseph's flat that night, the operators planned the final assault on No. 15. The three told the others of the cellar, the waving boy, the cops' loot, and the yad.

"It was glittering at the top, asking to be taken, but we had no time to go through the crates to see what else the bastards have stolen. We got the hell out of there," Sonny explained, but he didn't pull out the yad.

"Those assholes—skimming from Nazi thieves!" Mischa exclaimed.

"Won't the brass be pissed when they find out?" Otto mused.

"It's a sideshow," Emil growled at Sonny. "We've got a job to do, and it just got harder."

That got their attention. They shared the space with cops—and maybe a nosy kid. What they now knew made sentries even more important. Mischa would be one of two—Willy the other. Mischa obsessed about an early warning system. He began scheming—it was a challenge and a duty. Despite the eleventh hour, he was convinced his plan for a simple series of warnings would provide safety. It began with him and Willy in the alley as lookouts and ended with Gustav pulling on a rope tied to a small box filled with three or four metal pots on the roof. The commotion would warn them inside.

"Why not a bell?" Otto asked incredulously.

Sonny laughed so hard the others caught it and laughed too.

It was starting to get out of hand when Emil's rumbling voice cut through the mirth. "All right. You've had your laugh." When they quieted, he said, "Mischa's got part of it right."

Emil continued. "Though it's a bit complicated, and we'd never hear it in the cellar, Mischa is taking this seriously. And there's a kernel of a plan." Becoming thoughtful, he looked from Mischa to Willy. "Those crates tell me the cops have been around—recently. They might return when one of you is nearby."

The sentries looked at one another and nodded.

"Remember—*improvise.* We don't have the time or resources for anything else, so you might have to make it up on the fly. One of you should be in the alley at all times, if possible. We hope to be in a position to hear you, otherwise we're on our own. Hell, we might be anyhow."

"What about the kid?" Joseph asked.

"Who the hell knows?" Emil replied. "With luck, we won't need a warning or have to worry about the kid." Then he looked from Sonny to Otto and nodded. "We're ready, but now's the time if you want to back out, no questions asked." He looked at each in turn.

There was a knock at the door. Otto let Dix into the flat and an uneasy silence. Ignoring Dix, the men looked from one to another, the silence continuing until Mischa proclaimed, "To hell with the cops. I like our chances."

Everyone agreed. They briefed Dix, who liked Mischa's approach. Dix gave Emil the combination he'd memorized years before, wished them good luck, and departed.

Everyone had his assignment: Willy and Mischa were to take separate vigils somewhere in the alley, at Thiemann or Weser, at 8:30 the next morning. Emil, Otto, and Sonny would meet at Gustav's flat at 9:00, each carrying a satchel that by noon would be full.

Joseph and Dix would wait at the warehouse. Sonny's storage room was too exposed, so he had commandeered an empty one at the end of a winding corridor. They had discussed whether to use the warehouse at all, but there was nothing else. Half of them were familiar figures at the warehouse, though two of them might be on a wanted list.

Sonny was the last to arrive at Gustav's flat. On his way from Scheunenviertel, he had contemplated the job from every angle—the kid, Braun, the cops—and he liked their chances. He'd been in the game, as Emil called it, almost seven years, but you didn't pull a caper like this every day. He was smiling when he walked in, oblivious to the tension permeating the flat.

"What the hell's so funny?" asked Emil.

"Nothing," Sonny answered, but Emil wasn't satisfied. "Just a funny thought." Sonny tapped a finger on his temple.

"Now's not the time to get lost in there," Emil scolded, emulating Sonny's tapping. "Or the time to be funny. It's time to work." Emil was focused. "God damn it! Be alert." He looked from Sonny to Otto, and than to Gustav. "I mean all of us."

The flat fell silent. Gustav stopped pacing, nodded, continued to pace.

"All right! Gustav talked to some of the neighbors about Braun, casual like I asked him to." Emil looked at Sonny and Otto until he was sure they were listening. "Sure enough, he learned some interesting things. Didn't you?"

Gustav nodded as he paced.

"There are rumors about the cops and No. 15, so it's not just Gustav who's seen them. Braun's heard them, and he'd been asking questions, hanging around. That's unusual, so he must be spooked." Emil stretched his neck, then massaged it, but kept his eyes on both of them. "I don't like it that Braun is nervous—especially now."

"So, what do we do?" Otto's question hung in the air.

"Does Braun change anything?" Emil snapped back, his anxiety exposed. Then he spread his arms wide, begging the question.

"I say go!" Sonny shot back.

Buoyed by Sonny's enthusiasm, Otto nodded and pointed to the roof. "Can't get this thing done until we start."

"What the hell!" Emil settled it. There was no turning back this late in the game, and Gustav was in for the ride whatever they decided.

While the operators debated, Mischa and Willy walked Thiemann, Weser, and the alley joining the two streets, on the lookout for cops or the man described as Braun. To the casual observer there was nothing unusual about either man, though on scrutiny someone might notice each lurking aimlessly, in and out of the alley.

Emil looked at his watch. "It's 9:20. We should be out of here before 11:00."

The three burglars hurried onto the roof under ominous clouds that alternately darkened, then lightened, threatening rain. Sonny scanned the window from which yesterday's child had waved, finding no one. He did catch a glimpse of Mischa in the alley.

Quickly and wordlessly, they entered the shaft, grunted down the ladder, satchels over their shoulders, caught their breath at the bottom, opened the hatch, and entered the hall. Otto worked the hatch back onto its hole, and it looked good in the dim light. The only sound was the soft, repetitious pat of their boots hitting the floor. They started a quick inspection.

Suddenly they heard a voice—in the room with them?—and froze. Eyes widened, heads turned. Where did it come from? Sonny waved his arms, then pointed toward the boarded-up window facing Thiemann. They moved closer. The voices got louder, and they were captive to an unseen conversation.

"What the hell's the emergency?" An exasperated, raspy, phlegm-filled voice came through the window.

"It's nighttime only, remember?" Another voice, this one was higher, also impatient. Then a taunt: "You losing your nerve?"

"The rumors are thick—about cops coming and going. People are asking questions. I'm supposed to know about shit like that and do something." The third voice had to be Braun's. "Well, Putzy, Reinhard, what do you guys think we should do?"

Partners in mischief at No. 15, they huddled on the sidewalk, hypnotizing the three inside, waiting with Braun for the cops to answer.

Emil broke the spell with a shake of his head and a jab of his finger at the floor. If Sonny or Otto wanted to wait for the answer, neither said it.

"Shit . . ." was the last thing they heard as they moved. Time was closing in.

Within seconds they were in the small office, into the closet, through the door, into the musty dampness of the cellar. The cellar seemed smaller, more claustrophobic, with danger nearby. Each burglar pointing a beam of light, together they watched Emil pull three nails. The door swung free, revealing the safe. Emil stared, appreciating the design of its concealment, then knelt to twirl the dial of the lock this way and that. In fifteen seconds, the safe was open.

"Fantastic," Otto murmured after Emil reached in and pulled out a handful of jewelry and began filling his satchel—it was just as Dix had described! If any of them thought this was too easy, no one said it. There were voices, barely audible, from the alley—faint, like a whisper on the wind. They continued filling the satchels until the safe was empty.

Emil closed the safe, twirled the dial, and secured the wooden door. He and Otto moved toward the steps, clutching the satchels, but Sonny stopped at the crates. He opened one and began stuffing its treasures into his satchel. Otto saw what Sonny was doing and joined him.

Emil scowled, then quietly exhorted, "Quick. We gotta get out of here. Take what we can fence, leave the Judaica."

Sonny didn't respond, just took what was handy. Then Otto's hand shot up, and they went quiet. "Another voice," he whispered. "Closer."

"Ssh," Emil hissed.

They heard, "Heil Hitler!" Then a jumble of words, another voice, none of the words intelligible, until . . . "Now scram!"

"First one was Willy. Someone's at the back door," Emil whispered.

"Hell!" Otto's curse came out in a croak.

Their eyes followed the sound up the steps.

"Must be Braun!" Sonny said softly.

They were already up the stairs and into the little office when they heard the voices more clearly. They kept going.

"Move. Go. We could be surrounded." Emil pushed Sonny toward the shaft, and they heard a muffled shout but couldn't make out the words. Sonny pulled the hatch from the wall, and they clambered through. Otto was last. He started to fasten the hatch, but Emil put a hand on his arm and whispered, "Wait."

They listened for any sound—a voice or clatter—to tell them what was happening in the alley. Was Braun, Putzy, or Reinhart coming in? There was nothing. Thirty seconds, then a minute—the time dragged. Sonny pointed up, his eyes like fried eggs on a white plate, near panic in the enclosed space, head turning back and forth . . .

"Sonny, go up. Otto, wait," Emil ordered.

More noise from near the alley door. Nobody entered.

Emil squeezed Otto's shoulder: "Fasten the hatch and go!"

Sonny was already halfway up when Otto started; Emil followed, moving quickly and quietly. Otto paused to reposition his satchel and a tool flew out from a side pocket, glancing off Emil's shoulder and clattering onto the concrete floor. The sound ricocheted in the tight space.

"Sorry," Otto apologized.

Emil winced. "Keep going. Get onto the roof."

In less than a minute they were crouching in the lee side of the big box. Catching their breath, they listened for clues from the alley below. Hearing nothing, they duck-walked around to the side of the building, hesitated. If Braun was at the back door, all he had to do was look up.

"Now what, boss?" Sonny asked.

Emil stared at him, then raised his eyes heavenward and sighed. "Otto, the next time Sonny comes up with a grand plan, remind me to throw him out on his ass."

Otto smiled halfheartedly, still feeling the sting of his clumsiness.

"We're wasting time," said Sonny.

"First smart thing you've said," Emil shot back. He peered over the side until he was looking straight down. "Nothing." He jerked his head for them to follow and climbed onto the metal stairs. He forgot about the boy but stopped at the window. Several anxious seconds passed as Emil peered into the corridor. "It's clear."

They were in the flat in a matter of seconds, dropping the satchels with a clang in the corner behind a chair out of sight, as if that made a difference. Gustav stopped pacing as they entered. Ghostly pale, his eyes wide with fright, he apparently wished he were anywhere else but there.

"What the hell happened?" Emil demanded.

Gustav stared, unable to answer, so Emil placed a reassuring hand on his shoulder. Still, the words wouldn't come. Finally. "I-I-I don't kn-kn-know." Then what he said made them freeze: "Heard shots."

The men surrounded Gustav, but that clearly unnerved him. Emil pushed them back. Keeping his voice calm, he said, "Take a deep breath . . . good, now tell us what you saw and heard."

Gustav covered his face with both hands, and he sputtered, then gasped for the breath to say what he had to say. The words came in a rush. "Like you told me, I was watching the alley. From the Weser end comes Braun, and he's looking around like he's supposed to see something. But I don't think he looked up and saw you."

"Are you sure?" Emil asked softly.

Nodding but unsure, Gustav said, "I think so."

"What about Willy?" Sonny asked.

"We heard his voice, then another," Otto interrupted.

"Willy came up on Braun. By then Mischa was headed toward Weser. He must have seen Braun." Gustav stopped and looked to the window, replaying the scene in his mind.

He continued, "Braun was at the back door, too close for me to see what he was doing. That's when Willy came at him, yelling 'Heil Hitler.' There was some talk I couldn't understand. Then Willy yelled again, Braun yelled, and Willy sprung at him. I saw Braun squirming on the ground, trying to get up. Willy must have knocked him down . . ."

Gustav shook his head in astonishment: " . . . and then he bolted toward Thiemann. Braun was rolling around—he's so damn fat—but he finally got up and chased after Willy." Gustav bit his lip and looked down. "He had a pistol. Anyone could see it. Then the cops came, yelling, 'No Braun, no!' They chased after him . . . it happened so fast . . . then two shots . . . from the direction of Thiemann. That's all I know."

"Damn!" Emil cursed.

Sonny could only say, "He could be dying in the street."

"We don't know that," Emil snapped, his voice piercing the gloom, threatening their escape and Willy's life. "We've got to get out of here."

Emil grabbed Gustav's hand, shook it. "You've been terrific, and I promise you'll be well paid." Then placing a palm on Gustav's chest, he said, "Stay calm and out of sight—you don't know a goddamn thing." He put a finger to his lips.

Gustav nodded.

"I'll meet you tonight at the little tavern at 10:00 o'clock, okay?" Emil repeated the instructions until he was sure Gustav understood.

Gustav nodded again. The three men were out the door with their satchels, into the empty hall, at the Thiemann Strasse door in under thirty seconds. After a quick survey of the area, Emil nodded. As they left, he, grabbed the nearest arm—Sonny's—and said, "Keep an eye out for Willy and Mischa. And good luck!"

Sonny turned onto Weser and glanced down the alley just in time to see two uniforms heading his way. He turned left at Treptower without looking back at Reinhart and Putzy.

Mischa kept his head down, sniffing for danger. He glanced once or twice toward the roof but saw nothing. Keeping a steady pace, he tried to blend into the background. Neukölln shared its poverty and neglect with Scheunenviertel from the warehouse to Hirtenstrasse, so he felt on familiar territory. The H & S, a short walk down Weser, had shut down, giving him no reason to return. But the two neighborhoods were different in one respect—few Jews lived in Neukölln. Mischa shivered. It felt like rain soon, maybe even snow. Life had turned scary with the beating and gone downhill from there. He still tasted blood, though he knew it couldn't be there six years later. He never told anyone about that taste—not even Sophie. He was erratic and high-strung, and sometimes he thought he was crazy. At times he shook with fright, and Sophie held him until it stopped. Would they think him a coward?

But would a coward have tried to save the Reb? There hadn't been time for him to be scared. He'd just reacted, for all the good it did—a lump on his head, bruised ribs, and depression for weeks. Aside from the beating and a roughing up by a couple of SAs, he'd been lucky. That made him laugh.

He'd really been a mess that day at Paul's place when he argued with Sonny and limped out, angry, disillusioned. Every now and again he thought about the spoiled American, so far away. He envied Paul—he had none of this shit to deal with! When Hitler came to power and rounded up the KPD leaders, hope had evaporated, been replaced by fear, burrowing deep. The Nazis delivered on their promises.

He had survived—but hell, so had Otto and Dix. Then Sonny and Joseph had come up with the smuggling operation, bringing back hope. So Mischa had a second chance, but the fear lingered on. He clenched his jaw and mumbled, "Fuck the fear!" And a thin smile crept onto his face.

Emil said being scared was different from cowardice. Only a fool or a dead man wasn't scared. He'd said it so earnestly, it had to be true. Maybe Emil had read his mind—he had kept his eyes on Mischa longer than on the others: "Fear keeps you alert and in the game. Otherwise you get sloppy. Worry if you aren't at least a little nervous."

Turning from Thiemann onto Werra, Mischa repeated the words. A guy who's a Jew and a Bolshie should be afraid. Both were trouble.

Mischa had never hung around with goyim, non-Jews, until he joined the KPD. Well, there was Joseph—and Solomon—but they were honorary Jews. No one gave a shit—there were many in the party, including the martyred Liebknecht and Luxemburg. Mischa loved that he and Sonny were the only Jews in this operation to save Jews. Joseph, Otto, Emil, and the others were risking their lives to help people like him.

No, for Mischa, *goy* was not a pejorative. The word was merely descriptive, as in "Are you a Jew or a Catholic?" Once, his father got in his face, lecturing him that *goy* meant nation in the Old Testament. That meant everybody, including Judah. Some Jews had subverted the word into a slur. People were always fucking things up.

So Mischa kept his mind busy and supposed Willy was doing the same. They passed each other three, maybe four, times, acting like strangers. Their eyes met twice, and the third time he acknowledged Willy with a nod. There was no action—the street was quiet, boring. He saw no more than a half-dozen people in the alley, a few more on Thiemann and Weser. They paid no more attention to him than he did to them.

Mischa lost track of how many times he passed the back door of No. 15. At the corner of the alley, he looked toward Weser Strasse, then back to Thiemann—nothing. He fought the urge to look up. He tried to see above him without lifting his head, but it made his eyes hurt and he gave it up. Once, from the mouth of the alley, he spotted Gustav standing at the window . . .

When he got to Weser, Mischa turned left toward Thiemann. A fat, bald guy stood near the front door of No. 15. A tingling rushed through Mischa's body into his legs, like when he was a kid scared of shadows in the dark. Crossing Thiemann, he leaned against the nearest lamppost and lit a cigarette, watching. Braun scanned the street, hands on hips, as if waiting for someone. Within minutes, two uniforms came from Weser and met up with Braun; the three stood in a circle, talking. Braun gestured toward the building, agitated.

Mischa took a last drag on his cigarette, flicked it into the street, and looked at his watch. He walked back toward Weser and the alley, keeping an eye on the trio.

Braun jerked his thumb toward the back and left the two cops. The tall thin cop shrugged, took out a pack of cigarettes, and offered one to his shorter partner. He frowned, said something, and took a cigarette. Mischa forgot about them as he watched Braun disappear into the alley. Then Mischa saw Braun waddle toward the back of No. 15 and stop at the back door. He appeared to be inspecting the windows and the door. Movement from the far side of the alley caught his eye—Willy was coming at Braun from behind.

Willy was used to being cold, having worked most of his life outside. Still, he had to keep flexing his hand to keep it from getting stiff. He didn't like the waiting, hated the unknown, but he liked the camaraderie of the work at hand. It was a strike against the assholes for the unpleasantness they'd caused him.

Walking through the alley, Willy occasionally glanced at Gustav's window, keeping his head down for fear someone would follow his gaze, catch the operators on the fire escape, blow the whole operation. There was nothing much going on in the alley, but someone might be watching him. He leaned against a wall, lit a cigarette, crossed his arms over his chest as if he were waiting for someone, and watched the back door of No. 15. Mischa had just left the alley, turning left on Weser.

Maybe five minutes later, a fat man came waddling toward Willy. The man was bald and swayed from side to side. He looked at No. 15, at the windows and door but not at the roof. Willy took a long drag, exhaled, and watched—it was Braun.

Braun looked both ways, not noticing Willy, then pulled at the padlock on the door, backed up shaking his head, looked at the windows and back at the door. He took something from his pocket and put his hand on the lock.

"Can't let that happen," Willy mumbled, and without thinking, he trotted toward Braun, his mind churning for a plan. Within a couple of meters of Braun, he said innocently, "You can't go in there. The police say it's off limits."

Braun's shoulders jumped, and his head turned. Willy saw the open padlock swinging on the hasp. Braun turned back to the lock, sneering impatiently, "Get out of here! It's none of your business."

"Heil Hitler" was all Willy could think. He yelled it so the others could hear. Then he gave the stiff-armed salute.

"Ja, ja," Braun answered. Then seeing that Willy hadn't moved, he shouted, "Scram! Get the fuck out of here!"

"But . . . you aren't supposed to go in there. It's against the law," Willy protested.

"God damn it! I am the law, you idiot. Now get the hell out of here." Ignoring Willy, Braun seemed about to grab the padlock.

Improvise—the word bounced around Willy's head like an incomplete thought in search of an ending. To give warning was his only assignment, but what if it wasn't enough? Willy saw just two choices: scream and get the hell out of there, or take a run at Braun—and then scream and get the hell out of there. He improvised, lunging at Braun from behind, pushing him hard and screaming, "You're not supposed to go in there!"

Braun was flat on his back, stunned. He tried to move, but he was too fat and slow to get up. He rolled over onto one side. Squirming, he realized who had knocked him to the ground and yelled. "I'll get you . . ."

Willy was already around the corner of the alley, onto Thiemann and then left to Werra. He didn't stop. He didn't know where to go, but he ran like hell, hoping Braun was as slow as he looked. Halfway down Werra, Willy turned to see Braun at the corner in slow pursuit. There was something in Braun's hand, so Willy ran faster. He was turning left onto Treptower when he heard a crack, then another. He winced at the sudden pain in his left shoulder.

18

The man who runs may fight again.
—Menander

The pain was searing. Willy was knocked off balance but didn't fall. He kept moving, slowly, until he reached Kaiser Friedrich Strasse and started to cross. Looking over his injured shoulder, he saw that Braun had disappeared. Nobody was following, but that didn't mean no one would. His stomach churned at the thought of arrest, more torture. He felt his stiffened hand and twitching eye and knew he'd rather die than go through that again. He hurt like hell.

Horns honked and tires screeched, but Willy didn't hear them; somehow he managed to cross the busy street. Heading west, he came to a cemetery and stopped behind a tree among the grave markers. He winced when he stuck his hand under his jacket and felt the wet warmth there. Blood on his hand, he panicked, not because he might die but because he might die alone on the street—or not die and be captured.

Mouthing the words "Keep calm. All you have to do is walk five miles to Scheunenviertel," he kept moving. Five miles! Shit, that was a long way . . . He leaned against a tree, his eyes falling on the nearest gravestone. It read: "Loving husband, father, grandfather, now in the hands of God." Not yet! Taking another step, Willy doubled over from a jab of pain in his shoulder. Gasping, he straightened, then lurched in the general direction of the Mitte.

It started to rain, softly at first, in a fine mist that cooled his face. Then it came down harder, until Willy was drenched, and he shivered uncontrollably. Still he kept moving. Breathing was difficult—he opened his mouth and gulped. He felt some relief, then was quickly overtaken by the burn in his shoulder. His left arm hung limply; he'd lost the feeling in his hand. Crossing a street, he was nearly hit by a truck, but he kept moving past nameless shops and flats, encountering few people in the rain. He'd lost track of time. He stopped in a park to let the rain wash over his face.

Fear hit Mischa in the gut; he lit another cigarette as he watched Braun disappear into the alley. Where the hell was Willy? Then as if he had heard, Willy appeared at Braun's back. What the hell was he doing?

Mischa heard voices without words, saw Willy's one-armed salute, and heard an angry "Scram!" from Braun. Transfixed, Mischa silently urged Willy on—to do what? Send an alert to the men inside? Warn them, and get the hell out of there! Willy was to be admired—would he have done the same? His hand went to the knot on his head; he had his answer.

If Braun's angry response was any indication, Willy was improvising and doing a fine job of it. But his actions would only postpone Braun's entry.

Suddenly Braun was flat on his back. Like a turtle, his legs tread comically in the air. Mischa nearly laughed. Now Willy was leaning over, yelling in Braun's face. "Run!" Mischa wanted to shout, but Willy got the silent order and ran. Braun rolled on the ground, finally got to his feet, slowly giving chase. Mischa took the long way around and followed on Thiemann.

Both cops were running, yelling something at Braun, who had disappeared onto Werra. Mischa caught up enough to see Braun again, his arm extended in Willy's direction. Braun had a pistol! At the far end of the street, Willy was about to turn onto Treptower. One of the cops shouted, "Fool!" But it was too late.

Mischa heard two shots and saw Willy flinch but not fall, and then disappear around the corner. People on the street scattered as Mischa hid in a doorway, watching the cops confront Braun. They argued, and Braun put the pistol in his pocket. One of cops waved dismissively in the direction Willy had gone, then they headed back toward No. 15 and out of sight. The pedestrians reappeared, onlookers wondering what had happened.

Dazed but knowing what he had to do, Mischa flicked out his cigarette and started after Willy . . . At Treptower, he looked toward Kaiser Friedrich Strasse—no Willy in sight. Figuring he'd want to be on the other side, away from danger, Mischa crossed too. Willy needed help. That's all he needed to know.

At the cemetery, Mischa entered the grove of trees littered with grave markers topped with crucifixes. No Willy. But Mischa spotted something out of place, an irregular patch of crimson on a flat stone marker. Kneeling, he touched the spot and shuddered. It was damp. Willy had been here and that was reassuring, but the blood wasn't a good sign. Mischa ran from the cemetery as it started to rain.

Heading north to the warehouse, Mischa figured Willy would have to cross the canal and the Spree—but where? Gambling on the route, Mischa avoided busy streets, occasionally backtracking, scouring the alleys and side streets. Which bridges would Willy use? Ahead was another cemetery; to the west was Hasenheide Park with its thousand hiding places. But Willy wouldn't hide unless he was too weak to continue, and if he was being pursued . . . Mischa would never find him there. He kept moving, hoping that's what Willy was doing too. Skirting the park, he walked through the cemetery toward the river and Admiral Bridge, straight ahead.

All Mischa could think of was finding Willy. After that—well, he'd deal with it. Then it hit him. He'd completely forgotten about the guys inside No. 15. After the shots, he'd pushed everything from his mind. Nothing else had seemed important. Damn! Did they get Willy's warning in time?

Blind alleys slowed Mischa's progress, but he kept moving north, sweeping his eyes from side to side, searching for something, anything. The rain made it hard to see—it was a curse and a blessing. Something on the boulevard separating the traffic leading to a bridge, moved. Not certain, Mischa ran toward it. A hunched-over body came into focus, moved again. "Willy!" Mischa yelled,

Willy's head jerked and slowly turned.

Mischa reached him in a moment. "Can you make it? I saw everything. You were terrific."

Slack-jawed and breathing heavily, Willy tried to focus on the voice. With barely the energy to reply, he said, "Don't know." He coughed and spit. "Fucker . . . shot me."

"Where?"

"Left shoulder." Willy's voice was barely audible between coughing jags, and his breathing was shallow.

"How bad?"

"Get me back to . . ."

Mischa's eyes wandered to the round, dark red spot high on the back of Willy's jacket below his left shoulder. "Don't talk. Save your strength. We have to move."

Mischa supported Willy under his right arm, and they started across the bridge, a growing crimson circle visible on Willy's left shoulder. The rain helped, soaked his jacket, obscuring the spot, and the few people they encountered scurried by without a glance.

With effort, Willy put one foot in front of the other in a slow shuffle. He started coughing and nearly fell. Mischa, increasingly alarmed, kept him upright as the bloodstain grew. They stopped under an awning, their backs to the street, waiting for Willy to stop hacking. From behind, Mischa heard a woman's voice and glanced over his shoulder.

A middle-aged matron, her face clouded, asked. "Is he sick? He'd better see a doctor."

Glad she wasn't a cop, Mischa said, "He's drunk. I'm getting him home." He shrugged and forced a smile. Her sympathy wilted to contempt, and she left them without another word.

When the coughing stopped, they continued, Willy groaning with each step, his face frozen in pain. Stopping briefly now and then, they went on, in about two hours reaching the shadow of the New Synagogue's Moorish dome. Willy fell to the pavement.

Bending over his fallen friend, Mischa implored, "We're almost there—just five minutes, I promise. You can do it. You have to." Glancing at his watch, he saw the hands signal five minutes to three.

A cold steady rain added to the gloom as the other operators made their way to the warehouse, each taking a separate route. Their destination was disconcertingly similar to the one they'd just abandoned. Joseph and Dix patiently waited there, first to greet Sonny, then Otto, finally Emil.

Dix sat on a rickety chair in the corner of the small, musty room. By the time Emil appeared, it was crowded and hot. He leaned against the doorframe to watch the corridor for Mischa and Willy. The others stood or sat cross-legged on the cold floor. Three satchels lay in a pile, speaking of their success, but their faces said otherwise—something had gone awry.

"Can't we do something about that light?" Otto complained, shielding his eyes. Wordlessly, Emil tied a rag around the bulb.

Joseph watched the scene with growing apprehension. "What the hell happened? Where are Mischa and Willy?"

Dix looked from Emil to the satchels and back to the others. "By your faces one would think you had failed."

Sonny, Otto, and Emil exchanged pained glances, but no one answered. Finally Emil, as their leader, said, "We got the goods." Then he told them what had happened, with Sonny and Otto interjecting, until the picture came at least partly into view. At the end of what he knew, Emil sighed. "So we don't know what's become of Willy or where Mischa is. All we can do is hope they'll show up."

Dix stared at the satchels and pulled at his lower lip. "We should proceed, not all remain here. It is far too risky."

There were nods all around, but their thoughts were elsewhere. Finally Emil suggested they go through the loot, see what they had, and be done with it. Joseph went home, as there was no reason for him to stay. Sonny, Otto, and Emil agreed to wait for Willy and Mischa to appear.

In the meantime, they emptied the satchels onto the floor, separating the contents piece by piece into neat piles. After half an hour, they had five piles—of gold, silver, coins, jewelry with precious gems, and miscellany including watches, a small leather portfolio tied with string, and a leather-bound first edition of Mann's *The Magic Mountain*.

With a relieved smile, Dix plucked the portfolio from the floor, placing it on his lap and explaining, "Papers that have value only to me."

Emil and Sonny exchanged glances but said nothing. Dix removed the book from the pile, flipped through the pages, and smiled. Then he handed the book to Sonny. "Please give this to Joseph. I had forgotten it. He will appreciate having it. Tell him it came from an admirable library."

Dix leaned back in his chair. "Now all we have to do is convert the jewels and metals into useful exchange." He looked at Emil. "I will leave that in your capably larcenous hands." A grin spread across his face. "Of course, we will keep the gold and silver coins; they have intrinsic value."

Emil squatted to be at eye level with Dix when he spoke. They'd already agreed on the split, but there was something new. "Same deal. A third to you, the other two-thirds we split. But we get everything Braun and the cops stashed as incidental to our operation. It covers the . . ." Emil made a circular motion with his hand, " . . . aggravation." Emil's understatement was a reminder of their compatriots' absence.

Dix considered for several seconds, as if he had a choice. "Agreed." And they shook hands.

"What's in the portfolio?" asked Emil, his tone neutral.

"Look for yourself," Dix answered, handing it to him.

Opening it, Emil removed papers with the seal of the government of the United States of America, while Otto and Sonny looked on. Nodding his understanding, Emil handed the folio back to Dix.

"Wait!" Sonny spouted. "Can Joseph have them for a few days?"

Dix hesitated before nodding. "Of course. Guard them with your life; these are more important to me than all the silver and gold."

"Hasn't it expired after five years?" Emil asked.

"The dates are open, which I believe is unique. I made a valuable contact at the American embassy, despite my position in the KPD. The attaché feared Hitler more than he feared Thälmann. Truth be told, I am a bit of a chameleon." Dix smiled ruefully, then sighed. "I had intended to retrieve the papers in the days leading to Hitler's appointment as chancellor, but something more critical always intervened. As you will recall, we moved from crisis to crisis, and alas . . ." He shrugged.

Sonny carefully placed the documents in his satchel, which he'd take to Joseph's flat. Emil would take his satchel home; the one remaining would stay at the warehouse, in Joseph's storage room. The men divided the coins, Dix pocketing his share, and everything else remained for the marketplace.

"Please act with speed. I cannot leave until all the goods are sold," Dix politely requested.

"It could time to make contacts, but I'll move as quickly as I can," Emil told him. "We want the cash too."

Dix accepted the reality with a shrug. "After five years, what's another week? Thank you for your heroic work. I wish the missing men well. Remember to return my papers." Then he shook their hands and took his leave.

After Dix was gone, Emil said, "There are too many people; there's too much loot and no escape route. It makes me uneasy. We don't all need to wait." But they stayed.

After another ten minutes, they heard a noise in the corridor. Emil turned off the light, and Sonny quietly shut the door. The shuffling steps grew louder, then stopped. They heard a soft knock and Mischa's voice: "Help!"

Sonny opened the door expecting Mischa to slide in, but instead it was Willy, slumped against the wall, Joseph crouched behind him in shadow. The smell of wet wool and fresh blood, salt and copper, crowded out that of the musty air. Water pooled on the floor. Willy's eyes were closed, his face pinched.

"Oh, no!" Sonny groaned.

Quickly, they carried Willy in, gently propped him against the wall. Emil turned on the light, removed the rag from the bulb, and knelt next to Willy. "Where was he hit?"

"Once, somewhere around his left shoulder."

In the strong light, Willy's face was chalky and drawn, his breathing shallow. Emil opened his coat to look, and Willy's face contorted at the pain. "Can't tell from the front," Emil said. "But it's obvious he's lost a lot of blood."

Joseph leaned over to see and said, "Apply pressure to the entry to stanch the flow of blood. I'll look for some clean rags."

They gently turned Willy's body. Otto placed the palm of his hand on the bloody coat to apply pressure. Willy gasped, then settled down.

"Can you hear me?" Emil asked. "Just nod."

Willy's head moved a few centimeters.

"Good." Then speaking to Mischa, Emil asked, "What happened?"

Exhausted, Mischa had moved to the corner, out of the way, letting the others minister to Willy. Startled by Emil's question, Mischa took several seconds to focus on the scene. His lips moved, but nothing came out. He swallowed, licked his lips, and started again. As he told his story, the other just stared at Willy.

Sonny whispered, "He needs a doctor."

Stuck in a claustrophobic space with a man at their feet near death, the men were agitated, not thinking straight—not even Emil. They were afraid Willy might die, what that would mean to them. They had to do something. Finally Joseph took over. "He's right. Willy needs a doctor. Take him somewhere away from here. I spotted Willy and Mischa on my way home, but I couldn't take him to the flat."

Willy lay barely conscious on the floor, unable to offer an opinion.

"Okay." Emil rubbed his chin, trying to figure out what to do next, cursing Braun under his breath.

"Joseph's right." Sonny was chewing on his lip, staring down at Willy. He threw out his hands in frustration.

Emil turned to Sonny and Mischa. "You know this area. Tell us where can we take him."

They looked at one another, then Mischa's eyebrows shot up. "What about the shed?"

Sonny nodded, his mind momentarily occupied by a youthful liaison in that old shed. He recovered and said, "There's an abandoned shed in the back. We can take Willy there when it gets dark. Then get him to a doctor."

"Where the hell are we going to get a doctor?" Otto barked.

"Sonny?" Joseph's voice intervened. "Call Karl. He'll know a doctor. Come with me."

By agreement, Sonny and Karl discussed nothing by telephone. They customarily set meetings using code words for prearranged locations—Tegel Castle, Tiergarten Park, the warehouse, and others. But this was urgent. Karl would understand . . .

Not long after Sonny completed the call, darkness fell and Willy was moved into the shed. Sonny waited in the shadow of the warehouse entrance. An umbrella moved out of the darkness toward him. "Thanks for coming," he said, then led Karl through the narrow alley. Mischa nodded grimly at Karl, and the three men stood over the unconscious Willy. Karl knew about the operation, but he hadn't been involved—until now. He had offered a safe house for Dix and his family, but that was all.

Karl stared down at Willy and said, "We've got to get him to our safe house."

"What about a doctor?" Sonny asked urgently.

"Yes," Karl answered without hesitation. "I need a telephone."

They walked to Joseph's flat; Karl made his calls there and departed. Sonny returned to the shed and told Mischa that help was coming. Then Sonny rejoined Emil and Otto in the cellar.

Relieved at Sonny's news about a doctor, Emil stared at his younger, less experienced partners and slowly shook his head. "I hate it, but now that Willy's tended to, there's work to be done. The loot has to be dealt with quickly. With all the commotion we're making down here and out back, it's only a matter of time before someone gets curious."

Emil's words hit Sonny like a slap in the face, but he didn't know what to say or do. It wasn't right, not with Willy near death. He objected, "How can we? With Willy . . ."

"No!" Emil interrupted. "We've done all we can for Willy. He'll be safe in a few hours—the doctor will do what he can. When we're done you can see him, but in the meantime we've got to dump that loot onto the market." Emil maintained his stern, unyielding gaze until they nodded, mumbled agreement. That settled, a devious grin pushed its way onto Emil's mouth. "Now we get back at them."

Sonny stared blankly. "Huh?"

"We talked about it while you were busy with Willy and Karl," Emil said, nodding at Otto.

"We rat them out," said Otto.

"Braun, that malicious idiot, is especially vulnerable," Emil added.

"I like it," Sonny agreed.

Emil shrugged. "It's simple, to the point, and all we can do."

They had to act fast, since Braun, Putzy, and Reinhard might move the loot out of the cellar, if they hadn't already. Since it was Otto's plan, he'd make the call to the nearest Neukölln police station and hope Putzy or Reinhard didn't answer the telephone. They had already roughed out a script: "I saw a fat, bald, block warden, name of Braun—lives on Treptower—and some cops unloading boxes in the middle of the night into the old KPD office, No. 15 Thiemann Strasse. They're up to no good. If you don't do something, I'll call the Gestapo."

All Otto needed was the phone number, so he headed for Joseph's flat. Emil left for Wedding. Sonny would wait with Mischa and meet Emil around midnight in Wedding, after Emil's meeting with Gustav.

Alfred, one of Karl's trusted minions, parked at the back of the warehouse. He helped Mischa and Sonny carry Willy's limp body to the car. They were beyond worrying that anyone might notice. Sonny returned to Joseph's flat to wait for his meeting with Emil.

Mischa rode with Alfred and Willy to No. 53 Stuttgarter Strasse, Neukölln, an old boardinghouse. Alfred parked at the mouth of an alley, and they carried Willy through the back door to an upstairs room. Then Alfred left to fetch the doctor. On the way he dropped Mischa in the Mitte.

No. 53 was a near-perfect haven—one of two Confessing Church safe houses in Berlin. Sandwiched between abandoned buildings, it faced Stuttgarter Strasse. At the rear, across the alley from the house, was the flat, windowless wall of an abandoned warehouse. The alley dead-ended beyond the third building at another flat wall. No. 53 was narrower and shorter than its neighbors, making it appear smaller. Its many rooms and depth from front to rear made the place feel bigger, which created a fleeting disorientation. Its users came in from the alley—the front door was never used—into the kitchen.

No. 53 had not been used as a boardinghouse since the late 1920s. It still was the home of Frau Irina Moltke, a short, comfortably pillowed woman with gray hair tied in a bun. Her family had been members of Pastor Larson's church for many years, and Karl had known her most of his life. He was a friend of her son, Herbert. Her husband had died fifteen years earlier, and her two children had families of their own.

Until the law forbade it, Frau Moltke had cooked for a large Jewish family in the West End; she—and her husband and children—had become part of her employers' big extended family. She missed them all terribly, but now they were safe in America. Her commitment to the underground cause was such that she had volunteered the use of her big empty house.

Willy hovered between the living and the dead, unchanged. Within an hour, Alfred returned with a young doctor. Otto, who had made his phone call to the police and returned to Neukölln, waited with Karl for his verdict. Finally, the unsmiling doctor entered the kitchen, his face betraying their hopes for a good outcome. The doctor washed his hands and, while drying them, asked Karl for a glass of brandy.

He drank, grimaced as it went down, and shook his head. "He's lost a lot of blood—the bullet pierced the axillary artery—and without a hospital, I'm afraid . . ."

"Shit," Otto hissed.

"I know," the doctor said. "The bullet's out, and he's sleeping." Reaching into a pocket he put a packet and the small slug on the table. "Give him morphine for pain when he needs it, probably every three hours. Only water and soup, no solids, but I doubt he'll want to eat. I'll be back tomorrow." He pointed to the slug without comment.

"Thank you," Otto said quietly. He looked at the hand that he'd used to put pressure on Willy's wound. The little shed had hinted the stench of death—now No. 53 Stuttgarter Strasse reeked of it. He felt numb.

Karl touched the doctor's shoulder and led him to Alfred's car.

It was near midnight when Sonny pressed his ear against the door, heard nothing, and softly knocked. Emil motioned him into the flat, putting a finger to his lips. They walked silently to the kitchen. After handing Sonny a cup of coffee, Emil asked about Willy.

Otto had telephoned Sonny after the doctor left, and Sonny relayed his news.

"That bad?" Emil paced nervously, stopped suddenly, and said softly, "So he may not make it—I don't like losing a good man." His eyes softened, his words hanging in the air.

Sonny had been thinking the same thing. He whispered, "No. Willy's back in Neukölln—around the corner from No. 15."

"Have you seen the place?" Emil asked.

"Not yet—it's an old boardinghouse owned by a friend of Karl's."

"Must be a good friend to offer the house for such a dangerous game," Emil mused, then added, "one we're all playing."

"How did it go with Gustav?" Sonny asked.

"He's holding up better than I expected, no thanks to the cops showing up at No. 15 about 6:00. His wife saw them—or there's no telling what he'd have done. After they left, he saw the broken lock and knew they'd gone inside. He got so nervous that his wife got it out of him."

"What will she do?"

"Nothing—why would she? Gustav's looking at a fine payday and, if the word got out, we'd all end up in prison, or worse."

Frowning at the unwelcome prospect, Sonny asked, "Is that all?"

"No!" Emil answered, smiling wickedly. "A couple of hours later a truck pulled up with more cops, and they left with the crates."

"Hmm," Sonny hummed approvingly.

"Ja. It puts an end to Braun and his buddies," Emil surmised.

"So why this morning, of all mornings?" Sonny asked, echoing one of the four Seder questions.

Emil shrugged. "Who the hell knows? Braun heard the rumors and got spooked. Then Willy turned up, and that sent him over the top. But shooting twice in broad daylight?" He shook his head in bewilderment. "I figured Putzy and the other one . . ."

"Reinhard," Sonny supplied the name.

" . . . would at least have tried to clean the place out."

"Won't the cops talk to everyone in the building?" Sonny asked.

"I warned Gustav to be ready. All he has to do is play dumb and tell them what he saw, not give it a second thought. Hell, they were cops."

"And his wife?" Sonny asked.

"She's more together than he is."

"Good. Cops probably found our entry hole, but that won't make any sense to them unless they find the safe," Sonny speculated.

"Or unless someone saw us on the roof," Emil added. "And nothing can be done about it now."

Sonny thought about the kid in the window.

19

Naked in death upon an unknown shore . . .
—Virgil

Polly's work with Karl meant spending more time at No. 53, and she was there when Willy arrived. She helped the doctor remove the bullet and stayed in the room to watch him. When the doctor reexamined Willy in the morning, Polly was there too. Willy hadn't regained consciousness, and the doctor explained that without a massive blood transfusion there was little hope.

Polly stayed anyway, putting cold compresses on his forehead. She watched his labored chest rise and fall, then heard something terribly wrong. She brought a glass of water to his lips, recoiled, and dropped the glass to the floor.

"No!"

Willy's chest was still as stone, his face a serene mask. Polly hesitantly reached for his hand. It was still warm, so she felt for a pulse. Moving her finger along his wrist, she searched for a beat but couldn't find one. Slowly releasing his hand, she backed away and began to cry. She'd never been this close to death . . .

Otto and Sonny wrapped Willy's body in a bed sheet, then in a canvas tarp, and carried it to the cellar. That Willy should lie in a dank little space below the house awaiting burial seemed appropriate. Without a wife, parent, or child to console, they had no one to notify. Their little group was all he had.

Willy's death marked their first casualty in the war against the Third Reich; he was a martyr, their martyr. After suffering mightily, he had ignored the risks and provided shelter to Helmut Dix, Otto, and others. Willy had performed when it mattered most.

Now guilt, that familiar feeling, gnawed at Otto as he was pulled down memory lane. He hadn't taken Willy seriously. He'd been impatient and disrespectful. He'd leaned against a lamppost, sucking on a fucking cigarette, watching his comrades in shackles, another gunned down in a subway station.

Sonny slumped on the kitchen table, head resting on his arms, and cried for Willy, then for Uncle Simon, for himself. Willy's pain and the shock of his sudden death were awful reminders of Emil's warning that anything could go wrong. Sonny measured Willy's death against the worth of their escape, feeling only hollowness in their success. Was life so cheap? He wanted to scream: "How could Willy die for the greed of slimy cops and a fat block warden?" He hadn't been ready for this.

Work had ceased in the hours Willy lay in the cellar. They simply played their parts in a surreal play—nothing mattered, death permeated all. Willy's blood-caked jacket, his warning to them at No. 15, the bullet on the kitchen table—all that was real, but it made no sense. That the end of Willy's brave act was to protect the rest of them made his sacrifice a heavy burden. His death drew each of them to the realization of mortality—to what it meant for them to live in Nazi Germany.

Karl came into the kitchen, then Polly, then Frau Moltke. All knew the circumstances leading to Willy's death, and they didn't judge—or at least they said nothing. There was only silence until Otto muttered in anguish, "Are we worth it?"

No one responded. Sonny's thoughts were elsewhere. He suddenly got to his feet and said, "I've got to tell Emil."

Before he got to the door, Karl stopped him. "Sonny, wait. There's something we need to think about." They looked at him, expectant. "Willy's got to be buried."

Sonny, his coat half on, turned from the door and looked at Karl, then to Otto, to the cellar door. Nodding, he returned to the table. They couldn't call an undertaker, and no one in the house had disposed of a body before. They silently pondered the dilemma, repressing their thoughts until someone could find an answer. Finally one came—from the practical Frau Moltke, wiping her hands on her apron as she spoke to Karl.

"Willy is resting in the cellar, and that's where we shall bury him."

So Willy was entombed below No. 53 Stuttgarter Strasse. Late that day, after the final shovelfuls of dirt dropped onto his shallow grave, everyone but Joseph, who stayed away for security reasons, assembled in the front room to pay respect to Willy.

Sonny, Otto, Emil, Mischa, Karl, Polly, Dix, Alfred, and Frau Moltke stood uncomfortably, waiting for someone to begin, until finally Otto said, "I don't know if Willy was a Christian—or anything other than a Communist."

"I'm pretty sure he wasn't Jewish," Sonny dryly noted.

Then they spoke in no particular order, one taking a turn when another finished, saying a few words, a prayer, a remembered incident. Joseph's short note, read by Sonny, captured their feelings: "Willy died a martyr and a hero. Though there will be no epitaph or public grave or memorial, he will live forever in our hearts."

The mourners poured out some brandy and toasted Willy's short life, vowing to continue their work.

War had come before any of them were ready. What if they'd gone in No. 15 the day before, or waited a day, or . . . what? The questions nagged at Sonny, but it was no use—they'd gone in, and Willy had warned them in time to save them, and now he was dead. Willy's few possessions, proof of his existence, would land in the garbage bin when his rent went unpaid. It was up to them to keep his memory alive.

In the following weeks, Willy's death weighed heavily. They worked even harder—finding, meeting, and ferrying Jews and Confessing Church members to the border. Even then, Sonny's mind wandered into dark cul-de-sacs, which sometime led to inopportune silence. He met with a young couple in a hidden corner of Spandauer Vorstadt to provide final instructions on their departure. While he was explaining, he imagined Willy's voice from the alley behind No. 15, interrupting. Sonny jumped, almost ran.

The startled young woman, her eyes wide, asked, "What's wrong?"

"Nothing," Sonny lied, then finished his spiel.

A more positive consequence of Willy's death was a growing alliance—Karl's cell and Sonny's band of smugglers both made Stuttgarter

Strasse the heart of their operations. From the outset, Karl's help had been critical to Sonny's operation, and in the hours after Willy was shot, his assistance proved necessary again. Sonny had kept his end of the bargain by supplying Karl with forged documents and a pipeline. Both groups aimed to move as many vulnerable people out of Germany as they could. They complemented one another while continuing to operate independently.

Sonny's beloved warehouse had become toxic. Ownership passed to a Nazi crony, slowly forcing the Jewish vendors out of business. If the Gestapo was looking for Sonny, they'd look there—it was risky, even foolhardy, to use the warehouse after the burglary, and they wouldn't do it again. And with SA gangs increasing their harassment and bullying of Jewish neighborhoods in the Mitte, it was only natural that No. 53 Stuttgarter Strasse became the operation's base. Sonny and Otto spent more and more time there, leaving Joseph to work in peace.

Emil's remaining task was to dump all the loot on the market. To accomplish that, he spent a long day looking for Johnny of the late Katakombe and the even later Pink Slipper. Rumor suggested that Johnny had opened a tavern, keeping his hands in the game. After several time-consuming false starts, Emil tracked him down near Savigny Platz in the West End.

The Dove was a tavern on Pestalozzi Strasse. Emil found Johnny there late the next day. It was a comfortable little place—with a regular clientele that generated some cash—a good front for Johnny's fencing operation.

Over shots of whiskey, the two acquaintances talked old times, got up to speed. Having left the game behind, Emil needed an update on the market. Johnny was more than happy to accommodate: "The main problem for everyone is that the market is flooded, and that means depressed prices. With so many people desperate to emigrate, needing to raise cash, selling antiques, jewelry, porcelain, gemstones, to finance their escape, it's a buyers' market."

Emil didn't like hearing that conditions weren't favorable for the sale of the loot, but what Johnny said made sense. And, what Emil had to sell created another issue—too much merchandise for one man to fence alone.

"I need associates," Johnny said. "Otherwise, I could leave a trail. And more vendors enlarge the market. But I'll need a bigger cut to satisfy my subcontractors."

Emil was reluctant, but he understood. What made the deal possible was their mutual trust, and after some haggling over percentages, they shook on it. Each got less than he wanted, but both were satisfied. They arranged for delivery, and just before midnight the next day, Emil, Otto, and Sonny met at the Dove, each carrying a satchel.

Sonny hadn't seen Johnny for some years. Otto had never met him, though he remembered the name from the Pink Slipper bombing. He wisely said nothing. Johnny cautioned that it might take several weeks to unload the merchandise. So be it.

Standing behind the bar, Johnny poured what they wanted to drink, on the house. To Sonny, he looked the same as ever, just a little older. They toasted their enterprise, then talked about No. 15 Thiemann Strasse—and Willy. Johnny was sympathetic, but they had known the risks going in, and in the end it was just business. While for Emil that was true, Sonny and Otto couldn't separate their personal concerns from those of the operation. They weren't professional criminals.

Finally, they said good night and left through the back door.

Karl had invited Dix to stay at No. 53 to await the arrival of his family and their subsequent departure for Belgium. Sonny had returned the American documents, with thanks from Joseph. Now Dix roamed the house like a manic cat, his impatience wearing heavily on Frau Moltke, Polly, and Karl. Though less disagreeable than he'd been earlier, Dix had an innate capacity to annoy. But everyone appreciated what he'd brought to the operation, so they endured his antics with more tolerance than they might have otherwise. If Karl regretted his invitation to Dix, he never said so.

Almost two weeks after they had made the deal, Emil heard from Johnny. It was done. Emil collected the cash for the goods, and with everyone present but Joseph, he dispersed it among the operators. After giving Dix his one-third share, Emil paid Joseph, Emil, Mischa, Otto, and Sonny equally. In view of Karl's contributions, the use of the safe house, and future consideration, they agreed to cut him in on Willy's piece. Emil took a smaller but substantial share for Gustav. Finally, they set aside a sum to finance their future operations.

The death of their comrade cast a shadow over the satisfaction they found in the payoff. Dix deeply regretted what the execution of his plan had wrought, but nobody blamed him—why would they? While he grieved admittedly less than the others, he had reason to be optimistic. Within days, he'd reunite with his wife Grete, his nineteen-year-old daughter Mina, and his father–in-law Peter Cohn.

Grete had had five years, plenty of time to prepare, but still she didn't feel ready. Sitting on the bed, she looked back on her life—to the days Helmut Dix was on top, before he took flight. She had graciously accepted the commotion and tumult that went with being the wife of a high-level political operative, not to mention Thälmann's right-hand man. And why not? She'd led a comfortable existence, one commensurate with Helmut's position.

Gazing at her reflection in the mirror, she recognized that sadness and age had taken their toll. Anxiety had wrinkled the corners of her eyes and the area around her mouth. Yet she remained a handsome woman, her once fine features now a little softer. Long since having pushed politics from her mind, she nevertheless cursed them all—Thälmann, the KPD, the Nazis, and the failure of the Republic in taking her husband, for what that had meant in their lives.

As if it were yesterday, Grete remembered 3 March 1933 . . . They were at home that evening when the telephone rang.

"Who could it be this time of night?" Helmut had sighed, risen, and stretched his legs, before answering.

Grete heard half his conversation: "When . . . How do you know? . . . Thank you." Afraid to move, she heard the clunk of the telephone handset, saw Helmut turn ashen, as if the hangman had called.

"A comrade in panic." Helmut was dazed, his voice disconnected. "Did not say how he knew . . . no time . . . you must run . . . Gestapo . . ."

"Now?" Her voice was shrill.

"'It was Horstman. He said, 'Thälmann and the others were arrested. Run!' Then the line went dead."

"How do you know it's true?"

"Horstman would not lie, and I cannot take a chance. Anything to avoid arrest." Grabbing his coat, Helmut stuffed money into his pocket, hugged and kissed her, was gone.

Less than five minutes later, a black staff car stopped in front of the building on Agricola Strasse. Three men in uniform came to the flat, demanding to see Helmut Dix. After searching every room—waking Mina, giving them a terrible fright—the men left empty-handed but threatening to return.

Ten days later Grete took delivery of an envelope containing a summons for Frau Grete Dix to appear at the Charlottenburger Strasse police station on 18 March 1933 at 9 AM. That's all it said, but its purpose was obvious. Rather than worry Mina, Grete said nothing of the summons, just sent her to school as usual. When she sought the counsel of her father, he advised her to tell the truth—she knew nothing of Helmut's whereabouts. She swore her father to secrecy, rejecting his offer to go with her to the police station. She would make the distasteful journey alone.

At the police station, Grete handed the summons to a desk sergeant. "Follow me," he said and led her into a bare, windowless room containing nothing but a table and two chairs. "Wait." He pointed to the hard wooden chair.

She sat and stared at the blank concrete-block walls. Clinging to one was a photograph of the somber Führer; she avoided it by looking down at her hands, clasped tightly on her lap, struggling to hold fear at bay. She thought of the mischief that must already have been done in this room.

The door suddenly opened. Grete's head jerked toward a tall officer in plain clothes. He sat in the chair across the wood table and stared for too long without blinking. He had a big mole on his cheek. Without introduction, he peppered her with questions, one upon the other. Grete had barely enough time to answer one when he was on to the next, scribbling notes. His glare never wavered, though he wasn't rude—or polite either, for that matter. After a few minutes, Grete realized in his pattern the attempt to trip her, to make her give Helmut up.

"Where has he gone? Where did you meet after he left? Who would harbor your husband? What arrangements have you made for joining him?" And so on until she was exhausted.

After something less than an hour, he stopped. His eyes narrowed, and his face twisted into a sneer. "Your husband is an enemy of the Reich and must report for questioning. If he should make contact, you must inform us immediately. Your failure to do so will bring consequences. Do you understand?"

Wringing her hands below the table, Grete nodded weakly. In a barely audible voice she answered, "Yes."

The questioner's blank stare returned; after a minute he dismissed her. Grete was neither surprised nor reassured, only relieved that it was over. She shuddered in the chill air and took the subway home. A second summons never came.

Then one day, nearly six months into her husband's absence, outside the grocery, a man had quietly asked, "Frau Dix?"

Startled, she straightened, losing the grip on her bag. The stranger prevented the groceries from falling, and said, "Don't be alarmed. I'm an emissary from your husband." Calmed by his words, she nodded. Extending his hand in introduction, he passed a folded paper, whispering, "From Helmut. Return here tomorrow, same time." When she looked up from her closed hand, he was already walking away.

Back in the flat, she hungrily read the note, then read it again: "I am fine and miss you more than you can ever know. Trust the man who delivered the note. We will be reunited soon. Love, Helmut." Overjoyed at receiving some word, at knowing Helmut was okay, she set about writing a return note to give the stranger the next day.

However inadequate, their exchange evolved into a system of communication—where before there had been none. Grete assumed that Helmut had some plan for reunion, but nearly five years went by with only cryptic messages. Her hopes had begun to wane. She knew that if Helmut returned to the flat, he'd be walking into a trap. Their unctuous, occasionally civil, insincere neighbor downstairs was an informant; he feigned obsequiousness. Rebuffed when inviting confidences, he became cold and hostile. Helmut had known he was a Nazi—not for ideology or principle but for expedience and self-promotion.

"What a terrible disappointment for you, Herr Dix," he had ventured when they ran into each other in the hallway after Hitler's rise to power. His mocking sympathy came with a self-satisfied smirk: "I expect that you'll be leaving with your family for Moscow, now that real Germans are in power." His words oozed like refuse leaking from a sewer. Then he smiled, revealing his short, yellow teeth. Helmut had warned Grete to be wary—a man like that would watch and listen, report any irregularity.

After Helmut left, Grete spent most of her time in the Tiergarten flat, surrounded by antiques, fine china, and her mother's linens. Those objects, while a comfort, were also a constant reminder of what she'd lost. She was afraid of the world outside, of the forces that had compelled her husband to flee. She was prone to sudden fits of sobbing. Feeling captive in her home, she knew her life was less difficult than that of others . . . She still enjoyed the company of her daughter, Mina—lovely and intelligent if a bit headstrong—and of her steady father.

Only fourteen years old when her father fled, Mina had understood what his disappearance meant. An only child, she spent much time in the company of adults, enjoying their intelligent conversation more than silly adolescent games. Consequently, she was both spoiled by adult attention and more mature than others girls her age. Her father had taught her to camouflage her thoughts and feelings: "Never give anything away; never let the opposition know what you are thinking. A politician wearing his emotions on his sleeve courts defeat."

After the Gestapo finished their clumsy search and stormed from the flat, Mina saw her mother on the verge of collapse. Grete tried to explain but could not do it through her anguish. Terrified, Mina had shown remarkable poise in comforting her mother . . .

Outwardly, Mina's life had progressed normally—she attended school, performing well enough to please her teachers and her mother. At times she seemed distracted, even recalcitrant. Reticent about sharing thoughts with her mother and grandfather, Mina silently endured her loss. Despite her maturity, she lacked the experience to reconcile her own pain at her father's absence with her mother's present needs.

Both Grete and Mina were ill equipped for the roles foisted upon them. But in a stroke of youthful insight, Mina suggested her grandfather move into the flat.

Recently having lost his wife, Peter Cohn jumped at the invitation that came shortly after Helmut's disappearance. Robust and slightly balding at sixty-five years, Peter was a retired lawyer with a thick mustache that had tickled Mina when she was a child. He appreciated his relatively prosperous, middle-class life—before the death of his beloved Claudia—one moment vital, in the next inexplicably gone.

Like his daughter and granddaughter, Peter filled the empty space of his loss with the companionship of his new flat mates. After struggling for a while through their separate emotional deserts, they found support and understanding in each other. Sharing the large flat on Agricola Strasse, they took pleasure in providing one another the solace of a receptive ear, breaching the earlier, inevitable, family barriers. That their union also helped pay the rent was a bonus.

Mina's best friend was Monica Goldstyn. She lived in a big house around the corner on Solinger Strasse, with too many rooms and a housekeeper who gave them sweets and hot chocolate. Monica lived in such splendor because her father was wealthy, though how he had come to his fortune remained murky.

Mina had once overheard her father say that Herr Goldstyn was a shrewd operator. She took it as a compliment though his tone implied something less than noble. Monica's mother was nice, though remote, keeping busy with society friends. She would give Monica a quick peck on the cheek, Mina a smile, and leave in a cloud of expensive French perfume. Monica spent too much time in the big house with only the housekeeper—and often Mina—for company.

Nearly inseparable, the two girls had shared books, clothes, innermost thoughts, and long walks along the banks of the meandering Spree, through Tiergarten Park, at least when it was warm. Knowing that both of Monica's parents and Mina's grandfather were Jewish brought a greater connection. The two girls felt related in some way. None of that had mattered before the collapse of the Republic—but after the Nazis came to power, it mattered a great deal.

At fifteen, Mina had shed her awkward adolescence; suddenly she was a striking young woman with disquieting poise—she'd overheard her mother describing her that way to her grandfather. Grete worried that Mina's blossoming body would attract hormone-addled schoolboys. But she needn't have worried. Mina's affected aloofness sent the boys to more welcoming quarry.

Schoolwork came easily, and Mina excelled, but teachers who had once praised her work suddenly refused to acknowledge it—an unkind punishment for her father's political sins. Commendation ceased, though she continued to perform at a high level. One day, a sympathetic teacher quietly handed Mina a note for her mother, imploring her not to say a word to anyone. If Mina was concerned, she did not show it in handing the note to her mother. Chewing on her lip, she asked. "What does it say?"

Her mother frowned. "You're on a list of students no longer eligible for prizes or recognition."

Mina shrugged. "They can all go to hell! I didn't need their petty honors. Let them punish me for being Helmut Dix's daughter—I'll learn in spite of them." She took solace in not being alone—the same misfortune had fallen on Monica and all the other Jewish students.

That same autumn, Mina had arrived home from school and seen her mother and grandfather in earnest conversation. Fearing bad news concerning her father, she asked, "What happened?"

Peter and Grete hadn't noticed Mina's arrival; now they stopped talking. Her grandfather's face darkened, and his voice became formal: "I just obtained the copy of a new edict—'The Law for the Protection of German Blood and Honor.' It defines who is a Jew." Then he cited the definitions, as well as the prohibition on intermarriage and intercourse between Jews and Aryans.

Understanding only bits and pieces through the legalese, Mina asked, "What does it mean for us?"

Clearing his throat, her grandfather explained, "With one Jewish grandparent, you are a second-degree *mischlinge*; your mother is a first-degree mischlinge; and I, of course, am a full Jew, as all my grandparents were Jewish."

Mina knew the word *mischlinge,* or mongrel—she'd seen bullies chase a poor boy around the schoolyard, barking the term until a teacher stopped them. Now, putting her hands over her ears, she ran from the flat. She needed Monica, her last true friend in the world.

Running up the steps to the Goldstyns' front door, Mina's eyes stung from tears of rage. Catching her breath, she saw Monica's parents through the big front-parlor window, listening to a man talking, gesturing. She shrugged off the scene—it had nothing to do with her—and rang the bell. When Heidi opened the door, Mina ran down the hall, up the stairs, and into Monica's room, to embrace her friend. Mina told her what her grandfather had read, how awful everything was. She hated Germany, she missed her father terribly, and she wept.

Monica tried telling Mina that she already knew of the law, but she couldn't, and she wept too. They cried until their cheeks stung and their throats went dry and Monica got the hiccups. Words refused to come, her hiccups worsened, and they began to laugh—suddenly it wasn't so bad after all.

Then Mina noticed some clothes on the bed, the suitcases on the floor. Monica averted her gaze. "That man in the parlor is my father's lawyer," she said. "He's explaining the new law." Her eyes widened. "Come with me on a new adventure! It will be nothing like Tiergarten Park—that's familiar as an old shoe."

Monica was off on some crazy tangent, and Mina stiffened, confused. Friends were supposed to talk this out together, like the time that new teacher with the Nazi armband had scolded them for always having the correct answers: "You Jews think you are so clever." When Mina protested that she wasn't Jewish, he sneered, "We know who your father is."

Monica put a hand on Mina's. "The lawyer is getting papers for us to leave Germany. It's too terrible to stay. Anyway, I don't have a choice." Her face contorted as she searched for words that weren't there.

In Mina's agitated state, what should have been apparent to her obviously was not.

"Leaving a friend is unthinkable," Monica moaned, throwing the window open. "But staying in Germany with these laws, whatever they're called, would be idiotic and dangerous." She parroted her parents' words. Grasping Mina's hands, she begged, "Come with me to England, maybe to America."

Mina pulled her hands away. "Leaving? What about us?" Not again, she thought. Her father, her grandmother, now her best and only real friend! She felt the breeze become a gale, ripping off her clothes, leaving her naked and shivering. Friendships weren't supposed to end like this! The world was conspiring against her . . .

In two days the Goldstyns would go, leaving Mina friendless. She and Monica met the next day, made tearful farewells, hugged, pretending they would see each other again. Anything was possible, they agreed—now even Professor Einstein was in America! So they talked, as if it weren't final. Would each remember the other on that day, more than on the days before? Would their fun, their innocence, be lost in the haze of old memory? Would their love and shared experience survive? New memories would displace the old, and so history was made.

Having lost so much, Mina had developed a sort of recklessness merged with the notion that nothing was permanent. What she held dear simply would be taken from her. Small, individually insignificant actions—coming home late, talking back to her mother, occasionally skipping school—together became a pattern, a new way of being.

What had frightened Grete though, was her daughter's declaration, said almost in passing: "I'm going to find father. He's out there." Mina had heard rumors of an underground, and she'd figure it out. She would no longer sit idly by.

Grete reread the note: "Grete, Alexanderplatz, near Tietz by Viktoria tomorrow at 4 with grocery cart—Mina, Zoo Station clock tomorrow at 4 hold gloves in right hand—Peter, Tiergarten east side Floraplatz tomorrow at 4 carry a briefcase."

Staring at the scrap of paper, Grete thought about the waiting, the loneliness, the fear—it had finally come to this. She wept . . . But there was so much left to do! She jumped to her feet, then stopped—well, what? There was nothing to pack, just a few undergarments, a bar of soap, a toothbrush, and other small items in her purse, but there'd be no luggage. She'd wear something simple, several favorite pieces of jewelry, and a warm jacket and leave the rest behind. What were antiques, linens, dishes, even photos, in light of a family reunion, freedom?"

The note had come in a small envelope with three identity cards: Katerina and Bridgette Nielsen—wife and daughter of Hans Nielsen, though she didn't know his name yet—and John Frick. Her father hadn't thought he'd need a new identity, but if the Gestapo had all of Helmut Dix's relatives on their list, why take a chance?

Gripping the note, glad for the chance to start a new life, Grete thought she should be happy, but she only felt relieved that her long wait was over. Perhaps she was in shock—or simply overwhelmed by what might lay ahead. She thought about the man who had passed along those notes over the years, how she'd been too scared to look into his face. Not until their third or fourth exchange had she stolen a glance and noticed the tic in his eye. He was always the one. Why had it been someone else today? She folded the note, stuck it in her bra, and went to find her father and Mina . . .

Later, at the kitchen table, the three sat lost in thought. They'd memorized their assignments, and the ashes from the note were now a wet blob in the sink.

Mina, after straining to pull free for years, was like a rambunctious colt. Tomorrow everything would change! She could barely contain her excitement at the idea of discarding what she thought of as her cloistered life for a new one. Rumors of the underground were all she'd had, so she imagined a world in which heroic men and women took outlandish risks then retreated to hidden lairs. Eager for reinvention, Mina could be anything she wanted in her dreams.

In five years Mina had come to hate the comfort of their flat—it no longer mattered, especially when so many had so little. It was all just a reminder of the life she had before her father fled, before her grandmother died, before Monica was gone. Tomorrow she'd be hiding underground; she looked forward to meeting the man who had written the note. She smiled, thinking of the threat she'd made in a fit of pique about trying to find her father. Over several weeks she had walked every street in the Mitte or so it seemed, searching every face. Finally, with no idea where else to look, she gave up—much to her mother's relief.

But Mina hadn't forgotten her father. She imagined him trapped, like Valjean, in a hellish place, relentlessly pursued by a Nazi Javert. What exactly had he done to deserve banishment? Being a Communist apparently was enough for those beasts coming to power. Thälmann—Uncle Ernst she'd called him as a child—was likely now in prison—or dead. But there'd been millions of KPD supporters. Surely some had remained loyal enough—like the man who passed the note—to help her father. Mina closed her eyes to imagine a different world.

Closing the door for the last time would be a celebration. She would dance down the corridor, making obscene gestures toward the Nazi ass downstairs, and run onto the street, free. Just like—she searched for the right simile—Franz Biberkopf leaving Tegel Prison. She did not remember or care how it had ended for the hero of *Berlin Alexanderplatz* . . .

Peter ruminated too. Over the years since he'd moved in with Grete and Mina, they had rarely talked of leaving—they couldn't without Helmut—but he'd often asked "What if?" He thought of Claudia. How he wished she were alive, could be with him now! He sighed in frustration, but he was thankful that he and the two people dearest to him now would soon be free . . .

The next day Grete kissed Mina on the cheek and left the flat, pulling her small grocery cart. Passing the informant's flat, she smiled pleasantly at his door, hoping he would watch her walk down Agricola Strasse. Moments later, Mina put on her coat and walked out the rear door, gloves in hand. Forgetting the unctuous neighbor, she ran, cutting through to the next street toward the zoo. Peter had gone earlier—he had a stop to make on his way to the rendezvous . . .

Appearing to be simply a housewife with a few groceries in her cart, Grete stood in the late afternoon shadow of the massive sculpture of the goddess Viktoria. She ignored the traffic, the people passing, and the pigeons attracted like magnets to the public square. She glanced at her watch: it was 3:45. She smiled, thinking of her reunion with Mina, her father, Helmut.

"Good afternoon," came an unfamiliar voice at her elbow.

Sonny placed a hand in the small of her back. "Frau Nielsen, please come with me." Grocery cart abandoned, they walked at a comfortable pace across the plaza to the subway entrance . . .

Meanwhile, Peter walked in a slow arc along the east side of Floraplatz, in the shadow of Tuaillon's Amazon on horseback, surrounded by glorious bronze animals overlooking the pond. He'd miss the lovely parks and monuments but nothing else. He was neither expectant nor fearful. Since the death of his dear Claudia and during the wait for his son-in-law to surface, he'd become stoic. With little percentage in succumbing to grief, he'd chosen the comfort of his daughter and hers.

Peter had struck a Faustian bargain, sans the devil—joy must wait until his family was out of Germany. In the meantime, he'd kept his daughter and granddaughter safe—or they'd kept him. Thus far it had worked. The two women were healthy, he moderately so. On the brink of freedom, he began to contemplate their future.

On the way to his rendezvous, Peter detoured to the Jewish cemetery in Weissensee to bid Claudia farewell. Grete had pleaded with him not to go. It wasn't safe, she said. But he could not wave his wife goodbye from a street corner. He had to go.

Walking briskly past the Great War memorial and the mausoleums, he ignored the words "Death to Jews" painted on the sides of the desecrated headstones. Claudia's spirit did not inhabit this place—Peter didn't believe in such things—but her physical resting place was a point of reference in a chapter that needed closure. His knees groaned as he slowly knelt, put his fingers to his lips, and placed a kiss on the stone that bore her name. He closed his eyes, picturing his young bride, and whispered, "I love you." With a grunt, he got to his feet and left the cemetery.

He waited fifteen minutes at the appointed place, clutching the briefcase, until a man approached him from Flora Allee, his strong and purposeful gait signaling his youth. Peter waited until the young man faced him, saying, "Herr Cohn, my name is Karl. Please come with me."

Peter nodded. "It's John Frick."

. . . Mina, arriving five minutes early, watched the Zoo Station's busy entrance from across the street, scouring the faces. Sure her contact would be a man, she tried to guess which one. Good luck, she thought, then glanced at the clock and crossed the busy street, to stand at the entrance, gloves displayed. The excitement of the moment coursed through her in a shiver. Across the street a man seemed to meet her gaze, but he looked away when someone touched his shoulder, and they both walked away.

Then her eyes met those of a man approaching from her left, but she was used to men looking at her. He averted his eyes, but as he passed, she noticed a scar on his cheek. He was stocky, of average height, his hands stuffed into the pockets of a leather jacket. No, he had ignored her, so she shrugged and looked the other way.

A hand touched her arm: "Miss Nielsen, please come with me."

She turned to see the scar again, and to smile at how wrong she had been: "I'd love to."

20

Beauty like hers is genius.
—Dante Gabriel Rossetti

Otto returned Mina's smile, guided her into the station, and bought two tickets. Leading her onto the platform, he made sure that dozens of people stood between them and the policeman at the opposite end. Bending forward as a lover might, he whispered into her ear, "My name's Otto. Were you followed?"

Mina felt the warmth of his breath on her temple and glanced at Otto from the corner of her eye. She shook her head and said, "No, they stopped following me long ago. You learn to play the game."

"It's not a game."

Mina flushed, tried to say something, but the clatter of the incoming train drowned out her words. She closed her mouth and shrugged. Otto stared at her crimson lips, trying to read them as they moved without sound, and shook his head.

In the half-empty car, Mina fought the urge to explain herself or at least ask where they were going. But she didn't, and he said nothing. After fifteen minutes, the train slowed, and Otto nodded, got to his feet, taking Mina's arm.

The sign read Neukölln—she'd been there once, with her father when she was a girl. All she remembered was the shabbiness, how poor the people had seemed, so different from her neighborhood. From what she could tell, it hadn't changed. Her escort fit in perfectly with the unkempt, hungry look of the people there. He kept glancing over his shoulder, changing direction. Hurrying to keep pace, Mina felt flushed and breathless.

"Why do we have to walk so fast?"

"Oh. Sorry." Otto slowed.

Being cautious was nothing new, Mina thought, but this cloak-and-dagger act was something else. Hungering to know more about him, the organization, and what her father must have endured, she decided to make amends. "Listen," she blurted, her command drawing his eyes to her. "What I said—about this being a game—didn't come out right."

"Don't worry about it," Otto answered, without taking an eye off her. "Experience tells me to be cautious. You never know who's standing nearby. I've seen too much to be cavalier."

"Still, I had no right to call it a game. What my mother and I went through is nothing like what you and my father have endured."

"Like your father, I have survived." His head moved in a slow arc as he reached the corner. "You will understand."

"I'm usually not this shallow." Mina flushed again and shook her head, displeased with her behavior. "Thank you for being patient."

Otto nodded, but his eyes were on the path ahead.

"How long have you known my father?"

"Not long—I knew of him from the old days. We're almost there."

"I . . . don't know anything." Mina admitted haltingly, her confidence eroding. "What I mean is, I'm completely in the dark about my father, what you do, what's going to happen. And I'm a little frightened."

Otto stopped to face Mina, then said, "You should be. But in a few days you'll be gone, and all this will be a memory. I was scared for so long I didn't know what it was like not to be." He changed his tone, not wanting to make her more afraid than she was already. "A friend once told me that a little fear focuses your attention—that's a good thing, don't you think?"

"You're just saying that to make me feel better."

"Yes," he admitted, smiling for the second time. "But it's true."

Mina liked his smile—it changed his face, made it softer. Did he find it hard to laugh, to enjoy life? Then she felt foolish at such a frivolous thought. She had no idea of the hardships that men like Otto—and her father—endured to stay alive. She feared being in over her head—a new experience—and threw up her hands in frustration. Then she ran to catch up with him.

He slowed at the sound of her footsteps, turning when she was beside him. He couldn't ignore that she was easy to look at—her vitality flushed a pretty pink, her Aryan features perfect for Nazi propaganda. He laughed at the delicious irony.

"Are you laughing at me?"

"No. At the craziness of it all." That was true as far as it went.

"You have some explaining to do," Mina said sharply.

It was a long time since Otto had been with a woman—he shook the thought from his mind. Not with Dix's daughter! And she'd be gone in a day or two, anyway.

"Ja. I look forward to explaining," he answered, suddenly sheepish. With effort, he broke eye contact, thinking her mother must be a handsome woman.

They walked in silence onto Thiemann Strasse. The police sign was gone and the boards had been removed from the windows, though the door to No. 15 was still padlocked. There were plans for the old KPD office other than its storage of twice-stolen loot. "Over there," Otto pointed, "that's an old KPD office, where I first saw your father. It's been off limits, locked up tight for five years." His voice broke slightly.

Mina gave the building a cursory look—it seemed just one of several shabby structures—then back at Otto, but she said nothing. In several minutes they turned on Stuttgarter Strasse and into the alley. Otto knocked on the door. She heard a woman's voice.

"Who is it?"

"Two dear old friends."

Two eyes peered at them, the door opened a crack, and the woman let them in. "One can't be too sure," she said cheerfully.

After exchanging introductions with Mina, Frau Moltke took her upstairs—to be with both parents again . . .

Upon the successful delivery of Grete and Peter, Karl had told Sonny they needed to talk. Now Karl led him to the room where Willy had lain, closed the door, and got straight to the point.

"Polly's been a regular fixture here, helping Frau Moltke and me with other matters. I know it's over with you and Polly, but I don't want her presence to be an obstacle." Karl's voice gave nothing away.

Sonny bit his lip to keep from laughing—Karl could have been saying the wall was white. Polly's presence was obvious. Had Sonny been surprised to find his former lover ministering to Willy? Of course! But what, exactly, was she doing at No. 53? His search of Karl's face provided no answer. He didn't expect one.

"Yes. Polly and I are . . ." Sonny hesitated with a sudden emotion he'd long thought dead. He took a deep breath and finished, somewhat disingenuously, " . . . are over and done. You needn't worry. I have no interest in creating a rift."

Karl nodded. "Polly is here because she wants to help."

Sonny waited—there had to be more—but nothing came. Karl would have to tell him in his own time. They returned to the kitchen where Polly and Otto were talking. Frau Moltke was making dinner.

"Hello, Sonny," said Polly.

Suddenly uncomfortable, Sonny returned her smile. He could tell she was nervous too. They had greeted each other briefly at Willy's memorial service, but with so many people there it had been easy to avoid each other. Now they could not . . .

Dix and his family weren't the only guests at No. 53 Stuttgarter Strasse. Every day, a Confessing Church member or someone else needing help passed through. The guests had to be fed. Polly, Karl, Otto, and Sonny ate in the kitchen while Frau Moltke served her guests in the dining room. Karl and Polly sat together, talking quietly. Sonny heard Polly say she was leaving and would return later. She was just out the door, when Sonny decided to go as well. He caught her in the alley.

"Can I walk with you?"

Polly nodded, managing a tight smile, and they walked in uneasy silence, their eyes focused ahead. Sonny searched for something to say, something that wouldn't sound contrived. All he could think of was "Frau Moltke is a brave soul for opening her home to Karl and his group."

"Yes, she is." Polly was terse. The silence returned; his words had seemed interlopers—to be tolerated, not engaged.

After several minutes Sonny, unable or unwilling to withhold his feelings, blurted, "Imagine my surprise when I first saw you!" His tone was accusatory—out of line—and he knew it. He took a deep breath then exhaled, feeling frustrated and embarrassed. "I'm sorry. That didn't come out right."

"No, it didn't."

"What I meant was, I had no idea you were so involved in Karl's work."

"How could you? We don't see each other any longer. What I do should be a mystery to you . . . as your activities are to me." Polly saw Sonny wince and retreated.

She stopped walking and placed a hand on his arm. "Let's try to be friends, and, if that's not possible, let's at least be cordial. We're both doing the right thing—me with Karl's organization, you with yours." Her green eyes searched his with genuine warmth. "You and I are done. We need to work, so let's act like mature adults."

Of course she was right; the tension receded. Still, Sonny's sudden surge of regret, recrimination, guilt, dissipated only slowly. Neither spoke. History was written—they'd deal with it. She'd said the right thing, and he was relieved.

"Yes," he agreed. "The work is too important . . ."

. . . Mina's reunion with her father was tearful. Afterwards, she left her parents to search the house for Otto. She finally found him after several trips up and down the stairs. Leaning forward, her hands provocatively resting on her hips, she looked at him directly. "There's something about that KPD office you showed me. I want to hear the whole story. My father won't tell me, so you will."

Thrown off balance by the attack, Otto saw Dix's far less pleasing face in hers. Disconcerted, he recovered, then repressed the urge to smile.

"How much do you know?"

"Nothing, except that he retrieved our American documents from an office that's been locked tight since 1933. When I asked how, he refused to say." She took a breath and struck a more demure pose. Then she stepped closer, whispering.

"Listen, I know what you're doing. It's wonderful. I've grown up in the last five years, and now I want to help. But I need to know what it was like for him—and for you." Her eyes never wandered from Otto's. "I had it easy" she continued. "Grandfather took my father's place, and we had a home. The Gestapo let us alone, though we finally figured out that they were using us for bait." She paused, then spoke deliberately, like a shopkeeper counting change. "I need to know what it's all about."

Otto was hypnotized by her stare, unable to tear his eyes from hers. No woman had ever spoken to him like that, especially not one so distractingly attractive, even when she acted like her father. He felt a sudden urge to kiss her.

"Well," she said, "I'm waiting."

Momentarily confused, Otto realized his error. He cleared his throat to keep from laughing. Resistance was useless. He took her by the arm and led her to an empty room. They sat facing each other in darkness softened only by the glow from the streetlight seeping from the edges of the window shade.

"All right," he started. "I'll tell you." His eyes wandered over Mina's shoulder to the bed, distracted by the pleasant possibilities. This clean little room was the perfect place to live . . . He could help around No. 53, stay out of Joseph's way, continue in the enterprise. He'd talk to Karl and Frau Moltke . . .

Mina was looking at him oddly, so he started to explain about Willy at the zoo with her father, their near-disaster with the police. When Mina laughed, he said, "It wasn't funny." Then he told her everything.

When he was done, she walked to the window and raised the shade to look onto the street. "I've spent too much time inside, staring at the walls, looking out of windows in rooms like this," she said peering out.

"Not a room like this one," Otto corrected.

Mina turned her head and said, "A gilded cage is no less a cage." Turning back to the window, she asked, "What should I have done?"

Otto would not judge. "For most of the past five years, I've done little more than hide—a night or two under a bridge, in a flat with an old comrade, in a warehouse cellar, whatever I could manage. Staying free was a full-time job—fear, a constant companion. Still, we're not so different—I've done nothing worthwhile 'til now."

She nodded as if she understood. "Thank you for not judging me." Slowly she raised a hand and flicked her wrist, waving the past away. "All right. Like you, I've wiped the slate clean. So what do I do now?"

"Leave with your mother and father for Belgium. Start a new life."

She frowned and shook her head. "Run away? Now that I have a chance to do something worthwhile?"

"It's dangerous."

"You're still here."

The statement required no answer, but he supplied one: "True. I dreamt endlessly of leaving—that's what kept me going—but I couldn't. Now that I can leave . . ." He shrugged. "I have a new identity. Getting others out gives me something worthwhile to do. Maybe that sounds pretentious, but it's all I have. It's enough."

"It's not."

"What's not?"

"It's not pretentious." Then she asked, "Are you Jewish?"

He shook his head. "No . . . just an old Communist, like your father. I led a cell not far from here, but that's ancient history." He brought it back to her. "Your grandfather is Jewish, another reason to leave."

She turned back to the window and changed the subject. "It couldn't have been easy, the feeling of being relentlessly pursued."

"No," Otto's answer seemed woefully inadequate, so he told her why he'd quit smoking, how he'd left the flat to buy cigarettes and when he returned his comrades were in shackles. "Why was *I* free? Rationally, I understood, but it's taken me years to appreciate how lucky I am." He felt the warmth of her hand on his arm. "Just because I needed a smoke."

Mina's mouth curled at the corners, making her cheeks dimple. "Isn't that reason enough to leave?"

"I suppose it is," he said, barely above a whisper.

"Like you said, I am doubly at risk—a second-degree mischlinge, whose father's a big-time Communist the Nazis would love to put away. So I suppose I should leave as well." She laughed. "It's funny. Like you, now that I can leave, I don't want to."

She pointed to the floor. "When I got here and saw what all of you do . . ." She looked away, swallowed: "I have to stay. The work that you, Sonny, Karl, and Polly all do is so important."

"It's dangerous . . ." He saw her response and changed course. "Have you told your parents?"

Shaking her head, she smiled wryly. "They'll only try to stop me. I'm their only child, and a girl . . ."

"A woman," Otto corrected.

"Yes." Her eyes flashed and met his. "If I were a man . . ."

The Hager and Dix families anxiously awaited departure, their trepidation mounting with the wait. After what happened to Reb Friedman, Mischa's father had agreed to leave. That freed Mischa, and the realization that he'd never equal what he'd done in the aftermath of the Thiemann Strasse burglary spurred his own desire to go. Willy hadn't survived but, thanks to Mischa, he had escaped further torture. Then there was the lure of working with Dix in exile—whatever that might mean. And Sophie . . . Whatever the reasons, Mischa was leaving Germany.

Sophie, happier than Sonny had seen her in years, greeted him at the door. As they hugged, she whispered, "Thank you."

He had come to say goodbye, and after reminiscing about days long past and what lay ahead, Sonny pulled a parcel from inside his jacket and handed it to Mischa. "Give this to your father when you're safely in Belgium. Hide it and don't tell a soul."

Mischa carefully unwrapped the package and saw the yad that Sonny had inadequately described. He was rendered speechless by its beauty.

"Where did you get . . ." Sophie started to ask, then paused, suddenly realizing.

Tears welled in Mischa's eyes as he held the magnificent Torah pointer, its jewel-encrusted handle twinkling like stars come to earth.

"Thank you," he said. "But how do I get it across the border?"

Sonny smiled. "When you reach Aachen and the little café, you'll meet Fritz's cousin Günter. Give the yad to him; he'll pass it to Fritz on one of his trips to Aachen. Once you're in Belgium, the rest is up to you." Sonny hugged them both, kissed Sophie. "See you in Antwerp."

Content to remain in their little room, Helmut and Grete slept together for the first time in five years. Having yearned for one another so long, they met with an awkward hesitancy, soon dissipated into giddiness at their reunion.

Mina envied them the love that had endured their separation. Her own deprivation—of father, grandmother, and best friend, of trust after being spied upon by a neighbor, of security unsullied by the fear of eviction, of the good will of teachers, of political and religious freedom—compounded by the self-centeredness of her youth, made it difficult for her to comprehend the enormity of her mother's loss. More powerful was the feeling that she had simply been abandoned. Mina became a woman shaped by her swirling environment.

Watching her parents in tender embrace opened a window on those years when she was too young to understand. Her father's return reversed the tide, making her feel less alone, and stronger for it.

She knew Karl's rule for all who entered No. 53—to remain within its walls until given the word to leave. Duly warned, she nevertheless chafed at her continuing confinement. While others gladly complied, she pulled at her chains, emboldened by Otto's story. Nothing would keep her inside.

On her second night, after everyone had retreated and the only sound was the creaking of the old house, Mina moved silently from her room. Opening the back door, she slipped into the alley and around the corner onto Stuttgarter Strasse. She would wander the streets of Neukölln, find the canal or the cemetery where the wounded Willy had stopped in his flight from No. 15 . . . it really didn't matter where she went, so long as it was not inside.

As Mina crept down the stairs, Otto paced at the top of the house, unable to sleep but with no one to talk to. At times like these, he missed Joseph's cramped flat. Staring out the window, at nothing in particular but everything at once, he caught some movement, followed a lithe figure from the alley into the street, and knew it was Mina. Grabbing his jacket, he flew down the stairs two at a time and out the door into a light snow. He ran to the street, toward the hazy silhouette he saw ahead. She turned at the sound on the pavement of approaching feet.

At first startled, she quickly recovered when she saw who it was and smiled. "Walk with me." She seemed pleased that he didn't chastise her as they walked side by side. "I'm already sick of being locked up until my parents leave. I'll go mad," she said. She stuck out her tongue, put her hands to her head, and rolled her eyes. "Too much idle conversation and reading. No!"

Otto's laughter spurred her to say more, and she obliged.

"I want to see my new neighborhood. You may as well give me a tour, because I won't return to No. 53 until I'm damn good and ready." She beamed.

Thoroughly charmed, Otto said, "I'd love to." He might as well surrender, he thought. Short of carrying her over his shoulder, he couldn't stop her, fun as that might be. And he could be alone with her this way.

They passed beneath a streetlight onto the Teupitzer Bridge and leaned against the railing, watching the slow black water pass beneath them. In the distance the lights of the railroad yard glistened, as snowflakes like tiny crystals fell softly from the night sky.

"Isn't it pretty?" Mina asked.

Staring at her, he didn't answer.

"What?" she asked.

At a loss for words, Otto shook his head. With sudden yearning, his arms rose like wings about to take flight, then stopped. Standing a foot from him, Mina seemed to know. She said softly, "Don't stop."

And he didn't. After a few minutes, they moved across the bridge, her hand in his, and walked north along the canal. In no particular hurry, they walked farther from No. 53, Otto a willing coconspirator. The night was cold, but not too cold. The snow stopped. The low clouds reflected ambient light, bathing Neukölln in a soft glow.

Otto remembered something she'd said earlier. "What did you mean, until your parents leave?"

Caught off guard, she looked away, covering her mouth with her hand.

"Tell me," he gently goaded.

"All right," she said, standing taller. "I'm not leaving. I'm staying. Like I said, I admire what you do. I'd be abandoning you if I left." She was intense, as if she were practicing the speech she'd give to her parents.

"There's nothing romantic about it . . ." Otto started.

Mina's smile was coquettish. "You mean what happened on the bridge?"

Otto blushed, his face hot. "What I mean is, you can't know what it's like. Fearing the worst can be its own private hell."

"Please," she interrupted. "Don't patronize me. I didn't live it, but I was close enough. Now I need to work. I'm committed and, like you, I don't intend to get caught." Narrowing her eyes, she came at it from another angle. "Well . . . did I misinterpret that kiss on the bridge?"

"No," Otto answered, drawing out the word.

Mina shrugged. "Then we'll have to get to know each other better."

He smiled in spite of himself. "When will you tell your parents?"

"I don't know yet." Tears welled in her eyes as she shook her head.

She'd tell them in her own time, he figured. "Where will you stay?"

"Always the practical one," she teased. "At No. 53—with you, of course." Her laughter echoed in the empty street.

"Are you serious?" he asked. But he knew she was.

"Try and stop me."

Though flattered, he was a little disconcerted.

"Don't worry." She leaned forward and kissed him on the lips.

Otto knew she'd boxed him in, felt a need to think things over. Well, what the hell—why not go with it?

A few minutes later, as they walked across Wildenbruch Bridge, Otto spotted a big black sedan drawing near. He smelled Gestapo. Stopping, he pulled Mina close, held her head in his hands, and locked onto her lips. They held the pose until the sedan passed and longer . . .

"Oh, my. I'll take that as a yes."

"That sedan . . . looked Gestapo," he stammered.

"Never heard that one before."

Two days later, the exodus, as Mischa's father dubbed it, began. Dix would leave first, cross to Plombieres. Mischa and his family would arrive the next day. They'd await the arrival of Grete, Mina, and Peter before leaving for Antwerp.

Sonny wanted to be sure they crossed without trouble, so he made the trip, too, traveling separately. After an uncomfortable night on Günter's floor, he went with Günter to collect Emil and Dix at the railway station.

Driving up to the entrance, they saw Dix pacing back and forth. His deep frown warned of a foul mood.

"What's with him?" Sonny whispered, but before Emil could answer, Dix was in the back seat.

"It's about time," he muttered.

Emil looked at Sonny and rolled his eyes.

"What the hell's going on?" Sonny asked, too anxious to wait for an explanation.

Dix, his eyes on the moving cityscape, spoke to the window. "Mina is not coming, damn it! She is staying in Berlin to help your lot." Once it was out, his anger dissipated into an almost overwhelming sadness.

Sonny had seen them together, heard Mina's comments, but Otto hadn't told him. "Are you sure?"

"Of course, I am—God damn it! Fool girl thinks all this," he said with an all-encompassing wave of his hand, "is a romantic escapade. She has no clue as to the danger."

When Günter stopped at the little café with the blue curtains, Dix jumped out, slammed the car door, and disappeared inside. Emil followed while Günter waited in the car. Sonny hesitated, looking in both directions. Several men walked past the café and a delivery truck was parked nearby, but there was nothing else. It was normal and boring, just as he liked it.

Then he scanned the buildings and saw nothing, no movement, until something familiar registered. Retracing his visual path, he spotted a solitary figure gazing from a window above. A dim recollection . . . Had the old woman always been there? He smiled and raised a hand. She acknowledged him with a nod, slowly raised her right hand and crooked her forefinger, beckoning. Taken aback, Sonny placed his hand on his chest, and she nodded.

"I'll be right back," Sonny called over his shoulder to Emil. "An old woman wants to talk to me."

Emil looked around, saw no one, and turned back to Sonny.

"Up in the window," Sonny said, raising his eyes.

She was following their exchange, and she smiled at Emil. Without returning the smile, he told Sonny to be back in half an hour. Sonny leaned into the car and asked Günter, "You know anyone in that building?" He pointed.

Without looking up from his newspaper, Günter shook his head.

The building may once have been elegant—there was fancy stonework around the front door, and wrought-iron grills, carved woodwork at the entry. Benign neglect had given it a tired look, yet the building exuded a certain charm, and it was clean. Sonny walked quickly past the mailboxes, up to the second floor and the corner flat.

The door opened almost before he knocked onto an impossibly small, elderly woman with gray hair tied back in a bun. Her spine was curved like a question mark, making it difficult for her to look into his face. She moved her head to the side to get a good look at Sonny from the corner of her eye.

"Come in, young man," she ordered in a strong voice. "My body might be failing, but my mind works."

Sonny smiled at the vigor of her welcome and stepped inside. The aroma of lemon wax filled his head. He closed the door and walked into a stage set for a mid-19th-century drama. He suddenly thought of Paul's girlfriend, the actress Jenny Kino—for the first time since January '33. The last time he'd seen her on stage was the night Mischa had turned up, bloody and belligerent, at Paul's flat. He quickly discarded Jenny, to focus on his present hostess.

They were in a large sitting room filled with furniture in vogue about the time the last Kaiser had ascended the throne. The style was the height of Berlin chic in the 1920s. Against the wall was a beautiful, pear-shaped mahogany secretary. The woman shuffled to an easy chair with curved legs and slowly lowered herself onto its soft cushion.

"There. Now I can see you. Sit down, young man."

Sonny sat on the comfortably upholstered sofa with rolled arms. He saw fine Dresden china on the side tables, an ornate gilt frame displaying a handsome couple on the wall. Following his eyes, the woman said, "Those are my parents, and this was their flat. I have lived here nearly all my life. This was once a very nice neighborhood and, on the whole, I have no complaints."

"Yes, very nice," Sonny agreed, trying to figure out why he was there.

Pointing a bony finger at him, she said, "I have seen you before, with others, outside the café."

"Yes," Sonny acknowledged, wondering where this was heading.

"I am an old woman with nothing to do but look out my window. This is my neighborhood—I like to know what is going on," she said, almost defiantly. "Walking is difficult, so I rarely leave the flat. Someone brings groceries and cooks and cleans."

Sonny looked around for someone, and she said, "You may relax. We are alone."

Slightly embarrassed, Sonny said, "You're pretty sharp. What else do you know?"

"I know Aachen is on the border with Belgium. I know that our beloved Führer," her sarcasm was obvious, "and his malignant cohorts are the impetus for thousands of esteemed writers, playwrights, composers, artists, intellectuals, and scientists fleeing in haste. Is that enough?"

He nodded. "Whom of that lot do you miss?"

She closed her eyes and, as if the entire cast appeared, waved a hand. "There are too many, but Brecht, Einstein, and Grosz, to name three. I am sure you can name others."

"We could spend all day with the talent that has left Germany," Sonny agreed. "Is that why you beckoned me here?"

Her short, sweet giggle made her sound years younger. "Well, yes, in part. You remind me of someone." She placed a hand over her mouth, then continued in a different vein.

"I hate war, and just like the last one, this is where the next will be fought." She tapped her finger on the arm of the chair. "My husband died across the border. I never forgave the Kaiser, and I will not forgive Hitler. War is vicious and to be disdained by all civilized people. If my judgment is correct, you agree." Her sadness yielded to anger, but she held it in check. Pointing a finger at him again, she said. "Be careful. I want to see you again."

"I'm always careful," Sonny answered, enjoying her company.

"Good!" Then she introduced herself: "I am Frau Helga Freyer. What is your name, young man?"

"Sonny. Pleased to meet you."

"Sonny? Is that all? A curious name."

"Yes, simple and easy to remember—a childhood nickname—I have come to like it."

"Perhaps convenient in your line of work?" She paused for an answer she knew would not come. "The next time you must stay for tea." Not a question but a command. "Now, I know you must be going."

"Yes," he said. He walked across the room and took her thin hand in his. "Frau Freyer, until next time."

"Goodbye, Sonny. Remember—No. 74 Schiller Strasse."

21

For sufferance is the badge of all our tribe.
You call me misbeliever, cutthroat dog,
And spet upon my Jewish geberdine.
—William Shakespeare

Through spring, summer, and fall the operatives ferried Jews, Confessing Church members, and other opponents of the regime to Belgium in numbers as great as their capacity allowed. Karl's contacts gave Joseph greater access to documents that, well manipulated, meant freedom for a growing number of refugees. Joseph's friends delivered the stamp they had promised, making his task easier and immediately more prolific.

How many the operation could help depended on how many passports and visas Joseph could produce. So far as they knew, none of their clients had been rejected at the border. But the increasing human traffic convinced them of the need to use other border crossings to Belgium . . .

Joseph had only Sonny to contend with in the cramped flat. Otto had moved into No. 53 and was essentially living with Mina, though they kept separate rooms to maintain propriety. Mina kept busy helping Karl, Polly, and Frau Moltke with the flow of humanity passing through on the way to freedom or seeking refuge for a few days.

Otto had tried to convince Mina to leave with her parents, only to be pleased when she ignored him. His warnings steeled her resolve, so he gave it up. For the first time in her life Mina was working and helping people. With so much at stake, her old life—her interest in literature, art, and music—suddenly seemed frivolous.

Otto was falling in love, and he hoped Mina was too. He'd nearly given up on women before she appeared. In the dark days and darker nights underground, he had encountered an occasional coy smile leading to a lustful tryst. Mina was different. Still, he feared her romantic view of the underground would wane or that their ten-year age difference would turn her from him. He saw no evidence of that; rather Mina impressed him with a strength of purpose beyond her years, which pleased him beyond measure.

At a European conference in Munich in September, England and France had averted a crisis by capitulating to Hitler, handing over Czechoslovakia without a fight. British Prime Minister Neville Chamberlain's policy of appeasement meant doing whatever it took—anything to avoid war. And so Sudetenland, an area of Czechoslovakia that was host to many ethnic Germans, became part of Germany. The Czechs weren't even at the table when they were sold down the river.

Joseph had predicted this development after the Anschluss with Austria in March: "As day follows night, Czechoslovakia will be next. Then we'll see what France and England do." His fear that no foreign power would confront Hitler lay at the heart of his uncharacteristic cynicism. That he was right was little consolation.

The mischief with Austria had started as the operators planned the burglary at No. 15 Thiemann Strasse. News of the development careened from bad to worse. The Nazi propaganda machine demanded justice for the seven million abused, downtrodden Germans living in Austria. Clearly, Hitler had designs on the land of his birth—everything else was subterfuge.

Tiny Austria stood no chance for maintaining independence without England's guarantee, but His Majesty's government, in the face of this new crisis, cobbled together a response that—once diplomatic language was stripped away—meant only that, to avert war, it would give up Austria today or another small, middle-European state tomorrow. So be it. Those seeking to avoid German expansion swallowed a cruel lesson in the sacrifice of Austria and Czechoslovakia on an altar of illusory peace . . .

Otto spent many hours hiding out in darkened theaters, watching newsreels of Nazi rallies. The Führer pounded the podium, screaming for expansion, whipping the torch-bearing Nazis into frenzy. Otto had no doubt as to the outcome: Hitler would go to war. The only questions were where and when.

After two crises within six months, Joseph was resigned. "Peace in our time, my ass," he grumbled and, with effort, forced a smile. To Otto and Sonny he said, "Gentlemen, we have work to do. Let's focus on that."

By November 1938, life was so bleak for Germany's Jews that their number had declined by half, to about 250,000. Increasingly isolated, the Jewish community had nowhere to turn but inward—for services, welfare, information—and to groups such as Sonny's for refuge. That a German Jew would consciously decide to remain in Germany was, in his view, madness, the irony of his own situation notwithstanding.

The opportunity to flee appeared in many forms. But for the thousands with few resources, poverty consigned them to limbo. Sonny was glad that, thanks to the success at No. 15, the operation refused no one for an inability to pay. Funds from the burglary helped those in need to the extent they could. Sonny's group and others unknown filled the void for those without money and papers.

Still there were sons and daughters, husbands and wives, who had to abandon members of their families to a diminishing future—or what amounted to no future at all. How could they? And how could they not? Sonny saw their anguish in leaving behind loved ones—usually those too old or sick to travel.

Even now, some Jews obdurately denied their predicament; Sonny found it fatuous and bizarre. After five years of relentless Nazi attacks and stifling decrees, anyone doubting the precarious nature of the Jewish situation had to be in a coma. Scarcely a day passed without another Reb Friedman shorn, a man's hat knocked to the pavement, or far, far worse. Years of cruelty and deprivation punctuated by intervals of neglect, succeeding pogroms mapped in grisly pattern—this was the European Jewish experience, etched or should have been in the memory of every Jew in Germany. Whatever heights Jews might have reached in Germany were long since past. Sonny feared the bottom would be lower yet.

Clients came in a steady stream from Franz and his fellow runners—some were acquaintances, others chance encounters in the way Dix had come through Willy. Still other clients came secondhand—by word of mouth on the street or from satisfied customers. Sonny suspected that letters from distant safe havens sometimes mentioned one of the operators despite their admonitions not to do so. Discovery was their greatest fear; caution guided every move.

Prospective clients always got the same question: "How did you find us?" The answer varied—through someone long gone, through someone who knew Franz from the neighborhood, through some guy in a café in Spandauer Vorstadt. Ultimately, it didn't matter. The operatives weren't naïve, weren't blind to the problems in maintaining secrecy. Their protection—a leaky labyrinth constructed around Otto, Sonny, and Karl—was a fiction. That you couldn't get to them without a runner as go-between had no meaning for anyone who knew one of them and heard a rumor or two.

No buffer could succeed indefinitely; the need to peel back the layers to get to the center was simply their best hope of avoiding detection. Of one thing they were certain—Joseph must be protected. Without him, there was no operation.

How to get papers and whom to trust were thorny questions for the prospective émigré. Agents, as they were called, sold immigration services in Berlin, Cologne, Düsseldorf, Aachen, and other cities and towns along Germany's border with Holland, Belgium, and France. Securing a new life on the other side was possible for those with resources, leaving out those who hadn't any.

Sonny had seen prices at the warehouse market determined by competition among vendors, but the going price of a ticket out of the country did not exist in a market kept secret. Shopping around—comparing prices or the rate of a smuggler's success—was impossible. That put the hopeful émigré at a distinct disadvantage. The price was arbitrary; each group occupied a narrow, jealously guarded place.

Reliability—delivery across the border—was the only measure of success. But there was no way to know whether the guy in a bar in Cologne or the one on the street corner in Scheunenviertel would succeed. Some unsavory agents were only in it for the money, and you had to be prepared for the greedy border guard demanding a share—regardless of the quality of the documents . . .

Sonny met Herman Milberg in the fall of 1938. Crimson and gold leaves fluttered to the ground in the parks and the boulevards of Berlin, though there were few trees in Scheunenviertel or Neukölln. The earlier, chillier nightfall signaled the coming of winter and added to Sonny's growing melancholy. He had met Franz at the little café to go over a list of potential clients, including a fellow previously turned away at the Dutch border. Franz set an appointment for Sonny at the Rosengarten in Tiergarten Park . . .

Sonny stood behind an entrance to the rose garden at several minutes before 6:00. A young man stopped, looked around, then down at his watch, moving from foot to foot. Franz had described Sonny's contact as short, slight of build, dark-haired, a prominent nose. This forlorn fellow fit the bill.

"Herman?"

Startled, the man swung around, faced Sonny, hesitated, then nodded. Sonny smiled, took him by the arm, and silently led him into the barren rose garden. Herman scrutinized the man holding his arm, seeking answers to questions not yet asked.

When they were alone in a quiet corner of the grounds, Herman told Sonny that a guy at the train station had sent him to the spot.

"I had a bad experience with a crooked agent, so I'm leery." As soon as the words came out, he apologized, "I'm sorry, but I can't be burned again."

"I understand," Sonny responded. They arranged a second meeting.

In early afternoon the next day, Sonny and Herman sat in the corner farthest from the door in the nearly empty café. Sonny guessed Herman was in his mid-twenties, but his pale, tightly drawn face and stubble of beard made him appear older. His eyes were red-rimmed from lack of sleep, and he spoke in a whisper, looking from Sonny to the door. It was apparent that Herman had left his innocence at the border. He had a story to tell, and Sonny wanted to hear it.

Both men had grown up in the Mitte—they probably knew people in common, but they skipped over that. Some years earlier, Herman's family had moved to the West End, where his parents still lived on Pestalozzi Strasse . . .

Max, a waiter at the café long before Sonny discovered it, interrupted, took their order, and shuffled away. He returned in minutes with coffee and sweet rolls. Herman waited until Max was gone, then continued, "I learned a hard lesson when a greedy agent deceived me, so I'm distrustful. I was naïve, and I won't be again. This time I have to be sure."

"We provide documents, not empty promises. I'll show you a sample, but first I want to hear your story," Sonny said.

Herman nodded, blinked, and began. "Rumor told me Cologne was the place to find an agent, so that's where I went. It was early autumn, still warm when I left. Getting documents for America, France, Holland—anywhere—was beyond my family's connections, and time was running out. I'm an only child—my mother's too ill to travel—but my parents insisted I leave before it gets worse and Hitler goes to war. Then it would be too late. So with my parent's blessing and what I hoped was enough money to pay an agent, I left for Cologne."

He paused, brought the coffee cup to his lips, and drank. "I found lodging with a family in the Jewish quarter. The man told me about a Jewish nightclub where I could find an agent."

Several times Sonny had to ask Herman to repeat something he said because he spoke too softly or quickly. As the tenor of Herman's story changed, his features darkened. He rubbed his hands together, pulling at the fingers of his left hand, then his right. Distracted by Herman's fidgeting, Sonny asked him to stop, drink some coffee, try to relax. He nodded encouragingly, waiting for Herman to meet his gaze.

"Sorry." Herman sat back in his chair, took a deep breath, leaned forward, and drained his cup. "Mind if I smoke?"

Sonny shrugged, so Herman put a cigarette to his lips, fumbled with a match, and lit the cigarette with a trembling hand. Inhaling deeply, he watched two young women walking to the door. After exhaling a white plume, he started talking about other agents, assuming Sonny knew all about them.

Shaking his head, Sonny explained, "I know my own operation but no others. Assume I don't know a thing."

Herman put a finger to his lips, digesting that. He nodded and continued. "After several wrong turns, I finally found the nightclub, hidden in an alley. There wasn't a sign—you had to know it was there. It was early evening, and already there was a crowd of young and old—men and women but mostly men. A small band was playing, and several couples were dancing. That surprised me."

"What surprised you?"

"The band . . ." he answered, and pursed his lips, searching for the right words, " . . . was out of place, incongruous." He nodded as if he liked the way that sounded. "Everyone seemed desperate to buy or sell a way out. But all the noise made it feel like New Year's Eve. False gaiety—I can't tell you how disorienting . . . The room was full of smoke, people were drinking too much, and conversation was difficult because of the music. Someone would laugh or raise a voice—it felt manic. The scene was terribly wrong." After a long drag, he exhaled, coughing. "Sorry," he said absently.

"Never mind," Sonny said. "Keep going."

Herman nodded. "There were too many bodies—even more later—in that small space. A woman with too much perfume made me light-headed. But I settled down and got into the crazy rhythm. There was an undercurrent of expectation dragging everyone along. You know, like being on a conveyor, moving to only one possible outcome. Does that make sense?"

"I think so," Sonny answered. "I'll ask if I don't understand."

"Some people were there to enjoy themselves, others to make a contact, seal a deal for a ticket out. Hell, that's why I was there—departure and renewal. Everyone acted like yesterday didn't matter, and every tomorrow was today." He frowned, then explained, "I mean, only now mattered. Tomorrow might be too late, so you had to get it done today." Then he smiled sheepishly, and said, "I figured that out later. I didn't know what the hell was going on at the time."

Flicking his wrist, he left a jagged trail of smoke. "Everyone seemed equal—I figured that out the first night. Social status was irrelevant because everyone was a refugee in waiting; no one was better than anyone else. The club was a great leveler."

Max appeared—did they want more coffee? They nodded, so he filled their cups and shuffled away.

"Nobody gave a name; there were no introductions," Herman continued. "I can't remember one. But the atmosphere generated talk. I could have been anyone, made up a story—it didn't matter. After half an hour or so, I found an empty seat next to a well-dressed older man—the kind of arrogant ass who doesn't normally talk to someone like me."

Herman forced a brittle laugh. "But he did. He said he was Viennese, repeated it several times, even dropped Freud's name, like he was an old friend." Herman shrugged. "Maybe he was." For the first time a real smile came to his lips. "The old guy was leaving for Brussels to rendezvous with his gentile wife, who was still in Austria. They'd cleverly divorced to avoid confiscation of the family business, which she was selling. Then she would met him, but he was vague. I didn't want to know any of this."

He paused, then: "It was funny, like the sad way circus clowns are funny. This caricature of an upper-middle-class Viennese snob forced into a dingy nightclub, telling a stranger from the Mitte the intimate details of his life . . . sniffing the air disapprovingly, surveying the crowd as if he were somewhere else. That vain old man wanted me to believe he was someone special—he knew Freud, had a prosperous business, was conversant in all manner of human intercourse—sitting in that sleazy place. It's funny now, but it was confusing then. Finally, he was satisfied that he had said enough. He took a drink of his brandy and didn't say another word. I was dismissed, so I excused myself, and someone grabbed my chair. When I glanced back, Herr Vienna was going through the same gestures, probably the same spiel, to his new audience."

Herman went on. "I had a couple drinks at the bar and started seeing people differently, realizing I was more like them than I'd thought. There was a guy standing next to me, about my age, swaying to the music. He'd had a lot to drink. After about ten minutes, he leaned close, said he hadn't seen me before. He told me he was a traveling salesman from Berlin, had been in Cologne for a couple weeks but hadn't made a decision. His money was running out, but he wasn't going to let that keep him from having a good time. 'What decision?' I asked. He seemed to sober up, and he said, 'An agent, what else?' Then he said all agents were jackals—you couldn't trust any of them."

Herman threw up his hands. "Great! That's what I was there for—it scared me. So I asked what he meant. But he just waved his hand, shook his head, wouldn't say anything. I should have heeded his warning."

Sonny watched Herman's lips silently moving. "Then what?"

Regaining the thread of his story, Herman continued. "Ironically, minutes later the salesman pointed into the crowd and whispered in my ear: 'That one over there's an agent—one of any number who say they'll get you over the border if you have the money.' I followed the end of his finger to a man at a table across the room. He had shiny hair; he held a glass in one hand, a cigarette in the other. He was listening to a man in the next chair. I must have stared for more than a minute. Then I asked the salesman if I could trust a guy like that. He said, 'How the hell should I know?'"

Herman laughed and said, "Can you believe that?"

Sonny didn't answer. "So what did you do?"

"Nothing. I was too overwhelmed. Had I made a mistake in going to Cologne? I knew there were no guarantees; I'd gone to take my chances. I knew I had to calm down. So far I had one prospect—that slick-haired guy. I couldn't waste my money drinking, pretending the guy next to me was my best friend, so I left the club to get some fresh air."

Herman continued: "I spent the next day walking around the Jewish quarter, looking for answers. It almost felt normal, standing on a street corner, sitting in a café, talking to people. Some lived in Cologne. Others, like me, were from somewhere else. But everyone wanted out, and the sooner the better. Agents—or their runners—were everywhere, promising I could be in Amsterdam by the end of the week for 300 Reichmarks. One said he could get me good forged papers for 500 Reichmarks. They were carnival hawkers—how the hell could I trust any of them? How could I trust that slick agent? . . . The guy at the station—does he work on commission?"

"No, a salary," Sonny answered.

Herman nodded, then continued his story. "I couldn't decide. The agent at the club or the hawkers on the street? The club's false atmosphere—gaiety over despondence—it wasn't hard to peel back the confidence to find the core of fear. That's why they were in Cologne—the fear—why they drank too much, revealed too much. The agents played on fear. Hell, that's why I was there! I shouldn't have been surprised, but I was."

He made a fist and went on. "My parents were afraid for me; I was afraid, so I left. And now I'm afraid I've been beaten." His fist fell on the table without force, and he looked away. When he turned back, his face sagged with defeat. "While it's obvious now, it wasn't then. It came to me on the lonely train ride back to Berlin. I had to understand what had gone so terribly wrong to keep despair at bay."

An interesting insight, thought Sonny, but he wanted to hear the rest of Herman's story. "When did you finally decide?"

"By the end of the day I'd made up my mind, and I returned to the club. The agent sat at the same table, drink and cigarette in hand. I had rehearsed my spiel, but my mind went blank. His oily-haired head turned 'til his eyes met mine—I don't think he noticed. He squinted—from the smoke—and invited me to sit down. I did, but the words still wouldn't come. I had to pry them out."

Just then a man walked into the little café. Sonny nodded, though he couldn't fix a name to the face, and the man nodded in return. Herman followed the exchange and, as if it made a difference, asked, "Who's that?"

Sonny shook his head. "I can't remember."

Max brought the man a cup of coffee, and he sat alone, reading a newspaper.

Herman looked down at his hands, trying to recall where he'd left off. Then he said, "Oh, I was stuttering about needing to get out of Germany . . . The agent just stared at me, took a drag and a drink, but didn't answer me. Then his lips curled into an arrogant smile."

Herman closed his eyes, replaying the scene, and sighed. "Later I saw the schadenfreude in that smile . . . well maybe I'm reading something into it because of the way it ended. Anyway, the smile disappeared, and he said something could be arranged, almost anything could—for a price. He asked if I wanted a drink. I didn't."

Herman went on: "'Are you sure you want to go across?' he asked. This time I said yes. He warned it could be dangerous, but I knew that. His eyes scanned the club, looking for someone or something. Then he surprised me. He said, 'Everyone is desperate in his own way. Are you? Of course, you are.' He had me pegged, and I fell for his bullshit."

"Did you agree to anything that night?"

"No, I considered it for another day, then tried haggling over the price. But it was take it or leave it—others were waiting in line. So I agreed. I was to leave in a couple weeks, as soon as preparations were final. Two weeks passed without a word, and I was impatient. I considered finding another agent, since I hadn't paid anything up front. But I couldn't face starting over again. It was too daunting. Just when I reached the end of my tether, word came. I met him at the club, and just before closing the deal, he handed me a letter. He said it was from a client in Antwerp. It looked real, but the addressee was cut out—for security reasons, he said. That made sense, so I read how damn happy this guy was. I wanted it to be real."

He had more: "We were leaving late, so it would be dark at the border. I was told to report in two days at 5 PM to a commercial building down an alley near the club, to go inside and wait. When I got there, two women and a man were waiting with the agent. He demanded his 350 Reichmarks and then stuffed the notes into his pocket. He said our car would be there within an hour and wished us good luck. He left without looking back.

"We were staring at the door as if he'd come back and say everything would be all right. I hadn't thought of others making the journey with me. Both women were younger; they stood whispering, avoiding eye contact. The guy was about my age—we nodded but didn't talk. I was too nervous. After about twenty minutes I heard a car. The door opened and a voice told us to get in. Then two hours of cramped discomfort, silence. We didn't know where we were going, and nobody asked. I've never felt so anxious . . . When we finally stopped, it was at the town of Heinsberg, on the Dutch border. You know it?"

"No," Sonny answered. "There are so many. We mostly use . . ." He thought better of it and stopped.

Herman was distracted by a man walking near the table. Then he said, "Before I read the name of the town, I saw 'No Jews allowed,' but we didn't sully the place, not yet anyhow. We drove through, stopped beside a dimly lit house, and waited until the light in the window went out. The driver went into the house. Suddenly a caravan of policemen on motorcycles sped past, toward the frontier. They paid no attention to us. Five minutes ran to ten until a lone figure, not the driver, leaned into the car holding a torch. His smile was reassuring; he told us to follow him.

"We followed him in the general direction of the border, past strollers out for a walk, past the last cottages at the edge of town. Then the man turned into a stand of trees so dark we could barely see him. At the first clearing, I counted silhouettes—we were only four. The man had abandoned us. One of the women panicked and beseeched her friend, but I couldn't make out her words. Then, as if on cue, the four of us walked in the same direction, hoping something would materialize.

"We groped in the dark until we hit another clearing. There were lights, and a Nazi flag hanging from a pole. We ran. Then a squad of black-shirted SS came out of nowhere, surrounding us with rifles pointed at our chests, like they'd been waiting for us." The color drained from Herman's face.

"We were ordered into the shack, to face an officer not much older than me. He looked us up and down from behind his desk, then asked for our papers. Nobody moved, so he screamed, 'Now!' Our agent had given us nothing but a ride into the hands of the customs and border patrol."

Herman looked away to gather his thoughts. "The officer pointed at each of us, his eyes were piercing . . . awful. His hands moved in a strange dance, then he gave us a nasty smile. He lit a cigarette, blew smoke in our faces, muttered something. Then with a flick of his wrist he ordered the sergeant to search us."

Something in Herman's description triggered a memory . . . Sonny was in a café, drinking coffee, listening to someone. His eyes widened . . . it was Albert, talking about his hometown and all his plans . . .

But Herman was saying, " . . . After it was over, I realized it was a game, a fait accompli, the outcome already known. The officer and his men enjoyed the harassment—they'd probably done it before."

"So it seems," Sonny agreed, but he couldn't expunge the image of Albert's piercing eyes and dancing hands. If Albert was Gestapo, what was he doing at the border? That was under the jurisdiction of the Zollgrenzschutz.

"Did you catch the officer's name?"

Herman shook his head, "Of course not. Does it matter?"

"Tell me about his eyes."

Herman was perplexed. "His eyes! Why is that important?"

"Humor me."

Herman shrugged. "Like I said, piercing, lifeless, cold, what you'd expect from a Nazi officer." Then he seemed to remember something. "And his eyes darted from one to the other, as if he were unable to stay focused for long. That's all I know—what's this all about?"

"Forget it. Sorry for the interruption."

Herman frowned, confused by Sonny's digression, but he continued. "I was taken into a room, stripped and searched like a convict—it was humiliating. The troops had a good time scaring the 'fucking Jews.' Of course, they found nothing of value—except to us—a little money and tickets for transit. Then we were marched back to face the officer. What they found on us was stacked next to his ashtray full of butts. Riffling through the pile, he stopped and pulled out my ticket to New York on the *Rotterdam,* and waved it in the air. 'Whose is this?' he demanded. I admitted it was mine, figured I'd never see it again. He threw the ticket and all the other papers back at us and told us to get the hell out 'if you're so eager to leave the Third Reich.' And that's what we did."

Herman continued. "It was laughable to go to the border without papers, nothing, not a goddamn thing. What the hell was I thinking? What a damned fool I was." He looked forlorn. "But before it all went to hell, I was hopeful for the first time in a long time. All we had to do was walk from here to there." He pointed to the far wall. "And in minutes a Dutch immigration officer met us. Our little group hoped . . . and the Dutchman did nothing to dispel our optimism. He was polite, put us at ease, until he said, 'Papers, please.' And it all unraveled again.

"I showed him my ticket to New York; I'd be in transit, gone in a matter of days—no burden to Holland. The others did the same, but he was unmoved. 'There are regulations,' he repeated as we begged, pleaded, cajoled. When all seemed lost, the prettier of the women flirted with him, to no avail. She increased the volume, wiggled her ass, stroked his arm. We looked away, hoping she'd succeed. But he ordered her to 'behave like a lady.' I admired her courage . . . It might have worked with a different guard, but we had this one, who kept talking about regulations.

"Finally, my male companion tried to explain the reason for his, for *our,* flight and asked the guard to take mercy. My travel mate recited a litany of abuses that the Jews have endured . . . talked about the officer we'd run into on the other side if he sent us back. Apparently, he touched a sympathetic nerve. The guard dialed a number on the telephone. He spoke, then listened, rearranged papers on his desk, spoke again, listened, frowned, and looked at us. Dutch is close enough to German that I could pick out a word or two. It didn't bode well. He cradled the receiver, shook his head, and said there was nothing he could do."

Herman's voice fell to a whisper. "The women wept. I was in shock as the guard led us from the little building. When we entered no-man's-land, I thought about making a run. There were lights and endless coils of barbed wire. It would have been suicidal, but I didn't care . . . A harsh voice intervened. 'Come quickly. I don't have all night.' They'd been watching, waiting, knowing we'd be sent back."

Herman's head fell forward, his chin resting on his chest, his face in shadow. He sat like that until Sonny asked what happened next.

Herman raised his head and cleared his throat. "We were looking into rifle barrels, soldiers grabbing our arms, issuing commands. They shoved us into the back of a truck. I scraped my knee, and the flirtatious woman was nearly knocked unconscious. They swore at us and threatened to shoot us, but I was numb. By this time it was nearly dawn, the sky just starting to lighten. They drove us to the police chief in Heinsberg, and he locked us in the jail. Unhappy about being rousted from his bed, the chief pulled us out one by one, ordered us not to try again, and set us free."

Herman's eyes glazed. Then he raised his shoulders in an exaggerated shrug. "He told us where to wait for the bus, to get out of his town. The women cried. The other fellow was white as a sheet. I probably looked as bad. I had enough money for a bus ticket to Cologne and a train ticket to Berlin." Herman fell back in his chair, spent.

Working to keep his anger in check, Sonny asked whether Herman had confronted the agent who betrayed them.

Herman shook his head. "I thought about it, even had a speech prepared, but I didn't have the energy or the guts. Besides, what could I do? I still can't get used to it—that a fellow Jew betrayed me."

Sonny knew sleazy Jews, guys capable of nasty things, but this fit a whole new category . . . Someone in the café laughed. He heard clinking china and glass as Max cleared a nearby table.

Turning back to Herman, Sonny said, "That's one hell of a story, one I wish I hadn't heard." Herman had opened a window onto Albert—Sonny's gut said he was the man. Albert was working the frontier when Sonny was stuck in Plombieres. Heinsberg wasn't far from Aachen . . .

Sonny heard Herman ask, "What's wrong?"

"Nothing," he lied. He wouldn't trouble Herman with disturbing news that really didn't concern him. He changed the subject. "I can help you. Meet me here tomorrow at the same time. Bring a passport-size photograph. Papers will be ready in a week or so." He told him the price.

Herman moaned. "I spent nearly everything on the damned agent, but I'll get it somewhere."

"Can your parents help?"

Unable to speak, Herman closed his eyes and shook his head. Waiting for him to regain his composure, Sonny glanced at the man reading his newspaper across the room, was still unable to place him.

Finally, Herman said, "No, they insisted I leave—it was the hardest thing I ever did. They think I'm safe in Holland, and that's how it stays."

"I realize that, but you're here now."

"Don't you see? I can't go to them now . . . then leave again."

"Don't worry about the money. You're covered." Sonny told him. That's what the Thiemann Strasse money is for, he thought.

Bewildered, Herman stared and finally said, "I don't understand." As Sonny explained, the color rose in Herman's face. He managed a weak thank-you.

"I understand how you feel about your parents. I can get papers for them, too—just like that." Sonny snapped his fingers. "Think about it."

Herman pinched the bridge of his nose and spoke with his eyes closed, "Like I said, my mother's too sick to travel, so my father can't leave. They promised to follow, but I knew they wouldn't. Abandoning them once was bad enough. After what they've gone through, I can't endure seeing them again, not here. Let them think I'm in Holland." He looked away, then swept his hand over the table, the matter settled.

His parents must be struggling. Could his mother be that sick? To whom would they turn? Sonny had too many unanswered questions, but the answers were none of his business. Sonny understood Herman's response, but he'd work to change his mind in the days ahead. "Where are you staying?"

Herman hesitated too long before answering, "With a friend for a few days, but after that?" He shrugged.

Sonny considered. "I have a room for you until the papers are ready."

Herman brightened and thanked him again. Sonny wrote the address on a piece of paper, handed it to Herman, told him to memorize it, and to be there at 9 PM. Then he retrieved the paper and tore it to bits.

After Herman left the café, Sonny drank another cup of coffee. He thought about Herman's experience and about his parents . . . Helping Herman would be easy.

Then he thought about Albert—was Albert following him from one place to another? That didn't make sense . . . but there he'd been, in Aachen's main square, now at the border. Was Albert somehow connecting Sonny with the border? He couldn't see how, but the thought remained . . .

Sonny pushed Albert from his mind, replacing the thought of him with his satisfaction at being able to help a guy like Herman. That dissolved into smoldering anger as he thought about the kind of man who would abandon four people at the border. Probably he'd done it many times. That idea would lead only to despair, so he gave it up to think about what he could do. Smuggling was an ancient if not venerable profession, undeniably useful in these turbulent times. And it was what he knew best. Life in the shadows—having a false identity and no address—suited him, at least for now.

The man reading the newspaper was gone, so Sonny finished his coffee, said goodbye to Max, and left the café. On the way to Stuttgarter Strasse, his thoughts drifted again to Albert and where he might turn up next.

22

Cowards die many times before their deaths;
The valiant never taste of death but once.
—William Shakespeare

Sonny stopped at Samuel's newsstand to buy the latest edition of the *Judische Rundschau*, one of three remaining Jewish newspapers. A longtime Scheunenviertel hawker dressed in suit and tie, Samuel sang the headlines—a fire in Wedding or a bank robbery in the West End—in his Yiddish-accented tenor. In recent years he'd given up the burlesque—the bad news was too close to home. He was nevertheless a daily fixture, another thread holding Sonny's life together.

Sonny dropped several coins onto the tray, waved a greeting, and read the headlines. Two stories led: Poles were still stranded at the border, and Vom Rath was near death. The first story, ugly, was provocation for the second.

The fate of thousands of Polish Jews at the German-Polish border had dominated the front page for the past week. They were pawns kept in a state of limbo by hostile governments unwilling to yield. The crisis had begun in August, when Hitler decreed all noncitizen resident visas nonrenewable, setting in motion the deportation of Polish Jews. Many had long lived in Germany, the only home their children had ever known.

In Sonny's neighborhood, Polish Jews were part of the working, middle, professional, and business classes. Many were orthodox, but there were also the assimilated and secular Jews—indistinguishable from their German neighbors but for their Semitic features and, for some, their accents. Mischa and Sophie, had they not left the country, would have been among the deported. Sonny was relieved they were already gone.

In mid-October, the order had come: all Poles were to report to collecting stations. There they were loaded into trains like livestock. The order apparently was timed to force them to leave belongings behind, affairs hanging, friends with farewells unbidden. Twelve thousand displaced former residents—victims of a diplomatic stalemate—were mired at the Polish border. The German authorities expected Poland to grant the newly minted refugees entry. But it did not. The Polish government ordered them back across the river into Germany. A cold, drenching rain and a lack of services compounded the misery of the rejected Jews.

After days of diplomatic posturing and international handwringing, four thousand tired, hungry, and dirty refugees were granted entry to Poland. Still, the eight thousand remaining at the border languished in conditions too awful to contemplate. A front-page story in the *Judische Rundschau* reported Gestapo troops firing shots behind the refugees, trying to start a stampede. Other stories described further assaults—refugees being herded into cattle barns where fresh dung coated the floor, the elderly dying from exposure, increasing suicides. The misery centered in the village of Zbaszyn, Poland. Across Europe, the plight of the Polish Jews was a cause célèbre.

As the crisis built, Sonny saw warehouse stalls empty of vendors and heard of new vacancies where families once had lived. That feeling of powerlessness, of being preyed upon by a relentless Nazi state, returned to plague him.

Gripped by a seething anger, he nevertheless kept his cool. At first, he found proxies for the wretched suffering in Mischa, Sophie, and their families. He closed his eyes and saw them huddled, crying for help. The image stuck, then morphed into another, of anonymous black-suited, bearded orthodox men, scarf-covered women, and children peering out from behind their mother's skirts. Their faces remained in shadow, but their anguish was penetrating. He blinked to make them disappear, but the image morphed again . . . outside the station in Wedding another family around a bearded man in black.

Stopping at Emil's door, Sonny frowned, not remembering how he had arrived there but knowing he needed to talk. Someone walked by; Sonny kept his head down until the man was gone, then knocked.

Emil had returned the day before from a regular run to Aachen, delivering pay and making sure that the other end of the operation was in working order. Offering greetings from Fritz and Günter, he handed Sonny a newspaper from Liege.

"How's your French? There's a story on Vom Rath, something other than the bullshit we get here." Emil reached into his pocket and pulled out an envelope. "Oh, and before I forget, this is for Mina."

"My French is barely passable," Sonny said as he put the envelope in his pocket. "I suppose it's another plea from her parents to put an end to the youthful folly that might get her killed." The thought of her parents' torment, the images haunting him, the guilt in knowing his woes were few and that he had a way out, suddenly brought him to blurt, "It's the fucking apocalypse! I don't even know what to call this . . . this . . . situation at the border."

Emil's features softened; then his eyes narrowed to slits.

"What?" Sonny said, startled at his icy transformation.

"Why the hell are you still here?" Emil asked.

Without hesitating, Sonny shot back, "Same reason that Mina's here and that you're part of the operation."

"Don't give me that shit! You know what I'm taking about. There's no percentage in staying—for you or Mina. We'll keep the operation going. Hell, you're the only Jew left in the group. In fact," Emil leaned closer to Sonny and stuck his finger in his chest, "you've become a liability."

Sonny had heard that line before; they'd used it on Mischa. The irony of Emil's using it on him made him laugh.

That did nothing to soften Emil's mood, and he barked, "Nothing funny about it."

Caught off guard by Emil's vehemence, Sonny took a moment to gather his thoughts. He looked around the kitchen. Steam rose languidly from the spout of the coffee pot. Frost etched the corners of the window overlooking the old enterprise warehouse. And Emil's fingers tapped impatiently on Gustav's table. Calmed by the familiar surroundings, Sonny felt secure, the way he used to feel at the warehouse—insulated from evil.

Sonny looked at Emil, his mentor and friend, but did not respond. Another question popped into his head—how many times can you beat the system? Ignoring the thought, he shook his head and shrugged. Then, looking down at the table, he said, "Everything we've accomplished—the planning, all the nuts and bolts—we did at this table, late at night, with endless cups of coffee."

"Don't change the subject," Emil said irritably. "One of these days, you'll have to decide."

Their conversation had run into a dead end he couldn't get out of, so Sonny said goodbye and left with the Liege newspaper tucked inside his jacket, next to Mina's letter. He stopped at the kiosk outside a subway station in Neukölln to buy a newspaper. People eager for information surrounded the stall, so he couldn't get close.

"Führer sends doctor to Vom Rath," shouted the headline from a hanging newspaper. There were too many voices . . . Sonny heard only a smattering. "Just awful," from a woman, then a man: " . . . shot by a Goddamn Jew!" Murmurs, then another man, anxious, "What next?" And someone answered, "War!"

Annoyed, Sonny gave up and turned away, tripping over someone's foot: "Damn!" Falling free of the scrum, he floated downward, free of constraint. Before he hit the ground, he was jerked to a stop. Pulled by a strong hand on his upper arm, Sonny was back on his feet. He blinked into the face of a cop reeking of cigarettes and coffee.

"Be careful," the cop said.

Croaking his thanks, Sonny walked away, trying to clear the fog from his head. He cursed having put himself in danger for a goddamn Nazi newspaper.

When he got to No. 53, Mina and Otto were in the kitchen, so Sonny put the letter on the table. Unsettled by the haunting images of the border village Zbaszyn, by the voices at the kiosk, by the cop and Emil's probing, Sonny stood awkwardly to the side. The irony of Emil's questioning was that Sonny had already decided to leave—why hadn't he just said so? Inertia had set in, and he hadn't set a date.

Nobody spoke; the envelope lay untouched but not unnoticed. Mina stared like Pandora, mesmerized.

"Where's Herman?" Sonny asked, unaware of the letter's effect on Mina.

"What?" Otto asked absently. "Oh, upstairs—he wants to be alone. Can't blame him."

Mina was glad for the distraction, but the mention of Herman recalled his refusal to see his parents. Otto pointed to the letter, and Mina groaned, "I know what it says."

"Then tear it up," Otto suggested, knowing she could not—she owed her parents that much.

Mina sighed and looked up at the peeling paint on the ceiling. "What the hell!" She tore open the letter, fighting the urge to be alone with her anger—or tears—whatever it might bring. Deciding she had nothing to hide, she glumly read yet another of her parents' pleas that she come to her senses. Both men watched in silence as Mina read and reread the letter, then folded it into quarters, and returned it to the envelope. Her frown made her look older and even sadder.

"Well?" Otto asked softly.

"The same." Tears welled despite her effort to repress them. Otto softly caressed her shoulder and silently waited for her anguish to pass. Rubbing her eyes, she blinked back the tears, smiled weakly, then spoke to Sonny. "Have you heard any news?"

All they knew came from the German newspaper's description of a Polish Jew shooting a German diplomat in Paris the Sunday before. Every story concluded with an indictment of all Jews. Every negative event—a shortage of onions or the shooting of a diplomat—had a Jewish antecedent.

"Smuggled in from the front," Sonny said as he handed the Belgian newspaper to Mina. Knowing French well enough, she read hungrily, welcoming the distraction.

"How do we know this fellow Grynszpan actually shot Vom Rath?" Otto asked.

A reasonable question, Sonny thought, but he wasn't in the mood to be reasonable. He wanted to scream: God damn it! Who gives a shit about Vom Rath when thousands suffer! But his friends had done nothing to incur his rage. He bit his lip and simmered.

"How refreshing, not a single denunciation of the Jews," Mina said as she set the paper down. "Though it's essentially the story we've heard nonstop: Herschel Grynszpan, a Pole, fired a pistol five times into the body of an unknown bureaucrat named Ernst vom Rath, Third Secretary of the German Embassy in Paris, who hovers near death."

"Unknown until now," Sonny snapped. "Nazi propaganda is already preparing the comatose bugger for martyrdom. He'll ascend to the pantheon of German heroes from Siegfried to Bismarck, march shoulder to shoulder with the pimp Horst Wessel! Vom Rath's death in service of the Third Reich outstrips anything he could have done alive." Finally Sonny got it out, and he felt better. "To hell with Vom Rath. Fuck them all."

Otto nodded agreement. "Right. But beware! They'll use it as proof of a continuing conspiracy against the Third Reich. Every incident of Jewish violence, against any German anywhere in Europe, will be dredged from the depths as proof. Who knows what's in store? No good will come of it."

"I say good for him!" Mina exclaimed, pounding the table. Her sudden fury matched Sonny's, catching them by surprise. "At least Grynszpan did something." She read the Liege newspaper, translating the French to German. "Grynszpan went to the office of the Third Secretary Vom Rath . . ." She skipped ahead. " . . . Vom Rath was heard to ask Grynszpan, 'Did you have an important document to give me?' Witnesses said they heard the man identified as Grynszpan shout, 'You are a filthy Boche, and here, in the name of twelve thousand persecuted Jews, is your document.'"

"Suicidal," Sonny muttered.

At that moment, Karl entered, carrying several newspapers. They exchanged greetings, and he said, "I'm so ashamed and sorry."

They stared at him blankly.

"You don't know—the edict just came down. All Jewish newspapers are shut down immediately." He pointed to the *Judische Rundschau*. "No more stories on how to apply for a passport and visa, or on a family relocated in New York, or on the plight of the Poles at the border. None on the Vom Rath shooting and no editorial begging for calm. Without the Jewish newspapers, thousands will be denied vital information."

Karl read from the one of the newspapers he brought: "Jewish magazines, cultural papers, and community bulletins are to close immediately.

Jewish children are forbidden from attending Aryan schools . . . all Jewish cultural activity indefinitely suspended." He looked up. "It only gets worse.

"Worse?" Sonny muttered.

"Yes. A colleague informed me that a synagogue was burned in Hersfeld, in Hesse, southeast of Berlin." His voice cracked. "He didn't know whether anyone was inside or if scrolls were lost. Another colleague, with a brother in Vienna, told of Jewish shop windows smashed and synagogues burned. They're using Vom Rath as a fait accompli."

In shock, Sonny couldn't think straight. He spoke to the room, "Nothing's changed: expect the worst and we'll never be disappointed."

Karl broke the silence. "We have to double our efforts before . . ."

"Before what?" Mina begged the question hanging in the air.

Frau Moltke came into the kitchen, and everyone turned to her as if she knew the answer. Nonplussed, she asked whether they were hungry and began preparing a meal.

Vom Rath died the following day, 9 November 1938. Through the evening, radio broadcasts mourned the great hero's death with melancholy dirge and bellicose harangue against those responsible, despite Grynszpan's having acted alone.

Joseph, who had heard enough, turned off the radio, and returned to his work. Sonny paced the flat, feeling uneasy, mumbling, putting Joseph on edge. Finally, Joseph had enough.

"Go, get some fresh air. You're driving me crazy."

. . . Sonny walked beneath the dome of the New Synagogue through Oranienburg Gate, aimlessly toward the West End, the zoo, Kufurstendamm, and the favorite haunts of his youth. The streets were unusually empty, and he shivered in its eerie silence. As he passed the zoo, he saw something was missing. There should have been at least two cops at each gate, but he hadn't seen any cops, anywhere.

Ignoring the signs, Sonny circled to Unter den Linden. Drawing nearer, he could make out an ominous chanting: "Down with the Jews, down with the Jews, down . . ."

Still undaunted, he crossed the street near the French tourist office, now closed. People, mostly Jews, gathered there during the day for information on immigration. Brochures and pamphlets were available on racks outside the door, but a gang of thugs lurked in the area, intimidating anyone who dared come near.

The air was thick with mischief. Sonny had seen enough. Best not to press his luck. He headed back to the Mitte, frightened for any Jew caught on the street that night.

Back at Joseph's, he dreamt during the night of people huddled in a pouring rain. Every face he saw was Mischa or Sophie. He heard the evil taunts from the ugly, distorted mouths he'd seen the evening before. Waking from a tormented sleep before dawn, he quietly left the flat to take the subway to Neukölln. Pale shards of light broke through the darkness as he arrived at No. 53.

Frau Moltke was in the kitchen preparing breakfast. Sonny drank coffee at the table, his foot tapping an anxious beat. There was shuffling in the hallway, and Otto entered, offering a mumbled "Good morning." He poured a cup of coffee, and within minutes Mina walked in. She nodded to Sonny and hugged Frau Moltke.

Sonny told them about what he'd seen the night before. The color drained from Mina's face, and a hand went over her mouth as if she'd said something wrong. Anxious anticipation filled the room. The conversation was stilted, disjointed, until they tired of the attempt. Then no one spoke at all.

A pounding at the alley door roused them. Otto opened the door, and Karl burst in, flushed and out of breath. Small black and gray flecks dotted his shoulders and hair, but it was his eyes, flashing with a frightened passion, that scared them. He carried about him a slight suggestion of smoke.

Sonny had seen Karl like that before—something was out of order. Fear, like that of the night before but stronger, overcame him. Mina chewed on her lip, Otto reeled, and Frau Moltke raised a hand to her mouth as if to stifle a scream.

Finally, Otto exclaimed, "What the hell's going on?"

Gasping for air, Karl heaved out the words. "Synagogues are burning all over Berlin—shop windows are smashed—Jewish men rounded up and taken away." Overwhelmed by the enormity, he took another breath and continued. "Smoke's everywhere—the Fasanenstrasse Synagogue was burning—God help us!" Karl's fists clenched as he paced.

Dumbfounded, they waited for more.

"They let it burn, no fire trucks, no sirens. I saw idiots cheering as the flames leapt from the windows." He sniffed at the sleeve of his jacket and frowned. "Can't you smell the smoke? It's all over me." His voice lowered to a whisper, and he said no more as tears rolled down his cheeks.

Sonny's nostrils twitched, and he slowly nodded. Otto stepped outside, returning within a minute, bringing in the unmistakable stench.

"What about the little synagogue on Neckar Strasse, near the brewery? And the New Synagogue?" Sonny asked, sickened at the idea of either burning.

Karl shook his head; he didn't know.

"How do you know about the arrests?" Mina asked.

Sonny stopped listening—the words were background noise. Visions of a raging inferno filled his mind; it consumed everything Jewish—the neighborhood, the warehouse, Joseph, his flat and his documents, Samuel's newsstand, the old lady selling shoelaces, Max and the café.

Bolting from his chair to see for himself, Sonny did not hear their warnings. He was already out the door, coat in hand, into the alley, and onto Stuttgarter Strasse. Dark clouds swirled above, carrying the pungent odor of the burn.

How could he have missed it? Had the subway spared him? He ran until he saw pillars of black smoke above the buildings, pushed by the soft breeze. When he turned the corner, there were tongues of red, yellow, and orange flame darting from the broken windows, reaching up the sides of the buildings toward the sky.

Winded, he bent over, hands on his thighs, struggling to catch his breath but transfixed by the horror of a Jewish temple in flames. His eyes watered, a cloud of gray smoke drifted into his face, and a terrible smell threatened to leave him forever in the hellish glow of the Neckar Strasse synagogue. His rage nearly strangled him.

Frenzied citizens had gathered in the street; they screamed incoherently while others stood alone or in small groups, watching the spectacle in fascination, in horror, or in celebration. Fueled by the desecration, Sonny felt an urge to do something, but he was impotent. His anger turned to an overwhelming sadness, impossible to assuage. He could not tear his eyes from the scene, which stripped away his dignity. He was naked and alone.

The hoots and jeers of the mob grew louder. Sonny saw a woman, hand over mouth, tears filling her eyes. A man shook his fist and yelled. Children played in the street, throwing stones at the multicolored windows. Looking from face to face, Sonny saw no one he recognized, and like the night before, no police to end the madness, no firemen to extinguish the flames.

Thick gray smoke, like the devil's hot breath, billowed through the synagogue doors, rising into the sky, mingling with other acrid clouds moving through the city. Suddenly a window blew out, sending colored shards of glass raining onto the street. Orange and blue flames shot from the space where the stained glass had been.

Sonny's eyes lit on a fire dying in the street, its ashes drifting like gray snowflakes. Staring at the detritus, he came to recognize this shape and that, and then he knew—looted Torah scrolls and prayer books had been set aflame in the street. Distorted faces rejoiced in the conflagration, their inarticulate screams and chants punctuated by the rhythmic epithet, "Jew, Jew." Finally, when only wisps of smoke still rose from the sacred texts, he turned and retraced his steps to No. 53, the enormity of what he had seen only slowly sinking in.

A city he no longer knew had severed the connections, the symbols that for Sonny had meaning. He'd never heard of a Jew spared through prayer, and he'd given up on religion long ago. But saint or sinner, it didn't matter; in a pogrom you were simply a Jew. Still, he staggered under the loss. Profoundly grieved by the unleashed hell, he reached for a ritual he barely knew, silently reciting the mourner's kaddish, stumbling in broken Hebrew: "Yisgadal, v'yiskadash shmay rabo . . ." When he ran out of words, he whispered, "Amen."

Sonny had never even seen the little Neckar Strasse Synagogue, let alone sat in one of its pews, until he saw it burning. He had never appreciated the colored light reflected from its stained-glass windows. Ornate or simple? Orthodox or conservative? He didn't know. What did it matter? At least two synagogues had burned, and with all the smoke in the air, there must be more. He staggered, cringed, fearing for the domes crowning the most beautiful building in the city. Not knowing whether it was still there or not, he grieved and nearly tripped on a curb.

Moorish in design, its citrus-topped dome flanked by two smaller domes, the New Synagogue dominated the surrounding buildings of Scheunenviertel. Its stone façade held three huge, round, stained-glass windows above the arches enclosing its doors. Not having been inside for years, Sonny was indifferent to its status as a house of prayer, but he loved the massive temple—the wonderful pile of bricks, stained glass, and stone.

Images of his family's yearly visit for fall's High Holy Days, the Jewish New Year, flashed through Sonny's head. As a child, he had squirmed through interminable hours of prayer, been scolded to sit still. Light from above had shone through multicolored stained glass depicting Old Testament mythology. Higher yet, magnificent arches rose to the high dome where God, if ever he had thought one existed, certainly resided. Balconies lined both sides of the temple in which he sat between his parents, staring down at men in prayer shawls and women in their finery.

Over the years Sonny's parents had attended less often and finally not at all, releasing him from the belief that Hebrew chanting—the constant invocation of God—was anything more than superstition. His love for the building had remained; he needed to see it, to be certain it was still there. Sadly he squelched the impulse—the pogrom his father had feared was here—every Jew should hide.

Sonny closed the door, hearing Otto's voice, " . . . the targeting of synagogues, the looting, the arrests, has the fetid stink of orchestrated retaliation."

The question hanging in the air when Sonny raced out had long since been answered. Less than an hour had passed—they looked at him expectantly. His sad grimace told them what they needed to know about the Neckar Strasse synagogue, but he recited his story anyway.

After a respectful silence, Karl told Sonny that Polly had telephoned from Zwickau, where she was visiting her parents, with more bad news.

He explained that her parents had rented a flat from the Deichslers, a Jewish family that ran a little ground-floor department store. The family lived above the store, Polly's parents over them. Sonny knew all that, but he listened without interrupting.

Karl had more: "Looters smashed the windows and stole merchandise, but the worst is that Herr Deichsler was arrested and taken away, probably to one of the concentration camps. Polly is helping Frau Deichsler find her husband."

"What the hell can we do?" Otto muttered.

"We've got meetings, documents to deliver," Sonny nearly shouted. Then he uncoiled, knocking his chair to the floor. His instinct was to ignore the warning, the obstacles littering his path, and get to work.

"You can't," Karl said, but Sonny wasn't listening. Karl repeated what he'd said.

"What?" Sonny said.

"There are no men to meet—they've been arrested or they're in hiding. It's chaos out there. You'll be arrested." Karl pointed to the wall, beyond which fires burned and men were being thrown into trucks. "You are a Jew. You must hide."

Sonny dismissed the warning with a wave of his hand. "I live on the streets. I've got a new identity. I got it from you. Don't worry about me."

"Damn it, Sonny. Sit down!" Karl shouted.

Sonny flinched but did not move.

Karl looked from Sonny to Mina. "It's too late. Get out. Both of you!" He slapped his palm on the table. "When this blows over."

Otto put an arm around Mina: "He's right."

"And what about you?" She faced him. "You're a wanted man. For five years you've been one. Only since you've known these wonderful people have you even had a room of your own."

Otto did not reply.

Karl turned on Sonny, locking his eyes until it was uncomfortable. "You're a marked man."

A strangled laugh. "Hell, we're all marked."

Karl moved until he was inches from Sonny's face. "What good will you be if you're locked up? Go to the warehouse, walk around Scheunenviertel and Spandauer Vorstadt, see the broken windows, and ask, 'Where are the men?'"

"Damn it! That's what I intend to do." Sonny snapped back. He was up, moving toward the door.

Otto grabbed his arm, pulling him back. "Don't be crazy! Sit down and think about what we have to do."

But Sonny would not sit, not with promises to keep. Then he remembered. "Oh my God!"

"What is it?" Mina asked, fearing more bad news.

"Herman's father!" He looked at their blank faces. "Herman's parents don't know he's here, and if his father's been arrested—oh my God!" Now they understood. "I've got to tell Herman. I've got to help."

When Herman opened the door, Sonny quickly explained that all hell had been unleashed. Herman nodded as if he understood, but he looked dazed.

"Can you smell the smoke?" Sonny asked.

Herman sniffed and shook his head, so Sonny opened the window.

"Now I can smell it. That means . . . " He started but stopped, fear filling his eyes. "My father," he trembled, moving toward the door.

"No. Stay here. It's too dangerous." Sonny jerked his head toward the West End. "I'll go. What's the address?"

Herman staggered back onto the bed, as though Sonny had punched him. Putting his head in his hands, he moaned, "Oh my God! Oh my God!"

Placing a hand on Herman's shoulder, Sonny leaned over him. "Herman!" He shook him gently. "Give me the address."

In a flat voice, Herman recited, "Pestalozzi Strasse, No. 241, second floor in the back, on the right side, name Milberg is on the mailbox."

"I will keep your secret," Sonny promised, but Herman didn't hear.

23

I am a Jew. Hath not a Jew eyes: Hath not a Jew hands, organs, dimensions, sense, affections, passions? If you prick us, do we not bleed? . . . And if you wrong us, shall we not revenge?
—William Shakespeare

Sonny relented, letting his friends talk him into waiting until dark to venture onto Berlin's cruel streets a second time. Waiting was torturous. When he left the house, a sanguine sunset bled at the edge of the skyline, the clouds glowing like hot embers.

Sonny hoped Herr Milberg was safe at home. If not—well, he'd figure that out when he got there. Along the way he would pass the New Synagogue and the warehouse. He thought it would be spared, as Jews no longer owned it. Staying clear of the subway for fear of being trapped underground, he set out to walk the six kilometers to the Mitte. He would stick to side streets, pass through parks and cemeteries, and above all, avoid the roving bands of SA and Hitler Youth, surely out in force. For protection, he had his Aryan features and a false identity card.

Sonny followed the canal along a nearly empty street. The mischief was keeping most people behind curtained windows; the faint light seeping through projected a false calm. A lone barge moved slowly behind him as if it were following. Sonny noticed a faint outline at the helm, glowing intermittently, then fading. He stared, then realized the helmsman was smoking a cigarette, puffing in synch with the pace of the barge.

Within an hour, Sonny skirted Kottbusser Tor, Berlin's old southern gate, and headed toward Oranienplatz. Exposed in crossing to the other side of the empty expanse, he quickened his step. Jogging across the open square, he heard a deep rumbling, like an earthquake. Hesitating, he looked up and down and across the street. His eyes went to the narrow green space, a boulevard running from the canal all the way to St.

Michael's Church, and he froze. Coming toward him, in rigid formation, were hundreds of marching men. Incredibly, they were singing, but he could not make out the words.

The juxtaposition of where he stood and what he was seeing with the mayhem of the whole day made him feel crazy. The rhythmic stomp was hypnotizing. He hadn't lost his mind, not yet—he realized that storm troopers were marching toward him in perfect formation, torches blazing. Now he heard the song, praising the Führer, demonizing Communists and Jews. It was a world gone mad!

The slow, deep cadence of the voices punctuated by boots hitting pavement kept Sonny from moving. It was too late for escape, anyway—he was caught in the open. They didn't even look his way. Was he invisible? Led by a lone storm trooper holding a Nazi banner atop a pole, three columns of uniformed men, at least five hundred strong, marched smartly through Oranienplatz.

Then the singing stopped. The only sound was the collective thunder of feet striking pavement as one. Sonny's ears burned; he jumped as the singing picked up again:

> Deutschland, awake from your nightmare!
> Give foreign Jews no place in your empire!
> We will fight for your resurgence!
> Aryan blood shall never perish!
>
> All these hypocrites, we throw them out.
> Judah, leave our German house!
> If the native soil is clean and pure,
> We united and happy will be!

Sonny shuddered at the banal words, the incessant stomping. He had stumbled onto the perfect metaphor for man's perfidy. Five years of Nazi rule had conditioned him to avoid Hitler's henchmen—itching for a fight, tormenting old Jews, harassing shopkeepers—and now he was trapped in their fucking parade! If he hadn't been scared to death, he might have appreciated the absurdity of his position.

Once the troopers had passed and Sonny could breathe again, he cursed them and their songs. When he was certain they were gone, he hurried north toward the New Synagogue. Turning onto Oranienburg Strasse three quarters of an hour later, he sniffed the air—and smelled nothing. His heart leapt with joy and relief at the sight of the undisturbed majesty of the Moorish domes.

Heading for Krausnick Strasse, he took a left past the church to Sophien, left on Rosenthaler, onto Mulack. Looted merchandise mixed with twinkling shards of broken glass lay strewn on the pavement. Sonny made his way through the wreckage of his neighbors' lives to the warehouse. Stopping at the corner of Rücker Strasse, he watched the dark and foreboding, strangely empty, entrance. He clenched and unclenched his fists in the eerie silence, unable to recall a single time when there hadn't been someone on the threshold, in the entry, or loitering on the pavement. People were always coming or going—but not tonight.

That's when it hit him—the men of Scheunenviertel were gone! He ran to the door and into the building, casting a brief shadow until he was swallowed into its blackness. When his eyes adjusted, he made out the rough shapes of overturned tables and upended shelves. Despite new ownership, the vendors here hadn't been spared. There wasn't a stir as he moved deeper inside. Inching his way to the stairs, he took them two at a time, past the first to the second floor.

Moving toward a faint light, Sonny passed Solomon's booth and saw that it was untouched. The upper floors seemed to have been spared. The light grew stronger as he moved slowly toward Joseph's bookstall. He saw movement there among the bookshelves—it was Joseph.

"God! What the hell are you doing here?"

Startled, Joseph took several seconds to answer. "Checking on my books."

"Sorry—didn't mean it like that. I'm surprised to find you here, that's all."

All Joseph's books seemed intact.

"Were you here when the ground floor was ransacked?"

Joseph's face was pinched. Instead of answering, he said, "Why are you here? Where did you come from?"

"Neukölln. Karl told us about the burning synagogues and the arrests. I went to see for myself—a Torah was used for kindling, and the Neckar Strasse Synagogue was in flames. I haven't seen any men around." Sonny looked glumly into the dark space beyond the books. Then as if he'd just remembered, he said, "I'm going to see if Herman's parents are all right. I promised."

"What about them?"

Suddenly, Sonny felt dazed.

"You okay?" Joseph asked, concerned.

"Who the hell knows?" Sonny said, and he told Joseph about the marching troopers. When he was done, he rubbed his eyes with both hands, trying to exorcize the image.

Joseph shook his head. "Unbelievable."

Both men were silent for a moment, then Joseph asked, "Why are you risking your life like this?"

"I need to look in on them."

"Is that wise?" Joseph started, but he knew better than to try to change Sonny's mind. "Be careful. If his father has been arrested, there's nothing you can do."

Sonny nodded.

"Ja, I was here when they came." Joseph finally got around to Sonny's question. "I heard yelling, general commotion, faint at first, then louder. For an instant I was back in '19, but no Liebknecht or Luxemburg, only the SA ransacking the empty warehouse." Joseph looked away, staring into a corner. After a long pause, he came back to the present. "They didn't come up here, but that doesn't mean they won't come tomorrow."

He looked pained, and he closed his eyes. "I was in the flat," he started, pointing absently toward it, "when a truck pulled up in front of the building on the corner. An SA squad jumped out with rifles, like they were going to war. Then an officer—I suppose that's what he was—pointed, and they separated."

Joseph licked his lips and swallowed, and when he spoke again, his voice sounded disconnected, far away: "Starting at one end, they worked their way through the buildings until the street was filled with men." He met Sonny's eyes and shuddered. "I saw some older boys. They must have ordered their wives and children to stay inside, but I heard women shouting and wailing from the windows. Most of what they said was unintelligible, but one woman's scream pierced like a dagger—'Murderers!' I stopped counting at fifty—Goldman from down the hall . . . Stein . . . all of them." He took a deep breath.

"God damn," Sonny muttered. He ran a hand through his hair.

"That's only part of it," Joseph began, his eyes filled with pain. "My initial reaction—because I knew immediately—was to get Goldman, as many as I could, but," anguish clouded his face, "I couldn't. Instead, I stuffed everything—documents, paper, pens, ink—under the floorboards."

"I forgot about that." Sonny recalled how he'd pulled one, then two boards, until they had a space big enough for a stash. With the boards dropped back into place, you couldn't tell they'd been removed, but he'd never . . .

"My hands were shaking, passports fell to the floor, I spilled ink, but finally got it done. I had to clasp my hands together—like a man praying. I sat at my desk, waiting for the knock." He sighed and closed his eyes. "They left with the other men. I still couldn't move—too scared to leave the flat. I was suffocating . . . I had to do something, so I forced myself to come here." Joseph tapped a finger on his chest. "I learned what fear can do. I thought, 'You're not scared for yourself—it's for them.' But that was a lie."

"Only a fool wouldn't be scared. Besides, what could you do?"

Joseph wasn't listening. "I was a dangling, useless appendage."

"Never!" Sonny shot back. "All that you do? I'm just thankful they didn't burst through the door."

"Ja." Joseph was leaden, unconvinced.

"Have you seen Solomon?"

"No, I haven't seen anyone." Then he took hold of Sonny's arm and said, "Be careful."

"I will," Sonny answered before leaving his shaken friend.

Groping through the darkness, down the steps, through the debris, Sonny finally reached the front door. Pausing at the exit, he caught something on the street that sent a shiver up his spine. Retreating deep into the shadows, a slow-moving gray mass passed in front of the building—a storm trooper.

Sweat rolled down Sonny's forehead. Staying calm, he moved farther inside, toward the rear door. There, the street was empty, and he exited, his pulse quickening. He'd go to Solomon's flat, make sure he was all right, try to find out more. Turning the corner, he was surprised by two women: the younger one was sobbing—she had two small children clinging to each other. The older woman—mother, aunt, friend?—was comforting her.

"We'll get him out," the woman soothed, her eyes red-rimmed from tears shed for the younger woman—or herself. Her penetrating eyes met Sonny's. He felt inadequate, a spent force, a Jew caught on the street. Jarred by the poignant exchange, he suddenly needed encouragement, but there was little solace tonight. At least it's calm now, he thought as he took a breath of acrid air.

Solomon lived with his wife and two children; occasionally members of his extended family stayed with them for a few days. Keeping to the shadows, Sonny peered around every corner, scanning the narrow streets. When he came within sight of Solomon's building, his caution paid off. Ten meters away, a storm trooper leaned casually against the building, smoking a cigarette. Slowly retreating, Sonny went the long way around to the other end of the street.

Sonny watched the storm trooper flick his butt into the street, adjust his rifle, and approach. Thinking it might not be a good time to pay his old friend a visit, he was about to leave when he heard a shout, then silence, then a woman's voice. Sonny returned to the corner and saw a woman confronting the sentry. She was moving her arms and shaking her head. They conversed for several minutes until she turned abruptly into the building. That was it—a curfew!

Sonny had contemplated making a dash for Solomon's building, but caution prevailed. Now the SA strode purposefully his way, so he decided to run. He jogged quietly through the labyrinth of streets until he felt safe, then slowed. He ducked into doorways, avoiding anyone out of place—tonight that was everyone. Shards of glass littered every street in the Jewish neighborhoods.

Suddenly from the corner of his eye, Sonny saw a man lying in the street—legs stiff, arms at his sides. "Shit!" He recoiled, then moved in to help. He stopped. In the gutter was only a fedora-topped mannequin. Relieved, he laughed nervously and traced the dummy's flight back to its former home—a shattered store window now framed in jagged glass. Men's clothing lay on the sidewalk. From beneath the pile, just peeking out, was the boldfaced headline: "Vom Rath Dead!" For an instant, he felt dirty for laughing, as if complicit in the cowardly act.

Scanning the curtained windows of the flats above, he saw a crack of light and the downturned profile of a man's head. Above the window, a Nazi swastika fluttered. When Sonny looked back to the window, the head was gone. On every street, Jewish shops were marked by broken glass, looted merchandise, and coarse epithets scrawled on the doors. One shop was lit, and two women carried a board to cover the space that the window had occupied.

Sonny's impulse, again, was to help, but the women were leery. His offer met with suspicion. The older one, perhaps the mother, declined with a curt "No." The younger woman avoided his eyes. With their livelihood destroyed, a husband and a father likely arrested—why would they trust a stranger?

Sonny thought he knew the twisted logic behind Nazi cruelty, but the baseness of the attacks and their choreographed destruction left him adrift. Why had they done it? With complete power, they no longer needed a scapegoat. So why banish Polish Jews, who'd lived peaceably among them for years? Why destroy their neighborhoods and arrest their men? Do they hate us so much? Was all this carnage the result of a massive failure of imagination? The answer was too bleak to contemplate.

Leaving the narrow, winding streets of the Mitte, Sonny moved along the northern bank of the Spree toward the shelter of Tiergarten Park. He'd get lost in the woods, where men like Otto spent nights in warmer weather. Anyone out tonight was foolish—or compelled by fate. He wasn't surprised to see movement in the spaces between the trees. Hell, he was one of them!

Moving through a clearing, Sonny ran headlong into somebody crouched behind a tree and sent the fellow flying. He barely kept his balance, while the other guy seemed more shocked than hurt by his fall. Getting quickly to his feet, the man stared at Sonny. In a high-pitched voice filled with panic at discovery, he demanded, "Who are you?"

"A friend," Sonny assured him. "Hiding, like you."

The stranger was shivering, and when he finally spoke, he slurred his words. "All morning rumor ran rampant. And then I heard screams that SA were entering our building. I jumped out the window and ran down the alley until I got here. I've been here all day—cold and hungry, too scared to talk to the others in hiding. I'm not a religious man, but I've been praying." He grabbed Sonny's jacket in desperation.

Sonny pushed him away. "I know it's tough, but get a grip."

The guy went slack. "Sorry. I'm at the end of my tether." Then the guy started with questions, one upon the other: Was the SA still out, were synagogues burning, were Jewish businesses looted, was it safe to return to his flat?

Sonny told the man what he had seen . . .

As he listened, the man grew more distraught. "I'll never get my family out, not now. My cousin in America promised an affidavit. It didn't come, but even if it arrived today, I can't go home to get it." He buried his face in his hands.

Sonny knew he could help. With some questioning, he determined that the man had passports but no visas—that's what he'd been waiting for.

Suddenly animated, the man spoke of New Jersey, where his cousin lived. "Have you heard of Newark?" He babbled on about America, but as the complexity of his dilemma caught up with him, his enthusiasm dissipated. He shivered, then wrapped his arms around his chest, and began to jump up and down.

"Don't give up," said Sonny. Then he made his offer. When he finished, the fellow backed away and said not to kid him, not today. Trying not to show his frustration, Sonny kept at it until he broke through.

The guy laughed "This is too much—being offered a way out while hiding behind a tree!" Who could blame him?

Sonny arranged a meeting for two days later at 2 PM at the little café in Scheunenviertel. If that didn't work, the man was to return at the same time on the next day and again until someone met him there. His name was Henry Neuman, and Sonny swore him to secrecy. Hoping to God nothing would happen to either of them, Sonny wished Neuman good luck and left for Pestalozzi Strasse.

Less secure than he had felt in the park, Sonny headed toward the West End. There would be SA at Zoo Station for sure, so he went the long way around. Working his way north of Ku'damm, he repeated the word *Pestalozzi,* savoring its sound. At the same time a tenuous thought distracted him, and he nearly tripped on an overturned garbage bin. Then it came: Johnny's tavern was on Pestalozzi—but what was its name? No matter, he knew the location. He snapped his fingers, startling a pigeon—yes, the Dove! Knowing Johnny would be there, he decided to stop in just to get off the street.

Sonny kept walking. Savigny Platz lay just ahead when he heard a coarse voice: "Stop!" Preferring death on the street to life in the camps, he almost ran, but the thought of Henry waiting in vain at the café stopped him. He slowly turned. Standing three meters away wasn't an SA squad, or even a single storm trooper, but an older guy in street clothes. Listing like tall grass in a breeze, he smelled of alcohol and his eyes were glazed—the asshole was drunk.

Sonny let out the breath he'd been holding, quickly made sense of the scene before him, and barked, "What the hell do you want?" Then he moved closer, crowding the man until they faced one another in an oddly choreographed standoff. Sonny waited.

"I can smell a fucking Jew," the guy hissed. He puffed up his chest and looked Sonny up and down with drunken disgust. Seconds ticked by; the fellow looked away.

Sonny kicked him in the groin and punched his solar plexus. He crumpled like a tent in a windstorm. Sonny bent over him and shouted in his ear, "Fuck you! Fuck Hitler!" Flexing his hand, he walked away without looking back. Had the guy really sniffed him out?

In five minutes Sonny stood at the door of the darkened tavern. He knocked, but there was no answer. He walked through the alley to the back door where they'd delivered the No. 15 loot. Light shone in the lone window next to the door. he knocked again.

"Who is it?" That deep, rumbling voice wasn't Johnny.

"Sonny, a friend of Johnny's."

"Wait!" Then silence.

In about a minute, a different voice said, "Sonny, that you?"

"Ja. Can I come in?"

"Hold on." The bolt slid aside, and the door opened, revealing a sliver of light. "I'll be damned! Hurry. Come in." Johnny stuck his head out the door, then closed and locked it.

"We're all damned," Sonny muttered.

Johnny looked haggard, his smug half-smile fading. "Afraid so. What brings you out on a night like this? More trinkets to sell?"

"Nothing so banal. I'm on my way to check on the parents of a friend. I thought a safe harbor would be nice along the way." He pointed with his thumb back over his shoulder. "I ran into a drunken, crazed Nazi back there."

"They're all crazed." Johnny waved him to a table. It held a bottle, several glasses. Two men in suits were seated there, one older and nearly bald, the other with a scar on his cheek. Sonny introduced them as Blum and Mandel. Neither extended a hand—each just nodded.

The older man was Blum, and Sonny immediately saw in him a resemblance to Johnny's old boss. Two more glasses appeared, and Johnny poured while Blum and Mandel continued where they must have left off, cursing the fucking Nazis. What else was there tonight?

With no one else in sight, Sonny addressed Johnny. "Who was that at the door?"

"He works for me. Today he let in every Jew I know and some I do not." Johnny waved an arm toward Blum and Mandel.

Blum held out his hands in a gesture of thanks. "Johnny saved our asses."

"Never figured the Dove for a Jewish community center," Johnny said dryly.

"You did what's right, and I appreciate that," Mandel added.

Blum nodded.

"Where are the others?" Sonny asked, looking around but seeing nothing.

"Hiding in the cellar and a room off the back." Johnny waved his arm toward the rear of the tavern.

He was running a safe house, and Sonny was impressed. Guys like Johnny didn't give a shit about status or other superficial crap so long as there was money in it. But there was no money to be made tonight. He figured Blum and Mandel did business with Johnny, so they didn't have to hide in the cellar with the others.

"It's over." The deep, sandpaper voice Sonny had heard at the door echoed through the space.

Sonny automatically stood, thinking the SA was at the door. The others must have thought that too—anxiety pulsated through the room. A round, hairless head over a wide body emerged from the shadows. The man, like Emil but more fearsome, had a prominent scar on his forehead. His flat, unsmiling face seemed oddly familiar.

Only Johnny remained seated and calm. "What is it, Fred?"

The Hammer & Sickle's bartender had found a home with Johnny!

Fred spoke directly to Johnny. "That little shit called off his dogs—ordered a halt to action against the Jews."

"What?" Blum blubbered.

Fred turned his head in Blum's direction: "What I said. Goebbels told them to stop."

"It's safe to leave?" Mandel asked.

"How the hell should I know? I'm just saying what I heard." Fred's insolence recalled Sonny's first interaction with him.

Blum and Mandel started a conversation, and Johnny left the table. Fred turned to follow, but Sonny stopped him.

"Fred, from the Hammer & Sickle, right?"

Fred turned his head and eyed Sonny without recognition. He raised his heavy shoulders in a shrug. "Do I know you?"

"Ja. I'm Sonny, an old friend of Otto's," Sonny said, extending his hand. His mind's eye wandered to those fabulous Soviet posters. He wondered what had happened to them. Drifting back, he laughed and said, "The first time I came in, you scared the shit out of me."

A hum came from between Fred's lips, and he squinted, then a corner of his mouth rose a millimeter, in a smile. "Sure," he growled. "I remember you sat with Otto and a couple other guys, talked art and other shit, maybe even a little politics." Then the same corner of his mouth dropped. "Rumor was Otto got arrested in '33."

Sonny shook his head. "No. Otto went underground. Hell, he came here with me, six months back—just saw him."

"Must have been off that night. Glad to hear that. He's a good guy."

"How long you been working for Johnny?" Sonny asked.

Gears turned and lips moved before Fred said, "We both worked at the Katakombe—he was bartending and I was doing odd jobs—I came here with Johnny when it closed."

Sonny nodded.

"What have you been doing?" Fred asked.

"I used to deliver booze and cigarettes to clubs for a guy, but that fell apart. Funny I never saw you at the Katakombe." Sonny shrugged. "I started smuggling people out. Otto's part of the operation."

Fred extended his lower lip and nodded slightly. "Gotta go see if Johnny needs anything. Good to see you, Sonny." He stuck out an enormous hand, and they shook. "Give my best to Otto."

"I will. Good to see you, too."

Sonny watched Fred leave the bar, then turned to his drink. Blum and Mandel were gone, so he finished up and went to look for Johnny. Near the back door he heard voices; he was surprised to see at least ten people, almost all men, with the haggard look of hours spent in dark, cramped quarters. He read alienation on their faces, sensed distrust and fear—the night's common thread. Now suddenly free, they hesitated—the night was unpredictable.

He felt it too. None of the faces belonged to anyone he knew, though several looked familiar. He nodded as he passed long the tight, dark corridor, looking for Johnny. A small crowd huddled in a doorway. "Thank you, thank you," he heard again and again, until one of them said, "I'm taking my chances and going home."

"Be careful. If you need anything, you know where to find me," said Johnny from the shadows.

Pinched faces and bodies squeezed past Sonny, and he moved to the doorway. Johnny sat behind his enormous desk in the small space.

Empty, windowless walls of exposed brick stopped at the low ceiling. Squeezed into a corner was a tall file cabinet holding a lamp that cast Johnny's shadow across the desk. Though undeniably squalid, tonight this place was the home of a dignified hero.

"That was a good thing you did today," Sonny said.

The flicker of a smile appeared as Johnny waved off the compliment. "What could I do? Some are customers, friends; others are associates. Hell, most I don't even know, but what difference does it make?"

"It was risky."

"Risk!" He laughed cynically. "You and me been on the fringes for years. Shit, we're immune." More laughter, this time from deep in his throat. "You're a long way from home tonight, walking around like you're invisible."

"Ja. I carry a fake ID," Sonny answered, rubbing his bruised hand.

"Of course. You could put on a uniform—they wouldn't know the difference," Johnny teased.

"Not a bad idea, using a Gestapo uniform to get around. I could cut some brothers loose."

"Got one, if you want to borrow it." Johnny offered with a bemused smile, making the comment go either way.

Sonny let it slide.

"Even now, you can get just about anything. I used it a couple times. Nobody bothers you—they just give you the fucking, stiff-armed salute."

Sonny still didn't know whether Johnny was pulling his leg, so he changed the subject. "Never ran into Mandel or Blum before. What're they into?"

Drumming his fingers on the desk, Johnny seemed impatient—or nervous, after all. His answer was uncharacteristically circumspect. "Like you and me, they're into what pays. We've done business."

His curiosity piqued, Sonny asked, "What—prostitution, drugs, gambling?"

Johnny shrugged.

"Smuggling?"

Johnny's eyes gave the answer.

Sonny thought for several seconds. "People?"

"What difference does it make?"

"Just heard a nasty story about an agent leaving Jews at the border without papers. The group was out of Cologne, not here. Didn't like what I heard, wondered if that's what they're into."

Johnny shrugged. "They're into both, but recently they're into people. I can't speak to their success or their ethics." He refused to be drawn into Sonny's moral crusade. "They're filling a need—like you."

Johnny leaned back in his chair and rubbed his eyes. "Everyone who's hiding here tonight will start looking for a way out if they know what's good for them. Blum and Mandel are kicking themselves in the ass for not leaving yesterday." He looked at Sonny. "Why the hell are you still here?"

Sonny rubbed his chin and said, "You're the third person in the last couple of days asking me that. At least you haven't ordered me to go."

"Answer the question," Johnny pressed.

"Inertia, I suppose, and some crazy idea we'd get as many Jews out of Germany as we could before I left. We've succeeded to a degree."

"With a little burglary on the side."

"Sure. Spread the wealth."

Johnny doffed an imaginary hat. "I appreciate the business. That was quite a haul and a good story, and I do like a good story. Too bad about the guy who died."

Sonny felt a rush of guilt. "He died saving us."

"There's nobility in that," Johnny said, giving Willy his due. "But we're in a tough business. You can't get too sentimental."

These were harsh words from another realist, and though they were true, it was hard to hear them. "I never fully appreciated that until Willy died," Sonny said.

Johnny smiled warmly. "Think of it as a down payment on a new life in Belgium, France, England, or—think big—America."

They reminisced about the Pink Slipper, the music, the freewheeling good times, the bombing.

"Christ, what a night!" Johnny exclaimed, emotion sneaking through his cool façade. He stared at the blank wall, reached for a bottle, and filled two small glasses on a tray at the corner of his desk. He handed a glass to Sonny and raised his own. "To memories—and better times ahead."

They drained the glasses. Then Johnny started to talk: "It was Blum they were after, and if they couldn't get him, they were determined to close it down. Someone finally got him, but I don't know who." He rested his forehead on his hand, elbow on the desk, reminding Sonny of Rodin's *Thinker.*

Sonny set the glass on the desk. "I've got some matters to attend to," he said. "Are you leaving or staying?"

"What? Leave this empire behind?" The old Johnny was back, laughing. "Good luck." He stood and offered his hand.

"Thanks," Sonny said as they shook.

"Can I refer people?"

"Sure. I won't be around, so contact Emil—he'll make it happen."

Johnny nodded and sat down again. "Be careful out there."

Sonny waved a hand and headed for the door. Fred was alone in the hall with his back to Sonny.

"Fred, I'm leaving. You take care."

Turning, Fred said, "Ja, you too."

Residue of perspiration, alcohol, and tobacco filled the tight corridor. "How many people?" Sonny asked.

Shaking his head, Fred said, "Dunno, didn't count. Maybe twenty-five—could be more."

"Are they all gone?"

"Still some in the cellar, too scared to leave. Johnny says they can stay as long as they want," said Fred.

"You've done well tonight," Sonny said again, passing Johnny on his way out the door.

Like Fred said, the word was out, and everyone other than the Jews was back on the street, curious about the pogrom. They must have been glued to the radio—or perhaps they received a telephone call, then opened the door a crack, ventured into the hall and onto the street. They stood in small groups, like deer at a salt lick, skittish but curious. How would they react when they learned of the scope and brutality of today's pogrom? Would they sympathize with the Jews—or turn their backs?

Over the past five years they had all learned to keep their mouths shut. Since '33, Communists, socialists, religious leaders—anyone brave enough to protest—had disappeared. Some never returned, but those who did talked of camps, and rumors of torture had spread. Now, the Jews were disappearing.

People believed what they wanted to believe and what they needed to believe to survive, but they were fooling themselves. They'd handed power to a gang of thugs, were stuck in a morass of their own making—that much Sonny understood. Heads turned, looked at him suspiciously, but he kept his distance. While fear was the cost of doing business, it was a hefty tax for staying in a country gone mad. What did the good Germans have to be afraid of?

Still, what had happened today was a new chapter in cruelty. He couldn't even call it a nightmare—waking didn't make it go away. With a sudden spasm, Sonny flexed the hand that he'd swung at the drunk and winced.

As he approached Karl August Platz and the Pestalozzi Strasse Synagogue, Sonny's spine tingled. Years earlier, he'd met an architecture student and over coffee listened to him describe the building's Romanesque façade. Its form, typical of German medieval architecture, to the casual observer was a church or a school—but for the Star of David adorning its front and the mezuzah on the doorpost. Sonny had lost track of the guy, couldn't recall his name . . .

A fire truck was parked near the inconspicuous entrance to the temple, discreetly tucked away in a courtyard. Sonny silently prayed that the wonderful old building had escaped destruction. His heart sank when he realized the firemen were there to protect not the synagogue but the buildings around it. Children clung to their mother's jackets—he heard wailing. Among them were gentile tenants sent scattering as the firefighters fought to save their homes but ignored the burning temple.

"Fuck them. Let it all burn down," Sonny muttered.

He turned away, unable to witness the demise of yet another sacred building. He walked quickly, his shoulders hunched against the night cold, his hands buried in his pockets. Within minutes he stood inside No. 241 and found the name *Milberg* in the entry. With trepidation, he climbed the steps to the second floor, looked around, saw nothing, and walked to the Milbergs' door. He pressed his ear to the door but heard only the sound of his own labored breathing.

Fear of some awful truth made him hesitate. A neighbor's door opened slightly. A head emerged and Sonny nodded, though he couldn't see the shadowed face. The neighbor's door closed, and Sonny rapped lightly on the door before him.

He waited a long time, but there was no answer—no sound of footsteps or shuffle. Fearing the worst, he slowly turned the doorknob and pushed. To his surprise, the door opened into darkness. He stepped inside, closed the door, stood and listened. Again, there wasn't a sound—no breathing, no crush of fabric, no movement. He wouldn't go, not yet. In a voice just loud enough to be heard, he said, "Herr Milberg, Frau Milberg, my name is Sonny. I'm a friend of Herman's. I mean you no harm. I've come to see if you're all right."

When there was no answer, he thought to leave, but first he wanted to find a light switch. As he groped along the wall, he heard the thin voice of an old woman: "Who are you? What are you doing?"

Sonny jumped, took a breath, and strained to find the source. Finally, his eyes found the outline of a small shape seated in the corner no more than three meters away. He spoke to it. "Looking for the light switch."

"No! Why are you here?"

For some reason, he repeated his name.

"You already said that. I'm not hard of hearing," the woman said, apparently no longer afraid.

"Herman made me promise to check on you if there was trouble."

"Have you heard from Herman? Is he safe?" Her tone was expectant.

"No, I haven't," he lied again.

She made a clucking sound, perhaps of disappointment.

"I'm sure he'll write once he's settled," Sonny answered, this time telling the truth.

Turning the page, she said, "Herman never mentioned your name."

Eschewing another lie, Sonny said, "May I turn on the light?"

A cone of dim light suddenly revealed a woman whose feet barely reached the floor. Sonny squinted to see her face.

"Frau Milberg, are you all right?"

"Yes, I believe so, but I haven't moved for so long, it's hard to tell."

"Good. Is Herr Milberg here?"

"No," she answered, as if put out by his absence.

"Do you know where he is?"

"Maybe, but I can't be sure. He didn't know where he was going," she said, her voice quavering. "Without him, I'm lost."

Sonny moved to a chair nearby. On the table was the photograph of a barely smiling Herman flanked by his mother and a man Sonny took to be his father. He was about Herman's height, with a bushy mustache on a round face and pleasant eyes behind wire spectacles. Sonny stared at the image, memorizing his face, then closed his eyes and visualized Milberg. "Do you have any idea where your husband went?"

Instead of answering, she demanded to know the time.

Sonny blinked at her non sequitur and looked at his watch. "A quarter past ten."

"That late?" She stared at her hands, clasped tightly on her lap.

"It's been a long and terrible day," Sonny said lamely.

But she didn't seem to hear: "The telephone rang hours ago. I think it was still morning—we'd been up for some time. It was our friend Samuel, who lives down the street with his wife and two daughters. He told my husband to leave here and to hide. I heard only one side of the conversation, but that's what my husband told me Samuel was going to do. Someone warned Samuel that the SA was arresting the men. At first, my husband would not leave me . . . I'm not well . . . it's my heart. I have trouble walking . . . But I insisted. 'What good are you to me if you're locked away?' I asked."

Very sensible, thought Sonny. "Where would he have gone?"

"First, he made sure I was comfortable, and then he left. But he didn't say where." Her voice trailed off at the possibilities.

"Do you have any idea?"

Her face pinched in concentration and she took a breath, making a little rattle in her throat. She reached for a glass on the corner of the little table and drank before she spoke: "He may have found safety with friends in the next block, but other than that, I don't know." She pointed toward the window. "The Kuhns—they would have helped him—and others."

"Which building?" Sonny tried to keep the urgency from his voice.

"Let's see—second building from the corner, next block, same side of the street. They live on the third floor, in the front flat nearest to us."

She was too calm, perhaps in shock, too resigned to what may have befallen her husband. What could he tell Herman that wouldn't drive him deeper into despair? Sonny brushed aside the thought: he would find Herman's father, then worry about the message.

" . . . Perhaps that's what shock does to you." She smiled weakly.

She'd read his mind. Nodding, he asked, "Did the Gestapo come to the flat?" He didn't think so, but he had to ask.

"No, thank God." Her voice was barely above a whisper. Sonny had to concentrate to hear.

She straightened her dress and continued. "But I heard them screaming horrible epithets." Then she placed her hands on her ears to shut out the memory of what she'd heard. "They may have come in the building. I don't know." With effort she looked at Sonny with an intensity that hadn't been there before. In a tone just short of command, she said, "I need my husband. Please find him and bring him to me." Nothing else mattered—she was frail, alone, afraid.

"I will," he said and stood to leave, then remembered the face in the hall. "Has anyone checked on you?"

"Yes, the woman next door. Her husband hasn't returned from work, and she hasn't heard from him either. Her daughter lives with them. I hope she's all right. Will you check?"

Sonny nodded.

She looked into his eyes and said, "Good luck. You know where to find me."

24

Who ever loved that loved not at first sight?
—Christopher Marlow

Sonny knocked on the Milberg neighbor's door. He heard an angry woman's voice.

"Who are you? What do you want?" The door remained unopened.

"A friend of Frau Milberg."

"Why should I let a stranger in?" Now the voice sounded raspy, less hostile, younger.

"Frau Milberg asked me to look in on you. I'm a friend of Herman's, and I'm going to look for Herr Milberg. Please, let me in." He heard muted voices. The key turned in the lock, and the door opened a crack.

"Who are you?"

"A friend," Sonny whispered and waited again.

Finally, the door opened onto a striking young woman with flushed cheeks and an attractive overbite. Her eyes, dotted with patches of red, fixed on him like spotlights. "Who are you?"

Sonny stared at her but did not move or answer.

"Don't just stand there. Come in!"

He did as ordered.

She locked the door. "I saw you at the Milbergs' door. All right, what do you want?"

So that was you, Sonny thought. Tearing his eyes away from her, he saw an older woman, standing in shadow, wringing her hands. He sensed the resemblance of the two, but the daughter was taller and lovelier, her features more refined. Returning his gaze to the daughter, he said, "Herr Milberg is missing—I'm going to look for him. Frau Milberg asked me to make sure you're all right."

"Of course, we're not all right!" She nearly shouted, her bloodshot eyes flashing. "My father's somewhere out there." Struggling to retain her composure, she added, "He could be rotting in jail. So, you tell me how we're doing."

Sonny retreated several steps, raising his hands in surrender. "I'm sorry."

"Dear, don't take it out on this poor man," her mother admonished.

After a silent, uncomfortable interlude, the daughter spoke without apology. "It's a horror not knowing where he is. I've been saying for months . . . it's impossible living here. Now this." She shot an accusing glance over her shoulder.

Her mother looked down at her wringing hands. The accusation, like a spark of static electricity, must have stung.

The daughter's hands clenched, and her lips tightened. "At least Herman got out," she said, making one last swipe at her mother. Then she faced Sonny. "Now poor Herr Milberg is in hiding, Father is God knows where, and we're stuck in this hellhole." Her words rushed out in staccato force.

Sonny felt like taking cover. He'd seen too much awfulness today, and listening to this young woman vent her family's dirty laundry was more than he wanted to bear. But there was something about her, so he stood his ground, waiting for it to end.

She paused, caught her breath, and put a hand to her brow as if to steady herself. Then, in a surprisingly calm voice, she said, "You're a friend of Herman's."

"Yes," Sonny answered, thankful for the lull. "He asked me to check on his parents if anything happened. So I came and learned just minutes ago that his father is missing." Then he added, "I'm going to find Herr Milberg." He was surprised at his calm assurance.

It caught her attention too. She nodded approvingly, looking at him as if she had questions.

Before she spoke, Sonny asked, "Do you have any idea where Herr Milberg could be?"

She frowned and said, "No, unfortunately." Then she looked at her mother, who was shaking her head forlornly.

"Well, thought I'd ask," Sonny started, and without thinking, he blurted, "After I find Herr Milberg, I'll return and help find your father." Only after the words were out—such was the effect of this young woman upon him—did he realize their import. He was chagrined for a moment, but her smile extinguished all doubt.

Nodding at the prospect of help, she began, "I was . . ." She stopped, chewed on her lower lip as if to keep from saying more. Then she simply said, "Thank you."

Sonny felt the tension lessen—he wondered whether they even noticed—but he wanted to ease it further. "Frau Milberg appreciated that you checked on her. It was very considerate."

"Several times," the mother said. "She's not well, and she is alone—I have Rosa." She moved closer and placed a hand on her daughter's arm. "I offered to bring her here with us, but she refused to leave. She had to wait for her husband to return." Tears rolled down her cheeks, but she didn't seem to notice.

Confusing images of another Rosa from another, earlier time swirled in Sonny's head—another chance encounter in a darker, more foreboding labyrinth. "Rosa," Sonny spoke her name, provoking a fleeting sensuality, but the present Rosa's slightly husky voice roused him back to the present.

"Yes," she acknowledged, extending her hand. "This is my mother, Elise Fischer. And you are . . . ?"

Sonny's eyes fell to her hand, and he squeezed it lightly. She let her hand rest in his, then pulled it back. Milky white teeth showed through her faint smile. His eyes met hers, and slightly flustered, he said, "Uh—Sonny. People call me Sonny."

Moments before they had been complete strangers; unimaginable circumstances had brought them together, to face one another awkwardly in the middle of a room Sonny had never been in before. No one spoke. He felt as if they'd slipped through a crack as the silence stretched to fifteen, perhaps thirty seconds, of what seemed to be infinity. Nothing existed but Frau Fischer's quiet weeping for a missing husband, Rosa's desire for answers, and his own wondering about how he'd find the two missing men.

No answers came . . . so Sonny said, "Tell me about your father."

His voice must have startled Rosa, because her head jerked, and when comprehension came, her eyes narrowed with bewilderment. "What about him?"

"If I'm going to find him, I'll need to know something about him."

"I see." She shook her head, as if realigning its internal connections. "His name is Robert—Robert Fischer." Stepping back, her eyes traveled from Sonny's face down the length of his body, taking his measure. She moved closer—he felt her warm breath on his face—and said, "He's shorter than you, by several inches."

She turned, walked to a chest of drawers, took out a folder, removed what looked like a photograph. "Here, take this. It's quicker, much better than—you know—a thousand words, all that." Her smile was brittle.

Sonny looked at the photos of her father's thoroughly pleasant face, slightly crooked smile below strong nose and dark eyes—like Rosa's. He put the picture in his pocket as he softly repeated the name.

"I hope to return soon," he said, about to leave. But then he remembered what Fred had said. "Have you heard the news? Goebbels ordered an end to the pogrom."

Rosa's lips curled into a sneer. "I don't believe a word of it." The air moved as her hand flew close to his face. "It's probably a ruse to get those in hiding out into the open! God, how I hate this place!"

"I'm sorry. I didn't mean to upset you again." Sonny's apology sounded lame even to him. Of course, she was right—about the Nazis' arrogance in releasing the scum upon them, then cavalierly calling them off as if commanding a dog to heel.

Rosa put fingertips to temples. "I can't be more upset more than I am already." Shaking her head, she closed her eyes as if she were meditating. Then she opened them abruptly. "Sonny, be careful . . . and good luck."

Bounding down the stairs two at time, he was off to find the two missing men . . . they could be anywhere. By the time he reached the street, doubt licked at his confidence. Had a pretty face pushed him into making a promise he'd come to regret? It was one thing to make sure Herman's parents were safe, to offer to find his father, but his brash offer to Rosa and her mother? That was simple hubris, vanity.

Well, it was too late; now he couldn't get her face out of his head even if he wanted to, which he didn't. He repeated her name, "Rosa, Rosa," then whispered "Rosy." And from all those years ago that other Rosy came rushing back . . .

He was seventeen, helping his father carry cartons from the cellar. Tired, making his way through the maze of dark, narrow corridors, he turned a corner and collided with . . . someone suddenly filling the space. The body was Rosy's—she'd been as startled as he.

"I'm sorry—didn't see you—you all right?" Sonny's cheeks burned crimson. As her comely figure slowed into focus, his stammer increased. She was standing with her hands on her hips, one slightly higher then the other—a young woman, not a girl. He moved his eyes up her body to a face with a hint of a smile.

She said nothing.

He'd never seen her before—surely he would remember her if he had. Tall and handsome, she was Sinti . . . maybe. He wasn't sure. She had an unnerving poise. At rest, her body exuded a graceful ease, an inexplicable magnetism that he later understood as raw sensuality. After they'd known each other intimately, he realized that his initial response had met her expectations. He had passed the first test.

He forgot to breathe. As his discomfort grew to clownish proportions, she said with an assurance bordering on arrogance, "Be more careful. You could hurt a girl." Then her eyes flashed, and a bright, teasing smile appeared as she cooed, "I'm Rosy, Solomon's cousin."

"Sonny . . . er . . . I'm Sonny," he managed.

Her laugh was friendly. "Relax. I don't bite. Come up and say hello." As she moved around him, her hip provocatively brushed his.

Sonny was unsure the encounter was real. But her musky fragrance and the faint stirring in his loin were proof enough . . . When he got back upstairs to his work, his father asked, "What took so long?"

"I ran into someone," Sonny said, laughing . . .

After Sonny confirmed that the shapely apparition was real, his friend Solomon had pulled him aside. "Be careful," he warned. "Rosy has a certain reputation with men." He raised an eyebrow. "She gets what she wants—that's all I'm going to say."

Sonny shrugged, intrigued, but he wasn't sure what Solomon meant until his second encounter with Rosy in the cellar. Within minutes, they were groping and kissing, their bodies so tightly compressed that her nipples dug like fingers into his chest. After five minutes they were panting as if they'd run across the Mitte. Between breaths, she whispered in his ear, "You know the old shed? Meet me in ten minutes."

He nodded as she released him and walked away, moving her hand along the curve of her rump. Sonny tasted her on his lips and wanted more . . .

The old shed door was slightly ajar, and he went inside. Rosy was leaning against the wall. "Lock the door." Her lips were hot, her tongue probing every corner of his mouth. Sonny followed her lead, felt her hand on his pants. Her skirt was off, his pants down, her legs wrapped around his waist. They squeezed, thrust, and grunted with pleasure. Rosy moaned a rhythmic tune in a language he didn't know. Rapture came in a crescendo of erupting concentric circles, his body soaring above the shed. Then he fell limp, relaxed.

She murmured into his ear, "I will teach you how to wait longer, my love."

Dazed but elated, his breathing labored, shirt clinging to chest, Sonny zipped his pants and wiped his forehead with his handkerchief.

"We can't go back, not yet," Rosy said coolly, suggesting they take a walk.

Hell, he'd have hung upside down from the rafters had she asked. Aroused beyond his wildest dreams . . . vague yearning satisfied . . . he was unmoored, hurdling through space and time. She had taken Sonny over a threshold to a world he hadn't known only minutes before.

Passion was Rosy's greatest virtue—alas, the only one other than her physical attributes. With a limitless, lusty hunger, she titillated him beyond his youthful imagination. Before Rosy, sex was a mere string of letters, an abstraction. Now it exploded, red hot, a runaway locomotive thundering up his spine in fiery rapture. Something this intoxicating must be a sin.

Their unpredictable liaisons had no set routine. She would appear smiling at his father's stall, whisper a place to meet—shed or storage room—where they'd laugh and talk but mostly make love. Rosy made clear from the beginning that there would be no permanent attachment, and Sonny agreed—why not? He was having the time of his life.

But that their affair would end had never dawned on him, and when it did end—that was a sour and wrenching pill. Sonny had fallen in love, he thought, though he couldn't be sure—he'd never been in love before. There was that voice in his head hinting that love had to be more than lying on a hard floor or standing in a corner with his pants around his ankles. But the other, the wanting voice, had always won.

Then one day, and another, and days turned to weeks that she did not appear. Finally, Solomon said Rosy would not be back, she'd married, become an honest woman. So it ended as abruptly as it had begun—in and out. He should have known their relationship would be fleeting. Still, he longed for her, ached really, especially at night when he was curled up under the sheets. He'd reach out to touch her breasts, smell her skin, kiss her lips. That they'd never made love in a bed mattered little.

Sonny assuaged his pain by working harder and reading voraciously—Kafka, Doblin, Mann, and Zweig. One day rummaging in Joseph's bookstall, he found a slim volume of Shakespeare's sonnets and read until two lines rang true: "When my love swears that she is made of truth, I do believe her, though I know she lies."

And so it went, until over time the pain disappeared like the last frozen patches of ice in early spring. In the end, he realized that all they'd had was a sexual partnership—he meant little to her. She'd taught him a great deal but nothing about love or friendship.

Several years later, whenever his thoughts bled to Rosy, he realized she had given him a valuable lesson: take what life gives, learn from the experience, and move on. Rosy was a comet, streaking across the sky, appearing but once, disappearing. Within a year of the end of their affair, there came a new wound, deeper and far more profound—his father's death. And on top of that, his mother's . . .

Sonny frowned at his careening thoughts as he waited in the entryway of No. 241 Pestalozzi Strasse. Moving on from the distant Rosy, he embraced his parents, thought of Simon, then Willy, and wondered what misery lay ahead.

Then he turned to the task of finding the two men. He peered in both directions, not so enamored of the more recent Rosa that he'd be careless. Seeing nothing amiss, he set out for the Kuhn flat. The brisk air and his promises kept him moving.

In minutes he stepped inside the nondescript five-story building described by Herman's mother. After he knocked softly several times, the door opened onto a tall, slightly stooped, man with a thin face, and small, round spectacles. The man stared without blinking. "Can I help you?"

Slightly unnerved, Sonny began, "I hope so. I've come from Frau Milberg. I'm looking for her husband." His eyes moved beyond Kuhn into the flat, but he saw nothing.

"Come in." Kuhn closed the door almost before Sonny was past the threshold. "We've been worried about all our neighbors . . . But he's not here." His head shook back and forth and his lips pursed.

From under Sonny's breath, a harsh expletive escaped. He immediately apologized.

"I've uttered far worse many times today." Kuhn's attempt at a smile ended in a grimace.

After putting so much hope in Kuhn, Sonny's disappointment was palpable. He puffed his cheeks and slowly exhaled, then ran his fingers through his hair. He felt foolish, even naïve, for failing to consider other options. He needed answers. He lived underground, knew how to burrow into dark corners and hide, but men like Milberg and Fischer did not. Without much hope, he asked, "Where would Herr Milberg go?"

"I wish I knew," answered Kuhn, his small eyes darting to the sides and rolling back.

Sonny noticed and said softly, "I understand—back there," with a nod. "But not Herr Milberg?"

Kuhn raised a finger to his lips.

"How many?" Sonny asked.

"Five friends," he answered.

Sonny took Kuhn's hand: "Thank you."

"It's my duty," he said somberly. "Frau Kuhn is checking on neighbors and the families of the men. She hasn't returned."

Then Sonny reached into his pocket and showed Kuhn the picture. "Do you know Robert Fischer? Is he here?"

"I know him. I'm sorry—he's not here either."

Sadly, there it was. Sonny wearily shook his head. "Then I must be going."

Kuhn couldn't let him leave before giving him a glass of water and a thick slice of rye bread. Sonny wiped the crumbs from his lips with the back of his hand and thanked him. He heard a whispered "Godspeed" as he departed.

He raced through the possibilities stacked one on another in his mind—for where the men might be—until they collapsed in a heap. Realizing he was completely unprepared, he stood at the crossroads of Windscheid and Pestalozzi trying to discern where to look next for one or the other.

To the west a short distance was Lietzen See, the boomerang-shaped lake that might provide refuge in the way Tiergarten's forest had provided for Henry. But that seemed a thin possibility. Maybe Milberg had gone south to Kufurstendamm. But there wasn't cover—unless he knew someone there. His wife had not mentioned anyone. Perhaps he had gone north, deeper into Charlottenburg, toward Schloss Garten—but that seemed too far. That left the east, toward Savigny Platz.

With hands on hips, Sonny faced each direction in turn, realizing the difficulty of his task. If a stranger—someone like Kuhn or a guy like Johnny—Herr Milberg . . . Shit! Of course, that was it! Sonny squinted toward Savigny Plat—and Johnny's place. Why hadn't he thought of looking there?

No time to stand on the corner thinking he'd been an idiot. Suddenly Sonny's ears pricked to a distant sound, and he turned to the drone of vehicles bearing down upon him. A big black sedan, its two headlight eyes breaking the darkness, raced east on Pestalozzi. Trailing behind was a military truck, its diesel engine straining to maintain the pace.

Sonny realized that beyond his obvious problem, he was flauting the curfew. He froze. Exposed on the corner, he felt a tingling sensation in his hands, moving to his neck, settling along his hairline—the same unnerving sensation he'd felt in his encounter with Albert in Aachen.

For the third time that night, instinct told him to run, but it was too late. So he stared dumbly, as if watching from a window, at the driver's head in dark profile as the car passed. He imagined the driver hitting the brakes, the screech of rubber, the caravan skidding to a halt. He still squinted from the glare of the headlamps, but the vehicles didn't stop, and in the time it took to be scared shitless, they were gone.

Sonny fell against the streetlight, breathing heavily, tired of being scared. Balling his bruised hand tightly into a fist until it hurt, then rubbing the fingertips of his other hand along the smooth metallic surface of the pole until it felt hot, he welcomed the pain. And he headed to where dozens of men were in hiding.

Sonny ran with long even strides, imagining a frightened Milberg passing by the Dove, hesitating, then walking in. God, he hoped both Milberg and Fischer were there. And the more he thought about it, the less of a long shot it seemed. Hell! It was all he had.

Fred let him in, and Sonny went directly to the office. Johnny looked up. "Back for the uniform already?"

Ignoring the quip, Sonny began, his voice hopeful, "When I was here earlier, I should have looked for my friend's father, but I didn't know then he was missing. Name's Milberg—he lives on Pestalozzi. Do you know him?"

Staring at the blank wall where there should have been a window, Johnny repeated, "Milberg . . . Milberg. Is he a little guy, a mustache—a Hindenburg?" He made a motion with his forefinger under his nose. "Wears spectacles?"

"Sounds right," Sonny shrugged. "Never met him. I've only seen a photograph."

Johnny leaned back in his chair and stretched. "Don't know. I'll ask." He called out, "Fred."

In seconds Fred covered the door like a curtain.

"Was Herr Milberg here with the others? You know the little guy with the mustache and glasses, always has a brandy."

Fred, discarding one patron after another from his mental directory, nodded. "I know him." He shook his head. "He may have been. I never kept track—just let 'em in."

"Are some still here?" Sonny looked from Fred to Johnny.

Turning to Sonny as if noticing him for the first time, Fred said, "Ja. In the cellar."

"Wait. Do you know Robert Fischer?" Sonny handed the picture to Johnny.

Johnny shook his head. "Go take a look. Doesn't mean he isn't down there." Then he offered it to Fred, who did the same.

Fred led Sonny to the cellar door. The hushed voices wafted up memories like a breeze: Willy lying dead in the cellar, the operators descending into the bowels of No. 15. The images bounced around his head, gaining strength as he went down the groaning steps. Conversations stopped as heads turned to the descending body—legs, then torso, and finally his face. What news did he bring?

Through the expectant quiet, he said blindly, "Are Herr Milberg and Robert Fischer here?"

Several seconds passed before a voice softly answered, "I'm Milberg."

A long sigh whistled from Sonny's lips as he followed the sound of the voice to the man standing in the photo next to Herman. A small man, he looked pale in the poor light, and his face was tightly drawn. Sonny smiled with relief.

"Thank God, I found you. I'm a friend of your son, Herman. I promised I'd look in on you if there was trouble."

A voice came out of the dimness, "Trouble, the man says—what trouble?"

Sonny's face reddened, but he didn't respond. Instead he asked Milberg, "Have you seen Robert Fischer?"

Herman's father shook his head. "No, not down here—maybe upstairs." He took a long look at Sonny and demanded, "Who are you?"

Moving closer so that they wouldn't be overheard, Sonny whispered, "We can talk upstairs."

. . . They sat across the table Sonny had sat at several hours before. He could hardly believe his luck. He explained to Milberg that he had seen his wife and that he'd been to Herr Kuhn's. Elbows on the table, Milberg nodded. If he was surprised that a stranger should come looking for him, he did not show it.

"I didn't want to leave—she made me go," he said. "One man saw the SA arresting his neighbors with his own eyes, and he barely escaped." He shuddered, and asked in a low voice, as if afraid of the answer, "Are the rumors true?"

Sonny told him what he'd seen, omitting any reference to Herman's status.

Slowly tapping his finger on the table as Herman had done at the café, Milberg studied Sonny with a pained expression. "How come you're moving around while the rest of us are hiding? Are you Jewish? You don't look it."

Sonny knew the question that most Jews asked him was coming. "Can't help what I look like—though it makes me invisible, sort of. But yes, I am a Jew," he answered. "I'll walk you home. Goebbels ordered an end to the pogrom—Fred heard it on the radio."

Milberg kept tapping his finger; apparently he was in no hurry to leave.

So Sonny asked, "How did you end up in the cellar?"

Waving vaguely toward the front door, Milberg said, "Fred knows me." He stopped as if that explained it.

"And . . ?" Sonny prompted.

"I passed by with some other men, not knowing where to go. He literally pulled us in off the street, then ordered us into the cellar." He blinked, then asked Sonny, "How did you know to look here?"

"Johnny's an old friend, and I was here earlier."

"Thank you for being a good friend to my Herman." That was all he said, but his lips moved silently. Then, "Ach! It's hopeless." His words cut the tavern's still air.

Sonny cringed.

Then Milberg's eyes met Sonny's: "You met her. She's not well."

Sonny nodded—it was time, and as he'd done with Herman, Henry, and many others, he offered refuge to Milberg and his wife. Herman would have to deal with the ramifications, but at least they'd be together. Sonny explained that he would provide passports and visas and a secure place for him and his wife to stay. When it was safe to travel, they could leave for the border.

Milberg stared at Sonny, dazed. After thirty seconds or more had passed, he finally said, "This all feels like a dream—but my head's about to burst, my feet ache, and my back's sore." Taking off his glasses, he rubbed his eyes. "If I'm talking to you, it can't be a dream."

"No, it's real enough," Sonny told him.

Voices came from the back of the tavern, then the sound of a door closing. Both looked, but there was nothing to see—it was quiet again.

"How can we leave? My wife is ill."

"I understand that Frau Milberg isn't well. But after what's happened today, no one is safe here," Sonny said.

"No, it's not safe," Milberg mumbled, looking distraught for the first time. His gaze drifted away as he thought about the day's events. Having reached a conclusion, he asked, "Where will you take us?"

"We have visas for Belgium."

"Belgium? Herman is in Holland."

"Don't worry. At least you'll be out," Sonny said, doing his best, tried to gloss over the problem. But that derailed Milberg, so Sonny explained that they would rendezvous with Herman in Antwerp or Brussels.

"I'm overwhelmed," Milberg finally said; then he withdrew. After several minutes, he looked down toward the men in the cellar and asked, "What about them?"

Sonny leaned back in the chair, shaking his head. "Our group is small—there's only so much we can do. Helping so many would be impossible, so please say nothing to anyone other than Frau Milberg."

Milberg nodded hesitantly and began to mumble incoherently, head moving back and forth as if he were arguing opposing sides. Apparently having arrived at an answer, he said, "Staying will be slow strangulation, though traveling could be her death—I'll take our chances with you."

"Good choice—you'll be with Herman."

That seemed to please Milberg, but he became agitated. His lips moved, his hands rose, and his tone was apologetic when he said, "No offense meant . . . Do you mind if I ask Johnny, you know, for a reference . . . set myself at ease."

"Not a problem," Sonny answered.

When Milberg returned, he was smiling. "Johnny says you're okay."

"If you want to believe a guy like Johnny," Sonny quipped, and for the first time, the genesis of a smile appeared on Milberg's face.

Johnny's voice came from the hallway: "And after everything I've done for you."

Sonny laughed and asked to use the telephone. When Frau Moltke answered, he told her that the Milbergs needed transportation to No. 53, but that she shouldn't tell Herman about it. Everyone but Mina was gone, but she could arrange the transportation as soon as Karl returned. Sonny gave her the address and rang off.

Milberg thanked Johnny and Fred for their assistance. In ten minutes he was fawning at his wife's side, until she softly said, "Ernst, that's quite enough. Now sit down—tell me how you are. But before I do," she looked up at Sonny and with some difficulty said, "Thank you, young man."

Rosa's emotions had roiled from anger to fear to sadness and back until she was unable to separate one from the other. She'd forgotten to breathe, then gulped for air—coughed—paced the floor—straightened pictures—opened and closed drawers. Then the stranger she'd seen at the Milbergs' door had turned up at her own . . .

Sonny . . . what a funny name . . . She was unsure of what had happened after that . . . but he'd gone to find Herr Milberg . . . come back to find her father. Was it all real?

Hurrying to the window, she pulled back the curtain, glanced at her mother whimpering in her father's chair, and looked down to the street, hoping to catch a glimpse of him. There! He was out of the building, heading west on Pestalozzi. Yes, it was real, but would he come back? What if he was arrested? Today, anything could happen, and it probably wouldn't be good.

After Sonny's departure, her anger dissipated into anxiety, then panic. She couldn't stop thinking about her father. Her mother's tenuous hold was slipping—would she be next? Maybe Father was hiding somewhere—waiting until it was safe. Would it ever be safe? And if all she had heard was true, what was Sonny doing on the street? How could he find Herr Milberg? Would he look for her father? Would he even try?

Rosa yearned to leave Germany, had for several years. Anywhere west would do—France, England, America . . . Germany held nothing for her, certainly not now. She wanted a man to love, one who loved her, children maybe. Beyond that, she was less clear. She wanted a life free to do as she pleased—she could decide what that was later—one without a government set on making her life hard.

Rosa had no business or artistic aspirations, no profession. None of that mattered in light of her single-minded goal to get out. If her parents couldn't do it, she would do it alone. As life had grown more difficult, so had her anger at her parents grown—for not having the means or the connections to emigrate.

Her parents were partly to blame—they'd spoiled and sheltered their only child. Their paramount desire was to protect her, and after 1933 they had drawn their circle tighter, trying to shield her from the strangling edicts, the loss of jobs, the harassment at schools and on the streets. But it was impossible. How could they? How could anyone?

Their friends—and hers—became limited to those who were Jewish. They imposed a curfew; she generally obeyed. Gentiles were usually friendly—she could not recall an overt act of hostility because of her Jewish ancestry. She'd finished school in the waning years of the Republic.

She began working full time in her father's small store near Alexanderplatz, selling household goods. She had started in her early teens stocking shelves and soon was selling merchandise. The business thrived . . . until the boycotts of 1933. The store weathered that storm, but in the summer of '35, someone threw a brick through the window, disrupting business for several months. It never recovered.

Her father knew the man who did it—he had threatened as much after disputing merchandise he claimed was defective. Even if her father had had real proof, the police wouldn't help a Jew. When the doors closed for the last time and her father returned the keys to the landlord, it was like a death in the family.

Rosa's two close friendships ended when both girls left for America with their families in 1933. By then, Rosa had turned her attention to the young men around her. And she got all the attention she needed—sometimes too much—in return.

Like most adolescents, she'd endured an awkward stage but grown into an earthy beauty. With big brown eyes, and a generous mouth in a lovely face framed by thick, dark hair, she was destined to turn heads. She soon realized her attraction to men—boyfriends came and went, but disappointments were few and fleeting.

Rosa desperately wanted a life of her own, but the string of jobs she'd taken had ended six months earlier, when the stationery shop where she clerked shut its doors. Her mother's search for work was equally unsuccessful. Luckily, her father found a job with the wholesaler who had supplied his store. Though the work was menial, he was grateful to have a job at all.

For months after the store was shuttered, Rosa had pleaded with her parents to leave Germany, arguing that it was insane to stay, that they must go somewhere, anywhere, else—even Shanghai. But without money or documents, they could not. Rosa's disappointment turned to anger, and she came to see life in dichotomies—simple oppositions: My father built a nice business but lost it because he is a Jew. I was engaged to be married, but now I am not. We must leave Germany, but we cannot. The good suffer; evil triumphs. And so it went.

Rosa thought of Siggie, the man she was briefly engaged to marry but barely knew, with regret. Not because she loved him—she had willingly relinquished that requirement—or because he'd abandoned her, but for the lost opportunity.

Sigmund Froman was hopelessly smitten the first day he entered the stationery shop, and she knew it. He had stared so long that she thought he was in trance. Returning daily to buy pencils, paper, envelopes, whatever, after a week he screwed up the courage to ask her out for coffee. Over several weeks of coffee dates and dinners, she learned of his family business and his plans to emigrate. Then came flowers and chocolate, and after what proved to be a three-week courtship, he had proposed marriage, much to her surprise.

Several years older than Rosa, Siggie was ordinary in every way possible, though he dressed very well. Immature like most of the men she knew, he often looked like a startled little dog—the kind that sat on your lap, craving attention. Still, Rosa knew that her best, maybe only, chance to leave Germany was to find a man with the means—or allow him to find her. Siggie represented that opportunity; if that made her an opportunist, so be it.

Apparently having no particular skills or a job of any kind, Siggie was dependent on his parents. That gave Rosa justifiable pause. Then the stammering Siggie told her that the engagement must be put on hold. It was only postponed, he pathetically assured her. He would send for her as soon as he was settled. She knew it was a lie—she'd met his parents.

They hadn't tried to hide their disdain for her. They scrutinized her like a butterfly pinned to a board, searching for imperfection, anything to find fault with her, though they never spoke the words. Sipping tea in the sitting room of their Charlottenburg flat, they condescendingly alluded to the money they'd receive upon the sale of a business, as if it were still prosperous. They further alluded to leaving Germany as soon as possible, avoiding talk of their son's proposed marriage. Through veiled messages, they conveyed contempt for her family's status, their son's poor judgment in succumbing to her physical attractions, and his laughably short courtship.

By the end of her short and only visit, she had felt thoroughly debased, while Siggie seemed oblivious to her humiliation. Out of self-respect, Rosa refused to broach the subject, but she silently cursed their upper-middle-class snobbery. In a dark moment, she even rejoiced that most of their wealth was lost to the Nazis; they made her feel dirty. But she nevertheless despaired at her lost opportunity to leave. She might have been anywhere else but stuck in Germany with her father missing and Siggie God-knows-where.

She had cultivated that spineless creature until he flowered with a marriage proposal. She had smiled, looked down demurely, and told him such an important decision required a little time. They barely knew each other. She could never love a man like Siggie, but after the requisite interval, she had accepted. Rosa swore that if he'd had a tail, it would have wagged.

Then in the spring of '38, the bastard was gone, and she never heard from him again. For weeks after their engagement, she had endured his groping and bad breath, though she refused to sleep with him. She was saving herself for marriage, she said, shuddering at the thought of lying in the same bed with that weasel. Now Siggie was history and, like a toothache once past, best forgotten . . .

Rosa had learned a practical lesson from the experience: she must be more selective. Young and attractive, she was convinced someone would take her from this awful place, and she didn't stop looking for him. But with so many men gone . . . ? Well, that was yesterday, before her father had disappeared, before her mother's descent into fragility, before the hideous pogrom. The weight of an uncertain future and the thought that thousands of others were suffering the same fate did little to alleviate her pain or assuage her fears . . .

Rosa's mother sat, head in her hands, slowly sinking. Rosa had never felt more alone. She had to do something, so she began to call neighbors and family friends. As she spoke with half a dozen women, some who'd lost a husband or knew someone who had, a terrible, foreboding picture came into focus. The hope that her father might yet appear ran headlong into the fear that she would never see him again. A wave of panic followed each phone call, and after a particularly wrenching story, she wept inconsolably. She alternated between barely manageable anxiety and uncontrollable fear.

So it was, in the handful of hours after her father went missing, that she reached out for support that wasn't there. What she was only now coming fully to realize savaged her ability to cope. Rosa's world turned black . . . yet Sonny was reason for hope.

25

Nothing is so much to be feared as fear.
—Henry David Thoreau

For the second time, Sonny knocked on the Fischers' door. He had news, and he hoped they had some for him. Frau Fischer registered mild surprise when she opened the door. She managed a weak "Sonny's back."

"So soon?" Rosa asked, her voice revealing a thread of excitement as she appeared from behind her mother. After examining his face, her hand went to her mouth. "Oh, my God! You found Herr Milberg."

Her presence was a welcome antidote to the other events of the day. Sonny smiled, then nodded. "Yes, I'll explain, but first, tell me what you've found out."

Frau Fischer buried her face in her hands. Sonny grimaced and wished he hadn't asked. Rosa placed a gentle hand on her mother's trembling back and whispered, "We'll find him, I promise . . ." She glanced at Sonny. " . . . now that we have help." Gently taking her mother's hand, she led her to the bedroom.

After a few minutes Rosa returned, stifled a yawn, and gestured for Sonny to sit. She sat heavily, stretched her legs, and lifted her arms over her head as if he weren't there. Sonny watched with increasing interest until Rosa noticed, reddened, and quickly sat up. "How did you do it?"

She reminded him of Sophie when they were kids—she was unselfconscious, got straight to the point without wasting time. But Rosa wasn't a kid. He liked that she was a little embarrassed. "Are you surprised I returned, that I've found him?"

"A little." Her smile obscured her answer. Then she said, without sarcasm, "That was heroic." Her gaze was reassessing, and her smile turned to a faint smirk. "I can see that *you* are pleased. It's written all over your face."

"You haven't answered my question."

Shaking her head, she told him with a wave toward the window what her phone calls had revealed. "Several have missing husbands, others saw the shattered shop windows, and another watched the Schiller Strasse Synagogue burn. There's nothing to give me hope."

Despite what she said, Sonny noticed a calmer Rosa—perhaps her relative serenity came from a sense of shared purpose with friends and neighbors. Or maybe it was because he was there. Whatever it was, he was glad her emotions were in check, at least for the moment.

"Someone," she said, "I forget who—told me an SA ordered a neighbor to get her husband, who was hiding in back of their home. She lied, said he wasn't there. Then he asked, 'How old is he?' She answered without thinking, 'Eighty-six.' The SA said, 'Too old, orders are to arrest men from sixteen to sixty,' and was gone. She nearly fainted—her husband was born in 1886; he wasn't eighty-six years old. Do you believe it?"

Sonny cursed under his breath. "As young as sixteen?"

"Mere boys," she lamented. "If there's still a man in the house, it's luck—or he's hiding. Our neighbor downstairs said her husband hadn't returned from work when the SA came. When he did come home, those rats were gone. Now, like everyone else, her family is trying to find a way out. It's hard enough not knowing, but to watch my father be snatched away would be . . ." She took a deep breath and slowly exhaled.

"Several women said they're going to SA headquarters in the morning to demand their husbands be released," she continued, her faced hardening. "That's what I'm going to do." Suddenly unsure, she brought a hand to her mouth and gnawed on her thumb. "What do you think?"

"First, let's figure out where your father could have been, where he went . . . work back from there." Sonny knew it was a long shot, but it would keep her mind occupied. That was better than falling into despair.

Rosa leaned forward with an elbow on her knee and rested her chin on her fist. "It started like every other day. He left early for his job in the Mitte."

"Where exactly? I'm headed that way."

"Rosenthal Supplies. It's on . . ." She tapped a fingernail on a tooth. "How could I forget? Krausnick Strasse near Oranienburger."

"I know exactly—near the New Synagogue—but I can't place the business. I'll look for it tonight, then stop by tomorrow morning. What about your father's habits? Did he eat lunch out? Where? When did he get home after work?"

"Mother always made his lunch, and he was home by 5:30. Then we'd have dinner." She closed her eyes for another look at her father's day, then shook her head and groaned.

"Would he stop at a tavern?" Sonny asked, then saw that his question confused her.

She shook her head. "No, not to my knowledge. Why do you ask?"

Over the next twenty minutes Sonny told her how he had found Herr Milberg—about the Dove, about Johnny and Fred, about Herr Kuhn. "Luck was on my side."

Rosa's arms were folded across her chest, her eyes fixed on his as he painted a picture of Jews hiding in the Dove's cellar. When he finished, she softly repeated, "Johnny and Fred. How did you, and especially Herr Milberg, know of such a place?"

"I've known Johnny since my cabaret days," he answered, leaving the association vague. "I lost track of him and just recently discovered that he operates the Dove, near Savigny Platz. Herr Milberg liked to stop for a brandy now and then."

"Really?" she asked, wrinkling her nose. "I've seen the sort of men who go there."

Sonny laughed. "Men like me?"

Nonplussed, Rosa looked away, chewing on her lip. When their eyes met again, she said, "Don't know why I said that, but it's not the sort of place my father would patronize—Herr Milberg either."

Amused, Sonny wondered how she'd react when she knew more about him and Johnny. "It's just a place for a man to have a beer or a schnapps."

"Men who sneak around late at night are up to no good," she declared, closer to the truth than she knew.

"How would a nice girl like you know that?"

She managed a tired smile. "Maybe I'm not so nice."

"I'm relieved to hear that," Sonny winked.

"Don't be getting any ideas," she protested mildly.

Sonny sighed. "Don't worry. I've completely run out of ideas."

A slight blush rose on her cheeks. Rosa's eyes narrowed. "What about the big scary brute?"

Sonny laughed again. "He can't help how he looks. Would you have let me in the flat if I looked like that?"

Rosa's face screwed in horror, and she shook her head.

"Fred's really a prince of a fellow," Sonny offered. "He pulled Herr Milberg and dozens of other men off the street."

Rosa's hand went to her mouth. "That's Fred?!"

"Quite an imposing character, isn't he?" Sonny smiled at Rosa's confusion. "I met Fred years ago, at the Hammer & Sickle, in Neukölln. His glower could wilt a flower, and he's not much of a talker, but he saved a lot of men tonight. I hadn't seen him since '32." He laughed again.

"What's so funny?"

"My first impression of Fred wasn't much different from yours." Sonny told her about the beautiful Soviet propaganda poster, how Fred had frightened the hell out of him. "I spent a lot of time at the Hammer & Sickle." He told her how he'd met Otto. He missed those earlier days.

"Are you . . . a Communist?"

Shaking his head, he said, "No, I never joined, didn't believe in it, though my friends did." He told her about Otto's return from the underground and Mischa's exodus to Belgium with Sophie and his family.

Rosa's eyes widened at the mention of Belgium. In time he'd tell her more, Sonny thought, and he returned to his story: "Johnny let me in through the alley door, and I sat in the tavern with a couple of unsavory types he'd saved from the SA."

"Now you're teasing me," Rosa said.

"Just a little . . . That's when I learned that at least twenty-five men, maybe more, were hiding in the cellar and in a back room. What do you think of Johnny and Fred now?"

She smiled sheepishly but didn't answer. Instead, she asked, "How did Herr Milberg end up in the Dove's cellar?"

"I wasn't exaggerating. Fred—that scary brute—pulled him and others off the street. When I first stopped, I didn't think to ask whether Herr Milberg was there. I didn't know he was missing." Then he told her about his interaction with Herr Kuhn, another she could add to her list of heroes.

"Huh," Rosa responded. Then her eyes widened as she realized that Sonny might think her response tepid. "I didn't . . . " She stopped, then started again, "I'm completely mesmerized by your story, and by the people. For you to be on the street tonight takes incredible courage, far more than I have."

"Or stupidity," Sonny replied, recalling his various encounters in crossing Berlin. Then he grimaced. "I shouldn't have said that. Let me start over. Thank you for noticing. Like I said, I had more than my share of luck in finding Herr Milberg."

Her lips pursed, she nodded . . . her eyes traced the contours of his face.

Sonny sensed there was something more: "What?"

His question must have taken her by surprise because she started, then said, "Nothing."

"There's never nothing."

She sighed and smiled. "You're right. It's just that you said you'd come back and you did. But why did you come in the first place, beyond the line that Frau Milberg sent you? And why should you care about my mother and me?" She clutched her stomach. "I nearly bit your his head off when you first appeared at our door. But you didn't seem to notice. Now I realize my anger was misplaced. I'm sorry."

"Apology accepted. You're under a lot of pressure. As to why I'm here . . ." Sonny shrugged. "Helping people is what I do. Frau Milberg needed help, and so do you."

Rosa seemed satisfied, at least for now, with his answer. "Thank you. You are kind, and I enjoy talking to you. Though I shouldn't, not tonight." She looked pained. "I'm plagued by the thought of my father as hungry and cold, cowering in the corner of a crowded prison cell. I don't want to be disrespectful of my mother or my father. But after what you've done—finding Herr Milberg and promising to help find my father . . ."

"You're welcome," Sonny said simply, unsure of how to respond.

"Lucky or not, you seem to float unmolested . . . appear out of nowhere, leave, return. How come?"

Sonny shrugged. "You can see why. I look like them, not like us."

"Yes, but there's a curfew. Anyone on the street is at risk."

"Sometimes there are things more important than your own safety."

Rosa's dark brows arched. She seemed genuinely surprised by his comment.

"I've never met anyone who said anything like that." She tapped her chin with her forefinger, considering the implications. "Tonight has been a revelation—meeting you, then learning about men like Herr Kuhn, Johnny, and Fred. In my world, the Dove, or any tavern, serves no purpose but to provide refuge from domestic discord in a beer mug. Now, I see the Dove as a sanctuary, Johnny and Fred as heroes. Nothing fits the old patterns today."

Rosa closed her eyes and was silent.

"Are you all right? Sonny asked.

She nodded. "Considering what's happened." Then she reconsidered. "Of course, I'm not all right, but I feel better. When I just closed my eyes, I saw pure white light stretching to an impossibly blue sky, dotted with puffy clouds. Angels encircled a white-bearded old man in a toga—God sitting on a throne—like in a picture book I saw when I was little. Where is God now? Is it fair to ask that?"

"Yes. But I've given up on God. I can't square his existence with what the Jews have endured over the ages, over the past several days."

Rosa nodded. They sat quietly for several minutes. Then she said, "I'm embarrassed by my response to Fred and Johnny."

Sonny was pensive. "You had preconceptions that fueled your fears, and the Dove housed them. Now you know Johnny and Fred, or at least you know about them. Attitudes can change."

Then he told her about the orthodox Jews in long beards and black suits in the warehouse ghetto of his youth—and of his father's lecture. "They're different. It's the same with a man who looks like Fred or acts like Johnny. All you need to change your attitude are knowledge and an open mind."

That pleased Rosa. "Yes, I needed reminding. What you said about the orthodox, I've done that myself, heard others say it: 'Why can't they be like us? Then they'd leave us alone.'"

"I learned a long time ago that it doesn't work that way."

Rosa held his gaze and said, "Thank you . . . for staying when you didn't have to."

Sonny liked that she didn't avert her eyes. "You need help, and I don't want to leave. So many people need help . . ." He stopped short, not ready to tell her. Then he frowned, trying to recall . . . "My friend Joseph once read me some lines from Brecht: A former student complained of the lack of heroes, but Galileo was unmoved, and he admonished, 'No! Unhappy is the land that needs heroes.'"

"I can't imagine a less happy place than Germany." Rosa paused. "I feel like I've known you for years—if not in this world, then in another."

"Interesting. I feel it too," Sonny answered. "Though I don't know about the other-world part. Were we related? Were we friends? Maybe lovers?" Then he felt foolish. But when Rosa reddened to a pretty crimson, he didn't feel sorry after all.

A little flustered, she quickly recovered. "No, not that . . . just a feeling." Suddenly shy, she said, "That's a question left for another day."

Sonny smiled. "Yes, we'll pursue it in a happier time."

Rosa changed the subject. "Everything's a blur. I can't keep up."

"We were caught off guard." Then he returned to her previous thought, the part she was willing to pursue. "Time seems weird—so much is happening, but it's like you're standing still. People are thrown together; nerves are raw. That's why it seems we've known each other for years. We skipped a lot of the awkward part." Sonny waved his hand dismissively. "Chance threw us together," he continued. "Now we're trapped beside a churning river, threatening to drag us in at any moment. If I hadn't looked after the Milbergs, I'd never have knocked on your door."

Then he told her how Otto and Mina had met in the course of Mina's reunion with her father, after the two men had spent five years underground. "Now they're inseparable. Mina, a mischlinge, refused to leave with her parents. She chose to stay with Otto."

"Five years?" Rosa asked.

"Yes, Otto and Mina's father. Both were Communists."

She was still confounded. "She stayed . . . Why? After all that?"

"Love. Mina fell in love with Otto, and she wants to help."

Rosa's voice became husky. "How romantic. How lovely." Then her eyes narrowed slightly. "Help with what?"

Ignoring her question for the moment, Sonny said, "I don't pretend to fully understand what you're going through. Not knowing where your father is must be wrenching."

"Yes, of course," Rosa agreed, but she wanted an answer, and she pressed. "Mina stayed to help with *what?*"

Realizing she wouldn't be denied, Sonny saw no reason to keep the answer from her. Hell, he'd told Henry when he was hiding in the Tiergarten. "Otto and I and others smuggle Jews out of Germany. Mina's parents were among them, but she stayed to help with our operation." He held her gaze. "Rosa, I'm a smuggler, have been for years."

Rosa fell back in her chair and studied his face. Seconds ticked by, and after nothing came, she muttered, "Really?"

He nodded and smiled brightly. "You called Johnny and Fred 'shady' and they are, but so am I. I live in the shadows, where it's easier to do what I do. The first racket crashed and burned, but a new one rose from the ashes . . ." His words hung for several seconds, lending them import.

"At first it was a living, but now it's much more. There's nothing complicated about my motivation: I want to get as many Jews out of Germany as possible. Legal . . . illegal—it's all upside down."

Rosa stared as if he'd suddenly become someone else.

Sonny continued. "I was a smalltime peddler, doing a little of this and a little of that . . . starting when I was twelve with my father at a warehouse in Scheunenviertel. I never stopped until the smuggling operation shut down, just over a year ago. Then this venture fell into my lap—through circumstance and conviction. We're not in it for the money. Joseph would rather sell books, Otto would agitate for the KPD, and Emil—well, he'd rather smuggle goods in than smuggle people out."

"And you?"

"Years ago I dreamed of being a journalist . . ."

"What happened?"

"It didn't work out. I got lazy. Then events intervened . . ." he shrugged. "I didn't want it as much as I thought. I had just two little reviews on my resume, then Hitler came."

"Tell me about it," she said.

Sonny remembered sitting next to a reporter in a tavern near the office of the journal that printed his first review. It was a gallery exhibition. "In '30 or '31—hell, I should know—it's 1931. I reviewed a George Grosz retrospective at a gallery off Ku'damm. Counter Kessler actually read it. At least that's what the great man said when, by chance, we met a year later. We lamented the times like old chums. It was exhilarating. Anyway, by then, the Republic was on its deathbed . . . But the gallery show was before everything went to hell. George Grosz's *New Face of the Ruling Class* was published in 1921, and the show highlighted works from the book, plus other pieces. One was called *Five in the Morning.*"

"Let me think." He raised a finger, paused, and smiled. "I wrote something like '*Five in the Morning* shows corrupt, old, rich industrialists, one pinching a woman's breast, after a night of debauchery. Their oozing depravity is in stark contrast to the stolid laborers shown at the top of the canvas, marching to distant factories . . . Grosz's genius is in creating tableaus of alienation and depravity with crude, childlike drawings. In the foreground a man vomits, probably the artist himself.'

"I concluded with something like 'This prime example of Dada—anti-art—elicits indifference, a seeping despair, and speaks far louder than a broadside or a rabble-rouser's corner speech—a masterpiece from the master of political art.' Otto got a kick when he read that."

Rosa was laughing. "You remember all that?"

"Apparently so. I haven't thought about it in years." Then, "I also wrote about Grosz's portrait of the Jewish writer Herrman-Niese. But I can't remember what I said . . . something about the subject pondering a question, projecting an air of pessimism . . . blah, blah, blah. I was finishing it, felt insecure, feared it was overwrought. So I asked Joseph to read it. When he finished, he started laughing, and said, 'Of course, it is. You're a critic.' But I got it published in the back pages of a small magazine called *Art World*. I savored that for days."

"Congratulations," Rosa said.

"Thanks," Sonny said sarcastically, and they both laughed. "When they told me, I found a little tavern near the *Art World* office, not unlike the Dove. I'll never forget the old newspaperman who'd been drinking there long before I arrived. As soon as he saw me, he started complaining—publishing was going to hell. The guy didn't talk—he croaked—and he kept stifling belches."

He continued: "'Listen, kid. Munzenberg's name used to mean something.' He was hard to follow, but he warned, 'Words are out; it's all pictures.' If I wanted to work for the rags in this town, I should 'get a goddamn camera and take snaps of celebrities or unemployed workers standing in a soup line, staring forlornly into the lens.' He said the 'fucking camera'—pardon my language—'is wrecking journalism.' I didn't know what to think, but I thought the word still had a chance. So I thanked him for the advice and left."

"What a wonderful story! Are you sorry you didn't continue?"

Sonny shrugged. "Sometimes . . . but not often. I do wonder what happened to that ink-stained wretch and what he'd make of his profession now. All I know for sure is that the 'God forbid' moment my father feared is here."

He told Rosa about Aachen, Plombieres, Fritz, Emil, Karl, Polly, Joseph and his forged documents—everything but No. 15 and Willy. She didn't need to hear about that, not yet.

Then: "I'll take you and your parents out of the country as soon as we locate your father. You must promise to tell no one, not even your mother. Not yet."

"I promise," she stammered, shaking her head as if trying to jar her thoughts free. "Please, tell me more."

And that's what he did. Sonny unwound another fantastic tale to make her pulse quicken. His own mind raced at the possibilities, sweeping old disappointments away. If she hadn't known what to make of him earlier in the day—what would she think now?

She stared, her mouth slightly open. "You are . . . simply amazing."

"It's just what I do." Sonny could see that his story affected Rosa in much the same way it had affected Henry Neuman. She seemed taken by him—or his story—he wasn't sure which. But would he just be her ticket over the border, quickly forgotten once she arrived? Not about to spoil the moment with idle thoughts, he shoved the idea aside.

"You mean like a job?" Rosa sounded dubious.

"In some ways," Sonny answered. "Most of the time it's mundane—meeting people, delivering documents, making sure they cross safely. I won't deny it's dangerous, but we're cautious. If we're caught . . ."

Shaking her head, she said, "You're so matter of fact about it." She retreated for a few beats, then nodded. "And then there's the fact that I've been waiting for someone like you for years, and you turn up tonight." Rosa's gaze bore in on him . . . then she broke it off. Finally she said, "I don't get it." Her eyes turned back to his. "But I like it."

A sudden surge of heat colored Sonny's neck. His temples tingled until the feeling passed and the image faded. "Well, here I am—believe it."

"Great! Let's get my father back."

His throat parched from talking, Sonny licked his lips and swallowed. He looked toward the kitchen and asked Rosa for a glass of water.

"I'm a terrible hostess," she apologized and shot out of her chair. Within minutes cold chicken and rye bread sat next to his glass of water on the table. The two sat down and ate in companionable silence.

Sonny stole a glance or two between bites from across the table, liking what he saw . . . But he'd promised to find Rosa's father. What were the chances that he was hiding in a forest, too scared to move? That he'd walk through the door in the next twenty-four hours? No, he'd probably been arrested and was in jail or had been sent away. Then what? Sonny had made a promise he probably could not honor. Finding Herman's father had been too easy. He should have found Milberg an hour earlier. Now he was a hero, making for pressure he didn't need, though he enjoyed the attention. He sighed at the turn of events.

Sonny knew about personal loss—his parents, Simon, Polly, Willy—and about the pain of watching mentors and friends suffer—Joseph and Otto, especially. But he'd never had to endure not knowing whether or in what circumstances they'd gone. Still, he'd struggled through to try to make a difference.

His life seemed to hold no middle ground—people stayed or left. The losses quietly gnawed; they bred anger, loneliness, guilt. Abandonment was his natural state. He had recognized its effects, but would he ever fully understand, fully forgive? Could he be grateful? Though his father had kept him at arm's length, he'd given Sonny the tools he needed to survive.

And Willy—another man he barely knew. Sonny saw himself throwing dirt onto the shallow grave, Willy's blood-smeared torso sprawled in the cellar. Squeezing his eyes shut, Sonny willed the image to pass. It morphed into Albert, gazing at him from across the square . . .

He opened his eyes onto Rosa, apparently lost in her own hopes and fears. Sonny's voice pierced her veil. "Rosa, where did you go?"

"Nowhere really . . . Well, there's comfort knowing that good people like you still exist." She managed a smile.

Sonny nodded, accepting her praise but knowing that whatever he did in this hellhole of a country was not enough. "I feel particularly inadequate today." He was suddenly weary of the struggle, of life in the shadows, of being scared. And now, to search for an innocent man who in all likelihood was simply gone? He felt overwhelmed.

"You spoke of your father. Are your parents alive?" Rosa asked.

Sonny wiped his mouth with the napkin. "My parents died long ago. Like you, I have no brothers or sisters."

She looked to her parents' bedroom, then back at him. "Is that why you're so calm? I don't suppose you would be . . . I mean, if your parents were alive, you'd be with them."

"But they aren't. Most of my family is gone. My aunt and uncle and two cousins are still here, but we're not close. My friends are my family."

"They must be good friends."

"Yes. One friend who went through more than I'll ever know survived to call himself lucky. So am I—imagine my saying that today! But it's true. My oldest friend, the one in Belgium, is a Jew, but the others in our operation are not. They risk their lives daily to save Jews."

Rosa thought about that. "Your world is so different from mine, but I never thought that you weren't a Jew. Maybe it's your . . ."

"Aura of Jewishness," Sonny supplied, thinking of the drunk who'd had him pegged. "Most people are surprised to learn I'm a Jew."

"Of course. I can see that."

Sonny asked about her friends. She told him of the two girls who'd left the country.

"What about men friends?"

She shook her head but did not elaborate. He reached across the table for her hand. It felt warm. She let it rest in his.

"It's time I go." Sonny removed his hand. "I'll stop at Rosenthaler Supplies and talk with you in the morning. Don't decide about going to SA headquarters until we talk."

"All right," she murmured.

They stood near the door, neither knowing quite how to say good-night. Sonny stared at Rosa's hands as she wrung them nervously. Then he remembered. "I need passport photographs for you and your mother. I have the picture of your father."

"We have passports—the one thing I was able to get them to do . . ." she said, biting off her impatience.

"Until now," Sonny amended.

She brightened, walked to a chest of drawers, pulled out an envelope, and handed it to Sonny.

"I need the passports to forge the visas," he explained.

He turned to leave, but Rosa stopped him. "I don't even know your real name."

Sonny smiled sheepishly. "I never use it, but if you must know, it's Sigmund Landauer."

Rosa stifled something between a laugh and a cry.

"What is it?" he asked.

She shook her head and looked away, embarrassed. "I'm sorry . . . I just never imagined."

"You know someone with that name?" Sonny asked.

"Not really." She had never really known that other Sigmund, though after three hours she felt she knew this one well.

26

The Lord thy God hath chosen thee to be a special people unto himself.
—Fourth Book of Moses

Sonny entered the quiet of Joseph's flat and collapsed onto the sofa well past midnight. He immediately fell into a deep sleep . . . He woke with a start.

Joseph apologized for waking him, then: "When did you get in?"

Sonny yawned and shook his head. "Late." And over a cup of coffee, he gave an account of his activities since they'd parted at the warehouse.

Joseph looked at Sonny's swollen hand until he was satisfied it wasn't broken. Moving to the window, he saw his neighbors' ghosts and retold the story of the grim day before, as if repetition cleansed, soothing his soul. Sonny understood and let him continue without interrupting. When Joseph finished, he stared at Sonny and ordered, "Go!"

Sonny was startled, confused, then realized what he meant.

"Do I have to explain the danger you're in? You have a choice, not like those poor buggers." Joseph pointed to the window, his mouth an ugly grimace. "I'll prepare papers for the young lady. What's her name?"

"Rosa Fischer. And what about her father?"

Joseph shook his head.

"I have their passports, so they just need visas and . . ." Sonny laid the envelope on the table.

"Yes, of course."

"Thank you."

Then Joseph took Sonny's hand, this time in both of his, as if in the final scene of a long play, though grand gestures were not his wont. "Let this be our farewell. Don't come back, take what you need, get out while you can. You'll be in Aachen by tonight, Belgium tomorrow. Don't wait another day. Someone will get the papers to Rosa and her parents when it's time."

Sonny was moved by his friend's kindness; tears welled in his eyes. Looking at his hand, still in Joseph's embrace, Sonny stuttered, "I . . . I intend to, but not until . . ."

"No! I don't want to hear it." Joseph's voice rose in a burst as he pulled at Sonny's hand.

Sonny winced but managed a smile. "That hurts."

"I'm sorry," Joseph apologized, "but you're so damned stubborn."

"I know, and I appreciate your concern, but if you don't stop screaming, you'll bring back the SA."

With an exasperated sigh, Joseph waved a finger under Sonny's nose. "You're not taking this seriously. You'll wait until they release Rosa's father . . . but you have no idea when or whether those monsters will ever release him or anyone else. Go. Leave. And if—when—they release him, Otto can see to it." He grimaced. "Ach! What the hell am I saying? Otto should get out with you. Karl or Emil can handle this."

"Karl's got enough to do, and I don't want to get Emil more involved than he already is. I'll get Rosa, her parents, and Herman and his parents out. Then I'll follow. I promise," said Sonny.

Joseph cocked his head, examining Sonny as he would a rare first edition. Then he frowned. "Who is this woman Rosa? How did she suddenly capture your fancy?"

Sonny colored slightly, answering with more vigor than necessary. "I told you . . . She lives with her mother and father next door to the Milbergs, Herman's parents. I met her . . ."

"Stop!" Joseph interrupted. "You know what I mean. Everyone's a client—you're infatuated with this young lady."

"Well," Sonny started.

That answered Joseph's question; he sighed in resignation, recalling his own great love, but these were different times. "That's what young men do, but by God be careful. Falling in love can make a man blind and stupid, what you need least of all."

"I know."

"I doubt you do," Joseph countered.

"All right . . . it's impulsive. Besides needing my help, she's lovely. What else can I say?" Sonny would not admit to having some of the same misgivings.

But Joseph persisted. "Promise me you'll be cautious and get the hell out as soon as you can."

"I will. What about you?"

"Me?" Joseph asked, emitting a burst of bitter laughter. "I'm a good German, on no one's list. Why should I leave? Don't worry about me. Besides, I'm getting old, and I have too much work to do." He pointed toward an empty desk where a stack of documents should be.

"And if you're caught?"

"I won't be."

Sonny knew when to quit. "Okay. Then we'll both just have to be careful." He held out his hand.

Joseph grasped it gingerly, and they shook. "Then you'll leave."

Sonny laughed at his friend's persistence and, suddenly moved by the memory of himself at a younger age, put his other hand on Joseph's shoulder . . .

Again came the image of himself sitting on the floor of Joseph's bookstall, rummaging through a pile of magazines, mesmerized by photographs of tribesmen in Africa, nomads from central Asia, exposés of local celebrities, dreaming of the possibilities. After he finished a stack, Joseph gave him more. Sonny spent countless hours, his head buried in the magazines and books that inspired him to become a journalist . . .

"Remember when I was a kid? You gave me piles of magazines. I loved traveling to those exotic places."

Joseph smiled wistfully. "That was a thousand years ago."

"Not so long that we don't remember," Sonny whispered. He saw Mischa and Sophie running down the aisle, beckoning him to follow, giggling, waving . . . himself yelling to his father that he'd be back . . . the three friends exploring every corner of the warehouse, usually ending at the bookstall, watching Joseph stack books, dust shelves, sell a volume . . .

Sonny looked at his old friend, his happy memories battling the present reality. "I'm going to miss you."

"Me too," Joseph whispered.

"You've . . ." Sonny began, and the rest came in a spasm, surprising them both with its intimacy, "been like a father to me."

"Don't get maudlin," Joseph managed to say before looking away. They stood in the center of the room, hands joined . . . the seconds ticking away. Finally, Joseph released Sonny's hand.

Sonny pointed to the square table. "That's where we plotted our grandiose plans. What's with you, Emil, and tables? God, every time I see a table, I know there's got to be a scheme somewhere."

Joseph smiled.

"Back from disaster in Aachen, exposed by Albert, thrown on the woodpile by Polly—damn if you didn't save my sorry ass with a preposterous proposition. We made it work, didn't we?"

"Beyond my wildest expectations."

"There's risk. Not everyone's a joy to work with," Sonny said.

As if on cue, both said "Dix." They laughed.

"He was a pain in the neck, but it paid off. Not just Thiemann Strasse, but Otto and Mina," Sonny said. Then, anticipating Joseph's response, he said, "And there's Willy."

The mere mention brought back the cost, the burden that had come with their accomplishment. Sonny continued, "I'll live with his death the rest of my life—we all will. But the money from that crazy job helped a lot of people. And if I know you, Karl, and Emil, there'll be many more. Damn it! Willy didn't die without purpose."

Sonny gathered a few items, then stopped. He looked around the room that had been his home for a year. "To hell with it! Thanks to you I've got all I need right here." He patted the jacket pocket holding his identity card. Then he took another look, perhaps his last, at *Berlin Street Scene*—the town of his childhood.

"Go on. Get out of here. You've got work to do. There's little time." It was a command.

Sonny met a day promising acrid remains despite the hint of a clear, deep blue sky and the warmth of the rising sun. The scent of a thousand dead fires attacked his nostrils and the silent screams of neighbors sounded in his head.

Within minutes he was a lone sentry on Krausnick Strasse. Propping a foot against the door of an abandoned warehouse, he leaned back to watch Rosenthaler Supplies. Waiting reminded him of the hours of surveillance on Thiemann Strasse. He shivered, raised his collar, and stuffed his hands into his pockets. In daylight, Rosenthal Supplies looked even shabbier than it had in the dirty, reflected light of the city.

The night before, he had walked, run, ducked into doorways, under bridges, through the woods, back to the Mitte, staying clear of crazed Nazis, and singing storm troopers. When he turned onto Krausnick and scanned the Rosenthaler building, he saw exposed brick from beneath the stucco where the business sign was ripped from its mounting. Only the letters "Rose . . . Sup . . ." remained. Boards covered the window, and papers littered the pavement.

The front door had a newly attached hasp and lock. His knock had gone unanswered. He went around to the back, counted off the buildings, and pounded on the door—same lack of response. The windows on the floors above were dark.

He had turned to leave when a loud, demented laugh made the hairs on his neck bristle. Automatically crouching, he waited, but there was nothing but an echo. Someone had gone mad . . .

In the early morning light, Sonny had checked the doors—no one was inside. And for ten minutes he heard nothing but the hum of traffic, a horn blaring, a distant siren—as if normalcy had returned. No one approached from either direction.

Nearly every shop on both sides of the streets suffered some damage. Glass littering the sidewalks crunched underfoot. Sonny's neighbors were staying out of sight—though some brave souls had swept portions of the sidewalk, shuttered a window, secured a door—leaving the street desolate, forlorn. His neighborhood lay bleeding and breathless, its every building, every street, pulsing with loss. No one was secure. Loved ones had been plucked from their homes like chickens from a henhouse. What depths of despair the women must be in! Every one of them in the Mitte staring at a family portrait, a husband's favorite chair . . .

"Shit!" Sonny cursed, trying to think of something else, anything, as he waited for a sign of life at Rosenthaler Supplies—for Robert Fischer.

Then, as his eyes impatiently swept the street, a lone figure registered. He saw an old man slowly drawing closer, shuffling along with the aid of a cane. He stopped at every broken window and skewed door as if evaluating the damage.

Finally reaching Rosenthal Supplies, the old man stopped. Stepping back, he raised his head to look at the sign, down to the pavement, and back to the sign—reading the pieces. Then he moved to the door and fumbled in his pockets until his hand emerged. Nodding, he put a key in the lock, opened it, and returned the key to his pocket. He looked both ways, as if checking for traffic, and pushed the door open.

Sonny ran to the old man before he could open the door, and said breathlessly, "Sir, please, can you help? I'm looking for a man named Robert Fischer. I believe he works here."

Freezing at the sound, the man slowly turned, his liver-spotted hand still on the knob. Many years had etched his thin face. His small eyes were puddles of yellow behind tiny spectacles, but his posture was erect.

"What did you say?" His voice was shaky, slightly hoarse, but with a strong Berliner accent.

"Sir, I didn't mean to startle you," Sonny apologized. "I'm looking for a man—Herr Fischer. I understand he works here."

Without changing his sad, tired expression, the man asked, "What's that name?"

"Robert Fischer," Sonny repeated.

He sighed heavily. "I used to know everybody." He turned his attention to the door and slowly pushed. It refused to open. "Young man, help me get this door open."

Leaning on the door, Sonny pushed until it opened. Inside was a small office with several desks, one overturned; papers were strewn over the floor. There were holes in the wall. On the far side, a door stood ajar, opening onto the warehouse. The old man breathed heavily, shuffled to a lone chair in the middle of the room, and sat resting both his hands on the top of the cane.

Taking a good look at Sonny, he said, "I started this business before the war, built it into something, and now . . . " His shook his head, rheumy eyes circled the room. "I retired, handed the business over to my son. God! Look at the mess. Yesterday the filth ransacked the place, stole the merchandise, arrested my son. Why?" His angry question was rhetorical.

"Do you know where they took him?" Sonny asked tentatively, not wanting to agitate him further.

The old man's head moved slowly in an arc, taking in the room again, as if he hadn't heard the question. Then without looking at Sonny, he said, "My daughter-in-law is beside herself." He paused and shook his head. "Thank God, my wife is not alive."

Fearing the man might be moving to a world far removed from Rosenthaler Supplies, Berlin, November 1938, Sonny gently asked, "Do you know Robert Fischer?"

"Who?"

"Robert Fischer." Sonny waited and saw Herr Rosenthaler nodding as if he understood. "His daughter told me he worked here." Still no answer. "Herr Fischer had a store near Alexanderplatz. He bought merchandise from you until it closed in '35. You or your son hired him."

He shook his head. "The name is not familiar. It has been years . . . my son runs the business." He tapped his cane on the floor impatiently, looking about the room as if searching for something he could recognize: "Or what is left of it."

Sonny grabbed a chair, its back broken, and sat facing the old man. "Sir, my name is Sonny . . . You must be Herr Rosenthaler."

He nodded. "Sonny—what kind of name is that?

Sonny shrugged. "My father gave it to me when I was a child, and it stuck. I was born Sigmund Landauer."

"Landauer, Landauer," the man repeated, until a spark flashed in his eyes, for an instant making him appear younger. "Years ago I knew a Landauer." He rubbed his chin with a bony, spotted hand, coaxing the memory out. "Simon Landauer—yes, I knew a Simon."

Sonny brightened. "He was my uncle."

"Took his own life, did he not?"

"That's right."

A long sigh wheezed and whistled through his teeth. "Terrible. Dead like my wife—did you know my wife?

"No sir, I didn't," Sonny answered.

"I thought you did. I came to see that it is for the best."

"What is, Herr Rosenthaler?"

"That she died, of course. Who would want to be alive now?"

Sonny caught his sad gaze and held it: the old man had nothing but memories, and now this. Finally, he asked softly, "Can you help me find Robert Fischer?"

"My son was in the process of selling the business to a trusted employee so the family could leave. A gentile, a good man, with the firm almost from the beginning." His head turned to the windows, he seemed not to have heard Sonny's question. "Herr Busch covered the windows before he came to me last evening. He gave me the key." He patted his pocket and paused. "Yes, it was last night."

"Can you tell me what happened?"

"I do not remember the details, but if you will wait, Herr Busch will arrive soon. I had to see for myself." An indecipherable, nearly inaudible sound escaped his lips. Herr Rosenthaler closed his eyes; he had seen enough.

Sonny left the old man to his private misery and walked around the office. First, he looked at every corner; then he pushed through the door into the warehouse. Shelves once filled with inventory in neat rows were askew, bent, broken on the floor, as if a cyclone had gone through. Merchandise had been looted for Nazi cronies or the likes of Putzy and Reinhard. Sonny heard voices from the office and went there to greet Herr Busch.

About fifty-five years old, Busch was slightly rotund and had ruddy cheeks. He had an affable disposition not initially apparent, but eventually it surfaced. Waiting until Busch finished talking to the old man, Sonny then introduced himself and gave the reason for his visit. Before engaging with Sonny, Busch turned to the old man and said gently, "I'll show this man around and come back."

After they were out of earshot, he said to Sonny, "He doesn't need to hear the story again."

As they walked Busch tidied up. Pointing to the end of a large, overturned case, he asked Sonny for help in setting it upright. Then he stood with his hands on his hips and surveyed the wreckage of the once prosperous business.

"What happened?" Sonny's voice echoed in the empty room. The man slowly turned, and his ruddy face turned pale.

"I'm not a Nazi—always voted SPD," Busch said, suddenly sounding defensive, perhaps trying to assuage his guilt. "I have great affection for Herr Rosenthaler. He always treated me well. After his son took over, we both ran the business. I managed the inventory and warehouse, younger Rosenthaler the sales." His brow furrowed. "Who are you looking for?"

"Robert Fischer."

"Ja, ja, Robert. We reached a settlement: I'd buy the business and Fritz—that's the son—would leave for America with his family. Poor Herr Rosenthaler, he's devastated by all this." Busch swept his arm in a semicircle. "At least the Nazis arrested no one over a certain age."

"Then it's true? No one over sixty was arrested?"

"Yes, that's what the officer said."

Sonny felt Busch's eyes questioning him, wondering how he had avoided arrest, but he said nothing.

Busch continued: "We finished lunch around two o'clock yesterday afternoon, and then they arrived. Half a dozen soldiers—I suppose they're soldiers—in a truck. They arrested the men—Fritz, Robert, and Will, a young fellow who worked in the warehouse. Then they ordered the office girl and me to clear out. They'd already started loading the inventory onto the truck—over my complaint. 'Just following orders,' the officer said. When I told them I was buying the business, he shook his head, said the Jew Rosenthaler was the owner. That was it." Busch seemed genuinely stricken.

"Where were they taking them?"

"Wouldn't say, told me to go to SA headquarters to find out. Good lord, it was awful," he said and took a deep breath, his exhale an audible sigh. "So I went straightaway. After three hours of bureaucratic mess, a clerk told me they were taken to Sachsenhausen."

Sonny shivered involuntarily, then he took hold of Busch's sleeve. His words spilled out in a rush. "Did they say there's a way to get them out?"

Flinching at the contact, Busch said, "No. I asked how they could keep them locked up, but all he said was, 'Return tomorrow.'"

"God damn them," Sonny cursed.

"If . . . I mean when, they're released . . ." Busch coughed and looked away. "I did learn that to emigrate they need a receipt from the tax office to prove they've paid and a receipt from the finance department for property they take out of the country." He frowned. "Then there are the bribes—but maybe you already know that?"

Sonny thanked Busch, but he had one more question. "The young man, what's his name?"

"Will, Wilhelm Caro."

"Does his family know?"

Busch shrugged. "I don't know. Everything happened so quickly."

"Where do they live?"

Rubbing his eyes with thumb and forefinger, Busch said, "In the neighborhood." Then he shook his head toward the office. Rosenthaler was patiently waiting. "The address is somewhere in this mess." After ten minutes of sifting through the detritus, Busch found Will Caro's address. Someone—Sonny—had to tell Will Caro's parents.

The Caro family lived in a small, crowded flat, minutes away, near Koppen Platz. When Sonny relayed what he'd learned from Busch, Will's mother cried. The two children, like little lambs behind her, stared at the stranger with bad news and cried with her. Then the baby started crying, and Will's father gathered him in his arms.

Will Caro's father, not much older than Sonny, had eluded arrest by luck. When Will didn't come home, his father had wanted to look for him but was afraid to leave the flat. Sonny's news was devastating, dashing the hope that Will was in hiding.

"I'm sorry," Sonny began, "but as soon as Will is released, I can get papers for all of you to leave for Belgium." Caro, comforting the baby, didn't hear him. Sonny repeated the offer.

Staring blankly, he didn't seem to comprehend, but then his lips curved into a doubtful smirk. "Tell me again," he demanded. He glanced at his wife, then back to Sonny. "Even if what you say is true, we have no money to pay you, or to travel."

Sonny's assurance that money wasn't a problem only deepened the man's suspicion. His anger flared, as if he'd been made the fool. Then Sonny did something he'd never done before—he mentioned names. When Caro nodded, Sonny said, "I provided the documents."

Will's father stepped back and looked at his wife again. He shrugged and extended a hand. Sonny shook it, wished them the best, and left, nagged by the thought of the children clinging to their weeping mother.

Always careful, Sonny was more so today. He kept to back streets and alleys. When he saw men loitering on the next corner, he ducked into an apartment building. After several minutes, he exited the rear door and made his way through the alley. As he turned onto the street, he nearly collided with someone. Eager to move on, he mumbled, "Excuse me."

"Wait! I know you," came the man's faintly familiar voice.

Unable to escape, Sonny stopped. Caught by mutual recognition, they stood awkwardly, as if frozen in a photograph. Scrutinizing a face he couldn't name, Sonny finally remembered. The man lived near Joseph, was a fellow peddler whom he'd greeted in the past.

"Oh!" Sonny exclaimed, then relaxed. "Thank God. A familiar face."

The man let out a sigh of relief, grabbed Sonny's hand, and shook it vigorously. "Felix." His introduction came out in a rush as he hopped from foot to foot in a nervous minuet. "I was checking on my brother. I'm glad to say he's safe at home." Shaking his head in disbelief, Felix whispered, "I'm here by pure luck."

How many more times would he hear that? Sonny extended his hand. "Sonny. I'd like to say nice to finally meet you, but . . ."

"I know, it's crazy. If I hadn't been in the fucking subway . . . didn't know all this was going on, I'd be locked up like the others. Smelled smoke as I left the station . . . ran all the way home. Smoke poured from the synagogue off August Strasse; shop windows were smashed. My wife was hysterical—the SA pounded on the door and asked for me by name—just ten minutes before I arrived home."

Still clutching Sonny's hand, he muttered, "Goddamn ten minutes!" He shook his head. "How many times have you said timing is everything? God! Luck and timing!" Felix tried to smile, but his face twitched. Then he asked Sonny for his story because every Jew had one.

"Sort of the same, though not as dramatic," Sonny told him. "They didn't know where to find me." He slowly extricated his bruised hand from Felix's grasp.

"I heard that women—wives and mothers—banded together to enter SA headquarters and demanded to know where they'd taken their men. And damned if the SA didn't tell them." He leaned forward. "But that's all they said—nothing about releasing them. We're leaving for Paris—got family there—as soon as it's safe." They wished each other well and headed in opposite directions.

Through Scheunenviertel, street by street, were broken windows, doors knocked off hinges, twinkling shards of glass. Few of the shops were shuttered, though Sonny saw several women cleaning up the mess. Unnerved by the absence of people, of children in the streets, his journey was a walk through a lifeless, soundless dreamscape. Felix and countless others had avoided arrest in the subway, but Sonny stayed clear of confined spaces, where retreat was impossible. He walked to Rosa's flat, and when he saw two or more men together, he changed his route . . .

The pungent odor of a dead fire made Sonny turn away from what he might encounter before him. He couldn't face another burned-out synagogue. Block after block, the pattern of the pogrom's precise destruction repeated itself. Terrified again, he was also amazed. Only the Jewish shops were damaged and looted—adjacent gentile shops lay untouched. Only to prevent damage to their gentile neighbors were any synagogues left unburned. In the months past, Sonny had found it hard to maintain his spirits; today it was nearly impossible. Despair nearly overtook him at every turn.

When he entered No. 241 Pestalozzi Strasse, Sonny was comforted by the familiar smells of cooking, painted walls, and dirty carpet. Rosa practically pulled him into the flat, peppering him with questions: "What did you learn about my father? What's it like out there? When can we leave?" Coiled tight like a spring, she clutched the arms of his jacket. Her eyes searched his face for answers, her mouth slightly open.

"Rosa," Sonny said softly as he peeled her hands from his arms and held them. "Sit down. Then I'll answer your questions." Sonny looked for her mother, but she wasn't there.

Rosa kept her eyes on him. "It was a terrible night. Mother was alternately hysterical and strangely calm." She put her hands to her mouth. "I wanted to scream, but I couldn't—not with Mother in such a state."

"Try to calm yourself. You need to be in control," Sonny implored. Gently putting a hand on her shoulder, he guided her to a chair. Dark circles ringed her eyes, but she was hyperalert, running on nerves. He feared she would crash in a heap. "Did you get any sleep?

She shook her head, "I couldn't. After Mother finally fell asleep, my mind raced. I couldn't sit, couldn't lie down. I probably wore a hole in the carpet." She shot Sonny a quick, nervous smile.

Sonny nodded, placed a hand on hers, and held her gaze. "I've just come from Rosenthaler Supplies and have news . . . "

"What . . . what?" she interrupted before he could finish.

"Rosa," he spoke calmly and squeezed her hand. "We have to hope. That's all we have—that and your ability to function."

"Then give me hope."

"I'll try," Sonny began, and for the second time he delivered the news he'd learned from Busch. He told her he'd met Herr Rosenthaler and visited the Caro family. Finally he said, "According to what Busch learned at SA headquarters, your father was taken to Sachsenhausen."

Rosa stared blankly through Sonny into space, her lips moving silently. Then her chin quavered, she cupped her face in her hands, and her shoulders heaved into a sob. Rosa's misery—the pain of knowing and the fear of loss—was unbearable. He loathed what his words had done, hated this place where synagogues burned, where innocent men were thrown into camps. He hated this cesspool of depravity—from the goddamn warehouse cellar to Thiemann Strasse to this flat—and he especially hated God, for abandoning them.

Rosa had been dragged down with the rest of them. Sonny knelt, put his arms around her to console them both, and slowly her crying subsided. She raised her head and brushed the tears from her cheeks with a forefinger. "You delivered my worst fear!"

The intensity of her recrimination stung. Sonny flinched.

Seeing the hurt on his face, Rosa said quickly, "Oh Sonny, it's not you, not after all you've done." Anger drained from her eyes, and she reached for his hand and held it. "But to actually know . . ." Rosa averted her eyes.

"We have to hope." That was all he could think of to say. He had no plan other than to wait, and what was the solace in that? So they sat together for fifteen minutes, until Sonny said, "I have to go, but I'll be back."

He left for Neukölln to give Herman the news.

After the long trek across town, Sonny sat alone with a cup of Frau Moltke's strong coffee. He picked up one of the several newspapers stacked neatly on the table. He began to read but soon threw down the paper in disgust. Responsibility for the horrors of the past twenty-four hours was insanely placed on the victims, but he'd known that would happen. He left the kitchen in search of someone, anyone, and encountered Frau Moltke cleaning a room.

She saw him, wiped her forehead, and leaned against the mop. "Hello, Sonny. Mina gave me the message about Herman's parents. Rest assured, we didn't say a word. More guests are coming to join the others upstairs."

Muffled voices reminiscent of those in the hushed conversations of the Dove's cellar penetrated the doors at the top of the steps. One door opened a crack, revealing the sliver of a pale face, one eye peering at him. Sonny saw more faces in the background as the man nodded curtly, then closed the door. Sonny went up another flight and knocked on the door where Otto and Mina usually slept. They no longer kept separate rooms—there were too many guests for that. Mina let him in.

"It's a madhouse," she started, "but it's all we can do."

"Are you okay?" Sonny had asked the question so many times that it sounded mechanical, even trivial, to his ears though not to Mina's.

"Fine, normal, bored to death, scared, but these poor men and their families . . ." Her face was tight; she left the thought unfinished.

"Where's Otto?"

"Out there," she tossed her head randomly. "Like you . . . doing good." With a dry, mirthless cackle, she continued. "It's hopeless. I couldn't see it until yesterday. We've got to get out of this hellhole as soon as Otto can arrange it." She grabbed Sonny's jacket, as if it were a lifeline. "But he's so goddamn noble, so stubborn." Mina's voice was beseeching. "Sonny, you're the only one who can talk him into leaving. You're his best friend. He'll listen to you. I know he will."

Sonny shook his head. "I'll try, but don't be so sure. Whatever he decides, you've got to go. Hell, I'm leaving, as soon as I tie up a few things."

"What—save a few more souls?" Her tone was sarcastic. She paced around the tiny room, wringing her hands like Rosa. "I'm sorry. That was unkind. But you're just like Otto—always someone out there in need."

"That's why we're friends."

"Don't be so damned gallant. Think about *you* for a change!" Mina was headstrong, idealistic, a bit naïve, at least she had been. She'd eagerly joined the ring of smugglers, but the past twenty-four hours had made of her an unsentimental realist, her only desire to flee with her lover. Life in hiding, the chaos of the previous day, had soured her on the romance of the underground. And who could blame her?

Sonny had no answer, so he changed the subject, "I saw the men."

She shrugged. "They came on foot, others by car. We heard the pogrom was over, but we're not letting them leave until we're sure. We can't get papers for all of them, so Karl's talking to them about Shanghai, explaining what they have to do, that they don't need a visa."

She moved to the window and looked onto Stuttgarter Strasse, nearly empty: "The first night here I crept out of the house. It was against the rules, but I didn't care—I was free. Otto saw me leave, and he followed. We walked for hours. I can't tell you how exciting it was. The moment I walked through the door I wanted to help, and so I stayed. For the first time in my life, I was doing something important." Mina walked to the door, her confessional over. "I have to help Frau Moltke." Her footfalls echoed as she disappeared down the stairs.

Herman was sharing the small room with five men—all older, all frightened. Sonny greeted them from the doorway and beckoned Herman to follow.

"How are my parents?" Herman asked when they were alone.

"Fine," Sonny answered. Then he summarized the events of the night before. Herman took Sonny's hand in both of his and pumped it as if filling a pail of water. "Thank you, thank you."

"I was lucky," Sonny said, extricating his hand, by now an automatic response. His modesty went unnoticed. "Your parents will be arriving soon, so they'll need your help. Now's the time to bury your failure."

Tears filled Herman's eyes. He muttered again, "Thank you, thank you."

Sonny turned to leave, stopped, turned back, and said, "Tell me about Robert Fischer."

Surprised, Herman asked, "What do you want to know?"

"He's missing, and I promised Rosa I'd help—just like I promised you."

Nodding, Herman said, "I've known him as a neighbor for years, not as a friend, and as for Rosa . . . " His tone suddenly changed and he smirked. "She's a couple of years younger . . . Anyhow, Herr Fischer lost his business, and if I remember right, he went to work for a wholesaler somewhere in the Mitte. He's a nice man—that's all I know about him. It must be awful."

But Sonny wasn't ready to leave. "How well do you know Rosa?"

Herman looked down, suddenly shy. "Not so well now. You've seen her. I was still a kid next door when she blossomed. And I suppose I fell for her, kind of hard, but . . . " He made a face somewhere between regret and folly, then shrugged. "It's ancient history. I got over it. We were never friends after that—my feelings were hurt, but she was always cordial. Then I heard she was engaged."

Frowning, Herman shook his head and went on. "I didn't know the guy, but I heard his family had some money. Then he left for France or somewhere—without her. That all happened before I left for Cologne. I'm not surprised she found a guy with money. She was like honey to a bear." Herman's judgment came easily and without rancor. "She probably picked through them until he was the last one left— if you know what I mean. Anyhow, Frau Fischer told my mother that Rosa never heard from the guy. He probably fell in love with someone else. I guess if you have money, you can do anything."

"Ja, maybe," Sonny mumbled. But all he could think of was Rosa's response at the door. The other Sigmund, wherever he was, had nothing to do with him. He would deal with that later.

27

Whoever destroys a single life is as guilty as though he had destroyed the entire world; and whoever rescues a single life earns as much merit as though he had rescued the entire world.
—Mischna, Sanhedrin

For those with loved ones in the lowest of dungeons, the days passed slowly. They had no opportunity to visit, no information about the release of their husbands, fathers, brothers, uncles, friends. A fear so exquisite gripped the community that normal sights, sounds, and smells seemed the precursor of a second round of attack. The people retreated, their lives drastically circumscribed. Venturing only occasionally onto the streets, they tread lightly, glanced over their shoulders. Stuck in cycling anticipation and dread, they were anxious, short-tempered—their anger often erupting onto whoever was near.

Berlin's Jewish population was locked in the worst of two worlds. With the fate of the men unknown, the women were adrift, in a state of unrelenting uncertainty. They lived with unprecedented despair, terrorized by the demons of their worst fears. Thus passed the last three weeks of November into December.

People lived on the rumors making the rounds among family, friends, and neighbors. What little they knew of the camps came from the few who'd been released. Karl talked with a man named Fogelman who'd been at Dachau. The men were locked in a single room with 150 others for fourteen hours without food, water, or toilet, then ordered into the courtyard to stand at attention in ranks of 50, heels together, hands at their sides. The man in charge of his rank ordered veteran war officers "front and center and click heels," then whittled them down by wounds, decorations, finally to Iron Cross First Class. Of the nine remaining, he counted off the first seven, Fogelman's number. "Get the hell out of here," he ordered. Fogelman ran and never looked back.

Karl described Fogelman as "horribly torn, elated over his freedom but suffering from inexplicable guilt at having been let go. Perhaps the greatest irony is that he has papers for his family to emigrate—he just never had the courage to leave . . . until now."

As for the men who escaped imprisonment through luck or guile, they may as well have endured a hail of bullets. In the hours after the roundup, they searched themselves for injuries that weren't there, though they were certainly wounded. Their anxiety reached the level of that suffered during the Black Plague, when Jews were hunted like vermin. Everyone knew someone caught in the sweep. Sonny's Scheunenviertel neighbors held their breath until their men were safely home. Behind the façade of normalcy in the hallways, and on the streets when they did venture out, was an eerie stillness.

What had begun with insults, then kicks to the shin, had escalated to massive body blows and degenerated to submersion. Limbs wrapped in chains, bodies thrown into the river. People lived in fear of another pogrom, more vicious than the one before, begun for any reason or none.

Without Jewish newspapers, the beleaguered community lost its information lifeline. Then the government assessed reparations, cynically dubbed "atonement payments," upon the *victims* for damages. This financial load, on those already overburdened, was in the ludicrous amount of ten million Reichmarks. Further decrees prohibited Jews from attending theaters, movies, concerts, and exhibits, from owning stores and artisan businesses, even from access to the parks. The night of 9 November 1938—what came to be known as *Kristallnacht* for its shards of broken glass—marked a turning point. Jews were henceforth excluded from all cultural and economic activity in Germany.

Life was reduced to its most basic. Keeping one's wits was suddenly the most valuable commodity. No longer could anyone in a right mind say, "Conditions will improve. Germany is a civilized nation." For Sonny, the very idea was delusional—recent events obliterated it. After Kristallnacht, he thought, all Jews must reject the fiction that they could live under whatever privations, one by one, the Reich heaped upon them.

Several days after the pogrom began, after Göring and Goebbels called an end to the mayhem, it stopped. Karl dropped a copy of *Der An-*

griff on the kitchen table and pointed to the Goebbels column, reading: "We want only one thing, that the world love the Jews enough to rid us of them all."

Sonny and Otto waited for Karl to read further. Instead he said grimly, "Let's help him make that happen."

For two days there'd been no appointments set, no one to meet, but now they'd get back to work. Franz and the other runners, like Sonny, had escaped arrest and were back on the street. Two days after the arrests and the burning of the synagogues, Sonny kept his appointment with Tiergarten Henry. Then day and night, in dark corners of the Mitte, in flats, in the little café near the warehouse—wherever it seemed safe—Sonny and Otto met with men and women searching for a way out. They collected photographs and papers for Joseph and delivered his documents into grateful hands.

The operators retrieved documents from their hiding place under the floor, and the assembly line restarted. Joseph, pen in hand, hunched over his desk, focused on the details of forgery—weeding, watering, pruning his little garden toward a harvest of foolproof forgeries increasing in number but never quite enough.

They did what they could. But Sonny worried over Joseph's frequent breaks to flex his hand and remove his glasses to rub his eyes. When he mentioned it, Joseph rebuffed him: "There's too much work to be done."

Later on the day that Sonny informed Herman of his parents' pending arrival, Alfred drove them to the opening of the alley. When his parents exited the car, Herman broke down. Embracing them, he helped his mother into No. 53. No recriminations.

Smiling, Alfred told Karl and Sonny that Frau Milberg had refused to be carried down the stairs. She walked out with the aid of her husband and Alfred and by her own extreme effort—but not without paying a visit to Frau Fischer and Rosa, to bid them farewell and best wishes for Herr Fischer's return. When they were safely at No. 53 Stuttgarter Strasse, the three Milbergs sat in the kitchen, listening to Otto as he laid out the plan.

Nobody could leave until it was safe to travel, and the days dragged on until 16 November, when Karl finally came with the news that Reinhard Heydrich, head of SS Security Service, had issued an order for an end to the arrest of Jewish men. The pogrom was officially over.

Before that order, only a handful of the arrestees were released. Now rumors abounded—prisoners could go on their promise to leave Germany. Women flocked to the camps to retrieve their men. But in the days following, only a trickle of men reappeared. How long before a husband, father, or son was freed was anyone's guess.

Still, the operators agreed, it was now safe to travel.

Alfred drove the Milbergs to Kaiser Friedrich Railroad Station to board a train for Aachen. Each carried a passport, a Belgian visa, and a receipt for taxes paid, including the onerous Reich Flight Tax. Since they were taking only a few articles of clothing, permits weren't required. But a stack of forms was required for taking money out of the country that still might end up in the pockets of the border guard. The Milbergs carried several hundred Reichmarks among them, to be spent or given to Günter (Fritz's cousin and the group's Aachen operator) until each had only ten Reichmarks, the maximum allowed.

They made their farewells at the back door of No. 53. Frau Milberg planted a kiss on Sonny's cheek, and her husband pumped his arm energetically. Son Herman brushed Sonny's hand aside and embraced him, whispering, "I owe you much."

"Good luck! Buy me a drink in Antwerp."

While the Milbergs waited, Rosa set about her own, albeit shorter, journey. Standing at the mirror in a simple dress of black wool that complemented her eyes, she put on her coat and adjusted her cloche. Then she knelt beside her mother, seated with her head in her hands.

Kissing her cheek, Rosa said, "Everything will turn out all right. I promise." When her mother did not respond, Rosa made sure their eyes met. Her mother wept, and Rosa left the flat to the sound of her despair. She walked past the Milbergs' empty flat, vowing to be on that train, soon.

Waiting for the subway, Rosa looked confident, poised, but her heart pounded. Slightly lightheaded, she fought her fear with anger at having to make this trip. Staring down at the cigarette butts and dead matches, avoiding the gaze of others, she silently repeated that it would soon be over. She conjured memories of her father holding her little hand at the zoo as she shrieked with joy at the lion's den, of a birthday party with friends, of her parents dancing at a wedding.

Finally, she boarded the train; its rhythmic swaying calmed her. Rosa rehearsed the simple lines she'd recite to the clerk: "I am here to obtain the release of Herr Robert Fischer. Please tell me where he is being held and when he will be released." Saying the words again and again, she used the thought of seeing her father to ease the humiliation of having to beg for his release.

Rosa replayed in her mind bits of the two conversations she'd had with women who'd made solitary trips to the old Karl Liebknecht Haus, former KPD but now SA headquarters. The two told similar stories of seeking information about their imprisoned husbands from aloof, disinterested clerks who acted as if they were looking only for a misplaced glove. Enduring indifference, bureaucratic formality, endless forms, yet another clerk, more lines, straight-backed chairs in a windowless room, the two had separately wrung their hands, waiting near signs ordering "Quiet or Risk Expulsion," beneath portraits of the Führer hanging on walls threatening to collapse upon them.

When a corresponding name—if it was on the list—was called, each (there were many others) stood before a clerk who looked her up and down or not at all and announced the place where her husband or father or son was held. Rosa's two acquaintances had learned their husbands were in Sachsenhausen. How were they to gain their loved ones' release?

"Impossible. You must return. And maybe the Führer, in his generosity, will order the release of the criminal Jews."

Rosa's journey now was preliminary, the first step in obtaining her father's release. She and her mother needed formal acknowledgement that he was imprisoned, though they already knew.

When Sonny arrived at the flat earlier that day, Rosa had just finished speaking with the second woman. Pale as sculpted Carrera marble, Rosa chewed on her lip, telling him what she'd learned. He'd heard similar stories from Karl and Otto. He wished her good luck, they hugged, and he promised to call her later.

When he did, from the phone box near No. 53, the telephone rang four, five, six times. He was about to replace the receiver when he heard her breathless "Hello."

"How did it go?" There was an unnerving fifteen seconds of silence. "Rosa, are you there?"

She sighed. "Your information was correct. Father is at Sachsenhausen, but nothing was said about his release." Her disappointment traveled through the phone line like a foul odor.

"Were you harassed?"

"No. I wasn't alone. There were so many women. It was just boring, like waiting in the doctor's office. Only far worse."

There was nothing to do but wait. He said, "Papers will be ready. When your father's released, you will go."

The uncomfortable silence returned. Finally Rosa asked, "When are you coming?"

Sonny sighed. "Tomorrow. I have an appointment. I want to be with you, but there's so much to do."

Silence, then: "Of course, how thoughtless of me . . . Sonny, I'm lonely . . . afraid."

Sonny felt wretched. "I promise to come as soon as I can. Please be patient. There's nothing we can do but wait."

"I just want him back."

After ringing off, Sonny walked along the canal, staring into the slowly moving black water that looked as empty as he felt. To banish the guilt brought by Rosa's disappointment, he opened his jacket, welcoming the night chill. In minutes he was shivering, so he ran along the canal until his lungs hurt. Bending toward the ground, resting his hands on his thighs, he gulped air, aching to spend both day and night with Rosa. But he couldn't, not with all the work to do, not with her father locked in Sachsenhausen, her mother a wreck.

He winced. What was so wrong about being attracted to a beautiful woman? About his physical longings? Sure, she was alone, confused, scared, vulnerable. He sighed in frustration, knowing there was little to gain, much to regret, in going down that road. The prospect that her father might never be released staggered him.

A shapeless form lurched from behind a tree. Sonny backed away, then realized it was a man, his clothes torn and shabby. Unsteady on his feet, his hand was outstretched, begging. Reaching into his pocket, Sonny grabbed several coins and dropped them into his hand. The derelict grunted incoherently and shambled away . . .

Sonny was on his way to Joseph's flat for documents. Passing a bridge, he thought of his Uncle Simon: he missed the gentle misanthrope. He shuddered to think of Simon in Sachsenhausen with Rosa's father . . . Had it really been two years since Rudy's frantic voice had sounded from the other end of a phone line that Simon was missing? Squinting into the dark, Sonny was overwhelmed by an image of Rudy and Uncle John manhandled into the back of a truck. He sagged at having forgotten them. They had argued—the memory still stung—but they were family. Then Sonny brightened: Uncle John was well past sixty and would have escaped the sweep of arrest. But Rudy . . .

Sonny found a phone box, rummaged for coins, glad he hadn't emptied his pocket for the tramp. Concentrating until the telephone number came back to him, he dialed. One . . . two . . . finally on the sixth ring: "Hello." Rudy's breathless voice hit his ear.

"Rudy!" Sonny blurted in relief. "It's Sonny . . . you all right? And your father?"

Heavy breathing . . . "Sonny, I was down the hall . . . didn't hear the telephone. Mother, father, and Frieda are out, getting ready."

"Ready?"

"We're leaving as soon as we can." His voice was almost cheery.

Misdirected, fooled by a conjurer's sleight of hand, Sonny was thrown off stride. "When? How . . . how did you manage it?"

"Aunt Edith's affidavit for America arrived yesterday."

Sonny calculated the time Aunt Edith needed to find a patron to sign an affidavit and get it to Berlin. She would have had to start weeks before—long before Zbaszyn . . .Vom Rath's death . . . Kristallnacht.

"Sonny, you there?"

"You're leaving . . . I don't get it. We argued. What happened?"

Rudy was silent, then: "I regret what happened. You got us thinking. I wanted to contact you. Herr Wagner didn't know where you were."

That was the point, thought Sonny.

Rudy didn't ask why. "We were upset—I felt guilty about how it ended," he admitted, clearing his throat. "But then, Jews are wracked with guilt." His attempt at humor fell flat. "Ja. Well, I used to teach at a Jewish school in Charlottenburg."

"What happened?" Sonny figured he already knew.

"Weeks ago, well before the pogrom . . ." his voice thickened. "Nazi thugs vandalized the school—broke windows, destroyed books, painted threatening words on the walls. Parents stopped sending their children. We were all afraid. The school closed. They'd have shut it down anyway."

"I'm sorry," Sonny murmured.

"Ja. Nothing like the specter of death and destruction to focus the mind on what's important. Without work, no future, it was time to go."

"How did you avoid arrest? I mean . . ."

"And you?" Rudy parried, then laughed cynically. "I'll go first. Pure luck, like many others. Ten minutes before the SA came, I went for groceries. Smelled smoke, but still didn't know. The grocer was closed, so I knew something was wrong. Then I saw the trucks, heard screaming. I hid in an alley. Mother and father were in a terrible state." Rudy stopped short, then surprised Sonny: "You were right all along. I was wrong and . . . unkind. I . . . uh . . . want to apologize."

Sonny stared at the receiver. Faced with yet another attack, however benign, on his world order, he was speechless.

"Sonny, you still there?"

"Ja, still here. Just in shock." Sonny held a hand to his forehead.

Rudy's laugh came in a snort. "The whole world's upside down—why not me? What about you?"

"They couldn't find me. I've been underground for more than a year. My name's on a Gestapo list," Sonny answered.

Several seconds passed. "I had no idea," Rudy said.

"How could you?"

"When are you leaving?"

"Good question." Sonny shrugged into the telephone. "I'm too involved in helping others to leave—haven't had time to figure that out." He would say no more.

Rudy laughed. "That's just like you, so much like Uncle Simon."

The offhand remark, seemingly innocent, struck at the heart of Sonny's estrangement from his family. Had Sonny filled Simon's role, insulating Rudy from self-scrutiny as Simon had done for Sonny's father, for John and Sonny's Uncle Georg? Some day, Sonny thought, he'd set Rudy straight—but not now. He hadn't called to pick a fight.

"I miss Simon more than you can imagine."

No response, just an uncomfortable silence signaling an end to the conversation. Sonny sent greetings to the family. He and Rudy wished each other well.

Rudy said, "Maybe we'll meet on the streets of New York." Then the line went dead.

Sonny felt good about his family for the first time in years.

Rosa rarely left the flat—too many awful reminders were outside. When she did leave, it was for groceries or an occasional walk with Sonny. She spent the days caring for her mother, waiting for her father's release, and yearning for Sonny's next visit. But there was one task she'd kept putting off, intimidated by her lack of experience in such matters. About a week into her vigil, several days after her trip to the former Karl Liebknecht Haus, she made up her mind. Telling her mother she'd be gone for about an hour, she headed toward Savigny Platz. Walking briskly, focused on her mission, Rosa nearly missed a neighbor's greeting. In ten minutes, she reached her destination. She paused, then entered the Dove.

She waited for her eyes to adjust to the dim light. Several men sat at tables, a few more at the bar, most of them looking at her. But she was staring at the bartender, who was smiling at her. Nervously, she returned his smile, assuming he was Johnny. Her eyes drifted to the back, to the doorway leading to the cellar, and she walked to the bar.

"Good afternoon, miss. What can I get for you?"

Rosa cleared her throat. "You're Johnny."

He nodded, his smile broadening. "Have been for years. And you are?"

"Rosa. I live down the street," she answered, glancing in that general direction. "I'm a friend of Sonny's."

"Oh, I see," he answered, as if that explained everything.

"I . . . uh . . . I," she began then stopped, uncomfortable with the men staring at her. She leaned closer. "Can we talk in private?"

Johnny's smile remained fixed. "Sure, come with me," he instructed, and he led her through the rear door into the narrow hallway. He stopped and looked around, then spoke to nobody in sight. "Fred, cover the bar for me, please."

Rosa heard a door open; a big man carrying several bottles appeared. He closed the door and muttered, "What?"

"Fred, this is Sonny's lady friend, Rosa."

She flushed.

"Good to meet you, Rosa."

His gruff voice and manner were strangely reassuring. Her nerves receded. Being deep inside the Dove, where Herr Milberg and the others had found shelter, was comforting. She felt safe, no longer afraid of these men.

"The pleasure is all mine," she said and flashed him a bright smile.

"I don't argue with pretty women," Fred growled, as he squeezed by her into the bar.

Johnny had disappeared; Rosa heard his disembodied voice: "Rosa, join me in the office." She walked to the source, and he motioned her to sit. Rosa's eyes took in the small room while Johnny's eyes remained on her. He asked, "What can I do for you?"

Rosa's message was simple, one she could scarcely forget. "Thank you."

"Hmm." Johnny sat with his elbows on the desk, his fingertips touching. "I would say you're welcome, but first I need to know what I've done to merit the gratitude of a lovely lady. Normally, I'd remember."

She smiled, figuring he was just being Johnny. "I think you know . . . perhaps you're too modest."

"Modest! *Moi*?" Johnny threw his head back, laughing so heartily she laughed with him. Instantly, the little office filled with bonhomie. "I've been accused of many transgressions, but modesty isn't one of them." Leaning forward, his smile sagged to a smirk, and he asked, "Please tell me what I'm supposed to have done."

"You and Fred saved dozens of men from arrest," Rosa reminded him.

Suddenly serious, he pursed his lips and nodded. "True. But what else was I to do?" He shrugged and threw out his hands. "Leave them to the scum? No!" A self-deprecating smile then a "tsk, tsk" sound with his tongue: "Where are my manners?" He lowered his head in an abbreviated bow. "You're very welcome."

"How many were there?"

"I didn't count. Maybe Fred did."

Relieved, Rosa looked down at her hands folded primly on her lap and felt like a different person. She had said what she'd come to say, but there was more. "When Sonny told me that Herr Milberg was hiding here, I hoped my father was with him." She bit her lip and looked away. "Sonny promised to find Herr Milberg, and he did. He also promised to find my father. Thanks to you, he fulfilled the first promise. Now he needs to . . ." Rosa closed her eyes, fighting back the tears. "I promised I wouldn't do that."

Johnny let the moment pass then said. "I appreciate what you're doing, especially under the circumstances, but you needn't have come." He made a feeble gesture with his hand.

"Oh, but I did need to," she countered, her composure restored. "If not for you, then for me. On that awful day, you helped in ways that I couldn't have imagined. That opened my eyes. So I had to meet you and Fred. My father was arrested, and my mother has taken it badly. But we know where he is, and Sonny is there to help. He told me a little about your world, and his—one I don't understand but that I do accept, especially now. I'm a little wiser, maybe humbler too."

Johnny reached for the bottle at the corner of his desk. "Can I offer you a drink?"

"Why not? Yes, of course."

Johnny poured amber liquid into two glasses, handed one to her, and raised his. "To your father's swift release."

Rosa winced as the first sip went down; the second was easier. Emboldened by drink, she gave a quick, determined nod and asked her last question: "What exactly is it that you and Sonny do?"

Johnny drank, then licked his lips, and shot her a disarming smile. "It wouldn't be prudent for me to say. I suggest you ask him."

"I know that he smuggles Jews out of Germany, but . . ." she stopped.

"What else do you need to know?"

"He's a mystery, like you."

"That's life. We come from somewhere else, different from your world—no better, no worse—it just is. In times like these a guy like Sonny is a precious commodity. Don't let him get away." Johnny's smile evaporated, making him look tired. "For more, ask him."

She nodded, got to her feet, and offered her hand to Johnny. "Thanks for the advice."

He came around the desk and took her hand in both of his. "Free of charge." His smile returned as well as his charm.

"I'm so pleased to have met you and Fred."

"The pleasure is mine," he answered.

Rosa left the little office, strode through the narrow hall into the tavern, past the men drinking their beer. She smiled, waved to Fred behind the bar, and left the Dove. On the walk home, she felt comforted by what she had done.

But when she entered the flat, the feeling faded with the intrusion of the shattered pieces of her life. She'd become the head of the family upon her father's absence and her mother's decline. They shared the fear that father/husband would never return—and then what? She couldn't bear to deal with such a loss.

Thoughts of her mystery man, that "precious commodity," softened her distress. Sonny would appear soon, cheer her with his company, with a little coffee, tea, bread, chocolate—whatever he could manage. They would sit close on the sofa or at the table holding hands, talk of everything but what had brought them together. For an hour or two they would ignore the elephant in the room, almost forget they were waiting for some news.

The hours he spent with Rosa and her mother were happy ones for Sonny—an island of homely contentment divorced from reality. Bolstering Rosa's spirits and his own was creating a bond, bringing them closer.

What had long eluded him had returned—he was now part of a family—included by Frau Fischer, regardless of her condition, and embraced by Rosa.

Sonny had come to appreciate normal life—the repetition of the mundane, related, and isolated bits and pieces that gave form and meaning to a day—shopping for groceries, preparing meals, cleaning the flat, washing the laundry, planning for the future. Joseph, Otto, and Emil had long been his family, but this was different. Despite the turmoil visited upon her loved ones, Rosa made him feel he belonged in a way he'd sorely missed. And during the last weeks of November and into December, something dear blossomed.

Rosa would rise from the table after they'd eaten, walk behind him, place a hand on his shoulder, allow it to linger. Other times she absently touched his arm or rested her hand on his thigh as they sat quietly together. Then he softly touched her cheek, kissed her forehead. He loved Rosa's natural, unforced sensuousness, her throaty laugh, her raspy voice. She moved to the window, wrapped her arms around her chest, shivered, jerked her head, beckoned. He stood close behind her as she pointed down to the street: "My entire life, more than twenty years, that's been my view. Every curtained window, every door, the same, and the people below . . ." She stopped.

"That must be comforting," Sonny answered, recalling the suddenness of vacating his parent's flat, how it had ended with Herr Wagner.

She shook her head. "No. Everywhere I look reminds me of what I've lost. Over there," she pointed, "Father would come around that corner after work. People I used to know are gone, and the rest of them?"

On the pavement below, the faces obscured. What were those people thinking? Did they realize what was going on?

"Everything has changed," she started then paused. The only sounds were their breathing and the hum of the traffic below. "I went to meet Johnny and Fred."

Rosa had talked of going, but Sonny was surprised. "How did it go?"

She shuddered, so he wrapped his arms around her, pulled her close.

"Good. Johnny's smooth, self-assured—I liked him. And Fred, well, he's Fred."

"Johnny invented smooth."

She laughed. "I thanked him for what he did. Then I asked him what the two of you really do."

"What did he tell you?"

She turned to face him. "That I should ask you."

"Oh, did he?"

Rosa asked softly, "Sigmund Landauer, what is it you really do?"

Sonny pulled her closer and smiled broadly. "I told you."

"There must be more." She wouldn't let it rest.

"Let's just say I've done some things your parents might not approve of. I'll tell you when all this is behind us."

"Hmm," Rosa considered. "Sounds dangerous and romantic."

"Not exactly romantic, if what you mean is like what we're doing now."

"Still doesn't answer my question."

Sonny considered. "Let's make a deal. I'll tell you, but you have to tell me about the other Sigmund."

Rosa gasped. "No fooling you."

"Don't even try," he shot back, only half joking.

Untangling herself from Sonny, she chewed on her lip. "All right, it's a deal. But if I have to wait, you have to explain what all this means."

Sonny laughed. "Ask me something hard."

"Don't weasel out again. You're the worldly one. You must know." Her tone was light, but her expression was serious.

"Damned if I know!"

"When you showed up, an emissary from Frau Milberg, Father hadn't come home; Mother was falling apart. I was so afraid, but all that came out was anger. Others suffered as much, but I felt sorry for myself." She held up both hands as if to surrender to some unknowable truth.

"It was still happening; understanding had to come later."

"But you were so calm, so self-assured. What did you know that I didn't?"

"Nothing. Experience, that's all. But if my father were missing, I'd have . . . I could have been taken too—both of us."

"Don't say that."

"I'll never understand the twisted logic behind the pogrom. It's too monstrous. Its roots are so deep in darkness, I can't fathom the cause. That kind of hate takes centuries to cultivate. To them, we're not human. Look what happened in Zbaszyn."

"What's going to happen to us?"

"We'll get the hell out of here when your father's released. You were right to want to leave. Now we're caught in the aftermath of a firestorm. Survival, escape, loved ones intact—that's all that matters. Before my uncle threw himself into the river, I thought I knew what was going on. After that, nothing made sense." Sonny made a harsh sound, a short self-deprecating laugh.

He shook his head and continued. "The worse it gets, the less I know. Your comfortable life was turned upside down . . . then again by men like Johnny, Fred, and me, instead of . . ." Sonny stopped, recalling the deal they'd just made. "Trust me. There are surprises to come. But as to the larger why?" Sonny shook his head. "Damned if I know."

Rosa moaned and made a sour face.

He picked it up again. "After Plombieres, who knows? We could land in Antwerp, Paris, maybe London, even New York. My uncle, aunt, and cousins are well on their way by now." And he talked with her of the possibilities and of the family lore, telling anew his father's story of the shtetl, the newlyweds, the Cossack.

Rosa stepped back, tapping a fingertip on her lip as she studied his face. "Of course . . . But is it true?"

Sonny shook his head. "When my father first told me that story, I was enchanted. It took on a life of its own, became a running family joke, a punch line."

"Was it fun?"

"For a while, until it got old." Sonny sounded tired. "The story's apocryphal, but the larger story is our history: women raped, men murdered, villages uprooted. All I know is that Jews have been on the wrong side of history since the Romans killed that rabbi in the Holy Land."

Rosa giggled.

"All that's left is to get the hell out of here. I'll leave those questions to the philosophers, to another day."

Rosa sighed and, as if reading his thoughts, moved closer, whispering, "Hold me. I'm cold."

Sonny enjoyed the warmth of her body against his, but he couldn't help wondering whether it was for him or for Belgium. He was in her plans—she said it often enough. He believed her. Still, she was an enigma—simple but complicated. Sometimes demure, even reticent, she averted her eyes. Other times she was overtly sensual, brushing her hip against his, the softness of her breast resting against his arm like a pillow. Her movements were so natural, without guile—or were they? Sonny was stimulated, conflicted. Each encounter—small, self-contained—came with the sense that she wasn't aware something had occurred. If there was a pattern, a code, a message, he was damned if he knew what it was.

Of two things he was certain: Rosa was gripped by fear, and she bewitched him. Drawn like an addict to the promise of drugs, Sonny was hopelessly entangled in her thick, dark hair. Joseph's "be wary" was no match for her charms. She had to know the allure of her sensual beauty. Yet he had seen no proof she was using him to get what she desired. Ultimately, he didn't care. He enjoyed the attention, and he'd made a promise he intended to keep.

With a gentle push on his chest, she moved away, brushing his cheek with her hand. He pulled her back, kissed her on the lips, felt the tingling in all the right places. Then Rosa's soft, low voice roused him from his fog of desire, "I should look in on mother."

His eyes followed her as she moved toward the bedroom. Her hips swayed gently; she moved a hand through her hair, glanced over her shoulder. That little smirk. Sonny wondered whether that other Sigmund meant anything to her now.

Love was complicated at best. What chance had rationality or romance in times like these? What would happen after her father's release, after they left Germany? Nothing was guaranteed. Rosa and Sonny struggled for normalcy amid the specter of her father's imprisonment and the fear of another pogrom, like a metronome, marking time.

Such was their life together, at least for now—a gentle, mostly chaste relationship, built upon tragedy.

28

Andrea: Unhappy is the land that has no heroes.
Galileo: No. Unhappy is the land that needs heroes.
—Berthold Brecht

Meetings came at any hour, light and dark blurring to gray mass, obscuring day from night. Sonny operated like a second-story man, under cover of the dead, vast, middle of the night. Soldiering on, working to exhaustion, at times he floundered. Normal patterns of wakefulness and sleep, the usual mode of keeping time, eluded him—so he gave up trying.

Late one night, Sonny dragged into the empty kitchen of No. 53 and stared at the calendar hanging on the wall. His eyes stopped briefly at the snow-covered Bavarian Alps pictured above December before falling to the grid. It was Friday, December 2. Damn! Four weeks had passed since the revenge-driven Polish Jew had triggered the twentieth century's greatest pogrom. Sonny flipped the calendar back to November, saw the 9 circled in red, and whistled—it felt like months since then.

Tired, annoyed, hungry—he hadn't eaten since . . ? Not being able to remember annoyed him more. Rosa's question came to mind—"Why?" He didn't have an answer. Still, even in his weariness he'd seen the answer plain as the hunger screaming in his gut. How many burned-out synagogues, broken windows, looted businesses—merchandise scattered like seashells on the beach—had he witnessed in the past four weeks? God! Hundreds, and he hadn't even seen them all.

"Kristallnacht—Night of Broken Glass—hah," he sneered, as if a mother's shattered vase defined a pogrom. They hadn't figured the Nazis were this depraved. Who could have known? Simon?

Yet Kristallnacht had been good for the operation—Sonny and his associates were drowning in work. What before Vom Rath, Grynszpan, and Paris had been a trickle, now was stampede. People panicked, then scrambled to raise money to emigrate, sold jewelry, furniture, art, and businesses to Germans with money to buy. The sharks scented blood; their fins cut through the water's surface as they readied for attack. They were everywhere, and every Jew in Germany was ripe for extortion. Tonight that was Sonny's banal answer to Rosa's question.

He looked up to see Polly standing in the doorway, staring pensively. "I didn't hear you."

"I thought I heard a voice." She crossed her arms over her chest and hesitated before saying, "I'm glad it's you. We need to talk."

Sonny motioned her to sit down, sensing her discomfort. "I must have been talking to myself."

She dropped her arms to her sides, nodded. Her fatigue seemed to mirror his. Karl had long since replaced Sonny in Polly's life. Neither Polly nor Karl had tried to hide it—why should they? They'd known each other for years . . . After breaking off with Sonny, she'd started working with the Confessing Church. What followed had come naturally.

And now the two former lovers—Sonny and Polly—worked together, passing in the narrow hallways, occasionally eating together, discussing comings and goings, the status of documents. They reached an accommodation despite the lingering hurt of a love affair gone awry. The work necessitated their proximity—there was no time for distraction, for petty disagreement.

"Herr Wagner came into the store today." Polly got straight to the point.

That was the last thing Sonny expected her to say, though he smiled at hearing the old man's name. He had left Herr Wagner without goodbye or explanation. Well, there was no time for nostalgia. He'd let it pass . . . this must be important. "What did he want?"

"I'm still at the same old day job. It pays the bills," she said through a tight smile.

"I understand."

"I was doing something typically mindless, then looked up into his smiling face, his mischievous eyes. I knocked over a stack of gloves. He apologized for startling me, but I'd been clumsy. Then he took my hand in his, said how nice it was to see me, that he'd be quick. It was quiet so he needn't hurry, but I could tell he was nervous. He looked around, lowered his voice, and said a plainclothes Gestapo man came to the flat, looking for you—yesterday."

The blood drained from Sonny's head, making him lightheaded. He took several deeps breaths. From between his tightly drawn lips slipped the words, "Albert! What else did he say?"

She shook her head. "That he was looking for you. Herr Wagner didn't tell him anything."

"How did he know he was Gestapo?" Sonny asked.

"He gave me a sly smile, said he could smell it."

"Really?" Sonny said dryly. There was a lot of that going around.

"He also flashed his card, too quick to read, but it looked official. And he said he was Gestapo. He started asking questions—when did you leave, where did you go, where are you now? Since Herr Wagner didn't know anything, he had nothing to tell. He's to contact Gestapo headquarters if he learns anything of your whereabouts."

"Did he leave his card, a name, a telephone number?"

Polly shook her head. "No. That's the funny part."

Sonny frowned. "Makes no sense—no name, no telephone number." What the hell was going on? Why now? He tried to make sense of it. Was it something else, something personal? Tracking him to Herr Wagner would not have been difficult; maybe Albert remembered where he lived. Sonny tried to recall whether he'd been to the flat. No . . . his address must have been registered somewhere.

"Doesn't sound official," Sonny muttered under his breath.

"What?"

He ignored her question. "Did he describe him?"

Polly's lips pursed and she nodded.

"Albert?"

She nodded again. "Perfectly."

Where else would Albert look? Would he try to find Mischa or Sophie? Was he poking around the warehouse? What about Joseph and Solomon? Sonny muttered as he paced the kitchen floor. Then he stopped and exclaimed, "Shit!"

"What?" Polly asked, alarmed.

"Joseph! What if he looks for Joseph?"

Their eyes locked. For the first time in a year there was something other than anger, disappointment, resignation, forced sociability, between them.

"We've got to do something." Needing to be sure, he said, "Tell me how Herr Wagner described him."

"Blond hair, pinched face, a sneering mouth, hands constantly moving, a cigarette in one—oh, and a slight build. Who else?"

He stopped pacing. "That's him. Did Albert say anything—about me, about why he was there?"

She shook her head.

"Of course, he wouldn't." Rattled, Sonny kept talking. "In an official investigation, he'd have left a card, or it would have been a local man, not someone from Aachen. He'd have been bullied, threatened." Sonny stared at Polly. "Does he know about us?"

"I don't know. That's all Herr Wagner told me."

"It's been more than a year. He knows I live in Berlin." Sonny spoke quietly, talking to himself, trying to work it out.

"Whatever it is, I had to tell you as soon as possible. We're all at risk."

He nodded without comment. Polly's grasp of the obvious hadn't escaped him. Men were arrested every day in Neukölln and Wedding for small acts of resistance—distributing pamphlets, describing camp atrocities, quoting Roosevelt and Churchill. His group smuggled; Karl's group did more than that. Capture meant imprisonment or worse. He had to do something.

"Of course. Thank you," he said finally. His temples pounded like drums. He pressed his fingertips to the side of his head and rubbed, his hunger forgotten. What did Albert know? Was he just fishing?

But Sonny kept returning to Joseph and the documents. "We've got to get Joseph out of his flat to somewhere safe—fast—but where?" He leaned on the table, his face close to hers. "Does Karl know about this?"

"You're the first. There's another safe house for Joseph," said Polly.

"Good. I knew that . . . must have forgotten. I'm late right now for a meeting at Joseph's flat." Sonny looked at his watch. "Karl will be there.

We can figure this out." He calmed down, managed a smile. "How are you doing?"

Polly seemed surprised. Her answer came hesitantly. "All right, I guess. All the men are gone, reunited with their families. Otto and Karl must be at the meeting, Mina's here, helping." Polly returned his smile. "There's the brief update. I'd ask you the same, but I think I already know."

Sonny's eyes narrowed. "What does that mean? That I look depressed, exhausted, hungry. Oh! And scared shitless." He forced a laugh. "What the hell! It is what it is. If I can avoid that asshole, I'll be gone soon."

"Have something to eat." Polly pointed to the pantry, but Sonny shook his head. She changed tack and said, "Why wait? Get out now. I'll see that Karl gets Joseph to a safe house."

Another vote for his immediate departure, but he didn't respond. "Thanks. I appreciate that."

"Don't get formal with me!" Polly snapped. "I still care what happens to you. There's a crazed Gestapo on your ass. Is that not reason enough?"

Sonny raised his palms to stop the onslaught. "All right! I'm leaving as soon as Rosa's father's out of Sachsenhausen."

Mollified, she said was a smirk, "I heard you had a girlfriend."

"No secrets around here."

Unsmiling, Polly shook her head. "When will he be released?"

"Soon, I hope. Documents are nearly ready. When Rosa goes to Sachsenhausen to get him, I'm going with her."

"Is that wise?"

"I'm not stupid," he said too sharply. "I'll go as far as I can and wait. Anything could happen . . . I can't—I won't—let her go alone."

"My God, Sonny! We hid in the cellar for two years—look where it got us! Caught with a fake ID or with a Jewess, or as Sigmund Landauer, the Jew the Gestapo's looking for . . . I don't have to tell you. And Oranienburg is crawling with Gestapo."

They stared at each other. Polly was unyielding because she was right, and he shrank under her unrelenting gaze. That she, of all people, should be discussing this with him made him uncomfortable. Of course, there should be no secrets at No. 53, but that didn't mean he should endure her disapproval.

She waited for him to respond, but he did not. Her face softened. "Clearly, you have more than a casual interest."

He nodded.

Not done with him yet, she continued, "It's about judgment. We need to get our work done . . . nobody jeopardizes the operation." She put up her hands anticipating Sonny's objection. "Wait! I mean nobody—you, me, Karl, Otto, Mina—should be in a situation that makes it harder for us than it is already. Especially with Albert in the picture."

"Okay, I see your point. By the way, her name's Rosa. She needs help. Her mother's a nervous wreck and can't cope, so it's fallen to her. That I met her at all was pure serendipity." He told her the story, then waved impatiently. "Anyway, I promised to find her father and kept going back."

Sonny took a deep breath in an effort to maintain control. "They're leaving as soon as he's out. There you have it, the whole story."

"All of it?"

"Nearly." Sonny smiled sheepishly. "What are you, my mother?"

She ignored the gibe. "If you want to fall in love, that's your business. Frankly, I think it's wonderful. But keep your wits about you."

Sonny reddened.

"You'll leave when Rosa's father is out?"

He nodded. "I just don't know when."

"What do you mean, you don't know? You just said you'd help get her father out, then leave. What else do you need to know?"

"Ja, ja. Okay, I'm leaving."

Apparently satisfied, Polly asked, "Do you remember my parents' landlords, the Deichslers?"

Still leery but thankful for the reprieve, he answered, "Of course. Karl told us about your telephone call."

"I just learned that he was released. Several days ago, Frau Deichsler went to Dachau to get him. They're leaving for Palestine. Their youngest, a son, has been there since '33. A second daughter left in '36. The other day I met with the eldest daughter here in Berlin. She works in a Jewish nursery and is engaged to be married."

"That's nice. Does your friend need papers?" Sonny asked, unsure of where she was headed.

"An aunt in New York promised to send an affidavit for her and her new husband. Her parents leave for Palestine sometime after a February wedding, here in Berlin. To raise money, the Deichslers sold the building. My mother saw the deed, or whatever they call the phony document. It was extortion, plain and simple. A Nazi crony got the building for next to nothing, and—get this—under the terms of the sale, the Deichslers have to pay within two weeks for the damage done in the pogrom." She looked away.

"Bastards," Sonny cursed.

"Mother doesn't know whether they'll stay in the building," she said, tapping her fingers on the table.

Sonny had heard echoes of Busch's purchase of Rosenthaler Supplies and told Polly about it. But soon they ran out of words—like at the café when they first met—and were suddenly shy. They looked everywhere—at their hands, at the clock, around the room, in every corner—but at each other. That would be too intimate. They were frozen, unable to say what was needed, or anything at all.

Change, life's constant, comes slowly—with reflection or the suddenness of a Grynszpan's pistol. History might be understood, misconstrued, or forgotten—but it can never be undone. Now presented with the chance to make sense of their past or be forever stuck in the messy aftermath—why waste it?

"Sonny, Sonny." Polly sighed like the exasperated mother he'd accused her of being. "We know each other too well to dance around with our backs to each other."

Smiling at her metaphor, Sonny responded, "Sometimes I think about what might have been."

Polly shrugged, not from indifference. "Me too, but I couldn't get past the lie."

Sonny winced. "A hard lesson. But we might not have worked out anyway."

"That's too glib. If only you'd told me, we might have surmounted the problems, found this place."

"Maybe. But slinking around under bridges, in the cellar, was wearing us down. There was no life for us here. In the end, our only option was to leave, but you wouldn't do that. Then it was over. I discovered how lonely it can be."

Polly looked pensive. "I thought I loved you and you loved me."

"Thought you did?"

She nodded. "Now I'm not so sure. But you're probably right. Carrying on the way we did would not have worked indefinitely. What I do know is that my knees still hurt from the cellar floor." They laughed uneasily, and Polly looked away. When she turned back, a frown had replaced the smile. "I couldn't live with a lie—it was poison."

She kept her gaze on him. "Sonny, don't ever lie to Rosa. Don't hold back, regardless of the cost."

She was right—about that and the rest of it.

"I won't." He was amazed at how a few honest words could melt the regret, the recrimination. What had been so hard now seemed easy. "I wish you and Karl the best."

"Thank you. He's a wonderful man, doing great work. We share a vision of how the world should be," Polly said, shrugging at the obstacles. "The same to you and Rosa."

"It's funny. Despite the horror of the past month, I've been content just to be with her and her mother. Who knows where it will lead?"

Polly scratched an itch on her chin. "The great unknown."

"Life's a terrible mystery. We," he pointed to her, then to his chest, "went awry because of my secret, and now you're doing what I did, what I do."

"Like that Chinese curse," she recalled.

Sonny laughed. "We do live in terrible, interesting times." Then he hugged her, like a brother would a sister. Without another word, she ran up the stairs, gone.

Sonny looked at the clock. It was time to deliver more bad news to his cohorts . . .

Apologizing for his tardiness, he sat down next to Otto. They—Otto, Karl, and Emil—were talking about how to handle the wave of work threatening to drown Joseph.

Sonny could swear Joseph had aged in the past few days. Lines etched his face like an African mask, and his body sagged. Dark semicircles hung beneath his red-rimmed eyes, which seemed to be failing. His tremors had worsened from the delicate handiwork; he hadn't time for the rest that would heal. Like Sisyphus he struggled—but the boulders were winning.

News that Albert was sniffing around was the last thing they needed to hear now. It could wait until the work issues were resolved.

Joseph needed help, they decided. But sympathetic, expert forgers would not be easy to find. From whom, where, would they get it? Joseph gazed at a document as if he heard nothing they said.

Otto prodded, "Do you agree or not?"

"What choice do I have?" Joseph finally answered. He'd been loath to confront his limitations, especially now, when the need was so great. He'd been too damn stubborn. But he could not ignore their concern. He nodded reluctantly. "What are a few aches and pains?"

Otto tried not to show his frustration. "Well, that's a start." He looked to his fellows. "So, what do we do?"

No one answered.

Joseph absently flexed his hand, took off his glasses, and rubbed his eyes. "It's not just me. We're all stressed to the point of breaking. I admit having trouble keeping up." He shrugged at matters beyond his control. "Look at these piles of documents. As soon as I'm done with one, another two take its place." He looked from Otto to the others.

"Can you get help from your friends at the ministry?" Sonny asked.

Joseph surprised them: "I've already taken steps." He said no more.

"That's good." Otto said. "But you might have told us at the outset."

"We need to know enough for the logistics," Karl suggested.

Joseph considered his request. "I'll tell you this much. Several days ago, one of my friends came to visit." His hand swept over the papers on his desk. "We talked about a lot of things. I won't bore you with the details. Suffice it to say he offered to help."

"What does that mean?" Otto asked

"Like I said, help with the damned documents!" Joseph snapped. "That's enough."

Otto stewed but said nothing.

"We'll need some details," Sonny protested.

Joseph refused: "He's skittish . . . I won't compromise his identity. That's a condition for his assistance. Stay out of it."

Emil, quiet until now, said, "I appreciate your friend's reluctance, his vulnerability. Moving documents around is dangerous on its own, and it's time consuming." He didn't have to spell out the risks. He simply pointed to the pile on the floor. "Why not use couriers?" He looked at Karl, the man with the organization.

Karl thought briefly before answering. "I've got people." Then he snapped his fingers. "I'll see to it."

They spent the next half-hour discussing logistics. Otto suggested secluded spots—Tiergarten, Hasenheide, cemeteries—for drops, though they'd have to change them periodically. Everyone liked the idea. Karl said he'd work it out. Joseph would discuss it with his friend.

Otto and Emil stood to leave.

"Wait. There's something else." Sonny stopped them.

Four sets of eyes turned to him. Otto and Emil sat down. Sonny quickly relayed what Polly had learned from Herr Wagner.

"Shit," Emil cursed. "Asshole turns up like a bad smell." Then he asked Joseph, "How well do you know Albert?"

"Barely, but like everyone in the warehouse, I knew of him."

Emil pressed. "Did Albert know you were a friend of Sonny's?"

Joseph's face clouded. "Probably. It was common knowledge."

"We have to assume he did," Otto concluded.

"That settles it," Emil said. "It's foolhardy to stay here." He pointed again to the piles of documents.

Joseph rose from his chair, walked around the small flat, stopping in front of *Berlin Street Scene.* With his back to them, he said, "Tell me where to go."

They turned to Karl. Without hesitating, he told them about a secluded house in the West End. "It's perfect as a refuge, but no coming and going. Visits must be restricted, carefully arranged." He glanced at Sonny.

"I have to be able to communicate with my friend," said Joseph.

"Right," Karl murmured.

They thought about that until Emil said, "You're not the problem—the documents are." He turned to Karl. "Once Joseph and the papers are moved, he can come back and make what arrangements he needs to."

That seemed satisfactory.

Karl said, "I'll see to it straightaway, but before you leave, there's something you need to hear. I told you about Fogelman, the one who was released from the camp, but until now we've only heard rumors about the conditions there. Now I've heard firsthand. An old family friend, a lawyer, was released from Sachsenhausen. Last night, in my father's study, he told us of his ordeal. He hadn't even told his wife." Karl turned to Sonny and shook his head. "He didn't know a Robert Fischer."

"Thanks," Sonny mouthed silently.

Karl continued. "They let him out a couple days ago. He doesn't know why, didn't ask. He came to bid my father farewell. He and his wife are on a train to France—I hope—as I speak. What he described was a frozen hell, standing in the cold for fifteen hours straight with no relief. Groups of three hundred, lined up like Russian recruits—his phrase—holding their hats, valuables in the hat, no food or drink, no chance to step out of rank. Guards made them sing sentimental German songs as their limbs went numb. They had no coats or gloves. Did I say their heads were shaved?"

There was a murmured, "No."

He nodded. "He's not a young man, and he knew that if he faltered, he'd be beaten, maybe killed on the spot. Somehow there were newspapers in the barracks, and he stuffed them inside his jacket to keep from freezing, but he was always cold. Now he can't get warm no matter what he puts on. He shivered in our warm study. Three men died the first night, maybe from heart attacks or urine poisoning. And there were probably more—175 men piled in like sardines. When one turned, they all did. Sleep was impossible. The man next to him groaned, another snored. Knees stuck in his back, an elbow in his face. He lay somewhere between sleep and awake—in constant fear.

"Meals were black bread and pudding for breakfast, a little marmalade on Sunday. Soup for lunch, a little bread, a margarine ration, maybe cheese, herring, or pork. Ja, pork for the religious Jews. In the evening they got a hot meal, soup with lentils. He didn't starve, but some of the men couldn't eat, and after a week they looked to be made of wire. Most of the dead were from beatings, physical stress, exposure, lack of hygiene.

"Then the guards did their 'power jags'—I'd never heard him use slang before. He must have picked it up in the camp." Karl shook his head. "This hardly conveys the abuse. A guard jammed his rifle butt into some poor fellow's crotch. Then he got close and hollered, 'Damn Jew.'

"Men who didn't obey—who maybe didn't hear or were confused—were hung by their elbows or locked in what they called the 'standing cage'—so small you could only stand. Or they were beaten and shaken until their teeth rattled, muscles strained, bones broken. On the second or third night, everyone was ordered into the yard—to see a lighted Christmas tree flanked by two companions hanging on gallows, like human ornaments."

Karl paused and met their eyes, then looked away in shame.

"Then they were made to sing 'O Tannenbaum.' Mourning a fallen comrade was forbidden. There was no humanity. It was Dante's hell. That he could sit again in my father's den, or board a train with his wife, seemed an impossible dream."

The operators muttered curses, looked at their hands or away, contemplated the suffering. Over thousands of years, a thousand pogroms had evolved into a particularly vile, twentieth-century German strain. What could anyone say that wouldn't be trite, obvious, that could in some way diminish the facts? A shroud fell over them, sucked the air out of the room, and their anger turned to unremitting sadness.

Sonny and Joseph knew many of the men who were suffering. Surely this would be the first of many such stories they would hear.

"I thought you should know." Karl's voice broke the silence. He left to arrange for Joseph's move. Emil nodded and left too.

Sonny and Otto were about to leave, one then the other, when Joseph said, "I have something . . . a little speech I've been planning. Since I'm leaving, I better do it now."

Otto was attentive. Anxious about Rosa's father, Sonny was distracted. Joseph began anyway. "All my little aches, discomforts, are minor inconveniences. I'm a lucky man for knowing the two of you. For your friendship and help you have my never-ending gratitude and love. Without you my life will be . . . Every day you risk arrest, while I work in relative safety and warmth."

Looking away, he recited from memory: "'Noble be man, helpful and good! For that alone sets him apart from every other creature on earth.'" Tears welled in his eyes. "Our time is ever shorter, we're measured by what we accomplish. What you have done, both of you, will surely get you into heaven . . ."

He smirked and added with a shrug, " . . . which I doubt exists, but you never know." His smile was wry. "We must say goodbye now. I'll never forget you." Raising a hand, he stopped either from speaking. "Leave now. You're both at great risk."

To Otto he said, "For all of Hitler's rule."

He turned to Sonny: "For more than a year."

Then to both: "How much longer can you elude those bastards? You've kept them at bay thus far, but with Albert nosing around, you have to play the odds. You know what they're capable of. You have papers to take you into Belgium. Go, stay with Fritz, and help him, if that's what it takes. Go now, tomorrow, or the day after, but don't stay."

"Otto, take Mina. I know she's ready. Sonny, Rosa's papers are ready." He rummaged through a pile and put them in an envelope. "Here. Go with her or follow later. Just go."

Otto and Sonny took what Joseph said, each in his own way. They looked at one another, smiling ruefully. They'd been through much, accomplished much. Now their camaraderie was about to end. Suddenly, they spoke at the same time, each drowning out the other, and they laughed.

"Like brothers speaking as one—both unintelligible," Joseph quipped.

Sonny nodded to Otto.

"Joseph, despite your denials, you've always been our leader. You put this together and made it work. How many passports, visas, identity cards, have you forged?" said Otto.

Joseph shook his head. "Haven't kept track—many."

"What you started has changed my life. I'd fallen so far, I thought I'd never reach the surface again. You've given me something real and important."

Otto turned to Sonny. "Willy left prison with a lame hand and a bad eye, and he still considered himself lucky. I never understood that until he died." His voice thickened. "Life is what matters—I too am a lucky man, fortunate to call you both friends." He reached for Joseph's hand.

Joseph took Otto's hand, then hugged him.

"We're leaving as soon as things settle down," Otto told him.

"Good," Joseph said. He turned to Sonny. "And you?"

"When Rosa's father is released and they're safely on their way to Plombieres," Sonny answered. Then from a dark corner of his memory he pulled out a long forgotten piece of verse: "'One lives but once in the world, and I can't imagine not having shared it with you.'"

"Yes, Goethe always says it best," Joseph said, and he embraced Sonny. "Now go back to No. 53 and prepare to leave—both of you. Goodbye and good luck."

After they were gone, Joseph sat at his desk, ignoring the waiting document, thinking of the two men who'd just left him. One he'd known as a child, the other for seven or eight years. Both were now lost to him forever.

Well, he would forge ahead until he was caught or his eyes or hand failed. Leaving his Scheunenviertel flat would mean no more worry about the meddlesome block warden or Albert's knock. He'd always figured something stupid would lead to his arrest. The police would break down the wrong door, see him at his desk, surrounded by documents, and that would be his end—a serendipitous demise. That thought resonated, comforted him: he was too good at his work to be discovered . . .

Otto and Sonny left by separate doors and met on the corner. They moved quickly and silently past shuttered shops, burned-out buildings. Icicles hung from charred remains like long fingers pointing the way to hell.

Breaking the silence, Otto said, "We've had a good run—once I crawled out of the gutter, and we honed our act."

Sonny laughed. "I wouldn't call it the gutter."

"You weren't in it with me."

"True . . ."

They walked in silence until Otto asked, "What went wrong?"

"Everything," Sonny started, then shook his head. "Hell! I've asked that often enough . . . damned if I know."

Neither spoke for several minutes, until Sonny again picked up the thread. "But if you're looking for someone to blame, just take a stroll in Alexanderplatz or on Ku'damm. Look into people's eyes—if they'll look at you, if they aren't too embarrassed or feeling too fucking guilty."

His tone was harsh. "The banker, the worker, the housewife, the teacher—all of them. Ignorance and apathy, but worst of all the hate and lies that sustain Hitler and his sycophants." He threw up his hands. "All I ever knew was a little of this and a little of that, so what the hell do I know? You're the political thinker."

Otto answered with a short, brittle laugh. "Right! Lot of good it's done me. When we first met, you didn't have a clue, but as it turned out, neither did I."

"I guess that makes us even. Ask me again in ten years, when we're fat and have children bouncing on our knees." Sonny put a hand on his friend's shoulder. "You've been a good and loyal friend. I couldn't ask for more."

As they walked under a streetlight, Sonny saw the scar that had made Otto so dashing, so many years ago. It crinkled, strained, as a smile spread across his still handsome face. Suddenly Sonny wanted to reminisce, and he recalled the night they had met. Then they mused over long evenings at the H & S until their hopes crashed against the rocks of Nazi victory. Those had been heady times, they agreed.

Otto knew little about Rosa, only that Sonny spent a lot of time with her, that she was somehow linked to Herman, that her father was in Sachsenhausen. Now he asked, "What's with you and Rosa?"

Sonny told him, leaving out the part about going with her to Oranienburg. "I'm in love."

Otto slapped his friend on the back. "*Mazel tov*! Worse can happen to a man."

———

Several days passed, and Sonny's mood turned dark. He threw his coat over a chair in the kitchen, glanced up, and saw Otto. They exchanged exhausted nods, neither speaking, but as Otto turned to go, Sonny stopped him.

"Otto! There's a lot to do in the next day or two. We may not see each other before it's too late to say goodbye."

"We'll see each other," Otto started but reconsidered. "Maybe you're right."

"When are you leaving?" Sonny asked.

"I'm going upstairs now to figure out the loose ends with Mina—probably within a couple of days. Any news of Rosa's father?"

Sonny shook his head. "Soon, we hope."

The two friends embraced.

Shortly after sunset several days after Joseph's safe relocation, wet snowflakes fell onto Sonny's head and shoulders. Through a palette of red, green, and white lights in Alexanderplatz, he walked along on his way to a document drop. Automobile headlamps, flashing neon signs, traffic signals, streetlights, Christmas lights, reflected from the snow crystals, patches of ice, all the hard surfaces, creating a kaleidoscope of color. This made for a festive, swastika-wrapped city, should a person be so inclined.

But Christmas meant nothing to Sonny. Lights and decorations couldn't mask the dark hole Berlin had become. Still, the fresh sheet of snow helped cleanse his spirit. Such was his Berlin as 1938 came to a close.

Despite the horrors of Kristallnacht, most Germans entered the holiday season feeling good: unemployment was down; their Führer had given them reason to feel proud. The army had rearmed, reclaimed the Saar; *Anschluss* had brought Austria into the fatherland; and the Czechoslovakian Sudetenland was theirs. *Lebensraum*—territorial expansion to save the Germans suffering under foreign control—was official policy, seemingly Germany's destiny. Jews were excluded, completely isolated, subject to exorbitant taxes, their property appropriated, their men languishing in prison camps. Those remaining in Germany were being rudely ushered to the door. Passports and identity cards required prominent display of the letter *J* and the name *Israel* for men and *Sarah* for women.

A period of fitful calm lay over the Semites' fear that the pogrom would begin anew. The police had returned to their beats, though that brought scant solace. People took the measure of their streets, assessed the damage, found out who'd been arrested, who was safe.

Cleanup was underway—those lucky enough to escape the camps were ordered to sweep the broken glass from the pavement. No sooner had wooden planks covered the gaping holes of shop windows than signs appeared offering damaged businesses for sale. Vendors in the warehouse, who feared they'd be shut down or that their stock would be confiscated, sold their goods for what they could get. Desperate people like Rosenthaler and Deichsler sold their businesses for a fraction of their value and said farewell.

With the approach of the end of November had come official word of the release of the Jewish men. But December opened with few of them having returned home. Then, several days after the meeting at Joseph's flat, Karl learned that a man could be released if he had documentation granting entry into any of Germany's neighboring countries.

Sonny wasted no time in contacting Rosa. And they made their plans.

29

I am fated to a journey in hand with my strange heroes.
—Nikolai Gogol

Someone approached. Sonny waited until he passed, then left the alley. On his way to Rosa in the West End, he turned onto Stuttgarter Strasse, comfortable in his new neighborhood. Though shabby, it was now home. Scores of old Communist agitators lived in Neukölln, and it had harbored Otto and Dix over the years. Sonny felt safe, much as he had felt earlier at the warehouse. But he knew safety was illusory.

Within minutes, he reached the cemetery where Willy had rested, dripping blood onto a gravestone. He paused, paid silent homage to his dead cohort, then continued toward Hasenheide forest. He and Rosa would take the train to Oranienburg, she would collect her father, and they would leave the country. Otto and Mina were also leaving soon—maybe they were gone already. Franz and the other runners had departed several days before. Everyone else in the underground group was staying for the duration—however long, whatever the consequences.

Sonny would greatly miss Joseph and Emil—they would have to live in his imagination. He would soon make a new life, somewhere, with Rosa. That was the plan, but he was uneasy about leaving, about what the future might hold, though he knew they had to go. For the first time, he was forced to consider what change would mean for him and not just what it meant for others.

That was getting ahead of the game. First, he had to figure how to handle Rosa's trip to Oranienburg. He cursed the dilemma and the irony of the messenger who had warned him about Albert. He wouldn't—couldn't—be careless now. Swinging at the end of a rope wasn't what he had in mind.

While hundreds of women must have made the trip to Sachsenhausen, to Dachau, to Buchenwald, to get their men on their own, Rosa would not have to do so. He couldn't let her down, so he grappled with the problem while the pavement passed beneath his feet.

Two things occurred to him in rapid succession. The first, a simple, numbingly obvious solution: Rosa would not go alone because he would be nearby, watching her but not sitting or walking at her side. The second was the acrid odor of a dead fire. Sonny had paid scant attention to his surroundings when the stench eclipsed his relief at figuring out how to be and not be with Rosa. He frowned. Wet ash, burnt wood, and decaying matter percolated into that signature odor—like the garbage crisis but worse.

Intending to avoid the Neckar Strasse Synagogue, he had been drawn into its chilling orbit like iron to a magnet. Trying to avert his eyes, he nevertheless found his gaze pulled to the street, to the ashes of the burning Torah. Sensing a return of nausea, he breathed deeply as he scanned the street ahead. A group of young men loitered at the far corner, and he immediately knew.

"Shit!" he hissed, then muttered, "Hitler Youth," counting at least six of them. Another scourge. Relieved they weren't coming toward him, he was about to turn, when something moved in their midst. He walked closer, staring. There was a man on his hands and knees, like a small animal trapped by feral dogs. Now he could hear their taunts, though the words were inaudible. Several big boys moved from foot to foot, heads down, fists balled. Boxers eager for a fight or, in this case, a beating. Something in the unfolding drama kept Sonny from walking away.

Closing the distance, Sonny saw a bearded old man in black cowering in the middle, his arms covering his head. The Neckar Strasse Synagogue's rabbi? A wide-brimmed black hat lay askew on the pavement beside him. The odor of dead fire gave way to the scent of fear—Sonny's own. Distracted by the spark of a memory, he did not stop. Others on the street had evaporated into the chill morning air, sensing impending mischief, leaving the street corner to the boys, a pitiable old man, and Sonny. Grossly outnumbered, his mind raced for a rouse, a plan, anything to free the old Jew. In a flash of inspiration, he shouted, "Stop!"

Heads turned; hostile eyes bore into him. He had their attention—now what? Keeping the offensive, he said: "It's over! You fellows must have missed it. Heydrich made it official. The pogrom is over . . . no more harassment . . . Jews can leave." His mind worked feverishly, searching for what to say next, for how to fill the space, for a way to give them no time to think or act. "Anyone can see the old Jew is past sixty. Don't you fellows have something better to do?"

No answer—just the heat of their scorn. He had drawn their attention from the old man to himself. "What fun is there in beating on a defenseless old man? Would that make your mothers proud?" Sonny's taunt threw them off balance. His fear receded in his effort to keep up the front.

"Maybe we'll beat on you instead," one of them barked, drawing coarse laughter from the others.

"Me? A good German!" Sonny's feigned indignation projected as much confidence as he could muster. He'd play this to the end. What the hell? He would soon be gone.

Unsure of what to make of this guy spoiling their fun, several boys took a step toward him but no more. They were simply boys playing thugs. Moving his head from side to side, Sonny counted eight pairs of squinty eyes, eight sneering mouths. His eyes landed on the biggest, tallest kid, broad at the shoulder, who met his gaze with a malevolent grin. Figuring him to be the leader, Sonny challenged: "Why are you after the old man?"

Confused, the kid brushed a snowflake from his eyelashes, shrinking under Sonny's unrelenting glare. The battle was won—though a spark in the electric silence might still set off an explosion. The others watched, waiting. When the kid finally answered, his voice was too high to be menacing. "You a Jew or a Jew lover?"

Sonny nearly laughed at the cliché. Instead, he shot back, "Neither!" Moving into the circle, he stopped. He looked each boy in the eye, then pointed to the old Jew: "He's an old man. Leave him alone."

Frozen in fear, the old man's face melted into that of Reb Friedman. Sonny bent, picked up his hat, tossed it to the old man. "Go home—now!"

Hesitating, the man looked from Sonny to the biggest boy, and then he moved, running past Sonny, between two of the boys, his hat reunited with his head. Sonny thought he heard a hushed "thank you," as he raced by.

Discontented murmurs, sagging shoulders—the boys were defeated by the old Jew's escape. Sonny hadn't the caricatured features—hooknose or evil eyes—of Jews in the vile Nazi posters. That confused them. He wasn't their enemy, but his challenge made them tentative, weak, made him a foe.

"Why do you care?" one boy shouted.

Ignoring the question, Sonny barked, "Go have your fun somewhere else." He'd called their bluff, and he started to walk away. Now their squinty-eyed toughness, slack jaws, open mouths, seemed ludicrous. Sonny found the leader's eyes and disdainfully broke contact. Eyes straight ahead, he had moved nearly out of the circle when he took a blow to the side of his head.

The morning light dimmed, his knees buckled, and he staggered but managed to stay upright. Deliberately placing one foot in front of the other to regain his stride, gain distance, he fought the urge to pass out. He could hear laughter through the all-encompassing fog, no doubt at his drunken pantomime. Then there was a growl, deeper than the voice that had hit him: "Asshole."

Lurching around the corner, Sonny fell against the nearest wall. He touched his jaw and winced, fearing he'd lost a tooth—perhaps his reward for helping an old Jew—but somehow he felt redeemed. He examined his fingertips, relieved to see melting snowflakes, not blood. His tongue probed—all teeth accounted for. Dazed, he continued to hug the wall, the scent of its musty brick clearing his head. When the worst had passed, he slowly exercised his jaw, satisfied it wasn't broken. He pushed himself off the wall with both hands, relieved to feel nothing more than a nagging pain.

Within five minutes, Sonny regained his normal stride. He cursed his aching jaw, his bad luck, everything around him. Having to keep a better lookout wasn't his problem. He had turned into the Golem of Berlin—saving every Jew, righting every wrong. Brilliant! That would get him through the next day or two, then into Sachsenhausen or worse. Going to Oranienburg with Rosa would be a piece of cake compared to this. He tried smiling, but it hurt too much.

Once he felt safe, he stopped in front of a shop window. Tracing the outline of his face, he came to a bruise nearly the size of a walnut. It pulsed like a flashing cinema marquee: "For Mischa and Reb Friedman!" He managed a crooked smile, then saw the shopkeeper smiling through the window. Sonny waved and continued on his journey.

In an hour he stood outside Rosa's flat, his headache nearly gone, his jaw still aching—minor inconveniences, the price of freeing the old Jew. Sonny took a deep breath, gathering his thoughts, then knocked softly. Dim light from the corridor cast a shadow, obscuring his face.

Rosa invited him in with a toss of her head, and Sonny followed her to the center of the room. She stood chewing on her lip, not yet noticing his face. "Sonny, I'm anxious, scared," she began, her eyes taking in his face, passing over the bruise. She did a double take and moved closer. "What happened?" She reached out to touch the bruise.

"Don't . . . please," he begged, grabbing her wrist, trying to smile.

Rosa looked at him quizzically. "Does it hurt?"

"Not as bad as it looks," Sonny answered with a shrug. With self-deprecating smile comically misshapen, he told her what had happened.

"Oh, my God!" she exclaimed.

"I couldn't abandon the old man," Sonny said softly.

Rosa buried her face in his chest. "Hold me."

They stood for several minutes, Sonny slowly rubbing her back. "Where's your mother?"

When Rosa didn't answer, Sonny stepped back, saw tears like tiny silver threads running down her cheeks. He asked again.

Her voice husky, she said, "Mother cries all day, only brightens when we talk about getting father, then falls back into her shell. She barely eats. I can't endure this nightmare for another minute, let alone another day. Now you have to save an old man from a beating by children." Utter hopelessness infused her tone. "What fools we've been . . ."

She stopped short, moved away, then fell against him. After thirty seconds, she straightened, wiped the tears from her cheeks, and took a deep breath. "The worst part is not knowing, of being smothered by darkness. There may as well be no sunlight." She walked to the window, a gauzy chiaroscuro against the strong morning light. When she turned, the contours of her face melted into a ghostly outline.

"I used to feel safe. Now my world is filled with children who beat up old men, with burning synagogues and innocent men arrested, thrown into camps." Rosa pointed to the window. "You can live out there, handle thugs. I can't." Then, "How long have we known each other?"

"Less than a month."

"It feels longer," Rosa said softly. "I've lost all track of time, don't know if it's day or night . . . can't sleep . . . I'm so afraid. What frightens me most is that I might always be afraid, that it will never go away—that it will be a constant companion."

Sonny knew the feeling. He said softly, "It'll be over soon. You'll leave the fear behind."

Rosa laughed bitterly. "What? The scars miraculously heal on the other side of the border, in—what's it called?

"Plombieres."

She nodded. "No, Sonny. I'll . . . we'll face new problems—a new life, new language, new people, no money."

"It will be a challenge," Sonny agreed. He did not say everything would be fine—that would be glib. He smuggled Jews across the border, had saved an old Jew along the way. How the hell would he know? She was right.

She needed encouragement, so he said, "I know my little piece of the puzzle. Rumors fly. I heard about a man released from Dachau—he's leaving for Palestine with his wife early next year. You'll be leaving with your parents before the year is over, I promise. It won't be easy wherever you land, but it will better than here."

"What if there's a war?"

"Whoa!" Sonny raised his hand. "One step at a time. We've got enough on our plate already."

"I'm trying," Rosa protested. "There's too much time to think bad things—you know, that feeling you get when you lean over a railing . . ."

Sonny knew too well.

"... that's what I feel most of the time."

"It's going to improve," he said, putting his hands on her shoulders. "I promise."

Rosa searched his eyes and smiled. "I couldn't have survived any of this without you. You give me hope... but then you leave, do what it is you do. Then all the bad thoughts rush back. It's all a horrible joke. They won't let Father out—they'll come for mother, for me."

"No! Don't think that."

Sonny looked over Rosa's shoulder, out the window, onto the roof across the street. Three men were kneeling at an elevator shaft; holding satchels. He blinked and they disappeared. Then he was alone in the truck at the border in the dead of night, waiting for Emil. He was scared shitless, his only companions the wind whistling through the trees, a hooting owl, the sound of his own breathing.

"You said it. I *am* used to being scared—it never really goes away. It's a price I'm willing to pay. I hardly think about it any more, though I did this morning. It'll stay with me for a while... and there have been others." He felt Albert's eyes from across the square, saw Willy's body stretched out on the cellar floor.

"Like what?" Rosa asked, though her face said she didn't want to know.

"Not today. When we're safe, sitting in a little café in Antwerp," he answered and sighed heavily. "We'll get over this and move on. The moment you opened the door I wanted to help. And now," he said, "I'm in love with you."

"I know," Rosa said, putting a finger to his lips to keep him from saying more. "My world is upside down. I spend most of my time with a smuggler who saves old Jews. Things like that make it hard for me not to fall in love with you."

"That's good." His usual inclination was to wave off praise, but all he could hear was that she loved him.

They stood quietly, then Sonny reminded Rosa of their journey. Pulling the documents from his pocket, he placed them on the table and glanced at his watch. "We should catch the twelve o'clock train." She hadn't answered his question, so he asked again, "Where's your mother?"

Rosa was in a reverie, her eyes glued to the papers. Sonny took her arm, shook it gently. "Rosa, we have a journey to take. Your mother?"

She blinked, licked her lips, awakening to the fact that what she'd been waiting for was imminent. "She's downstairs with neighbors," she said absently. Fingering one of the documents as if it were a cherished family memento, she said, "I wish Joseph a long, healthy life."

"Yes," Sonny agreed, thinking of the flat filled with nothing but old furniture and memories. Folding the documents, he returned them to the envelope and handed it to Rosa. His smile was reassuring. "The Third Reich wants nothing more than to rid Germany of its Jews. Stay calm. Keep your wits about you. Everything will turn out fine."

His companionship, promises, documents, had brought Rosa this far, but he felt a chill at what lay before them. His aching jaw—and Karl's nightmare story—made him suddenly unsure. He shuddered at the specter of Rosa's father at the end of a noose. His confidence ebbing, he feared the limb they'd climbed onto might fail. But he plastered a reassuring smile onto his face, keeping his doubts to himself.

Rosa pressed the envelope to her bosom. "Finally, it's come."

"When you get to the camp, keep it simple—tell the truth. The only lie is that your mother got the visas at the Belgian Embassy; otherwise everything's kosher."

"Let's go then," Rosa muttered, resigned to her mission. She was about to put the papers in her purse, when Sonny intervened.

"Not a purse. Leave that here. Put them in a secure coat pocket."

Nodding, Rosa tried to force a smile. In that moment, Sonny saw the power he held over her, that he could choose who would get the papers needed to leave this place. Power over other people's lives could be a heady elixir, but it had never motivated him. He watched Rosa retreat within as she prepared for her singular journey. His mind went where it should not go—did those damn papers make him more attractive?

He sighed audibly; it was time to tell her of the change in plans. "Rosa," he started, then faltered. He absently wiped his mouth with the back of his hand, feeling a jolt of pain.

She winced sympathetically and moved closer to him.

"We need to alter the plan a bit."

"How?" She nearly spit out the word in alarm.

Sonny calmed her. "Don't worry, I'm coming with you. But it's too dangerous for us to travel as a couple."

Rosa moved from alarm to confusion. Her eyes studied his face for an answer. Not finding one, she said, "I don't understand."

"I'll be on the train, nearby but not so close that someone will think we're together. If we were stopped, it would be trouble for Paul Sander—not a Jew—and Rosa Fischer, who is one." He didn't mention the other scenario—himself a fugitive, in custody. "But you'll never be alone, except when you go into the camp. I'll follow you to the station . . . buy a return ticket . . . board the train. Don't look for me. We're strangers."

Putting a hand on his forearm, she said, "I hadn't thought of that."

Sonny pictured the station platform with other anxious women taking the same grim but hopeful journey. He encouraged Rosa: "If you sense a kindred spirit, sit with her for mutual support."

Rosa seemed unsure but nodded.

"It's only a suggestion. Stay calm; everything will fall into place. You can do it—I know you can." When he let her hands go, they fell to her side. He kept his voice confident. "When you get off the train, look for directions to the camp. I'm sure there will be signs. It's not far. I'll be trailing you, but don't look for me. When you're done, follow the same route. I'll be watching for you and your father."

Rosa fists were clenched, her lips tightly closed. Sonny helped with her coat and watched as she secured the papers in an inside pocket. He put his arms around her, pulled her close. "I look forward to meeting your father."

Then he kissed her forehead.

30

Avarice, ambition, lust, etc., are nothing but species of madness.
—Benedict (Baruch) Spinoza

Rosa boarded the train a few minutes past noon. Though it was only thirty kilometers to Oranienburg, the trip would take an hour with stops in Hermsdorf, Frohnau, Hohenneuendorf, Birkenwerder, and Lehnitz at the end of Lehnitz See.

Sonny took a seat in the half-empty car, several rows behind Rosa, on the opposite side. He buried his face in *Der Angriff*, the masthead evident to any observer. Emil had taught him this underground *trompe l'oeil* gimmick—it gave one an illusion of security. Sometimes that was enough.

Peering around the newspaper, Sonny stole an occasional glance at Rosa. She drew longer looks from several men, but she didn't seem to notice. And nobody stopped beside her. Once she turned her head, and he felt her eyes upon his face. He turned away, ignoring his faint reflection in the window to look onto the drab urban landscape—tenements, factories, warehouses in states of decay, clumped like livestock huddled against the cold. Curtained windows hid squalid lives, and fire escapes clung to the walls like spiders' webs, in zigzagging patterns.

Swastikas and red Nazi banners hung from walls, poles, and chimneys. "Jews Out," "Jew Scum," "Death to Bolshies," he saw scribbled everywhere, ad nauseum. He'd become numb to the epithets, though they were rough reminders of the journey's purpose. His gaze was drawn to a man smoking a cigarette, leaning rakishly on a shovel up the line . . . a picture perfectly still but for the languidly rising smoke.

Their eyes met. Sonny could read into them anything he wanted in that unlikely, intimate moment. Was that guy thinking about his wife, a girlfriend, job trouble? How good the cigarette tasted, Kristallnacht, the guy on the train? Sonny blinked, and the man was gone.

The urban industrial corridor yielded to affluent northern suburbs, then snow-covered fields and leafless trees. Craning his neck, Sonny could see the old castle in the center of Oranienburg, above the Havel River. That and the old brewery converted into a concentration camp were all he knew about this awful place. He hoped never to return.

Sonny waited for the car to empty, then stepped onto the platform. He kept Rosa in sight as several women passed by. He assumed they were on a mission like Rosa's. Coming toward him through the crowd was a woman holding the hand of, or more accurately, pulling, a thin, pale man. The couple disappeared onto the train that would take them to the relative safety of anywhere else. Ahead, Rosa was looking back, in the direction of the couple, a thin smile on her face. When their eyes met, she turned and walked into the station.

Sonny found the men's restroom . . . upon leaving, he asked the elderly attendant directions to Sachsenhausen. Sullen, his eyes flecked with tiny red veins, the man leaned on his mop, appraising his questioner with icy silence. Probably he had answered the question a hundred times: "Follow the arrow two kilometers north on Berliner Strasse."

When he reached the door, Sonny stopped. Rosa stood in hazy silhouette, just beyond the entrance to the station. Thick clouds, like a mask over the city, dulled the light to shades of gray, portending snow. Beyond her stood the sign, an arrow pointing the way. She seemed to study it.

Sonny stepped outside then stopped short. He watched Rosa stiffen, her head shaking. A man disappeared into the crowd. Who the hell was that? What had he said, or done, to affect Rosa that way? His eyes fixed on the crowd, the man reappeared, giving Sonny a better look. Then he was gone for good. Rosa hadn't moved—her shoulders were hunched, closing in on herself.

Sonny watched as she frantically scanned every face until their eyes met. Her mouth was open, her eyes wide with fright. Sonny smiled and nodded encouragement. Her shoulders relaxed, but her eyes locked on him. Then she walked in the direction of the arrow.

Keeping Rosa within sight, Sonny wove through the early afternoon pedestrians. He barely took notice of several boarded-up shops; he was stuck on the image of the disappearing man. What chafed was Rosa's reaction, her anxiety upon finding him in the crowd. So Sonny stopped at a men's shop, pretending to look at the display.

Closing his eyes, he waited for the image: a fedora on top, a long dark coat, about his height, maybe a little stockier—certainly Gestapo. But something else—his stride . . . uneven, with a hitch. Yes, he limped on the right . . . the left . . . no, the right leg. Sonny's face screwed into a deep frown; he didn't like the image he remembered. He wanted to think the man with the limp had offered assistance, but something about him gnawed . . . He turned and found Rosa ahead. She was walking alone, though other women nearby were heading in the same direction. Limping Man was nowhere in sight.

In fifteen minutes the commercial district yielded to warehouses and factories lining both sides of the road. Workmen gathered at some spots. Others were deserted. But a constant flow of trucks and black sedans moved in both directions. In another fifteen minutes a squat, typically Prussian-styled, white-clapboard building—apparently benign, though he knew of horrors there—dominated the view. Barbed wire ran along the perimeter from a large gate where people clustered, milling about. He caught a fleeting glimpse of Rosa just before she disappeared into their midst.

Sonny was too far away to see the wrought-iron banner over the gate, its cynical inscription, *Arbeit macht frei* (work makes you free), the fruit of a demented mind. Thoroughly disgusted just knowing it was there, he turned his back on the place and set out for a tavern.

Hungry and thirsty, he stepped into the first one he encountered along Berliner Strasse, wedged between warehouses. It was just past lunchtime, and the place had emptied except for a couple of down-on-their-luck regulars at the bar, a few others scattered at tables. Sonny nursed his beer, cursing softly as he gingerly massaged his jaw. Eating, drinking, waiting in the shadow of Sachsenhausen fit with the pattern of that morning—it was a bizarre day, to be sure. *Bizarre* barely captured its essence.

Now, he was playing Hansel to Rosa's Gretel, following her crumbs as she made her way to the evil witch. He might have laughed at the ridiculous comparison, but it was hardly funny. Scanning the dimly lit tavern in this Gestapo town while surrounded by regular drunks only confirmed the dearth of humor in his life. He retraced his day—Nazi Youth and old Jew, Rosa's response to Limping Man, the banal building housing a notorious camp, the pain in his jaw, the reason for Rosa's journey.

Somehow this fit into the arc of his life. And what was he to make of that? Of his little bit of this, little of that, of his father's deception, of Simon's sardonic prescience, of smuggling trinkets and people, of discovery by Albert, of Thiemann Strasse and Willy's sacrifice, of drinking and eating in the shadow of mankind's worst impulse—Sachsenhausen? Life had two meanings: the one he'd wanted, expected to experience when he was young, and the one left after the first one was stripped away. The ironies, heaped one atop the other, slowly yielded to a penetrating, absurdly dark humor. It was all a terrible, deadly joke!

Turning to hide his face, Sonny couldn't keep from laughing. Maybe he'd gone mad again. Yet there were tears running down his cheeks, and his shoulders shook. Finally, his jaw screamed—enough! And he stopped. After several deep breaths, he wiped his eyes, drank some beer, and looked over his shoulder. The regulars at the end of the bar stared quizzically, unsure of what to make of him. Then one of them gave him a toothy smile and raised his mug. Sonny returned the salute.

Sobered by the pain in his jaw, he turned his thoughts to Rosa in that monstrous place—where human ornaments hung from gallows and others died of exposure, where Jewish men were terrorized. Staring into an empty mug, he got the innkeeper's attention and ordered another beer, two hard-boiled eggs. After quickly devouring the eggs and half the beer, he found the world returning to its proper misanthropic alignment.

Sonny stared out the window onto the street where Rosa would soon pass with her father in tow. He would shadow them back to the station, and they'd get out of town. All he had to do was wait . . . He needed fresh air, so he drained his mug and dropped some money on the bar, nodding to the regulars on his way out.

Outside, a fog had descended to play tricks on his eyes. Buildings appeared hazy, surreal. Fanning his hand dispersed the fog, but like a swarm of mosquitoes, it quickly returned. He grimaced at his edginess, but he'd have to endure it until they returned safely to Berlin. If he had learned anything, it was that there was little comfort in any corner.

Sonny believed in reality, not omens. But everything was wrong—from the shuttered Jewish shops, to the graffiti, to the vacant warehouses and dark tavern, to the camp and its motto, to Limping Man—especially him. Being stuck in a Gestapo town with thousands of imprisoned Jews on a gray December day filled Sonny with a dark foreboding. Walking briskly in the cold damp air, he tried to dispel it. He came upon an opening, not much more than a stand of trees bounded on both sides by large buildings. From there he could watch the road through the fog, he could pace—and wait.

Rosa had been out of his sight for about an hour and a half when he saw her on the other side of Berliner Strasse, heading toward town. She was alone, but she appeared to be smiling. Perplexed, Sonny suppressed the urge to run to her side. Once she passed, he would follow.

He was about to turn onto Berliner Strasse when some movement caught his eye. Several people were on the street behind Rosa, yet nothing jumped out at him. But something was there—he kept looking. Impeded by the fog, he saw the hazy outline of a figure materialize. There was a hitch in his stride; he was gaining on Rosa. Now just across the road, a man in a fedora and a long coat moved quickly, his abnormal gait increasingly pronounced.

Sonny's eyes and mouth went dry at the disquieting scene. He'd been nagged by a bad feeling since he watched Rosa at the station. But maybe he was being too jumpy . . . maybe the man was simply trying to catch a train. Keeping in stride from across the road, Sonny tried to focus on the man's face, though his hat was pulled low. His imagination conjured a variation of Albert's predatory features . . .

Now the man was even with Rosa, but instead of passing her, he grabbed her left arm, jerking her to a stop. Rosa's head turned, her smile vanished, she recoiled. What was he saying—was he threatening her? Sonny couldn't see clearly. People passed. No one stopped to intervene in what might be construed as a domestic quarrel. The man seemed oblivious to everything but Rosa.

Sonny had come to protect Rosa, not to watch her squirm like prey in the talons of that freak. Now Limping Man was pulling roughly on her arm. Struggling, her free arm swiped in a slow-motion arc, and she screamed, "No!" He was dragging her to the corner.

Sonny watched in disbelief, impotent. He felt lightheaded, the pavement opening beneath his feet, sucking him into free fall. Grabbing for a hold that wasn't there, he heard Emil's voice in his head: "Be patient. Calm down. Don't show your hand early."

A convoy of trucks passed, and he lost sight of Rosa. Where was she? In his panic, he tasted eggs and beer, and he spit it out. Still unable to see her, he cursed himself for failing to act on his suspicions. But what might he have done? Abandoned her father? Taken her back to Berlin on the thinnest of hunches, on a vague notion of danger? Finally, the trucks passed. Sonny searched frantically until he saw two figures moving away from Berliner Strasse onto a side street.

Too far away for attack, Limping Man would surely have a pistol anyway. Sonny would not end his life and Rosa's, dead in the street. He'd keep his distance, watch, and wait for an opening. Limping Man didn't know he was being followed—that was Sonny's advantage. Clenching his fists so tight his fingernails pierced his palms, he welcomed the pain. It cleared his mind, let him search every memory for something, anything, with which to free Rosa. But nothing came.

The man limped into a narrow alley behind the first row of warehouses without a backwards glance. What arrogance! Rosa hadn't seen him coming or she'd have been looking over her shoulder, nervous as a cat. She had smiled, so there must have been good news at the camp. But where was her father?

When Rosa and her captor disappeared from view, Sonny ran across the street, barely avoiding a big black sedan, its horn honking. Fighting wild thoughts, he headed for the alley. Winded, he caught his breath, burped up more beer and egg. Spitting, he wiped his mouth on his sleeve and peered around the corner. Shadows played tricks on his eyes, until two forms came into focus some thirty meters away. Debris littered the alley that dead-ended at a blank wall. All the buildings looked vacant, derelict.

"Please!"

It was Rosa's voice. Sonny pounded his fist against the wall in frustration, again stifling the impulse to attack. Then he heard a high-pitched creak, like on the roof at No. 15. A dark rectangle moved in an arc—an opening door. They disappeared, and the door closed against the frame with a thud, then bounced partly open. Hugging the brick wall, he ran to the door and leaned against the wall, still as a statue. He listened, hearing nothing but his own panting.

Lyrical laughter, almost operatic, surprised him. It was so out of context that he thought his ears had betrayed him. He heard it again, was immobilized by its madness. Then silence, until he heard feet scraping against the concrete floor. They must be moving deeper into the dark building.

Sonny slowly pulled the door; it moaned not loud enough to betray him. He stepped silently through the opening and leaned against the adjacent wall, acclimating himself to the dark stillness of the cold warehouse. Several high windows provided just enough light for him to see several meters ahead. Moving from the opening of the alley to where he now stood had taken less than a minute.

For the moment, his only plan was to find them, get close but remain undetected, then use surprise to attack. His temples were beating like drums. He wiped his sweaty palms on his pants and surveyed the immediate area. In the dim light he could see a support column about a meter square, rising like a massive tree trunk from floor to ceiling. Probably there were more—he would use them for cover. He moved deeper into the warehouse, finding the next column, then the next, careful not to trip on the scattered debris.

From his left came faint shuffling, like sandpaper . . . then a whimper. Rosa! He crept toward the sound, but before he could reach the next column, he heard the jangle of metal, the scraping of a chain. Dirty white light flashed from the far corner. Dashing behind a column, he froze, then slowly peered around it. Some twenty meters away, a bare light bulb swung at the end of a cord.

When the ghostly shadows stilled, he saw two figures in what seemed a seedy bedroom: there was a bare mattress on the floor and a table with several chairs. Sitting on the table were a bottle, several glasses, and something reflecting light.

"Relax, my dear. It'll be over in a matter of minutes, and then you can go." Limping Man's calm, cultured tenor pierced the air. Sonny's muscles stiffened, screaming for action, and he nearly lost his balance. Then Rosa disappeared behind a column.

"Resistance only makes it harder. Why not enjoy it?"

Rosa returned to Sonny's field of vision, her arms crossed over her chest. Pure revulsion shone in her eyes. Then came the sound of shuffling feet. The man went to the table and poured from the bottle. He drank and walked in a circle around Rosa, appraising.

"No . . . please," Rosa begged.

Sonny balled his fists but stood his ground.

"Stop!" Limping Man's staccato burst of anger, his sudden change of tone, made Sonny jump. Then just as quickly, the voice regained its soothing banality. "Nothing you say or do will make a difference. If you want to see your father again . . . you'll do as I say."

With Limping Man's voice for cover, Sonny ran from column to column, coming to stand within three meters of the man's back. Sonny heard him grunt, and Rosa's coat flew from her shoulders onto the floor. She backed into the table—falling onto it, her back to Sonny.

"You're very pretty, and such a shapely figure. We'll have a very nice time."

Rosa did not respond.

The man sighed, and for the first time there was scorn in his voice. "Don't feel so damn superior *now*, do you?"

She did not move.

"Jews! Such a nuisance . . . why do we bother with you?" Exasperation framed the meaningless words. "At least the women are good for something." His lyrical laugh returned.

Rosa still did not move.

Sonny never doubted the man's intentions; time was running out. He started to move, was ready to spring, but his right foot hit something—

hard, immobile. Startled, he squinted at a solid mass, but he couldn't see what it was. Reaching down, he felt the cold sharp corners of a rectangle—he'd bumped into a pile of bricks. Smiling at his good fortune, he wrapped his fingers around a brick, but as he lifted it, a scraping sound carried through the empty space. Cradling the brick, he tensed, ready to attack should Limping Man come to investigate.

"Damn rats! Place is filled with the filthy creatures—like their Jewish relatives." His cackle made Sonny cringe. "Don't think someone will save you."

With a suddenness born of Limping Man's hubris, Sonny's pent-up anger escaped in a fury, nearly blinding him. Normally placid, he eschewed violence. But letting the rage overwhelm him, he exhaled fire. And he sprang like a man possessed.

In three long strides, Sonny was upon the man undetected. Sonny's hand, and the brick it held, moved in a fluid arc. When it reached its apex, a flash diverted his attention for an instant—so brief as to be almost beyond comprehension. He thought it may not even have occurred. But the man fell forward. Automatically, Sonny adjusted his trajectory, and the brick's powerful descent met the soft skin of Limping Man's exposed temple.

Sonny heard the crunch of cranial bone, followed in muddled sequence by a spurt of blood, a gasp. Limping Man fell in a heap to the concrete floor.

31

In revenge and love, woman is more barbarous than man.
—Friedrich Nietzsche

Bastard! Bastard!" Rosa screamed, her face distorted by rage. Blood splattered on her dress.

Dark crimson dripped from the corner of the brick. Sonny looked from Rosa to the brick and dropped it, his eyes fixed on her stained clothing. "Rosa, are you hurt?" he shouted.

Unhearing or yet unaware of his presence, she kicked wildly at the prostrate body, her arms moving in synch with the force of her attack. When Sonny finally penetrated her consciousness, her rage died as if smothered by a blanket. She stared at him in wide-eyed disbelief and muttered, "Sonny."

"Why are you bloody?" Sonny's voice was shrill.

Sonny was not a part of the nightmare forced upon her, but there he was. Her eyes moved from his face to the dead man at her feet, and she sagged. He caught her before she fell. "I stabbed him," she muttered.

"What do you mean?" asked Sonny. She wasn't making sense. Quickly, he went over the last few moments in his mind: he'd picked up the brick, heard the comment about rats, lost it, and rushed at the villain. Then he remembered the flash. He looked from Rosa to the dead man.

Rosa was equally perplexed. It was as if Sonny had been conjured, dropped in through the roof. She blinked, transformed by the change in circumstance. "Where did you come from?"

"I watched . . . followed. I was always close, waiting for the right time. But why is there blood on your dress?"

"You were?" Her voice was small, and a faint smile appeared. She hadn't been abandoned after all.

Sonny nodded, asked again, "Rosa . . . what happened?"

Rosa looked past Sonny's shoulder, trying to make sense of it. Finally, she said, "Over there," and nodded toward the table. "I tripped . . . fell . . . the knife was stuck in the table . . . I reached for it, couldn't . . . then."

Still looking at the table, she continued, "Something exploded inside me. He didn't see the knife until it was stuck in his chest." She seemed disconnected, as if someone else were talking; her arms hung limply at her sides. She scratched her palms, then raised her bloody hand, looked at the blood on her chest, shuddered violently, and vomited.

Sonny put a hand on her back. When she straightened, he moved toward her, but Rosa stopped him. "No! You'll get blood on your jacket." She worked her tongue, trying to purge the terrible taste from her mouth.

Remembering the bottle, Sonny poured some brandy into a glass. She drank, coughed, and drank some more. Sonny finished what was left in the glass and poured more. Then he looked at the dead Gestapo officer lying at their feet.

"It was self-defense. Rosa, you must remember that." That the Gestapo would not see it that way he hadn't yet worked out.

"Self-defense," she repeated. "Yes . . . that's it." Then she spoke so rapidly her words collided. "He was going to rape me . . . I had to let him have me, or my father would never be released. He had that power." She began to cry.

Sonny held her from behind, pulled her close, while she shivered in his arms. He heard her say, "Then you appeared like magic."

Everything was a muddle. What they'd done had not yet sunk in. Had he saved Rosa? Had she saved herself? Or had they both saved themselves? At any rate, she was safe, and relief washed over Sonny like a cool rain on a hot day.

Looking at the bloody skull atop that crumpled heap of a man, Sonny moved on to the thought of his sweet vengeance. The feeling quickly gave way to "What now?"

They had to get out of there, but first he had to make sure the man was dead. He nudged the body with his foot. When it didn't move, Sonny kicked harder, sending the corpse onto its back. The mouth was a distorted gash, the eyes dully opaque. Protruding from his chest, reflecting the light, was the stunning equalizer—the shiny object that had caught Sonny's attention just before the strike.

"That must have surprised the hell out of him," Sonny mused. He imagined Limping Man's arrogant smirk evaporating at the hands of this pretty Jewess. Sonny's eyes were drawn to the gory junction of crimson and clean white shirt. He looked dead, but Sonny had to be sure. He checked the pulse.

"Nothing . . . He's dead."

Then he grinned savagely as an epitaph for Limping Man popped into his head: "Siegfried, the golden boy of the Gestapo, wandered into the wrong opera and was brought low by a Semitic Valkyrie." His smile vanished as he looked up at Rosa.

Rosa's head moved slowly from side to side, her eyes wide as she tried to comprehend the surreal scenario, a sort of demented fairy tale. Her lips moved, but nothing came forth. Then with a start, she said, "It went in so easily."

She shook her head, still bewildered. "Is that when you hit him?"

"Yes. I saw the knife flash in the light, but I didn't know what it was at the time."

Rosa's eyes narrowed. "How many others has he ravished? It must have been easy with the women scared, with women who had no hope." Rosa spoke haltingly through her tears. "He was at the station . . ." She took a shallow breath: " . . . smiled that horrible leer . . . asked if I needed help. I shook my head, and he walked away. I'll never forget it." Rosa buried her head in her hands.

Sonny closed her coat, then looked for a rag. When he couldn't find one, he took the dead man's coat and cleaned the blood from her hands.

"I was focusing on Father." Rosa pointed to the lump on the floor. "Then he grabbed me." Her eyes went to Sonny. "I was so happy—I thought it was you."

"Ja," Sonny mumbled.

"I'm glad I killed him."

Sonny stiffened, alarmed by the truth. "No, Rosa. Never say that." He couldn't let her carry that burden. "No one must ever know. Forget what I said about self-defense. I killed him. Tell no one what you did. Promise me that."

Bewildered, she stared at him. "All right. If you say so." She sounded like a little girl—her voice small, eager to please. She was still shivering, so Sonny held her again. Her labored breathing smelled of brandy.

"We have to leave," he whispered as he looked around the warehouse, down at the dead man. Blood oozed from his chest and a small jagged scar on his cheek pointed like an arrow to the red gash on his temple. Sonny spoke to the corpse, "What are we going to do with you?"

Rosa pulled at Sonny's coat, then backed away. "Let's leave! Maybe he's not dead." She was in shock, but her urge to leave was fully rational.

"Oh, he's dead all right." Sonny felt a strange calm as he knelt down and searched the man's pockets. He found a wallet, several loose Reichmarks, a packet of cigarettes, a lighter, loose change, and a holstered revolver, and piled all but the money on the floor. That he stuffed into his pocket. He picked up the gun; it felt cold but good in his hand. He liked its heft and pointed it at the dead man, his lips curling into a mean sneer. "Bang, bang."

"Sonny, don't. You're scaring me!" Rosa's voice was shrill. "Let's go! Please."

"Sorry . . . Yes, of course we'll go," said Sonny. Then he opened Limping Man's wallet and found his Gestapo ID, more money, and a photograph. He put the money in his pocket and the other items on the pile. "In a few minutes." He read the ID. "Ah, his name is . . . was . . . Lieutenant Franz Walter."

Now what? But he was stuck on what they had done—what he had done. From one moment to the next there was a man alive, then a man dead. Killing felt nothing like he had imagined. He had no remorse, nothing—he was numb. Then a door opened on a pretty wife, children, loving parents. No! He slammed it shut. No sympathy for predators. He wouldn't credit the notion there'd be anyone to mourn Limping Man, wouldn't waste even a second . . .

Rosa, disoriented and scared, reminded him of his ancestor from the shtetl. The dead man on the floor was the Cossack. All Sonny cared about was that Rosa was safe—both honor and body preserved. It was that simple. But for what the Cossacks did to his ancestors, for what Braun did to Willy, for what the Nazis did to every Jew, and especially for what this Nazi had intended for Rosa, he felt the raw vengeance that had pushed Grynszpan to his deeply personal, desperate act. And like Grynszpan, he'd do it all again. Unlike Grynszpan, he'd get away.

"You're safe. That's all that matters," Sonny said, as he bounced the revolver in his hand.

"What will you do with that?" Rosa watched him with growing alarm.

Sonny shrugged, as he inspected the barrel, then thought of Emil. "Walther PPK" was etched into the metal. He dropped it into his pocket. "Lieutenant Walter has no further use for his Walther, so I'll give it to a friend." He smiled.

Then he looked down at the little pile and absently picked up the picture. His eyes moved over four faces then back to the lieutenant. The photo showed him very much alive—smiling, standing with three others in Gestapo uniform. Sonny's eyes focused on the other three men, and he froze. There, at the edge of the group, slightly apart, his eyes staring intensely at Sonny was Albert . . . again! Sonny's spine tingled.

Clutching the photograph, he wanted to tear it to pieces. He was cursed by Albert's very existence—an albatross pulling him down, a punishment for acts never committed. His mind flipped to that day at the café he'd been mesmerized by the sight of Albert, also with three others in uniform. Why had he stayed? He'd had no good answer when Emil asked, and he had none still.

He closed his eyes, retrieving the three-year old memory. The faces were hazy, unidentifiable but for Albert's—his was clear. Had Limping Man been there too? Sonny strained to retrieve an image that wasn't there. Only Albert, always Albert, remained in focus. He hadn't really looked at the others. Tearing his eyes from the photo, Sonny looked at the dead man. What did it matter? Limping Man was dead. Albert was not.

"Sonny . . . Sonny!" Rosa's voice roused him.

"You're right—we've got to go," he said. There were more important matters at hand—Rosa's state of mind, their escape—than his obsession with Albert. The picture and ID card went into Sonny's pocket, next to the revolver. He took several deep breaths to clear his head. Then he said, "Now, what are we going to do with him?"

They could flee to Berlin and be done with it. But Lieutenant Walter's Gestapo chums surely would find him. The investigation might connect him to Rosa. And there'd be hell to pay for Jews in the neighborhood and beyond. "This could start another pogrom," Sonny said absently as he rubbed his jaw.

"What?" Rosa was confused by his non sequitur.

"A dead Nazi by the hand of a Jew started the last pogrom. This dead creep could be the pretext for another, worse than the other." Sonny looked around the warehouse. "We have to hide the body . . . where?"

Rosa shook her head, too dazed, too scared, to follow.

Sonny gave voice to his thoughts. "Can't bury the body in a concrete floor. Can't carry it out." Using the cigarette lighter's flame for a torch, he walked around the huge empty space, between piles of haphazardly thrown wood, bricks, and scraps of paper showing little regard for German orderliness. In the corner were the mattress, chairs, and table among the mouse and rat shit that was everywhere, but there was nowhere to hide a body. He stared at the orange flame flickering in his hand, at a pile of wood, the paper, and burst out laughing.

Rosa recoiled. "Sonny, let's leave . . . I'm scared . . . please!" Her plea ended in a long, low hiss.

He ran to her. "We will, but I have an idea. Before we go, we'll give the lout a proper funeral pyre."

"What are you talking about?" Rosa's color had returned, but she was shivering uncontrollably. Now she looked at him as if he'd spoken to her in Hebrew. "I hate riddles!"

"We'll burn the building down—with Lieutenant Walter in it."

Rosa shook her head incredulously. "Don't joke."

"I'm deadly serious."

"Let's just get out!" Rosa's voice rose. She edged away from the body.

"Shhh . . . We will in a few minutes."

"Okay . . . but I can't take much more." Her eyes darted from Sonny to the dead man. Waiting in the company of a corpse she'd helped put in that state was too much. Then her eyes flashed with sudden realization. "My father! I still have to get my father," she moaned.

"Yes, of course, we'll get him," Sonny agreed. "With all this," he swept his hand through the air, "that got lost. What happened at the camp?"

"He'll be released tomorrow, but I have to get him." She shook her head at the thought of returning to the camp.

But Sonny heard only the good news. "That's wonderful." He squeezed her arm. "And that's another reason we have to burn this place down—there can't be a body to discover between now and then, or ever." Clearly she didn't understand the terrible possibilities, and there wasn't time to fully explain, so he said simply, "There's too much to connect you with him." He gestured with his chin toward the dead man.

Rosa refused to look at the dead lieutenant, yet the lines between the two of them seemed to grow and connect in her head. She would have screamed had her hands not already covered her mouth.

"We can't take the chance," Sonny started, smirked deviously, then lowered his voice, "but if we burn this dump to the ground, well?" He answered his own question. "They'll never find him. Besides, why should we care if this whole damn town burns down?"

"Okay. Start the goddamn fire," Rosa shot back, her profanity as unusual as everything else about their day. "Then we go!" Her hands were on her hips.

"Yes, just wait over there." Sonny pointed to the door, scared that one of Walter's compatriots, maybe Albert, would walk in. Quickly gathering kindling, he reconsidered. "Rosa, wait! Help. It'll go faster. Bring some wood." Pointing to a pile some five meters away, Sonny dragged the body between a column and the wall. He covered it with paper and several layers of wood, more paper, more wood on top of that, until the pyre engulfed the wall and column, and the body had long since disappeared. He balanced the musty mattress on top and against the column, lifted the table and chairs to the top. The kindling rose to his chest, threatening to tumble at any moment.

For his plan to work, the flames had to engulf the column, the wall, then the ceiling. Taking a step back, he inspected his handiwork and nodded approval. "Somewhat precarious, but once the fire starts, it won't matter." Sonny spun the wheel on Lieutenant Walter's lighter, sparking the flint until it lit. Then he kissed Rosa on the forehead. "Wait by the door. We'll leave as soon as the fire's blazing."

Rosa hid behind a column near the door. Her nostrils quivered—vomit and brandy had failed to wipe out the smell of that awful man's cologne. Musky and cloying, it lay upon her like a wet blanket. She rubbed her nose. She looked around for something, anything—ah, a bottle in the corner. Running, she retrieved the empty schnapps bottle and put the opening under her nose. Breathing deep, she took in the pungent odor until she gagged. Never had a foul odor smelled so good.

Falling against the column, she shut her eyes. The afternoon's events came at her in a fury . . . The leering, unctuous smile greeting her at the station. Finding Sonny in the crowd, nodding encouragement, and her walking . . . remembering nothing along the way. Women crying . . . she walked around them to a gate, where a man in uniform directed her. Then as if she were buying a rail ticket, the clerk at the desk, without looking up, asking, "Name?"

Confused, she said, "Rosa."

"His, not yours."

She must have said "Herr Robert Fischer," because he had asked for proof of emigration. She handed him the visa. Suddenly panicked, she searched her pockets. Her fingers touched the hard edges of the envelope, and she relaxed. She vaguely recalled the clerk telling her to wait. Other women waited behind her. After several minutes he returned.

"Robert Fischer will be released this time tomorrow."

She hadn't asked, "Why not today?" But she was happy and she was looking for Sonny so she could tell him the good news. Everything was fine until she turned, expecting to see him. Why is he hurting my arm? She saw the horrid smile, the scar on the man's cheek. "Stop hurting me." She tried to hit him, but he just laughed and dragged her into this place. Now he was dead . . .

What was taking Sonny so long? She scarcely remembered clutching the knife that had been just within reach. Then there was the blood—on her hand, on her dress. She was screaming; she didn't see Sonny smash the man's head with a brick. She hadn't known he was there until it was over. Putting her hands over her ears, blotting out the man's voice in her head, she spun around, but he wasn't there.

Sonny was silhouetted by the fiery glow. Covering her eyes, she peered between her fingers to the table, to the knife, now engulfed by flames. Then she looked for blood on her hands. Seeing none, she rubbed them together. Maybe she'd dreamt it all? No, she'd grabbed the knife, lunged, plunged it deep. Her fist struck his chest. He gasped—blood was on his chest, on her hand, on her dress, oozing from the side of his head.

"I killed him," she whispered, then covered her mouth with her hand. "No." She'd never say that again.

Smoke rapidly filled the enclosed space, and she breathed it in. Smoke covered the schnapps, the musk, so she breathed deeper, gasping for air. Coughing, she started to pace. Where was Sonny? She couldn't see him through the smoke. The tears flowed. She wasn't crying, just trying to breathe.

Then Sonny had his arm around her waist, and they were out the door. They stopped, looked inside as huge orange flames licked up and around the pyre. In a matter of minutes they would engulf the pillar, wall, and ceiling, seeking dry timber.

"Let's go." Sonny grabbed her hand, moving toward the street.

Rosa, her eyes watering, gulped the fresh air. They were free, waking from a terrible nightmare . . .

By the time they reached the mouth of the alley, Sonny expected to see smoke seeping from the open door. For a moment, he feared the fire hadn't taken. But he needn't have worried: a gray, rolling mass of black smoke soon rushed from the door like a train emerging from a tunnel.

"That's a beautiful sight," he declared, and they kept moving. By the time they reached the station, the crematorium would be burning out of control. By the time they arrived in Berlin, all of Oranienburg might be in flames. Sonny imagined a hellish night sky as the run-down neighborhood in the shitty Gestapo town turned to inferno.

They met little traffic, few people on Berliner Strasse. He glanced at his watch; it was a little after six. Rosa chewed on her lip. She looked vulnerable in the dim light. Could she hold it together until they reached Berlin? What if they were stopped—with blood on her dress, a revolver in his pocket? Well, they'd come too far to worry about that now.

He wrapped her in his arms and kissed her. "You were incredibly brave." Then he took her hand, squeezed it gently, and said softly, "Walk to the station. Use your return ticket. I'll be there."

"Okay. Sonny," she hesitated, "you're always near, even if I can't see you." Rosa's eyes searched his face, then placed a hand gently to his jaw. "Is it better?"

Sonny smiled and nodded.

"I'm glad." Then she took his hand in hers and turned it over and back, examining it. "No blood. That's good, isn't it, Sonny? They'll never know."

"That's right, and none on yours," he answered. "No one can ever know." He paused. "You can't tell anyone about him—that we killed him—not your mother, not your father, no one. You understand?"

She nodded. "But what about your friends?"

"Don't worry about them, but you must keep this a secret."

"I will." Her voice faltered. "And Sonny, we won't tell anyone what he was going to do to me." Noise from a passing truck drowned their voices. When it was gone, Rosa said, "Father will be waiting." Whatever resolve she'd gathered now crumbled like a sand castle in rising tide. She shook her head violently. "I can't return to this . . . this . . ."

Sonny put a finger on her lips and kissed her forehead. "Don't worry. Someone will come for your father."

"Promise."

"I promise."

Sonny nodded to the old man pushing his mop. Rosa was already on the platform about to board the train. No one approached either of them . . .

By the time they reached the flat on Pestalozzi Strasse, it was nearly eight o'clock. Rosa was in a trance, completely overwhelmed. But they had to get ready for her mother, still with the neighbor. Sonny guided Rosa into the bedroom, grabbed the nearest dress, and held it out to her. She stared at him blankly.

"Rosa, you have to change clothes," he said gently.

"Oh," she said, her voice flat. She began to disrobe. The blood-caked dress fell to the floor. Sonny turned to leave, but she said, "No. Stay . . . help me." Sonny handed her the clean dress, but she stepped back and shook her head. "I have to wash away his filth." She removed her undergarments and said, "My robe."

While Rosa bathed, Sonny washed the blood from her coat and put the bloody dress in a paper sack. He'd ditch it somewhere on his way to No. 53. He recounted the day's events in his mind, retracing the steps leading to Lieutenant Walter's end—and Albert's sudden intrusion. He regretted none of it but what Rosa had endured. He would take the blame or the credit—but deny she had any part in the act. She was free, her father would soon be free, and Lieutenant Walter would recede to history's ash heap.

He heard Rosa moving, and in several minutes she joined him fully dressed, apparently refreshed, managing a thin smile.

"Thank you . . . for everything." She walked to the window and pulled the curtain aside. The two, standing close, joined in a way few couples ever were, watched the street below.

Sonny detected a fleeting steeliness in her eyes that she hadn't had before. He searched for other signs that she'd passed the threshold into a cruel, unimaginable world—the set of her jaw, a flicker in her eyes, the way she held her head. But nothing overt betrayed her. The events were too fresh. Would she emerge unscathed? What torment might come? Whatever it was, he would be there to help. No one but him, perhaps a few friends, could ever know what she had endured—that a Gestapo officer had died for his lusty design.

Sonny's first duty was to Rosa. He would give his own emotions a shrug for now, deal with them later. Soon, he'd fetch her mother and arrange for transport to Stuttgarter Strasse, where they would stay 'til they left Germany. But Rosa had to be ready before she met her mother with the good news.

As they embraced, Rosa murmured, "It's over . . . it's over." Then she moved away, her face distorted. "Father! Someone has to get my father—you promised."

"Yes, plans will be made."

After half an hour of talking and crying, Rose returned to her old, though newly enlightened, self. She sighed and said it was time. Sonny brought a tearful Frau Fischer back to the flat. When he left—with paper bag, Walther PPK, and the specter of Albert hanging over him—mother and daughter were hugging, crying.

32

Evil is easy and has infinite forms.
—Blaise Pascal

When Sonny arrived at the alley door, he found that Otto had just returned. They stood in the kitchen without talking until Otto said, "Tell me what happened."

Sonny's shoulders sagged so that when he shrugged it was like a hiccup. His jaw was bruised, and veins like red rivers ran through the whites of his eyes. But what really gave him away was avoiding Otto's gaze. Despite his vocation, being furtive was not a part of his persona.

"Well?" Otto persisted.

Finally, Sonny said, "A day from hell." He sat down heavily.

"And?" Otto implored his friend to continue.

"I'm hungry. Is there anything to eat?" Sonny got up and rummaged around the kitchen for several minutes, in no particular hurry to tell his story. Then he ate in silence, Otto waiting.

Sonny finished eating, then said, "Rosa's father will be released tomorrow." But everything about him—his posture, sullen mood, and reticence—contradicted the joy and relief that might have marked the occasion.

"That's good news," Otto started, as he searched Sonny's face for a clue, an indication of what had gone wrong, because surely something had. "So why do you look like shit?"

Sonny checked the hall—no one was around. They could find an empty room, but—what the hell, he didn't care.

Not knowing how to start, he asked a question. "Have you ever wanted to kill someone?" His eyes were like darts. "I don't mean killing Hitler or Göring, that's easy—shit," he hissed, "they should all be dead.

And not just because some son of a bitch on the street did or said something you didn't like, where you'd think, 'What an asshole. If I had the chance I'd . . .'"

Frowning, he waved his hand, then shrugged wearily. "The feeling passes, you cool off . . . the next time you see the guy—if you ever do—you've already forgotten."

Straightening, he set his jaw defiantly. His eyes flashed as if he'd suddenly become mad. "No! I'm talking blood-on-your-hands killing."

Sonny shook his head, and his eyes wandered past his friend to a distant place. "I'm talking about murderous rage . . . grabs your head in both hands and tightens. All you hear, see, touch, smell, is boundless fury. Uncontrollable anger that won't, can't, release until he's limp, dead at your feet."

His fists clenched so tight his knuckles turned white, his pupils contracted. Then, shoulders relaxed, he leaned forward and asked in a calm, measured voice, "Well . . . have you?"

Otto backed off, flinching at the onslaught. He chewed on a question he didn't know how to answer, didn't know whether Sonny even wanted him to. Before it all crumbled and went to hell—sure, he'd brawled in the street with comrades at his side. They'd spilled their share of Nazi blood and some of their own, but so far as he knew, he'd never left a corpse behind. Some of the comrades had carried revolvers and used them if necessary, but he never had.

Otto assessed his friend waiting for an answer. He seemed a stranger. The Sonny he knew hated violence—never even went to rallies. Hell, he had refused to join the Communist Party! They'd been close friends for years, but Otto had never seen him like this.

An eerie calm descended on the room as Sonny waited for an answer.

Otto met his stare, opened his mouth, and shook his head. Finally he said, "I hate the Nazis for what they have done to my friends and to me—you know that already. I took to the streets, brawled just like the others, but did I kill someone? Sure, I've thought about it, but I'm not a killer."

He almost said, "And you aren't either." But then he remembered something about himself—in November '32, near the end, watching helplessly as a SA thug busted a comrade's head, blood streaming down his face. Without thinking, he'd picked up a pipe that someone had dropped, and he sprang, catching the Nazi behind the ear, knocking him cold. He'd been ready to hit him again—apply the *coup de grace*—but his comrade's groaning had roused him. He needed help more than the SA guy needed a shattered skull. So he dropped the pipe, and they got the hell out of there.

"Once. But I didn't do it. But could I?" He knew he could have. "What the hell's going on?

"Damn it! What stopped you? It's a simple, fucking question," said Sonny. His words came out in a slow, even cadence. Then he broke eye contact and began circling his friend. "That you could kill a guy and be glad you did?" He grabbed Otto's shoulders, and his eyes widened with savage intensity. "The bastard deserved it," he said quietly.

Over the course of nearly an hour, Otto extracted the details of Sonny's day, starting with the appearance of the Hitler Youth at the Neckar Strasse Synagogue, through the events in Oranienburg. At the end, Otto exhaled in a low whistle, then went for the bottle of brandy. He poured two drinks. "To life!" Otto raised his glass.

Sonny smiled weakly, and they drank.

They sat quietly for a few minutes, until Otto said, "I'll arrange transport for Rosa and her mother."

"Thanks, but I'll do it," Sonny said. "I'm all right."

Otto wasn't convinced. "Don't shed a tear for that asshole."

"I'm not worried about myself. I can deal with the nightmares, but what about Rosa? I was supposed to protect her. She was nearly . . . "

"Stop!" Otto slammed his palm on the table, making the glasses jump. "You saved her. What that piece of shit did was out of your control, just like everything else in this hellhole. Just be thankful you went along."

Sonny nodded, then leaned over the table, close to Otto, and said, "I killed him—alone."

"What?" Otto's face wrinkled in confusion.

Sonny tapped a finger on his chest. "I killed him—not Rosa and I—just me." Sonny stood up, put a hand on Otto's arm, and leaned inches from his face. "Promise me you'll tell no one—not Mina, not Karl, no one. I killed that Gestapo prick."

Otto nodded.

"Damn it! Say it!" Sonny's eyes widened to red-flecked, milky white moons as he squeezed Otto's arm.

Otto winced. "I promise."

Sonny forced an apologetic smile. "Good . . . thanks." Then he remembered the photograph and showed it to Otto.

"You're kidding," Otto started but saw the look on Sonny's face. "No, you're not."

Sounds in the hallway put an end to their conversation. Mina and Polly came into the kitchen. "What's going on?" Polly asked. "We heard shouting."

The men exchanged glances. Then Otto gestured with his head toward Sonny. "Something happened in Oranienburg."

Sonny told them, omitting all references to Rosa's involvement in the killing. They were horrified, though Polly took it better than Mina, who turned deathly pale. Sonny extracted promises that, as far as they were concerned, Rosa's parents would never know. Polly, without being asked, phoned Alfred and asked him to collect Rosa and her mother. He'd been to their door when he gathered the Milbergs, and he knew the address. Then she volunteered to travel to Oranienburg to get Rosa's father the next day.

Mina looked at Otto, and he nodded. Turning to Sonny, Mina said, "Rosa needs a woman she can to talk to. I'll be here when she comes." Returning to Otto, she declared with finality, "Then we're leaving."

Later the same day, Rosa and her mother left Alfred's car at the alley and entered No. 53. Sonny met them at the door and, after introducing them to the others, took them to a room upstairs. It was immediately apparent that Frau Fischer's malaise had lifted. Learning that her husband would return safely turned her into a different woman.

Not surprisingly, Rosa had withdrawn; her mother seemed satisfied, at least for now, to blame her condition simply on the trauma of the trip to Sachsenhausen. After they were settled, Polly and Mina joined them. Mina took Rosa's hand and led her to another room so they could talk.

As soon as Rosa left the room, Frau Fischer said, "Rosa isn't herself."

Sonny agreed. "It's all been a terrible emotional burden, as you well know, and it came to the top when she visited that awful place." He paused. "Forgive me for saying so, but neither have you been yourself." His words had the desired effect, and she said no more on the subject. Sonny adeptly turned to the logistical issue of collecting her husband the next day. Polly repeated her gracious offer.

"Thank you, Polly. That's very kind, but I feel much better now. It's my duty. I'll go," said Frau Fischer. They talked it over and in the end agreed that both would go.

Sonny excused himself to find Rosa and Mina.

Standing at Mina's door, Sonny listened for voices, then knocked softly. Mina's arm was around Rosa's shoulder; they'd been crying. One was fair, the other dark—like day and night—but they could have been sisters. He asked Mina for a few minutes alone with Rosa. After she left, they hugged without talking for several minutes, content to be close.

Rosa had been upset that Mina knew about Oranienburg, but in the end Mina's support was more important. Sonny assured her that no one save Otto knew of her part in the day's events. There could be no secrets among Sonny's friends and partners. Rosa's fears were fully assuaged when she learned that Polly would accompany her mother to Oranienburg. Freed from that burden, Rosa seemed resigned to an unclear fate.

In the few minutes they were together, Sonny noticed her eyes flickering vacantly, then fearfully, then softening. He read her responses with concern, unsure of what they meant. He was glad she wasn't hardened by her experience, at least not yet. He hoped she never would be. They talked of a life after Germany, where they'd go, how lucky they were to have each other . . . Sonny pulled her close, and they kissed. Then it was time for him to attend to errands. She clung to him. He promised to return soon. He found Mina, and she returned to sit with Rosa.

The next day Sonny was in the Mitte, meeting clients, delivering documents, when Herr Fischer arrived at No. 53. Polly met Sonny in the kitchen around five o'clock and gave him the good news. She handed him a newspaper, pointing to the headline, "Fire Destroys Large Swath of Oranienburg!"

He read: "A massive fire of unknown origin destroyed scores of warehouses and factories . . . no one was killed in the fire." A tight smile rose at the corners of his mouth. "That's true . . . bastard was already dead."

Polly explained: "It was chaos, but we walked unimpeded to the camp. I waited at the gate while Frau Fischer went inside." Her eyes misted as she told of women leaving the place downcast and demoralized, without husbands, sons, or fathers. "After about an hour, Elise emerged with Robert. He looked gaunt; his clothes were dirty, hanging on his body. I thought his condition worrisome, but he insists he's physically intact, happy to be free. All the way back, he looked out the window, held Elise's hand. It was only when he got here, washed up, and put on clean clothes that he started to talk."

"Did he talk about conditions in the camp?"

Shaking her head, she said, "No, not to me. He wants to meet you first. You're looking pretty good in his eyes." Polly smiled.

Sonny thanked her. He was about to go upstairs when Karl came in and put an arm around his shoulders: "Have no regrets, my friend. You performed admirably. One man hasn't done that much damage since Gavrilo Princip's shooting spree in Sarajevo."

"That's heady company," Sonny replied.

Karl got close and whispered, "It's one less creep to worry about and a mess for the authorities to deal with. You did well. Let's just hope Rosa comes out of this all right. And you too."

Sonny excused himself. He wanted to greet the man he'd been waiting to see for a month . . . Rosa's mother opened the door. "Hello, Sonny."

Herr Fischer was standing at the window with his back to the door. On hearing Sonny's name, he turned and smiled. Extending his hand, he said, "Robert Fischer . . . extremely pleased to meet you."

"Same here," Sonny began. He was looking at a tired, thinner version of the man in the picture Rosa had given him. His smile was slightly off kilter, his eyes dark like his daughter's. He was a little taller than Sonny had envisioned, though otherwise what he'd expected. "Herr Fischer, you gave us quite a scare. I'm glad you're finally safe."

"Please . . . call me Robert," then turning to his wife, he continued, "and Elise."

She smiled and nodded.

"Then Robert and Elise it shall be. Welcome to your temporary home."

"I don't know how we'll ever thank you," he began. "Elise told me you were a constant presence during our . . . separation, and a worthy companion to Rosa." His tone conveyed an understanding of the deepening relationship between Sonny and his daughter.

"It's what I—all of us here—do. And it's been my pleasure to get to know Rosa. She's an extraordinary woman." Sonny's declaration conveyed far more than Robert or Elise would ever know.

Elise stood with an arm around Robert's waist, as Rosa and he had stood the day before. Elise radiated a warm contentedness—vastly different from the woman Sonny had known before.

Speaking for the family for the first time in a month, Robert said, "We're ready to leave as soon as you give us the word."

"Can we talk later? I'd like to check on Rosa."

"Yes, I'd like to spend some time with you," Robert said. "Unfortunately, Rosa's not herself."

"Oranienburg was a wrenching experience. And of course, your detention was extremely difficult for her, as it was for Elise." Sonny turned to Elise. "I'm pleased you're so much better."

When Sonny knocked, Rosa and Mina were immersed in conversation. They stopped talking, and Mina asked, "Who is it?"

Sonny, pleased at their friendship, entered without answering.

"I'll be back," Mina said to Rosa.

When he bent to kiss Rosa, she pulled him playfully onto the bed. They embraced, and after several minutes, she said, "I feel better than I deserve to. Mina helps make the awfulness melt away, makes me forget what happened for a time. She hasn't had a close friend to talk with in three years, so it's good for both of us."

Lying on the bed, facing Sonny, an arm bent, head propped on hand, Rosa lifted her shoulder, as if shedding a burden. "She understands, in a way no one else could. We've talked about everything—why she stayed, why you and Otto stayed. I admire her, and I wish I had that kind of commitment."

"Don't sell yourself short. Look what you did," Sonny countered.

She shook her head. "I was pushed."

"Doesn't matter. Few would have acted so bravely. And soon you'll be gone. Mina's leaving any day now."

"I miss her already . . . Imagine how much I'll miss you," Rosa said as she wrapped her arms around him.

She looked better to him than the day they had met. Still, he searched for changes in her behavior. She seemed fine, at least for now. "I finally met your father. He seems well, ready to leave."

"That's an understatement."

"Did he talk about the camp?"

Rosa shook her head. "Not to me." She sighed. "I cry whenever I see him. So they walk on eggshells around me."

"It will get better . . ."

Two days later she was gone. They'd spent their last evening together sequestered in her little room. When Sonny was about to leave, reluctantly, Rosa tearfully refused to let him go. He could not stay, not with her parents across the hall. But she would not be denied.

"You proved your love, so will I . . . stay!" And she'd kept at it, her arms wrapped around him, until she'd worn him down. Once he agreed, sensuality overcame the sensible thing to do. She succeeded in seducing him without having to work particularly hard at it. They lay together nearly until the night succumbed to dawn, and he finally left her room.

It was late morning; Sonny drank his coffee, rapping his knuckle on Gustav's table. He'd come straightaway from bidding farewell to Rosa. After promising to join her soon, he'd watched her drive off with her parents in Alfred's car. He already missed her desperately.

"This is the last time." Sonny said, his voice breaking as he faced his friend and mentor.

"Don't go melancholy. You'll have us both crying," Emil protested, looking away.

"Since we first met out there,' Sonny pointed toward the old alley warehouse below, "I've spent more time with you than anyone, including Polly."

"Like an old married couple."

Sonny smiled. "But without the bickering. And it was right here," again he rapped the table, "that I told you of our scheme to smuggle Jews, then pitched the Thiemann job. Both times you said I was crazy. Now look at us."

Emil scratched at the back of his head. "Ja, it worked out well—would have been perfect if that asshole hadn't shown up."

"Poor Willy," Sonny lamented, his mind flipping to the image of another corpse. He looked away, waiting for the right time to tell Emil.

"So you're finally leaving." Emil changed the subject. Thiemann had been hashed, rehashed, with nothing further to be gained.

"You've been trying to get rid of me for months," Sonny said.

"Sure, why not? Otherwise, you'd come up with another harebrained scheme."

"Hell, I was just the messenger. We needed you—a seasoned second-story man—to make both work."

"Stop! You're making an old man of me."

"Well?" Sonny laughed. "Let's say . . . you were practiced in a specialty that suited our needs."

"Much better."

Neither spoke. The faint rhythm of the heating pipes textured their silence, punctuated by voices from the hallway. It seemed the right time. Emil hadn't seen Sonny since Joseph had agreed to move, and he hadn't noticed his jaw. The swelling was down, and the pretty shade of reddish purple had faded, though it was still visible. Sonny was jumpy, eager to tell his story: "That was quite a fire in Oranienburg."

Emil shot him a look, his eyes narrowing. He sensed the change in Sonny's mood, and whistled softly. "Ja, one hell of a mess."

Sonny cracked a devious smile. "You can thank me for that."

"What the hell you talking about?"

Sonny told him everything, just as he had told Otto. By the end of his telling, Emil was pacing the kitchen, shaking his head. Then he stopped and leaned over Sonny to examine his jaw. "Can't believe I didn't see that. Damn! That's one hell of a story."

"One we survived to tell, though I worry about Rosa."

"What about her father?"

Sonny told him. "He seems to have come through intact." Sonny brightened. "We get on well, and he knew my Uncle Simon."

"Good. That's nice," Emil said absently, stuck on the morbid affair in Oranienburg. "It's a nasty world we live in—when it's not a God-awful one." Shaking his head, he pointed a thick finger at Sonny. "You going to be all right?"

"So far no remorse, no nightmares—no bloody heads rolling around on the floor, bricks dripping blood, knives sticking from bloody chests. It's Karl's story, mixed with what Robert has told me about Sachsenhausen, that curses me at night." Sonny's lips curled into a sour smirk, as if he'd swallowed vinegar.

"There's something else." Sonny told Emil about the photograph, about Albert.

"Let me see it," Emil asked.

Sonny pointed out Albert and the dead man.

Emil examined the faces.

"It's out of control," Sonny lamented.

Emil hummed softly, considering, then said, "That's for sure—nothing to do about it now." Then he changed the topic. "Robert's story must have confirmed what Karl told us."

"More or less. The morning after he arrived, he asked Elise to excuse us, and we talked."

"Had he already told her?"

"I think so, at least in part, but not Rosa . . . said he wasn't going to."

"They're carrying terrible secrets. He may tell her someday, or not. Same with her." Emil walked to the window overlooking his corner of Wedding. "Experiences fade, hide in dusty corners," he turned to Sonny, tapping a finger on his forehead, "and pop out at night, drive you crazy. They'll have to learn to harness their demons, just like you."

"Don't like the sound of that," Sonny said. Then he gave Emil an abbreviated version of Robert's story. "He thought he'd never get out alive. Cold, shitty, overcrowded barracks, little food and water—all that was the same. Guards always screaming at some poor sod, once in his face. He witnessed several beatings, avoided them himself. Never mentioned the poor fellows hanging on the gallows. I couldn't ask . . . it would have felt like an intrusion after what he's endured."

"He must have seen it," Emil said.

Sonny nodded. "He stuck with several men he knew, and that helped to pull them through. Now, they're all safe. After two days, he shut down emotionally, though he didn't put it that way. Physically, he's unscathed."

"All he can do is hope for the best," Emil offered. "He may have repressed the worst of it—guys they hung, maybe some other stuff."

"How the hell does that work?"

"Damned if I know. The mind is a funny thing; it takes over, blots things out like they never happened. Especially something like that, but the experience never goes away. I knew a few shell-shocked guys in the war. They're all messed up."

Sonny's respect for the mind's tenuous hold on reality had grown after his little dustup during the garbage crisis. "That's why I'm worried about Rosa."

"You'll help her."

"Robert knows Rosa is different, though he doesn't know why. Hell, all she's done around him is cry. And he's got his own readjustment to work on. He probably has no idea how Elise suffered, though she probably told him." Sonny's face melted into a sheepish smile. "He thinks I'm some sort of savior, pulling Rosa and Elise through it all, now delivering his family to freedom."

"What the hell—go with it," Emil said with a laugh.

"Well, in the afterglow I got a little carried away . . . told him I love his daughter . . . want to marry to her."

"Good for you." Emil's smile broadened, his eyes closing to slits.

"Hadn't even asked Rosa yet," Sonny admitted.

"I assume you remedied that."

"Oh, ja. I pulled that horse from behind the cart—set it right."

"Well?"

Sonny grinned. "She said she would have asked if I hadn't." Then his smile faded, and he lowered his voice. "She was incredibly brave—thinking she was on her own with that monster. Not many would have done what she did."

"She's a fighter. By the time this mess is over, she'll wish she had gotten more of them."

Sonny laughed bitterly and pounded a fist on the table. Cups clattered, spilling coffee onto the saucers. "God damn them!"

"Ja, damn them, but take it easy, or you'll face Lisle's wrath," Emil warned. "You've done all you could—soon they'll be with Fritz."

"It's never enough! What about the others, the ones who won't get out?" He slowly shook his head.

They sat in silence, Sonny fingering his cup, Emil staring into space. Then Sonny's face lit up. "Almost forgot . . . I have a present for you." He reached into his jacket and pulled out the pistol, set it on the table.

Emil examined it—engaging, disengaging the safety, checking the load. There were four bullets. "I'll scrape off the serial number and hide it. Thanks."

"Here's his Gestapo ID." He put the card on the table next to the photograph.

Emil frowned. "That was dumb." His finger sliced across his throat.

Sonny reddened. He should have known better.

"You weren't thinking clearly." Emil grabbed the card, read the name and rank, then tore it into little pieces He burned them in a saucer.

Sonny watched the flames die, then said, "There's more. Yesterday I tried again to persuade Solomon to leave with his family. But I ended up bidding him farewell. He turned me down a second time . . . and there is more disquieting news. A couple of days ago, Solomon was cleaning up his stall when he spotted a guy talking with the manager. He recognized the man but couldn't attach a name. Then it dawned on him—it was Albert, with the dancing hands, dangling a cigarette, snooping around. Solomon didn't stick around to find out why." Sonny's eyes widened. "And something else—talk about timing—rumor has it that a couple of days ago there was a raid in Joseph's old building. Solomon couldn't confirm it, but if it's true . . ."

"That's too close—I don't like it." Emil said. "Another reason to beat a quick path to the border." He took another look at the photograph.

"Don't worry, I'll be on the train this time tomorrow morning. I've come to say goodbye."

But Emil was staring at the picture of Albert. "You going to keep this?"

Sonny considered, then asked, "Got a scissors handy? I'll trim the other three off, keep Albert's face—a reminder."

"What the hell for? A souvenir? Get him to autograph it when you two finally meet up?" Emil poured more coffee, drank, then said, "Do what you want. I'm just glad you're leaving." He sighed. "I wish you the best."

"Same to you."

"Back to Aachen, where your trouble began," Emil mused.

"If the little shit's here, he can't be in Aachen," Sonny surmised.

"If he's still here! That was two days ago. Maybe he left. And why did he come? Was he on temporary assignment, looking for you, or on personal leave in the big city? Come to have a little chat with your old landlord, a guy he doesn't know, then hang around the warehouse for old times' sake?" Despite the sarcasm, Emil's answers begged answers they didn't have. "Reasons don't matter—he's Gestapo, and he's looking for you." Emil pounded on the table, not hard enough to disturb the cups and saucers, or Lisle.

Discouraged, Sonny fell back in his chair, pulled at an eyebrow, and looked thoughtfully at Emil. "I don't know what to think anymore."

"It may come to nothing," Emil offered, trying to mollify him.

"Right," Sonny agreed, unconvinced, squirming in his chair like a three-year-old. "Except for making me nervous as hell."

"You should be nervous. Don't relax. Keep a look out. Stay a step ahead . . . understand?" The lecture over, Emil stared at Sonny. Then he nodded, apparently having made up his mind about something. "I've got to go to Aachen, pay the boys . . . wasn't going until next week. I'll keep you company."

Sonny liked that idea, and they made plans to take the 8:15 from Kaiser Friedrich Station . . .

Later that day, on a street corner in Neukölln, Sonny climbed into the back of a truck. Alfred drove to a fancy Charlottenburg neighborhood and parked in the back of a big house, relatively modest for the area.

"You've got an hour, then I go back," Alfred told Sonny. Carrying a box of documents, Sonny got directions to Joseph's room and surprised his old friend . . .

Joseph's face opened to a broad smile. "Hadn't expected to see you again . . . thought we'd already said our goodbyes."

"I needed to see you—your new room. Get a last look . . ." Sonny stopped in front of *Berlin Street Scene*—the home they'd taken away.

"Nostalgia does wonders for the psyche, but I'm too rooted in the present," Joseph said.

"It's all we have left," Sonny said sadly.

"Ach! You have a future," Joseph exclaimed, but he sensed a change in his friend. "What is it, Sonny? World-weariness? You're different."

"I am," Sonny admitted, then told him about the Jew on Neckar Strasse, Oranienburg, Albert's confounding connection with the dead man, everything.

"Christ!" Joseph muttered, putting a hand on Sonny shoulder. "I'm so sorry. Bear your burden well. How is Rosa holding up?"

Sonny shrugged. "She's holding up, or was when I said goodbye this morning. She'll be with Fritz soon."

"Relay my best wishes—her nights free of demons." Joseph's smile was forced.

"We plan to marry—when we're settled."

"Mazel tov!" Joseph exclaimed, and he embraced Sonny.

"Thank you."

"I'll miss you terribly."

Sonny nodded. "Me too . . . so let's say 'until we meet again.'"

"Yes, of course. Then I'll meet Rosa and the children," Joseph said. Now his smile was warm, genuine.

They were lying, of course. They would never see each other again, and they knew it. Their world was about to implode. But they kept up the charade.

"When sanity returns."

Joseph's smile evaporated. "That may be a long time coming."

"By the way," Sonny said, "we didn't get you out of the Mitte too soon." He told him about the rumored raid.

"Thank God for Herr Wagner."

"Ja . . . I'll still worry about you," Sonny said.

"Don't. I'm in a safe house," Joseph replied dryly.

Sonny laughed. "Nobody's safe, not anymore."

Joseph went to a bookcase, removed a book, and thumbed through its well-worn pages. Finding what he was looking for, he read, "'Whoever fights monsters should see to it that in the process he doesn't become a monster'—Nietzsche." He closed the book. "Sonny, you're a smuggler—a guy who always did a little of this, a little of that—not a warrior. Be careful that you don't like it too well." Joseph set the book down.

"War came to us when Willy died and again in Oranienburg. It's the card I've been dealt."

"Maybe so," Joseph agreed. "But I'll remember you differently."

"I'm still that guy."

"Of course," Joseph answered, trying to be persuaded.

"We've done a lot of good," Sonny said.

"It's never enough. Our little dribs and drabs barely make a dent. Hearing your story now, I'm dispirited."

"Try not to be discouraged. You've done more than could be expected of anyone. You're only human."

"Frail, vain, lustful, and lazy."

"You?" Sonny laughed at the notion.

Joseph, framed by the window at the back of the grand house, waved. Sonny waved back, climbed into the back of the truck, and was gone. Memories of the warehouse of his youth—frolicking with Mischa and Sophie, sitting for hours on the floor in Joseph's bookstall—dominated his thoughts, adding to his growing melancholy. Alfred stopped near Hermanplatz, long enough for Sonny to exit. Then he sped away.

Sonny spent his last night in Berlin at No. 53. He sat with Polly and Karl, lamenting the book burning, Willy's death, the hope of their founding alliance. Then Karl recalled his surprise at hearing Sonny's smuggler's tale, laughing with delight. Sonny glanced at Polly and felt his face flush. Though she managed to smile, her mirth was less robust than Karl's. That she was even present would have been impossible before . . .

Karl and Polly would continue the operation with Joseph and Emil, regardless of events. They were in too far to stop now. Confessing Church tentacles ran deep into every large city in Germany, into the countryside. Recently, they'd made contact with other groups, one purportedly providing intelligence to the Soviets. Karl was vague. How that would affect the operation remained unclear. And Sonny didn't want to know.

Living in an unrelenting police state that spent considerable resources in spying on its people made secrecy a paramount concern. They lived in a shrinking netherworld. Like-minded Germans were arrested every day for far less inflammatory acts than theirs. The friends Sonny would leave behind weren't so sanguine as to believe they'd go on forever, but they could try. Death was a real possibility, an accepted risk. Their commitment comforted Sonny but also made it harder for him to leave.

Finally, Sonny stifled a yawn to say goodbye for the last time. A sense of discomfort, not there earlier, gripped the three compatriots. No one spoke until Sonny broke the standstill. "Saying thanks for what you've both done is woefully inadequate, so I won't. And I won't try to convince you to leave. Stay well." They hugged, and Sonny went upstairs.

He'd already thanked Frau Moltke for opening her house to them. Otto and Mina had gone the previous day; now they were probably with Fritz. Sonny planned to catch up with them in Plombieres or somewhere in Belgium. When he said goodbye to Lisle, she kissed him on the cheek and told him to stay out of trouble, to take care of Rosa. Then she said, "What are we going to do for excitement without you?"

Sonny's last task had been to deliver documents to the Caro family. He was delighted to discover that Will had been released in good health. But Rosa's bittersweet departure had put him at loose ends. They'd had little time together at No. 53. Still, they had taken advantage of what they had, savoring their final night together. Rosa had pleaded with Sonny to leave with them, but that would have been too risky.

Especially cautious after the carnage at Oranienburg, he couldn't chance a walk with Rosa on the banks of the canal as Mina and Otto had done just months before. So they spent the hours remaining ensconced in the little room, succumbing to their passion for each other. Then she was gone, with another promise that they'd meet in a few days, in Plombieres or Antwerp. Sonny missed her terribly, felt out of sorts. For the first time in months, he had nobody to meet, no documents to deliver, no payments to collect, no instructions to impart.

After he'd limped back to Berlin from Aachen, been discovered by Albert, his world had collapsed. In the ashes, they had built something magnificent—an organization to be proud of. He went to the window, pulled the curtain aside, and peered onto Stuttgarter Strasse. That's when the realization hit—the game was over for him.

Gazing for the last time at *Berlin Street Scene* and hugging Joseph brought an ache to the pit of his stomach for all he'd lost, was losing. His father, his mother, the cabarets and clubs, American jazz, theater, art, the old life of the warehouse, his beloved Berlin—now a hostile place.

Uncle Simon had understood the danger earlier and more clearly than most and succumbed to the oppression—and his inner demons. Sonny had wanted to see his uncle's death as noble, the ultimate protest, but it was not. Though he'd long forgiven him, Simon had failed. But perhaps that was too harsh a judgment for a man ill equipped for Nazi villainy. Sonny was more resilient, bore his burdens more lightly and in a different way. He'd always choose life over death, and he had reason for hope: a new life with Rosa in Antwerp, Paris, maybe London. He looked forward to whatever there might be.

One step at a time. First, he had to get to Aachen, then to Reinartzkehl, without confronting Albert. His hope for an alternate life course, one without Albert dogging his every move, one in which the KPD and the SPD coalesced to defeat the Nazis, had been in vain. In his imagined world, the Republic endured, consigning Hitler to history's dung heap. Cabarets flourished. Brecht and Weill, Grosz and Einstein, produced, delighted, and challenged the frontiers of music, theater, and science—in Germany. He and Emil brought contraband into Germany for Franco, still presiding at the warehouse.

Sonny wondered whether in that alternative world he and Polly would still be together. There would be no Rosa, no dead lieutenant, no Sachsenhausen. Would he make such a trade? Sonny shuddered. He gave it up, no more enlightened than when he'd begun his musing. He was leaving tomorrow and should be glad there was nothing left to do.

33

All have not the gift of martyrdom.
—John Dryden

The brim of his hat pulled down, Sonny leaned against a post. The big clock read 7:50. He swept the railway platform, looking for a thin, nervous man smoking a cigarette. The faces blurred. A hand fell on his shoulder, and he jumped.

"Easy, it's me," Emil whispered.

"Don't sneak up like that."

They boarded the train, found an empty compartment, and Sonny immediately closed the curtain to the corridor. He faced the window. Though his identification card said Paul Sander, Albert wouldn't be fooled...

When they reached Aachen, the sun had long since set. Sonny shivered, more from frayed nerves than from cold. Following in Emil's ample wake, he snaked through the exiting passengers.

Self-quarantined, Sonny hadn't left the compartment but sat with his face hidden in a newspaper staring out the window, Emil shielding him from the passageway. He had allowed Albert to get under his skin. He couldn't shake the feeling Albert was somewhere nearby. Every lurch of the train, every sound, had Sonny on edge.

Before they reached the terminal, Emil stopped suddenly, and they nearly collided. "Hey, what?" Sonny asked.

"Not sure," said Emil. "Settle down. I'm going to check on something. Wait for me across from the 'Gents.' If I'm not there in ten minutes, meet me at the café."

Günter would be waiting at the blue-curtained café across from Frau Freyer's flat. He would collect the payment for passage and drive Sonny to Reinartzkehl. Now, Sonny was standing in shadow, keeping the restroom in sight, fretting over what Emil's leaving him might be about.

Ten minutes turned to fifteen, and reluctantly Sonny crossed the street to stand in a shop entry, his eyes glued to the station entrance. People came and went—still no Emil and no hint as to what had spooked him. After twenty minutes, a rush of panic rose from Sonny's chest to his head. His nostrils filled with the memory of dead, burnt-out synagogues, further fanning his fears. He tapped his foot on the pavement.

Where the hell was Emil? He never did anything without a reason. He must have seen something or someone—it had to be Albert. That's what Sonny had figured all along—he'd just been afraid to admit it.

After waiting too long, he headed toward the square, keeping to the shadows. His footsteps echoed on the cobblestones. He stopped, glanced back. The sound stopped—no one was there. Across from the square, two men left the tavern he and Emil had vacated months earlier, right before Albert had intruded. Sonny turned and walked the long way around.

Once past the square, he'd be at the café in ten minutes, no more. Across the street, a man approached. Sonny held his breath until he passed . . . Exhausted, he finally stood in the doorway of Frau Freyer's building, watching the little café. All he could see between the curtains of its fogged-over windows were vague outlines.

About to cross the street, Sonny heard an approaching car and slid back into the doorway. A black Mercedes 260D, the kind favored by the Gestapo, crept by, then turned left, giving the occupants a good look at the café, though they wouldn't be able to see inside any better than he. Sonny stiffened. Would he be walking into a trap?

Still moving slowly, the black sedan took another left turn at the far corner. In a few minutes, he heard the familiar diesel coming toward him, repeating its trip past the café. Just as the sedan reached him, a flickering light ignited in the back seat. Sonny saw someone lighting a cigarette, but he couldn't make out the face. *Shit*! Someone in authority was interested in the café.

Now was a good time to pay Frau Freyer another visit, to get off the street. She was always home, so he knocked twice, waited until he heard a faint "I'm coming." The door opened onto the tiny, smiling woman. Once he was seated and she had poured him a glass of sherry, she said, "Frankly, I've been expecting you."

Comforted by her company, Sonny relaxed for the first time since leaving Berlin, his fear waning to tolerable. Though old and frail, she had sparkling, intelligent eyes, now fixed on him.

"How have you been since we last met?" he asked.

She nodded almost imperceptibly. "As good as can be expected under the circumstances."

"Yes, of course, the past month has been . . ."

" . . . an abomination."

Sonny nodded, then asked, "Am I that predictable?"

"No, but considering the events of the recent past, you should be heading west. Like their pillaging Hun ancestors, the miscreants have had their way with our Jewish neighbors. The police stand by and do nothing, and from what I've heard, too often they assist in the mischief. I assumed you would make haste to leave our blessed fatherland had you not already done so." She was sarcastic though deathly serious.

She went on: "Herr Glaser avoided arrest, thank God." She pointed to the floor. "He is a widower and lives, rather *lived*, on the floor below. His children emigrated to America some years ago, and he is now on his way to them." Distracted, she sighed and took a sip of sherry.

She returned, though not to the present. "I nursed casualties from that miserable waste of human life beyond the border—the Great War." Her hand fluttered in a halfhearted wave in Fritz's direction. "Such terrible carnage, now this. I'm ashamed of my government. It is run by fools." Frau Freyer took another sip of sherry and set the glass down carefully. "I am glad you are well—and for your company."

Sonny raised his glass. "Thank you. I wish you the same."

Instead of raising her glass, she slowly rotated her arthritic hand, like a wobbly spinning top. "I am an old lady who never leaves her flat. Any visitor, especially you, is a welcome diversion. Where was I?" She paused. "News reached me . . . I hid Herr Glaser and several others until the insanity blew over."

"That was brave."

She shrugged. "What can they do to me?"

"Nevertheless, your bravery is admirable."

Relenting, she acknowledged his compliment with a barely perceptible nod. "I could not sit idly by while old friends were arrested."

"You said there were more than one." Sonny drank his sherry, looked to the window, his mind drifting to Emil, the black sedan.

"Six in all," she answered. "Now they are all safely out of Germany."

"Good," Sonny offered absently, then changed the subject. "Just moments ago, while I was waiting to cross to the café, a Gestapo staff car—at least that's what I think it was—drove by slowly, twice. I didn't go in." Sonny waggled two fingers in the air. "Made me nervous . . . that's a funny way to do surveillance. They don't normally advertise their presence. Of course, none of this may have anything to do with my friends or me. Can you shed any light on this curiosity and our little café?"

Frau Freyer cleared her throat. "I have seen that automobile or one like it, and I conclude it has nothing to do with your operations."

"Really?" Sonny was impressed.

"I believe it is an affair of the heart." She coughed and looked away, slightly embarrassed. "A young lady and her suitor rendezvous at the café. He arrives in that automobile, and they leave together. He is generally in uniform, though I have no idea whether he is part of the Gestapo."

"He may be army," Sonny acknowledged.

"Perhaps . . . I can tell you that they meet twice a week at the café." She paused. "I believe it is on Tuesday and Friday at seven o'clock, and they have met for the past several months. What time is it now?" She craned her neck to see the clock on the table.

Sonny glanced at his watch. "It's nearly eight—Tuesday." Then he added, "13 December . . . I believe." If she was right, the officer wasn't his concern, but he didn't like the idea of sharing the little café with an army or Gestapo officer and his mistress. "So why didn't he stop?" he asked.

"Who knows? Sometimes he enters the café. Sometimes he waits for her in the sedan near the door. She is much younger—pretty, with dark hair . . . I suspect he is an unhappily married man."

"What does he look like?"

"Older, heavyset, jowly—thoroughly awful." She made a sour face.

"He didn't go in or stop . . ." Sonny left it hanging.

Frau Freyer finished for him. "Maybe she did not come or she was late, and he gave up or has come a third time to collect her."

Sonny smiled. "Maybe."

She took another sip of sherry, and they sat silently until she asked, "Are you leaving now?"

"Yes. I wanted to say goodbye."

"And so you have. I wish you Godspeed." She smiled and had the good grace not to ask how the black sedan fit into his visit.

"Thank you. The problem is that my friend disappeared at the station, said he'd meet me over there." He pointed toward the café. "He's a very prudent fellow, so he must have seen something, but he didn't say what. Otherwise he wouldn't have given me the slip."

Her brow wrinkled. "The slip?"

" . . . eluded me."

"Ah," she sang. "The slip. I like it. Herr Glaser gave them the slip."

"Exactly," Sonny agreed. Maybe Emil had been in the café with Günter all along. "Thank you for the sherry. I better look for my friend, actually two friends. The missing one's from Berlin, and the other lives here. You've probably seen them both."

"I recall the big man, but the other . . ." She shook her head. "He is less memorable. So where will you go?"

"First to the café . . . then?" Sonny frowned and shook his head. "Regardless, it's been my pleasure to know you."

"Mine as well." Frau Freyer's smile faded. "Be careful, Sonny. Remember you are always welcome here." He walked across the room, took her hand in both of his, and kissed her cheek.

Outside, he walked to the café and pressed his nose against the windowpane. Günter sat alone. There was no one in uniform, no pretty brunette, so he walked inside.

"What the hell happened?" Günter whispered before Sonny had a chance to sat down. Cold coffee sat near an ashtray of dead cigarette butts and a folded newspaper. Squinting at the smoke from the cigarette stuck in the corner of his mouth, he glanced at his watch. "You're an hour late—scared the hell out of me."

"Sorry. Couldn't be helped," Sonny looked around the café. "Have you seen a pretty brunette?"

"What are you talking about? No. Now tell me what's going on."

"But first, did a family named Fischer—mother, father, daughter—come through? And Otto, with a striking blonde?"

Günter took a drag, exhaled, and calmed down. After several seconds he asked, "Good-looking daughter?"

Sonny nodded.

"Ja, no problem. And it was good meeting Otto and his girl. So she's the daughter of the grumpy big shot we took across in the spring."

Sonny sighed with relief. "Good! I've got a personal interest in all of them."

Frowning, Günter folded his arms across his chest. "I'm waiting."

"Okay . . . I was watching from across the street—to be safe—and a Gestapo staff car drove by, slow, twice . . . like he was looking for someone in the café. I got spooked."

"Why were you watching?"

Sonny told Günter about Emil slipping away at the station, his own visit to Frau Freyer. " . . . . It's nothing to do with us, but I don't like sharing our little café with a Gestapo officer and his whore. I suggest you find a different place."

"Ja," was all Günter said.

"I don't trust coincidences. First Emil vanishes, then the Gestapo drives by." Sonny's eyes drifted to the door. Still no Emil.

Carefully removing the cigarette from his mouth, Günter dumped the long ash, played with a corner of the newspaper, and rubbed his chin stubble. "So what do we do?"

"I'm not crossing over until I know Emil's safe—and what's going on," Sonny said with finality, glancing again at the door.

"I think we should get out of here." Günter started. He'd been checking the door with compulsive regularity since Sonny told him about the black sedan.

"What if Emil comes?"

Both stared at the door in silence until Günter gestured with his head toward the street. "Does Emil know about the old lady?"

Sonny shook his head. "No, he wouldn't go there. Would he go to your place?"

"He'd never find it."

They were discussing their options, forgetting the door, when a shadow covered the table like a cloud blocking out the sun. They looked up at Emil's smiling face.

"Good evening. Sorry I'm late," he said cheerfully, as if he were only late for dinner.

Both men were talking at once, so Emil ignored them, sat down, and nonchalantly drank Sonny's coffee. Then he sat back, crossed his arms over his chest, and waited until they were silent. Günter lit another cigarette, and Sonny fingered his now-empty cup. They stared expectantly until, unable to bear it any longer, Sonny blurted, "Well?"

"Not here," he replied bluntly.

"Let's go," Günter responded, his relief palpable . . .

They sat in Günter's automobile behind an abandoned warehouse in the industrial section where Emil had taken Sonny on his first trip to Aachen. Sonny was just as afraid as he had been then, but he said nothing. Instead, he and Günter turned to face Emil in the back seat. Ambient light from the cloud cover muddied Emil's face. The hum of the idling engine was the only sound.

"When we got on the train in Berlin, I made out two men as Gestapo—they weren't trying to hide it."

"Then why did you say you didn't see anything?" Sonny protested.

"You were already too scared."

Sonny didn't respond.

"One was older, but the other one looked like Albert. I recognized him from the photograph, but I couldn't be sure. So I followed him, discreetly," Emil said.

"*And*?"

Emil shook his head. "I lost him."

"Still, you should have told me. What if he came through the car and saw me?" Sonny's glare was piercing; his hands were shaking at the thought.

"Would have made matters worse," Emil argued.

"Who the hell is Albert?" Günter's question broke through their bickering.

"You checked him out for us last year—found out he was working the border. During the war games, he spotted Sonny from the Aachen square," Emil explained.

"Now I remember."

"He's Gestapo, knows Sonny from the old days—been looking for him."

Günter whistled through his teeth. "Shit! For how long?"

Sonny shrugged, thought about his conversation with Polly, remembered looking at the calendar. "Couple of weeks ago . . . first of December, that's when he paid a visit to my former landlord, asking questions. I found out the next day, immediately told Emil and the others. We moved Joseph. Then I heard Albert was poking around the warehouse where I used to have a stall. We lost contact sometime in '32. Saw him once three years ago, but we didn't talk. Then with all the bullshit happening . . . there was always something more important." He waved his hand, as if that explained everything.

"Sure, an avenging angel doesn't have time to worry," said Emil.

Sonny didn't bite at the sarcasm. Instead he spoke to Günter: "Albert sent me underground."

"Why now? I got the information more than a year ago." Neither had an answer, so Günter asked another: "What does he look like?"

"I'll show you a picture later," Sonny answered, then quickly described him.

"It makes no sense for the Aachen Gestapo to send a guy to Berlin," Emil said. "It's a damn bureaucracy. If they wanted Sonny, an agent in Berlin would handle the investigation. And not be polite doing it."

"Albert didn't even leave his card," Sonny interjected.

"Proof it's personal," Emil offered.

"Then why?" Sonny asked.

"Who the hell knows," said Günter.

"And if it's not personal?"

Emil shrugged. "Makes no sense . . . but those assholes never give up. Priorities may change, but if there's a file, they'll eventually get to it."

They fell silent. Then Emil squinted at Sonny. "You were jumpy enough after Oranienburg—that's why I didn't say anything."

"Oranienburg . . . that's Sachsenhausen. What the hell does that have to do with this?" said Günter.

They were distracted by a sound outside the car, maybe a small animal. Their heads turned toward the noise, but there was nothing to see.

"Cat. Or a rat," Günter surmised.

No one spoke. All were fixed on the noise, on Günter's question, on Albert. Then a match scraped on the box and flared an orange and red flame. Günter's face glowed as he lit a cigarette. Smoke filled the car.

"Damn," Emil cursed. He rolled down the window.

"Sorry," Günter muttered, opening his window and waving his hand in the air. The smoke dissipated. "You're going too fast, changing directions. I was with you about Albert stalking Sonny, but now you're talking Oranienburg—that's something else. I don't like secrets!" Günter spat out the word. "What the hell's going on?"

"Settle down," Emil soothed. "We'll tell you everything." He looked from Günter to Sonny. "Give him the short version."

Sonny sighed and wiped his mouth gingerly with the back of his hand, "I couldn't tell you in the café. Besides, I was too caught up in Emil's disappearing act—and Albert." He spent the next ten minutes telling Günter about the old Jew, about Rosa, Limping Man, the fire. "It's not every day a fellow gets the chance to square things with the Gestapo—and get away with it."

"Shit! I'd be jumpy too."

"Sonny's been a busy man. Now throw another fucked-up Gestapo into the mix—one obsessed with our very own fair Jew—and it's a real nasty Nazi stew."

"Hmm," Günter nodded.

"Albert's here and so am I," Sonny said under his breath.

Emil spoke to Günter. "All we know for sure is that Albert's looking for Sonny."

Günter's face glowed crimson as he took another drag. Stocky and shorter than Sonny, he shrank in his seat. "All this talk—suddenly I don't feel safe—let's go to my place."

"Go," Emil agreed.

Günter made sure they weren't being followed, then headed for the edge of town. In fifteen minutes he parked behind the small house in the clearing carved out of the forest. Under a starless sky, they could see almost nothing. Preoccupied, Sonny had paid little attention to Günter's route. He had only a vague idea of where they were—despite having visited the area before.

Günter's wife, Katrina—a plump, pleasant woman—met them at the door. She started a pot of coffee and put a plate of sweets on the table. They sat down to finish their talk. Katrina joined them but said little.

"Let me see the photograph." Günter held out his hand. "I'll use my contact to find out what I can about . . . what's his last name?"

"Schwarz."

"Sounds familiar," Günter said, handing the photograph to Katrina.

Rubbing her finger along the cut side, she studied it, then shook her head. "Never seen him. Where's the rest of the photo?"

Sonny sighed and told the story again.

"Oh, my dear God," Katrina lamented.

"One hell of a story," Emil agreed.

"If you're leaving, why do you need to know about Schwarz?" Günter asked.

"Good question," Emil said. Then he nudged Sonny in the ribs with an elbow. "Go. First thing in the morning. I can smell the chocolate and taste that good Trappist beer. You and Fritz can have some for me. Once you're gone, Albert's got nobody to find . . . if he's got something more, we'll deal with it."

It was tempting—that's why he was here, to leave. But Sonny's confidence was eroding. "What if he's on duty at the Reinartzkehl station?"

"What are the odds?" Günter asked.

"I could go, look around. Say I forgot my papers," Emil offered.

Shaking his head, Sonny said, "Too dangerous . . . won't let you do it."

"Ja." Then Emil turned toward Günter: "Can we find out where he's stationed?"

"I'll try."

They agreed that first thing in the morning Günter would visit his cousin Vincent at the courthouse, take the photograph with him. He'd tread carefully so as not to put Vincent at risk. In the meantime, Sonny would get comfortable at the farm—until they had some answers.

"There's no reason for you to stay," Sonny told Emil. "Go home."

Emil considered. "Not yet. If Albert's on to us, I want to know."

"And then what?" Günter asked.

"I don't know." Emil rubbed his eyes with the heels of his hands and yawned. "Probably have to shut down the operation, at least for a while. Then find a new crossing. It would be too dangerous here."

"With Belgian visas, that's a problem. Germany borders Belgium for what? Sixty kilometers? Albert could work any of the crossings."

"Let's not get too far ahead of ourselves," Emil responded, his eyes bloodshot, his smile brittle.

"Even if he knows about us—and I don't see how . . ." Sonny pointed a forefinger at Emil. " . . . He can't know who we're sending across. Our documents are perfect, foolproof, the best." He wasn't boasting—it was true. "As far as we know, none of our people have been sent back."

"How would you know? Would someone check in with you if it turned out badly? Say thanks for the help?" Emil countered.

Sonny didn't answer.

"Even if he, or she, could find you, why would he?" Emil countered. "What if the border authority starts digging, cross-referencing numbers, going back to Berlin—wherever?" He listed the possibilities.

Sonny thought about Herman, frowned, and made a fist. "Damn him! We're going in circles. We need a plan. I don't want to close another operation because of Albert, especially not this one. It's too painful to think about."

. . . When Emil and Sonny woke up, Günter was already gone. Katrina was in and out doing chores. They'd just finished breakfast when they heard the Opel come to a stop, the door slam shut. In seconds Günter was in the kitchen exchanging worried glances with Katrina.

"What is it?" asked Emil.

"We walked in the square. Vincent does the best he can with bits and pieces of office gossip, the occasional fact," Günter started.

"Yes, of course," Emil agreed. "But what did he say?"

"I'm getting to it. Vincent identified Schwarz from the photo. It probably was him on the train. He returned from leave the same day you got here. But that's not the worst of it."

Suddenly the room fell silent. Sonny scratched his palms with his fingertips and waited. Times like this he missed the sounds of Berlin—honking traffic, clanging pipes, noisy neighbors—covering the uncomfortable silences, filling the gaps.

"A man's been arrested. They've got him in the courthouse jail. We don't know if he's one of ours."

One of ours? What did that mean—someone holding one of Joseph's documents? Robert! Sonny counted backwards on his fingers, lips moving, trying to figure just when the Fischers would have crossed.

"What the hell are you doing?" Emil asked, perplexed by Sonny's behavior.

"What if it's Robert?"

"Who?" Günter asked.

"The family I asked you about—the Fischers, Rosa's father. Today's the 14th, Wednesday—that's right, isn't it?"

Katrina confirmed that it was.

"And Rosa left on the 12th, two days ago. When did they cross?"

"Not yesterday, but the day before," Günter told him. "I remember your girl didn't say much—her mother did most of the talking. Then I drove all three to the border and watched them go across." He shook his head. "No. I saw them only as far as the shack, not across."

Sonny had been holding his breath. "You're sure about the day?"

Günter nodded. "It was Monday, the same day they arrived. You guys came yesterday—nobody crossed."

"Last question. What day was the man arrested?" Sonny asked.

"Don't know," Günter answered.

"About when?" Sonny pressed.

Günter shook his head, his sigh echoing through the quiet kitchen.

"Albert was still in Berlin," Sonny said absently. "Could still be Robert, but I don't think so. If it was, they'd have arrested all three." Sonny was stricken.

"No!" Günter objected. "One man, no one else." Then he looked away and said quietly, "I never said the arrest was at the border—Vincent didn't say where."

Startled by Günter's outburst, then relieved, Sonny emptied his lungs in a long, slow exhale: "Still, some poor sod's wallowing in a jail cell. There are so many agents, so many groups working the border. He could be anyone—our faceless man. I'm having a hard time shaking the image." Sonny felt sick with fright for the poor fellow . . . How it affected their operation was less clear.

"What about Albert? What's going on at the border?" said Emil.

"He's still working the border. Rumor is he's constantly angling for a promotion—it's a running joke," Günter said.

"That's him," Sonny snickered.

"He's on loan to the border patrol. They rotate personnel at the border in a radius of about fifty kilometers," Günter said.

"That explains why Albert was working the Heinsberg crossing—into Holland—when Herman tried to cross," Sonny noted.

"Where's that?" Emil asked.

"About thirty kilometers north," Katrina told him.

"Who's Herman?" Günter asked.

Sonny explained. When he finished his ears pricked to a rough guttural sound, like that of a growling dog. He walked to the window, heard it again, this time from behind. It was Emil.

Emil cleared his throat. "He's free-lancing."

"Still a guess," Sonny countered.

"An educated one—everything points to it," Emil replied, then reiterated their discussion of the night before. "If it's Albert—not the Gestapo—looking for you . . ." Anticipating Sonny's reaction, he cut him off: "Ja, ja, I know it doesn't make you feel better, but it's not as bad."

"Maybe there's nothing to get—Albert's crazy," Günter speculated.

"Could be, but let's leave him for a moment. What if the guy they're holding has one of our documents? Could he name any of us?" Emil looked to Günter and Katrina.

Pulling on his lip, Günter looked furtively at Katrina. Sonny noticed the exchange.

Emil picked up on it too: "Is there something else you want to tell us? No secrets, remember."

Günter colored while Katrina stared at the floor. Emil waited.

"If there's something you know, tell us, for God's sake," said Sonny.

Günter lit a cigarette and said, "We've got our own little operation with people along the border. We send them across using papers we get hold of, sometimes by other means." He didn't elaborate.

Emil was aghast. "Why didn't you tell us? It might have saved some time, not to mention worry. I don't give a shit—but for you to keep it from us..."

"Sorry. We didn't want to confuse matters with your operation, and we're so used to secrecy."

"What do you mean, *your* operation? You've been with us from the start," Sonny objected.

"All right. It's out in the open. Let's deal with it," Emil said. "Could he be one of yours?"

Katrina looked stricken, and Günter was looking at her when he said softly, "Could be, but we don't know."

Emil nodded, then listed the possibilities: "He's part of your group. Or some poor guy who stopped at the border with bad papers and may or may not be one of ours." He glanced at Sonny. "Almost surely not Robert. Or it could be some other possibility we can't account for... say another smuggling outfit."

"If I drove him to the border," Günter's eyes widened. "He'd know my car."

Emil said to Günter, "Ja, he would." Then to Sonny, "Could he identify you?"

Sonny nodded. "If it *was* me. But it could have been Otto or one of the runners. Toward the end I didn't have time to meet with everyone." He paused, mentally removed Robert from the picture, then continued. "Nobody knows my real name." Then he slammed a fist into his open hand. "But Albert knows Sonny." He combed a hand through his hair, closed his eyes. "That leads nowhere, since now I'm Paul Sander. Albert would have to see my face." Toying with his thoughts was the image of some poor guy in a cell, his face—*his* face—buried in his hands.

"Now everything is different. They might not be so quick to release a guy like Herman. But if it's an operator, someone with real information, then it's . . . bad," Emil noted soberly, sending a chill through the room.

"Since we don't know who, where—for all we know, he could have started shooting like Grynszpan," Sonny offered.

Günter shook his head. "No. Vincent would have known something like that."

"I was just . . . never mind," Sonny said impatiently, his nerves raveling. "Whoever he is, I can't stop thinking about him."

"There's nothing you can do. Forget him. We've got our own problems!" Emil's cold assessment made them all uncomfortable.

"Maybe you can, but I can't," Sonny snapped, recalling a similar order at the time Willy was laid out in the old shed.

"I agree it's not easy," Günter said. "We need to know."

"And then what?" Emil asked the more important question.

"Save the operations," Sonny answered.

"And ourselves," Günter added urgently.

Both made sense, but that meant dispersing, getting lost. Günter and Katrina would find shelter with their own, Emil would work his way back to Berlin, and Sonny would head to Plombieres. But like dogs chasing their tails, they were stuck, unwilling to act without more information. For all they knew, the guy in jail was a red herring, but for Sonny it came back to Albert. They were staring at him.

Feeling the heat of their eyes, he asked in a low voice, "What?" No one spoke, so he did. "How the hell should I know what's percolating inside his Nazi skull? It's enough that he's dogging me." Their short friendship had ended, without confrontation or argument, on its own, like a dying fire no one had bothered to feed—then years later at the café? None of it added up.

"Maybe he's got a crazy score to settle that I know nothing about. Or he's figured out what we're doing?" His hand cut the air in frustration.

"We could be overreacting," Emil said, trying to calm Sonny.

Everyone in the room seemed restless. The room pulsed, ready to explode. Emil paced. Günter lit a cigarette from the end of one he'd finished and blew thick smoke rings above his head. Katrina, her back to the room, washed dishes, her face and thoughts hidden. Sonny sat, his leg bouncing in a mad rhythm.

So it went until Günter squashed out his cigarette and announced, "I'm going back to town, to find out what I can about the man in jail and about Albert's posting."

"Don't—it's too dangerous," Katrina objected.

But Sonny and Emil agreed it was the thing to do. As Günter drove off, she wrung her hands, avoided their eyes.

The whine of the Opel dissipated, and Emil waved to Sonny. "Let's take a walk."

"Sure. Why not?" They hadn't been out of the house since they arrived, and it gave them a chance to get some fresh air, to talk privately.

From outside, the house and large shed appeared to have been dropped into a forest clearing. Only a narrow lane connected the house to the road, and its rear opened onto a field. Isolated, they could be anywhere within a ten-kilometer radius of Aachen. They walked up and down the plowed troughs of the frozen field. Recently fallen snow had cleansed the landscape to a pristine white. Their problems should be so easily surmounted.

Sonny felt he was in another place and time, and then it came to him—he was trailing Bismarck, Fritz's old brown dog, his tail wagging, nose to the ground, stopping at every tree to leave his mark. Sonny smiled, took a deep breath, stretched his legs, and tried to think about the future, about Rosa. But it was hard . . . Albert kept getting in the way.

He imagined Rosa walking the old, cobbled streets of Antwerp's Jewish quarter, missing him as much as he missed her. Or maybe she was still with Fritz, walking in the field with Bismarck, or sitting in the kitchen with Marlene on her lap. In every imagined scenario, she was flawless. Then his face clouded—the man in jail was Robert. He shook his head. "No, it's not him." He forced himself to believe it.

Try as he might to stop them, Sonny's thoughts, like a rampaging river, went where they went. Images of Albert's creepy face morphed to the man slumped in the barren cell, head between his knees. Trepidation, downright fear, controlled his mind, kept the thought of Rosa from comforting him.

Sonny watched another old dog—his loyal and steady friend—navigate the path ahead. Something else was troubling . . . He caught up to Emil and asked, "Why do you figure Günter kept his operation from us?"

"I wondered about that too. But we have to take his answer at face value. What else can we do? If it's one of theirs in custody, that could be worse than Albert."

They'd been gone for about an hour, cleared the thick stand of trees opening on to the field. White smoke from the chimney formed random designs, then dissipated beneath the grey overcast sky. Random flakes of snow drifted onto their heads, their shoulders, the ground. Soon it would fall harder, obscure the path and the view. Sonny looked for Günter's battered Opel, but Emil's hand on his arm stopped him short.

Emil pulled him back to the woods and pointed. "That sedan shouldn't be there."

Sonny scanned the area near the house, looking for what he had missed. "Oh, my God!"

34

Worst of all, continual fear and danger of violent death; and the life of man, solitary, poor nasty, brutish, and short.
—Thomas Hobbes

With several strides, Sonny and Emil were out of sight. The snow was coming faster, providing more cover but also making it hard to see more than a few meters ahead. And it felt colder. They tramped through deepening snow, through the woods, toward the house, came upon a fallen tree and climbed on top. Nothing stirred outside the house. Only the black sedan was visible.

Suddenly things were so complicated. Exchanging an anxious look with Emil, Sonny noted, "We'll freeze if we don't get out the woods soon."

"Fucking Gestapo," Emil cursed.

"What brought them?" Sonny's question was rhetorical—he knew the answer.

Soon they were covered in white, nearly indistinguishable from the small evergreens dotting the forest, except that the humans were moving. They were breaking a trail—the only sounds were the snapping of branches, muffled footfalls, heavy breathing. They put their minds to a plan of action.

Emil stopped to catch his breath and turned to Sonny. "Now we know they're onto Günter. Either he's in custody and they're looking for us, or they're waiting for him."

Sonny shook the snow from his head and shoulders. "I'm betting Günter's still out there, and they don't know about us."

"Ja, maybe."

Sonny started to say something, then his eyes widened. "Katrina!"

Emil winced. "How much do you think she knows?"

"Everything . . . she was part of the meeting. Remember the look Günter gave her?"

"Don't want to think about what's happening inside." Emil batted snowflakes in the air.

They'd heard too many stories of the horrors the Gestapo, the SA, could inflict—of Willy, Robert, Karl's friend Herr Fogelman, and others. Awash in his visions, Sonny was again overwhelmed by circumstance. He'd never been this vulnerable—in a snowstorm, in unfamiliar territory with no route of escape, the Gestapo blocking their path, one of their own at risk.

"We can't just leave her," Sonny exclaimed and took a step, then stopped. "Damn! Wherever I go, there's nothing but trouble." He stomped his feet to keep warm.

"It only seems that way."

"That makes me feel better," Sonny muttered.

"Give me a plan. That's what you're good at." Emil's challenge was real; they had to come up with something. "Remember what you did in Oranienburg."

"Hell! I was improvising."

"It worked. What do you think this is?" Emil put a big hand on Sonny's shoulder, smiled wryly. "Don't sell yourself short. We'll come up with something. If nothing else, we've got the element of surprise."

"Man, that sounds familiar," Sonny snorted. He flashed on Rosa's blood-spattered dress, Limping Man on the floor, Albert staring at him from the photo. Emil was right. The possibility of surprise was their only advantage

"Günter's been with us from the start. He's a good man, and Katrina doesn't deserve what they're probably doing to her." Sonny shuddered. "What do you think they're doing to her?"

"Nothing good, that's for sure—better not think about it," said Emil, jerking his thumb toward the road. "Günter's out there . . . doesn't have a clue. Otherwise they'd have taken Katrina to headquarters."

Suddenly Sonny waved toward the house, "Our satchels are in there." His hand went to his pocket for the documents. He felt their hard edges and exhaled.

"Nothing we can do about that," Emil replied.

In the fifteen minutes since their lives had crashed down around them, nothing seemed to have changed outside the house. Nobody had gone in or come out. Now the snow fell harder. Only the lone black sedan was visible, but perhaps another vehicle was hidden from view. "They're waiting for Günter. I doubt they even know we exist."

"Do we make a run for it or fight?" Sonny asked. Rolling in the snow, grappling with a Gestapo soldier had little appeal, but neither did running away.

"I don't like our odds in a fight," Emil said with a harsh laugh. "But let's stick around awhile, see what happens."

So they talked it out, figuring there were at least two in the house, more in the lane—but how many? "We need to know how many are out there before we decide what to do next," said Emil.

"Not exactly a plan, but a start," Sonny conceded. "We've got to act quickly. Günter could return any time and . . . " He didn't have to finish the thought. "Standing out here in the cold is getting old, fast." He jumped up and down.

"Before barging in on their little party, we need a plan," said Emil.

"You keep saying that," Sonny replied through chattering teeth. He traced the line of trees flanking the house with his hand. "If I can get to the house, to a window, see what's going on inside . . ."

"How you going to do that?"

Sonny thought for a bit. "Circle through the forest, toward the road. Then I'd be . . . what? . . . ten meters from the house, maybe closer, still hidden from view. With the trees for cover, all I'd have to do is scurry to the window for a look."

Following Sonny's gaze, Emil frowned.

"What?"

"No." Emil shook his head. "First, we find out how many are out there." He pointed to the road. "For all we know, there's a squad. Then we run. If not, we'll figure what's next."

"All right. Let's go," Sonny said.

They moved deeper into the woods toward where they thought the road would be. Oversized snowflakes filled the air, so thick they were nearly blinding. They kept the house behind them, then turned right in the direction of the road. Slogging through deepening snow, climbing over fallen trees, ducking under branches, they eked their way. Sonny slipped into a depression and fell on his butt, disturbing a white rabbit. Startled, it hopped wildly out of sight. Smiling, he got up and went on.

After fifteen minutes of fighting the undergrowth, Emil stopped. "Let's see where we are in relation to the house." They made a ninety-degree turn and went forward. Emil broke some branches to mark the return trail. In minutes they were at the edge of the woods, the lane separating them from the house. To their left, the lane cut through the trees straight to the road. They backtracked, using their markers for a guide.

They counted on the falling snow, trees, dense brush, and undergrowth to cover their movements. With only a vague notion of the distance from the house to the road, they broke a trail, each using one hand to protect his face from snapping branches.

After another ten minutes of slogging, Sonny was breathing hard, sweating under his jacket, tired but not cold except for his feet. They stopped to catch their breath, Emil nodded, and they started toward the road, or so they hoped. Without a reference point, they could well be trudging in a circle.

Sonny's foot caught on a fallen tree trunk, and he fell against a branch. It broke with a loud crack, so close to his ear that it sounded like a gunshot. At first he froze; then he scrambled behind a tree. Emil, several meters ahead, did the same. Both crouched, still. After a few seconds, they heard rushed footsteps—and a voice.

"Who's there?"

Emil put a finger to his lips, pointed down, and waved both palms. Sonny didn't need Emil's pantomime. He nearly stopped breathing. The sentry moved closer, mumbling as he came, then stopped. At least five meters of thick brush, tree trunks, and a wall of white separated them. The sentry, seeing nothing, apparently gave up: "Must be an animal." The sound of crunching branches receded into silence.

Sonny moved quickly to Emil's side. They were confident the sentry was alone. And they had proof Günter wasn't in custody. They still didn't know how many were in the house.

"Strange there's only one," Emil mused. "You'd think they would come with more backup."

"Our lucky day. I thought we were dead meat."

"Shut up!"

"So, what about him?" Sonny pointed.

Emil's curse came in a long low hiss like air leaking from a tire. Then his face settled into a frown. "Too risky to leave him be. If Günter returns, it's too late. We've got to narrow the odds." He flicked his thumb toward the sentry. "He's got to go."

Days earlier such a brutal assessment would have been unthinkable. But Oranienburg had made possible the unthinkable. Sonny knew by the sentry's voice that he was just a kid. Unlike the monster at Oranienburg, he'd done nothing to them. Sonny grasped for an alternative. "There must be another way."

"Then tell me," Emil demanded. "You think I want to kill a kid not much older than Eric? Stop thinking of him as an innocent—he's Gestapo. He won't hesitate to gun you down." He leaned in until only inches separated them. "And think of what they've planned for Günter and Katrina."

"Can't we disable him? Tie him up?" There was urgency in Sonny's voice. Killing again scared him, especially like this.

"Too risky—he's armed, could be onto us before we got that far. And if we did, then what? Tie him up with a rope we don't have? Stash him in the woods so he can get loose, start screaming, come after us?" Emil shook his head and stuck a finger in Sonny's face. "These pricks have no conscience. I shudder to think about Katrina in the house with them. And that poor guy locked up."

Emil paused, glanced in the sentry's direction, then clinched the deal. "Think about Willy, what that prick tried to do to Rosa. Think what Robert and all the other poor sods in Sachsenhausen have endured." Emil grabbed Sonny's jacket. "Listen! To free Katrina and save Günter, not to mention you and me, there's going to be bloodshed."

Sonny raised his hands in surrender. "All right, all right. You win." He looked in the direction of the sentry, thought about what they had to do. "But I'll never like it."

"There's no choice, unless you want to walk away."

"No."

"Good. We need to distract him, so one of us can deal with him." Emil put a gloved hand to his chin.

"You'll have to . . ." Sonny couldn't say it, and he changed tack: "So long as there's only one."

"Only one," Emil agreed.

They needed surprise . . . Sonny came up with a diversion. "How's this? Say one of us—me—walks innocently down the road, comes upon the sentry and engages him. You sneak up from behind and . . ."

"You'd have to give me enough time."

Sonny nodded, ignorant of what Emil needed time to do. "I suppose you have a plan?"

"Ja, sort of, but I'll be improvising," Emil said.

"What do you think I'm doing?" Sonny protested, then pointed away from the lane. "I'll go through the woods, get on the road far enough over there, and start walking back. When he comes to investigate, I'll think of something, give him a load of shit, keep him occupied. That's all I've got so far." He kind of liked the plan, though he was less than keen to carry it out it. "After that . . ."

Emil scratched his chin. "It might work."

"What do you mean—*might*?"

"Nothing's perfect. We don't know how he's going to respond. He might just shoot you."

Sonny's jaw dropped.

"Just kidding."

"Didn't need that," Sonny said testily. "You come up with something better—that's all I've got."

Emil's fingers worked at his beard, then he shook his head. "It'll work—let's be positive."

"All right. The . . ." Sonny was going say kid, but he swallowed the word, " . . . he won't suspect anything from a sweet guy like me." He smiled innocently.

"Right. You start. I'll head for the road after a few minutes. When I hear the two of you talking, I'll wait for an opening. Good luck."

Sonny chewed on his lower lip and shrugged. Putting a hand on Emil's shoulder, he said, "We had a good run."

"Just go."

Sonny set off through the woods. Would the plan work? He'd need a script—or maybe it didn't matter—all he had to do was keep the guy occupied. What was he doing on the road? He was a neighbor, surprised to find Gestapo at the Giradet farm. What if the sentry knew the neighbors? Or asked for his identity card with its Berlin address? Christ! Emil would have to be on the guy quick . . .

After ten minutes, Sonny figured he'd gone far enough. He left the cover of the woods and stepped to the edge of the road. He looked for the sentry but didn't see him. Walking at a normal pace, he saw what had to be the lane to the house. Still no sentry. Damn! Where was he? Sonny started to whistle the first tune that came to mind—the opening to Beethoven's Fifth. He repeated the same familiar few bars. Then he heard that voice he'd heard in the woods.

"Who is it?"

"What?" Sonny acted surprised, searched for the source.

"Stop!" The sentry stepped out from behind the line of trees. In three long strides he was in the road, his rifle at the ready.

Sonny assessed his adversary as he had the Hitler Youth. Taller, thicker in the torso than Sonny, cheeks rosy from the cold—he couldn't be more than twenty-one. He looked nothing like Albert or Limping Man. His eyes darted from side to side, then back to Sonny. He was clearly uneasy at this development.

Sonny realized he had more combat experience than the sentry. He stopped as ordered. A look of concern replaced his smile. The sentry advanced until he was two meters from Sonny. His glare only made him seem stern, unhappy.

"Who are you? What are you doing here?"

"Taking a walk. Why?" Sonny's voice was calm, despite the vein pounding in his neck.

"None of your business," the sentry answered. "Just keep moving." He swung his rifle in the direction he wanted Sonny to go.

"Have business at the Giradets?" Sonny asked.

"You know them?" the sentry asked.

"Of course. We're neighbors," he answered, gesturing over his shoulder, stalling for time. "Ach, now I get it." Sonny nodded thoughtfully, as if he understood.

That piqued the sentry's curiosity. "What's that mean?"

"My suspicion was right." Sonny leaned confidentially toward the sentry, as if to say something important.

Taking the bait, the sentry lowered his rifle, ready to hear what Sonny had to say. At that moment, Emil bounded from the woods. The sentry heard him and turned, but Emil was already on top on him, one arm around his neck. With the other, Emil snapped the sentry's head sharply to the side. There was a sickening crack. The soldier went limp.

Emil was breathing hard. "Quick. Help me get him off the road."

"That was impressive," Sonny said once they had him in the woods.

"Learned it during the war. I'll teach you later. It may come in handy." Emil averted his eyes from the dead kid. "You're the one with all the ideas. What next?"

Sonny stared at the dead German at his feet. He looked older now, the color drained from his face, a frozen grimace. Sonny knew he was as guilty of the killing as if he'd broken the man's neck. Suddenly nausea struck and, like Rosa, he vomited. Then he ate some snow to clear his mouth.

In the meantime, Emil was examining his rifle . . . Sonny closed his eyes, piecing together the events on the road: Sonny engaging the kid, Emil pouncing, grimacing, grunting, the kid going limp, dead. It was that quick. He'd seen that glint in Emil's eyes. He'd seen it in Rosa's. He probably had it himself. "Now we've each taken a life—like soldiers."

"What did you say?"

"Now we've each taken a life. Does that create a new bond between us—that we're at war?" That made sense in this demented world.

Emil kept fiddling with the rifle but looked up. "Don't get carried away. We've got a lot more to do."

"Carried away? God damn it! I never wanted any of this."

"Neither did I. They've forced our hand. Who gives a shit about two dead Gestapo?" Emil lowered the rifle.

Sonny looked toward the road, then back at Emil. "Have you done that before? You know . . ."

Emil lips curled with distaste, and he met Sonny's gaze. "Yes—didn't like it then, still don't. In war, you do what's required."

Sonny accepted his answer with a nod. Then he looked toward the house and back at the dead body. "What about him?"

"Leave him. Let's go." Emil started toward the house.

Sonny hesitated, then said, "Wait! The night I found Herr Milberg, Johnny told me he had a Gestapo uniform. Said I could borrow it, that it might come in handy."

Emil stopped, looked down at the body, back at Sonny. "What the hell are you talking about?"

Sonny explained.

Emil smiled. "You surprise me more every day—you're a hell of a good soldier!"

They stripped the grey Gestapo uniform from the dead soldier, and Sonny put it on. He pulled on the boots and lowered the cap, obscuring his face. He wrapped his pants and shoes in his jacket, asking, "How do I look?"

Emil looked him up and down. "Not bad. It's a little big, but you'll pass a casual glance. Now we figure out how to use you."

Sonny shrugged, then pointed to the rifle. "We can pick them off one at a time when they leave."

"Sure. They'll come outside, one at time, and wait patiently for you to shoot them, Katrina standing by."

"I'm trying! You come up with something."

"Take it easy." Emil stopped. "All right. I'll teach you how to shoot." He explained how the rifle worked and handed it to Sonny. "It's got a real kick, so be careful. Hold it tight against your shoulder just above the armpit when you pull the trigger. It's loaded, so don't rest your finger on the trigger—got it?"

Sonny held the rifle and sighted down the barrel. "Bang, bang."

"Lesson over."

They slogged through the woods to where the lane opened onto the clearing, less than ten meters from the house. Against the backdrop of fresh snow they would be easy to see, so they kept under cover of the forest. Sonny tapped Emil on the shoulder.

"What?"

Cocking his head toward the house, Sonny whispered, "Now's the time for reconnaissance." He liked the sound of the word he'd heard Emil use on the Thiemann Strasse job. "I'm in uniform, so if they see me they'll think there's trouble and . . ." Sonny frowned.

"And what? Surrender?" Emil shook his head.

"Hell, we've got to do something."

They were coaxing out their next move when they heard the Opel coming down the lane.

"Günter's back—no time for planning, got to act," Emil muttered.

In seconds, the Opel stopped next to the house, and Günter got out. He didn't seem to have seen the Mercedes. Before he'd taken two steps, a uniformed Gestapo appeared, pointing a rifle at his chest. Hands in the air, Günter moved out of sight. Before clearing the house, the soldier looked down the lane, apparently for the sentry.

"That's your cue, Sonny," said Emil. "We have a plan. Improvise where you need to, keep your finger off the trigger until . . . I get there."

Sonny swallowed. "Promise?"

"Run like you're catching up, go inside, keep your head down. Remember what I taught you about the rifle. You may have to use it."

Sonny had run out of choices. "Wish me luck." He ran to the house. At the door, he stopped to catch his breath. Beyond frightened, he embraced his new identity, opened the door, and went inside. Acting the lowly sentry, he stayed near the door, blended into the background, held the rifle as Emil had instructed, hoped he'd be ignored . . .

Rifle barrel pressed into his back, Günter stared open-mouthed at Katrina. She was tied to a chair, her arms bound at the back, her ankles to its legs. A bright red welt shaped like a flower seemed tattooed on her left cheek. Her eyes were wide with fright. As soon as she saw Günter, she began to cry. He knelt in front of her as if praying. An empty chair awaited him. No one noticed the sentry.

"Welcome, Herr Giradet. It's about time you got here." The voice, an insincere baritone, came from Sonny's right. "I have had the pleasure of meeting your charming wife. Allow me to introduce myself: I am Captain Albrecht of the security police. You stand accused as a traitor to the Reich—I suspect your wife as well. We have been talking—rather I have been doing most of the talking, and my patience is wearing thin. I have given Frau Giradet the opportunity to save herself. She must tell me everything she knows."

Sonny kept his head down. The bill of his sentry's cap pulled low, he took a good look at the captain before averting his eyes. He was shorter than Sonny and a little heavier, his face nondescript. The captain seemed rather ordinary but for his deep voice. Recalling Limping Man's tenor, Sonny wondered whether a distinctive voice was a requirement for every Gestapo officer.

The baritone intervened. "Alas, she plays the heroine. Now that you are here, we shall move forward with more convincing measures." Albrecht nodded his determination. He moved to within a meter of Günter. He pointed his pistol at Katrina's temple and stared impassively into Günter's eyes. "Perhaps the pain we inflict upon your wife will convince you to talk about your ring of traitors?"

He held up a hand, his fingers splayed, like a cop stopping traffic. "Do not bother to deny it—we know. Sergeant, tie him up. Private, keep your rifle on him. If you have to shoot, do *not* kill him." His lips curled into a nasty smirk, his eyes never leaving Günter's.

Sonny pointed the rifle as ordered, kept his head down, and waited. Why wasn't the captain taking them to headquarters? Was he grabbing the glory, playing the dilettante? Günter's voice brought Sonny back to the moment. He managed to keep his composure.

"Katrina, I'm so sorry," Günter said, his voice breaking. "I won't talk—they'll kill us anyway."

"A hero, how tiresome!" Albrecht scolded. "You are both traitors. Talk or the pain will be exquisite."

The sergeant had lowered his rifle onto the floor so as to tie Günter to the chair. The captain returned to his former spot, his Walther PPK now aimed at Günter. No one took further notice of the sentry.

"You are part of a dangerous circle plotting against the Reich. After a long, unpleasant session with one of my associates, your fellow conspirator was convinced to talk." An unpleasant, guttural sound—perhaps a laugh—escaped the captain's mouth. "You have been named a part of his ring of vipers. Sadly, your compatriot is barely clinging to life." Albrecht's head moved from side to side in an exaggerated show. "Unless you both talk—and quickly—your wife shall meet the same end."

Günter's ring was compromised—the man in custody had nothing to do with Sonny's operation! He knew that Robert was with Rosa and Elise, safe in Belgium. He glanced from Günter to Katrina, from the kneeling sergeant to the captain, whose attention was fixed on Günter. Sonny might as well not have been there at all.

"I will count to five," Albrecht began. "If you do not start talking . . . that bruise you see on your wife's cheek will be joined by others. It is your choice—what shall it be?"

Sonny licked his lips, figuring it was time. Hoping Emil was nearby, he raised his eyes to the captain's face—he was counting. "One, two . . ." The captain morphed into an image of Limping Man, disappearing into the crowd, reappearing . . . as Albert. Five years of pent-up frustration, humiliation, anger, broke to the surface of Sonny's consciousness just as it had in Oranienburg.

In one fluid motion, his charade crumbling, Sonny swiveled the rifle, adjusted his aim at his target's chest. Holding tight, he pulled the trigger. There was a deafening roar, and the recoil thrust Sonny back, though he didn't fall.

The force of the impact knocked Captain Albrecht off his feet and against the wall, sent a picture flying from its hook. His head jerked as if he were looking for the source of his demise. But the essence of the man had already disappeared; he was dead before he hit the floor.

A second explosion, unexpected. As Sonny realized Albrecht's pistol had discharged, Emil crashed through the door. The sergeant's head turned toward the captain, mouth open as he watched his commanding officer die. Before he could get to his feet, Emil pounced. Within seconds the sergeant was gone, too.

Günter watched as the captain dropped to the floor, then turned his startled gaze on the Gestapo private, still pointing his rifle at the fallen officer. Günter's head fell to his chest.

"It's me, Sonny!" the private screamed. But in the noise and confusion Günter and Katrina didn't hear. Sonny's ears screamed from the gunshots in the small crowded kitchen; his nostrils twitched from the discharged cordite. Emil still crouched by the dead sergeant. Günter was slumped in the chair, Sonny frozen by the sudden carnage.

"Günter, Günter," Katrina screamed. Her wails penetrated the air. She pulled at her ropes.

"What?" Then Sonny saw that Günter was injured, though he had no idea how. In two steps he was at Günter's side, rolling him off the chair onto his back. Blood had seeped through the front of his jacket, but he was breathing.

"Oh God, no!" Now Sonny knew what had happened.

Emil found a knife, cut Katrina loose. She fell to the floor, her head to Günter's chest. His face was ashen, his eyes unfocused. No one spoke, though Günter moved his lips, trying.

"No. Save your strength," Katrina whispered. Their hearing slowly returned to normal.

"Too late." His voice was hoarse, barely audible. "Go . . . to Fritz . . . not safe for you."

"No!" Katrina wailed.

"Emil . . . Sonny, take her . . . Gestapo knows . . . run."

"Do they know about us?" Sonny asked.

Günter's head shook slightly, and from between labored breaths came a faint "Water."

Emil filled a glass, lifted Günter's head, and let him drink. He coughed, water spilling from the corners of his mouth. His eyes narrowed to slits, and after several labored breaths, he whispered, "Vincent Albert . . . Katrina . . ." He shuddered, his face compressed in pain.

"What?" Emil tried to keep the urgency from his voice.

Günter tried to speak and couldn't but then words came. "One of ours . . . better you didn't know . . ." He winced, closed his eyes. "Go" was his last word before he lay still, barely breathing. Five minutes passed. With a final breath rattling in his throat, he died.

Katrina bent over his body, quietly weeping. After no more than a minute, she raised her head. "I never imagined it would end like this. He told me to go to Fritz." She kissed his lips and wiped the tears from her eyes. "We must leave, take Günter with us."

They wrapped Günter's body in a tarpaulin. Before they closed it, Katrina kissed her husband for the last time. Then they placed the package in the trunk of the Opel. Sonny retrieved his clothes and put them on again. He tossed the sentry's uniform onto the dead sergeant. Katrina packed a few items, and they were out the door with their satchels, into the Opel.

Emil was starting the car when Katrina said, "Wait. I have to call Rita, Vincent's wife. She has to warn her husband." She got out of the car and went back to the house, quickly returned, and Emil drove them away.

35

Show his eyes, and grieve his heart, come like shadows, so depart.
—William Shakespeare

Darkness was several hours away. Emil figured they had until the next morning before the Gestapo began scouring the countryside for Günter and Katrina—and maybe two strangers. But there was no guarantee they would take that long to discover the three dead men at the farm. He drove past the sentry entombed in snow and turned onto the road, toward the main highway, away from Aachen.

The reality of death and their own escape brought an awed, bewildering, guilty silence to the present company. Three men lay dead behind them—four including the sentry, of which Katrina yet knew nothing. Barely twenty minutes had passed since Günter's last breath. A trusted associate and husband lay dead in the trunk. There was much to digest.

Sonny, still disturbed by the ringing in his ears, kept his eyes on the lane, refusing to look into the woods. He'd worn the sentry's uniform, for God's sake—how close was that? He shuddered. Stripping the body had been his idea. Emil had said there was no choice. But Sonny couldn't get that kid's cherubic face out of his head. God, he hated this!

He was sick—not to vomit again but sick of life. No. Sick of death. And war. Emil said war had come to them. He'd said it himself, and surely it had. But Sonny wanted it to end, to be over, so he and Rosa could start anew. Something deep inside said it wasn't going to happen soon. Real war was coming . . . massive armies. He nearly laughed. Where had he been if not at war? Sonny felt the automobile change direction and flushed the thought from his mind.

After driving about twenty minutes, Emil turned off the main road onto a track, stopped, and shut off the engine. He faced Katrina, broke the silence. "Günter was a good man. We'll miss him. He didn't deserve to die, not like this." They sat quietly, thinking about Günter, what had just happened. After several minutes Emil asked, "You have papers?"

She nodded but didn't speak.

"Where will you go?"

Through her tears, she managed to say, "Family . . . will hide me . . . until I cross."

Sonny leaned in to tell Emil what he'd heard the officer say before the carnage began. When the silence returned, Katrina looked at them through red, swollen eyes, hands clasped tightly. Taking short breaths, she began, "All the information that officer had was correct—they must have one of ours. Rita told me Vincent called with the same information he'd given Günter . . . at their second meeting."

"What information?" Sonny asked.

"We're Huguenots—like Fritz. It's our heritage to help the Jews, anyone in need. You know we worked the border, like you did. We don't have a forger, but sometimes we get papers, usually smuggle them over. The people disappear into Holland or Belgium. We also circulate anti-Nazi literature, which probably bothers them more than the smuggling, when they know about it."

"They do now," Sonny noted grimly.

Emil glanced at Sonny, then asked, "Is Fritz involved?"

"Not directly, but he provides shelter to some of ours." She looked down at her hands. "All I know is that whoever is in custody knew about Günter. They must have tortured the poor man until he talked . . . don't know how he was captured. We're so careful." She dabbed at her eyes with a handkerchief. "Poor man." She might have been talking about Günter.

"Is Vincent part of the group?" Sonny asked.

"No. He was an occasional source of information. Only Günter and I knew. Vincent is a party member—for his job—so I suppose he's safe. But as Günter's cousin . . ."

"A Nazi?" Sonny asked incredulously.

She sighed. "Yes. I know it's a terrible irony. He wanted to keep his job."

"Hmm," Emil grunted. "It was good cover but a dangerous game."

"Now that's ended," Sonny said.

Katrina cringed. She slumped in her seat and broke down.

Emil placed a light hand on her shoulder and kept it there. Facing Sonny, he spoke in a low voice. "Günter seemed to say that they're not looking for us, but we need to run."

"I heard that too. I'd like to know what he learned about Albert."

"If anything," said Emil.

When darkness fell, Emil drove north along the main road for a half hour. Lights of the farmhouses, scattered like a string of broken pearls, were dimly visible in the near distance.

Katrina directed them to her cousin's farm. "Just ahead, there's a big tree on the right. You'll see its outline against the sky. Turn right onto the lane after the tree."

The deeply rutted track, sheltered by a line of trees, ended at a house. Lights shone through the windows, and when the Opel stopped near the back door, an outside light came on. A dog bounded from the house and ran around the car, barking. A man appeared, and the dog stopped. Katrina introduced them to Jakob and wept again.

"Quickly into the house," Jakob ordered. He turned to the strangers for answers.

Emil gave him a rough outline of what had happened. Slumped in a chair, Katrina grieved a world forever gone.

"Oh, my dear God!" Jakob cried, embracing Katrina.

After a few moments, she said, "Günter is in the automobile."

Dazed, Jakob opened, then closed his mouth, unable to speak. Finally he muttered, "I'll find a safe resting place until he can be buried in the spring."

Katrina, sliding deeper into personal grief, didn't hear.

Jakob, unsure of what to do to next, turned to the two men but did not speak. No one else did either . . . Finally Jakob roused from his stupor and offered them food. Sonny and Emil hadn't eaten since morning and gratefully accepted. Katrina refused.

Sonny and Emil felt safe for the moment. Jakob welcomed them to stay the night, but they would have to leave early in the morning. That meant deciding where to go. Katrina heard them talking and became anxious. Wide-eyed, she suddenly stood, grabbed her satchel, and headed for the door. She was going to another relative—this one north of Düsseldorf.

Clearly, she was in no condition to drive. Jakob blocked her path and led her back to the chair. They convinced her to wait until she felt better. After an hour, she had eaten something; still bleary-eyed, she was ready to leave. After an emotional farewell, she drove off in the old Opel. Then the three men sat down to talk.

Jakob, like Fritz, was a bachelor farmer, and he too hosted émigrés—on their journey to Geleen, in Holland, or to Plombieres—sometimes overnight. "You gave me the bare bones. Now I want all of it," he demanded. "Tell me exactly what happened!"

Sonny and Emil took the better part of an hour to tell it. When they finished, the three men retreated within; the house became quiet. Sonny was downcast. Emil was harder to read; his expression said little of what roiled inside. He knew they'd upped the ante—no place was safe, no one secure, time was short.

Jakob broke the silence: "If I hadn't seen Günter's body, I wouldn't believe your story—it's too horrid."

Before Oranienburg and Limping Man, Sonny probably would have agreed. But he was in a new world. What he'd done and seen at the Giradet farm was weaving itself into the pattern that had begun with Willy's death and continued with Grynszpan's pull of the trigger, with Kristallnacht. He saw his future, and it scared the hell out of him.

Jakob fetched his bottle of brandy and three glasses. He toasted: "To Günter, a good man, and to the hope that I never hear another story like his."

"Amen to both," Emil agreed and emptied his glass.

"I've been part of the underground since '33, smuggling people for three years, and like you," Jakob looked at his two companions, "I accepted the risks. That man in custody could have been me—or you. Would I have given up Günter, Katrina, the others? I'd like to say I would not, but if they tortured me? I don't know . . . I grieve for the poor soul in custody, for Günter, for all of us in what lies ahead."

"Any idea who that man is?" said Emil.

"No. Günter knew him. He's probably a stranger to me. Did he name others?" Jakob shuddered at the question. "I never planned for a moment like this, never figured it would happen." He shook his head and looked away. "Should I wait for them to kick in my door? Make a run for it? Katrina's running, you two will be running tomorrow, but me?" Jakob sighed as he ran a hand through his close-cropped hair.

He answered his own question: "I'll stay. They won't run me off the family farm. Besides, where would I go? To Fritz?" His smile turned wistful. "No, it would be too crowded."

"You're Katrina's cousin. Be prepared for a visit from the Gestapo," Emil warned.

"I'll deal with that when it comes." Then he asked his guests, "Where will you go?"

Both men frowned. They exchanged glances. They hadn't had a chance to talk in private about their plans, about Albert, the killings, anything. Their original plan had been lost somewhere back at the farm. Neither answered.

Jakob waited, increasingly perplexed. And he asked again.

Emil stared at Sonny. He finally answered, "Aachen."

Sonny, chewing on his lip, seemed only mildly surprised. "Why would you risk it?"

"Unfinished business, I suppose," Emil answered tersely.

"You suppose? You have to do better than that. You're not thinking straight," Sonny shot back. "There's no reason for you to go to Aachen. You've got family in Berlin. For God's sake, think of them. It's bad enough that I have to go through there to get out. But you don't have to."

"What about Albert?"

"Forget Albert—it's too late," Sonny argued. "We'll never find out why he's looking for me—not now." He paused to think about that, then asked, "All right . . . say we find out . . . then what?"

Emil did not respond.

"Kill him?" Sonny snickered. "Sure! Why not? We're just getting started. I'm good at it. So are you. Soon we'll have Himmler in our sights. Emil! Germany's dead for us—give it up. Once the manhunt starts—hell!" He wasn't done yet. "There's nothing you, me, Jakob, anyone, can do—not now. Normal men scatter in the wind after what we've been through."

Emil's eyes never left Sonny's, but he still said nothing.

Jakob spoke, "Sonny's right, but I'm not going to try to change your mind—it's up to you. When they find the bodies, the Gestapo will go crazy. It will get very hot around Aachen. I'll drop you both near a bus stop on the main road, early tomorrow. Go north, south—your call."

Emil finally spoke: "They'll be looking for Günter and Katrina, for their Opel. Not for us."

"Unless they know about us," Sonny said. "Though I don't see how they could. We didn't leave anything at the farm. Once Katrina's over the border—I hope by early tomorrow—they'll be looking for two people they can't possibly find."

"For your sake, I hope to God that's true," Jakob offered. "But the Gestapo won't confine their investigation to one couple—any stranger will be suspect. And what if the prisoner divulged other names? With three of theirs dead—one stripped of his uniform, nearly naked in the woods—they'll be vicious. There could be mass arrests—remember Kristallnacht?"

The color drained from Sonny's face.

They agreed the investigation probably wouldn't begin until the next morning, when the officer and his two men failed to report to headquarters and men were sent to the Giradet farm to inquire. Whenever it came down, everyone in the area would feel the presence of the police. The area near Aachen would be sealed off; the manhunt would begin.

"Your ability to move will be restricted," Jakob noted grimly. He finished off his brandy. Then he took them to a small room with two beds and bade them goodnight. He would wake them at dawn.

Nerves ragged from too much death kept Sonny and Emil from sleep. They didn't even try but instead put on their jackets and followed the dog out for a walk in the dark. The cold was energizing; it cleared their heads for thinking. They walked under a clear, starry sky along the track leading to the road. Neither spoke.

After several minutes Sonny said, "What a mess! Get away from me. I'm bad luck. I leave a trail of dead bodies . . . Now it's one of our own—I can't face another."

Emil kept walking with his hands in his pockets, shoulders hunched against the cold.

"Go back to Berlin, back to your family," Sonny implored.

"Ja, everything's turned to shit, I'll grant you that," Emil agreed, then stopped to face Sonny. "It's not your doing that a guy was caught, forced to talk. Don't carry that around. Günter and Willy are the only ones who matter. What happened at the farm was beyond our control—a terrible hazard of our work . . . what we hoped would never happen. It was simple—them or us." He let out a long, low whistle, bringing the dog to his side. He patted its head. "It's been twenty years since the big war. I hated it. My opinion hasn't changed."

Sonny looked up at a million twinkling stars, hoping he'd find an answer to what had happened to his life. All he'd ever wanted was a little of this, a little of that. Well, he'd made his choices. That he didn't like the result did not matter. Now life was at its most basic. He'd survive and make damn sure those closest to him did too.

Emil's burst of cynical laughter startled Sonny, and when Emil spoke, his voice was hard. "They pushed. We pushed back. So far we've gotten away with it—you've gotten away with it twice. But next time?" He might have been reading Sonny's mind. "What if Alfred is caught moving someone to No. 53, or the cover's blown at the big house where Joseph's holed up, or Karl's group is infiltrated? They've had five years, tentacles deep into every neighborhood. It's probably just a matter of time."

Sonny didn't want to hear it, but Emil was right. There was no point in arguing. "I hope to God you're wrong."

"Me too, but I'm a realist. Hitler wants war—first rearmament, then the Saar, the Rheinland, Austria, Czechoslovakia. What next? At some point England, France, or the Soviets will push back, or Hitler will eat Europe whole. War will put us out of business, if we're still operating." Emil slapped Sonny's shoulder. "Like we've always said, our personal war against the Third Reich started when that fat asshole shot Willy." He shrugged. "It's just escalated. And you got your military training on the job."

Sonny and Emil had worked together seven years. Sonny's reality met Emil's bleak prescription—both were sour. That they thought the same thing brought a measure of comfort but also a measure of despair. Joseph and Otto had predicted war. What Sonny had experienced in the past month said they were right. With his lover waiting in Belgium, he should get out of Germany fast. But going back to Aachen was crazy. "It doesn't make sense," he said finally.

"What?" Emil asked.

"None of it does, but I mean you going back to Aachen. Sometime tomorrow morning they'll know for sure. It's too dangerous." The dog loped ahead, nose to the ground, wagging its tail. It stopped, walked back, and did it again. Watching the dog amused Sonny; nothing had amused him for days—not since Rosa left. "If we were only dogs."

They walked in silence until Sonny said, "Sorry about losing it earlier. I just don't want to see you do something we'll both regret."

"Don't worry about it—you're right," Emil told him.

"Hell! Why didn't we take off right away—as soon as we got here? Jakob could have dropped us on the road. We'd be gone, away from this mess—you'd be on a train to Berlin, and I'd be in Plombieres. Or you could have gone with Katrina, then on to Düsseldorf."

Sonny's questions hung in the air.

Finally Emil answered. "You said I wasn't thinking straight—neither of us were. How could we, after what's happened? Maybe we should have burned the house down, dragged the sentry inside, set everything on fire, then driven the black sedan down the road."

"Seems I've heard that before."

"As for leaving yesterday, Albert may have been at the border . . ."

"Ja," Sonny agreed.

" . . . and you'd have had to deal with that." Emil paused, then continued. "Despite everything, I'd like one last shot at him."

"Interesting choice of words."

Emil snorted. "Like Jakob said, they'll round up strangers, spend a lot of time looking for Günter and Katrina, maybe not go farther 'til we're long gone. Still, we'd never get close to Albert. And Vincent, after what happened at the farm, will be too spooked even to talk to us."

Sonny put a hand on Emil's arm. "All reasons for you to beat a path back to Berlin. Warn everyone—Karl, the others. He'll find a new safe house. Joseph's well hidden, but maybe he needs to keep moving. Forget Albert. There's no reason to believe he knows what I'm up to. How could he? If he reported what he knows, it's too late. If he hasn't, then let it be. Maybe the whole Albert thing is personal. He wants to apologize for snubbing me at the café."

Emil laughed and walked away. From behind him, Sonny said, "Well, you never know."

Emil, barely visible against the dark sky, seemed to nod in agreement.

"One more thing," said Sonny. "Teach me that stranglehold."

. . . In the morning Sonny and Emil told Jakob of their plans. Emil would go north to Düsseldorf and catch the train to Berlin. Sonny was to go to Belgium as originally planned. It would have been easier to head north into Holland, but his visa was for Belgium. The closest crossing was Reinartzkehl . . . or he could continue south to another one. Either way, he would have to change buses in Aachen.

After a simple breakfast, Emil and Sonny went outside to make their farewells. Soon they'd be faced with the demands of escape. With the dawning of a new day, the carnage of the recent past yielded a sorrow banishing even their fear. One last time they felt compelled to examine their actions—to figure out what went wrong, what they could have done differently. In the end, no new insights came.

"Events caught up to us," Emil said. "We're survivors. That's good for something."

"A trait that will come in handy, I suspect," Sonny answered.

"Always a good thing. There'll be hell to pay around here. The Gestapo will take out their anger on countless innocents, I'm certain. Sorry for that."

"That's the worst part. War is like that, I guess." Sonny spoke so quietly Emil had to lean close to hear.

They walked in silence until Sonny started to say something and stopped. Then: "I want to reminisce, but there's no time."

They didn't even try. "Someday, you can write down our exploits, send me a copy," Emil told him.

They shook hands and wished each other well, then Emil wrapped his arms around Sonny in a hug. "Take care of yourself and Rosa, maybe drop me a coded line from Antwerp. There'll always be a pot of coffee awaiting your next outrageous proposition."

Sonny smiled, then got serious. "We'll probably not see each other again."

. . . Jakob had them lie down in the car. In ten minutes he pulled into a lane, stopped behind a line of trees, and said to Emil, "There's an inn, half a kilometer north, where you can catch the bus to Düsseldorf—only forty kilometers away."

As they drove away, Sonny turned and waved. Emil smiled and nodded. Jakob headed back toward Aachen. Fifteen minutes later, Sonny stood in a clearing, watching him drive away. There was a tavern, just ten minutes from there, where he'd catch the bus to Aachen. Jakob warned him to avoid the owner, a prominent local Nazi.

After an uneventful half-hour, the bus arrived. Sonny boarded, paid the driver, and found a seat at the back. The other passengers glanced at the stranger, then away. He sat watching the oncoming traffic. His watch read 7:35. Did the authorities already know? Jakob had told him to look for a general store just before the turnoff to the Giradet farm, about thirteen kilometers down the road on his left. In twenty minutes, Sonny saw the store—no sign of police or the Gestapo.

In another ten minutes, the bus pulled into the station. He'd put off the decision about whether to chance the familiar but potentially dangerous Reinartzkehl crossing or to head south—until now. He bought a ticket for Reinartzkehl, figuring every crossing posed a danger. His bus left every forty-five minutes—he'd just missed one. The station clock read 8:09. With time to kill, he'd take a walk, stretch his legs.

Aimlessly he passed the railway station where Emil had given him the slip. Then he walked to the shadow of the courthouse clock tower, stopping to take inventory. Everything seemed normal—as it should—people heading to work. But the killing of the sentry and the sergeant disturbed him beyond what he'd felt after Oranienburg. Rationally, he accepted the necessity of what he and Emil had done, but he wasn't a killer.

"War is like that." Emil had taken the other side.

But the killing chafed, forcing Sonny to endure the running commentary in his head. Still, he stayed in the shadows, walking the narrow winding streets, skirting the openness of the main square. He hadn't planned to be here. But while he was, he'd watch the comings and goings at the courthouse.

He was there less than five minutes when he heard automobile tires screeching, then a siren. Within seconds, an ambulance and several black sedans drove toward him at high speed. They knew! The grim realization was like cold water on his neck, sending a shiver of fear down his spine. Every eye turned on him, fingers pointed—he looked for a place to hide. No . . . no one paid him heed. The caravan sped past and disappeared, surely on its way to the Giradet farm.

What would they make of the multiple deaths? The young sentry nearly naked, dead in the woods, his uniform dropped carelessly over the body of the sergeant? The captain's blown-open chest? The blood? Gestapo would run roughshod over everyone, turning over every rock to find Günter and Katrina.

Well, they would never find Günter, and he hoped they wouldn't find Katrina. Sonny feared the brutality of the frustrated authorities. He worried about how the Gestapo would deal with Jakob—and how he'd respond. Emil had convinced Jakob that it was unsafe to stash Günter's body on his property. Sonny hoped he would take care of it soon. All of them—Jakob, Vincent, Rita, others he didn't know—were at risk.

Suddenly, Sonny realized how exposed he was, standing on the street in the shadow of Gestapo headquarters. Being out in the open was foolhardy. He'd been drawn to the headquarters, just as to the Neckar Strasse Synagogue, as if he were in a trance. Maybe he wanted to trade places with Albert—be the pursuer and not the pursued. He might have appreciated the irony were he not so frightened. He was breaking all the rules.

Glancing at his watch—still time to catch the bus—he started walking briskly, better a moving target. By now Emil would be in Düsseldorf, maybe on the train to Berlin. Otto and Mina would be with Fritz, Joseph putting final touches on a document. Maybe Karl and Polly had spent the night together, making love. And where was Rosa? What was she doing now?

An unwelcome thought elbowed Rosa out of the picture: the Gestapo would cast their net in a twenty . . . thirty . . . seventy-kilometer radius from Aachen. Sonny kept walking, but he didn't know where to go. He had a bus to catch, didn't he?

They'd eventually look beyond Günter and Katrina and, like Emil said, every stranger would be suspect. He was a stranger, leaving town. He didn't intend to stick around. He was glad he'd left the station, hadn't boarded the bus, as he surely would have been detained. He quickened his pace, cursing his failure to see the obvious.

Somehow, he would get to the border. He changed direction, headed toward Reinartzkehl—away from the courthouse, away from the bus and railway stations. Would the border be open or closed? More sirens sounded in the distance—a speeding sedan, a squad of Gestapo headed to the railway station—to do what?

Needing to blend in, Sonny slowed down. He sensed nothing from those around him. Why weren't they curious about the sirens? They couldn't know the reason for them, not yet. But word of the Gestapo-killing traitors would trickle out. He appreciated that he was vulnerable and considered a change in plans.

In the twenty minutes it took Sonny to get to the little café and Frau Freyer's flat, he worked on a plan to cross the border. Every potential move seemed dangerous, and without more information he couldn't leave. Was Albert working the Reinartzkehl crossing? Would anyone attempting to cross the border now be detained? He needed to know. Vincent was the only one he could turn to.

But even if Sonny could find him, would Vincent be willing to help?

36

Out of this nettle, danger, we pluck this flower, safety.
—William Shakespeare

Sonny stood nervously at the door and looked down the corridor. Nothing stirred. Frau Freyer registered surprise as she let him in.

"Sonny, I assumed you were gone. Has something gone wrong?"

"Nothing to concern yourself about," Sonny began. "A slight change of plans. I'll leave soon—after I deal with . . . several matters. I'm sorry to inconvenience you again."

Waving a bony hand, she said, "It is nothing. I am always glad to see you, though I fear mischief is the cause." Then she instructed, "Pour yourself a brandy, some sherry for me—the time of day be damned."

Sonny took a mouthful, leaned back in the comfortable chair, and let the alcohol calm his nerves. "Yes, events have conspired against me—require extra caution." He purposely remained vague.

"How are your friends?"

Sonny winced but said nothing.

Even her weakening eyes took it in. "Is there anything I can do?"

He shook his head. "My friend is safely on the train."

"Good! He gave them the slip," she said with a straight face.

Sonny managed a smile. "Yes, he did. I hope to do the same."

"I don't expect you to tell me why, but you must have a good reason for returning."

"It wouldn't be prudent for you to know," Sonny said, then took a sip of brandy and licked his lips.

She looked slightly disappointed.

He went on. "I have a request that you should feel free to reject—it's risky and I can never repay you. Think it over before you respond."

She straightened, a soldier reporting for assignment. Her readiness to help slightly unnerved him. With her elbows on the arms of the chair, she brought the fingertips of her hands together, waiting. "Sonny, I am at your disposal. I will do what I can."

"Thanks." Sonny smiled sheepishly. "How could I think otherwise? I need to lie low, stay off the streets. May I spend the night?"

Her smile was enigmatic. "That's easy. I was hoping for something more dangerous."

"You're a gem."

She shrugged. "As I am sure you recall, Herr Glaser is gone, his flat is empty, the rent has been paid for several months." With effort, she rose from her chair and shuffled to the secretary against the wall opposite the window. She opened the door and reached inside. "This is the key to Herr Glaser's flat. You may use it as long as you like . . . though I don't recommend more than several days." She told him where in the building the flat was located.

Sonny took the key without comment, then asked, "Do you have a telephone directory?" He didn't know Vincent's surname, but he hoped it was Giradet, like his relatives.

She pointed to the secretary. "You will find it there as well."

Sonny turned the pages, located "Giradet, Vincent," and sighed with relief. Finding paper and pen, he wrote: "673290, 57 Frei Strasse." Returning to his chair, he asked, "Can you direct me to Frei Strasse?"

She thought a moment and, without questioning, provided its general location.

His work for the moment accomplished, Sonny spent the rest of the day in Frau Freyer's flat. They talked, ate lunch, and he took a nap. Upon waking, he tried to read but found he could not confine his mind to the page. He paced, anticipating what he was about to do.

After several minutes of this, Frau Freyer said he was making her uneasy. He sat down, and they talked intermittently until the sun disappeared from the sky. Excusing himself from her company, he set out to find Vincent Giradet . . .

After an hour of walking and missteps requiring him to retrace his path, Sonny found Frei Strasse in a comfortably middle-class section of

Aachen. He'd never been there before. The bulk of the neighborhood consisted of turn-of-the-century, architecturally uninteresting but well-maintained three- and four-story apartments. The few people he encountered along the way seemed in a hurry to get off the street. When he reached the intersection of Arbeiter Strasse, he breathed a sigh of relief—57 Frei Strasse was just a short walk away.

Spying "Giradet" on the mailbox adjacent to flat 2B, Sonny mounted the steps wondering whether Katrina had mentioned Emil and him to Rita when they spoke the day before. Barely twenty-four hours had passed, though it seemed an eternity.

Vincent would be surprised if not dismayed to see him. Sonny figured Vincent to know something about his group. Günter had pumped him for information at least three times—twice in the past thirty-six hours. Given his position and the risk, Victor would be skittish, maybe hostile, but Sonny had run out of options.

Sonny stood facing the door, about to knock but suddenly hesitant. Was he being foolish? Was this too risky? Too late now . . . He knocked, and within seconds the door opened just to the end of the inside chain. A pair of eyes set in a bland face looked him over.

"Can I help you?" The man's words came out in a rush. Perhaps he expected trouble.

Standing in the well-lit corridor, Sonny was eager to get into the flat. "Please, let me in. My name's Sonny. I'm a friend of Katrina and Günter."

Upon hearing Günter's name, the man blinked rapidly, closed the door, slid off the chain, opened the door, and pulled Sonny in.

"Quickly," he said as he closed the door. He moved to the windows and pulled the drapes closed, then stood in the middle of the room, his hands balled into fists, glaring at Sonny. His eyes were filled with suspicion and fear, mostly fear.

Sonny saw a slightly built, middle-aged version of Günter. The man—Vincent, he presumed—was in coat and tie the picture of a mid-level bureaucrat. The strong overhead lighting accentuated the furrows etched in his frowning brow.

Suddenly the man spoke in rapid-fire staccato: "How did you find me? Why did you come? Are you crazy? It's far too dangerous."

Sonny nearly ducked for cover. He waited a few seconds, then answered lamely, "You're in the telephone directory." Vincent glared at him until Sonny realized his response had hardly been illuminating. "I need information . . . have nowhere else to turn."

Sonny waited, but Vincent said nothing. Finally, Günter's visibly shaken cousin beckoned Sonny deeper into the flat. He motioned Sonny to a seat at the dining table. Apparently no one else was there.

"Who are you?" Vincent demanded.

Sonny explained his connection to Günter, saying that Günter's questions about Albert Schwarz had been asked on his behalf. At the mention of Albert, Vincent put his fingertips to his lips and wilted in his chair.

Without looking at Sonny, he said, "Tell me everything."

When Sonny finished, Vincent closed his eyes, then tilted his head back. He began rubbing his face with both hands. He remained so for several minutes, then abruptly stood and silently paced. After several times around the table, he spoke.

"I know three dead security policemen were found at my cousin's farm . . . they failed to report for duty this morning. I've already been questioned . . . couldn't tell the man anything . . . I know nothing. I think he believed me, but of course, I don't know."

He stopped pacing and faced Sonny. "After Rita spoke with Katrina, she called me and told me what she knew." He licked his lips and looked away. "Then she left to visit her mother—she lives in a town nearby. We agreed that would be prudent. Rita's call was short on detail. I assume you were with Katrina when she called. And after?"

Sonny told him about spending the night with Jakob.

Vincent cut him off, putting his hands over his ears. "I don't want to know." Then he patted his thigh and pursed his lips as if to speak. He must have thought better of it because he only continued to pace.

Sonny waited, not knowing what to say.

Finally Vincent asked, "What do you want from me?"

Relieved, Sonny began, "My final destination is Plombieres—Fritz." He noticed the flicker of a smile, but it immediately disappeared. "I missed my bus, then took a walk, heard the sirens, saw the swarming

Gestapo. I figured they'd cover all departing buses and trains, question someone like me, a stranger, maybe seal the border . . . Listen, I'm eager to get out, but I'm afraid to cross at Reinartzkehl without knowing it's safe. Before it was only Albert. Now I have to worry about the whole fucking Gestapo."

Vincent stopped and stood with his arms extended toward Sonny. "Of course, I understand, even sympathize. But I've got my own problems." His voice was shrill, infected with fear, but sorrow filled his eyes. "I can't imagine anything worse, but . . ." He fell back into the chair.

Sonny feared Vincent might have fainted, but he looked up suddenly and said, "If I agree to tell you all I know, will you promise to leave?"

Sonny nodded. "Yes, of course."

"Sometime this morning, when the captain and his men failed to report for duty, a team was dispatched to the farm. They found the bodies. Rita told me in her call yesterday that Günter was dead, Katrina was going underground, and something about two visitors."

He nodded at Sonny. "You heard the sirens on the street this morning. That's when the courthouse started to buzz with rumors of trouble. A high-ranking Gestapo officer—a man I've been friendly with—paid me an official visit. Of course, he knew Günter was my cousin, and he asked questions about him, about Katrina, about the Underground."

Vincent shrugged. "He was formal, distant, spoke without a hint of our friendship, but he wasn't hostile. I've always feared such questions, and I rehearsed my answers so often, my lies sounded true, even to me." Clearly he was replaying the scene in his head. He smiled wryly. "You couldn't invent something this awful."

Vincent's smile evaporated, and he shook his head, then continued. "That's when I learned that the man in custody wasn't some poor soul apprehended without papers but someone who was part of Günter's network. I was glad I didn't know him. I was told he'd been *convinced* to divulge names—and one of the names was Günter's. The officer's smile was ironic. He watched for my response."

Vincent visibly shuddered. "I mumbled something about being appalled by my cousin's treachery. I must have passed the test because he left without pursuing it further—at least for now."

Vincent rose and resumed his pacing. He rubbed his neck, thinking out loud, piecing together what had happened at the farm with what he knew from the courthouse. Apparently reaching the point where he thought he understood, he stopped and faced Sonny. "Why is Albert Schwarz stalking you?"

"I don't know—all I know is that he is. We were friends in Berlin, before Hitler . . . Then he spotted me here last year—that's when Fritz had Günter ask you about him." Sonny paused, then asked what he needed to know. "What else can you tell me about Albert? About the border? Is it safe to cross?"

Vincent must have sensed his anxiety because his eyes lingered on Sonny's face, searching. He shrugged and shook his head. "I told Günter everything I knew. Now that three Gestapo men are dead, there's chaos at headquarters. Every man available is looking for Günter and Katrina, maybe others—I don't know. Albert Schwarz was on loan to the border patrol, but he may have been called back. I've haven't heard of any change at the border. More I can't say."

Sonny chewed on the realization that the poor guy may have given up names beyond Günter's. But his own name couldn't be on a list, could it? He saw a squad of Gestapo surrounding him, his arms in the air . . .

Then Vincent's voice roused him. "Günter killed those men—with Katrina's help—when they went to arrest him. That's the rumor. They found the bodies at his place, so it makes sense. Now they've both disappeared." Realizing what he'd said, Vincent averted his eyes. "I can't believe he's dead . . . If they knew I talked to him yesterday . . ." He shook his head and was still.

Vincent's quandary was all too obvious. Sonny waited for him to continue, but he remained silent. Sonny asked, "Did the officer ask when you'd last seen him? Did he give any indication he knew you had?"

Vincent seemed not to hear. He looked past Sonny, then his eyes drifted back; he seemed to be processing the question. Finally, he shook his head. "He asked . . . I pretended to try to remember, then told him it was at least several days ago. But if anyone saw us together . . . Ah, Christ!" His eyes closed, as if he'd fallen into trance. But then his head jerked. "Go. I've told you all I know. I'm in enough trouble already."

"Maybe no one saw?" Sonny said encouragingly, but Vincent wasn't listening. He had his hand on Sonny's arm, was dragging him to the door.

Vincent peeked into the corridor, saw nobody there, and pushed him out. "Good luck," said Sonny, but the door was already closed.

Sonny left the building, ruminating on what he'd heard: The Gestapo may have extracted names beyond Günter's, they were shorthanded for the murder investigation, and Vincent hadn't heard anything about the border. What did it mean? If they took every available man for the investigation, the border checkpoints would be undermanned—or closed, though Vincent thought not. But the guards probably would interrogate anyone waiting to cross.

Sonny had learned little, though he'd put matters into perspective for Vincent, if that was any consolation. His choices remained as before, though his perception of choice seemed substantially narrowed: Cross at Reinartzkehl, or go south as far as Ihrenbrück or the village of Urb, and cross to Saint Vith. He knew of the crossings because of the operation's research as their numbers increased. But that was all he knew.

Were he to catch a bus on the main road, he would stick out as a stranger. If only he knew how to hotwire a car, he could steal one, drive to any village along the way . . . But even if he could, there probably would be roadblocks . . .

He would have to walk. But that would leave him in the open, vulnerable. And it would take him a couple of days—rather nights. Sonny felt stymied at every turn. The sad fact was, he'd have enough trouble getting the few kilometers to Reinartzkehl, let alone sixty kilometers to the border. Nowhere would he be safe. Then it hit him—Reinartzkehl, Ihrenbrück, Urb—it didn't matter—every choice posed its dangers.

Sonny was exhausted, hungry, couldn't think straight. Mostly he was afraid he'd never get out, that he'd eventually be arrested. He passed a busy tavern, hesitated, then went in and got lost in the crowd at the bar. To his surprise, the chatter at the bar was calming. He got an earful of what he already knew and something new: a nine o'clock curfew would go into effect the next day.

"Everybody drink up," someone said. Another voice cursed the criminals responsible for the curfew. Others joined in. Sonny felt his neck burn, so he buried his face in his beer mug, lingered a few minutes, then left for the safety of Herr Glaser's flat.

On the way there, he agonized over not heading directly to Reinartzkehl from the Giradet farm. Emil could have dropped him at the road to the crossing hours earlier, then driven Katrina to Jakob and gone on to Berlin. The thought kept returning until he thought he'd explode. Finally, he'd had enough. He decided there was but one rational course.

Despite settling on a plan, Sonny spent a fitful night, dreaming of Albert, Günter, Katrina, and the calamity at the farm. He woke before dawn, unsettled. Unable to piece his dreams together, he rose and quickly dressed. He pushed the key under Frau Freyer's door and left the building just as the sun was rising over Aachen.

He had decided to walk to Reinartzkehl, then the last five hundred meters to the border. The shorter the way, the greater the chances for success. All he had to do was avoid the police and the Gestapo.

The city limits extended about halfway to Reinartzkehl. He'd have to pass through suburban neighborhoods, then disappear into farmland and woods dotting the countryside. If all went well, he should be there in an hour, maybe a little longer. He was guessing . . .

Sonny moved along the city streets with a sense of purpose, as if he were supposed to be there, as if he were not a stranger. In the morning cold, the few people he encountered probably were on their way to work—no one loitered. His self-confidence wasn't wholly contrived. He had convinced himself that, with caution, he would make it. When someone approached him or was in his path, he took an alternate route—turning into an alley or another street when he could. He remembered Emil's advice regarding the Thiemann Strasse burglary—he would not run unless someone was after him.

He passed through an unfamiliar area of factories and warehouses, comfortable in that setting. Several laborers came out of a building ahead, so he turned into an alley to avoid them. Littered with debris, the alley showed no evidence of human activity. Sonny felt an overwhelming sense of déjà vu and staggered. Then the image of Limping Man, dragging Rosa, crept into his mind, stiffened him. The events of Oranienburg, then of the Giradet farm, rushed through his head. He leaned against a building for support, trying to control his paranoia, with limited success.

Sonny had always found violence abhorrent, but he had changed in the doing of it, of that he was certain, and he didn't like it . . . But he couldn't agonize over his lost innocence, not just now. He continued through the alley.

At one of the warehouses ahead were boxes stacked on a loading dock, evidence of human activity. Sonny hid behind a light pole to get a better look. Within a minute, a man came out, picked up a box, and carried it inside. Then he repeated the process. Sonny waited again, but the laborer didn't return, despite the remaining boxes.

He walked over and looked around, counted at least a dozen boxes and a covered cart before he spotted a small bag of tools. He looked to each end of the alley, then into the warehouse. No one was in sight; the tools were within easy reach. He grabbed the bag, slung it over his shoulder, and quickly walked away.

At a safe distance, Sonny ducked into an alley, found a sheltered corner, and rummaged through the bag. Inside were the tools—hammer, screwdrivers, pliers, wrenches, saw—everything one would need for minor maintenance. A tag attached to the handle identified the owner as Ernst Dreske, No. 133 Büchel Strasse. Sonny had found the perfect cover. "Thanks, Ernst," he said, and he continued on his way.

He slowed near a little café at the edge of the warehouse district. Several men stood near the door, another joined them, and they all went inside. That reminded Sonny that he hadn't eaten, and he fought the urge to stop for coffee and a pastry. As he passed the window, he glanced inside and saw a cop at a table, reading a newspaper. He didn't break stride.

Soon the warehouses yielded to a commercial district with shops and small businesses. It was too early for shoppers, and only a few of the places yet showed signs of life. Then he was in a middle-class neighborhood of apartment flats similar to Vincent's. With the tools slung over his shoulder as a prop, he played the part of a laborer on his way to a job. He figured, hoped, that anyone seeing him would think he had good reason for being there.

Sonny had passed the first block of flats when he happened to glance between two buildings onto the next street. A slow-moving black sedan disappeared behind one of them, reappearing on the other side. It was keeping pace with him, going in the same direction. Knowing he'd be stopped and questioned, he felt a familiar jolt of fear. What could he do?

He casually turned into the nearest building, as if that's where he'd been headed. Good! The door was unlocked, and he was able to go inside. Inside the foyer, he waited and watched. Within minutes, the sedan slowly passed in front of the building. The driver's head turned as he scanned both sides of the street, looking for anything, anyone, out of place.

As soon as the sedan was out of sight, Sonny heard a door closing behind him, then a child's voice. Without looking behind him, he pretended to study the list of tenants and rubbed his chin.

In seconds, he heard, "Can I help you?" He turned to a young woman, holding the hand of a boy no older than three, standing at the door, ready to leave.

"I'm looking for . . . " he paused, momentarily nonplussed, until Otto's alias popped into his head, " . . . George Heinrich. He has a job for me." Sonny returned to the list, this time using his forefinger to better review each name.

From behind him, he heard her say, "There's no one here by that name. Are you sure you have the correct address? This is No. 75, Dresden Strasse."

Sonny's shoulders sagged, and he turned to face the woman. Smiling sheepishly, he feigned embarrassment, then laughed. "I'm in the wrong building. Thank you for your help."

She looked at him. "Really?" She seemd skeptical, but she said nothing more. The child ignored him.

Sonny politely held the door for her and the boy. She turned to the left, the child skipping at her side. Throwing the tool bag over his shoulder, Sonny followed them but turned to the right. He wondered whether he should walk into another building, but he kept going. When he reached the corner, he looked back. The woman, the little boy at her side, was talking to someone. She was pointing in Sonny's direction—at him!

Who the hell was she talking to? The block warden or just a neighbor? Sonny tried not to react, just kept walking, focused on the man. But what would that accomplish? Sonny was too far away to make out his face or hear what he said. Now Sonny fought the urge to run. He kept walking along as if nothing was wrong, though everything was. He turned to the left, toward the street vacated by the sedan. Within seconds the man, woman, and child disappeared, blocked from view by the building on the corner. Then he ran.

He figured the black sedan was continuing its leisurely surveillance of the neighborhood, moving in the other direction—away from where he was running. He couldn't know for sure, but he was heartened that the car did not return—at least he hadn't seen it. He doubted it would make a second pass unless . . . Whatever the case, he wouldn't wait.

At the next corner, he turned right, in the general direction of Reinartzkehl. Nearby stood the last row of flats, a road, and beyond that, an open field. Several farms like that of the Giradets bordered the road, which now saw a steady flow of commuter traffic. Eyeing the line of trees bordering the farms, Sonny turned into the lane of the first farm.

Had he been seen? Leaving the lane, he slogged through the snow that had fallen the day before. It slowed his progress, but he needed the cover of the trees. A dog barked from somewhere on the farm to his right. God, he hoped it wouldn't give chase. He kept moving; the barking stopped. He trudged to the edge of the woods to get a look at the traffic on the road. Within a few minutes he saw a black sedan, driving slowly toward town, holding up traffic. It looked like the vehicle he'd seen earlier, but then they all looked the same. Was the Gestapo looking for him?

He saw a man walking on the shoulder of the road. The sedan stopped and the driver got out, approached the man. The cop or Gestapo turned and beckoned someone. The woman in the foyer with the little boy got out of the car and joined them. He knew it was she, even though the boy wasn't with her. She'd gone along to identify the stranger.

The man on the road raised his arms, probably in a plea of innocence. The woman shook her head, confirming he wasn't the man she'd seen. They left him on the road, got back into the sedan, and drove off.

That was all the proof Sonny needed. The woman had found the cop, told him about the stranger looking for someone who didn't exist. They were looking for him, but no one had pointed in his direction. In fact, he'd retreated into the trees and was hidden from view.

He knew they would keep on looking. She'd had a good look at his face and would provide a description—man with a short beard and dark coat, maybe gray, maybe black, like a thousand others, his cap the same. Sonny was sweating, breathing hard. His heart was pounding. But they didn't know where he was—that was good.

Would they bring out more men, drive up and down every road within a certain radius of that building of flats, look for George Heinrich? They would spend some time poring over the city directory, then what? Vincent had said they were short-staffed—what could they do? Finding Günter and Katrina had to be their priority. Would they think *he* was Günter? Sonny ran through the options—there was nothing to do but head for the border.

He stuck to the perimeter of the village, walking through fields and woods. After about three-quarters of an hour, he could see the road again, but he stayed within the protection of the trees. A familiar sign pointed the way to the border—now in full view. His confidence returned, though he still had some doubts. Would they be waiting at the border, the woman and child?

No . . . he was being paranoid. Vincent said they had called for reinforcements. How wide a net could they throw? Did it make sense to look for a guy who had walked into the wrong building? Or were they looking for Sigmund Landauer, Günter's co-conspirator? Was Albert part of the team doing the search? Too many questions. Too late. He had to keep going.

Before leaving his cover, Sonny tossed the tool bag behind a tree. Then he walked onto the road he had traveled countless times with Emil, never alone. A gust of cold wind made him shiver, made his eyes water. Ignoring the momentary discomfort, he reached into his coat pocket, feeling for his passport and visa. He felt along the edges of both documents, sighed with relief, and managed a smile. At just the right spot, he returned to the cover of the trees, to where he could watch the border.

All that separated him from Plombieres, Rosa, and Fritz was a ten-minute walk. And the border patrol.

A healthy fear returned—he could handle that, he had expected it. He wondered whether Ferret Face was on duty, whether he would turn him in. Sonny decided he would not—he had too much to lose.

Sonny couldn't make out the faces of the guards in the distance, though the guardhouse and customs shed were visible. He counted three trucks, several people standing in line, waiting to leave. He did not see the black sedan or the woman with a kid. His plan was to watch and wait for at least half an hour to satisfy his suspicions. That should be enough time for the people and trucks to cross—or not. Still, he wouldn't be able to tell whether they were looking for him.

Several men in uniform stood in a cluster. One walked in, then out, of the customs shed. Nothing unusual happened—no one was denied exit. More trucks and automobiles passed by. He saw no one on foot. When he next looked at his watch, forty minutes had gone by.

Now, it was his turn. Sonny took a deep breath, left his hiding place, and began the slow walk toward the checkpoint. Watching his feet hit the pavement one after the other, he tried to empty his mind of Albert, Kristallnacht, Oranienburg, the farm, the woman with the kid. All he wanted to think of was crossing over, being with Rosa. Getting to her was all that mattered.

"Keep going, keep going," he muttered to himself. Breathe in and breathe out. He stifled the urge to run back to the safety of the woods . . . and suddenly the polished boots of the first guard were at his feet.

"Show me your papers!" the guard commanded, searching Sonny's face.

Sonny realized that a photo or least a description of Günter had been circulated. Returning the guard's gaze, he saw the unlined, ruddy face of youthful inexperience, not unlike the one he'd snuffed out the day before. His eyes drifted to the solid stripe on the guard's uniform, the same rank he had appropriated then. He almost looked away, but the guard snatched the papers from his hand.

After a perfunctory examination, the guard handed them back, pointing to the customs shed. "Over there."

Sonny followed his finger, hesitating, trying to appear as if he'd never been there before. Several men, huddled in conversation about fifteen meters away, stood between him and his destination. "Thank you," he said as he walked away.

The group of men was too far away for him to hear what they were saying—actually only one of the men seemed to be talking. In a matter of seconds, Sonny would pass them on his way to the shed.

He bent slightly forward so that the brim of his cap obscured his face but not so much as to draw attention. As he made the lonely walk, he stole a glance or two at the group of men, painfully aware of their authority. They were all in uniform. The one standing with his back to Sonny was slender. Something about him drew Sonny's attention, and he fought the urge to stare. It was the cigarette fixed in the man's hand—his slicing of the air, the jagged trail of smoke . . .

Sonny's knees nearly buckled, but he shortened his steps to keep from falling. His mind raced. The two men in a position to see him must not have noticed him, or if they did, they hadn't responded. Somehow Sonny managed to keep his expression neutral. It was far too late for subterfuge. He just kept walking, head down, toward the shed. Each step took him farther into the abyss, toward no possibility of turning back.

Ironically, the knowledge that there were no options brought him a strange calm. He relaxed, accepted what he could no longer control. He remembered the day that he and Emil had witnessed the Wehrmacht parade through Aachen—the moment he and Albert had locked eyes. Emil had said, "People don't recognize the familiar when it's out of context."

Emil had been wrong that day, but he was right in general. Now Sonny put his faith in Emil's statement, even offered a prayer: "Please God—if you're out there." In seconds he would be even with the group of men.

Albert—surely it was he—still stood with his back to Sonny. He spoke, waving his arms; the others listened. Sonny heard fragments of his lecture, a familiar voice, words without context: "Maintain vigilance . . . murderous Underground." His audience engrossed in what he said, Albert was engrossed in them.

Should any of them glance Sonny's way, they would see a man with a week's growth of beard, eyes shaded by his cap, collar raised against the wind—they would see nobody, just as Albert had looked through him in the café three years earlier. Now he would welcome the slight.

Clutching his documents like a lifeline, Sonny moved past them. Slowly, he exhaled the breath he'd been holding and breathed in, keeping his eyes on the waiting border guard, who extended a hand. He did not have to ask for a passport. Sonny handed over all his papers at once.

If Albert paused, casually glanced to his right, he would see Sonny's back. Surely he would turn his gaze to the passerby. That was Albert, perpetually distracted. Would he see just any man, or would he see Sonny?

Then Sonny felt it—Albert's certain gaze. He felt his neck burn as Albert's eyes passed over him—the eyes that had locked onto his in Aachen, that had looked through him at the café. The absurdity of the situation screamed at Sonny—the man who had pursued him for a year now stood a few meters away, unable to see his face. He had taken every precaution, only to stand within reach.

The guard turned the pages of Sonny's passport, then of his visa. He seemed to be reading every entry. He reviewed the stamps, looked at the picture, then to Sonny and back. He frowned. Turning to his superiors nearby, the guard hesitated, then asked a question.

Sonny did not hear it, though he held his breath. He was trapped. He wanted to fold in on himself, to disappear. The vein in his temple pounded a rhythmic warning. His sorry world melted into the surreal. Floating safely over the border, he embraced Rosa, buried his face in her hair. Taking her hand, they walked, with Bismarck leading the way. Birds sang in the trees, puffy clouds dotted an azure sky. It was too perfect . . .

Now he saw Albert dragging on a cigarette, grinning . . . Willy in his shallow grave, a trail of dead Germans, smoldering synagogues, looted businesses, Günter dead on the floor, Katrina weeping . . .

Sonny fixed his gaze on the Belgian flag fluttering in the distance and shuddered, steeling himself. His ears pricked to the sound he would never forget—a voice reedy, thin, and high—a voice he hadn't heard in six years. He lowered his head, hunched his shoulders, hoping against hope.

"Private . . . can't you see I'm busy? Use some initiative, for God's sake!" Then an exasperated sigh. Albert was so close Sonny could smell the smoke from his cigarette.

Stung by Albert's rebuke, the young guard stiffened, his face turning crimson. He held Sonny's papers closer, scrutinized them further, lips moving silently. He went from one document to the other in what felt to Sonny an endless cycle. The guard was playing his part, playing vigilance.

Seconds turned to minutes. A bead of sweat formed on Sonny's upper lip. He dared not react, but he feared Albert would be provoked should the charade continue. He might walk over, snatch the documents from the guard, then fix his eyes on Sonny . . . see him. And taunt: "Well, well! Look who we have here . . ."

Sonny's skin could barely contain him. His muscles, nerves, organs seemed about to break through. He nearly looked at his watch and asked, "What the hell's taking so long?" Then he heard the guard clear his throat and, with false confidence, say, "Go."

Clutching his papers, Sonny swept his mind of all things Albert and began the slow walk to Belgium. He'd gone no more than ten paces when he heard shouting. The voice, inarticulate and vague, came from far behind him. Then silence . . . another shout. A command: "Stop!"

He kept walking, his gaze on the road ahead. He would not turn to look at them. He would not give them the satisfaction. He imagined Albert, turning to the source of the shouting and back to the guard, to the man now on his way to Belgium.

He shivered and kept walking. Damn them! He fought the urge to look back, to see what was coming. He was the mythic Orpheus, but he would not repeat that Greek poet's mistake. If he did, Rosa would drift away . . . He focused on placing one foot before the other. God damn them! They'll have to shoot me.

He saw himself stagger as bullets tore through his torso. Losing his balance, he fell, arms outstretched to Belgium, his blood spurting onto the frozen no-man's-land. He saw his father and mother in happier times, though he couldn't make out just where they were. They were laughing . . . There was Uncle Simon telling the joke about the two old Jews on the park bench. Sonny laughed. Did that mean he was still alive? Then they were all at Willy's memorial service, all but Joseph. He was in his flat, bent over a visa. Looking up at Sonny, Joseph said, "Your time has run out . . ."

"No, damn it! I'm not ready," Sonny said aloud. A black bird swooped by, breaking his reverie. The bird landed on the ground in front of him, looked up, then flew ahead, and landed again. "Maybe there is a God!" The bird was leading him to freedom.

Sonny heard another indecipherable shout, more silence, but he just kept walking. Beyond the border, he saw movement. Was it Rosa? Fritz? Waiting for him? More shouts. Someone—not Albert—answered. Coarse laughter. Shouting "Stop!" was someone's cruel joke, but no one had fired. He hadn't been shot—he was alive.

Sonny took a deep breath of fresh Belgian air. In thirty seconds he was standing under the tricolor. His hand shook as he handed his papers to the Belgian guard—not his old friend Claude but someone friendly just the same. His smile was genuine.

"Good morning, sir. Welcome to Belgium."

About the author

Steven Muenzer is the son of parents born in Germany, who with the aid of an aunt living in New York fled to the United States at the end of 1939. World War II had begun by the time they left Holland on the *Rotterdam*, the last boat out. The author's exploration of their experience as the Republic died and the Third Reich rose to power was the genesis of *Farewell Berlin*. This, his first book, is thus a work of fiction that includes some family lore. Muenzer practiced law for thirty years before starting his writing career. He lives in St. Paul, Minnesota, with his wife, Jeanne Scott, a psychologist.